The House of Ribbons

By

Keith Slade

First Edition

Dedication

I dedicate *The House of Ribbons* in memory of my friend, C. Dean Andersson. He was and still is an amazing influence. Although he left us too early, his amazing body of work perseveres. Rest well, my friend, and know that you are greatly loved, as you were a kind, loving person. Thank you for being such an amazing mentor and friend.

This is not goodbye; this is simply until we meet again.

Wooden Man Productions

Proudly Presents:

The House of Ribbons

Table of Contents

Chapter 1

We All Have Our Beginnings

When I opened my eyes, all I saw was darkness at first. I was standing barefoot in the grass, and a warm breeze blew in, caressing my face. I didn't know where I was or how I got there.

As I regained my sight, I heard something. Turning around, I could see a few people off in the distance sitting around a fire. I started feeling dizzy, and I became very unsteady. My eyesight was blurred, and the world spun violently.

I reached out my hand and attempted to call out, but my throat constricted. A thick, choking fluid erupted from my mouth and nose. My eyes burned so badly that I wanted to dig them out of my head, and I felt like my insides were on fire, which forced me to drop to my knees. I clawed at the ground with my bare hands as I desperately strained to catch my breath between intense stomach contractions—but to no avail. My efforts seemed to only make it worse. At that point, I could no longer see again and could barely get enough air to stay conscious. My head was still spinning with a frightening disorientation that was overlapped by pain.

I was so scared and confused. All I could think about was the intense pain. Was I dying? When would it end? But I could hear what sounded like laughter. My stomach continued to twist, but the pain soon subsided. After emptying my stomach, I saw nothing, only darkness, as I fell to the ground. Although I was still aware of my surroundings, I felt like I was floating.

When I opened my eyes, I was held by a woman. I was too weak to lift my own arms. I tried to speak, but no words came out.

"Relax and gather yourself. You're safe with me." The unfamiliar blue-eyed woman smiled.

I tried desperately not to pass out as I reached up to touch her moonlit face. A warm, caring smile and light-blue eyes were the last things I saw before the thick void of darkness enveloped my consciousness. But eerily, I could perceive them.

"Sunako, he's out again. The sun will be up in an hour." She ran her fingers through my hair. I didn't let her know I was awake, as I enjoyed the way her fingers felt.

As the sun cast its light on my face, the two women smiled. "Sofia, we should talk about you-know-who."

The two propped me against a tree and walked a few dozen feet away. Unbeknownst to them, they were being watched.

I was floating again. I could hear someone softly speaking. The words came and went in undulating echoes that compelled me to follow. As I moved toward the beautiful sound, I saw a faint light, then I suddenly felt as if I couldn't breathe. When I opened my eyes, the light and water violently rushed in. Someone was holding me underwater. I could barely make out a wavy face as someone straddled me. One hand was firmly wrapped around my throat, sharp nails digging painfully deep into the back of my neck, while their other hand hindered any attempts to grab anything. I began to feel weak.

As I fought to survive, the face came into clear view. Deep blue eyes were surrounded by wild blonde hair and pale skin. Her grip intensified as her gaze was transfixed on me; our eyes were locked. She wore an insane ear-to-car smile. My lungs burned. I needed just one breath. I was fighting for my life, and all the while, the void of unconsciousness beckoned me back again. Certain death would follow.

With the last of my strength, I took hold of her hair, which only seemed to anger her more. When she squeezed harder, her nails pierced my neck. Suddenly, she was gone, and I was being pulled out of the water to the shore. I was choking, throwing up what felt like water and sand, but it didn't last long. Soon, I could breathe again, but my breaths came out as gasps. As soon as my breath stabilized, I could see two girls fighting in the water. Surprisingly, I felt good while regaining my strength.

I rose to my feet and moved back toward the water, but a voice from behind me said, "Leave them be. Let them work it out. You'll only make things worse if you interfere."

I turned toward the voice to see a woman black haired woman standing on the beach.

"Hello, I am Sunako. Who might you be?"

I thought for a moment. I must have looked confused because she asked again.

"What is your name, boy?"

"I don't know." I tried to think but nothing came to mind.

"Well, you're very lucky because she had you underwater for a while. I thought you were going to die when I grabbed you. Thankfully, you started to cough up all that water. Come lie back down."

"Why are they fighting?" I asked. "Why did she hold me underwater? I haven't done anything to her."

"That is Cheri," Sunako said. "You're lucky. If she'd had anything sharp, we wouldn't be having this little talk. Where do you come from?"

"I don't know," I replied.

"What House do you belong to?"

"I don't know."

"How did you get here?"

"I don't know."

"Who are your people? What land do you come from?"

Sunako had more questions than I had answers.

"I have told you all I know." I met her gaze.

Sunako seemed frustrated but remained gentle. "Then, what *can* you remember? You have to give me something because I'll need to explain you to the head of our House."

"It was dark when I opened my eyes. People were sitting by a fire, and I remember the grass felt soft and cool against my feet. Then, I immediately became sick, and my eyes were burning."

"I was there for that." Sunako smiled. "You were a mess, like a fish out of water, and in so much pain. When you passed out, I honestly thought you were going to die."

As I lay in Sunako's arms, she ran her hand through my hair.

"Are you the one who held me earlier?" I asked.

"No, that was her." Sunako pointed at the taller of the two women coming toward us. "That's Sofia. She's the nice one. You already know to watch out for Cheri."

The two walked toward me. Cheri said nothing, but her eyes told me all I needed to know.

Sofia extended her hand and said, "Hello, I'm Sofia of the House of Ribbons. What's your name?"

"I think Cheri might have done a little damage because he can't remember his name or where he came from," Sunako explained.

"No, I remember last night."

"Please tell us what you remember," Sofia said.

"I opened my eyes, and I could see a fire. Then I became sick and passed out. I could hear laughter, then someone singing. I woke up, and I was underwater with her on top of me." I pointed to Cheri.

"What is that on your wrist? May I see it?" Sofia asked.

It was a flat, silver metal band with a very small gap at the wrist. "Batch Slade," Sofia read off the bracelet. It had eighteen small holes drilled into one side and something else.

"I don't know what kind of writing this is. Sunako, is this Japanese?" Sofia asked.

"No, I have never seen anything like this." Sunako studied the bracelet. "I'm not even sure if this is writing."

"What could it be then?" Cheri asked, looking around. "I think it's time to inform Lady Silk. Look, clearly something is wrong with him."

"We'll go see Lady Silk. Cheri, come with me. I don't want you around him right now. Sunako, take him back to our cottage. Hold his hand the entire time, and talk to no one. If he tries to run away, kill him. If he stays calm, find out what you can. Boy!" she addressed me. "You will stay with Sunako. Do as she tells you, or I will finish what Cheri started in the lake. Do you understand?"

I nodded.

"Very good! Now, off with you two, and act normal," Sofia said.

I wondered what they were going to do.

We started to walk off.

"Wait. His backpack and boots are by the tree. Don't forget them."

"Cheri, why in the hell did you try to drown that boy?" Sofia hissed. "He was in my care, and you had no right to attack him! He was no threat to any of us! Lady Silk will not be pleased if she finds out."

"No, please don't tell on me! I'm already in so much trouble, and you know that. What do you want to keep quiet?" Cheri pleaded.

"I want you to promise not to attack him again. If Lady Silk allows it, I want you to stand with me when I ask for him to be placed with us," Sofia demanded. "And you'll be nice to him."

"What? No! Gross. Do you like him?" Cheri seemed very unhappy.

"No, it's just something about him," Sofia said. "But he does have beautiful blueish-green eyes. Maybe I'll name him Ocean Eyes." Sofia smiled as she daydreamed. Cheri shook her head in disapproval while they walked to Lady Silk's house.

The main house was a splendid, four-story, light-tan stone plantation house with twin wraparound white balconies and four mighty pillars in the front. The shutters were painted in House colors: the left shutter was yellow, the right one purple. The main house could easily be defended and had enough room to house all the members of the House of Ribbons. The cellar was more reminiscent of catacombs, with an area with four separate jail cells, a different huge section for a wine storage area with other storage areas, and a large steel vault.

Sofia and Cheri stopped in front of a stained wooden side door with decorative iron hinges and one huge door knocker that doubled as a pull ring for the handle. Sofia banged on the door. Soon after, a woman answered.

"Hello, Elma. We have an urgent need to speak with Lady Silk. It is a matter of great importance," Sofia said.

"What did hothead Cheri do this time? Is someone dead or dying?" Elma asked, folding her arms against her chest while her eyes narrowed.

"I found a boy by the lake when Sunako and I were out for a walk late last night. He just appeared out of thin air, and I walked right into him," Sofia explained. "Soon after, he became violently sick, and then he passed out. I kept watch over him until he woke up this morning.

Cheri helped me clean him up, and now he's resting in our cottage with Sunako."

"Wait, are you telling me Cheri helped you clean up a strange boy? Now I've heard everything," Elma said. "Come on, Sofia. Don't bullshit me. I bet she tried to kill the boy, and by the looks of it, that would explain the state of your clothes. You two are *filthy*, and it looks as if you've been fighting again! Do you know if he's a runaway slave?"

"I don't believe so," Sofia said.

"Good, that's a headache we don't need right now. Lady Silk will be back in a few days. I will inform you when she arrives, and you can explain this mystery boy. She'll send for you at her earliest convenience. Until then, you're in charge of him. Wherever you go, he goes. Inform him of our ways and rules. If he breaks one, you'll pay for it. Have him dress as to blend in. If anyone asks who he is, just tell them he's a guest of Lady Silk and you've been assigned to escort him around. You three take time off from your duties until you're called on. Now, off with you two. I have other duties to attend to."

Elma shut the door swiftly behind her.

"Thank you, Sofia, for not telling on me." Cheri sighed in relief.

"Don't thank me just yet. Lady Silk might have a different opinion. She could be very displeased that we helped the boy," Sofia said.

"We? *We*?" shouted Cheri. "We didn't help him! You and Sunako helped him!"

"Yes, *we*! Now keep your voice down! Unless you want me to remember how you tried to see if the boy could breathe underwater. I believe that might be something Lady Silk will look down on harshly. It wasn't our job to execute him. Only the lady of a House can decide that, and you're painfully aware of this rule. Come on, let's hurry back to the cottage."

Sofia took off like a flash, but Cheri beat her home.

"I hope someday I'll be faster than you," Sofia said.

"I don't think so, Sofia the Snail." Cheri poked her in the ribs, and they both laughed as Sofia opened their front door.

Chapter 2

Discretion in a State of Undress

"Sunako? Sunako? Where are you? Sunako!" Sofia yelled.

"We're in the bedroom. Come quick!" Sunako shouted.

Sofia and Cheri sprinted into the room.

"Why is he nearly naked?" Sofia screamed.

Sunako smiled. "Come look! He has no scars, birthmarks, or tattoos. Only this bracelet, which I haven't figured out how to remove. This silver ring with little designs will not come off. I tried using soap and oil, but it still won't come off. These boots were attached to the backpack that was near him, so it must be his. There is one set of clothes that look identical to what he was wearing when we found him, plus a pair of pants."

"Wow, all of his clothes are really soft, like sleepwear, yet strong," noted Sofia. "What about his other stuff?"

"He had one dagger attached to his right hip with etchings on both sides of the blade. A smaller, similar knife was attached to his right leg just below his knee. The dagger has a clear green jewel held in place at the bottom of the hilt. Then, there is this wide, tan leather belt with a big buckle. He came with weird clothing: a smoke-gray shirt and a pleated blue-green skirt made of a durable material that stops two inches below his knee with this dull silver emblem with letters on it. The back-right pocket is this odd pink color. So, this must be a woman's dress, right? Oh, he was wearing this satchel around his neck—look inside!"

Sofia opened my small brown satchel; it was clearly made of animal hide. She removed a large silver coin, which was inexplicably heavy and oddly shiny. But it was also well-worn with a man's face on one side with unknown marks that were possibly words. The other side revealed a strange symbol and more marks.

Sofia smiled. "I wonder what far-off place these things come from?"

"See?" Sunako said.

"Sunako, what did I tell you? Put his shirt back on! This is the opposite of what I wanted! Why did you undress him in the first place?" Sofia asked.

"You asked me to find out what I could about him, and I was very curious. Besides, look at him. Don't you see it? He's not like anyone here. Look at his face! No one in the four Houses looks like him, and he is so good-looking. I mean, you can feel the way he is looking at us. It's like he can see our souls."

Sofia growled, "Yes, he's very pretty, but that still doesn't explain why he's in a state of undress!"

"Like I said, I was curious and still am." Sunako's smile spoke of other things.

"I bet you were!" Cheri snapped, leaving the room.

Sofia asked, "Why is he just standing there like that? He looks like a statue. Well, Sunako, what—if anything—did you learn? Or are you going to just sit next to him drooling with that goofy look on your face?"

"What look?" Sunako flushed red.

"The look you have on your face right now—it tells me more than I care to know."

Sofia seemed skilled at verbal jabs.

"Well, just *look* at him. He has all this muscle tone, but no scars." Sunako pointed at me. Then, her finger delicately danced across my skin.

"It doesn't make any sense. He looks perfectly shaped for combat, but shouldn't he have at least a few scars from fighting, training, or punishment? Then, I thought about it. What if he's a brand-new clone?"

Sunako patted the bed, and I sat next to her.

"A clone? At his age? No, if he were ten years younger maybe. People generally don't make clones of this age group. My vote is against him being a clone," Sofia said.

"Why not?"

"Sunako, he has no marks. All clones bear a mark. Just look at Cheri and the three Myers girls. The list goes on. All five have a mark at the base of their necks. We also saw the three boys that Lady Silk bought last month. They have tattoos on their necks and whip marks on their back. Plus, some male clones are eunuchs. Did you check him?" asked Sofia.

Sunako smiled as she said, "No, I thought you would want to be here for the final inspection."

"Sunako, you have him sitting in our bedroom shirtless and in a skirt, and you didn't peek?"

Sunako said, "I was waiting for you to check further, honest. If he has a mark, we'll find it together."

"Cheri, come in here! Now!" yelled Sofia.

"What! Why is he still like this?" Cheri looked displeased.

"Cheri, I want you to go see Tomaz. He's about this guy's size. Ask him for two sets of clothes. Tell him that Elma asked for this, and you're in a hurry. Say nothing else. Then, come right back," Sofia instructed.

Cheri ran off.

I spoke up and said, "She looks angry."

"She always looks angry. Just ignore her. We do," Sunako said with a mischievous smirk and a wink.

"Are you uncomfortable undressing in front of us?"

"No, should I be?"

"No, it will be fine. All right, stranger. Take it off. We need to check you for marks."

With that command, I removed my last garment. My eyes danced back and forth from each woman's face as I tried to read their expressions.

Sunako's almond eyes went wide, her face turning bright red. Then she covered her mouth, her eyes darting over to Sofia, whose face showed the same reaction.

Sofia asked me to turn around then asked, "Are you still comfortable?"

"I'm fine."

"Damn straight, you are!" Sunako exclaimed.

"Sunako! A little decorum would go a long way right now." Sofia turned to me. "I mean, are you embarrassed to be naked in front of us?"

"No. Should I be?"

"No, you have nothing to worry from us," Sofia replied.

"Is everything okay?" I was curious as to why they were staring. It made me feel weird and tingly in my stomach.

"You're looking fine. I mean, you're doing fine," Sofia said. Sunako laughed.

As Sofia went through my pockets, Sunako tapped Sofia on the shoulder, then whispered something with a huge smile on her face as she pointed at me.

"Oh my, will you look at that. I think you should cover yourself up before Sunako's eyes fall out of her head or she dies of shock." Sofia grinned.

I smiled. "As you wish."

Sofia handed me my clothes, and I redressed right there.

"I like the sound of that," Sofia said with a devilish smile. "You can speak like that all you want around me." She moved her hair over her ear.

Sunako bumped Sofia.

"I mean, *us*, in this cottage." Sofia's smile was large and warm, her eyes never leaving mine.

Cheri returned with clothes. "Here you go. What did you learn, girls?"

Sunako laughed. "Hey, Cheri. He's definitely not a eunuch, that's for sure. You should see the size of his—"

"Damn it, Sunako!" Sofia yelled.

Cheri's hand flew out to slap Sunako across the face. But just before contact, I grabbed her wrist.

"No! You will not harm Sunako!" I commanded.

"Let me go, you filthy animal! How dare you touch me!" Cheri fumed.

Sofia said, "Boy! Please let Cheri go!"

Once I let go Cheri's wrist, she wrapped her hands around my throat and pushed me back onto one of the beds. She straddled me, but it didn't feel the way it had when I was in the water. The pain was minimal, and I could breathe fairly easily.

I smiled, and Cheri went wild, yelling and drooling on my face while straining to bite me. I placed my forearm under her chin to stop her, but she bit down into my arm, her teeth disappearing beneath my skin. Blood spilled out of the sides of her mouth; her eyes locked on mine. She seemed to hate me. Seething, she breathed heavily through her nose.

"Cheri, let him go!" Sofia screamed.

Sunako shouted, "Boy! Stop her! Stop her now!"

I decided to do as I was told. I reached for her throat with my free hand and squeezed until she let go. Her eyes stayed on mine up until they rolled into the back of her head. Not wanting her to fall off the bed and hit the floor, I caught her as her body went limp.

Sofia looked shocked, while Sunako clapped excitedly. I gently placed Cheri on the adjacent bed, her face smeared with blood. The crimson was a sharp contrast to her pale skin and golden hair. In that moment, I found her deeply attractive. I wanted to kiss her, but I didn't understand why.

"I'm sorry. Is that not what you wanted me to do?"

Sunako jumped into my arms, hugged me tightly, then said, "I've wanted to do that to her for a long while."

Her lips were only inches from mine, but Sofia pulled her away before we connected.

"Sunako, attend to his arm, not his lips. Does it hurt? Let Sunako take care of your wound, and I'll deal with Cheri."

"Cheri! Cheri!" A light slap to the face woke her.

Cheri said, "What? What happened?"

"You attacked the boy again. This time, he stopped you! What is wrong with you? Do you want to be punished again?"

Cheri began to cry. "No! I'm sorry. Please give me one more chance. Please!"

"Now sit and calm yourself. Remember who you are. Know your place, or I shall inform Elma that you are out of control again. You might want to go wash your face. You have blood all over it."

"I'm fine for now. Besides, I like the way he tastes." Cheri sat on the edge of her bed with a scowl, crossing her arms and legs. Her dark-blue eyes filled with tears, and she fought to hold them back. I could feel her looking straight into me; she was seething. She wanted more of my blood.

"Boy, why did you stop Cheri before she could hit Sunako?" Sofia asked.

"I did not want to see her in pain."

"Are you angry with Cheri in any way? Can I trust you will not try to harm her or get even?"

"I'm not mad, and I will not harm her so long as she does not attack anyone in this room. I promise to protect you three from any harm."

"Excellent. Then I should not have to worry about either one of you getting into it," Sofia said. "Are you hungry?"

"I am." I felt more than hungry. I would have eaten almost anything. My stomach felt so empty, and my mouth was dry from thirst. "May I have some water, please?"

"Sunako. Sunako! Hello?" Sofia snapped her fingers in front of Sunako's face.

"What? Oh, sorry. I was miles away."

"Clearly, you were. I swear! You're acting like you have never seen a boy before! Just—" Sofia brought her hands up to her face, rubbing her temples. She muttered something to herself and spoke directly to Sunako, "Get. The. Boy. A. Cup. Of. Water." Sofia threw her hands in the air, dismissing her.

Sunako was only gone for a moment. She reentered the room with her hands wrapped around a cup of water. Her footsteps were hurried but made almost no sound on the wooden floor. I was standing by the bed adjacent to Cheri. Sunako handed me the cup with a smile and a wink. She took her right hand and brushed her hair back, exposing her ear. She gazed deeply into my eyes, biting her bottom lip. I could feel my face becoming warm in a way I was unaccustomed to.

Sunako returned to Sofia's side and asked, "Do we have to call him 'boy?' Look, there are two words on his bracelet: *Batch* and *Slade*. Let's pick one and call him that."

"Good point, Sunako," Sofia said. "Boy, which do you like: Batch or Slade?"

"I don't know. Which do you like, Sunako?" I winked.

"I like Slade," Sunako squeaked. "Okay, all in favor of Slade, hands up?"

Sofia and Sunako raised their hands, while Cheri held up her middle finger.

"Sofia, what does that mean?" I asked.

Cheri said, "It means fuck y—"

Sofia yelled, "Cheri! Finish that sentence, and Elma will be the least of your worries tonight!" She exhaled. "Slade, it's a terribly rude gesture, and you would do well not to copy Cheri because she sets a bad example. All. The. Damn. Time!" Sofia clapped loudly for each word. "Cheri, now be a dear and help Slade get dressed while we whip up something to eat. I, for one, am famished, and I can only imagine how Slade feels."

"*Me*! Why the hell should I?"

"Need I remind you so soon? Or shall I tell Lady Silk how you mistreated our guest before and after Elma told us to watch over him?"

"I believe Elma said he was in *your* care."

"You are correct, Cheri, but as I am head of this cottage, that makes me in charge of you and Sunako. So, do as I ask, please. No more of this nonsense."

"Why don't you have Sunako get him ready? I bet she would jump at the opportunity," Cheri said.

A hopeful look flashed across Sunako's face, her eyes wide and eyebrows raised.

"No! This will be a great learning experience for you. It will show us that you can control yourself, as you're in desperate need of some control."

With a long and labored sigh, Cheri said, "Fine. This day just keeps getting better!"

"Bring him to the table as soon as he is dressed. Come on, Sunako," Sofia said. As they rounded the corner, Sofia placed a finger to her lips and shushed Sunako. She led Sunako upstairs to one giant bedroom and pointed at an area of the floor above their bedroom. "We can secretly watch them from here." Sofia pointed toward a rug, sliding it away to reveal two small holes. Sunako smiled, and Sofia whispered, "I'm not sure I trust the boy. I just want to watch them for a bit."

The two girls slowly lowered themselves to the floor. Their view was at a perfect angle to see the whole room, and they could hear the conversation perfectly.

Back in the bedroom, Cheri mumbled to herself. Her words were barely audible, but none of them sounded good.

"Look here, boy. I don't like you! I want to smash your face into the wall and taste your blood again. Then, I want you to leave and never come back. I hope Lady Silk sends you away, sells you off—or better yet—has you killed."

Sofia whispered, "Did you notice how good he smelled?"

"I thought I was the only one who noticed. It's so good. I just want to snuggle him."

Sofia said, "You just might get your wish tonight."

"What do we do if she hits him and he fights back?" Sunako whispered.

"We will not intervene unless it looks like one of them might kill the other."

"I hope he kills her."

"Sunako! That's an awful thing to say."

"It's true. Cheri has treated me like shit for the last few years. She's a bitch, through and through!"

Sofia said, "First off, language! Second, yeah, she can be hard to handle sometimes." Sofia remembered a time before Cheri became problematic, and she smiled. "Just give her a little more time. Please? For me?"

As I got dressed, I asked Cheri, "Why do you dislike me?"

She got close enough to my face to where I could feel the heat from her skin.

"Why? Because I don't like the way you look or the way you smell. It makes me uncomfortable," Cheri said. "I don't like the thoughts I have about you. I, I, I want to—" She grabbed me, almost in a hug, as she ran her lips across mine. She lightly bit my bottom lip and whispered, "You can't understand the way I feel. I'll have to kill you because I can't stand this feeling within me."

I looked up and noticed the sneaky little spies and winked in their direction.

Cheri pushed me hard into the wall with one hand. "Come with me, boy."

Sunako asked, "Is he looking at us? Can he see us? Sofia, let's get that food ready. They're almost done. I really think he saw us."

"Sunako, don't be foolish. There is no way he could have seen us. Cheri probably said something disgusting to him, which caused him to smile, and he just happened to be facing in our direction." Sofia and Sunako exchanged guilty looks.

Chapter 3

Warm Food and Icy Glances

Cheri and I walked into the dining room. "Sit here, boy! Sofia, I have the boy dressed. What now?" Cheri yelled to the two in the other room. She sat down opposite of me, and we were the only ones at the table. "What are you staring at, boy? Come on then. Out with it."

"Your eyes are very pretty. Your hair is like the sun, and you look like an angel." I smiled.

"What? Why would you say that to me?" Cheri said, stunned.

"You asked me to tell you why I was looking at you. I'm sorry if I offended you. Please accept my apologies. I should have known better."

"You didn't offend me. Did you really mean what you said? Do I really look like an angel?"

"Yes."

Sofia and Sunako walked in. "Okay, you two, I see that you are both still alive. So, that's a good start, and it's nice to see you getting along."

Sofia and Sunako placed a bowl of soup in front of Cheri and me, then placed the other two bowls on the table.

"Eat up. It's deer meat stew. We bought some meat from the hunter who comes by a few times a month." Sofia smiled as we started to eat.

"It is very yummy! What do you think, Slade?" Sunako asked, taking another spoonful.

"It's very delicious. Thank you for sharing your food with me. I hope I can repay you for your kindness." I wondered if I'd ever had deer meat before. Either way, it tasted amazing. "Did he teach you how to hunt?"

"Jim and his wife taught a handful of us to hunt, skin, and set traps for small animals, like rabbits. In return, his family lives under our protection. Jim makes spiced deer jerky, and the young children make arrows in their spare time to trade for it. We've made more than a few arrows for trade. The jerky is delicious. Occasionally, he will hand out pieces of smoked deer, rabbit, and on the super rare occasion, bear heart. Over time, he was given the name Mr. Treat, so now they're known as Jim and Kim Treat." Sofia smiled.

Sunako added, "If you're still here next week, you can come with us to hear Jim tell stories about the old gods and goddesses. He comes once every two weeks and tells stories. Some are scary; some are dramatic; and others are plain crazy. Kim tells the romantic stories of love and loss." As Sunako talked, she brushed her hair over her ear, twisting and playing with a long black strand. "During story time, you can sit next to me if you want."

Cheri cast an icy glance at me and said, "Sunako! If you like him so much, why don't you just wildly rub yourself on his leg right here in front us, you filthy creature?"

Sunako stood up. "What did you just say to me, bitch? You know what? I'm sick of your shit! Why don't you just shut the hell up for once?"

Sofia spat out her drink with laughter, banging her fist on the table. She tried to compose herself to no avail, her laughter startling Sunako and me.

"Holy hell, Cheri, that was hilarious!" Sofia continued to laugh loudly, adding some heavy clapping as she stood up from the table. "Cheri, I think that was the funniest thing I have ever heard you say. Sunako, your comeback was great—real sharp."

"Cheri is always so mean all the time, and I can't stand it!" Sunako crossed her arms.

Sofia wiped tears from her eyes and sat back in her chair, beginning to wipe up the mess she'd made. "Now, we're all at this table together. Our new friend is our guest, and we have two days to get to know him. So, I suggest we make the best of our time together. I, for one, feel comfortable around him, and I trust you will as well, Cheri. Please give him time," Sofia said. "Sunako, please pass the bread."

We finished eating without any more fighting.

"Slade, would you mind cleaning up with Sunako?"

"I will do my best, Sofia. Thank you for all that you have done for me and thank you again for the food."

"You're very welcome, Slade. It's our pleasure to have you as our guest. Please don't hesitate to ask for anything," Sofia declared.

Sofia and Cheri stood up, walked into the other room, and sat on the couch.

Sofia took Cheri's hand in hers and asked, "Cheri, why was there was blood on his mouth and his neck? Can you tell me what that was about and how it got there?"

Cheri softly said, "I was so confused with the way he smelled—even his blood was sweet, not thick and gross. I felt like I couldn't help myself. I felt compelled to kiss him, but I managed to just touch his lips before I went for his neck. I still have that feeling. What does it mean?"

"Can you tell me why you seemingly hate that boy if you feel this way?" Sofia rubbed the top of Cheri's hand.

"I didn't like the way you looked at him when you held him on the beach. He could have been a spy, an assassin, or a filthy skin changer. I didn't want to lose you. Sofia, you're the only one that understands me. You're my best friend. You have always looked out for me, and the thought of losing you filled me with crazy thoughts."

Sofia turned and hugged Cheri tightly. "I'm here for you now and always. I miss the old you. Where is calm, loving, happy, and peaceful Cheri? You used to always be so cheery. What happened, honey? Why are you so angry lately?"

"It's nothing. I'm just trying to adjust to the change. It came late for me, and I'm unsure how to deal with these newfound emotions. You and Sunako went through the change one right after another when you were twelve, and I didn't get it until sixteen. I felt left behind."

A single tear rolled down her cheek, and Sofia leaned in to kiss it away.

Cheri laughed and said, "You always know how to cheer me up. I love you."

"I love you, too. I thought you first got your period with us and just didn't want to talk about it. I'm sorry that I never asked you." Sofia must have felt bad for not knowing.

Cheri jokingly said, "No worries. Now, let's get back to Miss Lovey Dovey and Mr. Dreamy Eyes before they get too close and she loses her virginity on the kitchen table."

"Yuck! On the table where we eat? Well, it could be worse. We could wake up in the middle of the night to them screwing loud and hard," Sofia said. "Hey! You called him Mr. Dreamy Eyes. I think you're the one who wants to screw him hard! You're a naughty girl." Sofia laughed and slapped Cheri on the shoulder.

Cheri smiled. "He is very polite; he sounds very educated; and his muscles are toned. I want to see what he can do in the pit. Oh yeah, maybe against Richter or William, those two bastards! Yeah, I would like him better if he defeated one of them."

Sofia asked, "What would you do if he took one or even both down? Would you kiss him?" Sofia made a kissing sound.

Cheri smiled. "If he took both of those bastards down? I would take him into my bed! So, yeah, I would kiss him." Cheri flashed a smile at Sofia.

Sofia covered her mouth, her eyes wide.

"Don't give me that look! You asked a good question, and I gave you the only truthful answer. Oh, and I forgot to mention it, but he said that I look like an angel," Cheri said.

Sofia said, "Between Sunako's eagerness to be at his side, your filthy thoughts, and my curiosity about his identity, I think it might be an interesting two days."

Cheri said, "None of his clothes look familiar. Where do you think he's from? Maybe the mountains or the deserts. Either way, it must be pretty far away." Cheri rubbed his shirt on her face. "Sofia, feel this."

Sofia took the shirt. "Oh, it's soft! This is softer than our blankets. All his clothes are incredibly soft. Look at the stitching on his boots. It looks brand-new, and I don't know what kind of material they are made from. Look at the bottom of the boot. He must be from the mountains, and these protect his feet from the jagged rocks."

Cheri smiled. "I have never met anyone from the mountains. I have only heard the stories that they rarely come down and have ships that can fly past the clouds. Oh, wait. Do you think he is one of the people from the stars?" Cheri's mind raced with excitement.

Sofia said, "No, I heard none of them look human. I bet we will come across a few more from his tribe, house, or whatever they call themselves soon. His people will come for him. Yes, I am sure we'll find out more tomorrow. For all we know, they're out looking for him right now. He probably hit his head, fell into the river miles upstream, floated all the way here, and washed ashore not too far from where I found him. He did get really sick. It must have been all the water he swallowed. He was throwing up so much. That must be why he was so weak and unable to fight you off." She was sure of it. "Looks like we might have just figured it out. Only time will tell."

Chapter 4

Friends with Benefits

"Slade, come in here, please."

I heard my name being called. Then, Sunako took my hand and led me toward Sofia's voice. Sunako's hand was so soft. I swore I could hear little whispers as we walked into the bedroom. I played it off to an excited imagination and my surroundings.

Cheri asked, "How was the kitchen table? I hope he got that wet spot."

Sofia laughed loudly again. "This! This Cheri! I could get to like this, Cheri!"

Sunako and I looked at one another, confused.

"I did not see a wet spot. Sunako must have gotten it."

Cheri and Sofia looked at one another and started laughing again.

"I'm sure she did," said Sofia.

Sunako blushed. She let go of my hand and sat on her bed. When her heat left my hand, I became a little sad. I looked in her direction and smiled. She smiled back.

Sofia and Cheri got onto their respective beds. All three were sitting with their legs crossed and hands in their laps.

"Slade, do you remember anything at all?"

I shook my head.

"I have a great idea. Help us push the beds together. We do this kind of thing all the time. Come get comfortable with us. No point in standing all night."

With the beds together, I sat on the end of the middle bed, all three facing me. "How long have you three lived here?" I asked.

"Sofia has lived here the longest, then me, then Cheri," Sunako answered.

"I just noticed we have not formally introduced ourselves," Sofia said.

Sunako went first. "I am Miss Sunako. I am Japanese and come from the deserts of Japan. I was six when a female from the Jotanfo Race found me clinging to my mother's body. We had been attacked; my village had been destroyed. The Jotanfo's name was Notnair'e, and she was very kind to me. She treated me like a daughter. When I turned seven, I developed my gifts. I can rapidly heal people and animals, and I can move really fast. Notnair'e explained that I needed to go live with my own kind because she had to leave and go back to her home planet. Her home world's air is thin like that of the top of our highest mountains, so it would be difficult to live there. Notnair'e knew Asya, the witch who visits the House of Ribbons. So, we traveled to see her, and she left me in her care. I stayed with her for two years until she brought me here to the House of Ribbons. I soon moved into this cottage with Sofia. I am not the only healer who lives here in the House of Ribbons. I am treated very well and have a great job. All I have to do is hold hands with people when they get a boo-boo." Sunako smiled. "I am seventeen years old."

Sunako had an exotic beauty to her with beautiful, almond-shaped eyes that were light mahogany in color. She had long, straight, raven-black hair and light-tan skin. She looked nothing like Sofia or Cheri. Those two could pass for sisters, or at the very least, cousins, but Sunako looked wildly different. She spoke with a soft yet direct tone and had a slight accent, which was very pleasant on the ears, as it filled the room like butterflies. She was five foot five. I found it hard to look away from her face.

I asked, "Are Jotanfo the only non-humans that live on this planet? Is Asya a witch doctor?"

"Asya is a real witch that controls our territory and keeps us safe. She visits us often and has the best candy. There are a few other non-human types that live on this planet, but we have almost no contact with them. Some, like the Jotanfo, easily pass for human."

Sofia spoke next. "I'm Mistress Sofia. When I was eight, I was sold to Lady Velvet of the House of Dreams. I lived with them for a year before I was won in a bet by Lady Silk. I have the gift of extreme acrobatics with unrivaled balance. It also makes me a really capable fighter as well as dancer. I am very strong and almost as fast as Sunako. I can redirect the pain I receive back onto the person that is trying to hurt me, which makes it much harder to fight me."

Sofia closed her eyes and smiled, balling her hands into fists while pumping her shoulders and hands up and down a few times. I didn't know what that meant, but it looked like she was celebrating or asserting her dominance. "I'm a ranger, trainer, and a fight instructor with Mr. H. I'm eighteen years old."

Sofia had fair skin and medium-length, wavy black hair. Her eyes were a very light blue and stood out against her dark hair. Her voice was direct, but she controlled the volume with ease and was smooth as a feather. Maybe it was because she was the first one I'd seen, but I would follow her anywhere just to be close to her voice. Just to be in the same room with her made me happy.

"I'm Miss Cheri. I was given to Lady Velour when I was seven, but I displeased her greatly, so I was given to Lady Silk. If it were not for my abilities, my head would have rolled off by now. I can see perfectly in the dark no matter how dark it is. I can fight better than most because I have a modified muscular and skeletal system that makes my bones hard to break. Plus, I'm far stronger than a natural-born human." Cheri looked away, then slowly back at me. "I'm a clone."

She moved her hair to show me her mark, a number two next to a symbol.

"My natural gift is that I can understand any language and speak it as if I were born with that tongue. I'm also very fast. I was sold in a group of five to Duke Esben. He gave me and my sister as gifts to Lady Velour. As you can see, I ended up here. I never had a name before I came to live here. I was always just called Two. Then, one day, Mistress Saffron named me just after I became a ranger. I'm also a fight instructor. My clone sister, who was better behaved, went to continue to live with Lady Velour before she was sold off. I dislike being a clone, and I have a hard time liking other clones. I'm seventeen."

Cheri had wild, curly, sunshine-blonde hair that hung just below her shoulders and deep blue eyes. Her skin was very pale, almost snow-white, which made her lips stand out in a natural crimson. She was five foot two. I hardly knew her, but my feelings for her were confusing.

"Why do you dislike clones?" I asked.

"I hate being no more than something that was made to be bought. Created to be nothing more than a tool. I'm a person—I have thoughts and feelings. You can't imagine what it's like to know you are nothing more than just a copy of someone that lived a long time ago. It makes me feel like I have no identity. So, I hate seeing others with my face."

Sofia reached out and rubbed Cheri's back. "Slade, some people can demonstrate things that will seem like magic. Please don't let it scare you. It's not magic. They are abilities, gifts that some of us are born with, and some of us have more than one gift. They come out as early as age five or as late as thirteen. Take Richter and William. Richter can make you feel more pain than you're really in. A small cut will make you feel like you're dying. William can make you feel great sadness. Both are strong and become super aggressive at the drop of a coin. They oversee and carry out punishments when someone breaks a major rule."

I asked, "Why are they super aggressive?"

"They enjoy what they do, and they like throwing their weight around. Lady Silk likes to take them with her when she meets with others outside of our area. Mistress Saffron is an oracle, just like Mistress Topaz. They can sometimes see paths for different outcomes, and sometimes, they can see the gift or gifts a child will get. I bet they'll want to see you as soon as Lady Silk gets back."

Sofia said, "The three sisters have unique gifts, each one different from the other. Lady Silk can take possession of a person's shadow—any shadow really—then make it do her bidding. It's very scary. Lady Velvet can influence a person's dreams. Lady Velour can raise the dead and compel them to speak. They have other gifts, too, but more common ones like speed, strength, and healing."

Cheri said, "Slade, your clothes are not like ours. They're so very soft." Cheri huffed and ran her fingers through her hair. She glanced at me. "Seriously, is nothing triggering your memory?" She frowned.

"No."

"Would you like to see our area tomorrow, meet some new people?"

"Yes, that would be nice."

Sofia yawned and asked, "Nothing at all, not even a flash of a memory?"

"I'm sorry. Nothing reminds me of anything. No people or places before meeting you. I wish I could be of more help."

Sofia smiled. "You're doing fine, Slade. I feel you're more than what you know, but hopefully, Mistress Topaz or Mistress Saffron can see something that will lend a clue. Or better yet, tell us who you are."

"Maybe he teleported here, and it jumbled his mind," Sunako suggested.

"Ha ha! Only the witches have that gift." Cheri laughed.

Sofia smirked at Cheri, then said, "How do you know? Have you met everyone everywhere? I thought not. Besides, the facts are that he is here, and no one has any answers. He could be part of the Oncari, but I hope it's not true. Slade, please don't be an Oncari. Wouldn't that just be my luck? The prettiest boy just appears, and then we find out he is an Oncari assassin with memory loss. Slade, you can steal my heart. Just don't stab me in it."

Sunako started laughing. "Look, who remembers the old campfire stories of the faraway tribes and witches from other planets? But they are just stories. It has been so long that I almost forgot about the Oncari, shapeshifting beings that are older than our sun. They're just spooky stories to make the children stay in their beds at night so they don't become a snack for one of the Oncari child-eaters." She stood on the bed with her arms outstretched, her expressions changing constantly.

She had my full attention with her story. I was full of questions about the Oncari.

Sunako looked at me. "The old stories describe a way to tell if an Oncari has become whatever creature. You could be an Oncari in disguise. Slade, do you trust me?"

I smiled as she pushed me down.

As I lay on the bed, she crawled on top of me. "Can we watch you bleed?"

"Didn't I bleed enough when Cheri tried to take a bite out of my arm? But if it will put your mind at rest, then do what you feel is necessary."

Sofia asked, "Sunako, can you get me a knife?" She looked at me. "I'm going to cut you behind your ear right here. You will bleed a bit, and then Sunako will work her gift on you." When she lightly touched the spot, it forced my eyes closed, and I started to feel warm. "Did you like that?"

I nodded.

"Good, very good."

Sunako returned with a small knife.

"The Oncari, as the stories go, will change back into their natural state when injured here."

I said, "I apologize, but that sounds completely wrong. What a poor design for a species! And why not move the spot to a harder-to-hit spot? I don't like this idea. Please don't do this."

Sofia said, "I don't see why you would protest. Just a little pain, and Sunako will take it away. Please, do this for me. Then, we will know that you are safe to sleep next to. I mean, you wouldn't want to sleep on the floor like a dog, would you?"

I smiled. "You have a way about you, Sofia, that makes it hard to say no to you."

Sofia smiled. "Here we go. This might hurt a little." She held my hair tightly but not painfully, her face close to mine. The heat of her breath was heavy on my face, and I swore I heard whispers again in my mind. The knife parted the skin with a sharp pain. I reached out and took her in my arms.

"Damn it! Quick! Shit, don't get blood on my bed. I need a rag! I think I cut him a little too deep. Never mind." Sofia placed her mouth behind my ear and rolled me over onto her until Sunako could stop the bleeding.

Sunako asked, "Slade, are you okay?"

I smiled. "I'm fine. It stung a bit, but it was not your intention to cause me pain. Did I pass your test?" I noticed my blood was on Sofia's hand and mouth.

Sofia said nothing. She grabbed Cheri's hand and left the room.

In a dark room, Sofia kissed Cheri, and Cheri got what blood was left in Sofia's mouth. "Cheri, is this what you meant about his blood?"

Cheri said, "Yes, and it tasted better in your mouth. Kiss me again. I want another taste."

They kissed again.

Sofia and Cheri walked back into the room. "Good news. You're not Oncari."

I asked, "Sofia, were you and Cheri kissing?"

Sofia said, "No, I needed to speak about an idea with Cheri. Why do you ask?"

I smiled. "Cheri's face was clean before you two left the room. You have my blood all over your lips, and now she has blood on her lips."

Sofia laughed. "Well, I should tell you that we are together, in a way, and your blood doesn't taste like blood at all. Trust us, we have been in more than a few fights where the other person was bleeding onto our faces while we were on the ground."

I said, "Okay, that's a bit strange."

Sunako took Sofia's hand and sucked her fingers clean. "Oh my, you are sweet. Well, this is bullshit. You both got to taste him, and all I get is leftovers. Barely a taste. What happened to last month's talk of equality, sharing when we get something new and yummy? This is not fair."

Cheri laughed. "Sunako, that was about food. We have never done anything like this before. It's not like we're vampires. But, Slade, you're definitely different than the rest. You're like wine."

Sunako tried to hide her smile. "We'll take you around tomorrow and introduce you to our little group of friends. Oh, we could have breakfast with Mistress Lethe. She makes the best eggs and bacon. Cheri, please run over and ask Mistress Lethe if it would be okay for us to come over. Tell her about our new friend. You know how she loves to meet new people. I'm sure she will be more than happy to meet him, but we cannot tell anyone that we drank his blood. It might look weird, and I would like to keep it between us, please. We all agree?"

Cheri was off like the wind.

Sofia said, "Well, let's get you cleaned up and ready for bed. I'm tired, and it has been a long night. I bet you're worn out as well. Now, what to do about the sleeping arrangement?" Sofia crossed her arms, thinking.

"Come on, Slade. I want to wash the blood off you. I can heal it faster if it's clean. Then I'll rub on some salve to dull the pain, and by the morning, you'll be good as new," Sunako said.

Sunako led me out of the room as Sofia's eyes followed me. Her lips were cherry-red, and I wanted to kiss her. Then, we were alone in the bathroom with the door closed. Sunako was delicate with her hands as she worked the salve into the bite mark. She looked into my eyes.

"Sunako, I feel bad that you are the only one who did not get a real chance to have some. If you want, you can taste me."

Sunako's face was blank. "Really? I don't want to hurt you, but I do still have the knife."

I bent my neck, and she cut deep, which hurt more than I expected. I began to bleed a lot. I met her mouth, and she latched on, holding me tightly. I felt her gift inside of me, and the pain started to go away. I held her in my arms. I would let her drink as long as she wanted.

After a few minutes, Sofia walked in and exclaimed, "Sunako, what are you doing?"

Sunako looked over at her and replied, "Enjoying myself. Oh, Sofia, I want him. I want him to live with us. Please, Sofia, get him to live with us. Lady Silk loves you. Please, ask this of her for me."

"I was already going to. Now, please don't suck the boy dry. Shit, I didn't mean it that way. Just finish up in here. I have to piss." She paused for a moment, then said, "Never mind."

She sat down and did her thing as Sunako went back to kissing me behind the ear. Sofia and I were locked onto each other's eyes.

"Sunako, you should stop. What we did to him, what *you* are doing to him, is unnatural. I think we were wrong to have tasted him."

Sunako stopped. "Yeah, I guess. Besides, he stopped bleeding right as you came in, so I'd have to cut him again. That was amazing. I feel amazing. Slade, I'm sorry if I was too aggressive and caused you pain."

I smiled. "I really liked it, and it wasn't fair that you didn't get your chance in the room."

Sunako's eyes were wide and looked into mine. I barely felt her rubbing the salve on.

"There you go. Thank you for letting me have some of you." Sunako smiled at me.

"Thank you, Sunako. You have done nothing but make me feel welcome. I greatly appreciate your kindness and your tender touch."

"You're welcome." She kissed me on my cheek. "We should get back." She looked nervous and grabbed my hand. She hugged me once more. Then, we walked out and into the dining room as Cheri strode in.

"Good news! We're having breakfast at Mistress Lethe's cottage. She said just bring—Sunako? What is on your face?" She moved toward Sunako, and I stepped in front of them. "I won't hurt her.

Sunako, is that blood on your mouth? Did you drink his blood? Wow. Look at you! Our little mouse is growing up. Good for you. He tasted amazing, right?"

They smiled at each other. Cheri walked into the bedroom. We followed her, and the girls chatted quietly about daily life. It felt so good with the attention off me for the first time since I woke up. Sunako held my hand as they spoke, and I could feel my wounds stitching themselves back together. A knock came at the door, and Cheri went to see who it was. She came back in with a guest.

"Mistress Sofia, I just had to come straight over to meet your stranger. Oh my, by the looks of him, Cheri did him almost no justice in her description."

Cheri gestured to me to stand up, so I did.

"Oh, just look at him. You know, Mistress Sofia, I would be more than happy to take him off your hands if you're not ready to have a male living in your cottage. We are hoping to get one assigned to our cottage within a month, and if you don't want this one, I would like to place dibs on him." Mistress Lethe was tall with long black hair in two braids, wild brown eyes, and very dark skin.

"Mistress Lethe, I'm sure that if Slade is able to stay, Lady Silk will place him where she wants. He might go to one of the other two Houses. Either way, he's in my charge until Lady Silk comes back." Sofia leaned back against the wall and yawned as she stretched out her arms. "Mistress Lethe, I hope you don't find me rude, but I'm simply wiped out, and my eyes grow heavier by the second. I look forward to joining you for breakfast. Your eggs are amazing, combined with all the questions you could ask and all the answers that I can provide."

"What is that smell?"

Sunako pointed to me.

Mistress Lethe walked up to me and ran her face along my shoulder and up my neck, exhaling softly in my ear. "Oh my! Any chance I can take him home for a few hours? I'm sure I have a job that he could help me finish, a chore that requires an extra body." Mistress Lethe's eyes were half shut with a predatory smile that I was a bit uncomfortable with.

"I'm afraid your bold yet revealing request must go unanswered tonight. Elma gave me strict orders that he not leave my side until he meets Lady Silk." Sofia smiled and shrugged.

"Then, please, allow me to invite you both. You know, the more the merrier, and I am sure he could easily finish us off and come back for more."

"Oh, you filthy thing! With that, we will see you in the morning and not a moment sooner."

Mistress Lethe smiled and took her leave.

Sofia smiled, shaking her head. "Slade, it looks like your cut is all healed up, thanks to Sunako. Wait, shouldn't this have taken at least a few hours? Where is the scar?"

Sunako said, "Weird. That should have taken longer. Perhaps my ability is getting stronger."

Sofia asked, "Slade, do you think you would you be comfortable sleeping in bed with us? We could make up your own bed if you want. It's your choice, after all."

I wanted to say yes.

Cheri stood on the bed and chimed in with, "If he sleeps in a bed alone, he could get up and go anywhere or kill us in our sleep. I vote he sleeps next to Sunako. That way, if he tries to gut us in our sleep, we will be woken by Sunako's shrill, desperate screams as she clings to a life that is rapidly approaching its end."

Cheri acted out the imaginary death as she fell on the bed, shaking and twitching, while making deep gurgling sounds from her throat. Sunako crinkled her nose and gave Cheri the same rude gesture with her finger Cheri had made earlier.

I yawned, crawling on top of Cheri and locking eyes with her. "I was thinking I could sleep next to you, Cheri. I could hold you tight all night long." I winked.

Both Sofia and Sunako burst into laughter. "Holy shit! Did you just make a joke?"

Sunako ran out of the room.

"I think I did. Was it funny? And why did Sunako run out of the room? Did I offend her?"

Sofia was still laughing. "It was very funny, and no, you did not offend anyone. You made her laugh so hard, I think she was going to piss herself."

"I didn't think it was that funny. I think it was creepy with a hint of funny. Now, do you want to get off me before I drink from you again?" Cheri squinted.

I replied, "I will let you drink deep if I can taste you." I breathed slowly into her ear, and she shuddered.

"Sofia, please get him off me before I drink from him again."

Sofia took my hand, and I crawled off Cheri. Her eyes never left mine.

Sunako came back in the room. "Creepy? We all drank his blood like a bunch of depraved vampires." She hugged me from behind, placing her face against mine, and said, "You're my new best friend." Then, she kissed me on the cheek and jumped back onto the bed.

Sofia said, "Time to get some sleep so we can have a fun day tomorrow. I know I shouldn't have to say this, but no one try and drink Slade in the night."

Cheri got up and turned off the lights. The glow of the moon came through the window. I saw the silhouettes of the girls as they changed.

"Slade, put this on, and get under the covers." Sofia handed me the same thing they wore: a full-length night dress. Then I got into bed, and the girls followed, Sofia on one side and Sunako on the other. Cheri asked Sofia to sing us to sleep. I lay flat on my back, Sofia's voice filling the room with its beautiful sound.

When it was over, Sunako rolled toward me and put her leg over mine. Her arm was across my chest; she laid her face on my shoulder.

She whispered so low that I thought I might have imagined it if it were not for the heat of her breath, "I have you safely in my arms. I will protect you as you dream."

I suddenly could not hold a thought. My eyes became too heavy. I fought to say thank you, but I lost control of my mind. Sleep crashed, and I dreamt of water, blood, tears, and a long fall into love with a strange, dark-skinned, green-eyed woman who fell with me. She whispered things I couldn't hear and disappeared just before I hit the ground.

Chapter 5

Meet and Greet

Suddenly, the room was too bright. Sunlight violently flooded the room and blinded me as someone threw open the shades. My arms were uncomfortably tingling. I felt like I was being held down, and my vision was a little blurry. I could barely make out Cheri and the figure standing next to her at the foot of the bed.

Cheri said, "Rise and shine, people!"

My vision returned to sharp focus. The girl next to Cheri was covering her mouth, her eyes wide. Both Sunako and Sofia were nestled under my arms. Sofia's head was on my chest, and Sunako's face was against my neck with her arm just above Sofia's head. Sunako was breathing rhythmically in my ear.

Cheri yelled again, "Time to get up!" She kicked the bed.

Sunako jumped up, rubbing her eyes with a big yawn. She said, "That was the best sleep I've had in a long time." She giggled as she got out of bed. "Well, will you look at this?"

I tapped Sofia on the shoulder. The only reply was a tight squeeze as she snuggled closer. Then as her mouth was about to meet mine, the unknown girl called out to Sofia loudly.

"Mistress Sofia! I bid you a good morning. Mistress Lethe will be ready to receive you in ten minutes. She requests you bring the stranger and milk."

Sofia raised her free arm and waved at the girl.

"Let's give Sofia a few minutes to wake up, lest she become grumpy," Cheri told everyone. I heard the door close not too long after.

"Sofia. Sofia, wake up." I rolled her onto her back so that I could get up, but her arms came around my neck, her eyes still closed.

She asked, "Would you kiss me if I asked you to?" Her eyes opened slowly, a smile gracing her beautiful lips. Her fingers gripped my neck tightly. Without warning, she had me on my back and sat on top of me. Her hands on my chest held me down with surprising strength—her gift had not been exaggerated. "Slade, tell me what you see when you look at me." She slid the straps off her shoulders, her top sliding down to her midsection.

"I see the angel who saved me. I see the woman who I would escape death again to impress. I see my past in your future. I see *you*!"

A single tear spilled from her eye. I didn't know why I'd said it, but I felt like I knew her. She was strange yet familiar, and I had been waiting to say something that would impress her again.

She leaned in to kiss me, pausing a mere inch above my face. I felt the heat from her lips. Her black hair tickled the sides of my face as she angled her mouth to connect with mine.

"Will you lov—"

A loud coughing sound cut Sofia's words off, and our heads turned to see a smiling Mistress Lethe.

"Mistress Lethe! Your arrival could not have been any more ill-timed," Sofia hissed.

"Mistress Sofia, have I come at an inopportune time, or am I just in time for a little snack before breakfast?"

Sofia looked at me and said, "To be continued." She looked frustrated with Mistress Lethe's timing and comment. "Come on, Slade. Put on the clothes Cheri brought you, and let us get some food before Mistress Lethe tries to have us for breakfast."

"Don't forget the milk, Sofia. I'll see you at my cottage in a few."

Sofia handed me the milk. "Let's get going. I can only imagine what Lethe is telling the girls right now."

I opened and held the door. "After you, Mistress Sofia." I bowed slightly as she walked by.

She took my hand and asked, "Who are you really? Where do you come from?"

I smiled and leaned in close to her ear. "I seem to be no one, but I can yours. Wherever I came from could not be as good as being here with you."

Sofia shuddered, and we stepped outside. The other cottage was so close that we could see it as we left ours. It seemed even brighter outside. A warm breeze carried the scent of food that beckoned me forward as if an invisible hand were leading me by the nose. We arrived and knocked on the cottage door, which opened instantly.

"Good morning, I am Miss Aelia. Please come in. Mistress Lethe is waiting for you in the dining room. Right this way." Miss Aelia escorted us to the table, where upon entering, the room's occupants fell silent, all eyes directed toward us.

Mistress Lethe spoke, "Mistress Sofia, please accept my apology. As our food would have begun to get cold, we proceeded to dine without you and your handsome guest. May I remind you that etiquette dictates punctuality in matters such as these?"

Sofia smiled. "Mistress Lethe, it is I who should apologize. Tardiness has no real excuse, especially when one is invited into the cottage of one of the best cooks in the community. I hope I can make it up to you."

"Where are my manners, Sofia? I trust you have worked up a healthy appetite from this morning's workout? Even if your belly is full, I am sure you could make room for some eggs and fried tomatoes. We chopped up some potatoes and fried them up as well. The eggs were made in your favorite way: sunny-side up, if I remember correctly."

Laughter erupted from the table. Mistress Lethe's eyes were locked with Mistress Sofia's for a long moment. Out of nowhere, they both started to laugh. Then Sofia hugged Mistress Lethe.

Mistress Lethe whispered in Mistress Sofia's ear just loud enough for me to hear, "Mm-hmm! I can smell the sweet, sweaty scent of your arousal—it's dizzying. And I can smell him on your skin. You wear him well, like a fine perfume." Mistress Lethe's eyes bore into my soul as she smiled. "Slade, as my personal guest, please sit here at the head of the table so that we may all easily enjoy your company. Mistress So—"

"Do you think it would be okay to dispense with the formalities due to the informal gathering?" Sofia questioned.

"I thought you'd never ask. Now, Sofia, please sit across from me. I want to hear all about your man-slave. How did you come to be rewarded with such an exotic prize? I don't believe I have ever even seen or heard of you talking about a boy in all the years I have known you. I always thought you were interested in Cheri with the way you two are joined at the hip. Or is that due to Cheri's reckless abandon for rules?"

"Lethe, I'm sure I don't know what you are saying. Cheri is the model of civility, and her kindness knows no bounds. I'm sure that anyone with a pair of eyes could see that she holds a certain grace in the way she speaks and flutters about." A huge smile began to grow, not only on Sofia's face, but also on the other girls' faces at the table. I slowly sipped my coffee.

Lethe stood up to get the milk. "Oh, my dear Sofia, if you're going to bullshit me, at least allow me to put on my work boots."

The room began to laugh, but I just sat there, trying to understand. The joke had escaped me. A plate was placed in front of me, and I thanked the young girl who brought it to me.

"Slade, welcome to my little cottage. Allow me to introduce my friends. The one that greeted you at the door is Aelia. This is Phoebe, and this is my little kitty cat, Chloe."

Everyone was staring at me.

I didn't know if I was supposed to speak, so I stood up and said, "Mistress Lethe, Chloe, Phoebe, Aelia, thank you for being such welcoming and kind hosts. Your warmth fills me with happiness. I am humbled to be in your presence."

They looked shocked, so I nervously took my seat. I looked back and forth, noting Cheri's small smile and Sofia's flushed cheeks. Sofia started smiling, but the room was silent.

"Did I say something wrong? Because it was not my intention to offend."

"Sofia, I have never seen such a well-refined slave, and I have never heard that accent before." Lethe slowly shook her head. "Sofia, Slade is not a slave, is he?"

"He is a guest of Lady Silk and will be treated as such." Sofia winked at me.

Lethe stared at me. "If he's not a slave, then he must be a royal with the way he speaks. The clothes I saw him in last night were a bit day-to-day, but his looks? Yes, he must be a royal! Master Slade or *Lord* Slade. Oh, feel how it rolls off your tongue. Have you come here to secretly inspect our little House, its inhabitants, and slaves? Maybe you have come to pick the best of the best for a bride or maybe a harem? Oh, please let it be a harem. Maybe he is a prince like in the stories of the old days, from the far-off lands."

I asked, "Are you all slaves?" I was having a hard time with the thought of them being owned. *Am I a slave?* "Please tell me you're not slaves."

"Does he not know? I think I will let you have that talk with him. I'm sorry, Slade. I truly did not mean to upset you," Lethe apologized.

I just smiled at her, but my head was spinning. *Who am I? Am I a good person or a bad person? Freeman or slave?*

Sofia put her fork down. "I will tell you, but you must keep it a secret until Lady Silk has a chance to meet with him. Slade has no memory. Nothing before I found him. I think he fell in the river, hit his head, then washed up on our bank. He could be anything, and with the way he speaks, he's clearly educated, so I don't think he could be a slave."

"Anything but an Oncari," Cheri said with a smile. "So, that is a plus."

Lethe said, "Oncari? Are you daft? They're just a scary campfire story about shapeshifting child-eaters. They're not real. I must say, you three are anything but boring."

The food was delicious, and I offered to help clean up, much to my host's protests. The rest of the women retired to the main room.

Chloe and Phoebe moved around like two little hummingbirds.

Phoebe said, "Slade, you're staring. Have you never seen clones before?"

"Cheri is a clone, but, no, I haven't seen two at the same time until now." I had to have looked dumb.

"Think of us as twins. Slade, what are you wearing? It smells great." Aelia took hold of my arm and sniffed my hair.

"I don't smell it, but Sofia likes it."

Chloe spoke, "It's not so bad, you know, being a slave. It's not like the old times where being a slave was terrible. Here, we work and train; we are given free time and the choice to pick our mates. Those who are paired up are never separated. The ladies are very kind to all of us so long as no one harms anyone else, and the rules are few."

Chloe's talk made me feel better. We finished our chores.

They led me to the main room where the others were sitting.

Lethe asked, "How did you like doing chores?"

"I find it to be a necessary evil of sorts, but the girls did most of the work, I will admit."

"Oh, honey, we are women. There are no girls here. Once a girl turns fourteen, they're considered an adult. Worry not. We know you meant nothing by it." They'd seen my face turn red. "Sofia has filled me in on the rest of your story. I will say, you could not have been taken in by a nicer person."

"I feel blessed. I promise to one day repay the kindness I have been shown."

"Slade, may I smell you?" Lethe walked over to smell me while her fingers traced my face and lips. "Sofia, you're right. He smells wonderful. I thought it was just last night. You're so lucky."

"I'll feel lucky after we see Lady Silk and she lets him stay." Sofia smiled.

Lethe returned the smile and said, "I have a feeling they will find a way to satisfy that promise and themselves at the same time." A pillow flew across the room toward Lethe, but it hit thin air. Lethe was sitting on the couch one second, then standing next to me the next. She gave my backside a little squeeze. "I'm sorry. I simply could not help myself. Slade, can you guess what my gift is?"

"I take it that you are very fast."

Lethe moved around the room as a blur. The only real detectable movement was a trail—the color of her clothes.

Sofia stated, "I'm sorry, but we must take our leave. We're going to show Slade around the grounds. Thank you for the amazing breakfast and wonderful company."

"It was our pleasure. I hope you get things squared away with this fine young specimen." Lethe offered her hand.

I slightly bowed and kissed it.

"Oh my! You're a real Prince Charming. Sofia, I'm so envious of your find. Slade, it was very nice to have met you, and I look forward to seeing more of you again. Don't forget how well I can cook. I will always have something for you to eat here." She winked.

Sofia smiled. "Lethe, I trust you will keep what you have seen and heard today to yourself. I would hate to become salacious gossip."

"You have my word. These lips will be sealed. Hey, if you get to keep him, you could bring him over for a little Welcome to the House of Ribbons Party. We could break him in properly to the ways things are here." Lethe kissed Sofia on the cheek.

Aelia, Phoebe, and Chloe waved goodbye, and we left.

As we walked, my new friends pointed out people and things. We ended up at an area where two young boys were fighting.

"They are training. It begins at age ten. Everyone learns to fight in case we need to protect ourselves or our House. Do you want to watch for a bit?" Sunako held my hand.

"Yes, please. Sofia, may I ask a question?

She nodded.

"Are you, Sunako, and Cheri slaves?"

She smiled and took my other hand. "I guess it's time to have the talk. Clones are bought and sold sometimes. Lady Silk will come home with a natural-born sometimes, but yes, they are owned. They serve her, and she takes very good care of them. She never calls anyone a slave, and they can earn their freedom. But where would they go? The ones that have been freed have stayed with us, like Mr. H. There are people out there in the world that would put clones in chains or make them do the work of a prostitute or sex slave. No thank you. I like it here where I'm safe, well-fed, and loved. You look uncomfortable."

I replied, "The word *slave* makes me oddly uncomfortable and angry at the same time. What if I'm someone's slave or a royal? If that is true, I would have to leave this place. I want to stay here with you three."

They were all smiles.

"Slade, what would you do if we find out that you're a royal?"

I answered immediately, "If I were a royal, I would buy Cheri, and I would grant her freedom. Then, I would give you two whatever you wanted to come with me, even if I had to beg you three to stay with me." I could tell my answer surprised Sofia.

Sunako laughed. "I think we would take you up on that offer, provided that you are really a good guy. Last thing we would need is to find out that you were an evil overlord."

Cheri looked at me and said, "Why would you free me? I'm just a clone, and I've only been wicked to you."

"Cheri, you deserve to live free. I want you to be free. You're a person, not a clone. No one chooses how they are born."

Cheri smiled. Then Sofia called out to get a man's attention, waving him toward us.

As he walked up, Sunako said, "You will like this guy. He is like you, Slade. Very nice. He is one of our best fighters and an excellent ranger. Just don't play cards with him. He's a real snake in the grass."

"He said he has the gift of luck. It makes him a better fighter and a great teacher. He trains people to be unpredictable in a fight. He is much more free-form in his style, but he makes it more fun than it is meant to be."

I liked how Sofia explained everything to me.

"Ah, Mistress Sofia, Miss Cheri, Miss Sunako. Good afternoon."

"Helge, good afternoon. This is Slade. He's a personal guest of Lady Silk and will be here a few days, maybe longer, if the fates have anything to say about the matter." Sofia grinned.

Mr. H extended his hand. "Welcome to the great House of Ribbons."

I shook his hand. His smile was both soft and genuine. He had a slightly slanted scar on his right cheek that was roughly an inch and half long.

"I received word earlier that you were given some time off. Not to worry, I told the class some old stories and asked some questions to help sharpen their minds. We're about to do a three-on-one fight then some sparring. Do you think Slade would like to stay and watch? Maybe get a round or two?"

I could feel him sizing me up but not in an aggressive way.

"As much as I would like to see what he can do, without Lady's Silk direct permission, he is only allowed to sightsee. Is your wife home today, or is she still at Lady Velour's? I was hoping to speak with her as soon as possible."

"Then you're in luck. She came home this morning. Slade, it was very nice to meet you. I hope to see you again."

We left to seek out Helge's wife, and after a short walk, we came upon a reddish-brown cottage. Cheri knocked on the door, and a small child answered the door.

"Hello, Kai. Is your mommy home?" Sofia's voice was different when she spoke with the boy.

"Mommy, Sofia is at the door!" He stared at me silently until his mother came to the door. She had pretty silver hair that shined in the sun.

"Run along, Kai. Sofia! So, the rumor I see standing before me is true. Welcome, I am Mistress Dawn. You must be Sofia's stranger."

Sofia inquired, "Dawn, I was hoping you could help me by using your gift on Slade. What can you tell me of his intentions?"

"Oh! I see. Come in. Have a seat." Her table was long and could seat eight people effortlessly. "Sofia, may I have a word with you in private, if that's okay?"

Sofia got up and escorted Mistress Dawn into the other room. I sat and looked around the room, which was covered in paintings. One looked just like Sofia, Cheri, and Sunako. In another, Dawn was with her family. They looked so lifelike that I stood to get a closer look. I don't think the ladies knew I could hear them.

"Sofia, you look worried. Are you feeling well?" Dawn placed her hand on Sofia's.

Sofia told Dawn the story of how she met Slade and everything that had happened since. "I don't know, Dawn. The second I laid eyes on Slade, I had a weird feeling in my stomach. It feels, well, I don't know how to explain it. Like I look at him, and I want to throw up, but not out of disgust or anything like that. I see that Sunako has taken an unusually deep interest in him. Cheri has been more aggressive toward Slade than I have ever seen her be toward anyone. Please, tell me: do you think he is using an ability on us?"

Dawn laughed, hugging Sofia close. "Oh, my sweet little fool. Have you overlooked the possibility that you are crushing on him? And by the looks of it, you're crushing hard. So are the other two."

Sofia was shocked and silent for a bit. "I did try to kiss him twice. I can understand Sunako, but Cheri? I think you might be wrong about that one. I think she hates everyone."

"Oh, my dear Sofia. Who knows matters of the heart better than Mistress Dawn? Now, let us do what you have come here to do and look into his heart."

Dawn and Sofia walked back into the room.

I asked Dawn, "Did you paint these?"

"I painted them, so I could always see the ones I love. I can paint something as if it's right in front of me, even if it was years ago, down to the smallest detail. I have painted all three ladies, and a few lords have traveled from afar to have me paint them. It is a great honor to have people come from far and wide. Slade, may I hold your hand? I would like to see something."

I gave her my hand. She probed inside, which felt much like a feather in my ear. Then she stopped.

"I have what I need. Sofia, one more minute in the other room if you please?"

They hurried out of the room. Cheri looked agitated again.

"What did you find out? Tell me, tell me." Sofia clasped her hands together as if praying.

"My word, Sofia, I have never seen you this excited. What you want to know is how he feels, if it's real, and what you should do about it." Dawn smiled, running her hand down the side of Sofia's face. "That boy feels so deeply for you that he does not even have the words yet to tell you of the song in his heart. Give him time so that he can sing you into his arms. Until then, he is yours. But he is also deep in his feelings for Sunako and confused about his feelings toward Cheri.

"Based on your story, I believe I know why he has these feelings. But it's all just a theory. I think you're his first—his first woman—and you showed him a great kindness. You showed him unconditional love. I think he can sense it. Then, you have Sunako. She used her gift on him, while you sang to him. It must have made him feel like a baby in his mother's arms, so warm, soft, and loved. How many times have we had someone falling for a healer? I think it comes with the gift, but it always wears off in a few days. I think you have enough to think about. Please use proper judgment in this matter."

As the sun went down, we returned to Sofia's light-blue cottage. We had some more stew, and Cheri traded for some honey bread, which was delicious. They told me stories about the people I'd met and a few I'd not yet met. We laughed a great deal.

Is this what it feels like to be home? Do I have a place to call home? Does anyone miss me out there, or am I completely alone? With that, loneliness tried to rush in, but I pushed it out of my mind. Sunako and I washed the dishes, while Cheri and Sofia showered. When they were done, Sunako went for a quick shower. She walked by, wearing only a smile. Her hair looked like wet silk, and I wanted to touch it.

Sofia said, "Your turn, Slade. Don't forget to wash behind your ears."

Cheri called out to me, "Yeah, don't forget to wash that cute ass."

I added, "I was hoping you would wash it for me."

Cheri winked and threw a small pillow at me. I caught it and gently tossed it back. As I showered, the loneliness came back, only much stronger. The idea that I might be no one was eating at me. The heat from the water brought me no comfort. After the shower, I worried about meeting Lady Silk. I climbed into bed, and both Sunako and Sofia claimed their spots closest to me. I tried to force my mind to give up my secrets. *Who am I?*

I asked that question hundreds of times as I drifted off into the inky blackness of sleep. I dreamt that I was yelling for help in a mirror, my reflection mimicking me but just slightly out of time. I kept yelling, “Help me!” But even when I covered my mouth, I yelled and banged on the mirror. I was asking for help, and no one came. I was left alone, lying on the ground with only my reflection looking down on me while beating his fists on the mirror. My mirrored self wouldn’t stop screaming for help.

Chapter 6

Playing It Cool

The ladies and I woke to a loud knocking at the door. A nervous look shot across Sofia's half-awake face, and the women rushed to the door, falling over one another to open it.

A young boy stood barefoot at the doorstep. "Mistress Sofia, Lady Silk will see you all at nine a.m. Miss Elma says he is to come dressed in what he arrived in."

Sofia asked, "Was there anything else?"

He said, "Lady Silk came home early with Lady Velvet and Lady Velour. Everyone seems upset."

"Is that all, Cooper?" Sofia asked him as if she knew there was something else he wanted to say.

"Mistress Sofia, may I please have a treat?" He smiled.

Sofia asked, "Cheri, can you please get two pieces from a jar in the kitchen?"

Cheri obeyed and returned in a hurry.

"I will give you two pieces. One for doing great at your new job as messenger, and the second is for being a little cutie. But, please, in the future, don't use a stick to knock on the door. It makes a scary sound so early in the morning. I almost died of fright."

Cooper smiled, running off to wherever he came from. The door closed.

"Shit! We have less than forty-five minutes. Sunako, Cheri, get dressed. Slade, put on the clothes you came in. Take everything you own." Sunako and Cheri looked very worried as well.

My new friends were moving fast, getting dressed in light-brown clothes with brightly colored stripes on their shirt and shorts.

"Hey Slade, would like me to explain the colors on our clothes?" asked Sunako.

"I was just wondering about that?" Slade said.

"I wear a three-quarter sleeve tan shirt with bright yellow and purple stripes on the right shoulders that runs from my elbow down my back. I also wear tan shorts with red trim and black lace-up boots that can handle rough terrain."

"Cheri wears a three-quarter sleeve light-blue shirt with bright yellow and purple stripes that run down the right shoulder to her elbow then down her back; tan shorts with green trim; and black boots. Sofia wears a three-quarter sleeve hunter-green shirt with bright yellow and purple stripes that run down both shoulders to her forearm then down her back with gold trim on the neck and shoulder cuffs; hunter-green shorts with gold trim; and black boots with silver tips that look more like weapons than a fashion statement. The gold trim on her shorts indicates Sofia is a mistress. Any color could be worn on the trim of the shirts, shorts, dresses, or pants, but a mistress always has to wear gold trim."

When they were dressed, each one braided the others' hair. The braids were all different. I was dressed but felt out of place.

"Ladies, you all look so beautiful." I fought not to stare at them, so I looked around the room like I'd lost something. "Are these your uniforms?"

"It's kind of like a uniform, but this is our formal dress for seeing Lady Silk or visiting another House. Don't worry, Slade. You look good. Now listen to me. Speak only when spoken to. Never lose your head for any reason, no matter what happens!" Sofia looked worried.

I wondered if she knew something I didn't know. Either way, I would find out soon enough.

"Stop, Sofia! You're going to scare him. Lady Silk just got news of the stranger. That's what the others are calling him. I think it sounds awesome." Cheri walked up to me and said, "Hey, *stranger*. See, it sounds awesome."

Sunako smiled and winked, so I winked back.

"What is the worst that can happen? They make him leave?" Sofia was pacing back and forth.

Sunako started to laugh. "They could execute him then the rest of us. I think that would be the worst that could happen."

"Real nice, Sunako. Way to help relieve the tension." Sofia paced faster.

"Sunako, that's not helping the situation right now!" Cheri said while chewing a bit of a treat.

Sunako said, "I'm sorry. That was not what I meant to say. I meant only to imply the worst could happen." She was eating a piece of rabbit meat. She pulled some from her mouth, then offered it to me. I held out my hand, but she shook her head. I opened my mouth, and she placed a piece in there. She whispered, "I'm glad to have met you, and I hope you get to stay. I don't want you to leave us." Sunako held back tears as she reached her arms out to hug me. While in my arms, I felt her heart beating thunderously.

Sofia walked up to me and said, "I want you to stay as well." She hugged me and kissed me on the lips and ear.

Cheri looked at me and said, "Don't look at me. I'm not a hugger. You would have to really impress me to give you a kiss, but I agree with Sunako and Sofia. I would like you to stay. Maybe not in this cottage but somewhere here within the House of Ribbons where I could see you here and there."

"Slade, do you remember what we talked about? How to be silent and only speak when spoken to? If someone is talking to you, always look the person in the eyes. If anyone asks a question, tell only the truth. Lady Silk should have one of her oracles with her. You will be able to hold no secret from them," Sofia spoke quickly.

"I remember what you said yesterday about the people with magical abilities."

"No, it is not magic. They have a natural ability, like a gift. Magic users learn from books, and other magic users utilize crystals candles and enchanted items. Not everyone can learn magic, but those who do will stick together or keep to themselves. We are born with these abilities. We practice and strengthen our gifts." Sofia looked worried again.

"How do I know if I have an ability?" I looked around at the girls.

Cheri shrugged.

"I guess we'll find out sooner or later," Sunako said.

Sofia said, "We know nothing about where you come from, who your people are, or if you're some kind of clone. You could be a slave. More importantly, in your case, a runaway slave that hit his head, then got amnesia. I really hope you're not a runaway slave."

"Why? What happens to runaway slaves when they get caught?"

Sofia was silent for a few seconds.

"They are executed. Most of the time, in the most horrible way to set an example to other slaves." She cleared her throat. "It's time to leave. I would rather be a little early than late."

She seemed a bit calmer.

We left the cottage, and I wondered if I would ever see it again. I shouldn't worry—I'd done nothing wrong. As we walked toward the large house, no one spoke, but people waved when we passed by. We arrived at the main door, and Elma was there waiting for us.

"Ladies, I trust you told the stranger our rules. Lady Silk is almost ready to see you. Boy, use your manners. Lady Velour and Lady Velvet are here today, so be mindful of your tongue. Please, come in. Wait right here until you are called, whether one at a time or as a group."

"Elma, is it true? Is Lady Silk upset today?" Sofia spoke in a low but direct tone.

Elma nodded. "Lady Silk is upset, but not because of the stranger. Something happened at the House of Dreams a little over a week ago. That is why Lady Silk has been back and forth so much lately. But you did not hear that from me. I will let Silk know you're here. Please have a seat and relax until I call you."

We sat in uncomfortable silence.

Chapter 7

First Impressions of Lady Silk, the Master of Shadows

"Time to come in, girls. Bring the stranger." Elma held the door open as we entered. "Sofia, you know where to stand."

It was a large banquet hall. I half expected to see Lady Silk on some giant throne, but no, she was on a couch flanked by four women, who appeared important. They were on a platform a few feet higher than everyone else. Two banners on opposite sides of the room were yellow and purple—the House colors.

When Lady Silk spoke, her voice was strong and dark, like tinted glass, which belied her delicate feminine form. "Sofia, I am told that you have found me a stranger, then nursed him back to health, with Sunako's help, I presume? He has lived with you for the last few days. I hear he has no memory of who he is, where he comes from, or who his people are. Are these things true, as to the best of your knowledge?" Lady Silk was completely still and looked more like a statue than a living, breathing person.

Sofia spoke with confidence, "Yes, Lady Silk. I found this boy very close to the water's edge. Sunako and I nursed him back to health. I held him while singing as Sunako healed his body with her gift. The boy indeed stayed with us, as per Elma's orders, and he has never left our sight. He has been a perfect gentleman every second, and yes, as far as we know, he is telling the truth about not having any memories from before I encountered him."

Lady Silk asked, "Does this boy know his own name, or have you three given him a name? Did he have any weapons or personal effects on him? Does he bear the mark of a slave or clone? Lastly, and more importantly, has he demonstrated any abilities?" Lady Silk threw one leg over the other, then put her clasped hands on her knee.

"I found Slade wearing what he's wearing now, minus socks and boots. His dress is blue-green. It has no patterns, although the back-right pocket is colored a strange pink. A backpack was found a few feet away from him with identical clothes and boots attached. Slade wore one tan belt, larger in width than any I have ever seen, with a large buckle. He has two dresses, two smoke-gray shirts, four pairs of black socks, and one pair of tan boots that are reminiscent of heavy-duty combat boots. The belt is an identical color to the boots. He also had two weapons. One is a dagger with etchings; it has a five-inch handle wrapped in leather with a thirteen-inch, double-edged blade. The whole dagger is made of one piece of metal that makes a strange sound when you tap it with your nails or against other metal. It bears no scratches or signs of use. Embedded at the end of the handle is a greenish jewel.

"He also has a six-inch, single-edged knife with etchings along both sides of the blade. It was strapped to his right leg a few inches below his knee. He has a small animal hide satchel with one large silver coin inside. He was wearing a silver ring with little designs all around it on his left hand, but it won't come off. We tried everything we could think to remove it. He has a silver bracelet with eighteen very small holes with some unknown writings or designs. We identified the words *Batch Slade*. With that information, we have elected to call him Slade. The strange thing is, the bracelet is not removable except by his own hand. We've had no luck trying to get it off ourselves. Lastly, he has a dull silver emblem that is attached to his skirt. It's a few inches under the belt on his right pocket, which has letters on it. We have inspected him from top to bottom. Oddly, this boy bears not a mark, brand, or even a scar, for that matter." Sofia held the room's attention. Her hands remained at her sides the entire time. "As for any abilities, we've yet to observe any."

Lady Silk asked, "Slade, is it? To my left is Lady Velour, and to my right is Lady Velvet. They are my sisters. I believe you are aware of that fact by now. Behind me is Mistress Topaz and Mistress

Saffron. I trust the newly titled Mistress Sofia kept you fed, comfortable, and entertained?"

"I am very honored to meet you, Lady Silk, as well as you, Lady Velour and Lady Velvet." I bowed my head to each woman. "Sofia is a credit to this great House. For me to ask for anything more would have been an insult to her generosity."

Lady Silk studied me like a hawk—she would miss nothing. She looked half-relaxed, half-ready to strike.

"Well said. I see your education has escaped the black hole of oblivion that has consumed your memories, while you hoard other memories away like a treasure. With that said, I would like to officially welcome you to the House of Ribbons. Welcome to my House. I wish I were there to greet you when you first arrived, but it was Mistress Sofia who welcomed you and treated you as I would have. She is the shining example of a lady-in-training. She is the head of her cottage, which includes Sunako and Cheri. Henceforth, you will refer to Sofia as Mistress Sofia in public. Behind the closed doors of her cottage is up to her. Please, bring me your bracelet, ring, the coin, and both weapons. Then, let me have a close look at you. Hopefully, I will be able to recognize something that can lend a clue as to who you are and where you might be from."

As I approached, Lady Silk extended her hand. "First, the coin." She rolled it around with her slender, delicate fingers. "Interesting. It's oddly heavy. I've never seen a coin like this, and I do not recognize the man on it. He must be a king. I don't recognize these words or letters or this symbol."

She passed it to Lady Velvet then to Lady Velour. They all agreed about the weight, indecipherable writings, and symbol.

"May we see your bracelet? I mean, may I try to remove it?" She tried, but all she managed to do was move me around a bit.

I effortlessly removed it and placed it in her hand.

"Wow! This foreign metal is as light as a feather." Lady Silk tried again to bend it open. "Slade, what is the trick to this thing?"

I opened the gap, and Lady Silk extended her wrist to me. "May I?"

I placed it on her wrist.

She inspected it closely, looking at the holes. "Only a machine could have done this. It's just too precise to be done by hand. The lettering is engraved with smooth ridges. I have never seen a piece of jewelry like this. It's much too fine for a slave, besides the fact that only he can take it off. So, what good would that do for a master? A slave is identified by a clearly visible mark on the neck or forearm, nonremovable collar, bracelet, or anklet that tells everyone that the slave is owned by someone. In the case of a runaway, they can be identified and returned. Now, let me have a good look at this ring of yours." She looked at it as she moved my hand around. "May I try to remove it?"

I nodded, and she slowly spun it around in a circle, trying to pull it forward. When that didn't work, she pulled a bit harder and smiled. "Topaz, come put his finger in your mouth and try to remove it."

Topaz held eye contact as she put my finger in her mouth; her tongue danced around the ring. Then, she slowly pulled my finger out of her mouth. She pulled on the ring, but it wouldn't come off.

Lady Silk smiled again. "Strange indeed. Topaz, tell me, what was it like having him inside your mouth?"

All three sisters laughed, but Topaz turned bright red, her crystal-blue eyes never leaving mine.

"Well, Topaz? I'm waiting. What did you feel?"

"It was exciting in a foreign way to me."

The three sisters laughed again.

"No, my sweet Topaz. I mean, what did you see? But I do thank you for that frank description of your personal feelings."

"I'm sorry, Lady Silk. I didn't try to read him, and I wasn't thinking straight. Shall I try again?"

"Soon, my beautiful Topaz, soon. Wait a minute, and I will set you loose on him."

They laughed again, and Topaz looked away from me, still red.

"Now, turn slowly, and let us have a good look at you. Sofia, his skirt is a color called teal. This spot is coral, not pink. These are rare colors, so I am not surprised you couldn't identify them. Hand me your weapons."

As I did, I swore I saw shadows move in an unnatural way.

"This is a beautiful dagger. My sisters, look at these wondrous etchings. Oh, the metal does make a strange sound when I tap it with my nails. By the gods, look at this jewel. It looks like a large emerald, but it is closer to teal in color. Does the emblem detach from your skirt?"

"Yes." I removed it and handed it to her.

"These are English letters. Slade, can you read this?"

"Yes. 'Vero Nihil Verius.' It means 'Nothing truer than truth.'"

"What about the weapons? What do they say?"

"The dagger has a design on one side, but the other side reads, 'When blood flows, tears follow.' The smaller knife reads, "'Last resort in desperate times.' The other side is just a design."

"What language is this?"

"Latin, my lady."

"Excuse me, Slade."

Lady Silk spoke in a low yet audible tone with Lady Velvet and Lady Velour for a few minutes. Then, she turned to address us:

"We believe Slade must be a non-worker, not a slave or clone. But let's not rule out that he could be a new or special type of clone, one from a faraway royal family. His bracelet may indicate rank and title. These holes are either his number as a clone, or this is his age. If this is his number, then we will encounter more of them within a short time. If so, he will go back to where he came from. He does look about right for the age of eighteen. His weapons are foreign and functional, and with a jewel like this, he must be of some importance or rank. We believe his clothes may be a uniform, due to the elegant look and how they don't restrict movement, much like the Ocil women from where the deserts meet the forests. For those who don't know, the Ocil are made up of mostly warrior women. Only females are allowed the honor to fight, and they only wear a skirt while doing so. The men are mostly used as workers and for breeding. My father has a very good relationship with them.

"Slade, we do not know who you are or where you came from. I have a woman here who can enter your mind, but with your permission, of course. You may refuse, but then I will have to ask you to take what is yours and leave at once. You will then be escorted to the nearest town and told not to return. Please take a moment to think it over," Lady Silk said. "My throat is parched. Elma, please have two bottles of white wine brought to my sisters and me."

Elma snapped, and two little figures scurried away, returning with wine. The young blond boys were about ten years old and dressed in House colors. One held the glasses, while the other poured the wine. They both handed out the three glasses, their movements flawless, like a dance. Then, they receded back to the corners of the room. They had to be clones.

"What say you, Slade? Will you allow Mistress Topaz to read your mind like an open book? We may very well learn everything that we desire to learn about you."

I nodded.

"Excellent, then we can begin. Richter, William take your positions."

I turned to see the two young men move, one behind me, the other on my left.

"No need for concern. This is just a precautionary measure. I trust you understand."

I nodded again.

"Mistress Topaz, you have the floor and an audience. Time to shine."

Topaz's face was still beet-red. I didn't believe her to be more than nineteen years old. I noticed her grace as she walked up to me. Her hair was light blonde with a long snow-white strip on the left side. Her eyes were like crystal-blue jewels.

Mistress Topaz said, "Please relax. This might feel a bit strange."

She took my hands in hers, and we interlocked our fingers.

"Are you ready?"

I smiled and nodded. Suddenly, we were falling through bright empty space. I shut my eyes tight, expecting the ground to rush up and remove my soul.

"Slade. Hey, Slade! Open your eyes. You're safe on the ground with me."

I opened my eyes. We were in a dense forest with no sound, no animals, and no wind.

"Slade, we're inside your mind. Please take me to your earliest memory, and just relax."

We were falling again, and her hand tightly gripped mine. She smiled as we made our way through the clouds. I saw the ground and thought of my feet firmly planted on the grass, and then we were.

"Slade, how did you do that? How did you take us to the ground that fast?"

I looked at her and pointed to a cave in the distance. I started to walk fast, almost dragging her.

"Slade! You're pulling me. Stop now!"

I stopped and placed a finger to her lips. We entered the cave and were transported to the scene three days ago.

"Slade, is this your first memory? In this place, one's mind cannot lie. Nothing is hidden from those of us with my gift. How can this be your first memory? How could you only be three days old?"

I looked at her and said, “Topaz, tell me about Lady Silk. Tell me about the rules of the House of Ribbons.”

Topaz said, “Lady Silk is a Lady of Shadows. She can give temporary life to any shadow. She can be very kind but is a firm believer in rules and the enforcement of them. She is the strongest of her sisters. Slade, how are you doing this to me? I’m supposed to be in control in here.”

“I don’t know how I’m doing this, but I have my own questions. What are your thoughts about me? Are you the only mind reader in the House? You will tell no one about this interaction until we figure it out. Understand? Now, answer my question.”

“Slade, I think you look so different than the others. The way you walk like you don’t have a care in the world, the way you speak and your unfamiliar accent, now this? You make me nervous, curious, and dizzy at the same time. Mistress Saffron can do what I do, and we are called oracles. I will keep our secret if you promise to kiss me here and now.”

The mental projection of your lips touched, but it felt real. It was like a lightning strike—painful and hot. I could see her thoughts. She had been watching me before our first meeting.

As our kiss ended, Topaz said, “I have never done that before. That was amazing and scary at the same time, but please don’t look anymore.”

I pushed past her will. *He is so attractive* and other thoughts that would make most blush slid past my focus.

“That’s not fair. I need just a little privacy, please. I have what I need, so let’s disconnect.”

“Who am I? How can I do this? What did you learn about me?”

“I only know what you know. You are three days old with no memory before that time. Only blackness, which means time before life, yet you have intelligence. We should keep what you can do between us. I will tell Lady Silk that I will need to see you soon to slowly work you. To disconnect, just think of the room where our physical bodies are, and we will wake up.”

I thought about Sofia standing next to me, and my eyes opened.

Topaz and I were back.

Chapter 8

We Might Not Get Tomorrow

"Topaz, please share what you have learned. Who is he? Who are his people? What are his intentions?"

Topaz looked dazed.

"Topaz, are you feeling okay?"

"Yes, Lady Silk. I'm fine. I have been through his entire mind, and he is what he says he is. He is no one. He did not exist before Sofia found him, at least not to his knowledge. No thought was hidden from me. At first, I thought he had amnesia, but those with amnesia still have their memories. They just have a hard time finding them. This is not the case. Slade had nothing before coming here, absolutely nothing. It really is like he just came into existence at that moment."

"Then tell me about his time while here. Do you think he can he be trusted? How has his behavior been? What are his intentions?" Lady Silk seemed annoyed at the lack of answers.

"I will say on my name in this House that he can be trusted. His behavior is that of a well-refined gentleman. He has only been helpful, kind, and honest in these past few days. One can lie with the tongue, but the mind will only speak the truth."

In that moment, I knew could trust Topaz.

"He has no intentions but to stay with Sofia, Sunako, and Cheri. His loyalty to them is astounding. The only troublesome thing I saw was about Cheri."

"Cheri? What has she done now?"

"Lady Silk, after Sofia found Slade, Sunako started healing him because he was violently ill. They put him against a tree to speak, and that is when Cheri got ahold of Slade and tried to drown him. He was then saved by Sofia. Sofia and Cheri fought, while Sunako used her gift on him for a second time."

Lady Silk glared at Cheri as she stood up.

Lady Silk was livid. "Cheri, you've been a pain in my ass one too many times. Your aggressive attitude will stop here and now! This boy could have been an envoy from a far-off place. What if you achieved your goal in killing him? We would have had a problem. First off, I would have had to give you to them. Second, it could have been seen as an act of war, and there are people out there that greatly outnumber us. We're not a fighting House. We work with those who need to find lost people and various other things. We only have a small defense group. You could have endangered us all! You will be punished here and now. Five lashes, and you will not be allowed to be healed for three days. Richter! William! You know what to do. Slade, if you are to stay with us, take this as your first lesson that this type of behavior will not be tolerated. Cheri, this will be your very last chance before exile or worse!"

Cheri walked next to me, then removed her shirt and stood topless. She made no effort to cover her breasts. She was told to remove the rest of her clothes and did as she was told, tearing up. She looked humiliated. I felt her fears, and it made me angry.

Richter moved into position, undoing the clasp that held his whip. I felt his excitement. The look on his face suggested that he both loved and really disliked Cheri. Sunako and Sofia moved to one side to be out of striking distance, but I remained at Cheri's side.

Lady Silk said, "Slade, I would move if I were you, or you might catch a stray strike. Richter, you may begin."

I spoke loudly, "Allow me to take her punishment!"

Richter paused as Lady Silk raised her hand.

"I do not believe what she has done should be considered a punishable offense. I believe she was acting in the best interests of the safety of the House of Ribbons." I took Cheri's hand in mine, and we interlocked our fingers. I said, "Do you trust me?"

"Don't do this." She shook her head.

"I am sorry in advance."

Lady Silk asked them to proceed, and Richter reared his arms back. He thrusted his wrist and hand forward. The whip extended as the tip sought to kiss its target.

I spun Cheri away from the strike, the whip splitting the air. It hit the right side of my face from forehead to ear, just missing my eye. I felt the pain, but what upset me most was the amount of warm blood it drew. It flowed into my right eye, obscuring my vision. One eye, two angry men, and one young woman who'd tried to drown me stood around me.

"Cheri, I have a bad feeling about this. Now do as I command."

William quickly moved toward me.

I shouted, "Kneel!" to Cheri as I kicked my unsuspecting attacker in the stomach. He dropped to the ground with a loud *oof.* Richter tried again to hit Cheri, but I swung my body to block him. The tip angrily bit my skin again, like red-hot metal pressing hard against my upper back. I succeeded in defending her, and she looked up at my face. With my one clean eye, I saw Cheri smile.

She said, "Get them for me!"

As I turned to face Richter, I saw him trying for a third time to hit Cheri. I caught the whip in midair. It stung so much I wanted to yell out, but I would not give that bastard the satisfaction. I wrapped the leathery end around my hand and wrist and yanked hard. Much to Richter's surprise, his instrument of pain had been pulled out of his hand.

I turned my head and handed the whip to Cheri, saying, "A gift for you, my sweet."

Richter ran at full speed with his hands out. He grabbed me by the throat. The sound of my body hitting the wall echoed throughout the large room. He squeezed me so hard I almost blacked out. All I could do was kick him. My foot met his groin, and gravity made him a slave to the cold marble floor. Then I kicked him in the face for good measure.

I did not see nor hear William come up from my side. He wrapped his arms around mine, sticking them at my side. He had the upper hand, and I could feel his breath on my neck. I pushed my chin as hard as I could into my chest, and focusing all the strength I could muster, I thrusted the back of my head into his face. I heard his nose break, his scream silenced with my fast open-handed strike to his esophagus. He hit the floor, unconscious.

Richter had recovered enough strength to make another pass at me. He moved slowly, watching me as he found his footing. I faked a hard right, and he took the bait, swinging his fist out. I spun around to his back, catching him off guard. I reached around his neck with one arm and used the other to lock my wrist in place. Richter twirled around, but all good things had to come to an end. I used all my strength and squeezed. He went to his knees first, and his hands were palm-first on the floor like he was attempting a pushup. Soon, he was asleep on the floor and began to snore loudly.

I did my best to dust myself off, my eye still clouded with thick, drying blood. I reached out my hand toward Cheri, as she was still on her knees.

"Take my hand and get off the floor. That's no place for you."

She took my hand and said, "You must know that we're fucked now, right?"

I said loudly, "Lady Silk of the House of Ribbons, if those were the best you have, then you have my sincerest apologies. I made a promise to these three young ladies. I promised that I wouldn't let them come to any harm due to my arrival or actions."

Lady Silk stood up. "A promise that was not yours to make! These are my girls; you're a stranger. I have half a mind to kill you where you stand."

In the moment, I could count at least five shadows that began to move as if given life.

"Lady Silk, you have every right to take my life, but I ask only this one thing. Please, allow me a few seconds to say thank you to Sofia, Cheri, and Sunako."

Lady Silk nodded.

I walked up to Cheri and said, "Goodbye."

She hugged me tightly.

Then over to Sunako. "Goodbye, my sweet."

She began to cry as she clutched onto me, and I hugged her and kissed her ear.

I moved to Sofia. "Sofia, thank you for caring enough to help me when I could not help myself."

Sofia jumped into my arms and kissed me so hard that our teeth bumped each other. Our tongues danced about, and I felt a foreign emotion that started in my stomach and made its way to my chest. As we finished kissing, she bit my bottom lip gently. Her eyes were wet, and she would not let go of my hand.

I asked her, “Why do I feel this way?”

She began to sob loudly, the tears streaming down her cheeks.

“Time’s up!” Lady Silk had seated herself. Two of her shadows came toward me.

I closed my eyes and thought of my new friends and the strange feelings I had for them. *What will happen to them when I’m gone?* I became angry and opened my eyes. The shadows were standing still, right in front of me. They had no features, not female or male, just black as night. One shadow placed its hand on my shoulder. It was not warm or cold, but it had weight. The one in front thrusted its hand into my chest. At first, there was no pain, just an odd tingle like when my legs would fall asleep. Then, I felt it take my heart. I screamed. I would have dropped to my knees if I weren’t so stiff, but I was losing total feeling throughout my entire body. I reached out to grab its arm, but my hand passed right through it as if it were not there. The pain reached a point where I screamed again, louder that time.

I heard the girls crying. *They must be having the same thing done to them!*

I yelled, “No! No, not them. Let them be!” I felt cold and sickly, but I was fueled by anger.

I reached out to the shadow again, finding it was solid. I pulled its hand out of my chest. It tried to push against me, but it felt more like a small child. I closed my eyes and smiled, punching it in the head, which felt like hitting water—but without the wet feeling. I opened my eyes, and it was gone. The shadow at my shoulder reached in through my back, but as I turned around, I moved back just far enough to hit it in the head. It exploded into shadow-like dust. A third one came at me, and I rammed my hand into its chest. It disintegrated in front of me, and other shadows receded into the black corners of the room.

“Slade! Stop! Where did you learn to fight? The way you moved just looked flawless, like you knew where and when Richter and William would strike. Tell me, how did you touch my shadows? How did you resist their touch? How did you fight them off? Tell me, Slade, would you stay with us after what has happened?”

“Lady Silk, if I may answer the last question first?”

“By all means. You have our undivided attention, and we are all waiting with bated breath.” Her fingers tapped rhythmically on the side of the sofa, her nails clicking one after another on the ornate wooden design.

"Lady Silk, if given the chance to remain and rectify this problem, I feel that you would make a rewarding choice. One that, if not given, would surely be sorely missed based on what you have seen today and what might come of the future. My skills, whatever they are or however they manifest, may be of invaluable use to this great House. Would not a union only benefit you, Lady Silk? I don't know who I am; I don't know if I have any gifts or skills. I do know I would serve at the pleasure of the House of Ribbons and its noble lady, placing all before myself. Because if I don't, we might not get tomorrow."

"Well said, Slade. If you come to have no other abilities outside of fighting, at least you have your silver tongue, and I doubt it will ever let you go hungry. Slade, you are hereby granted temporary admission to the House of Ribbons. Learn our rules well, and do not step out of line again. Consider this your admission fee. Sofia, step forward. I'm assigning Slade to your cottage, regardless of the wants of any member of your household. This includes your desires on the topic, and by the looks of the kiss you gifted him, I would hazard no objections on this matter will be entered. Now, take your leave. Return to your cottage and see that this young man is attended to. Slade, you will always obey Mistress Sofia, no matter what she may ask of you. I will call on you four within a week. Let my words be heard. No violence that has happened today in this room will continue from this point on! Hear me well, Richter, William, and you, Slade! No grudges will be held, no scores to settle, no revenge! Is that understood?"

All three of us answered in unison, "Yes."

"Last matter of business. Slade, this bracelet is your property, and I will give it back, but in the meantime, may I show it to a few friends? With their help, I may be able to decode it and find out who you are and where you come from."

I nodded.

"Excellent! Now, begone with all of you. I have other matters that require my attention."

With that said, Lady Silk unexpectedly flipped my coin in the air toward me, and it was spinning wildly. Time seemed to slow to a painful pace. In fact, everything seemed to be moving at the same speed—not frozen, but as if the coin were met with a great deal of resistance. I could see the little details on the head and tail, and for some reason, I knew its trajectory. As it approached me, I reached my hand straight up and snatched my coin out of the air with two fingers, all without taking my eyes off Lady Silk.

Lady Velour covered her mouth, hiding her facial expressions. Lady Velvet clapped, nodding approvingly. Lady Silk uttered just one word.

"Marvelous."

The four of us took our leave before we wore out our welcome.

Chapter 9

New Friends and Bedsheets

We started the walk back to the cottage, and an odd howl could be heard. There was a cheer from a few people who had been watching.

"Slade, does your face hurt? Because that looks really painful," Cheri said in a low voice.

I said, "It was worth it, as you are unscathed. I will be fine once I can get a drink of water and wash the blood out of my eye. Thank you for asking."

I was in pain, but I was afraid to tell them. It felt right to hold it inside. She reached out and took my hand, giving it a little squeeze. It brought me comfort. Sunako took my other hand as Sofia led the way home. More than a few women gawked as we walked past.

The little boy, Cooper, ran up to Sofia. "Mistress Sofia, is it true? Did Slade really take on both William and Richter at the same time?" As the little man spoke, he acted out his words with a punch here and a kick there, which made me laugh. "Wow! Look at his face!"

"Cooper, not now. Please run along." Sofia shot me a glance, and I was unsure what she was thinking. She opened the door to the cottage and asked Cheri to get something to clean my wounds. Cheri left immediately.

"Sunako, go find Otho. Ask him for three bottles of cherry wine. See if Tova is working and tell her we need her. I will bring Slade in, clean him up, and have him ready for you. Now hurry, honey. Come on in, my bloody prince. Let's get you cleaned up." She got the hot water ready. "Remember what Lady Silk said to you? To obey my every word?"

I nodded.

"Good. Now take it all off, and get into the tub."

I did as I was told.

The water was almost too hot, but I settled into a comfortable position with my head on the back of the tub.

Sofia said, "Slade, stay here and relax until I come back. I'm going next door to get my friend, Mistress Lucy. They should have something for the pain. Do not try to wash yourself, as I want to clean your wounds." As she walked away, she paused at the door, looking back as if to say something. She went to move again but stopped just outside the doorway, staring at me while biting her bottom lip. As she left, she murmured, "Such a prize."

I sat in the hot water, which was tinted crimson. My whole body became relaxed, and I fell asleep. I dreamt of Sofia's face looking down at me while she held me. The look in her eyes was one of love, warmth, and happiness. Without warning, I was in a field, and I saw myself sitting cross-legged under a tree. I was holding a human head, but I couldn't see the face. I was crying in anguish, unable to stop my tears as my pain and rage grew stronger. I was the embodiment of grief.

I stood there and observed myself for what seemed to be almost two days, but in fast motion. As it began to rain, I felt every cool and refreshing drop. I bent over to speak to myself, but when I reached out for my knee, I looked up, and our eyes locked. I could suddenly feel all my pain as if it were mine from the start, which was a significant and terrible mixture of deep sadness, loss, and anger. I was consumed with hatred and grief simultaneously. We were both wedged together in the deepest pit of sorrow. I recognized myself in that moment, as we were the same person at different times of our lives. Our pain was stuck in some kind of loop, and my abhorrence for myself made the eyes glow white on the other version of me. I hated him as much as he hated me. I wanted him dead right there on the spot.

He shouted, "It was you! You did this!" Drool spilled from his mouth, and tears stained his cheeks as he rose to his feet. Each hand looked like they were holding an invisible ball, ready to grab me. "You did this to her! You took her away from me! I will kill you!"

He was howling mad. I almost didn't see him jump for me. Before I could react, I was within his grasp. He was ferocious and strong, like a wild animal, as he squeezed my neck, and tried to bite my face. I did my best to block him, but it only resulted in him biting my hands and arms. I told myself it was only a dream, but the pain still felt real to me. I called out to Sofia for help, but he only became angrier.

As I was slowly losing consciousness, I looked over in the other direction. That was when I saw it: a head that looked like it belonged to Sofia. Her wet hair stuck to the side of her face, her eyes lifeless and mouth agape. My anger deepened, and my strength returned. I had his hands off me and was pushing him toward the tree. I got in a swift kick, pushing him hard against it.

"How did this happen? We promised to protect her!"

"I did, but you did this. You let this happen. I will kill you to save her!"

He pulled out a large dagger, and I could not stop him as he moved with such speed and grace toward me. I failed to grab his arms, and he plunged the knife up until the hilt was in my chest. The pain was unlike anything I'd felt, a white-hot metal burn inside my chest. I was too weak to push him backward. I immediately started to cough up thick blood. Breathing became a burden. I wanted to wake up from the nightmare.

He withdrew the dagger, and the pain became more intense. Even if I wanted to say anything at all, I couldn't. The blood that flowed out of my mouth prevented any noise other than gurgling. I was drowning again, but in my own blood. As I knelt on the wet ground, I watched him recover Sofia's head, then sit back down as he began to cry again. I placed my palms down on the wet grass as I waited to die. My eyes began to close, and my last thought was of Sofia, how she took me in and how I must have failed her. I deserved this for breaking my promise. I fell face-first into the grass, and darkness overtook me.

Suddenly, I gasped for air. I was racked with pain, but at least I could breathe. Cheri was sitting in my lap, covered in blood. My friends were all around me, yelling, moving fast, and calling my name.

I heard one of them yell, "He's awake!"

Another shouted, "What's wrong with his eyes?"

I was in and out of consciousness. Every time I opened my eyes, there was a different person hovering over me. I could feel Sunako's hand holding mine, her gift coursing through my body. Someone else was at my other hand. I finally passed out, sleep taking hold. I had no dreams.

Cheri broke the silence. "What the fuck was that? Can anyone tell me what the hell just happened?"

I rested, Sofia and the other women in the room breathed a little easier. But they were so frozen in silence that one could hear their collective heartbeats.

Forty minutes earlier, Slade had only been asleep for ten minutes. Sunako had been the first to come home. She had put the three bottles on the counter and called out to see if anyone was home, but no one answered. She went to use the bathroom and noticed Slade asleep in the tub. With it being a two-person tub, she thought to herself, *I want to get in and heal him while we're in the water.* She was lost in thought when Cheri popped up behind Sunako and gave her a little poke in the ribs.

"Boo!" Cheri had startled Sunako. "You know, Sunako, I see how you look at him like a hungry animal. Why don't you just go up and touch him if you want to? We practically own him now. Just look at him. Even with all that blood on his face and in the water, tell me you don't want to get in there with him. I don't even like him, and I want to climb on top of him."

"I want to start the healing, so, yes, I want to get on top of him. I mean, in with him, next to him. I meant, next to him." Sunako smiled as she bit at her index finger.

Sofia had arrived with her friends, Lucy and Tova.

Sofia laughed. "Sunako, I found Tova. Wait, what are you two doing? Are you both staring at our naked guest? Sunako, you I can understand, but Cheri? How is he doing?"

"He has not moved in the last few minutes, but Sunako was here before I got here," Cheri said. "Oh, I have these for you." She handed Sofia some salve.

"What do you think?" Sofia asked Lucy and Tova. The two gazed at the silent, incapacitated mystery that was Slade.

"Is it really true? You know almost nothing about him?" Tova asked.

Lucy walked up to Slade. "Can I touch his face?"

"Yes, but keep your hands out of the water, Mistress Lucy."

Lucy walked around Slade, looking at him from every angle.

"He looks like a statue. I've never seen looks like his before, and he's so lightly tanned. No one here looks like him. His hair's an amazing color blond—not too light but with a hint of silver—and look how the light hits it over here. There's slight hint of red. I have only seen one redhead before. You know the old woman who comes a few times a year? She has fiery red and blonde wavy hair."

"Do you mean the old witch? I have never seen her without that cloak she wears. It covers her whole body, her head, and most of her face. They say she isn't human. She scares me," Tova spoke softly.

Lucy laughed. "You're scared of a magic user? Come on. Tova, she is super friendly. Remember the candy I shared with you last month? I got that from her. She says that she enchants the candy to always taste completely different to each person. I still have two pieces left. Oh, I'll trade you both for a night with him. But let's clean him up first," Lucy said. "On second thought, leave him dirty. It will give Momma something extra to do before and after."

"Ten pieces, and you have a deal." Sofia's hand was out, awaiting a shake.

"You know, I only get two to four at a time. Besides, I'm almost twenty, and trust me, I know what to do with him. I could break him in just right for you. It's a damn shame the water is so dark. I can't see what he has to work with." Lucy rubbed her hands together as if to warm them.

"Like I said, ten pieces—take it or leave it. Until then, he's mine. I mean, ours."

Sunako shot Sofia a dirty look, and Cheri was shaking her head with disapproval.

Sofia looked at both of them. "What? It's good candy because it's enchanted."

Just then, Slade began to twitch, shaking violently in the water. He was grabbing at his throat with one hand and the side of the tub with the other.

"I think he's choking!" Cheri jumped in the tub, lifting Slade's head to clear his airway. Just as Cheri lifted Slade's head, he coughed up a chilling amount of blood. Cheri kept trying to clear his airway. Then, Slade opened his eyes, and they were black as night. But still, Cheri was undeterred. Lucy and Tova were shocked, frozen in horror.

Cheri yelled, "Sunako! Tova! Grab his hands and work your gift! He is losing too much blood. He needs you two more than any of us."

They did as they were told. A tear opened in his chest with even more blood spewing from the fissure. Cheri was now covered from head to waist, her hair soaked crimson. It was in her eyes and her mouth. She tried not to clean her fingers in front of Lucy and Tova. Slade's body soon began to settle down as the shaking stopped. Whatever was happening to him was over. The room was as silent as a morgue.

Cheri broke the silence. "Damn, that was intense!"

"Damn it, Cheri! I both literally and figuratively pissed myself with your outburst!" Sofia said, embarrassed and upset.

Sunako and Lucy laughed and said in unison, "I did as well." A part of the bathroom looked like they had just committed a savage murder.

Sofia, still shaking, said, "Okay, let's drain the tub, rinse him off, and draw him some clean, hot water. It will help speed up Tova and Sunako's healing gifts. As soon as he can be moved, get him dried off and put him in bed. Miss Tova, I'm sure you won't mind a sleepover. Mistress Lucy, you're more than welcome to stay for dinner and the sleepover, if you would like?"

Two hours passed as I remained unconsciousness. I slowly opened my eyes, and my head was pounding.

"He's waking up," said Sunako.

My mouth was incredibly dry. I turned my head. Unfamiliar green eyes were staring at me. Then I turned my head.

Sunako said, "Welcome back to the land of the living."

I looked at her as she walked toward me. She was so very beautiful.

"This is my friend, Miss Tova. She is a healer, like me, and you needed us both at the same time."

I slowly got up to get some water. Sunako and Tova followed me. I had the worst taste in my mouth, and my throat felt like it was on fire. I walked into the dining room where the rest of the group was gathered. There was a pitcher of light-brown water on the table. I could barely speak so I pointed to my throat, then at the pitcher. Sofia smiled and poured me a cup. I drank it down, then two more. Cheri and friends looked shocked, with wide eyes and jaws agape.

"Slade, are you feeling well?" Sofia asked.

"Better now, Mistress Sofia." My voice was soft yet thick and gravelly.

Sofia coughed loudly into her hand. "Slade, maybe we get some clothes on or, at the very least, a pair of shorts."

"As you wish, Mistress Sofia." I had been oblivious to my nakedness, not that I would have been ashamed.

Tova said, "Wow, did you see how much iced tea he drank?"

"You said ten candies, right, Sofia? Consider it paid. Because whatever the old witch wants, I can do it or get it." Lucy did not let her feelings go unnoticed.

Sofia ignored Lucy and said, "Sunako, be sure he's okay. Look in on him without being noticed."

Sunako ran off.

"Food should be ready in twenty minutes. Miss Tova, can you lend me a hand?" Cheri asked.

Later, Sofia and Lucy set the table, while Cheri and Tova served the food. Everyone took their seats and waited for Sunako and Slade to come to the table and sit. Cheri made roasted turkey breasts with potatoes and corn on the cob. Sofia poured everyone some cherry wine. The dinner was wonderful and the company even better. At first, I felt overwhelmed and overly questioned. They spread it around as if I'd been a part of their group from the start. Then, I felt more comfortable.

After dinner, as the cherry wine was on its last bottle, Lucy asked, "Slade, can you tell us about what happened in the bathroom? More to the point, what was happening to you? Provided you know."

It was Mistress Lucy's first solid question of the night that held no innuendo, and her inflection marked real interest. I was just starting to think of how vapid and droll she was. I was imagining all our future conversations would be tediously woeful with a heavy salting of her sexual prowess. No, the question might just have potential for real depth. I sensed a real person hiding underneath that mask of sexual depravity. She was well acquainted with the knowledge of her overly cute face and matching body. I wondered if she would ever realize that she was much more than a cute woman within a jumble of dirty words.

"I remember Sofia leaving, how the water was just right, and how relaxed I was. So comfortable, but something was pulling me into sleep. Next thing I knew, I was standing in a field not too far from an unusual tree. It had a large canopy that reached to the ground in some places, about forty feet tall with soft, little green leaves. Sitting underneath was a man with my face, and he was holding something in his hands and crying. His pain was so great that I was a slave to it, and I felt like I was there for almost two days. I approached him, but he did not seem to notice or care that I was there watching him. But his pain grew more intense the closer I came. That is when I noticed what he was holding. He had a severed human head, and he had allowed himself to embrace true sorrow and despair." I paused as I took a drink. The room hung on my every word.

"Only when I touched his knee did he acknowledge my presence. He became enraged. He blamed me for her death. He said I failed my promise, and now he had to kill me to stop her from dying. He started to choke me with one hand, and he was impossibly strong. Then, he stuck me in the chest with a large knife and let me go. He picked up her head and went back to crying and cursing the gods. He left me bleeding on my knees. The last thing I remember was falling over onto my face. I awoke to Cheri covered in blood before losing consciousness again. Then, I woke up next to Miss Tova with Miss Sunako standing at the foot of the bed. Does that answer your question, Mistress Lucy?"

All eyes were on me, and the room was still. I was uncomfortable.

"Is everyone okay?" I was glad I didn't say whom the head belonged to.

Sofia said, "Yes. I mean, you don't know or remember what happened in the bathroom?"

Each one took a turn in explaining all the gory details. The more they spoke, the more I silently begged them to stop. I was mortified. I was afraid to get up and leave the room to escape my shame and must have gone into shock because Cheri came over to me, covered my mouth, and commanded me to "Wake up," which knocked me out of the unintentional daze.

Lucy said, "I think the day's activities and the wine has been too much for young Mr. Slade. I can only imagine what's going on inside his pretty head. Poor thing." She changed the subject. "Pie! Who wants pie? Tova made pie today, and I want pie! I'll be right back." Mistress Lucy stumbled away from the table, banging her shoulder on the doorway, while giggling all the way.

Miss Tova ran after her. "She might need my help." She moved much more fluidly through the doorway. Within a few minutes, the pair returned. Tova held two pies, and Lucy brought over two more bottles.

"It's Saturday night. That means no duties for us tomorrow, and I have strawberry pie and white wine." Lucy extended her arms and twisted the bottles in opposite direction.

Tova said, "We have three pies. One is apple, one strawberry, and the other is pumpkin."

I could smell them as they entered the room, which made my mouth water.

"Here you go, Slade. You look like you could take all three at once." She placed a slice of all three before me. "Tell me what you think." Tova smiled and moved around the table with the grace of a dancer. She seemed so reserved compared to Lucy.

I had no words to describe the apple pie. It was just amazing, but the pumpkin pie was the best and so wonderful that I missed it when it was gone.

"Thank you very much, Miss Tova. That was possibly the most delicious thing I've ever eaten."

She was still chewing, so she simply smiled and nodded. The rest of the ladies wore huge smiles.

Lucy commented, "Wait until you try me." She winked, then blew me a kiss.

Sofia looked shocked and said, "Mistress Lucy, you're too forward. So, are you two still staying over tonight?"

"Mistress Sofia, I'm sorry, but I feel bewitched by his looks. And of course! How could we possibly say no to you?"

Lucy had a cute smile and wore her wavy dirty-blonde hair right below her shoulders. With wide brown eyes, she looked like a pixie. Her size from a distance would make anyone believe they were seeing a child because of her height at five foot one. She told me about her abilities. She could predict the moves of her opponents during a fight and foresee the best way to fight an opponent off in seconds before she threw a punch. She also had high energy and endurance.

Sofia smiled. "Good, then I think it time to take this circus into the other room. Go get into your nightwear, but first, I must use the bathroom."

Cheri, Sunako, and Tova made short work of cleaning the table and dishes, and I watched them work in near perfect synchrony. I felt like I was in the way, so I meandered into the bedroom. Lucy was the only one there.

"Hey, Slade, are you having fun tonight?" Lucy walked up to me and whispered in my ear. "Want to have a bit more? Want to have a good waking dream?" She ran a finger down the side of my arm, then lightly rubbed her fingertips on mine, making them tingle.

"Siren! Get away from him! I might have to take him to stand guard outside of the bathroom, lest he gets taken advantage of." Sofia took hold of my hand.

"Oh, Sofia, you exaggerate! It's not like I had enough time to do anything. This one should be devoured slowly, like the meat of an endangered animal."

The girls changed into their nightclothes while chatting. They walked right past me. I sat in a chair in the corner of the room, watching them talk and laugh, which made me happy and comfortable. I guessed I was a little too comfortable because I fell asleep and saw his face again at an unfamiliar, bright place.

He was talking to a mirror, and he said, "I will find a way kill you. I will save her." Then, he ran up to me, grabbed me by the arms, and shook me. He turned into an almost eight-foot, light-blue creature, but the voice never changed. "Listen to me! To save her, kill the one with your face first! You will only bring pain! You must be willing to kill yourself to save her. Do what has to be done. Please, I miss her so badly. Only you can save her now!"

I asked, "Who are you? What is your name?"

He replied, "I used to be you. Now I am no one, and this is what we become, regardless of whether or not she dies." He let go and walked away, his tail waving back and forth. "My name is unimportant right now. All you have to remember is that skin color is teal. Don't worry. You will see me again. I'm the only real one here. You are just a memory that haunts me."

He disappeared, and I stood in the room alone.

The door slid to the side, and a beautiful woman with silvery-blonde hair said, "Is everything okay? I heard yelling. Slade?" I felt like I was being pulled backward. "Slade, don't go. Let me help you save her. See past the manipulations, and don't make a killing blow!" the mystery woman yelled.

I just missed grabbing her hand. Then, she was gone.

My eyes slowly opened, but the light was off. The room was lit by a few well-placed candles. Shadows danced about the walls in all directions, which was sinister and imposing. Those silent figures could effortlessly attack if Lady Silk were around or just outside the window.

Cheri said, "Hey, look who is awake. Did you dream?"

I was afraid to say what I saw, so I shook my head. "I was just resting my eyes."

Laughter broke out.

Sunako said, "You were out cold for about an hour. Tova told a story of a woman who turned into the world's first dragon. It was called 'Teardrop Dragon.' I shook you, and you slept through it. We thought it best that you sleep for a bit. It's time to get into bed. It's almost my turn to tell a bedtime story."

I said, "I should get into my shorts. I'll be right back."

I was about to leave when Lucy spoke, "Honey, please don't get modest on us now. We've all seen you completely naked."

Cheri laughed.

Sofia said, "I almost hate to say it, but Lucy has a point. No reason to be shy now. The mystery has been revealed, and you're a sexy beast." Mistress Sofia might have the wine to blame for that slipup.

Lucy laughed. "Mistress Sofia! Mind your wicked tongue before it leads you to dark places and sweaty kisses. Save your words before you find yourself spending your last amount of energy writhing in ecstasy."

Tova softly said, "Yeah! Why are you scared now? With what happened in the bathroom… One simply cannot unsee that."

"Seeing it, I can handle. At least, you weren't covered in it. I mean, it got into my hair. In my mouth, I don't care, and I think I can still taste it." Cheri made a face and took another drink. "Yep, that was definitely the taste."

"That was just an excuse to take another drink," Sofia said.

"Maybe?" Cheri smiled.

"*Him*! You think you still taste him, not it," Sunako corrected Cheri.

Sofia yelled, "Oh, shit! That means he is inside of you, Cheri, and not in the fun way. Oh, you dirty girl!" Sofia was laughing so hard she fell backward off the bed. I was able to catch and cradle her head before it hit the wood floor. "You really are a hero, aren't you?" Sofia looked up into my eyes as she lay on the floor, her head in my hand and my other hand on her hip. Her hair was soft between my fingers.

I got a violent flashback of her severed head. In the background, I could hear the girls chanting something, but I was held fast in the vision.

"Kiss me!" Sofia demanded.

I was back.

"Kiss me now!"

I leaned closer, and her lips met mine. She took control, taking the lead. I was pulled into her mind and was awash in strange thoughts, fireworks exploding in my mind, a tickle in my belly. I was falling, knowing full well I would land safely. When we were done, she was all smiles, and I was dizzy.

"Wow! I've never kissed a boy before." Sofia's voice was soft as her body trembled. Her hands were firmly locked around the back of my neck and the small of my back.

The world came crashing in at the sounds of the girls clapping and cheering. I was confused for more than one reason. We slowly rose to our feet, mine less steady than Sofia's. I still felt dizzy, confused, and hungry. I was hungry to kiss again. She turned to get back onto the bed, returning to her original spot, but I took her hand.

"We kissed in Lady Silk's house. So, this was our third kiss." I smiled.

Sofia laughed. "Oh yeah, that is right. I was so scared you were going to die."

"So, how are we going to do the sleeping arrangement? I vote he sleeps next to me, as I'm a guest. The host should be inclined to make their guests as content as possible, and I seem to have forgotten my teddy bear at home. What else would you have me hold?" Lucy grinned, her eyes holding me in her sultry gaze.

"Why, Mistress Lucy, I stand corrected. Proper etiquette dictates that I do accommodate your wishes. So, on that note, I am inclined to—"

"Come to Momma! Girls, get ready to learn from a master." Lucy pointed to me and said, "Slade, get that sweet ass over here and submit to your newest mistress. I have an itch only you can scratch."

Sofia said, "At least, allow me a second to finish my thought, Mistress Lucy. I am inclined to put your needs ahead of mine in this situation. So, for starters, if you want to hold something, you can hold my ass! Secondly, I will grant you full permission to think on him in any way your mind can come up with, but I loathe the very thought of you and your lecherous ways and your inglorious self roughly teaching him the improper ways to act while in the company of women. I must decline your request unless you have the ten pieces of candy hidden somewhere in your sleepwear."

Sofia's response shocked and amazed me. I wanted to be in her arms and kiss her that much more. The girls laughed more as the two mistresses' verbal sword fight had come to a swift climax. Lucy yielded her advances for the night.

Lucy laughed. "You win this round, but I will have some part of him between my legs at some point."

Sofia laughed and said, "I bet you will, but not before I have him. Slade, it's time to cuddle up between Sunako and Tova, so do not go and die on me—I mean, *us*—in the night."

I crawled up between Tova and Sunako as they pulled the sheets over us. Then, Tova took one of my hands, and Sunako snuggled up to me, placing her head on my shoulder. I felt their gifts course through my veins, making my skin tingle. Cheri extinguished the last of the candles, enveloping the room in darkness, with only a hint of light forcing its way through the windows. It was a very dark night with the clouds hanging thick in the sky.

"Sunako, will you please tell the last story of the night?"

"Yes, Mistress. Tonight's story is an old favorite of mine. It was told to me by my adopted mother, Notnair'e, so I tell it for Slade, who has not had the chance to enjoy it. I present for your enjoyment 'The Diamond-Eyed King and the Child of Whispers.'"

I listened and enjoyed every second of the story. When it was over, my mind raced with the thoughts of a place like that with a hero king and a child that helped end a war. The way she told it was very fun and exciting. Everyone was asleep except for Sunako and me, and she finished the story solely for my benefit.

"Thank you, Sunako. That was a great story. I hope you have more because I want to hear them all."

She thanked me, and I carefully got out of bed, needing to use the bathroom. I had to walk slowly because I did not realize how badly I had to pee. As I relieved myself, I could not help but imagine what it would be like to meet such a noble hero like the Diamond-Eyed King. I wanted to be a hero like that, a true good guy, selfless to the core. I was no one yet someone at the same time. Maybe a slave? A lost boy? Someone's trash they'd discarded? Last survivor of a destroyed village, like Sunako? I finished and headed back to the room.

As I made my way in the dark, an invisible hand grabbed mine, while another covered my mouth.

"Come with me."

I breathed a sigh of relief, knowing it was Sunako and not Lucy. She led me to the living room. Sunako pushed me up against the back wall and spoke in a whisper so low I swore I was reading her mind.

"Slade, please kiss me. Kiss me like you did with Sofia. Please, I can't tell you why, but I burn for you. You've been on my mind since I first laid eyes on you. I know Sofia likes you, but please kiss me. Please, let my first kiss with a boy be you." She slid her hand from my chest to my face, while her other hand gripped firmly onto my hip. "Tell me you want me. Tell me that you want to stay with us. Tell me anything that is true. I would listen to anything that your tongue and lips can say. Please, take me in your arms. Protect me as you did Cheri. Please say something, *anything*."

The room was so dark I could scarcely see her face, but I could smell her salty tears. "Sunako, I will protect you as I will protect Cheri and Sofia, but I don't understand the feelings I have for you, Sofia, and Cheri. Sofia kissed me, and I am unaccustomed to the ways here. If I don't talk with Sofia first before kissing you, then I would betray what little trust I may have earned with her. Trust is very important to me, and I want to be a good guy. Please, give me a chance to speak with Sofia. I hope you understand."

Suddenly, I felt we were not alone.

"Show yourself!"

The figure shifted to the little light that shone through the window.

"Slade, go to the dining room, and wait for me. Go now!" Sofia sounded odd.

I left without another word.

"Sunako, did you mean what I heard you tell him?"

"Yes, Mistress Sofia. I can't explain why I am taken with him. When we first helped him, then after what happened in Lady Silk's house, I have been drawn to him. When you kissed him, you claimed him as your own in front of all of us. Please, Mistress Sofia, don't keep him to yourself just because you can. Let him understand how things here can be. Give me a chance to show you that I have strong feelings, too."

"Follow me," Sofia whispered.

They walked quietly to the dining room.

"Slade, did you mean what you said in the other room about trust being very precious to you?"

I was having a hard time reading Sofia's tone.

"Yes, Mistress Sofia. Because I know nothing of myself, I must trust that I'm a good person or, at least, better than whatever I was before you saved me. If it turns out to be that I am a bad guy, then I must become strong enough to kill him, so I can remain who I am now: honest and true."

"Sunako, hear what I am about to say: we will talk about this tomorrow night, not a second sooner. Do you understand? Slade, do you understand as well?"

We both nodded in agreement.

"So, with that said, I'm going back to bed. I suggest you two do the same, if you know what's good for you. Oh, Sunako, you should both have some water because kissing with a dry mouth can ruin a first kiss. I wouldn't want your first kiss with him to feel anything but fantastic, understand me? I'll take my leave now. You two take your time but come to bed soon. And no hands below the waist!"

As Sofia talked, Sunako got herself water. Mistress Sofia yawned with outstretched arms and walked away and said, "Goodnight, my loves."

Sunako was up against me in the blink of an eye. "Sit down!" she commanded.

I did, and she straddled me, placing one arm on my shoulder with her hand caressing the back of my neck. Her nails gave me chills. "You look thirsty. Are you thirsty for me?" She lifted the mug to her face and took a slow drink. The hand on my neck tilted my head back as she lowered her mouth to mine. Our lips touched, and I anticipated her kiss. Instead, cool water slowly flowed from her mouth into mine as she held my face with one hand. The water felt wonderful as it tickled my tongue. The feeling was unfamiliar. It did not taste or feel like water as it slid down my throat, but it was magnificent.

"I knew you were thirsty. Do you want more?"

I nodded.

"Good, I have something even better than water for you tonight." She then placed her lips on mine, her tongue gently passing into my mouth. Our tongues lovingly massaged one another. I greedily held her to me like a coveted secret lover, and I could feel her using her gift, which made it more intense, more personal. My thoughts were awash with her eyes and her gentle voice. We kissed for what felt blissfully longer than forever. When it came to an end, it was not long enough.

As she rose from my lap, she took my hand and said, "Time for bed."

She led me back to the bedroom. I got into bed first, and Sunako straddled me while pressing her finger to my lips to silence me. I could feel the heat between her legs—I hadn't felt that in the chair. She moved slowly back and forth, and my body reacted to it in an unfamiliar and wonderful way.

"I hope the water tasted good. Now, please go to sleep before I need some water… or something sweeter," Sofia said.

Sunako slowly moved her body as she lay at my side, lightly nibbling at my neck and ear. Tova's hand found its way back to mine slowly, and she ran her fingers in small circles on the palm of my hand, which tickled in a strange yet pleasurable way. The two of them sent new and confusing thoughts through my mind as I fell asleep. I wanted to enjoy the feelings a little longer, but I could not fight sleep.

That night, I dreamt of the man with my face, the pain, his words, and how twisted he became in his metaphysical transformation, which frightened me. Was this a glimpse of my future? Or a product of a restless mind?

Chapter 10

Kissed with a Fist, Knocked Out by Love

I woke up to the smell of eggs and something salty beckoning me to rise to my feet. Sunako's head was on my chest, and her arm was draped over my stomach.

I tried to move her, but she said, "Five more minutes, please?"

"Get up, Sunako. We're waiting for you two, and food is almost done!" Cheri wore a smile as she left the room.

"I am very hungry. Last night, I only had a snack." She was gazing at me with her chin planted on my chest. "Race you!"

With that, Sunako was in the air with a small flip. She hit the ground, and her feet made almost no sound. Then she was out of the room in a flash.

From the other room, I heard Cheri yell, "Damn it, Sunako! No running in the house!"

I got dressed and made my way to the table.

Tova, Cheri, Lucy, and Sofia chimed, "Good morning!"

"Slade, we made something special to celebrate your triumph over William and Mr. Jerkface Richter. People are talking, and everyone wants to meet you."

Sofia added, "Mr. Treat had some pork, and I bought three pounds. So, today we have bacon and eggs with spicy cubed potatoes.

Now if only my head would stop pounding. Anyone else feel like that?"

Everyone shot a hand skyward.

"Water, three cups worth, and your head will feel better." It just slipped out of my mouth.

"How do you know that if you have amnesia?" Lucy asked with a raised eyebrow.

"I just know that water will cure a hangover and a headache. Obviously, dehydration is at the root of the problem in both cases. Besides, I've been speaking since I met Sofia and Sunako. I have a lot in my head. I just don't know where I'm from or anything pertaining to who I am."

"Holy shit! You lucky bitches! The one we have is dumber than shit, is a terrible cook, and not good at all in the bedroom. Clumsy stupid bastard. I really think he doesn't even like us. I mean, what is the point of owning a man and getting nothing but shitty work out of him? On top of that, yours is something to look at. I am envious through and through." Mistress Lucy sighed as she looked at me.

Sofia smiled at me. "We don't own him. Lady Silk is going to determine what to do with him and whether he can stay or leave. Until then, he is a guest and will be treated as such. No one can force him to do anything."

"Well, that sucks. Slade, you're a lucky guy. I would have had you over and over until we had to call a healer to bring you back to life. Real backbreaking work in my pleasure mines."

"Mistress Lucy, you have me at a disadvantage. You know so much about me, and all I know about you is your weakness."

"Ha. Really? Is that so, boy? Would you be prepared to place a wager on it?"

"Mistress Sofia, would you mind if I did? I will respect your wishes."

"Slade, at least for now, you're a free man, so you may do as you please. But if you're asking because you think I may become upset or displeased with you, then worry not. Besides, I wouldn't mind Mistress Bighead over here being taken down a peg or two. By all means, give us a show."

"What will the game be?" Cheri asked. "First to pass out is a good one."

"It would not be fair for two reasons. One, he knows almost nothing about my gifts, and second, I have already won because he is cocky fool." Lucy smiled at me.

Sofia asked, "What are the stakes?"

Lucy said, "I want him for one—no—*two* weeks, and he obeys me as if I were his queen. I get every little thing I want."

"Slade, what do you want?"

"I want two favors to be asked and granted at a later date, and you will grant it as if you were before your king."

Cheers rang out.

"Deal?" Lucy held out her hand.

"Deal." I took her hand and shook it.

Cheri said, "But first, we eat! Breakfast is served."

Sofia was right. The bacon was excellent, and the spicy potato cubes were amazing as well. Everyone laughed and joked, made silly faces, and some food was thrown. It was a good time.

After we ate, we cleaned up. Everyone pitched in. Then, we took a half an hour to relax, and more jokes were told. After that, we slowly got up and went outside behind the cottage. The weather was nice with a cool breeze.

"Okay, boy, are you ready to become my new toy?" Lucy winked and blew me a kiss.

I caught her kiss, turned around, and patted my ass with it. Our friends lost their minds with laughter.

Someone yelled, "Ready?"

I said, "I thought it was already over and you were about to fall to your knees in praise for your king!" I raised my fists in the air to signify my readiness.

"Okay, first to pass out or get knocked out loses," Sofia said excitedly.

"Please hold my shirt." I handed it to Sunako and winked.

I darted at Lucy, and she introduced me to her right fist then its sister. My cheek stung, and her next two landed on my stomach and forehead. So, she was strong and a skilled fighter, her hands moving at speeds that would make hitting her a bit of a chore as she blocked all my strikes.

"Come on, kid. I thought you would have more than that for me. Momma is going to break you in more than one way today." She smiled as her fists danced about my face and body. "Sofia, I wonder if

Slade is going to want to come back to you after he's had me. If he does, at least you know how he became a good lover."

She was slowing a bit, but it was a ploy. I went straight in, and at the last second, twisted my body as she slammed her right hand hard into my temple. I became dizzy, but I caught her arm and swung up behind, catching her hair in my left hand and gripping her throat with my right one.

I said, "Yield now to your new king, and I will be merciful!"

She struggled hard against my grip as she tried her best to swing her foot back and up into my groin, which would have been the truest test of fortitude on my part. I gave her a light squeeze, showing her that I was not going anywhere. I loosened my grip for her to announce her surrender.

With the little air I allowed her to have, she said, "I hope you choke me harder than that in bed, my soon-to-be lover."

With that, I sailed through the air. Somehow, she'd found a grip on me that took me by surprise. I watched her find her mark before I hit the ground. Her foot slammed down on my chest, stealing whatever wind I had. I could barely hear the women going wild. I just lay there for a moment before she returned the favor by grabbing me by the throat. Her strength was a bit disconcerting.

"Don't pass out just yet, lover. I want to tenderize your meat before I devour your flesh." Even during a fight, she had a one-track mind. "Come on, say it! Say my name!" My eyes rolled up into my head as she squeezed even harder. "Say my name, bitch!"

Just then, I felt a second wind arrive, and my eyes snapped back to look her in the eyes. I winked, put my hands together like I was praying, and thrusted my arms between hers, breaking her hold on my throat. I wrapped my arms around hers, pinning them at her side as she gritted her teeth. I got ahold of her neck again. I held her throat and shoulder, biting down on her neck.

I could hear her thoughts as she felt my lips and teeth on her neck and immediately knew it was over. She shook violently, and her body went limp. Her legs turned to jelly, but I did not stop. I loosened my arm and slipped out from under her arm to better hold her tightly against my chest. I slightly moved my mouth, gripping her tighter with my teeth, and hit the spot I was seeking. Lucy started to moan and spasm, her free arm reaching around my shoulder onto my back. I moved my mouth again for a better grip. Lucy began to scream, deep and guttural. Her nails gripped and tore across my back, leaving a burning, bloody trail with every rake. Another deep scream, and she was out cold, her body seemingly lifeless in my arms.

I lifted my mouth from her neck and looked at my friends. Some new people had gathered I had not noticed before. All were in a sort of stunned muteness. I lifted Lucy into my arms and brought her into the cottage.

I placed her on the bed, went back outside, and said, “Who’s next? I’m still hungry.”

One of the women in the group raised her hand and said, “If it’s going to end like that, then let’s just cut to the end of the fight.” She walked forward.

All I heard was, “Bitch! Get back! That is our house boy, and this match is over! Thank you for stopping by, but now, piss off!”

Sofia took my arm and brought me into the kitchen. “What the hell was that?”

I thought she was mad.

“I’m sorry, Mistress Sofia. I’ve crossed a line. I will leave if you wish it.”

Sofia said, “Leave? Why would I want you to leave? I want to know what you did to Lucy. I have never seen anything like that before. You took her out with a kiss, and she looked like she was in ecstasy. I honestly think I’ve now seen the craziest thing in my life to date.”

“Maybe he’s a vampire.” Tova hid behind Sunako. “We were all sleeping in bed with him. He could have taken any one of us.”

“Don’t be stupid!” Sofia shook her head. “Besides, he was out in the sunlight. We have a better chance that he is a sparkly werewolf. See how that sounded, Tova? It sounded stupid.”

Tova spoke, “What about last night and how his eyes went all black? We all saw it, and with what we just witnessed outside, we can put two and two together.”

I laughed. “You mean this?” My eyes went completely black. “Yeah, I can do that as easily as I can wiggle my ears. Look, and lose yourself in them.” I stepped toward her.

“Slade! That is horrific. Stop that. Make them go back to blueish-green! Please don’t do that again unless we ask. I really thought I just imagined that yesterday. I mean, no one said anything about it after it happened. I need to sit down first. Let’s check on Lucy. Oh shit! Please tell me you didn’t kill her.”

They all sprinted past me into the bedroom.

Sofia yelled, “Mistress Lucy, are you—oh, shit!”

Lucy seemed about half awake with one hand down her pants and the other pulling up the bedsheets, her breathing labored and loud.

“Someone wake her up.”

“She is your mistress, Tova. You do it,” Cheri hissed.

I walked past them to lean over and whisper in Lucy’s ear, “Wake up, Lucy. Everyone is watching.”

Lucy spoke loud and strong, “Let them watch us. Let them join for all I care. Just keep it up. I’m almost there again.” She moaned loudly with rapid short breaths. “Oh, yes. Oh god yes!”

I placed my hand on the side of her face and spoke louder, “Mistress Lucy, open your eyes!”

She did and slowly pulled her hand out of her pants, sat up, and said, “Was that a dream? That could not have been a dream. If so, that was the realest dream I’ve ever had. Wait, who won?”

“By the looks of it, you won,” said Cheri.

Lucy had a big smile.

Sofia then laughed. “No, no, honey. He won, then carried you to the bed, and came back outside to us. Tova thinks Slade is a vampire.”

“Well, if he is, please bite me any time you want. My head is still spinning. I swear I have never felt anything like that before. It was so intense, so raw. Nothing comes close to whatever he did. Sofia, you have to try it. He is your house boy—I mean—guest.” Lucy looked at me and said, “Thank you, my king. I owe you two favors, which I will happily fulfill when you ask.”

I thanked her as a knock rattled the door. Sunako ran to see who it was and returned with a letter in hand.

“A letter came for you, Slade. It is addressed to you with the House seal on it.”

“Wow! This came straight from Lady Silk. Open it, Slade. Tell us what it says,” Sofia said.

I read it aloud.

Slade, you’re a good fighter. Please report to Helge Monday morning. Then, meet with me at four p.m. that same day. Show this letter at the front door. I greatly look forward to our meeting. P.S. Please bring Mistress Sofia, Miss Sunako, and Miss Cheri with you as well.

Yours truly,
Lady Silk

"Well, let's have fun today because it's back to work tomorrow." Cheri had a point. "Come on, we can go swimming. All in favor?"

Everyone raised their hand, so I did as well.

"Is Damara back yet, Mistress Lucy?"

"No, she is still at Lady Velour's, helping with the training of a few new rangers. I know she is going to like Slade. You know how she loves to meet new people. You will like her, Slade. She's very funny."

"Pack some food, and we can have lunch by the water. I'll go back to my place and gather some nibbles."

Lucy went off with Tova.

"Girls, I need to talk with Slade alone for a minute. Slade, come with me."

Sofia seemed off. Not mad, not happy, just off. We went into the living room that seemed larger in the dark. She closed the door, then got close enough so that when she spoke, I could feel the heat of her breath.

"What did you do to Lucy?"

"I just used her weakness against her."

"That isn't what I meant, and I think you know it. So, don't play coy with me. What happened to her? Show me."

"Oh, you mean this?" I gripped her tightly and breathed heavily just below her ear. She shuddered as I grazed her neck. Then, I withdrew, snapping my eyes black. We stood almost nose to nose, and she slowly opened her eyes. She saw me staring back at her with the black orbs in place of my eyes.

"Damn it, Slade! That is really horrific. Come on, turn them back, or I'll be forced to ignore you while we swim today." Sofia crossed her arms.

"If you ignore me, then I'll be forced to talk with the other women who are enamored with me." I smiled and shifted my eyes back to normal.

"Don't be a bastard! It's not a good look for you. You will show me what you did to her."

She walked out, leaving me alone in the room. I realized it was the first time I'd been alone since I first opened my eyes. Then, it was just a minute or two until Sofia found me. Alone. I didn't know if I liked the feeling. A rush of emotions filled me, and I wanted to run from them. I didn't know what I wanted to do. All those thoughts were like a tornado, everything spinning too fast to catch anything. My hands were tingly, and I just wanted to run and hide. I was scared of who I might have been.

"Slade, are you coming?" Cheri called out from the front door. I hurried toward her voice and met the group. Two men I hadn't met had joined the group. As we walked barefoot, I counted every time I stepped on an uncomfortable stone. I regretted leaving my boots at the cottage. Tova introduced me to Gavin and Bryce, who were clones and very tall at about six feet with pale skin, pink eyes, and short, almost white hair. They looked about eighteen.

"Hi. My name is Bryce, and this is my clone, Gavin."

Gavin laughed and pushed Bryce. "You're *my* clone, you stupid dummy!" Bryce set off after Gavin. I watched them run down the road a bit, then back.

"Race you to the lake, Slade. Last one there is an old woman."

Well, I didn't need a push with that challenge, and we three took off, each trying to outdo one another. I pushed out ahead of them, and I could see the lake. So, I pushed harder and harder. I made it to the shoreline and leaned over to catch my breath. The air seemed to burn my lungs, but in a good way. I looked for Bryce and Gavin, but all I saw were the women coming toward me.

"I seem to have lost the guys. Did they run off?"

They started to laugh and pointed.

I pivoted, but all I could see was the lake.

I turned back toward Sofia and asked, "Where did they go?"

I heard a whisper. "Behind you."

I turned again and didn't see them.

"Tag, you're it."

Still, I saw nothing.

"We are everywhere."

Someone flicked my ear. I spun around in a full circle, but I still didn't see either of them.

Another whisper: "Oh no, too slow. Look out, son. I got your nose."

My nose was lightly poked. Invisible laughter echoed in such a way that I couldn't get a read on its origin. All I could see was a little dust getting kicked up here and there. I felt more pokes, then I snapped my eyes black. The colors were different with that vision, so maybe I could see something.

They were moving at an astonishing rate of speed and looked as if they were using no effort, like walking on air. One of them came in for another poke, and I leaned back while extending my leg. He saw me and made an odd face before tripping over me. I felt like I'd whacked my leg on a tree. His brother came in almost at the same time, and I reached out. But grabbing his arm was a bad idea, because as soon as I got ahold of his arm, he pulled me clean off my feet with the sheer force of his speed. I flew through the air, crashing hard to the ground, and slid across the grass. It felt like my arm was pulled out of the socket.

I rose to my feet, cradling my arm. I could see Sunako running toward me with Tova.

"Slade, you think maybe you can go an hour without getting hurt? We're here for fun, not healing. Now, let me look at that arm." She touched my arm. "Yep, it's out of socket. Mistress Sofia, I will need you to hold him. Slade, I am going to pop it back in, okay?"

Sofia grabbed me from behind. Her strength could easily crush the ribs of most people.

"Tell me if I squeeze you too hard." She did, but it felt nice for some reason.

"On the count of three, okay? One—" With a fast, hard pull, my arm was back in, but it hurt like hell.

"Sorry about that, but never go on three. If you do, you would've tensed up, and it would've caused more pain than what you just felt. Now can we go swimming before someone else gets hurt again?" With that said, she was off to the water.

"I thought I said to tell me if I held you too tight."

"I didn't notice. Were you squeezing me?"

Sofia laughed and pushed me down.

Lying on my back, I watched Sofia run into the water. Things look so different upside down.

"Slade! Hey, man, how did you do that with your eyes?" one of the guys asked. "It's me, Gavin. You can tell because I have a vertical scar above my eye. Bryce has two horizontal scars."

"Oh man, you have to spill it. How did you see us?" Bryce asked.

"Okay, I'll tell you, but you have to keep it between us because I just figured it out myself. I can see in different spectrums of light, and things move differently with my eyes like this." I snapped them black, and the guys recoiled a little bit. "Don't tell me you two are scared of this!"

"Damn, that's creepy as hell. Let's go swimming."

Before I could blink, they were in the water and far out from shore.

I walked up to the water's edge and watched the women splash and swim. Lucy called me to join them, so I slowly walked into the water. It felt oddly familiar, but I couldn't place why. Probably because I might be in the place Cheri had tried to drown me. I got chest-deep when something brushed my leg. I assumed it was Cheri swimming underwater.

I heard my name and looked over toward the sound—I received a full face of water. Sofia had splashed me, and we laughed. I wished I knew who I was, but I liked that feeling I had with them in the water. In a short time, I felt like I fit in. After a few hours of play, we took to dry land to have some cured meat and fruit for lunch. I enjoyed the way the sun felt on my skin.

I talked with the guys a little longer throughout lunch. They called themselves specters because of their skin and ability to move so fast. They said that no one could see them until I had. After lunch, the guys had to leave for their upcoming duties.

"See you soon, Slade. Thanks for the invite, Mistress Lucy." Gavin and Bryce waved as they seemingly disappeared into thin air.

Tova said, "So, Slade, what do you think of our two specters? They, and a few others, keep us safe, day and night."

"I really liked them. Are the other people like them?"

"More or less. Only Richter and William are big assholes. They enjoy what they do. Watching Slade hand them their asses has been the best part of my life so far." Cheri smiled and patted me on the back and whispered, "My hero."

That small gesture made me feel very happy. I felt like a hero.

We went back to swimming, laughing, and more splashing. After another two hours or so, calmness set in as we lay half-in, half-out of the water. The women took turns singing different parts of songs.

"Okay, people, the sun is setting, and I have to get this young man to the safety of our cottage before the beasts of the night descend and tear him from our arms," Sofia said.

"Mistress Sofia, I have never known you to be so dramatic. I can't place my finger on it, but I guess you hear the call and the beating of the drums of desire. It calls to you, doesn't it?" Lucy stared at Sofia.

"Mistress Lucy, I believe that you are a free spirit with an even freer tongue. Well, yes, I will admit that your stories make for a great Friday or Saturday night entertainment, but a little decorum would go a long way as not to contaminate the poor boy's mind. At least, let us get him properly settled in and familiar with the ways of the House of Ribbons."

Lucy smiled. "I am nothing if not honest. This boy you have is so much more than he seems. I see him as a great thing who has fallen from the sky, and the gods have favored him with a kiss upon his forehead. Just remember our deal. Ten pieces of enchanted candy for time with Slade."

"Don't I get a say in this?" It just came out of my mouth.

Lucy laughed. "Welcome to the House of Ribbons, my fine-as-hell new friend. Sofia, you might want to have the new guy talk with him tonight, so he does not have a heart attack by finding out from one of the other guys tomorrow." Lucy stood up and stretched. "Tova, my sweet. How does a hot bath sound to you right about now?"

"Wonderful, Mistress Lucy."

"Slade, it has been one of my greatest pleasures to have met you. From seeing you at Lady Silk's house to this very moment, you're nothing if not amazing. You could not have a better mistress than Mistress Sofia." She walked up, hugged me, and said, "If you ever need anything, I will only charge you but one kiss on the neck."

We all walked back with plenty of laughs as the warm sun began its journey to the underworld. We parted ways when we reached our respective cottages. Sofia, Sunako, Cheri, and I got to our cottage, and I sat in a chair at the table.

"Slade, there are some things you should know about the House of Ribbons. First, what would you like for dinner? We have some stew left."

I smiled and rubbed my stomach.

"Good. Cheri and Sunako will take care of that quickly. So, I will start from the beginning. You should know that the House of Ribbons is not a fighting House. It's a House that could provide insight and aid to those who visit. Arts can be learned here, and clothes can be bought. Our objective is finding missing people. We have two sister Houses: the House of Dreams and the House of Whispers. There is one that is controlled by their father—the fourth House—but let's just focus on the sisters. Our three Houses help one another, as the founding members of each House are sisters. The House of Ribbons has the smallest numbers, totaling around high fifties. With permission, people are allowed to pair up with someone from one of the other Houses. Not all are allowed. Those with rare gifts and the ones with multiple abilities have to stay with the House that they swore loyalty to, but they have more privileges then most."

"Why do you have fighters if this isn't a fighting House?"

"Hand-to-hand combat is a stable routine for almost everyone who belongs to the House of Ribbons and the other three Houses. Practice with a sword starts at twelve years old, whether you have an extraordinary ability or not. All will learn to fight and defend, regardless of gender. The rangers and the oracles have the most privileges, but rangers have the most dangerous job. To be a ranger you must have one of these abilities: speed, strength, healer, or silver tongue. Never more than five people per team. If you stay with us, then you will be our first silver tongue if that is an ability you possess. You would shoot up the chain overnight, and you seem to be able to speak very well. But, to answer your question: everyone needs fighters just in case the House comes under attack. Plus, it's great exercise.

"Slade, almost all the clones here are slaves, but they are not treated badly. It's us, the women, who have the most freedom. Yes, some of us belong to Lady Silk, which makes us her property. But it is the men who serve us. But understand it's not like real slaves. If you were placed with us, then you would be ours, like a live-in boyfriend. Cook, clean, and service whatever needs we might have. Please don't make me go into detail about that."

I sat for a few seconds, not saying a word. "I understand."

The thought of being a slave, to be bent to the will of another, made me angry. Whether born a clone or a natural human, no person should be forced into chains. My heart wept at the thought of how big the world must be and how many souls were born only to serve at the foot of a master against their own will. I didn't understand why I had such a hatred for the concept, but I did.

"I have not been forced to do anything against my will, so I should not have to worry. Plus, I do not foresee you becoming a ruthless, nearly unstoppable tyrant hell-bent on ruling it all any time soon. Besides, how bad could it be, being a slave to love—I mean—you?"

Sofia smiled. "I was supposed to teach you all this last night, but you had to go and bleed all over poor little Cheri." She and Sunako laughed.

"Hey! That was not funny. That was scary. I thought he was going to die. Slade, I didn't want you to die." Cheri walked out of the room.

"Did Cheri just admit that she likes him?" Sofia asked. "Sunako, stay with Slade. I need to speak with Cheri."

Sunako looked at me. "Did you have a fun day? I like that everyone who has met you likes you."

"I like this place. I would very much like to stay here with you three, but I have a fear."

Sunako got up to sit next to me, taking my hand in hers. "Tell me of your fear. Share it, so I might be able to ease your mind."

"I would rather say it in front of all of you at one time. I have to get it off my chest before I make a mistake and lose what I have earned."

Cheri and Sofia reentered the room, and it looked like Cheri had been crying. I got up and walked over to her.

"Cheri, I know we had a rough start, but please know that I hold no ill will to our first meeting. I think it was perfect, but I don't understand why yet." I extended my hand, and to my surprise, she jumped into my arms and hugged me tight.

She said, "Promise us that you will stay with us." She looked me in the face. "Become the man that shares our life and our cottage." Her tears began to flow.

I held her face, and the more I wiped away her tears, the more I inadvertently reinforced them. Her tears were like an army that let nothing stand in their way.

"If Lady Silk allows me the privilege to stay in this cottage, then you have my promise that I will stay here with you three."

I held Cheri close to me. I would not let her go until she wanted me to.

Sofia spoke to break the silence, "So, I have been thinking about this all night and today. Cheri, please take a seat. Slade, sit here. I think now is the perfect time to lay bare what I'm about to say. There is no reason to fight over Slade. I will not lay claim to him, even though I do have the right to do so, but I will not do that. Instead, I think we should share him like a fine, exotic-aged wine." She looked around the table. "With whom better than my closest friends, my cottage sisters? Slade, if you agree, then you will be ours as we will be yours."

"That was my fear that one would be upset due to my feelings toward each one of you."

Sunako raised her hand. "Then who gets the first drink of this fine, exotic wine?"

"I guess we can put our names in a box, and he can draw a name." Sofia looked pleased with her idea.

Sunako's eyes sharpened to slits. "No, I think I should be his first, as I healed him at least four times already."

"Really? The small cuts from Cheri's nails? Yes, you healed him, but I don't think he was going to die from that."

Sofia had a good point.

"He could have gotten an infection, which in turn, could have prematurely ended his life. Not to mention what happened in the bathroom." Sunako folded her arms and sat back in the chair with a smile.

"You're right. What a fool of me to doubt you!" Sofia rubbed her temples. "Cheri, you have not said a word this whole time, so that means you really must have something to say on this matter."

"Slade, I want you to kiss me until I can't speak. I want to surrender in your arms. I want you to always make me feel protected like you did at Lady Silk's house so I don't have to be so tough all the time." Cheri wore a look that made me want to save her from whatever haunted her.

"Cheri, is that why you have been this way for so long?"

Sunako and Sofia got up and hugged her. All three were crying.

"Don't I get a say in this matter?"

Cheri got up and said, "Sofia has not told him the biggest part about the three Houses."

Sofia looked nervous.

"Slade, the men here are the real slaves. Yes, as a clone, I am owned, but we own the men. All the Houses are that way. A man's job here is to work to protect us, and they are used in other ways. But it is us females that get the most freedom. I am sorry, Slade. You may have gone from one set of chains to another. On the bright side, we want you to stay with us, and we will treat you like a husband like Dawn does with Mr. H."

Sofia added, "There is one House that has no slaves. The House of Thorns, which is run by the father of the three sisters."

I said, "Then I will happily live with you three without complaint. Now I understand why there are so few men around."

The rabbit stew smelled great. It had carrots and onions, served with apple slices on the side. The dinner was excellent and the company even better. After dinner, we sat in the front room and talked about light stuff, as the last few days had been overly eventful, to say the least. Sofia laid her head on Cheri's lap, and Cheri caressed Sofia's hair, twisting and combing it, then braiding it on one side. Sofia was the first to fall asleep, then Cheri. Sunako laid her head in my lap, and I mimicked what I'd just watched Cheri do with Sofia's hair.

"Slade, would you kiss me again if I asked you to?" Sunako asked in a soft voice.

"Why would I deny such a simple request from one as beautiful as yourself?"

"You know, you don't have to sweet-talk me anymore. You already know I like you… But I do like it." She touched my face.

Cheri woke up and carried Sofia to the bedroom.

"I say it because I mean it. I see no need to lie, and I honestly think you three are the most beautiful I have met since I have been here."

"There are more women than men here, and you have only met a few women so far. What about Topaz? She and Sofia are very close."

"Sunako, my sweet, beauty is what comes from within. I'm just lucky that all three of you are beautiful, inside and out."

Sunako got up to straddle my lap, slowly kissing my ear and neck. "Can you do two things for me?"

"Name it. Your will is mine."

"I want you to look at me with those black eyes of yours and kiss my neck. I want to feel what Lucy felt."

I stood up while holding her. I placed her in the chair, standing in front of her.

Then, I snapped my eyes black. "This doesn't scare you?"

"I want you more like this."

She jumped up, and we kissed, a soft and slow kiss with her tongue deeply probing. After a few minutes, she bent her neck to me. I could see the pulse just underneath her skin. How could I resist her?

I started softly kissing her neck. Then without warning, I latched on and started to nibble and bite lightly. But when I bit her, something took over. I covered her mouth, feeling her gift kick in, which drove me a little too wild. I clamped down harder and pierced her skin. She began to bleed into my mouth—not an awful taste, but I wasn't after her blood. I could feel her wound healing. Sunako was so much stronger than Lucy. I stopped only when I lost my balance and we fell over. Sunako was out cold, and I was so dizzy. It was hard to crawl out of the room. I couldn't stop my head from spinning, and I passed out in the dining room.

Chapter 11

My Eyes Do More Than See

"Slade, wake up! Wake up!

I opened my eyes and wondered why Sofia was standing over me.

"Damn it! What did I tell you about those eyes? Make them go away."

I tried, but it did not work. I saw Sofia's skin glowing. There seemed be a smoky substance slowly coming out of her eyes, and somehow, she was still radiantly beautiful.

"Slade, can you hear me?"

"Yes, Mistress Sofia. I'm sorry. My eyes are stuck, but I see you so much differently. You're glowing. Even in the light of this room, you're glowing, and your eyes… your eyes are magnificent."

"Why do you have dry blood all over your mouth?" Sofia questioned. To Cheri, she ordered, "Go find Sunako!"

I could still taste Sunako. "May I have some water?"

She returned with a cup, and I gulped it down.

"Thank you."

I thought about Sunako and sprinted past Sofia, barging into the living room.

"Sunako?"

There she stood, dressed in the uniform from Lady Silk's house.

"Are you okay, my sweet?"

Sunako smiled. "Okay? I have never felt better. I think you gave me the best night of sleep I've ever had. Where were you? I woke up alone and feared you'd left. Slade, you might want to wash up. I think you might scare the children."

"My eyes, I cannot make them go back."

She looked like an angel, and I could see the faintest outline of wings that swayed back and forth when she turned around. I swore she had a tail with what looked to be a snowflake for the tip, but I had to be seeing things.

"Sunako, hold still." I reached out, expecting my hand to pass through the beautiful illusion, but it was solid. I took hold of it and gently pulled.

"Slade, what did you just do? What was that? Do it again! Sofia and Cheri, come see this," Sunako said.

Cheri said, "We have a few minutes before we have to leave. What's up?"

I pulled a little harder, and Sunako was tugged toward me.

"Is that some sort of weird trick?" Sofia moved toward me. "Slade, you have to make a good impression on those you meet today, and those eyes are horrific. So, please bring back the pretty blueish-green eyes for me." She placed her hand on my arm, then jumped back so fast she fell over. "What in the hell was that?" She was shaking her hand, a shocked look frozen on her face. "Cheri, did you see that?"

"All I saw was that you touched his arm, then you jumped back and fell over. Honey, are you feeling well? You look pale, like you've seen a ghost." Cheri looked puzzled, obviously not used to the levelheaded Sofia acting so out of character.

"Sofia, you saw it, too? Sunako has a tail," I remarked.

Sofia spoke while still on the ground, "Slade, I don't know what I saw, but can we address whatever this is later tonight? I didn't see a tail. I saw wings. Bright-white wings."

"Are you serious?" said Cheri as she helped Sofia up off the floor.

"Slade, do I really have wings and a tail?" Sunako looked over her shoulder at me.

I tugged her tail again a little harder. "You sure do."

Sunako spun around, stopping right at the point where our lips met. She gave me a quick kiss right as Sofia began to speak.

"Hey! Come on, we have to go. We will have plenty of time to kiss him later."

Sofia's voice took me by surprise, causing my eyes to revert to normal. But it felt different, like my eyes were tired and sore, and I was staring at a bright light. The world looked a little bland, its colors restrained.

"Come on, kids. Work now, playtime later. We need to go." Cheri's voice was direct with a happy tone.

Due to time, I stayed in the clothes I'd worn the day before. I put on my boots. Then Sunako and I went out the front door where Cheri and Sofia were waiting.

"Slade, I will escort you to Helge. You will stay with him until the time on your letter. I will gather you beforehand, so time does not slip away. Lady Silk greatly dislikes lateness. Do you have your letter?"

I searched my pockets. "I think I dropped it."

"You did, and I held it for safekeeping. I will give it to you when I pick you up later today. So, learn what you can while you're with Helge, and don't be afraid to let loose. Now, let's go. But first, a bit of business as your mistress. I must insist that we each get our good morning kiss. You understand? This will start the day right and bring us good fortune."

Sofia stood with her arms outstretched, and I slid in between them to kiss her. Cheri's arms were out as well, and I moved slowly up to receive a peck on the lips.

"Maybe, if you're lucky, I will give you a real kiss later."

I moved to Sunako, who was all smiles.

"Goodie, I get seconds." Then, she grabbed me, pulling me into her kiss, which left me a little breathless. Her kiss was very enjoyable.

"Right then. Off we go."

Sofia and I went one way, while the other two went in a different direction.

"Slade, are you nervous about today?" Sofia bumped me with her hip and smiled.

"Well, since I've arrived, I've had one woman try to drown me, then choke me, all the while dining on my arm. Then, there was William and Richter and Lady Silk's very own shadow creatures. And last but not least, Mistress Lucy, the succubus and her hammer hands. She really could hit so damn hard and nearly knocked me down. So, should I be nervous about today? Compared to the last few days, today should be as enjoyable as your kisses."

Sofia asked, "What is a succubus? Is it like a vampire?"

"No, it is a female demon that enjoys the company of men while slowly eating their soul. Over time, they use their feminine wiles and beauty to lure in men, teaching them the language of lust. I don't really think Lucy is a demon; I think she is more of a vixen who is used to getting her way and gets what she wants by using her sexuality. It can be a useful tool or a dangerous weapon."

"Come on. How can sex be used as a weapon? You just made that up." Sofia hip-checked me again, and I tripped over my own feet and fell, trying to recover.

"Get up, clumsy boy. We have someplace to be." She reached out her hand, and I took it, pulling her down on top of me.

"While you are down here, may I have one more kiss before the long hours of the day leave me dehydrated from your lips?"

We kissed. Her lips softly rubbed on mine as our tongues danced.

When it was done, Sofia dusted herself off and asked, "So, how can sex be used as a weapon?"

"She could make her way into the arms of a whoremonger, a king, or a high-value target, then kill him at his most vulnerable moment."

Sofia looked at me. "How do you know that?"

"I don't know; I just do."

Sofia laughed and said, "I bet you have all kinds of things rolling around in that beautiful head of yours. Or maybe you're just crazy. Either way, it's my problem now, and that sounds like a good problem to have. I guess I'm lucky that way. You could have been a real pain in the ass, like Cheri."

We arrived, and Mr. Helge looked to be meditating. A handful of other people were there stretching and talking, while others were training with staffs. We waited until Mr. Helge opened his eyes, as Sofia did not want to disrupt him.

"Hello, and good morning, Sofia and Mr. Slade. Sofia, will you be joining us today, or are you training the young ones today? And where is Miss Cheri?"

"Miss Cheri has a ranger's meeting for the newest members and will fill me in on what I missed. She will be here after that, and I was thinking, with your permission, that I could take the young ones to watch the strangers fight today, if that is okay?"

"Yes, of course. Now about your stranger—Mistress Sofia, may I speak with you in private? Please, I mean you no offense, Mr. Slade."

“None taken, Mr. Helge. Please call me Slade, as I have not earned a title yet.”

“Thank you, Slade. Please call me Helge or just H. Either one is welcome. I was never one for titles myself.”

Sofia and H walked about twenty feet away.

“Sofia, I received a letter yesterday regarding Slade. Lady Silk wants to see what he can do. She wants to know what his limit is. She wants to know if he is a danger to this House. Look, Sofia, I think Lady Silk was a little spooked by what he did the other day. Up until then, she was untouchable. We are here today, and so is he. I’m very sorry, but I will have to do as I am instructed. Please, bear me no ill will about today’s events.”

“Mr. Helge, I have known you for many years. I know you’re a kind soul, so please don’t concern yourself with the feelings of others. Our job is to make the best fighters so they can fight at their best.”

“Thank you, Sofia.”

Sofia called out to Slade, “Slade, will you come here?”

“Yes, Sofia.”

Sofia’s smile seemed to hide something important.

“Save that kind of talk for later, or you’re going to make me feel like the day will stretch on too long. We have to focus now. No more pillow talk until tonight. Do you understand why you are here today?”

“I am most likely here because of what H was saying.”

“You could hear us from that far away?” Sofia looked confused.

“No, I could read his lips. Not entirely, but I got the gist of the conversation.”

“Do you mean you can watch a person’s lips and know what they are saying? I have never heard of that before now. Don’t tell anyone that you can do that. I mean *no one*!”

“Mistress Sofia, bring Slade in a few minutes. I will gather the group.”

Sofia waved to H, signaling okay.

“Are you ready? Please try not to show off too much today. I fear you might get a following, and that’s all you need right now, more women trying to sweet-talk you out of your clothes. I mean, just the thought of it makes me want to sweet-talk you.”

“Sofia, whether I’m surrounded by a thousand women or every lady that rules doesn’t change the fact of the matter: I have promised my heart to you three, and that is the way it will stay until you three don’t want me.”

Sofia smiled. "You talk as if you're something we own and can be easily discarded. Slade, we have never liked a boy, let alone kissed one before. You're our first, and I could not be more pleased with you. You'll never be treated like a slave. Slade, you're a perfect gentleman, so keep being you, and we will keep being greatly enamored with you. Now it's time to get into a fight. Get out there and don't give me too much of a reason to baby you tonight."

I didn't need any more reasons to get into a scuffle. I loved the way Sofia spoke so confidently.

"Mr. Helge, I am ready for today's class."

I was sizing up all that I could see. More women than I would like, and I really didn't want to hit a female. I saw a few of the guys eyeing me like I was food. Good. Hungry animals were reckless and took unnecessary risks to become the alpha.

H said, "Slade, I'm going to begin to teach today's class. Please, sit at my side. Today's class will be solely about unexpected circumstances and improvising on the fly. Slade is that unexpected circumstance. He is the wild card; he is the old woman who is done taking shit from everybody. I have trained some of you for the last five years, so I expect you not to embarrass me today. Fail today, and you have only failed yourselves. We will also study Slade—how he reacts and how he moves. So, either way, today we will learn something.

"Today will be nothing like you have ever done before. Today, you all will have a chance to stop this man right here in this circle. Slade, stand up. This man is a stranger! He is foreign, even to himself. He knows nothing but his own name, so your job today is to jar his memory. All we really know is he is handsome, and he has fought and defeated William and Richter. But those two were not trained by me, and you all are an extension of me. Make him submit, and you will all have the day off. Be the one or ones that bring him down, and you will get one week off. This is from Lady Silk herself. Any questions? No? Slade, say hello."

I stood up. "Hello."

"Twenty minutes, people. Stretch, get mentally prepared, do what you need to get into the right headspace. Slade, this is not how I normally train, but this comes from the top. Just try to last as long as you can. There is no shame in losing. We have all been on the wrong side of better opponents. I don't know what you do before something like this, but now is the time to center yourself. If you pray to a god or two, feel free. We are accepting of all forms of worship here, but I strongly suggest you stretch."

He walked away to greet Cheri and Sunako. "Cheri, it's about time you showed up. I thought you were going to miss all the action."

"Wouldn't miss it for the world." Cheri waved at me.

"Miss Sunako, will you be watching, or are you here as a healer?"

Sunako smiled. "I'm here to help those unfortunate enough to go up against my man."

"I was not aware he was yours. I was under the impression he belonged to Sofia."

"He is all three of ours." Sunako laughed.

Mr. H took me to the side and said, "I couldn't imagine being owned by three at one time. Dawn picked me shortly after I arrived. I will understand if you are a little tired this coming week."

"I am with them willingly. I'm not a slave."

"I meant no offense, but aren't we all a slave to love?" Mr. H smiled and patted me on the back. "Today will be informal, but we will have special guests. Lady Silk and Lady Velour will be here to watch, so no pressure. Ah, here comes Lady Silk and her merry band."

Lady Velour seemed to be alone, while Lady Silk had four people with her. Two I recognized, and two were females I had never seen. The first two were Richter and William, and the other two were easily six feet tall and built for battle. I would have bet my only coin they were clones.

Lady Silk walked up to me. "Slade, I trust you have enjoyed the last few days here. I would hope that all your needs have been taken care of, and I would like to see what you can do today either way. I still look forward to today's meeting. Oh, Slade, I have showed your bracelet around to a few of my oldest friends, and none of them have seen one like it. The writing still remains a mystery. The strangest fact is that no one could remove it from my wrist, so if you would be so kind as to take it off for me? Not being able to take it off it makes me feel uneasy."

Lady Silk extended her arm, palm-up, and I reached for her wrist. I intentionally let my fingertips softly glide across the palm of her hand. She reacted favorably.

"Careful, boy. You might not welcome my advances if I call upon you."

I smiled and touched my bracelet. When it loosened, I slipped it off her wrist.

"Thank you, Slade. I look forward to an interesting rest of the day."

William and Richter never took their seething eyes off me. The other two acted like I didn't exist, which was fine by me. As I turned around from our brief one-on-one, I noticed many people had gathered. Everyone was around. *No pressure, my ass.*

As I put my bracelet back on, I couldn't help but wonder what it looked like in another light. I snapped my eyes, and what I saw was so unreal. It softly glowed the color teal, and I could read some of the words. All the while, the designs moved like snakes intertwining, the whole thing seemingly alive.

"Slade, anything said in the circle will be heard by everyone, so feel free to be entertaining," said Mr. H.

First up for the match were two Egyptians clones: Eros and Clete. Their skin was an amazing bronze color; both were five foot nine. Their movements were like that of a cat, no movement wasted—cautious but intimidating. Clete lunged at me with one fist poised behind his ear, while the other was balled up at his side. Eros was charging up behind him, maybe pushing him into me for added force. The only thing to do was close the gap fast.

With my outstretched hands, I darted forward. Clete's eyes widened with bewilderment just before I caught him by the throat. I instantly wrapped my open hand around his throat. The force was so hard, a jolt of pain shot through my wrist. I knocked Clete unconscious as I pushed him backward into Eros's face for a dual knockout. Clete's body hung from my outstretched hand. The crowd stood in stunned silence.

Mr. Helge raised his hand, and two more opponents stepped forward. One male, one female. Zale and Martina, one of the few married couples. He was tall at six foot two and broad-shouldered with a strong chin. She was very petite and short at four foot seven. They both had long black hair with deep olive complexions. They split up. Their footsteps were clunky, and Zale seemed unsure of his next move. He waved his fingers like he was playing an invisible instrument. Maybe it was a signal to his wife. Martina was surefooted, and she had a plan she soon shared with me. Martina made a strange sound, and I expected her attack. So, I focused only on her, but it was a diversion for Zale to grab me in his arms.

I tried the move I did on William, but because of his height, I hit his chest with no effect. He squeezed tight, then knelt down, forcing my knees into the ground. Maybe he was anticipating a kick to the groin. I held my breath, hoping he would tire as I struggled against his grip, but Martina took advantage of my situation. She was running at me at full speed. Her small stature would suggest a light attack, but whichever way she hit me while I was held down would have been hard. But for some reason, Zale stood up at the last second, and I took full advantage by raising my foot as fast as I could. Then, Martina crashed face-first into my foot, and with that momentum, her body slammed into my groin, reminding me of the huge external weakness we males were born with.

Zale yelled and tossed me like a ragdoll, picking up his bloodied wife. He was pissed, but in the time that he looked my way, I was on top of him with my arm wrapped around his neck. He stood up, and my legs just dangled—I was like a child on his father's back. I tightened my hold, and he began to spin around. The mad bastard spun so fast I feared I'd fly off. I had no choice but to pull with everything I had left, which was probably not much. Then, just like that, I was flying through the air again.

I could see Sofia in slow motion as she blew me a kiss. I was sideways then upside down, eating grass and dirt. I tried to pick myself up because I'd rather lose on my feet than on my knees, but defeat was not mine. Apparently, my choke hold and all that damn spinning took it out of the big boy. I threw up my hands and whatever I had in my stomach. The crowd went wild.

Mr. Helge, who had been sitting with Lady Silk, walked up to me. "Slade, do you want to continue, or do you concede?"

"I don't think no is a real option today, so I might as well give the lady of the House the show she craves."

"Okay, kid, round three. Drink some water, and take your place in the center."

My next opponents were Aelia and Acacia. Aelia was blonde with two long braids, deep dark-blue eyes, and a fit body. Her pale skin made her cherry lips stand out like a rose. Acacia had short black hair with a black strip painted across her blue eyes. Both women were five foot seven. They kissed like old lovers. I felt like I was the only one who'd noticed.

They walked within spitting distance, and Acacia said, "He is smooth-looking, like a girl. What do you think, Aelia? Want to try a boy for once?"

Aelia laughed. "I hear they don't last as long, but he is cute in a new puppy kind of way. Hey, boy, want to be our puppy? I'll give you something to eat. Then I'll make you sleep on the floor."

"I'm sorry, ladies. You see, I'm not housebroken, so I will just end up pissing all over everything, including your dreams of winning today. But thank you for the offer. I think I will take you up on being the first man inside you, here and in front of everyone."

They looked at each other and laughed loudly.

Aelia was first to attack. She landed her first few hits to my chest and face; each one was surprisingly solid. Acacia was so fast and kicked like a mule. I swore she ran over me twice before I could finally stand up, just in time for Aelia to help me check if I had anything left in my stomach with a punch. I fell to my knees, and I could hear Aelia laughing. Acacia kicked me in the back, and the ground rushed up to kiss my face or maybe the other way around. Either way, I was in a tough spot, and Acacia standing on my back was a bit embarrassing.

Aelia said, "Let's hurry this up. I have to pee. Oh, wait. I'll just piss on you and 'your dreams of winning today.'"

I rolled hard to the right, and Acacia fell on her back. I grabbed her by the wrist and throat, lifting her up to use her like a shield. I blocked three of Aelia's punches with the back of Acacia's head before she noticed that she'd hit her lover.

"Bastard!" If Aelia didn't look mad before, she was now.

I squeezed hard, and Acacia went to sleep. I gently laid her on the ground, then stuck my finger in her ear.

Aelia shot me a confused look.

"So, you said something about pissing on me. Well, here I am, feeling a bit dry."

"For that, I'm going to knock you out and piss in your mouth. Then, you will always know who owned you!" Aelia was furious.

I yelled, "I will knock you out without hitting you, and you will be the one pissing yourself! So, you will always know it was Slade who kissed the piss out of you."

The crowd's cheering rose to a deafening roar. I figured they liked the taunting better than the fighting.

Time to risk it all. Aelia threw a punch, but I moved my head slightly so that her hand slid right past my sweaty cheek. I wrapped her up in my arms, trying to get a better hold as she struggled. I could hear profanity-leaden quips from her: something about me having a little something or other, how my mother was a whore. If Aelia were as skilled with her fists as she was with her razor-sharp remarks, then I would have surely lost already. I kicked the back of her knee, and she fell to both knees. I managed to get one hand under her chin, working hard with my other one to stop her from landing another blow to the side of my head, which was, frankly, starting to hurt. I slipped one finger into her nose.

"I told you I'd be inside you."

Four sharp nails raked from my forehead to the right side of my chin. Damn it all! It was painful as all hell and drew blood. I had no choice but to play a bit of a rougher game, so I grabbed her flailing arms and gave them a solid twist. Aelia screamed, allowing me to bend her head to one side. I bit her between the neck and shoulder, and she was mine. Her arms went limp, and her scream changed. She tasted different. She was like honey wine, and I felt an energy flow into me the more and harder I kissed. I shook her violently from side to side as I began to feel fully awake, super charged. I wanted more, but it slowed to nothing.

I took my mouth off her, laid her on the ground, then said, "Aelia, my sweet, you seem to have pissed yourself."

Lying on the ground, Aelia looked up at me. She could hardly talk, but she managed to choke out, "Worth it!"

I stood up and raised my fist in victory. I didn't just feel good. I felt *amazing*.

Mr. Helge walked up. "Lady Silk has offered a better set of fighters. If you wish this to be over, all you have to do is knock them both out."

Lady Silk spoke loudly, "The prize you will be fighting for is entrance to the House of Ribbons as a free man with a title and your choice of lovers. Lose and you willingly give yourself to me and the House of Ribbons as a slave, or you can be allowed to leave my House forever. Which do you accept?"

It wasn't even a choice—that was a great offer either way. I got to be with the ones I wanted to be with.

I yelled, "Either way, I'll be a slave to love!"

Mr. Helge leaned in and said, "Kid, I think we'll get along swimmingly. Now, whatever you do, don't show any emotions. Do not let this fight shake you! Everyone is watching, and between you and me, there are those you cannot see that are watching you today." Mr. H bellowed to the crowd, "So without any further delay, I present to you the fight of the day! Here stands The Beast from the Void! Some call him The Vampire; some call him The Stranger; and yet others call him Slade! But today, I'll call him Meat for the Grinder!" In a low voice, he asked me, "Do you think I oversold it?"

"Yeah, a little thick, don't you think?" I smiled.

He laughed and continued, "Next up is The Ranger with No Fear of Danger. The Hidden Blade, The Mistress of Mayhem, The Beauty That Bashes, The Rose Queen herself. *Thorn*! Last but not least is The Queen of Mean, The First to Fight, The Heartless Heartthrob herself. *Bloodshed*!"

I saw two fully robed individuals step forward. They wore the House colors: purple and yellow. Their hoods completely obscured their faces. I bet that scared most people, but all I knew was that I was fighting to remain free and fear only hindered one's ability to focus.

Lady Silk stood up and said, "Fighters, if you do not fight to your full potential today, I will sell each of you to different faraway places. I will not see either one of you two go easy or throw this fight. I want to see blood. Shed it for me today in honor of the House of Ribbons. Show that no matter your feelings, no matter where your heart may lie, you will do as commanded without thought or hesitation. You will fight to remain a part of the House of Ribbons. Now begin."

I thought that was a bit dramatic. She was just trying to shake me. The fighters pulled their hoods back and disrobed.

"Ah, shit! You have got to be kidding me!"

Damn it, I said that out loud. Both Cheri and Sofia looked right through me like they didn't know me. Cheri came up fast and hard with her swing. I dodged the first two attempts, but she landed her third punch. If she was holding back, then I might be really screwed. Directly after that hit, Sofia kicked me in the back, knocking the wind out of me, which sent me into Cheri, who was waiting with a kick of her own right in the center of my chest. Whatever air I had left flew out of me, and I fell to my knees, clutching my chest. They must train like this to be so coordinated. Cheri kicked me again, sending me back into the ground.

They both put a foot on each one of my hands, pinning them to the ground, while Sofia held her arms in the air, playing to the crowd. I struggled to free myself, making them push down harder. I was sure my fingers were going to break. I did the only thing I could think of: I lifted my legs up and grabbed Cheri's waist, stiffening my body. She fell backward, freeing my right hand to ball up, which hurt more than Cheri standing on it. I punched Sofia in the side of her knee, which freed my hand. She was not kidding about her ability. I felt everything I would have to do to her, but so would she. All I had to do was endure what I did to her and what she did to me. So, fighting her was like getting damaged by two people in one. She grabbed her knee and yelped. That was the only way to win. I had to really fight back. I heard Cheri's angry breathing and turned around just in time to dodge a hit to the face. Cheri's strikes were relentlessly pushing me back toward the crowd and Sunako. I wished she were somewhere else as to not see the fight.

I was dodging most of her light blows, but Cheri was just the distraction. She was pushing me, so I did not see Sofia slide up to deliver a punch to the side of my head. Sofia hit my head hard. It was all I could do to regain my balance and gather my bearings—my head was swimming from the hit. It looked like there were easily four of them as I stumbled around, only to take another blow to the head. The world was spinning as the crowd yelled encouragements and taunts. All I knew was that I couldn't get knocked unconscious. I had to fight on. Someone's foot made contact with my groin, and I felt like something had leapt into my throat. I took another punch in the ribs. Throwing up was not an option when I couldn't breathe. They paced around like wolves looking for their next hit.

Okay, they might not be able to knock me out as quickly as they'd thought. I would have to be the one who ended it and fast because I was starting to hate every second of the fight. I took another hit to the face by Cheri. Damn it, her knuckles felt like they were made of metal. Sofia jumped and grabbed me in midair, using her body weight to violently spin us around. We hit the ground harder than I wanted. Well, there were the acrobatics in her fighting style. I managed to get up and land a few good hits on Cheri, but she shrugged them off like they were nothing. Hitting her was like striking a punching bag.

Then I saw it. She had a pattern: push back and let Sofia hit me.

Cheri hit me and started her push again, but I used both arms to block her. Just as we reached the kill zone, I jumped forward and grabbed her throat, taking her by surprise. I applied real pressure and squeezed the ever-living hell out of her. Sofia got me from behind, placing me in her own chokehold. By the gods, she was strong. I honestly believed she was trying to pull my head from its resting place.

Her grip was intense, and Cheri was putting up a fight. But I gripped harder, and Cheri finally passed out. I was about to follow her into a deep, dark slumber, as Sofia had her legs around me and was pulling backward so hard that all I could see were stars. It was all I could do to bend slightly forward and jump backward, slamming her back into the ground with me on top of her. The maneuver must have knocked the wind out of her because she completely let go. I, too, was feeling the fall. Her gift was becoming a real pain in the ass. I rolled around between her legs and snapped my eyes black. She was frozen, and I grabbed her hands and held them above her head, stealing a kiss. When I did that, the crowd must have loved it because they were clapping and yelling even more. The kiss must have either made her angrier or given her an adrenaline rush because she popped me up and over her head, and I hit the ground headfirst. I lay on the ground, trying to command my legs to move, but they were numb.

I could hear Mr. H yell out, “It looks like the Beast has lost to the Beauty.”

Sofia came at me with full speed. I didn’t even have time to get off my ass before her foot kissed my face, and I spat up more blood. I must have bit the hell out of my tongue and cheek—there was more blood that Lady Silk wanted. I wasted no time finding Sofia, but she wasted less time, landing a solid punch to the stomach. I was about done. Most of the blood rushed out of my mouth and nose as I tried to breathe. I stood up, or more likely, Sofia *let* me stand up. I took a shot at her, and she dodged it while returning a punch of her own. I faked a punch and then landed the real one right in the left eye. She stumbled back as I did the same. Holy hell, that hurt, and I was so done with being hit in the face.

She came at me again, and I braced for the impact of her fists or feet, but I slipped to one side, sticking my foot out and tripping her. She hit the ground, and I was on top of her with my hands locked around her neck. I seemed to use choking a lot, but it was a great go-to move that worked—it was my only real move. I felt the pain I was inflicting, but I didn’t have the air restriction she was enduring. I hated it, and as I looked into her eyes in that moment, I wanted to be kissing her, not choking her. I would try my best to make it up to her if she weren't too mad later.

I said, "You're so beautiful. I think I love you."

I squeezed as hard as I could in the moment. Her eyes rolled back, showing only the white, and her hands fell away from my wrists and hit the ground with a low *thud.* I stood up, lifting one arm in the air. Victory was mine. I just wanted to not be in more pain. Sunako and another rushed to Sofia's side.

"Slade is the winner of the day!" Mr. Helge came up to me. "Son, that was mighty fine fighting, but you could use some real training. Then, I could see you becoming an excellent fighter."

Lady Silk said, "Slade, come to me."

I shuffled over to her.

"You have truly amazed me today. I expect to see all four of you at the meeting. Your cottage mates should have more than enough time to get cleaned up and healed."

She and her group turned and walked away.

Sunako rushed up under my arm to help steady me. "Hey, cutie, you look like shit. Sofia is awake. How do you feel?"

"I feel like I must look. Are Cheri and Sofia mad at me?"

"Tova had them picked up, and they're on their way to the cottage. I don't think they will be mad, although Sofia has never lost a match." Sunako laughed. "You were amazing out there; people will talk about this for days."

As we got back to the cottage, Tova was drawing a bath.

She and Sunako were talking about who was going to heal who when I spoke up and said, "Please heal Cheri and Sofia before me, I insist. Besides, this looks worse than it is." I was lying my ass off, but I wanted them healed first. "I'm just going to sit here and relax a while, if no one minds."

I pulled out the chair and sat down. I wanted to cry out because my whole body hurt so much, but I just half smiled at Sunako and Tova as they walked into the bathroom. I had to have fallen asleep because I could feel nothing, but my thoughts were still aware.

"Good job out there. Damn, you are exciting to watch." A woman's voice was inside my head. I had to be dreaming. "Keep up the great work, and soon, you will find what you are looking for. Then, you will find me."

I felt dizzy, like I was moving. A figure made of darkness was talking to me, and it was embracing me with both arms.

"Rest well."

Chapter 12

On the Destiny of the Soul

"Wake up, sleepyhead."

I opened my eyes. I was face-first on Sunako's chest. Her skin was soft and warm, and I could hear her heartbeat.

"You're a cuddly thing, and it's a good thing I like you, or I would say you're barking up the wrong tree. How does your body feel?"

"I feel really good. Really strong, absolutely no pain. Thank you again."

Sunako said, "Tova and I double-teamed you."

Tova laughed.

"What does that mean? Why is Tova laughing?"

"In this situation, it means you had two women at the same time because Tova and I healed you at the same time. Our gifts can combine to become stronger and more effective." Sunako smiled. "You should get dressed. We will have to leave to see Lady Silk in less than thirty minutes."

"Was I out that long?"

"Yep, about five hours," Tova answered. "Let's try not to make this a habit of you getting hurt and Sunako and I riding in to rescue you. People might think I like you as well."

I laughed.

"The one thing I find weird about you is that your heart rate is oddly all over the place—strong one minute, then soft the next. I will ask Lady Silk if I can call on the old witch to see you."

"Why do you call her an old witch?"

Cheri walked in, leaned against the door frame, and folded her arms. "Because she is an old witch, by which, I mean she is *old*. She's a real witch with magic. Lady Silk has sought the witch's council for as long as I have been here. She's really friendly. The kids here love it when she comes for a visit. I once heard that she mentored Lady Silk when she was a child."

I got up to get dressed. As I walked around the corner, Sofia was standing on the other side of the wall. She wore an unfamiliar look, and she placed her hand on my chest to stop me. She pushed me backward until I fell into a chair.

She straddled my lap and said, "I have never lost a match, but somehow, you won. You're lucky I like you so much, or I would have to slide something sharp under your chin as you slept."

"I didn't feel so lucky while you two were beating me like I wronged you in another life. Hell, it felt like you were trying to pull my head off, and Cheri was doing her best to give me brain damage. I did not want to hurt either one of you. I most certainly did not want to get hurt by you two, but both of you forced my hand by pushing me to the limit with a challenging fight. I honestly thought I was done for more than once. Your gift makes you someone to be reckoned with, a true warrior."

Sofia sat up straight and smiled.

"And you, Cheri, your gifts are ones I would like not to be on the other end of again anytime soon. You hit like a landslide and kick like a mule. Your strength is scary, by which I mean, who would think that you have a heart like a lion? Your strength is that of a dragon! And all that is wrapped up in this innocent young lady's body?"

"Your words tickle my ears. I thank you for the compliments." Cheri, who was standing behind me, leaned over and kissed my cheek, and whispered, "I wouldn't mind a little more physical contact later on tonight."

"Get in line, baby. If anyone gets him first, it should be me because I found him first and I went the longest with him in the pit." Sofia was very direct.

"I believe I am a free man, and didn't I win the right to choose my partner or partners?"

They both laughed.

Sofia said, "Oh, Slade, until Lady Silk pronounces you a free man, we still own you. So, until then, we might have a need or three to tend to."

"Needs?" I wondered what she was getting at. No sense in looking like a fool by assuming the meaning of her coyness.

Sunako walked in and tapped her foot. "What is this? We have somewhere to be in twenty minutes, and all you want to do is play kissy-kissy? We can talk about who gets him second after me when we get back."

"Remember, I get a say in this, too."

I was immediately interrupted by all three of them with, "Shut up, Slade!"

Sofia said, "We were not talking to you. We were talking *about* you and how you will best serve us. It is a simple concept, so get on the same page with us."

A knock on the door brought everyone to their senses. Sunako opened the door. "Hello, Topaz. How are you today?"

Topaz walked in. "Good evening, everyone. I was wondering if I could have some time with Mr. Slade?"

The ladies looked at one another.

"We have a meeting with Lady Silk in twenty minutes. Can't this wait until later?" Sofia asked.

"I fear it cannot. I'm here with Lady Silk's blessing. I promise none of you will be late." Topaz handed a letter to Sofia. Topaz said, "Hello, Slade. I watched you fight today. I will say I was more than impressed. May we speak privately?"

Topaz sat next to me and held out her hand. I took it, and we were alone together in a place within the mind.

"Slade, I wanted to see you again. You're in my head when I don't want you to be and not in my arms when I want you to be. I can't stop thinking about how intense our short time was, but I believe I have come to learn something about you, so keep an open mind to what you're about to see."

Soon, I saw a mental copy of me.

"See, it is a complete copy of you, inside and out."

I didn't know what to say.

"Hello, Slade. It's me or you or us. Either way, you and I are the same person. I am just the mental copy of you, and you are the living mind inside the living body that is Slade. I hope that made sense."

"In a weird way, it makes sense. So, what do you want?"

"That is the same thing I would've said. Yeah, so, I have learned a lot living here inside Miss Topaz's mind, and we have become close. You see, time does not really exist where we are right now. Well, almost no time. Like right now, outside of our conversation, almost no time is passing. I really thought I would be trapped in Topaz's head for the rest of her life. So, at first, I lived in her library, absorbing her memories until I came to her ability. Then, I began to understand what I was and how I was alive. Slade, we are one, and we have the gift of an oracle. I believe we're more than just that. I think we are from someplace special, and that is the reason that we have no memory. This is why it has been cut out. At first, I thought it was suppressed, but no. It's just not here, just a blackness where memories should be."

My doppelganger made sense.

"What have you learned in the last few days?" It was so odd to speak with myself, especially because he knew more about me than I did.

"A few days for you is years for me. I will help you unlock the sight—that is what they call it. Oh yeah, the eyes… I think I know what they are for. You're going to love this."

"Seeing in other color spectrums and seeing the things unseen. I figured that out the other day."

"Damn, I worked on that one for what seemed to be a year, but I cannot change my eyes in here. Can you?"

I tried. "No, why won't they work here?"

"I think it's because they would have no purpose in this place. Technically, we're just merged minds without physical form so we have no eyes to turn black, but I could be wrong."

"Can I see this library?" I asked.

Topaz took my hand or more like the mental projection of my hand. Either way, I could feel her hand. My doppelganger opened a set of large, ornate wooden doors.

"Here you go, Slade. Please, I am an open book for you. You can look at anything; you just have to ask. I will not say no to you." Topaz pointed toward a table with large tomes.

"Thank you. I'm just trying to take it all in."

Topaz said, "Exactly! What I want is to take it all in. Take you in me. I have had your mind, and now I want—no—I *crave* your body, your skin pressed against mine. I want to feel you inside of me. I don't have a thought without you whispering to me. Now, I want to feel your hot breath in my ear. I want you to hold my hips while you press into me. Please, I need your mind and body at the same time."

I put my hands up and said, "Whoa! Slow down! I didn't even know that I had a copy, let alone that I left it within someone's mind. On top of that, learn what they know on the most intimate level. Then you have to say what you just said to me? Yes, it's flattering, but I promised Sunako, Cheri, and Sofia that I would be theirs, so you would have to start with asking them."

"Slade, I somehow cannot come home unless she allows it. Her mind has learned from me, and now she is so much stronger than when I first met her. If I don't come home, then this information cannot be absorbed, and you will not know what I know. I don't see this being that big of a request."

"Topaz, what if I promise to kiss you, then kiss your neck, and let you have this copy of me here and there for sleepovers? Then, if and when the ladies are okay with it, I will be with you in the way you want, but not at the risk of breaking my promise to those three. What do you think?"

Topaz looked at the copy of me and said, "I will miss you. Hurry home to me."

"It will feel like forever, my love."

Topaz and Batch embraced with a deep kiss and a tight hug.

"Come on, handsome. We have to see Lady Silk," said Topaz.

He walked over to me, and we held hands.

I said, "Damn, this feels odd."

"Slade, I expect you will get all the information in one torrent. I will do my best to hold the floodgates. Just try not to freak out if it comes too fast. Just sit back and take it all in."

"Thank you. Good, now let's disconnect. Are you ready, Miss Topaz?"

She said, "Yes," but her sad eyes said no. She asked, "Any chance I can have you both at the same time, right here, before you leave?" She made a large bed appear out of thin air.

"Good evening, Miss Topaz."

With that, I was back in the real world. I could see Sofia, but I felt dizzy.

"Slade, I can't hold back all the information. Have Sofia knock you out. I fear it might drive you mad if you take it all at the same time. I had years to absorb it all, and I fear it could send you into a coma. I really don't know how you will handle it, so better safe than sorry."

"Sofia, knock me out fast! Sunako, my sweet, heal me."

Sofia looked confused. "What?"

I was running out of time and could not explain. "Just do it!"

I guess that worked because I felt a few fists and then the wooden floor and stopped feeling dizzy.

"Slade, welcome to the inside of your mind. Wipe your feet, and come on in."

"First off, if you are going to be a separate mental part of me, then you're going to need a name."

"Sure, sounds good. Why not Batch? It's written before Slade on our bracelet."

"I'm happy that you picked it because I had no idea what to call you. So, Batch, how is this going to happen? Will it be painful?"

"No, because it's all done. Now, I am going to a place you cannot go, a place very deep into the recesses of our mind. There, I will build a better library and a better way to process all the new info we are going to collect. Give me some time to make some order of this new information. I expect to see Topaz when I'm done. I will tell you when I have everything ready. Until then, you will start to remember and understand what I let out, so don't let it freak you out."

Great. I had a little me running around in my head and building a place to store and process new information. What the hell was I going to do about Batch falling for Topaz? How did I tell the girls about that when I didn't even understand how that worked?

"That is your problem, brother." His laughter was haunting. "Slade, I can hear your thoughts. I don't know how I would get any work done around here if I had to hear you think all the time. Let me fix that—hold on. Okay, that should do it. Now, when you need me, just call my name, and we will be able to communicate. But most of your thoughts will be yours."

"Is it always going to be like this?" I didn't know which was worse: not understanding who I was or having a second me in my brain.

"I will work on a way to give us a bit more privacy. I think your endless prattling on would drive me crazy because it's louder for me than it is for you." Batch sounded irritated.

"Slade, wake up!" A hard slap brought me back.

"Hey, sleeping cutie, we have about ten minutes to be at Lady Silk's. If you can't walk, I'll have to carry you over my shoulder. Topaz, if we are late, you will explain that to Lady Silk." Sofia seemed aggravated with her.

"Lady Silk will be more understanding than you think. This boy is a treasure chest of secrets in more ways than you know." Topaz made dreamy eyes at me.

"Just remember, it's us who hold the key to this treasure chest." Sofia placed her hand on my shoulder.

Topaz got really close. "Just remember the promise you made to me, Slade. A person is defined by their word, lest his tongue be forked, only tasting dust, and forever speaking backward. Now, come on. We can all walk together."

As we walked, people waved and wished us a good evening, and the few children we saw followed us, laughing and talking with each other.

A child came up and said, "Look, I have a bracelet like you." He showed me his wrist. The boy couldn't be a day over six, maybe seven.

I said, "Wow, I like yours better than mine. Do you want to trade?"

He smiled and said, "Yes, please."

"Well, you can have it if you can get it off my wrist."

I stopped and let him wrestle with the silver bracelet. He did what he could to get it off, and at one point, just hung from my arm, energetically trying to solve the puzzle to unlock his prize. He would be the envy of his little friends.

"Valens, honey, we have to go to the big house, so I am sorry to say goodbye. Slade can't play any longer. Now, run along."

Valens said, "But Slade said I can have it if I can remove it."

The kid was funny. He was like a squirrel in the way he seemed to weigh almost nothing and the way he could climb all over my arm, my shoulders, and down my back.

"I'll see you later then. I'll get it off." He ran out of sight.

"How can he move like that?"

"How can you do what you do, Slade?" Sunako said. "It's his gift. He's an early bloomer. We call him Raccoon because he likes shiny things, and sometimes, he bites. You're lucky he didn't bite you."

"Sometimes? He just bit me the other day for no reason. He is lucky he's fast, or I would have kicked him in the tail," Topaz said.

I laughed and said, "You mean his ass?"

Topaz laughed hard. "Oh no, that little monkey has a tail. Valens keeps his tail tucked away because another boy made fun of him. He is a hybrid clone and a sticky-fingered little pickpocket, so watch his eyes when he is around you."

"What next, people with wings?"

"Don't be stupid!" Topaz's tongue became sharp as if I'd offended her.

We were at the front door, which looked a lot like the door inside of Topaz's mind.

"Topaz, why does this door look like the doors to your mind?"

"I love this door. Every time I see it, I feel useful; I feel loved; I feel needed. It feels like home." Her smile was warm, but her eyes held sadness and did not see me. She was looking at something far away, and a small part of me wanted to touch her face just to remind her that she was loved. The door opened, and as Topaz crossed the threshold, I reached out, placing my hand on her shoulder.

"Topaz, I will find a way to honor my promise. Just give me a little time."

She placed her hand on mine. "Thank you, Slade. I'm sorry I snapped at you. It's just so silent since you left my mind."

"Topaz, he picked a name. It's Batch."

She smiled. "I like that."

"What's that all about?" Sunako asked.

"Who knows? She's a weird one." Cheri's words were cold and unwarranted.

"Sofia, I will need to talk to you alone tonight." I just needed to tell her about what happened with Topaz.

"I was hoping for a little alone time with you." She smiled.

"It's about Topaz."

Her smile disappeared. "Okay, tonight, but not before a kiss."

"I wish it was tonight already."

Her eyes sparkled and grew very wide.

Topaz smiled. "Hello, Elma. I have Lady Silk's guests."

"Topaz, you can escort them into Lady Silk's private reading room." Elma walked away.

Topaz thanked her, and we walked up the right side of a beautiful wooden staircase to the second floor of the mansion. It had so many doors, and I was told each floor had different colors for each door to find one's way around. I just thought it looked very pretty.

"Well, we're here. Anyone want to take a deep breath before we enter? No? Okay then, let's go." Topaz was being a little too dramatic for the moment.

"Hello, and welcome to my house again. Slade, I'm sure these women have kept you fed and satisfied to your heart's desire." Lady Silk's shadows peeked around from behind the curtains like a curious child would watch its mother. No doubt, they were guardians. They did make scary bodyguards.

"Lady Silk, these fine young women should be commended for their sheer generosity. Cheri, Sunako, Topaz, and Sofia are wonderful and loving. It is I who should be thanking you. I feel less like a poor houseless bastard and more like a nobleman."

Lady Silk sat back in her chair. "I like the way this one kisses my ass. You four should take notes because this is my new favorite boy. Tell me more, my young, attractive, houseless bastard."

Shit, I might have laid it on a bit thick.

"What can I say other than what has not already been said by better gentlemen than I? Lady Silk, you and your shadows are as beautiful as you are deadly. Only the most stouthearted of gentlemen could ever slide up next to you for even the briefest of moments to try in vain to win a kiss and the feel of your cheek on their fingertips. Yes, a truer rose, full of thorns, with a sweet scent like a siren's call to those who have not the faculty to resist the fall before the rocks, if not only to glimpse but the face of a goddess."

Lady Silk leaned in, perched on her elbows. "Holy shit! Ladies, this one is a keeper. If his tongue is as smooth in bed as it is in this very room, then I might just have him over a few times a week to help me with a spot that eludes those I deem worthy of searching for my hidden source of pleasure. Sadly, only I can uncover my secret spot. I do lead a lonely life in that way."

I didn't intend to be so wordy. Better watch my tongue, lest Lady Silk put it to whatever use she might have for it.

"Now, on to the more pressing topic at hand. What to do with the eloquent young Slade? This will be a first for me, so if my words do no justice, please forgive me this one time. Slade, if you were so inclined, then please be my guest and join us in the House of Ribbons as a free man. How do you feel on this matter?"

"Lady Silk is an amazing specimen, isn't she? A true anomaly like us. Don't you think, Slade?"

"Batch, I thought you would be away longer."

"No, work was easier than previously thought. You have some great stuff in here. I mean, what you just said would have taken years to learn, let alone master. Someone did this to us for a reason, and I hazard to bet that they're watching us closely."

"I can't hold two conversations at once!" Batch was becoming a nuisance.

"I heard that, Slade! Maybe it's you who is a nuisance to me. Have you ever thought of that? No! I did not think so! Manners can go a long way with me, and it looks like we are going to be roommates for a long time."

I ignored Batch, as I was well-aware he knew I would.

"Lady Silk, I would be a fool to say anything other than yes. Thank you very much. Any other combination of words would fall flat and lose their meaning."

Lady Silk smiled.

"Good, Slade. I believe you could become a very important person here. Topaz believes you to be an oracle, but I have never heard of a male oracle. I think Miss Topaz is wrong, but I'm not an oracle, so I have called for someone special on behalf of both Topaz and Tova, as they know her well. Both believe you to be different than any other male we have met. This woman, I trust with my very life including the life of every member of this great House. I believe she will know better what you may be and how best to put your gifts to use. Now, on matters of wants and needs—where do you want to live? I have two cottages open that are empty, and you would be the first male to run a cottage out of my two sisters and me."

"Thank you, Lady Silk. But would it be possible for me to stay with Mistress Sofia, Sunako, and Cheri?"

Lady Silk looked around the room at each one of us. She was silent for longer than would be comfortable for most. "I believe that can work, provided that Mistress Sofia would be comfortable with a male living with her that she held no power over."

"I think I speak for those in our cottage that we would very much enjoy Slade living with us." Sofia placed her hand on top of mine.

"Slade, have you been taught why a male is in each house?"

"Yes. Males, more or less, serve at the pleasure of the mistress and her misses of that cottage." I found it to be slavery within slavery, but I'd keep that thought to myself.

"Excellent, so you do understand our ways and rules. So, with that said, I trust you have picked the woman or women you would like to be with?" Lady Silk gestured toward my three cohorts.

"Yes, I am very fond of these four women."

"Four!" Cheri jumped up. "Do you mean Topaz?"

Sofia removed her hand with a scratch of her nails.

"Cheri, remember your place and where you stand with me, young lady." Lady Silk was fast to shut Cheri down, but unfortunately, all eyes were on me.

Three pairs seemed to be extra intense, while one had dreamy eyes.

Lady Silk was bewildered. "Well, young Slade, I can clearly see that three of the four women in this room are a bit shocked with this revelation, but I'm sorry. I cannot let you be with Topaz in that way. An oracle can never be with a man. She can only ever be with women—so say the witches. If you turn out to be an oracle, then I will allow the conversation to continue. But, then again, I've never heard of an oracle being male, not even in stories. This will be something I can address with the old witch when she arrives. If she allows the two of you to be together, then I'll be fine with it."

I said, "I hear she is a magic user. Or is it an ability?"

"Both. She is also gifted with an almost unnaturally long life." Lady Silk looked off to the left as if enjoying an old memory.

"If I may ask, is she just called the old witch?"

"Don't you remember? I said her name is Asya. If you're extra lucky, you may get a piece of her special candy. Trust me, there is nothing like it anywhere."

"Mistress Lucy and Mistress Sofia told me about it."

"How did that come up, Mistress Sofia?" Lady Silk propped her elbows on her desk and rested her head on her hands. She wore a curious smile.

"Mistress Lucy is quite taken with Slade. She wanted to have him for a night or two for her sweet tooth, so to speak." Sofia searched the floor as if the right answer were lying at her feet.

"I'm not making the connection. Could you be more specific?"

Sofia took a deep breath and said, "Mistress Lucy wants Slade's company and all that he can do for two nights. We came to an agreement for ten pieces of candy that she can have him for two nights."

Lady Silk laughed. "Let me get this straight: you would sell him for two nights for ten pieces of enchanted candy?"

"Yes, Lady Silk." Sofia hung her head.

"You see, ladies, this is why I made my dear Sofia a mistress. She saw a way to make the world work for her. Sofia, you have the making of a true lady. I see you having your own great House one day, making our area better, stronger, and safer. With that said, I would hope that now you know that as a free man you can no longer rent him out as you please."

"Yes, Lady Silk."

I asked, "Is that a lot in candy?"

Lady Silk smiled. "Let's just say that with ten pieces she can get a great deal in trade. I very much like the idea. Ladies, please give Slade and I a chance to speak in private. Topaz, please stay. I will need your gift. Thank you very much, Mistress Sofia, Miss Cheri, Miss Sunako. I will send him back to your cottage when I have concluded our meeting."

They got up and left without a word. I thought my timing was off with what I'd said about Topaz. I wondered if they were upset with me.

"I would like to reiterate what I said about your relationship. If I find out that you two have crossed me on this, then I will be forced to punish and sell you, Topaz. Then, Slade, I will throw you out. Am I clear?"

We both answered in unison, "Yes, Lady Silk."

"Look, I know what it is like to be young and in love, but young love is often driven by lust, and lust can cloud your thoughts and make people do stupid things. Topaz, your gift is so important, and they say an oracle can lose that gift because her heart is no longer pure due to the impurities of men and their lack of control that leads to times of war. Matters of the heart are things most are either blind to or simply don't care about. But I will speak with Asya. If she gives her blessing, I will as well. So, until then, keep your clothes on. Wait. Better yet, Slade, you are not to enter her body in any way other than to kiss her mouth with your mouth. Other than that, everything is off-limits."

"I clearly understand and promise to honor your request and Topaz's virtue."

"Good, Slade. I love a person I can trust, and I do not know you well, but something tells me that you are not a danger to me or my people. So, earn my trust and be richly rewarded. Topaz, what I am about to say stays in this room and is to never be repeated. Slade, I greatly want to know what you are. This is the real reason that I sent for Asya. She may be able to provide me the answers I'm seeking. Word could spread about the man who fought off my shadows. This is unneeded attention that I would not like. I would like it to be put out there that it was merely a rumor. So, what I'm asking you is, when the time is right, I would like you to throw a fight. I want you to lose to my shadows in front of those who would see me as weak, due to there being a way to fight my gifts."

"Lady Silk, for your generosity in letting me be a part of this wondrous House and the fine people who serve and love you, I would do this for you in a heartbeat. If I might add, your gift is as marvelous as it is intriguing. It must be a terrible burden to have such a unique gift. I'm happy to have met you."

"Having a gift like this makes for more lonely nights than I care for. Some men are too scared that I will cut them in half. I'm treated more like an assassin than the lady who controls the eastern land. Well, I'm more than pleased with our meeting and confident that you and I will have a very long friendship," Lady Silk said. "Oh, I almost forgot. Slade, your title here will be mister. So, you will be called Mr. Slade. Now, off with you two. I have someone else to see tonight."

Topaz and I took our leave and descended the opposite stairs. I paused a moment to look at the beautiful painting of Lady Silk and her sisters, artwork clearly done by Mistress Dawn.

We walked through the door, and Topaz took me by the hand and softly demanded that I kiss her right then and there.

"I'm sorry, Topaz. I truly want to, but I must speak with Sofia first. Otherwise, I feel I would be breaking a promise."

"She does not own you, Slade. You're a free man, and I don't think you understand how big that is around here. Even I'm not free, but my heart is. But I want you to catch it."

I took her by the hand. "Come on, we have to sort this out tonight."

We walked silently, holding hands, while Topaz tried to get into my mind. I had to fight to close it off to her, lest she wake up my irritating other half. We got back to my cottage, and I turned to kiss her on the cheek.

"I wish I could do more, but this will have to sustain you for a while."

Topaz hugged me tightly.

Chapter 13

Witches and Kisses

I knocked on the door. A few seconds later, Cheri opened it.

"Why did you knock? You know you live here. Sofia, it's Slade. He is back with Topaz."

"Why is she here with you, Slade? We want answers, and we want them now!" Sofia looked very angry.

"Sofia, please let Slade explain before you become upset and do or say something that you will regret," Topaz suggested.

Sunako moved toward Topaz. "Bitch! If I were you, I would shut up and take a seat. We don't want to hear a peep from you and your witch's tongue."

Sunako was shockingly fierce, and it was sexy. I didn't know she had that in her. It made me want to kiss her right there, but I feared that would only make things worse.

"Slade, you better do two things real fast, or we are going to spill some of your blood tonight." Sofia was poking me in the chest and rather hard.

Topaz said, "Mistress Sofia—"

"No! No more titles in this cottage!" Sofia tightly crossed her arms but stared intensely into my eyes. She had that cute little thing she did with her forehead and eyebrows when she was really upset, which hinted at a vulnerable heart.

I waved my hand toward a seat and pulled it out for her. "Please, my sweet, I know you will understand better than I do about what I'm about to tell you. Can I hold your hands?

She said, "Yes."

I spent the next twenty minutes explaining what I barely understood myself. The only way I felt they'd understand was to show them.

"Hey, Batch, time to shine."

Topaz helped me enter Sofia's mind.

"Hi, my sweet. As you have already been told, I'm Batch, a part of Slade, and can exist outside and separate of my host body. Please think of us as two people who coexist."

Batch and I stood next to each other.

"Does this make it easier to see us like this? I think it would be easier to show you something amazing—with your permission, of course."

"By all means, Batch, show me." Sofia looked cautious.

"Here are our memories. Sofia, you don't have a clue what it is like to be next to you. My heart races, and I feel sweaty, nervous, and off balance. We share this feeling for you, Sunako, and Cheri. I am the one who caught feelings for Topaz. I thought I was stuck inside Topaz's mind, never to return to my body. Now you know everything."

Sofia's image jumped into Slade's arms and said, "That is all you needed to say."

We disconnected from Sofia.

"Well, that was something. Can you give us a moment? I want to speak with my girls alone."

I excused myself from the room to go lie down and observed the beds had been moved back to the way they were. I picked a bed and lay down. It felt so soft and smelled too good. I figured it had to be Sofia's bed because it smelled like her hair. I must have drifted off to sleep.

"Slade, can you hear that? Hey, man, wake up."

"What do you want, Batch?"

"Do you hear that whispering?"

"What I hear is you interrupting a nice nap."

"You're still asleep, but I am awake, and so is your mind. There is so much that you need to learn about this place inside your mind."

Batch had a point. I really didn't know anything about myself.

"We should wake up. I think they're talking about us."

But I was not in control of the moment because someone else had plans to cut my nap short by crawling onto my lap. As I woke up, Topaz was straddling my waist, and Sofia, Sunako, and Cheri were at my sides.

"Good news. We have come to a decision."

Each wore a smile as Sofia spoke, "You will be allowed to see Topaz, but only if the old witch says it is okay. Until then, you are solely ours. You may kiss Topaz when you wish. This, we will not mind."

"Thank you, but I'm a bit confused. Why were you mad earlier?"

Sofia softly smiled. "Yeah, I was, and so were they. But after what you showed me and then talking with Topaz, we understand that this was not you trying to bend us to your will, but rather that you feel something for us. Then you found out that you had some kind of ability like hers. She also said that there is not a mental version of her in her head that can go out into other people's minds. That being said, we can still be together if you still want to be with us." Sofia batted her eyelashes.

"Why would I not want to be with you? I literally fought two of you for the right to be free and stay here with you three, and I took a beating to prove that. I truly hated the idea that I had to fight both of you."

Sofia smiled. "Really? I loved that fight. It was weird, intimate, sexy, and dangerous. Besides, Sunako fixed me up real fast; you were more of a mess than either one of us." Sofia had a playful tone in her voice. "Yeah, so I lost my first fight to date the new guy. That was a bit embarrassing, but I get to enjoy him later, which is right about now. So, I hope you had a nice nap because it's playtime and we have come up with a fun game."

Sofia stood me up and kissed me passionately for a bit. Then, she pushed me into Sunako, who took me into her arms. I put my hands in her hair, and as we kissed gently, her fingers slid under my shirt and all over my back.

I felt a second pair of hands on my hips, then I heard, "My turn." I was turned around, and Topaz said, "Hello, I waited for this all night." She grabbed my arm and pushed me to the wall. As we kissed, her hand traced the side of my face, softly biting my bottom lip as our kiss came to an end. I looked around, expecting Cheri to be next, but she was not in the room.

I asked, "Where is Cheri?"

"Slade, I don't think she understands the feelings she has for you yet. Just give her a little more time." Sofia smiled.

As I started to walk out of the room, Sunako called to me, "I wouldn't go out there. Cheri was crying as she left. She enjoys her privacy. She might knock you down."

I said, "Please give me a little while to talk with her." I left the room and walked to the front door, which was half-open, so I took it as an invite. It was pitch-black out. The clouds were blocking any moonlight. I could barely see my hand in front of my face, so I snapped my eyes black, and an ocean of colors spilled from the nothingness. When I saw Cheri, it was too late to react. She hit me right in the face, and I was sent to the ground with blood in my mouth. But before I could react, she was on me, crying silently. Her tears shined like diamonds against the blackness that made up the space between her cheek and my chest.

She looked as if she were on fire: deep blues, reds, and yellow flames poured from her skin and rose high, illuminating the area around us. I was truly amazed at what I could see with my black eyes.

Cheri slammed her fists into my chest. "Why? Why do I feel this way about you?"

The flames grew to a scary height and were white with hints of gold. The pupils of her eyes glowed a bright blue. I was in awe of what I was witnessing and became lost in the moment. Her fists brought me back to reality.

She lay down on me, and we were chest to chest. I could feel her heartbeat as if it were my own.

She sobbed into my ear and said, "Why did it have to be you? How have I lost so much control of my heart? What are you doing to me that makes me feel crazy when I'm around you? Lost, scared, angry, and happy at the same time? I want to kill you to escape this feeling, but I fear I would die without you." She sat upright and slowly pulled off her shirt and wiped her face with it. She sat there bare-breasted for a minute or so. She wore the smile of a girl at a funeral saying her last goodbyes. "I know I don't know you, but I want you so bad!" We shared our first kiss right there, and it was magical. Frenzied, our lips slid across one another as our tongues danced.

She held my face with both her hands, while I glided my hands up and down her back. I rested my hands on her perfectly developed bottom and lightly squeezed. She let out a little moan. She grinded her body against my lap. I was beginning to feel oddly sleepy and awake at the same time, my breathing quickening, as my heart threatened to fight its way out of my chest and into her hands. It felt like our tongues were melting into one. It was hard to concentrate on anything other than her salty lips and my want for more.

She ran her hand behind my neck and rolled us until she was lying on her back. I was on top between her knees, our bodies pressed together, undulating as if dancing to our own music. She held onto my neck and shoulders as we kissed. I tried to reposition myself, but she wrapped her legs around me.

"You're not going anywhere until I get my fill, and now, I want you to fill me up."

I couldn't think straight, like I was being overtaken by some deep primal urge. I began to feel more lightheaded as Cheri's hand disappeared under my skirt, taking firm hold of my manhood and sending me into what I could only describe as frenzied insanity. All logic left me as I was driven to taste her.

I placed my left hand on the side of her face, and she put my thumb in her mouth. As I turned her face, revealing her neck, I could see her pulse. I could feel it like it was a beating drum, and I was a slave to the rhythm. All I knew was that I had to be inside her. We needed to become one in the only way that felt natural. So, I bit her gently at first, but the more she moaned, the more I lost control. I pressed my body against hers and bit her deeper and harder.

"Make love to me right here, right now! I need to feel you inside me. Please, I'm starving for you!"

The rest of what she was saying was incoherent, like she was speaking in tongues.

I resisted my desire to continue kissing her neck. I sat up on my knees as she grabbed and pulled at me, trying to free me from the confines of my clothing. I pulled off my shirt and watched as she frantically tore at her pants. Her eyes were rolling to the back of her head.

That was when I heard it. A little giggle caused me to turn my head to see both Sunako and Topaz staring at us. Topaz's hand was down her pants as she was biting her lip. Sunako was covering her face, but I could see her smile.

"By all means, please continue," said Topaz.

Cheri had her pants on only one leg, and she was pulling me down to her.

Sunako whispered in my ear, "Don't stop. Can't you see she needs you right now?" Sunako's eyes looked intense, like a hungry animal in a cage just out of reach from its prey. Her tail whipped around.

"Sunako, what is taking so long? Holy shit! Are they? Bring them in! Quickly!"

Sofia tried to help me to my feet, but she got too close, and I locked onto her neck. Then, she went limp in my arms, and I kissed a little longer. I carried her into the cottage and sat her in the chair, continuing to kiss her, which felt more like feeding on her energy. I stopped because my head started to spin. I wanted something else, but I couldn't put my finger on it. All I knew was I intensely hungered for more.

Topaz walked by, carrying Cheri. "Slade, I'm going to put her in bed for when you need her later."

Sunako asked me, "Are you okay?"

I told her, "I just need the room to stop spinning. Can you take Sofia to her bed for me?" I exhaled. "Batch, what the hell is happening? Batch!" I sat down and put my head on the table.

"You don't have to yell. There are a lot of stairs in this place. What may I help you with?"

"You can start with why the hell is everything spinning?"

"It will be fine. You just took too much at one time, but you should get used to it. I call it essence drain. Cool, huh?"

"How is that cool? Sounds like I could have killed her."

"No, nothing like that. That would be lifeforce drain. Then you would be a vampire. So, you're like a vampire but not the burst-into-flames-in-the-day kind." He laughed. "I name you Count Slade."

"You're not a big help tonight."

"Hey, put me back into Topaz. I have to research this gift. Besides, I miss her."

"How do I do that again?"

"Just kiss her, then kiss her neck. She will link with us, then boom. You get some privacy."

"Sunako, please get Topaz. I need to give her something before she leaves."

"Yes, my sweet, as long as you save some for me." Sunako kissed my forehead.

I smiled and looked her in the eyes. "My dear, I have saved the best for last."

Sunako ran off with a bounce in her step. Damn, she was cute.

"Yes, Slade? You sent for me? I have been patient. Is it my turn?" Topaz bit her bottom lip as she tilted her head.

Lucky for me, my head had become steadier. "Come with me, please."

I led her into the living room, and I sat down. She straddled me. Then we started to kiss, softly and slowly at first. I just wanted to transfer Batch, but as we kissed, I noticed that each one of the ladies kissed differently. Topaz was a soft kisser as if she were studying my mouth and slowly savoring it as if it would be our last.

Topaz whispered, "I missed you so much. Take me until I have no more to give." She then removed her shirt. All she wore was a pretty, clear stone on a leather cord. I kissed her neck until I found the right spot. Then I held her tightly to me as I kissed her deeply. Her taste was so much different from the others. She was like dark coffee with almost too much sugar. We linked up as I bit her harder. Transfer was all I wanted, but I was being washed away in a torrent of passion.

"Wow, Slade. Is this what you feel every time you do this? Truly a special gift. I wonder what its true purpose is. If you think this feels good, wait until you make love for the first time."

"How can it feel better than this?"

Batch had already gone to Topaz, but he answered, "I will gather that information from Mistress Lucy. She seems to understand it better. The only info I have is that Topaz has only ever been with women, but she has heard a few stories of sexual intercourse between a woman and a man. I do not understand enough, but Lucy seems likely the key to the information we seek. What I can tell you is women like to be kissed all over their bodies. Just look for the warmest points on her body and kiss there."

"Thank you, Batch. See you soon."

No reply was given as he faded away into Topaz.

"Slade, you can kiss me anywhere you want."

I found it a bit wild to be able to kiss and speak with our minds with the only downside being that she knew my truest thoughts.

"I'm afraid that I don't understand what Batch meant."

"Where do you feel the most heat coming from on my body?" Topaz and I danced together in her mind.

"I feel it in my lap." I was sure of that.

"That's where I want you to kiss me, but it is not like the neck. You must be very gentle. Absolutely no biting. After you do that, kissing will be so much more pleasurable, but it will come in third place compared to other things."

I slowly stopped kissing her neck, and we disconnected.

"I'm sorry, Topaz, but I made a promise to Lady Silk that we would only kiss."

Topaz took my face in her hands, forcing me to look her in the eye, and declared, "It's only a kiss, just like on my mouth, but down here." Topaz took my hand and placed it between her legs. I just wanted to give in and touch her, but I knew I shouldn't. What if it was a loyalty test?

"I want to, Topaz, but I made a promise, and I feel too close to breaking it. I don't feel fully in control, and I have to live by my word, or I will be nothing but a liar with no honor. Please, help me stop before I ruin what we have. Please, Topaz, be my strength, and I will make you happier later than if we cross this line now."

"Sunako, come in here, please. I fear that Mr. Slade's mind is more on you than me right now. Can you take over for me?" Topaz kissed me as she got up. "Sunako, a minute before you mount him."

They left. I snapped my eyes black. The room was vividly dark but with deep splashes of color. Then Sunako walked in, lighting up the room. She was bright white with her wings straight out, and her tail was moving like a cat's tail with fast, jerky movements. She was fully naked and climbing onto my lap. Topaz had also removed her bottoms and sat on the end of the couch. She had just enough room to stretch her legs out to touch my hip with her foot.

"Don't mind me. If I can't join, at least I can watch and enjoy myself." Topaz wore a wicked smile that dripped with mischief.

Sunako moved slowly back and forth, side to side, while her hair covered my face. It tickled as she held onto my shoulders. She seemed to be dancing to music in her head. I caressed her back and hips as we started to kiss. I found a spot on her back that made her quiver and inhale deeply.

"Touch me like that again. Oh, that is wonderful. Your fingers are like feathers. I have goosebumps all over my body. Do you like touching me?"

"Very much so. You're soft as an angel."

Sunako took my hands and placed them on her breasts. I gently held them as we kissed. Soon, her mouth moved to my neck, and I braced for the feeling they got when I kissed their necks. She hungrily kissed and bit at me. I felt wonderful, but it was nothing like when I bit them. *Was I the only one who could do that? What would that mean? What would that make me?* I wondered what it really felt like.

Topaz got up and stood behind Sunako, whispering in her ear.

Sunako said, "Oh, I like that idea."

Topaz started to kiss one side of Sunako's neck. I started on the other side as Topaz's hand found its way to the back of my neck, holding me tightly to Sunako's neck. I liked watching Topaz as her hands traced Sunako's body. I could feel their energy moving between them and into me. I was going to have Sunako right there, but the lights came on.

"Hold the hell up! First of all, we have not had that talk, and we never decided on who goes first and in what order!" Sofia yelled.

Sunako laughed. "I think his body has chosen for him." She reached down and grabbed a little too hard. "It seems to have chosen me."

Sofia looked upset. "Of course that is going to happen. Between you and Topaz, I'm astonished he does not have you two on all fours on the floor and humping you both like a wild dog in heat!"

"Don't be gross, Sofia. Besides, he's not like that, and if he were, then I would have nothing to do with him." Sunako seemed offended by Sofia's remark.

"Well, by the look of it, you seem completely intent on having sex. I mean, you're buck naked and grinding all over his lap." Sofia was speaking with her hands.

Cheri walked in. "What's with all the noise? I was having a wonderful dream. Sunako, why are you naked? Why is she naked? Why the hell is Topaz naked?"

"Don't you try to shame me! You and Slade were mostly naked outside on the ground and just about to become one."

Cheri blushed. "I thought—I thought that was a dream. Is that true? Sofia, is that true? Was I?"

Sofia tried to hide her smile. "You were, yes. If given a few more seconds, you would have lost your virginity right there in the grass. You were like an animal. Your eyes were wild, and you tried to remove the rest of your clothes. Your pants were on just one leg. Topaz carried you to bed."

Cheri said, "All I remember was seeing you kissing him then pushing him toward Sunako, and I felt left out. So, I went to get some air, and Slade came out. I hit him, and the rest is a blur. I thought it was a dream. A really nice dream. So, why were Sunako and Topaz naked, looking like they were going to double-team Slade?"

"Because we were before Sofia walked in," Sunako said arrogantly. "I was this close to losing my virginity in his arms."

"I can say that I started out only watching, but then I began to caress Sunako. I just wanted to be close to them as they became one. You can't fault me for that." Topaz winked at me.

I said, "What about what I want? I seem to have no say. Every time I turn around, I'm either kissing someone or being attacked, which leads to kissing. Don't get me wrong, I love it, but I must confess something. I know nothing about what is going on from minute to minute! I'm just winging it. I barely understand the feelings I have and the desires I get when I am near any one of you.

"When we're kissing, those feelings and desires seem to take over in a great and heavy way. It feels like something inside of me takes over, and all I want to do is touch, kiss, and press myself on one of you. I don't expect any of you to understand because I scarcely understand it. It's almost like a language that I am so close to understanding, but then the light goes out on me."

Each of them started to laugh, which embarrassed me. I wanted to leave the room.

"Please don't laugh. I was being honest. There is no need to further humiliate me with your scornful laughter."

I stood up and started to walk out of the room.

"Slade, don't leave."

I disregarded Sofia's request. I headed into the bedroom, wishing I could take back what I said. I felt so stupid. I lay back and studied the wooden ceiling. I remembered seeing Sunako and Sofia spying on me through those little holes near the center light. Why did I tell them? I should have just acted like I knew what I was doing until I could get with Lucy. She had to have the answers I sought. I pretended not to see the girls in the doorway.

"Slade, may we speak with you?" asked Sofia.

I nodded, and they came in and sat, two on each bed.

"Slade, we meant no harm in our laughter. Honestly, what you are feeling is what we all feel."

I laughed because it was like Topaz and Sofia had been in my mind and knew my feelings.

"I'm just as scared as you are, but I want to touch you and be touched by you. I want to kiss you every time I see you. You make me feel like I have butterflies in my stomach, and I have never felt that way about anyone, let alone a man. I have—I mean—*we* have never been with a man, and we know only a little more than you. We only know Lucy's naughty bedtime stories. Poor Topaz, she is never allowed to be with a man because they believe it will taint her gift. She said that Lady Silk said you can if you are like her and if the old witch gives her blessing. That is why we said it was okay, that we will be more than fine with her and you because she has it the hardest out of all of us. Slade, can't you see she is crushing on you something crazy?"

Topaz lightly pushed Sofia. "Shut up, Sofia. I think he knows better than all of you how much I like him."

"So, Slade, how do you think we should proceed?" Sunako was very direct, and I liked that about her. "Because I want to have you like cake."

"What the hell does that mean?" Cheri was laughing.

"I heard Mr. Helge say that to Mistress Dawn last week. Then he slapped her on the ass, and they kissed in a very tender moment." Sunako smirked at Cheri.

Cheri shook her head. "He meant he wanted to kiss her between her legs, you goof."

Everyone laughed except for Sunako.

"And he said, 'I want to have your pie tonight.' He says that all the time. They're very much in love."

Sunako smiled and said, "Okay, Slade, I want to give you my pie. Peach. Have you ever had peach pie before?"

"Sunako, I have never been with a woman before I met you four, so no. And I have never had peach pie before. Only the ones from the other night. Can I have pumpkin again?"

The women laughed so much that Cheri and Sofia fell off their beds.

"Oh my, Slade, she didn't mean real peach pie, like the kind a baker would make. She wants you to eat her kitty cat."

I was half-surprised that Sofia got the whole sentence out because she was laughing so hard.

"You eat cats here? Are you savages? You know, there is almost not enough meat for a small child on those dirty little things."

Their laughter was boisterous. Topaz had tears in her eyes, and Cheri was facedown banging her fist on the floor, which made a weird echo in the room. The fit lasted long enough for me to get up, have a piss, and come back. I got changed and into bed. I pulled the covers over my head. I wondered if all the guys were laughed at.

"Oh, my sweet Slade, you misunderstand us again. Yes, you made us laugh, but not *at* you—we promise. Come on out from under the covers, and we will help you understand."

I pulled down the sheets to my chest but held them with a firm grip, waiting to be laughed at again.

"Topaz, will you do us the honor, please?"

Topaz took off her clothes, and she stood there fully naked. She was something to behold in the light.

"I will start from the top, so forgive me if you know, but these are her breasts." Sofia stood behind Topaz and ran her hand slowly over her. "This is her stomach; we love being kissed here." She glided her hand around Topaz's belly button. "This is where it gets good. This is her kitty cat, but it has many names. Some sound great. But some are downright disgusting and will not be used in the cottage unless you want to be slapped." She slid her hand between Topaz's legs toward the back then the front and did that a few times. Then, they kissed.

"Why is it called that? And what are the other names?" I was very curious because I never knew it had a name, and I had never seen what a woman had down there before.

"Thank you, Topaz. We'll finish this later. I think maybe he should learn those words from other men. Slade, you might understand it better from watching and listening to some of the guys, and if you use a word we don't like, we will politely ask you not to repeat it. You only ever get one time to say it, so stick to calling it a kitty. Trust me, you'll do fine. Just try not to pick up some of their filthy habits," Sofia said.

I had a lot to learn. "Can I just have a few days to learn about and understand these feelings? I want to at least be able to control myself around you ladies. I feel like I lose myself to more primal urges. I want to know the words and how to better explain myself."

"It's called sex or making love. Talk to Lucy tomorrow. She should set you straight. Don't lose yourself with her, and no kissing." Sofia pointed at me.

"Hey, I have a great idea." Topaz jumped back up in all her glory. "Slade, you could take Batch and have him research her mind on the topic of sex, making love, and many positions of intercourse."

"Damn, Topaz, that is a brilliant idea." Sofia hugged her. "I'll have Lucy over first thing in the morning. So, yes, you can have a few days to learn and understand what you have learned, but I warn you: I can't hold myself and them back at the same time. So, we're all going to learn one way or another."

The way she said that made me nervous.

"So, I know right now I can't sleep in the same bed with you tonight. Neither should Cheri and especially not you, Sunako! Topaz, will you sleep here tonight and be the keeper of his virtue? I know I just want to tie him down and make him mine."

"I will do my best to fend off you savages in case you find yourself sleepwalking and trying to get into the wrong bed."

They laughed again.

Topaz got into nightclothes and into bed with me. "Slade, go kiss them goodnight, and turn off the lights."

I got up and kissed each one slowly and wished them pleasant dreams. I turned off the lights, then crawled back into bed with Topaz. She grabbed me, pulling me tightly against her, and we lightly kissed. Her hand reached down and grabbed hold of me. I gripped her wrist and pulled it up to my waist. I didn't know how much more I could take.

"Please, Topaz, I don't want to sleep on the floor, but I will if you keep trying to rub me there. Just let me fall asleep in your arms."

"Sorry, but you're just so tempting."

We kissed a little before she drifted off, but sleep eluded me. My mind was awash in thoughts, mostly of how much I wanted to have them all. It didn't help that it wouldn't go soft. Then, my mind became foggy, and I was in the void with unfamiliar voices asking me questions, but I couldn't hear all the words. It felt like floating. I was so comfortable and relaxed.

"Slade, wake up!" I could hear Sofia, but it sounded like I was underwater. "Slade, damn it. Wake up!"

I opened my eyes, and the ladies were standing together, but I was higher than them and slowly rotating.

"Slade, can you hear me?"

"Is this normal? It feels very strange, like I'm in invisible water," I said.

I was trying to not freak out, but I was possibly reaching my limit on too much strange stuff in so few days. I started to move in a direction toward the dining room, and Sunako ran ahead of me to close the front door just before I sped up and slammed into it headfirst.

"Damn it!" It really hurt, but whatever had me moved me back, slamming me into the door about five times. I begged Sunako, "Please open the door!" I was afraid I'd become a part of the door.

She opened it, and I floated out and up about fifteen feet in the air. The sun was just peeking over the horizon, ready to bathe the land in its loving warmth. I could barely see the robed person with arms outstretched and wiggling fingers.

"Tell me your name, boy!"

I could not see the face because of her hood, and the figure was flanked on both sides with similarly dressed, smaller figures.

"My name is Slade. Who might you be?"

"A witch is all you need to know right now, and you will be up there until you get yourself down. But I warn you: my patience will wear out very soon. Then, I will lift you much higher, and I will let gravity teach you a valuable lesson. One you won't soon forget!"

I saw the ladies head to the nearest tree behind the strange woman.

"How am I supposed to get myself down when you clearly have me at your mercy?" I crossed my arms as I floated upside down, acting as if my dilemma was an everyday occurrence.

"At my mercy?"

I had risen at least ten more feet in the air.

"Now you're really at my mercy. It is a long way down. It will happen fast, and the sudden stop will be unpleasant."

"Maybe, but this is the unpleasant part. The fall will be a minor inconvenient romance with pain, nothing I will not brush off with ease. So, as not to waste your time, can we please get to the crux of this demonstration, or is this something you like? And you will find that I'm already spoken for by these four beautiful ladies."

"Arrogance is not an attractive quality. Besides, you could never measure up to the standards of my ideal man. Now, boy, you have eyes, yet you do not see."

Up I went again. I was now higher than the tallest trees. The rising sun looked beautiful. At least I could enjoy that.

Shit, she meant my eyes! I snapped them black, then saw that I was in a bubble of water-like substance. There was a little red dot that stayed at the same spot no matter how the water moved. So, I touched it. The water was gone, gravity finally claiming me. I held my breath so as not to yell. There was no sense giving anyone the satisfaction in knowing I was scared. The sudden rush of speed felt sickening, and I was shocked at how many thoughts I had in such a short fall. I stopped just before I hit the ground.

"Thank the gods, I thought your stupid ass would have been up there all day."

I was rotated in a way that my feet were just off the ground, and without warning, I was no longer held by an invisible force. I was back on the ground. I said nothing to the hooded figure and did my best not to throw up, as I felt it would have been a sign of weakness.

"Boy! Do you know who I am?"

I smiled and paused. "With all due respect, should I?"

"I would have thought you would at least guess as to who I am by now. What if I told you that I could restore your memories? Would you want that?" The strange woman stepped forward as she spoke.

"I would like that very much."

The two strange figures approached and shed their hoods, revealing that they were children no older than ten.

"All you have to do is defeat my two apprentices. Then, I will attempt to restore your memory."

The two stepped closer.

"Be careful. The smaller one tends to be a little biter, so I would watch those fingers if you're attached to them." She snapped, and the children walked toward me.

I smiled. "If this is what I have to do to get my memories of who I was back, then I don't want them. What kind of bastard would I be to fight a child, or better yet, what kind of bastard was I? And if I were that bastard, I would want to keep him buried deep within me, never to be let out. So, in short, I thank you for your offer but respectfully decline. If that is all, then I ask to take my leave now without further delay."

"I was informed that silver tongue of yours was something to behold. Yes, you may take your leave. Or you could be my guest for the next few days, and maybe, just maybe, we can sort you out. Would you like that?"

I thought about what I had just been offered. "Yes, I think I would like that."

"Excellent. May I come in?" Her voice was distinct: very feminine with a subtle rumble.

"I would invite you in, but I lack your name for a proper invite, and we would not want to be rude and accidentally offend you."

The stranger reached out and removed her hood and cloak. She was at least six feet tall with long light-blonde hair, piercing green eyes, and snow-white skin. On each finger except her thumbs, she wore a ring. A long necklace hung between her breasts, and it seemed to reflect an unknown light.

"I'm the old witch, Asya, at your service."

No! How could that be? She was described to me as a kindly, old woman. Asya could have not been more than twenty-five. I bowed and extended my arm toward the door.

"Please, would you be my guest and come inside our humble cottage?"

Asya placed her hands on her apprentices' heads and made a peculiar sound. They were reduced to mist, slowly settling to the ground, only to vanish around my feet. Asya moved with such grace. It could be argued that her feet did not move, but that she merely floated into the cottage. Once inside, I asked her if she would like to sit at the table or the living room.

"The living room will do just fine."

I showed her the way.

"Will it be okay if my cottage mates come back in?"

"I would think it a bit rude of us to deny them entrance to their home, wouldn't you agree?"

I was caught off guard by her answer. "Yes, a fool of me to waste your time with a question as feebleminded as that one was. I am sorry. Any further questions will be more precisely thought out as to not insult whoever took the time to educate me in the ways of communicating with my betters, as to not be viewed as a common, barbarous imbecile."

"Well, I wouldn't go that far. I would have thought poorly of your educators, but not of you, my boy."

I excused myself to get the ladies. "Sofia, are you all okay? Because you all have a look on your faces."

"Really? A look? Do you know who that is in our cottage?" Sofia looked at the other ladies.

"I do. She is the witch, Asya."

Sofia stepped forward and said, “Duh. We know that! Why is she here, in our cottage?”

“It would seem obvious that Asya is here to visit with me.”

Sofia’s look changed. “Are you being a smartass right now?” She poked me in the center of my chest in a very dominant way to remind me that I might have been a bit curt with her.

They went into the house, each giving me a little kiss on the cheek except Sofia, who gave me a peck on the lips.

“We will talk about your tone later, mister.” With a smile, she disappeared into the cottage. I wondered if she knew that I had to fight not to smile any time I looked into her eyes. I walked into the living room but stopped in the doorway.

The ladies got dressed in our room for the day and came to say goodbye.

Sofia spoke as she walked by, “Slade, we will be home after our duties. We hope to see you then.”

“Please, Sofia, a moment. Asya, may I introduce you to Mistress Sofia, Miss Cheri, Miss Sunako, and Mistress Topaz?

The ladies, including Asya, giggled.

“Oh, I see you have all met before. Of course you have. I’m the new person. I am embarrassed.”

Asya smiled. “Save your embarrassment for when you do something embarrassing, young Mr. Slade. Of course I know each and everyone’s name who lives in the House of Ribbons. I have known Lady Silk and her sisters in the time way before they had the title of lady.”

“May I speak openly, Asya?” I sat opposite of her.

“I’m an open book, brimming with knowledge. You only need to do two things. First, ask the question the right way, and second, never fear the answer. Now, come sit beside me. Let me have a good look at you, but only after you see these beautiful ladies off to their day.”

I got up and exchanged a small kiss and smile with each one.

“Miss Sunako, Mistress Topaz? Please stay with us. I believe that Lady Silk will grant you the day off from regular duties to attend to what I may need while I visit. Besides, Lady Silk is with Lady Velour for the day. I usually don’t come this fast when I get a non-urgent message, but I had to see you with my own two eyes, and now here you are—here *we* are. Shall we begin?”

Chapter 14

The Things Unseen

"I would like to start with your first memories. Now, please give me your hand. Topaz, you as well. You know the drill. Sunako, would you be a lamb and make us some tea? I brought a special type this time."

Sunako took the hand-sized bag and then disappeared into the kitchen.

"Good, now relax your mind and join me."

We sat on the couch, completely motionless and silent. To the casual observer, we looked like we were asleep, but that was not the case as our minds intermingled.

"Hello, Slade. Welcome to my mind's library."

Asya was floating above the ground in a flowing, sparkly, bright white gown. It was at least twice the length of her body in the back. In the front, I could see her knees, and her dress still didn't touch the ground. As she spoke, flowers appeared and disappeared all over her gown.

"Asya, this place is so enormous. I never thought someone's library could be so massive."

It was the largest thing I've ever seen; it stretched higher than I could see. I couldn't even glimpse the other side of the wall from my vantage point. There were books on every shelf, books on the floor, books stacked ten feet high, and some books just floated around as if carried by invisible students.

"Slade, this is the accumulation of all my knowledge. The size of a being's library is based on their age, their pursuit of knowledge, and new discoveries. My dear Slade, I live for these things."

"There are so many colors here. I don't even know what those colors are over there, and why do these books have a keyhole?" I traced my mental fingers over the book and the lock.

"I think the better question you want to ask is how to learn to make locks like this for your books. What do you do when you have a guest inside your mind? Do you let them just mill around and sneak a peek at this and that?" Asya asked.

"I never thought of it like that, and I have only had Topaz inside of my mind until today. The question I have is: how do I make locks like these? How can I best protect myself?" I floated up and gazed at all the wonder around me. "Why don't my black eyes work in these places?"

Asya laughed. "Simply put, you have no eyes here. This place is the mental projection of what I want your mind to see. Watch this." She snapped. The room became a field of flowers with a stunningly colossal waterfall about a half-mile away. "If you like that, then keep your eye on me."

She snapped again and quickly transformed into a terrifyingly monstrous dragon, easily big enough for me to walk straight down her throat. Each tooth was six feet long. I tried to walk back, but I fell backward, covering my face as she drew near. Her chin was in the grass, while Topaz looked scared and frozen to her spot.

I was very frightened in that moment. "Please stop! I get it! You're the master in the world that is your mind!"

The dragon laughed. "I would run if I were you, little snack! Run or stop me. If not, I will show you a horror that your mind is not yet ready to handle!"

With that, she let out a deafening roar that made me feel as if my heart was rattling. She snatched Topaz up with a massive, clawed hand and said, "Run, boy, run! You don't have what it takes to make your stand here, let alone fight me!"

I stood my ground until she let slip her flames. Then I did as I was told and ran to one side as the heat kissed the back of my neck with an unfriendly bite. I knew the pain was not real, but my mind made it authentic enough. I ran, but she stayed in her place. I kept my eye on the waterfall. With the simple theory that water beat fire, I figured I should be safe from it as long as I reached the water. Soon, I felt the mist on my skin, which made my neck feel better. Even at that distance, she was massive. Her wings were double her body length. She truly looked impossible. Nothing could ever be that enormous while living on a planet with humans.

"I said *run*, boy!" Her thunderous voice shook the ground beneath my feet.

Asya started to gallop toward me with an astonishing speed. I backed up into the water until I was chest-deep as she leaped into the air. With a mighty flap of her wings, she was airborne. The wind hit me with such force that it caused me to be pushed back into the water. She flew by, and I could see Topaz struggling to free herself.

"Help me, Slade! Asya has gone mad."

Was that why the old woman had come unannounced so early in the morning? Had she gone mad? How were we going to get out if we couldn't disconnect?

"Boy! Save her before I drop her or worse." Asya ascended again, and I heard Topaz scream.

I had to do something, but what?

Asya stopped and hovered. She roared and let Topaz go—her screams were heart-wrenching. I was helpless; all could do was watch her fall. I tried to float, like back in the library, but it wouldn't work. I attempted to use my willpower to get me off the ground, but nothing responded. The best I could do was get under her. Maybe I could break her fall, or at least, we would die together. So, I ran to where I believed she would hit.

Topaz screamed for me to get out of the way.

I yelled to her, "If you die today, then I will die trying to save you!"

But her body was snatched up mere feet from impact, and the force of the wind pulled me off my feet.

Topaz yelled, "You must find it within yourself to stop her!"

But how could I stop a mountain of teeth and claws hell-bent on eating me? Wait, if she wanted to, she could do anything she could think of. So, why couldn't I? Mountains only feared water, so I had to become water.

Asya landed just a few lengths away from me. I slowly left the water.

As my clothes clung to me, I yelled, "I will give you one chance to let her go and release us from your mind, or you will be sorry—this, I swear!"

She tilted her head and began to laugh, loud and long. I will admit it was more than a bit demoralizing being laughed at by a behemoth dragon witch.

"How is a tiny tick like yourself going to stop me *here*, in my own world, no less?" She continued to laugh. "What are you going to do, make me laugh to death? Because you're killing me right now."

Asya released Topaz, who ran into my arms, and we kissed. "I'm sorry, Topaz. If I never came to the House of Ribbons, you wouldn't be in danger. Is there any way we can disconnect from her?"

Topaz said, "No, she owns this place. We will die here if she wills it, and our bodies cannot live without our minds. Before we die, will you tell me that you love me, just once? Please, I want to hear it from your real lips."

"Wait, can you reunite Batch and me?"

She kissed me and transferred Batch back home to me.

"Batch, do you have any ideas?"

"I have one, but you are not going to like it. I think you should run at her, try to climb upon her back, then look for a weak spot. She will not be able to get you in that form, and if she changes, then maybe we can get her between changes."

"That's a shitty idea, Batch, but it's better than anything I have." I ran toward what could only be described as a living horror.

"Hey, man, what can I say? I'm the smart one, and you're, well, you're just the body with a pretty face."

I told Batch, "Shut it, jackass. If I die, you are definitely coming with me."

I reached Asya's front leg and started to climb as she was running, which made it almost too hard to hold on. She took off and away into the sky.

"I hope you're still with me, little tick. I wouldn't want you to fall off. I still have plans for you, my tiny chew toy. When I'm done with you, I'm going to swallow Topaz's mind and slowly digest her thoughts and add them to my library. She will become just another book with a pretty lock. I'll do the same to you as well. Then when I'm all done with you two, I will devour Sunako and Cheri. I will get Sofia, but I will make it slow for her. I will tell her how you had the chance to save them all, but you failed! You failed yourself, and they had to pay for it!"

The image was so upsetting, but that anger fueled my climb. I finally reached her back and noticed how high we really were.

"Where are you, my little tick? I hope you don't mind a little acrobatics."

She leaned to one side and rolled at a sickening speed. I held onto one of her scales, but my hands became useless against the centrifugal force, and I involuntarily let go. I was in free fall.

I rolled to see Asya descending toward me. Her mouth opened as she got closer, hungrily preparing to gobble me up. I gave in to my only thought. If I were a dragon of that size, I would be able to fight back and maybe save Topaz. I could die happy knowing that I freed her from such a prison. Maybe she could get help to fight the crazy witch in the real world. We were at least a mile up and still gaining speed. The sound of the air rushing by was deafening. Her jaws snapped shut, opened, and clicked shut again. At that point, she was just playing with me. I thought about my current size and my steering abilities. I found that I could, so I shifted to the left and spread out my arms and legs. The air shot me up past Asya, just narrowly missing her spiked tail. Either way, I was out of range of her gaping jaw.

Well, that was one problem down. Next was how not to become a stain of meat and bones after I smashed into the ground with the force of a falling star.

How did she become that monstrous beast? Did that mean I could be whatever I wanted? If so, then I wanted to be giant, so big that she looked like a knee-high dog. Asya flew off to the right, and the ground was rushing up to give me my final farewell kiss. When I hit the ground, I was confused because it felt more like I'd fallen from five feet, not a few *miles* up. I rose to my feet, and as I did, everything seemed oddly small, especially Asya. She looked smaller. No, I had become huge—a huge human. I was taller than the waterfall, but Asya was growing by the second.

"I see you, little tick. Remember that you live in my world, and here, you will die by my claws."

I took off as quickly as my legs could start, and we hit at full speed. Just as I threw my shoulder into her, she grew bigger. The force of my body mixed with the speed I'd gained caused me to hit her harder than I expected. She was thrown backward onto her back, and I jumped up onto her abdomen knees-first, grabbing her by her scaly neck. I squeezed with everything I could muster. Her eyes were fixed on me, and her mouth opened. I could see a faint glow, so I freed a hand and grabbed her mouth just as a small amount of fire escaped, burning my hand and fingers. It only fueled my rage and desire to twist her head off. Her claws tore into the flesh of both forearms, and I struggled to apply more pressure. I felt as if my wrists were going to break.

"I hate this place, and I will not let you harm my friends." I sent a thought out to Batch.

"What can I do, Slade?"

"Batch, in this place of the mind, shouldn't you be able to come out and wander?"

"I didn't think about that, but, yeah, it should work."

"Great, now get your ass out here. We have some work to do."

With that, he was standing there, but was really small.

"How is that supposed to work with you so tiny? Stop being a jackass!"

"Sorry, Slade, but this didn't come with a manual, so give me a second!" Batch rose and grew until he was my size. "How is this, brother?"

"Just grab her. I want to try something."

I envisioned a set of chains wrapped around her body and a muzzle for her face. I found it easier to concentrate when not struggling so much.

"Slade, what now?"

"I guess we wait for this witch to release us, or we can beat her to death."

"Oh yeah! Or we could just beat her until she is too weak to fight back. Then we might be able to get past the locks on her books. Imagine what we could learn."

"Batch, you have a good point. She was going to kill us anyway, and you know the old saying: 'Do unto others.'"

Asya laughed. "Good! It's about time. You two are a bit slow, but I think I can work with it." The dragon disappeared, and only her voice remained. "Would you like to go back to the library or stay here where I can show you that I own this world and you're just a first-day student?" Asya's voice echoed seemingly from everywhere.

I asked, "How do I know that you are not just afraid to continue because we had the upper hand?"

Just as I finished my sentence, Asya appeared out of nowhere and took my arm. With a small twist, I was on both knees. Batch came to help, but with little effort, she kicked him farther than I could see.

"Oh, I'm sorry. Did I interrupt your thought? Did I just steal your thunder? It's okay if you have nothing more to say. So, shall we adjourn for now? I believe our tea is just about done." Asya snapped, and we were all back in her library. "I hope this, our first-time training, was eye-opening for you and what you can do if you use your mind. It's a very powerful tool and weapon to wield. Here, Batch, take a copy of this book and study it. You should find it very useful."

"Thank you, but it is in a language I cannot read." Batch flipped through the pages.

"No, you just need time to learn to read it." Asya smiled.

"Topaz, did you know that we were not in danger?"

Topaz shook her head. "I did not. I really thought she went crazy."

"Well, I smell a warm cup of tea, and that means our time is up. Batch, get back to your home, please."

I opened my eyes and stood up. "So, what was that all about?" I almost bumped into Sunako.

"Watch it, Slade. You almost got me wet." Sunako winked at me.

Topaz laughed, and Asya raised an eyebrow. I hoped to find out why girls always laughed at that.

"Slade, if you spill my tea, I swear I will stick you to the ceiling overnight. This tea is rare and hard for even me to get." Asya reached out, grabbed her cup, and took a sip. "Oh yes! Sunako, you know the perfect time to steep tea. You're a true angel."

I whispered, "You have no idea."

"Slade, do you think you are the only one with eyes like yours?" She made her eyes go black with the snap of her fingers. "I was born with mine, and they're just like yours. And, yes, she's an angel with one hell of a story of how she came into existence, but that is another beautiful tale for a later day. I will tell it to you, my sweet Sunako."

I asked, "Why do I have these eyes?"

"My child, you were born with those eyes. I think you may be rarer than you could ever imagine. Stories tell of a boy, an orphan adopted by a king who had special eyes himself—just different. He was seemingly a normal boy with blue eyes, and on his thirteenth birthday, his eyes fell out, and the gods wept for him. Theia, one of the twelve Titans and the Titan goddess of sight, traveled to the boy that night and bathed him in her tears. She took her right eye and made them into two, then kissed the boy on the forehead. Then she told him to open his eyes to see the world for what it really was. The boy opened his new eyes and marveled at what he was seeing. My child, witness all the old magic mixing with the new magic, and see the magic yet to be. Theia is an oracular goddess; she also gifted his heart the ability to divine the future. A male oracle, the first of his kind, due to the fact that they only selected women who were pure of heart. They carried the light that can peer into eternity's darkness without going mad. It was said that the three Sisters of Fates are some form of gods who whisper the future into the ears of the truly gifted. It's said they visited the black-eyed boy often. He later became the first mortal friend to the Sisters of Fate."

I sat and took in the story as we sipped the delicious tea.

"This boy had been such a great success that many lifetimes later, Theia convinced Nyx—one of the primordial goddesses—to help her conceive a child with Ares, who was one of the twelve gods of Olympus and the god of war. Nyx insisted that the child would be kept secret from the world until Nyx knew the time was right. A child with the strength and physicality of Ares, clarity of sight of prophesy from Theia, and a kiss from Nyx—he would represent balance and help bring that balance whenever called upon. He would serve the Sisters of Fate with unquestioning loyalty. He would become their hammer. He would learn to walk the many worlds while seeking out the other lost and secret children. He would be able to open the doors forbidden to even the gods. Those doors are only accessible to the thirteen primordial gods, Chaos and her children, six goddesses, and six gods. Nyx is Chaos's firstborn daughter, greatly beloved and feared by all."

"How many stories are there about this boy?"

"A few. In another story, he becomes husband to one of the sisters, then a god himself."

"Then what purpose do my eyes serve?"

"My child, I just told you. It helps you see the true world around you. As you get used to them, you might find a few more uses for them." Asya took a small sip of her tea and said, "Yum. Oh, how long I have waited to share and enjoy this tea with new friends. My boy, you have questions, so please waste no time. Ask away."

"I don't really know where to start."

Asya smiled. "Start where you want. Your mind will put it in order later."

I didn't know why, but I liked her. She seemed like she really cared.

"The story you just told. Who are Theia and Ares?"

"Theia is a Titan goddess and the mother to Eos the dawn, Helios the sun, and Selene the moon. Ares is the god of war, and he lives on Mount Olympus. He is an Olympian, a sheer force of nature; his only true love is war. Not victory, just war. But you forgot about the most important goddess. Without Nyx, the mother of all oracles, you, Topaz, and I would not have these amazing gifts."

"What does that all mean?" I had no clue what to think.

"Well, Slade, it seems that you were at least personally kissed by the primordial goddess. Nyx is the second oldest goddess, which makes you blessed beyond that of a regular oracle. In all of my travels, I have never seen or heard about a male oracle. Plus, you have the black eyes. You only get them if they are gifted to you. Do you want to know what they are called?"

"Yes, I very much would like to know what they are called."

"The Eyes of Nyx," said Asya.

I was silent, expecting a better name.

"Look at his face, Topaz. He was expecting a better name." They were laughing together. "Slade, the blessing from Nyx comes after a woman has proven herself loyal, usually after ten. Don't look so glum, my young friend. As you get older and understand the importance of the gods, you will see that the Eyes of Nyx sounds better than it does now."

"Asya, is the story true? Was there a boy born of a Titan and an Olympian? Am I that boy? Do I get to meet my mother and father?" My excitement caused my heart to race.

"I'll be honest, Slade. It's all just a story from a very old, dusty book. Some stories tell tales, and some tell of how to be a good person through a colorful story."

"But my eyes? My gifts? Asya, are the gods and goddesses real?" I had a tear in my eye that I fought to hold back, but it spilled out. "Asya, I must know who I am and why I was thrown away! I need to know what I did wrong."

"Slade, I have never met a god or goddess, but I have faith in their invisible presence. Just look at us and what we can do. If that is not a gift from the gods, then I don't know what is. Come here, my child."

Asya took me into her arms, and I silently cried on her shoulder. "I have you now. You're safe with me, my child. Just give it time, and all will unfold before your special eyes. Oh my, is that smell coming from you?"

Sunako said, "Yes, from the first second I held him, he smelled like that, but now he smells stronger than ever and even more beautiful." Sunako stood up. "Give him to me now!"

"Sleep now, my children."

Topaz and Sunako fell over.

"Slade, what are you doing? Whatever you're doing, stop it."

I was crying, full of anger and sorrow.

"Slade, sleep now. Sleep now!" Asya stood up and disappeared when I wouldn't fall asleep. I was so angry that I could not control my eyes. They periodically switched on their own. I couldn't breathe, so I went outside to calm myself.

"Slade, wake up. Slade, wake the hell up!"

I slowly opened my eyes to the blurry outline of a long-haired woman with her hand out.

"Take my hand, and I will wake you up, but not before I tell you that I love you. I am waiting for you to find me. Come find me. Come fall in love with me again. I promise to keep you safe if you're honest and true."

"Who are you? Why can't I see you very well?" I asked.

"Your eyes are stuck between here and there. I need you to find me by voice alone. I love you."

"Slade! Wake up!"

With a hard slap, I woke up.

"Welcome back. Now let's get you back inside."

"Asya, what happened? Who was that woman? Why are the ladies on the floor?"

"Slade, you became a little too emotional. You will really need to control the sadness inside of you because it seems to trigger your amazing smell. I got away just in time."

"Got away?"

"Your smell was clouding my thoughts, so I needed fresh air. Look, I'm going to wake the ladies up. I'll tell them the tea was a little too strong. Are you ready?"

I nodded.

"Ladies, wake up. Looks like the tea was a bit strong. I took the liberty of watering it down a bit." Asya sipped her tea. "Ah, so much better. Now where were we with your questions? Something about me, I think?"

I asked, "So, about what you called training: what was the purpose of not telling me that it was training? Why did you make me feel that Topaz was in danger? Then you said you were going to get my friends."

"Okay, not a question about me, so let's jump in with both feet. If I told you it was training, I would have never been able to see what you could do. I needed you to feel that you had something to lose, like your life or the lives of your friends. Best part is, like a true hero, you only cared about your friends and lovers. You would have sacrificed yourself for them, and you only recently met them. In your chest truly beats the heart of a hero. I am proud of you. Many fail their first test."

"Why can't I remember who I was before I came here?" I felt like she was holding something back.

Asya took a long sip, stood up, and stretched her long arms high in the air. "Slade, while you were training, I was researching your mind and memories. What I gathered is you have blank spots, no different than if it had been cut out. I'm sorry, but whoever did this to you did it on purpose. For what reason, I don't know. Maybe it is to protect you, the world, or maybe them."

"From whom or what?"

"Maybe from you, Slade. Maybe you're so particularly important that you need to be hidden away until the time is right, or maybe you're a dangerous beast from the void sent to devour the universe, and trust me, we don't need another one."

"You mean like the boy in the story?"

"Okay, Mr. Slade, what if you are the boy from the story? And that is a huge *if*." She studied my face.

"Okay. What if?"

Asya smiled and took my hand. "Then you will find your life will be blessed. You don't seem to care if you're a beast from the void or a mad god intent on conquering the universe?"

"No, I don't. How old is that story?"

"I found a book that was over two thousand six hundred years old, and that story was in it. Based on the time of the Greek god Ares, that could have been another few hundred years. So, let's say close to three thousand years ago."

"I'll be honest: I don't feel that old. If I was, why do I seem so young?"

"Time means almost nothing to the gods; you may very well have been asleep. You could just be one lucky guy, and you will not age after a certain point. And that was the 'if.' Besides, it does make for a fun campfire story. The fact is you're a male oracle with the Eyes of Nyx. So, let us focus on the here and now. May I see your bracelet?"

I extended my arm, and she smiled, trying to remove it for a few minutes. "Nice trick. Be a dear and remove it for me."

I took it off and handed it to her. My wrist felt naked.

Asya studied it for a few minutes, and I excused myself to use the bathroom. It had only been about a week, and so much had happened. I was overwhelmed. All I wanted to know was who I was, but all I'd found was that there was only a hole and that someone had put it there. Someone stole the parts of myself that made me *me*. Someone stole me. I tried to push the thought out of my mind, but it kept returning. So, I splashed some cold water on my face before returning to the living room.

"Did you make any discoveries while I was away?"

Asya said, "I believe I have. Could you stand over there?" She pointed to the far end of the room, and I found my mark.

"Slade, I think this was made for you, and it, like you, is one of a kind. I believe it will lead you home one day. In all my years, I have never seen writings like this. Now, hold out either arm and watch this." Asya threw the bracelet at my face with remarkable speed. I almost didn't get out of the way in time.

"Hey! You could have put my eye out with that thing! If you were testing my reflexes, okay, but we don't throw things at my face. Some would find it rude."

The three women laughed.

"Please, someone tell me what is so funny! I understand a lot, but there are times you laugh and I have no clue what is funny. Like now—what did I say that was funny? What joke am I missing now?"

They all pointed at me, and Asya said, "Slade, look at your wrist."

I raised my arm and saw my bracelet nestled comfortably around its home. "How did you do that? Was that magic?"

"No, not magic. It only recognizes its owner's touch. I first thought it to be a simple enchantment because some items like that are something that can be easily imbued with magic, but I see now that this is not the case. Slade, I believe your seemingly inconspicuous silver bracelet is hiding a huge secret. One being it's no doubt a piece of advanced technology, and two, I think it either knows your name or this writing is important to only you. Maybe everything you need to know is within it."

"Advanced technology?"

"You really have no idea what I mean, do you? Think of it as a form of magic that runs on electricity, but this seems to be from a place far away."

"Did you look at it with your black eyes?"

"No."

I laughed. "Go on and look." I handed it back to her.

"Slade, I don't see anything different."

I placed my hand on hers and snapped my eyes black while looking at my bracelet.

"Holy shit! I don't, I don't know what to say. Look at it move and snake around itself as if alive, like living metal… And the colors! If I didn't see this with your eyes, I would have called you a liar to your face."

I took my hand off hers.

"Well, you are my newest and most important person to study. With your permission, of course."

I smiled and said, "Of course. It would be rude otherwise."

"Why didn't you see it with your eyes?"

"I would very much like to know that myself."

We both looked at one another for a minute, and I felt strange, like I knew her. Was she someone I knew but didn't remember? Was she testing me? Asya broke our staring contest.

"I hear you have an unusual coin. May I see it?"

I handed over the satchel I wore around my neck. "It was in this when I woke up."

"It's clearly leather, but the cord feels stronger than it looks. Oh my, look at this. In all my years, I have never seen a coin like this, and this symbol on the back is strangely familiar. I hear you know Latin as well."

"Oculos pulchros habes."

"You pronounced that perfectly as if Latin was your first language. Thank you for the compliment. Now, I am hungry, and I am sure you three are as well. Sunako, I hear you make delicious eggs?"

"Yes, but we are out of eggs, I'm sorry to say."

"I think I saw a box on the table. It should have more than enough for us and a week's worth for you all later."

Sunako said, "I don't remember you having a box with you, but thank you very much." Sunako got up and saw the box on the table. "Oh my. Topaz, come give me a hand."

"It's my pleasure, dear child, and no, I didn't have that box with me. The two little ones brought it in a few minutes after Mr. Slade used the bathroom. You would not have seen them because they're very good at being unseen."

"What happened to them? It looked like you turned them into smoke or mist," I said.

Asya smiled. "I only moved them from one place to another, and the mist is just for show. It adds to the *wow* factor. It's a witch and wizard thing." She winked. "Slade, while we have a true moment alone, may I ask you something?"

I nodded.

"How do you feel about this place? Would you leave if you could?"

"I won my freedom, so I can leave if I wish, but I like it here."

Asya slowly looked around the room. "Is it because of your little harem you have gathered here?"

"I don't know of what you speak. If one could clarify their true intentions, then one would be able to articulate the correct retort."

Asya's eyes went wide. "Well, I see your years of being a great pupil have not been taken from you. I would hazard a guess that whoever your teacher is or was would hold their head up high, knowing that your intellect not only stayed intact, but that you flaunt it like the royals do, with gold and other pretty trinkets. I take it you have some fight training buried beneath your pretty blond locks, because when I look into your ocean eyes, I see something untamable and consuming." Asya slid closer until our legs touched. "I understand why they flock to you. Not to mention the smell that radiates from you. It must be very hard to be around you for long periods without touching you."

"Yes, it's a bit overwhelming. I don't understand what they want and when they want more. I lack the knowledge of what I should do."

"May I be so bold and ask which one of them have you made yours yet, or is it all four of them?" Asya was very interested.

I smiled. "Asya, I have not been with any of them. I have a plan to learn what I need to know from the mistress next door. Mistress Lucy has knowledge on the subject of how best to be intimate."

"Mistress Vixen? By the gods, not her, my boy! I take it you have met her, and it would be safe to assume that she wanted some time alone with you? I'm right, aren't I?"

"Yes, she offered to buy or rent me from Mistress Sofia, but Sofia's price was too high for Lucy to pay in the moment."

"Really? And do you know what this price for you was?"

"Ten pieces of some kind of candy. When Lady Silk found out, she laughed and said that the price was too high because it would make her well-off. Tell me: if this candy is so precious and ten pieces is a lot, then would not it be wise of me to make sure my mistress is well-off?"

"I don't think you understand what is being asked of you. Do you really have no knowledge of the game called love?"

"I know that love in an intense feeling between two people, but there is more than two people I feel intensely for—that is what confuses me."

"I think I understand your confusion. You're hung up on monogamy."

"I don't know that word."

"Interesting. Monogamy is love or intimacy between two people. It's an outdated practice in places like this. The word you should get used to is polyamory, love between multiple partners."

"That makes sense, but it still seems like someone would get their feelings hurt."

"You just worry about you. They know what they're doing." Asya paced about the room and appeared to be talking with someone. She stopped, sat with me, and sipped her tea.

"What of the woman from my dream?" I asked.

"Dreams, most times, are just that. Dreams. Our mind enjoying a bit of playtime."

"But it was so real. One time, I got a good look at her, and she had deep tan skin with piercing green eyes like yours."

Asya spat her tea on me.

"I hope this is not a custom from where you are from because that was a bit unpleasant."

"I'm sorry. Did you—did you say green eyes and tan skin?" Asya asked while her voice shook.

I nodded.

"Yes, it must have been a dream. You know, with your newfound intense emotions and desires."

"Asya, why are you lying to me? I can hear your heart speed up when you speak. Is she real?"

From just outside the doorway, Topaz called, "Asya, the food is ready." Asya jumped up and walked by Topaz, whispering something into her ear.

Topaz smiled, walked up to me, and said, "Asya said you wanted to speak with me."

"Close your eyes, please. Batch and I want you to have this."

I took her in my arms and kissed her deeply and walked away, but she followed a few minutes later.

We all talked while we ate a strange type of meat and eggs that tasted sweet and salty. I drank some berry juice. We laughed, and Asya sang a song at the end of the meal. She said it was to honor the food we ate in hopes that it would bring us strength and vitality to fuel the mind. It would let the soul soar high enough to be blessed by the gods from times long past. As Asya sang, she made butterflies appear that fluttered around the room, each a different kind and color. Her song was pleasant on the ears, and I felt it in my chest. It made me feel warm and loved. When it was over, I missed it like a lover's kiss drying on my lips.

We spent the rest of the day talking. Many hours passed until Sofia and Cheri arrived home, the setting sun following them.

"Go to them. Greet them with what they longed for most today," Asya ordered.

So, I walked up to Cheri and hugged her and whispered to her that I missed her, and we kissed. Then, I walked up behind Sofia and asked for her hand. She gave it to me, and I spun her around. We danced for a few minutes around the kitchen, kissing lightly. I rested my hands on her hips, her hand settling on my back, while the other caressed the back of my neck.

Sofia said, "You remembered that I like to dance."

I smiled, "I waited patiently from the moment you walked away this morning to dance with you. You're so light on your feet that you seem to glide across the floor."

"Slade, I thought of you all day. I missed you so much. Thank you for being you. We'll be in the shower if you feel you need a kiss."

They walked off, leaving a trail of clothes behind them. They both stopped at the bathroom door, looking over their shoulders at me. I took their winks as a second invite. As I was taking off my shirt, I did not see Asya behind me.

Asya coughed. "Slade, I believe you have company that you need to attend to. Don't you think?" Her height made me feel small. She leaned down to meet my eyes and gave me a warm smile. She took me by the hand and led me to the bathroom. She walked us up to the shower, which was large enough to fit four people. The water flowed from the ceiling from what looked like two metal flowers. Both could be used at the same time, or they could employ just one.

"Mr. Slade will not be joining you two in the shower. As much as he would like to, we invite you to sit with us tonight for a talk and maybe some stories."

"Thank you, Asya. It's our pleasure to have you in our cottage."

Sunako and Topaz prepared dinner as the other two showered and got dressed.

"Mistress Sofia, would you mind if I added a bit more company for tonight's dinner party?" Asya's hands were together as she spoke.

Sofia looked around the room as she dried her hair with a small towel. Whipping her hair back, she said, "The more the merrier."

"Slade, go next door, and ask Tova and Lucy to come over as my guests."

I left at once, but as the door shut behind me, Asya startled me.

"How did you get out here? I just left you in the dining room. Was it that disappearing thing you do?"

"Maybe I'll teach you one day, but this night, I have one smaller request of you. Dinner will be served in forty minutes, and I want you to spend at least thirty minutes of that time with Lucy in her cottage. Ask her for a tour, seem interested in whatever she might say, and flirt a little. Welcome more sexual advances, but refuse. Mind yourself as to not get out of hand. Do not lose yourself to her, but kissing here and there will not hurt. This will be your perfect opportunity to fish out the knowledge you seek from within her filthy little mind. Remember my words: do not let it get out of hand over there. Leave after you obtain this newfound information. Now, be off with you. I'll tell Sofia what you're doing."

I walked off toward Lucy's cottage while enjoying the beauty of the setting sun.

"Sofia, after you are fully dressed, grab a backpack and escort me to Mr. Otho's cottage at once."

"Yes, Asya."

A short five-minute walk and they arrived at their destination. Sofia knocked on the door, and Mistress Acacia answered.

"Ah, Mistress Sofia. How are you this night?"

"Mistress Acacia, I am well. May we speak with Otho?"

"Of course." Acacia called for him. "Sofia, how is your new toy? Is he as enjoyable in bed as he was during the fight?"

"A lady never tells of such debauchery." Sofia tried unsuccessfully to hide a wicked smile.

"Yours and Cheri's fight with him was one of the best fights I have seen in long time. Well, if he can make love half as good as he can fight, then, my sexy Sofia, your nights are filled with good times. Don't forget to invite us over for dinner or maybe a late-night snack. Don't go forgetting us now that you have a man." Acacia had one arm extended to the top of the door as she spoke.

Sofia smiled and said, "I will definitely keep you two in mind. Thank you for the offer. I look forward to taking you up on it."

Otho came to the door.

"See you later, Sofia."

"You as well, Acacia."

"Otho, how are you tonight?"

"I am well, Mistress Sofia. How may I be of service to you?" Otho bowed as he spoke.

"Cut that, Otho. You're always so silly. We are here to see you and procure some of your delicious wine."

"We? Lady Silk needed twenty bottles before she left yesterday. What do you have for trade?"

Asya stepped out of the shadows. "Hello, Otho, how have you been? I trust the recipe I gave you a few years ago has worked well for you. I trust they have yielded a much better taste?"

Otho dropped to his knee. "Asya, forgive my bumbling mouth. I did not mean to waste your time."

"Otho, get up! What have I told you about that type of behavior? You will speak to me as if I were your equal." Asya helped Otho to his feet.

"I'm sorry, Asya. You're like a goddess who walks side by side with our kind. What do you two need? I have a selection that is a far superior selection than the other two Houses. Please, come inside and have a seat."

"Otho, please. I'm not a goddess, but you're the cutest thing for saying so. I am having a dinner party that seats eight. What would you suggest for type and quantity? And yes, a little tipsy would be nice tonight."

"Ah, yes. Then may I suggest my new sweet cherry wine? This is not to be confused with plain cherry wine. No, no, this is magic on the tongue, I assure you. I have white and red wine. I have broken them down into names. They're Blood of the Moon, Ageless Smile, Fighting the Break of Dawn, Soul of an Angel, Tears of the Fallen, and Laughter in a Glass. For the times you want a little lightheaded giggle, go for Blood of the Moon and Sweet Cherry. Those are reds, and the rest are white. I named Ageless Smile after your smile, Asya."

"Oh my, Otho, you have been a busy little bee, haven't you? I knew you were the right soul to give those recipes to, and your names are so delightfully imaginative. May I gift you a kiss on your cheek?"

"It would be such an honor, thank you."

Asya leaned toward Otho, kissing him gently on the cheek. Otho turned a deep red with the ear-to-ear smile of a child.

"Well, for that many guests, may I suggest eleven bottles? I find it better to have a little more than too little. Shall I select for you?"

"Please do, Otho."

He left the room while Sofia and Asya exchanged small talk.

Otho returned with a wooden crate. "Here are eleven of my newest and finest. I hope that you will find them to your liking. The whites were already chilled, but the red needs at least thirty minutes to chill but no longer than one hour."

Asya said, "Thank you, Otho. How much do I owe you?"

Otho looked at Asya and said, "Your money is no good here. If it were not for you, I would have just been a basic winemaker. You have elevated me to a legendary winemaker almost overnight. No, I cannot accept any money."

"Well, then. Will you accept this instead? I mean, who would turn down a handful of candy?"

Otho's eyes looked as if they would fall out.

"Go on, Otho. You wouldn't want to offend an old woman, would you? Be a sweetheart, and please call on Acacia and Aelia for me."

Otho took seven pieces of candy, and they disappeared into his pocket. Soon after that, Acacia and Aelia entered the room.

"Ladies, thank you for always being kind to one of my very favorite young men. I have a gift for each of you. Now, open your hands if you would, please."

Asya gave each woman two pieces of candy.

"Now, I trust you two will continue to look after my dear sweet boy with great kindness for me. Yes?"

"We love Otho as if he were our very own brother. Always have." Acacia stared at the candy as if it were pure gold.

"Asya, may I carry this crate for you?" Otho reached for the crate, but Asya twitched her fingers, and the crate started to float upward.

"Thank you, Otho. You're a true gentleman through and through, but I have this."

The door opened on its own, and Asya and Sofia took their leave, the crate floating along with them.

"Otho, my dear. I could use your help on something."

Otho moved quickly toward Asya. "Yes, Asya."

Asya floated Otho up to her eye level.

"I wanted to give you this." She handed him an unraveled piece of cloth. "This has five new and two very old directions for new wine to add to your list. I will have a box delivered to you with something to add to the soil. I will send one of my sisters to instruct you on how to use everything. Maybe you two will hit it off." She handed him another piece of candy, and he went back inside.

"Sofia, I trust you will keep Otho's secret winemaking tricks to yourself?"

"Asya, I do not know what you're talking about. I was busy looking at something off in the distance in the other direction while thinking of Slade's lips."

Asya handed Sofia a piece of candy as they walked back.

"Just in time. Dinner will be on the table in ten minutes." Topaz moved to accept the crate.

"Where is Slade?" Sofia noticed he was not in the cottage.

"I sent him to retrieve some information for me and to fetch our guests. Now, while the boy is away, tell me all about him and spare no details. You know I like to live vicariously through you all."

Chapter 15

Dinner Party with Angels

I knocked on Lucy's cottage door.

Tova answered. "Hi, Slade. How are you this evening?"

"I am well. I was wondering if your mistress is home? If so, may I speak with her?"

"I will get her at once. Wait here."

She returned with Lucy by her side.

Lucy slowly licked her lips. "How can I be of service to you, Mr. Slade?" She leaned her head on the doorframe and widened her eyes, which gave her pretty face a whole new look.

"I am here to invite you two over for dinner and drinks as personal guests of the witch, Asya. But first, I need to speak with you in private. Tova, you're expected soon after you get this message."

Tova jumped up and down, clapping. "Wow, dinner with Asya! Let me put on a better shirt and throw my hair up." Tova had a bounce in her step as she hurried away.

Lucy invited me in as Tova rushed round.

Tova exclaimed, "See you over there!" She exited and left the door open.

Lucy moved to close the door, but before she could turn around, I stepped up behind her and murmured, "This is nice, just you and me. I like it better this way. No sharing, and I get the one-on-one attention from you that my body is craving." I pressed my chest to hers. As we kissed, Lucy's hands wrapped around me, holding on tight as if we hadn't seen each other in many years. I moved my mouth to just below her ear where I softly nibbled and kissed her neck. I felt her shudder.

"Not here. Come with me." She led me to the back of the cottage. "This is my room."

Their cottage was set up with a room for each person. Lucy took off her shirt then pants with a speed that, if I had blinked, they would have appeared to have vanished. As she stood there, the light danced about her bare skin, making her body inviting to the touch. Lucy lay back on the bed.

"Are you ready for this? I'm going to make you a slave to my touch." She held up her hand, motioning slowly with her index finger for me to come to her.

I told her, "Get up on your knees and turn around."

"I like this side of you. Taking control is sexy, but at some point, I want to be on top so I can show you the way I like it. So, this is just to start, then I'll get on top." She sat up on her knees, and I came up behind her, taking her by the throat with one hand and grabbing her hip with the other. She slowly grinded her bare bottom against me.

"You're very sexy," I said.

"Thank you. Now take off your skirt. I want you completely naked."

"I need you. I need to learn from you. I need to be inside you right now!" I exclaimed. I could smell her sweet perfume, and I began to feel lightheaded. I inhaled deeply and kissed her neck harder than I'd expected—we were connected.

"Slade? Where are we?"

"Lucy, we are inside your mind. This is where I can learn what you know on the topic of pleasure. Oh, meet Batch. We are the same but a little different."

"Hi, I'm Batch."

Lucy's jaw hung open. "There are two of you? Wait, the last time you kissed me… Was this the place I went?"

"Yes, it was."

"I remember it like it was real, but I know it wasn't. So then, how did everything *feel* so real?"

"May I answer this one, Slade?"

I nodded and grabbed a book.

"You see, Lucy, what happens in the mind triggers all sorts of amazing feelings and memories. We can make you feel intense pleasure, intense fear, and we could trigger anything from here, but tonight, we seek what you know about the many forms of intercourse."

"Do I have to give it to you? If I say no, will you just take it?"

"Why would you say no?"

Lucy said, "It's mine. If you take it, then that would be stealing, would it not? Should it not be paid for because I own it and you need to learn?" Lucy made a good point.

"I did tell you that I wanted to be inside you."

"I thought you meant you wanted to have sex, not sneak around inside my mind."

"So, what do you want in exchange for your knowledge on the topic we desire?" I looked at her, and she smiled.

Lucy rubbed her hands together. "I want what you did to me the other day three more times. I want to get to know you, and I want you to *want* to make love to me at least twice at a later date."

"I will do the first and the second, but I can't promise the last one, as only the four can agree to allow me. You can ask them for permission."

"Okay, I will hold you to your word. Batch, you may do whatever it is you do to understand." Lucy spread her arms out and tilted her head back. "Tell me when you are done."

"I'm done." Batch smiled. "Slade, you have to see this! It is going to change your whole world. There are at least one hundred plus words that are not in our vocabulary."

"How is it possible for you to learn so fast?" Lucy asked.

"Imagine the information you store is in many different books that makes up your mind. While I am in your mind, I can move really fast, and in here, time moves normally for us, but the outside world almost stops. To the people watching, it only looks like we are touching for a few seconds."

A wicked smile crept across Lucy's face.

"Well then, why not let me have you and Batch at the same time while we are in here? I've never had two men at the same time."

"Thank you for the offer, but as I said before, my promise includes the mind as well, and Batch has paired with Topaz."

Lucy asked, "Then can you show me how to control my arm and hand in the real world so I may enjoy myself?"

"Okay, think about your hands."

"Wow! It feels so odd. Can you feel me touching your hand?"

"No, I cut myself off for maximum concentration."

"Kiss me before we part." Lucy's arms opened, and I stepped into them as we embraced. Our lips touched and tongues intertwined. When we were done, she whispered, "I have you in the palm of my hand, and now I really can't wait to have you inside of me."

"Slade, somehow she has made time match time in here."

We disconnected.

I suddenly realized why Lucy wanted to control one of her hands. She had reached back and taken me in her hand, gripping my manhood firmly.

"Can you please let it go?"

"Why? Don't you like it when I do this?"

"Very much so, but please, if you don't release me, then my promise to you will be void, and this will be as far as we will ever go."

Lucy reluctantly let go. She smiled as she said, "You're lucky that you're taller and I could only move my hand because if I could have moved my body, you would have been in a very tight spot, if you know what I mean. I couldn't get my body to raise up and insert you. I just want you to know that I'm not like this with just anyone. Just because I talk freely, my body is mine and mine only and not something that is easily given out."

I stood up and did my best to make myself relax as to not be tempted further.

"Tell me, Lucy, why are you so sexually aggressive toward me if you are not like this all the time?"

Lucy ran her hands through her hair. "I don't know, but something about you drives me crazy. When Tova mentioned you earlier, I got goosebumps. The way you smell, the way your eyes burn with this insane intensity, your ability to enter the mind. Oh, and trust me, what you have right there doesn't hurt, unless you push wildly without care for the lucky woman. So, be gentle with that sword, okay?" Lucy winked and bit her bottom lip.

"Yeah, about that. How do I make that go away?"

"It needs a kiss, and look at this, I just happen to have lips. You do not want to go walking into that cottage with that all hard like that in front of all those hungry women. Plus, I bet Sofia will have some questions of her own."

"Very funny. Now, can you be a little helpful for once?"

"Well, I could hit you in the stomach. That might work. Either way, it would be fun because you keep me in this cage shaped like a heart."

"You know, Lucy, if you spoke more like that, I would like it more than the dirty jokes." I smiled, and she smiled back.

Lucy requested, "Okay, for this, I want one more time added from two to three times, or you can see what happens when you walk through the door and everyone gets a look at that." Lucy crossed her arm, waiting for my answer.

"Fine, I agree. But it better work if you want to get paid."

"Trust me, I know how to shut a man down when he has one of these. Wait, I want to see it one more time before I do this."

"Why?"

"Because I asked nicely, and I didn't get a good look at it."

I pulled up what I was wearing.

"Oh, I'm going to count the seconds till I ride you."

"Are you satisfied?"

"Not as much as if you were to leave me in a sweaty, wet coma."

I rolled my eyes.

"Don't you roll your eyes at me! Now, raise your hands to the sky, close your eyes, then say, 'Mistress Lucy, you're very sexy, and I want to taste you.'"

"What?"

"It will stop you from tightening up."

I did as she asked.

Her knuckles cracked as she clenched her fist. *Bam*! It was a swift kick to the groin, not a punch. I dropped to my knees, struggling to breathe. I felt like she'd kicked something into my throat. Lucy walked up to me, took a handful of hair, and pressed my face up against her bare-skinned hip.

She looked down at me and said, "I told you it would have been more pleasurable if I kissed it away."

In that moment, I nodded in agreement.

"Give it a minute or two. Then you will be right as rain, but I do like the way you look down on your knees in front of me. So humble, so cute at the same time. I'll see you at your place. I think it would be better to arrive separately, so give it about five minutes, then come over."

Lucy put on some clothes, helped me up to sit on the bed, and kissed my forehead. She left without a word.

"Batch, what do you think about the new info?"

"I think the topic should be explored further due to a few things being incomplete, like the intersecting lines between love and intercourse. Love crosses many lines, like friendship, lovers, companions, and something called a one-night stand. That last one might be a sexual position. I will need a better source on these topics because Lucy has not been in love. But be careful. She does have deeply intense feelings for you. At first, I thought it was because she was used to getting her way like a spoiled, self-centered child or how the alpha eats first thing. But no, I think she may have real feelings outside of lust, and this could cause interpersonal conflict that will add undue stress to our otherwise new life if handled incorrectly."

Batch made it clear that, even with the new information, it was a topic that was immensely deep and complicated. I stood up, and although the pain was fading, I still felt nauseated. Full use of my legs returned, so I made my way home.

Before I opened the door, Batch added, "I will work on a better way to extract information, much like Topaz can do. Besides, how would it look if you could run around kissing the necks of those we want information from?"

"Good point, Batch. I see how that might look odd. Thank you. Where would I be without you?"

"There is a word that fits perfectly for this. In fact, that word fits so many different situations: good, bad, indifferent, happy, sad, and almost everything in between. If used right, it will start a fight or make one want to have sex. It can also cause disgust or laughter. But for now, let me keep this powerful word under lock and key due to its barbaric nature and lowborn attributes. We wouldn't want you to look more out of place by incorrectly using this word, even though said word is so very multifaceted. I feel it will be a word we'll both greatly love to use."

I turned the doorknob and walked into the cottage. I was greeted with an amazing smell and the sounds of joyful laughter. The table was set, and there were a few candles in the center.

"Hello, Slade. Did you get what you needed while you were out?" Cheri was all smiles as she spoke. She leaned in and gave me a small kiss on the cheek. I winked before heading to the bathroom to relieve myself. I was still a bit tender. I thought I should ask Sunako for a quick healing session before we sat down to eat. I had to hand it to Lucy because I did not see that one coming, and it did work. I walked out of the bathroom and right into Lucy.

"Ah, Lucy. I was just thinking about you."

"Really? I hope it was something pleasant." Lucy looked me up and down.

I laughed. "I was thinking of how you took me by surprise and helped me with a slight problem. Thank you again for that."

"I wouldn't call that *slight*. You had what you call a large problem that needed to be handled right, but you have this adorable code of honor, so I helped you by putting my best foot forward. How are they by the way? I could still give you that kiss to help with the sting."

"Did I hear someone say a kiss?" Sofia's middle finger caressed her bottom lip.

"Yes, Mistress Sofia, I was just reminding your fine young man that if he ever needed a lesson on kissing, that I would love to be his head mistress and teach him some tricks that I know you love."

"I think he kisses just fine, but then again, I learned what I know about kissing from you."

Sofia and Lucy smiled, and they began to kiss. I felt a stirring, and my problem was back—there was nowhere I could go. With Sofia and Lucy occupied and my back up against the bathroom door, I was trapped. But I was saved by Asya as she called out that dinner was ready.

Asya walked up and said, "Without a drop of wine and already teasing the poor Mr. Slade. Just look at the state you two have put him in. You two are making things *hard* for him." Smirking, Asya suggested, "Mr. Slade, please take care of that because you could start a riot by parading that thing around at a dinner table fully of horny women."

"Hey, Slade, I can help you with that if you want."

Sofia said, "Lucy, don't be gross. Can't you see that he looks embarrassed? Slade, look me in the eyes. It is nothing to be embarrassed of. I should have known better than to do that in front of you before dinner. I'm sorry. Now, make it go to sleep or whatever you need to do to come to the table. Okay, just follow me. Lucy, just be you, and be a distraction."

We reached the table, but before I could pull out my chair, Lucy said, "Everyone, may I have your attention? I would like to thank Asya for throwing this wonderful dinner party. I'm thankful for my beautiful sisters and to our new friend, Mr. Slade, who should have sat down while I had everyone's attention so no one would notice his huge erection."

Everyone looked at me and smiled.

Asya burst out in laughter. "Lucy! Please show a little decorum, or at least, let the wine flow before we revert to crude humor. Slade, please sit down."

I sat down between Topaz and Sunako. On the far end was Lucy, then Cheri, who was in front of me, Tova next to her, and Sofia and Asya at both ends of the table.

Sofia stood up with her glass.

"Please, raise your glasses up toward the heavens so the gods may bless this meal, this drink, and my loved ones that sit with me this night. Thank you for allowing Slade to find his way to us and into our hearts."

When Sofia was done, all seven of them raised their glasses and said, "To the heavens and back."

I raised my glass with them but only smiled. I enjoyed how their combined voices made one beautiful sound. Everyone engaged in a bit of small talk on who was liking who and upcoming things that included the other two sisters' Houses. Dinner was a soft white meat called turkey breast, gravy, corn on the cob, mashed potatoes, peas, and a delicious thing called corn muffins. I had no memory of seeing so much food before. Every bit of something was an adventure in taste. As I ate, the newly acquired information started to make its way into accessible thought, which made me smile periodically.

"So, Slade, what has it been like for you these past few days?" asked Tova.

"Every day is a new experience that I slowly analyze and savor. So much wonder. Take this meal, for example. To you, this might be something you have had, and therefore, it's great but not the best thing you have eaten. But everything that I have eaten so far has been an explosion of flavor."

Lucy spoke up. "Slade, soon you will know that each woman has a different taste."

Lucy, Cheri, Tova, Sunako, Topaz, and Sofia laughed.

"I did notice that already. Cheri is saltier than Lucy."

The whole room went dead silent.

Sofia stood up. "What did he just say, Lucy?" She looked enraged. "Did he go down on you?"

Asya interrupted loudly, "Sofia, please allow the boy to clarify his poorly worded statement before you say something undignified and unbecoming of a mistress. Mr. Slade, the spotlight is all yours. Can you feel all these pretty eyes on you?"

I swallowed my food with an almost comical gulp. Then, I took a not-so-steady-handed drink as I scanned the room and settled my gaze on Sofia, who managed to look even angrier.

"Well, Slade, we're all ears. I'm most interested in your explanation, and I will have it here and now!" Sofia's knuckles were turning white as she squeezed the handle of the knife.

"I'm not sure we're talking about the same thing. When I kiss you on the neck, depending on what you were doing or if you just got out of the shower, you would taste completely different, as each person's skin has its own taste, due to my aforementioned statement. Did I answer your question?"

The room went from silent to uproarious laughter in a heartbeat, so much so that it startled me.

Sofia stared at me. Her expression softened as she laughed.

"Why? What did you think I meant?"

Sofia smiled. "Don't worry. I will show you later."

Topaz whispered in my ear what Sofia had thought I meant and why she was mad.

"Batch! What did Topaz just tell me?"

"Calm down, Slade. It is perfectly natural, and most of them do it amongst themselves. So now would be the best time to release this new piece of information, but I warn you, this may be very intense due to subject matter that is directly tied to powerful emotions. Mental and physical reactions might occur. This is why I wanted to do this later while you slept."

Batch spoke with his hands in exaggerated movements. I didn't do that when I talked. I found that to be odd. Batch released the information on what Topaz said. A sudden rush of feelings and emotions were happening, and it was a bit too much.

Tova asked Asya, "Is Slade okay? He looks frozen."

Asya got up and placed her hands on both sides of my face. I became calm and clearheaded. "Slade, can you hear me?"

"Yes, Asya. Is everything all right?"

"You might have taken too much information at once. I see you are reviewing the topic of sexual intercourse, the dynamics of love, and loving more than one person. Wow, I do not envy you right now.

Trust me, it will become more or less clear. As long as your heart is without lies, never say love unless you are in it."

Asya's words held weight, and I thanked her. We disconnected, and I observed Sofia smiling and talking with Lucy. I got the sudden urge to have her right on the table in front of everyone. So many new thoughts ran with words and meanings that made me hungry, but not for food. I began to wonder if they could hear my heartbeat.

I was unaware that Asya was behind me and touching my neck, so as I attempted to stand up, her hands forced me back into the chair.

She whispered to me, "I would enjoy dinner first and drink deep this wine. Do not let yourself become overwhelmed with emotions. Control your body. Don't let it control you. So, take a deep breath, and enjoy these moments."

I placed my hand on hers and looked up at her smiling face. I felt better and more controlled. I would admit that I found her incredibly attractive, physically and mentally. Oh no, I just thought that while touching her hand. *I hope she didn't hear that.*

"I did, and thank you, Mr. Slade." She sat back down, winked, and shot me a sultry smile. Someone threw a piece of corn muffin at me, hitting me in the head. I started to laugh, which was exactly what I needed in the moment. I felt so much better and able to think. I stood up and raised my glass.

"To Asya, this dinner is more than I deserve. To each one of you that sit here with me, I could not have been delivered to a better place than here." I took a series of small bows.

Sunako said, "I have a great question for you, Asya." She paused, then looked up and tapped her fork on the table. "If Slade has had his memories cut out, then how does he retain his repertoire of impressive manners? His vocabulary is the highest of any man that lives here in the House of Ribbons. Even when a lord visits with their entourage, none of them seem to have Slade's silver tongue, and his way with words is something to behold. I believe I'm not the only one who thinks this." Sunako raised her hand, and each person raised theirs as well.

"I don't know, Sunako. I have the same questions about the boy as you do. If I had to guess, whoever did this to him could remove only what they did not want him to remember but allowed him to operate as if he had no memory loss. I mean, he clearly has had a very high-level education but only remembers that and not the day-to-day things, people, and places between those days. It is truly mind-boggling. I believe, in time, we might just find out."

Topaz suggested, "Hey, Slade, say something that would sweep even the most jaded among us off her feet." She grinned.

"Topaz, you must have someone in mind." I saw only two at the table she could be speaking about, and I believed I knew who.

"I do. I want you to sweep Tova off her feet. Tova doesn't believe in love. She is jaded to its existence."

"I believe in love, Topaz. I just don't think I will ever feel it. Besides, love is overrated. But I will raise to the challenge. Slade, you think you can sweep me off my feet?" Tova stood up.

"Oh, may I raise the stakes higher?" Sofia giggled. "If I'm correct, Tova, you have not kissed Slade."

"You are correct. I have not kissed him. I just don't see what some of you see in him. Yes, he is attractive and smells amazing, but I see no reason to fall all over him. In truth, I find you all a bit embarrassing the way you covet him like a new toy. Yes, I know we have so few men, but there is no way I am going to get the giggles over this pretty boy."

Sofia laughed. "Okay, I have a good test. Slade, get Tova to want to kiss you without touching her neck or any part of her body. If you fail to get her to want to kiss you, then you have dishes for a month, two weeks here and two weeks at Lucy's house. Oh, and you have to do it without help from Batch, so give him to Topaz."

"Deal, but I thought this was supposed to be challenging." I wiped my mouth with my napkin, leaned over, and kissed Topaz to give her Batch.

"So, boy, do you have what it takes to make me surrender to your kiss with your voice alone?" Tova was direct with her tone and gaze. "I'm not so easily persuaded as some of these overtly sexual creatures."

"Yeah, Slade, can you? I have a better idea. Cheri, please get me something to blindfold Tova in case it's his eyes and voice that lull us like a siren's call. So, no sight, no touch—just words alone." Sunako gave me a mischievous grin. She was trying to make it a challenge.

"With Tova's permission, of course."

"Are you scared that you will have no effect on me?" Tova asked.

Cheri returned with something to blindfold Tova.

"Careful, Tova. I have seen his mind, and it does not work like others. His ability to think on his feet is impressive. He stands poised, silently planning his assault to win a kiss from you," Asya warned. "To raise the stakes, I will give you a piece of candy if you resist kissing him."

I walked toward Tova but stopped about ten feet in front of her.

"I think you might be a little far away from Tova to kiss." Cheri smirked.

I just raised a single finger to my lips to silence the room. I said nothing for two whole minutes.

"Slade, is it your intention to bore me into a kiss? Because if that's your tactic, then your silver tongue has been vastly overexaggerated, and I won before you ever stepped out of your chair."

While she spoke, I took my time and walked around the table, approaching her from behind while I used the sound of her voice to mask my footsteps.

I placed my mouth next to her ear. My voice was just above a whisper, but with a heavy breath, I said, "Tova."

She gasped, and everyone saw her shiver. I moved back to my original place, then closed my eyes.

"Tova, it is true that you and I have never shared a kiss, but you do long to kiss me? Your desire escapes through your breath while you hide your passions. I only want to enjoy you like the unique wine you are. Would it not be a terrible waste of such a perishable moment that would be better spent in the deep embrace of self-discovery? What is unknown will give way to the known with all manner of feelings set loose from their cages long cast away to your cynical depths." I paused for a moment in hopes that she might anticipate what I might say next.

I moved closer.

"Tova, if there were a hole in front of you and you were in love, would you not let that love help you jump over it? Because I would climb down and then back up for the briefest second to know the song that your lips sing to understand the whispers of your heart. I ask you to take a leap of faith, knowing you will land in my arms. Let me keep you warm, if only for a passing second, while you etch your kiss upon my heart. Or would you let my unanswered heart fall forever into the abyss of loneliness, knowing only your lips could soften the impact of a reality, a reality I could never have because your heart is blind to my words? So, like a flower freshly picked, I will dry up without the water of life that is your kiss. Now, Tova, will you grant me a single sip of water so I do not become like dust to be swept away, lost to time?"

She stepped forward, and I felt the heat from her mouth as she breathed slowly on my lips with only the smallest space between them.

"Tell me the truth. Do you really want to kiss me, or is this just a game?"

"I spoke with a truthful tongue. I don't just want one kiss. If so, then I would rather never be haunted by a kiss you should have never been so reckless with. Knowing your lips just once would be torturous every time I hear your voice."

The room was so silent, I could hear every heartbeat chanting in unison, *Kiss, kiss, kiss, kiss, kiss, kiss*. Tova closed the gap and gifted me a warm drink of her water as we embraced. She kissed differently, her tongue moving around mine like it was slowly searching for a way to hold on. Our tongues danced, encircling one another with soft, smooth tickles. As our joining came to an end, Tova slowly bit and held onto my bottom lip for a split second.

"If you won the challenge, why do I feel like the winner?"

"I never challenged you, so I think we're both winners. I'm very thankful for that kiss. It was wonderful."

She turned to sit down, but I held her hand, pulled her back, and asked, "May I have one more kiss? Because I'm feeling dry again."

We kissed, and somehow, she was more passionate. She made it feel like we had been apart for some time, which made me lightheaded. Tova removed the blindfold and winked before she returned to her chair. When I sat down, the room was still silent.

Lucy broke the silence, "Was it just me, or was that super exciting?"

The room raised their glasses and toasted our kiss.

"So, Slade, what's it like to be an oracle?" asked Cheri.

"I don't know yet, but I will tell you when I find out."

Lucy said, "You're a lucky bastard, do you know that? You're going to get the most attention and the most privileges from Lady Silk."

Tova threw another piece of food at me.

"Well, all I have done with it so far is research the topic of sex."

"And what have you learned so far, Slade?" Sofia asked.

I smiled and took another drink. "That I can't wait to taste you." My right hand found Sunako's left thigh, and my left hand discovered

Topaz's right thigh. The ladies laughed while Lucy and Sofia clinked their glasses. They both kissed me on the cheek, and Sofia winked.

"Tell me, Slade. What was it really like when you woke up? And how are you dealing with the things you are learning on a daily basis?" Asya seemed to have that question lined up.

"I felt it was a dream for the first day because something was off, and I could not find a real balance. Then, I woke up the other day, and I felt strong—I felt *good*. I really did not feel alone, and I think that was key to adjusting as well. I also have much to be thankful for."

"Slade, if you could get your memories back but find out something so awful about yourself that we would turn our backs on you, would you want to know or stay as you are now?" Topaz's question was a very good one.

"I would forsake whoever I was to hold onto this life because I could not have been liked or loved to be missing this long with no one looking for me. Where I'm from, I'm obviously not missed, and that is their loss."

"It hasn't even been that long. What if their out looking for you." said Cheri.

"I think I'd rather stay lost so long as I stay here."

Multiple ladies said 'Aw.'

"Slade, does it come natural to speak the way you do, or do you have to focus? I mean, no offense, but you're just so smooth. Your words flow when you speak. It's like you know what we are going to say, and therefore, you have the perfect answer. Is that an oracle thing? If so, why doesn't Topaz or Saffron speak like that?" Sofia placed her hands under her chin.

"No offense taken. Honestly, I open my mouth, and it comes out. I don't think about it. I don't think it's an oracle thing. I think I was given a great deal in the way of education, and whoever I was learning from spoke much like this. I must have really admired that person."

"Slade, I bet you a back massage that you can't walk over there and say something that would make every woman at this table smile and/or shudder. That includes Asya." Lucy crossed her arms with a smug look.

"How is there a loser in that? Okay. Here we go." I walked to a spot in the corner and raised my glass. "Each first kiss is a last chance to be brave."

Everyone, including Asya, smiled.

"Damn, you're smooth. He's really good." Lucy raised her glass and said, "To Slade, the soon-to-be hardest working man in the House of Ribbons."

"Slade, what do you think of the corn muffins?" Sunako asked while she refilled Asya's glass.

"I hope you will make these again."

"I don't think you'll have to wait very long for muffins!" Sofia exclaimed.

Everyone laughed, but Asya laughed so hard that wine came out of her nose. She even laughed while wiping her face.

"I think they go perfectly with the turkey. If you take a small bite, then a small sip, it makes a new taste. Which wine is this?"

Asya snapped, and the bottle raised off the counter and floated over to me.

I took the empty bottle by the neck. "Soul of an Angel? Clever name, even better taste. Asya, may I ask you a personal question?" I was a bit nervous to ask. "Are you really a witch, or are those just abilities?"

"See, ladies, this boy is very inquisitive. I like that. Yes, it is true. I do have natural-born abilities, but I was taken in by a real witch of the woods. She was something from a time long forgotten. Her name is Galya. You see, my gifts are that of healing, just like Tova and Sunako. I also have a photographic memory, so I can read something and never forget it. So, this witch took me under her wing. I learned a great deal in a year, even though I still had no ability to use magic. So, one day, we set off to see one of her oldest friends to see if I was worthy of this gift. It took two weeks to get there by foot, but I never complained. When we arrived, we were greeted by some of her students.

"Then Galya brought me before Zyra who saw that I had a hidden ability that had just recently manifested. Zyra saw that I was an oracle and said I should be trained in the ways of how to generate and control magic. She wanted me to hone my newly developing ability. They worked their magic and called down an angel and a demon to decide if I was worthy. I was. Then, they blessed me, and I could use magic. Ever since then, I have dedicated my life to helping find the lost people, like ourselves, and those who would be better off with their own kind. That is the story of how I became a witch. But you should know that there are still places in this world that hate and fear our kind.

"Did Topaz tell you that I'm the one who found and named her? I think she was about four, and she was alone in the woods. Not too far from here was an old man, lying facedown and dead. I suppose of old age or illness. Soon, I took a real liking to my new little squirrel. Then, when she was ten, she started developing her gift. Later that year, I was called away, and I was not able to take her with me. I brought her here. I wanted her to have a stable life with others of her age, and Lady Silk would not have said no to having an oracle. Here, Topaz has been loved by Lady Silk. Topaz made many friends because of her witty humor. She is very much a daughter to me, and I love her greatly. I miss her while away."

Topaz blushed.

"Asya, is it true that oracles make better witches?" asked Topaz.

"Yes, in a way. It helps that an oracle is more of a magical ability because it is a gift from the old gods. If the person is worthy, then they, too, could become a witch. Mind you, there are the bad types as well, because the universe will always have balance. So, beware the bad witches because they will try to eat you up."

As Asya finished, she held out her hands and made fire rise violently from her hands.

I was put into fight-or-flight mode, and I chose to fight. My eyes went black on their own. I jumped to my feet, held out my hand, and spoke in a language I did not understand. The fire went out.

Asya said, "Slade, calm down. As you see, no one is in danger. I'm sorry if I frightened you. How do you know those words?"

"I don't know. I'm sorry for my behavior. What you did caught me off guard. Something about your hands creating fire frightened me. I apologize for my rude behavior. Please forgive me."

"No worries, young man, but I see I might need another visit with Mr. Batch and your library soon, but not this night. We are having too much fun, and the party must continue. Now, Tova, how has Damara been? I did not see her today."

"Damara is out on ranger duties. There was a murder at the House of Everlasting Tears, and three people are missing. Lady Silk sent six to find them. We received word two days ago that they should be back sometime tomorrow."

"Please tell her to find me. I have something for her," said Asya.

"What's the main function of the House of Everlasting Tears?" I asked.

“They train royal guards, butlers, chambermaids, and the like. Their people are top notch,” said Tova.

“Why is it called Everlasting Tears?”

Asya smiled. “It sounds nice, and one doesn’t forget a name like that. Take your name: Slade. That’s a name that lingers on the mind, not easily forgotten.”

“Does anyone want some more wine?” Lucy held up a bottle called Tears of the Fallen.

I held up my glass and said, “I ponder the vast emptiness, things of the past, and how the void consumes me.”

Lucy poured a few glasses and came to me last. “You’re an ass, but I want you to fill my void. Mind you, you’re a beautiful-looking ass, but still an ass. Save the poetry for the ears of young women.”

Laughter broke out.

I smiled. “How then, would I get your attention otherwise?” I looked her in the eyes as she filled my glass.

“Well, I really like the way you say my name. You have this cute but hard-to-place accent.”

Asya noted, “He definitely has an accent that is unknown to me, and I know this whole planet. I liked the way he asked for another glass of wine. I found it very cultured and refined. All he was missing was his pinky in the air.” Asya closed her hand, leaving only her pinky out.

The ladies laughed some more and talked amongst themselves about the accent that I hadn’t recognized I had.

“Yeah, it really comes out when he is tired,” said Sunako. “It’s just so sexy.”

Sofia chimed in with, “I hear it when he makes his voice really low and gravelly.”

“I heard it too when he whispered in my ear,” Tova said just before taking a bite of her food. She slowly pulled the fork out of her mouth, all while staring at me with half-closed eyes.

Cheri laughed. “I notice it when Slade is being direct. I also hear a low rumble from his throat. What about you, Topaz? What do you hear when he speaks?”

“I hear it, but I can’t place my finger on where it comes from. But it is sexy as hell. I could listen to him read a food list and love it.” Topaz blew me a kiss.

Asya asked Lucy, “Do you have anything else you would like to add?”

"All I want to know is what he sounds like on top of me, bringing me to the edge of my own death over and over again."

All the ladies raised their hands, saying, "Here, here!"

Asya added, "Lucy, I swear you must be the horniest woman I have ever met. So infatuated with sex. I don't envy any of you, and Slade, you clearly have some long, hard nights in front of you."

Again, the beautiful women raised their glasses and said, "Here, here!"

Plates were emptied as each of my new friends had asked their fill of questions. We all had enjoyed the jokes and tales of unbelievable things. When dinner ended, Asya then asked if we wanted to enjoy some time relaxing and hearing some stories, but only after everything was cleaned up.

I was the first to volunteer for dishes, but Sofia said, "I think you would find it boring."

"I want to pull my weight, and I should start learning the chores tonight. Besides, it will get done faster with an extra pair of hands."

Laughter spilled from Sofia as she walked into the living room.

"I will show you what I want you to do." Sunako handed me a stack of eight dishes. "Follow me."

We went into the kitchen. It had a long, ten-foot counter with a good-sized sink, about three feet from the end. I set them down and gave Sunako a little kiss on the cheek.

She said, "Save that for story time."

With help from Tova, Topaz, Sunako, we washed, dried, and put away the dishes quickly. It was time to relax and hear Asya tell some stories.

As we settled in, Cheri started a fire in the fireplace. It was our only light source, and it set the mood of the young night. There were stories to hear. Five bottles remained, and no one wanted the night to end.

"You did a great job cleaning up, but I need Mr. Slade for a moment in private. So, carry on as you were. We'll be right back."

Chapter 16

The Demon King and His Love in White

Asya and I walked outside, far enough from the cottage as not to be overheard.

"Slade, how do you feel in this very moment?"

"I feel good, happy, and a little lightheaded, but nothing that would cause me to do or say anything stupid." I didn't know if that was the answer she was looking for.

"That is not what I meant, but thank you. I mean this new life, all the new things that you have learned. You must have and or will soon have complicated questions, and these questions should not be left unattended. So, think of me like a close friend. Feel free to ask me anything. And thank you for what you said about me at the table—it was a very welcome compliment."

"Thank you, Asya. I do have a question, but I'm not sure that I will be able to word it correctly. Where are all the men? Not that I am complaining about my situation. Is it like this everywhere, and if so, why?"

"Great questions, my boy. You're asking the right ones. Well, yes and no. In some places, there are many more men than women, and other places, there are an even mix. Then, you have places like the House of Ribbons. Sometimes, less men means less fighting for control of land and its resources, which means less wars, unnecessary pain, suffering, and death. Think of it this way, Slade. You're one of ten males who are sixteen and older with forty-four women in that age group. I am amazed they don't have a waiting list to sleep with you. I have seen that in other places. You're blessed with intelligence, a silver tongue, and extraordinarily good looks.

"Now, I will look out for you because I believe you're very special. I would like to think that however you arrived here, it was by the hands of the gods. So, enjoy this life. Take nothing that is not offered, and never bully anyone. Just because you have power does not mean you should flaunt it or force it on anyone unless it's information that is needed to rescue someone. If you were a ranger and you needed information but did not trust the source, then you should use it. Remember, I will teach you ways to see through the lies to free the truth. You're about to become very valuable to Lady Silk after the talk I will have with her. Once she fully trusts you, almost nothing you ask for will be denied because you might become her prized champion. In the meantime, just be patient and follow the rules.

"Before we go back inside, I would like to speak with you about how you turned off my fire. I want you to know that you did nothing wrong and have nothing to be worried about. I'm not upset, rather the opposite. To see you use such a high-level command of that type of magic was amazing, and it gives me a clue on who to ask about you. But for now, say nothing about what happened at the table. I will speak with the ladies about forgetting what they saw until you and I can understand better who you are and where you come from. Now, let's get back in there before the drinks disappear."

"Thank you, Asya. I feel better about a lot of things now. I'm very happy to have met you." I wanted to hug her as a thank you, but I was unsure of how she would take it.

"Slade, come here." She hugged me and said, "Never fear what you don't know. It's better to try and fail than to fail because we never tried."

"Asya, you can read minds?"

She placed a single finger to her lips and made a small whistling sound. She faded into heavy mist. I was alone outside, and I drew in a deep breath, enjoying the cool air in my lungs. I walked back in and heard laughter, which caused me to smile. Asya was inside. She could have walked the twenty feet. I guess I would do the same if I could teleport.

I sat on the couch. Sofia and Sunako came to sit at my sides.

"Get comfortable because story time is about to begin," Asya spoke as she sat on the floor cross-legged and rose in the air. I felt she enjoyed a bit of flare.

As if we were children, we smiled and clapped at the truly magnificent display of power.

"Now, my friends, what story will I tell tonight? Should I start with a love story, or shall I take a request?"

I held up my hand and waved it like a child. Asya silently pointed at me.

"I would like to hear the story of Lady Silk, Lady Velour, and Lady Velvet. They're so young, so there must be a story to tell. I would like to know how the three sisters became three separate Houses."

Asya smiled. "Does anyone here know that story?"

The six girls shook their heads.

"Grab a drink and let me take you on a trip back in time thirty-one years ago. A newly pregnant woman named Haley was with a group on the run after her village was destroyed by a group of slavers. They were captured, but Haley and a handful of others killed some of their captors, including the leader of the slavers, and made a run for the woods. Haley became badly injured and came very close to dying, but she was a fighter and willed herself to live. I happened upon the group by chance. I helped keep her alive. We made a six-day journey to the House of Thorns. It was run by a high lord who used to be a battle master. His name was High Lord Dutch, and he had a large village of a hundred or so freed slaves that paired up and married. Most had children. High Lord Dutch was instantly taken with Haley and she with him. He promised to protect her with his life if need be.

"Please excuse me." Asya took a long drink. "Haley gave birth to triplets, and they lived happily for seven years, but one day, Haley was murdered by Rhonda, the wife of the dead slaver. The assassin was stopped by a man named Herrick, but he was badly stabbed in front of his daughter while stopping the assassin. Mr. Cyril had a healer save the man. Lord Dutch was so grief-stricken that he and twelve freed slaves-turned-fighters located the slavers' base. That night, they snuck in and killed every man, woman, and child except the slaves. They released them.

"Lord Dutch turned Rhonda into a slave, his own personal dog. She would spend her life as a slaver and now spends the rest of her miserable life as a slave. Lord Dutch raised those three young ladies to be just that: ladies with their own Houses. They call him Lord Father. He never remarried or took a lover because his loss was too great. Lord Dutch had a lot of land, and he had all that you see built for his adopted daughters. Silk was made a lady of this place. Then, he built two more nearly identical villages for Velour and Velvet while granting them the title of lady. The House of Thorns is the main House that can be called on for defense if need be, and I visit often."

Everyone clapped. Sofia stood up and stretched.

"Thank you, Asya, for the history lesson. I always wanted to know where the sisters were from, and it's not something so easily asked without fear of accidentally offending Lady Silk," said Sofia.

Asya said, "You're welcome, my sweet. Now, ladies, what do you say? Thirteen minutes so we can all hit the bathroom, then right back here?"

Everyone agreed.

Sunako was the first to come back, and she demanded a kiss. I stood up, took her in my arms, and we kissed. The other girls followed closely behind.

"What did I tell you, Slade? Some nights will be filled with love, and you should love in return. Love is the oldest and greatest magic there has ever been. Is everyone ready for a tale of love, a demon king, angels, and a secret gift?"

We all raised our glasses and said, "Yes, please."

"Long ago, in a place like this, there were people who lived under the rule of one simply called God. God had many angels. Angels come in many colors, but they all have pure-white feathers. After a failed takeover by one known only as the Devil, just under half were cast out after a war in a place called Heaven. They were sent to live in a place called Hell. These fallen angels were renamed demons. Most shed their beauty, taking hideous appearances as to further shun God. They became the things of nightmares, the eaters of souls who sin against God.

"A small handful of demons remained beautiful in the way only an angel can be beautiful. Some switched back and forth, but a sole demon dreamed of only one thing. His was the dream of true love, something only the children of God could attain. His name is Abaddon, and he was one of five kings in the new realm called Hell. He was the third-most powerful. Abaddon cared not for a crown because what was a crown and a place to rule if he had to rule with an empty heart? So, one night, Abaddon hung up his crown and set out to walk the land of mortals. As he stepped out and onto the land, he was stopped by an angel that he had never met before. Mind you, Abaddon was one of God's first angels. Then he created fifty angels called the Seraphim then many more, but Abaddon had never laid eyes on that beautiful angel before.

"'Hello, I am Abaddon. Who might you be?' Abaddon went to one knee as he extended his hand.

"'I am Kael, guard of this gate, but you can save your forked tongue, fallen one. I'm not concerned with you or anything you could ever say to me. You may come and go as you wish, but all sinners trying to escape will be punished at the end of my sword.'

"'I only wished to ask you who you are because I have never seen you before. I thought I knew all my brothers and sisters. I am sorry to have bothered you.' Abaddon then walked away from Kael. For more than two hundred years, he saw her thousands of times. Each time, when he returned, he always left her a flower from a far-off place and, sometimes, something sweet to eat. He would never say a word to her, but he always smiled while in her presence.

"One day, while Abaddon was leaving, Kael asked him, 'Where do you go when you leave this place?'

"Abaddon said, 'I travel the world and watch over the people of this planet. I right the wrongs done, like those of unfaithful lovers and humans that sin in the face of my God, my Father.'

"'How can this be? You're a fallen one. God has turned his face from you. Why do you care about unfaithful lovers and those who sin against my God, my Father? Remember, fallen one, you chose to turn your face from our Father. Then, you were cast out forever, to never know His love again. You are less than the dirt that we walk upon. You're not worthy to stand upright, and the very sight of you disgusts me. Foul thing, plague me no more with your pathetic gifts and attempts to catch my eye because I would sooner go blind than look at you for a second longer!' Kael turned her back on Abaddon, and she straightened her wings out as far as they would go. That was the thing that an angel would do to greatly disrespect someone, but it was not the worst gesture she could have done. However, it cut Abaddon deeply.

"Abaddon fell to his knees and proclaimed, 'Yes, I feel the loss of my Father's love, the loss of my brothers and sisters' love, but I have love. It still lives in my heart. I know love's true curse more than most, and I hope you never know its icy kiss.' As Abaddon spoke, he silently wept tears that began falling from his eyes to the soil below. He'd never felt alone, but that night, for the first time in thousands of years since his expulsion from Heaven and God's love, he felt alone, truly alone. The weight was too much. Abaddon spread his wings, then took to the sky, reaching a speed that only an angel can reach.

"He flew straight and true on a path known only to the original angels, a secret road built by God's own hands. Abaddon reached a speed so great he would have outflown a lightning bolt. With the doorway in sight, Abaddon pressed on faster, but instead of breaking through the door and begging for the mercy of his Father, he slammed himself into an invisible wall so hard that he was knocked unconscious. Just so you know, angels and demons never sleep.

"For the first time in Abaddon's very long existence—including his excommunication from God's love—he was at peace. His sleeping body fell from such a great height that it took two years of falling before Kael even saw him coming through the clouds high above. But in those two years of Abaddon's absence, his tears had grown into flowers that were unlike any ever grown before on Earth. A few became many different kinds until the area had become a gigantic garden that would have surpassed any that had ever come before it. Kael tended her garden with care and great love. So, when Kael witnessed Abaddon falling, she knew that there was one thing she could do.

"Kael had to save Abaddon from hitting the ground to save the flowers so that Abaddon could see the beauty that his tears had created. Kael crouched down and sprung upward. With a mighty flap of her angelic wings, she sailed through the sky toward Abaddon. Right before Kael caught Abaddon, she saw his real face for the first time. Not as a demon, the fallen one. She saw him as he was, an angel of God, his first right-hand. In that moment, Abaddon was reborn in her eyes and soul as her love.

"Kael caught Abaddon, but he was falling at the speed of a falling star. Kael was caught in the impact of the fall, and she knew that they would destroy the ground below. The surrounding areas would be wiped from existence. Their garden of love would end. Her wings, for the first time in her life, were useless. They just flailed around as she became a slave to the sheer force of the wind, and they fell as she tried in vain to wake Abaddon.

"She whispered, 'Dear Lord, my God, my Father. Please, save not us, but save these flowers, flowers born of your loving son, your son who never forgot you, never forsake you, never stopped loving you. Your son who did good work in your name while seeking nothing in return. His wish was to feel your love, if only for a moment more. Please, my Father, save these flowers.'

"With only a few seconds before the two would hit the ground, Kael spoke Abaddon's name and confessed her love for him. Kael took a deep breath and held Abaddon as close to her as she could and squeezed her eyes closed. *Impact!* Nothing—no sound, no pain, no dust cloud. Abaddon still in her arms. When Kael looked up, she saw her Father smile at her. He had caught them in His hand and held them in His arms. God held them close to His chest.

"'Child, do you hear that? It is my heart, and it sings to you. Now, please wake up and come take your place back at my side. Abaddon! Rise up, redeemed in My eyes.' Abaddon woke up, and upon seeing his Father's face, he began to smile. God placed them on the ground. Abaddon fell to his knees.

"'My Lord, my Father, I have missed you. Without your light, my heart would not beat, and every day was dark. Please forgive me, your child, for what I did was wrong all those years ago. I know I am not worthy of your love again, but please know that I will never stop loving you.'

"'Kael, why did you try to save Abaddon? Why did you risk everything for him? You risked your very soul to save one deemed unworthy of the love of God, the love of his brothers and sisters, and any love he might have had for himself. Love would escape him for all time. Why do this?'

"'My Father, my God, I speak the truth when I say that I love Abaddon. I caused Abaddon a great pain with my wicked tongue, and his tears gave life to these wondrous flowers, found nowhere else in all of your creation. These flowers are like my children, and that makes Abaddon their father. How could he be so bad and still create such works of art? How could he inspire me to love him?'

"'Child, would you give your wings for Abaddon? Would you give up your place in Heaven for Abaddon? Would you go blind to My love for this wretched creature? What would you do to prove your love for him? Choose your next words carefully, child, because you may never hear My voice again!'

"'Kael! Please don't do this! I'm not worth it! You have everything, and I am nothing! Please turn your face from me, *please*! Do not do this. I will only drag you down. Please don't make me suffer more by making this mistake! It would drive me mad knowing you would have to share my fate! Please, my God, my Father, take her away from me! Please don't give her this choice! She deserves your love. Mine could never compare, and it would only mock me even further, knowing you lost another child to their own impetuous actions! Please! I beg you my Lord, my Father, take her away from me! Take her back to Heaven! I will guard this spot for all eternity. Just don't let her choose. The only path is the one that leads to you; the only love that matters is your love, my Father, my God.' Abaddon gave it his all. He placed his face to the ground and silently prayed for Kael's angelic soul.

"'What say you, my child, Kael? The choice is yours and yours alone. Stay with Abaddon or return with me to My kingdom and never set eyes on him again for all eternity? I will have your answer now.'

"Kael stood tall with her brilliant white wings out like open arms. 'My Father, my Lord, my God. You have given me a life beyond that of so many, but I must follow my heart, the same heart you created just for me. I love you my Father, my God, my Lord above all others, but I also love Abaddon. I wish to be with him and to have your blessing on this matter. I want to stay with Abaddon. My Father, my God, my Lord, before you go, please know that I thank you for everything. I will spend forever showing you that we can make you proud, even if we never know or feel you.' Kael bent the knee, placed her sword on the ground, and lowered her head, waiting for her Father, her God, to depart.

"With a loud snap of his fingers, they were transported to the front gates of Heaven. 'Rise, my son, Abaddon. Rise, my daughter, Kael. Follow me. I have a job for you two. Abaddon, I know your heart, your every thought, and I am most proud of you, my son. You have shown this old being that even I can make a rash decision. Allow me to rectify that one with my blessing on Kael's hand in marriage. When you two decide to wed, I want you two to help usher in a new age of mankind. I want you to grant those who deserve it the power of this.' He stopped for a deep inhale and conjured a book that fit perfectly in His large hands. 'This is a grimoire, a book of magic. The grimoire holds the smallest fraction of the power all angels wield. Balance has to be allowed to exist. So, Kael, I entrust you with the knowledge to show selected humans how to read these powerful words and not be consumed by them. These humans will be allowed to decide to become good or evil after they learn the words. This will be the balance, so punish them, not because of their choices—free will must be at their very core.

"'Abaddon, you and Kael will go and teach my other children to understand us as we do them. Abaddon, you will guard my coming son so that he can be the intermediator between us and humans. Abaddon, welcome home, my son.' With that, God caused Abaddon's once great and feared sword to appear, which he handed to Abaddon. God kissed him on the cheek and hugged him tightly. 'Welcome home, my son. I have missed you greatly. Remember, when you two are ready to join souls, a great feast will be had at your wedding, but please come enjoy some time in Heaven. I want all those to see that forgiveness can be given.

"'Abaddon, my son, you have shown this old fool the most valuable lesson: that is, to love unconditionally, even if that love is not returned, as you did with Kael.' God stood silently as the weight of sadness enveloped Him until a single tear rolled down His cheek. Then, He took that tear and changed it into the universes first and only tear stone diamond. He gave it to Abaddon. 'My firstborn son, take this gift and bestow it to your love. If Heaven ever needed a new leader, this ring will be all you two will need to govern and control all the power that comes with the thrones of Heaven.'

"'Father, no. You are the One above all. You're the power that drives our religion. Only you could govern Heaven, commanding the cosmic power to keep our enemies at bay.'

"'Abaddon, I will tell you something from my heart. The seat next to me has been empty for too long, and I don't know if she will ever return to it or me. I govern as a lonely old man. I dine alone. Abaddon, love Kael. Hold her close, and never let anything divide you two. Losing my love is my only real regret.'

"Soon after, Kael and Abaddon went on to become married, and for the first time, Heaven and Hell stopped fighting and rejoiced as one family. Soon, they spread long life and magic to the first of us."

Asya finished her story, and all I could hear were my friends quietly crying. Sofia's tears soaked a spot on my shirt, while Sunako's tears covered my shoulder.

"Okay, ladies. Time to get up and stretch those bodies and hit the bathroom again. Slade, can I see you for another moment?"

We walked outside.

"Slade, I see you want to ask me a deep question. So, do it before I die of anticipation."

"Asya, I thought you could read my mind." I smiled and crossed my arms.

"It looks like Batch has put the book I gave him to good use. That book helps you prevent thoughts from being easily read. Trust me. It will be of great use to you in the future. If I have now answered your question, then answer my first question." Asya tapped her foot with a quick rhythm.

"First, I need to have a piss, if you don't mind." I turned to the nearest tree, and as I attempted to relieve myself, Asya pulled me into the air and hung me upside down.

"My boy, if I wanted to wait, then I would have let you piss. But making me wait is not what I desire, so how about I call these beautiful ladies outside? I can hold you up there until you piss all over your own face. How about that? I would hate for you to get a harsh nickname, like, I don't know, maybe Piss Face?"

With that statement, Asya summoned all six beauties.

Sofia said, "Oh, look at Slade!"

Topaz and Tova laughed with her.

Cheri asked, "Asya, can you make him bounce a little up and down?"

Topaz asked, "Asya, can you make him fly around but upside down?"

The wine had gone to most of their heads. Sunako kept stumbling to one side or the other. In truth, it was very cute.

"Lucy, come kiss me."

She came to me with her own clumsy feet, only falling twice. "Slade, you're too high to kiss. Stop screwing around and come down to me."

I reached and took both of her hands, but I was still held by something invisible. I was hoping to pull myself down with Lucy's body weight.

"As you can see, Asya, I have Lucy, and we wouldn't want to make things more awkward than it already is. This is a bit of a strain if you get my drift."

"Really? Will you ask me your question then?"

"Yes, Asya, but after my break. Deal?"

Asya squinted and smiled. "No deal."

Up I went, taking Lucy with me. She was about three feet off the ground, but my hands somehow had become locked into hers.

"Ladies, your attention, if you will, please. Mr. Slade has kindly called me out on something. In short, he would like me to wait until he has relieved himself before answering my question. Now the young lad hangs upside down with a great eagerness to relieve himself, and his bright idea was to bring Lucy into this. I would hazard a guess that he thought I would not make him piss, not only on his own face, but also on Lucy as well. Is that right, boy?"

"Yes, that is right. Now please, I'm having difficulties holding it back, and yes, I called your bluff. I don't want to piss on Lucy. Lucy, I'm sorry I got you into this."

"If it gets me into the shower with you, then feel free to piss on me. It will be well worth it." Lucy was making it harder as she intentionally started to shake about. "Come on, big boy, it's almost shower time." Her smile was as wicked as her laughter.

"Okay, Asya, you win. I will ask. Just let me down."

Gently, she lowered Lucy down and released our hands. But Asya held me up. Lucy sat underneath me. Her stubbornness was going to bite her in the ass.

"Asya, how is there one god, but you reference many gods? See, it was nothing big."

"Slade, you just asked one of the biggest questions of the night and one I can answer after you go wee-wee."

She started to laugh hard and brought me to the ground. She turned me right side up. Returning me to my feet made me feel like I was going to explode. I rushed over and placed my hand on the tree to steady my dizziness. I did not want to have a piss in front of my friends, but I figured only Cheri could catch a glimpse since she could see in the dark. Holy hell, did it feel good to relieve myself. I really thought I was going to piss on my own face. The thought of it made me laugh out loud, drawing the ladies to crowd around me as they poked me in the back and messed with my hair. I felt like I was having the longest piss of my life, and it probably was. When I was done, I felt so much better.

"Come on, girls. Let's move this party back inside." Cheri motioned everyone inside.

I gave Lucy a hand up, and she walked by me. I said, "Hey, I owe you a kiss, right?"

She jumped up and into my arms as we shared a nice kiss.

"I still want that shower, and maybe I'll piss on you." She started to laugh and ran into the cottage. Lucy could move really fast.

As I tried to follow, I tripped and fell over. I lay on my back, looking up at the star-filled night. I snapped my eyes black and noticed some of the stars looked like they were moving slightly in different directions. Some of them seemed to blink or twinkle. *How odd. It must be the wine and all the excitement.*

"Slade, take my hand."

"Thank you, Asya. I hope this doesn't sound rude, but is the Abaddon story from a book? It's not real, is it? It sounded like a love story for women."

"It's never rude to ask a valid question. The Abaddon story is real. It was shown to me rather than told to me. Abaddon himself, then Kael, showed me her point of view. I have a feeling they will want to meet you at some point to see if they know how you used magic that may have not been taught to you. Now, take my arm so I may steady myself, and we can do our best to hold each other up and enjoy the rest of the night."

As I came in, I saw a new plate of corn muffins and Sunako and Topaz kissing in the corner. I acted like I did not see them and walked into the living room where Lucy and Sofia were kissing and Cheri and Tova were kissing. I waved to Asya, and I led her into the bedroom.

"Well, look at you. I have to say, I didn't expect this from you so soon." She removed her shirt, then pushed me against the wall. "I must say: you smell so delicious."

"What? No, I wanted to know about the ladies. Is this normal? Or are you doing this?"

"That's why you called me into your bedroom?" Asya's smile was diminished somewhat.

"Oh, I'm sorry. Asya, you're beyond beautiful, and I can't help but think you know me more that you lead on, but I promised the ladies."

"Yes, I know. Blah, blah, blah, promise to be faithful. Yes, the wine helps them to loosen up and let their hair down a bit."

"What?"

Asya smiled at me. "It is an expression that means to relax—something you should do more. You didn't know? You didn't know that these girls were all together?" Asya laughed as she fell back on the bed. She was hauntingly beautiful as if she were from far beyond this world. "Boy, you're going to get a lesson in love that you will remember for ten lifetimes. I did tell you they were going to wear you out."

"Asya, do I not seem relaxed? Why does sex seem so important?"

"Great question. You see, at your age, males go through a change, causing deep desires to exchange its DNA with females. In essence, you're being driven by your DNA. Does that make sense?"

"No, not really. If that were the case, then why are they becoming intimate with one another?" I felt like I should understand, but I did not.

"It is perfectly natural. With so few men, the women tend to find a way to relieve the day's stress. Some are in love, and some dislike men due to mistreatment in their pasts. Others, like Lucy, love the act, but she secretly has always wanted to find real love. Don't tell her I said that." Asya laughed. "As for you, my boy—well, think of it like this. You have six females who want you and are willing to share you. I have known lords who do not have it as good as you have, my lucky little friend. But I caution you that a heart won can be lost forever if mishandled."

"I think I understand."

"My boy, you're doing great, but give the ladies a little space because I think you could get attacked." Asya patted my shoulder. "I will give them a little while longer, and I will call their attention."

"Why would they attack me?"

"You need to not take things so literal. You know you're safe, but if I called their attention toward you, then would they not hesitate to remove your clothes and have their way with you? Do you understand? If not, I will add it to our upcoming lessons."

"Thank you, Asya. I will not let you down as a student. I am grateful that we met and that you are pleased enough to want to teach me."

"No, it is I who should thank you for coming into my life. I learn just as much from you, the student, as you will learn from me. Hey, how about you escort me on a small trip? It should last up to two weeks. What do you think?"

I thought about it. "Yes, I think I would like that. May I bring someone with me?"

Asya said, "Well, I was thinking more like three. I like to have a bit of an entourage when I visit the other Houses. So, Slade, are you ready to really expand your mind?"

"Yes, very much so."

"Great, I will speak with Lady Silk. I know she will want you taught at the same time as Topaz. Lady Silk prizes oracles more than a dragon loves gold. Slade, at the risk of sounding out of place, would you kiss my neck and show me what you did to Lucy the other day?"

"What if it gets out of hand?"

"How so? Is there something you want to say?"

"Something about you is causing a deep arousal within me. Your, smile, eyes, and smell beg me to kiss you—no, I want more." I stood up. "Forgive me, the wine mixed with your hypnotic gaze have me thinking thoughts."

"By the looks of you from the waist down, my exposed breasts aren't helping the situation."

"Yes, they're wonderful—I mean, great. Asya, please, I fear I'll touch you and give in if you get any closer."

She slowly put her shirt back on, all while keeping eye contact. "You're right. The wine was strong, and you have passed my test."

"Asya, you never answered my question about the gods."

"Slade, yes, there are many gods from all around the world and time periods. Think of it like this: At different times, different gods rule, and depending on the deity you follow or worship, they all have their 'I created the Earth and all the stars' story because mankind gobbles that shit up. Writings from ancient times helps humans feel closer to their god of choice. They pray to whichever they call their deity, and theirs is always the all-powerful one. In truth, they rule in three, meaning there are always three gods ruling different parts of the world. The Greek gods gave Christianity a chance to shine, but no religion is ever gone. There will always be devotees praying to the old ones."

"Asya, you're pulling my leg. How can there be so many gods at once? Wouldn't that be too many kings at once? People go to war, and one rules over the conquered time immemorial."

"Slade, I love the way you think. This might be the wine talking, but you're very attractive, and your smell is so intoxicating. No, wonder they want you so. You know, I briefly loved a man who smelled wonderful. I met him after Haley's death. He was the one who was stabbed while stopping Haley's assassin."

"What happened to him?"

"Herrick and his daughter had to leave one night. I never saw them again. He was my very first love. I would have married him. One smell would make me drunk. You both have the same eyes. I wonder if you two are from the same place."

"Asya, please, not you as well. Honestly, focus!"

"Yes, business before pleasure. I'm sorry. So, time means nothing to the gods. They can have overlapping ruling kingdoms that almost never fight, but it has happened in the past. New gods rule, then fall out of favor, only to be replaced by different gods. Is that a bit clearer?"

"Yes, thank you, Asya."

"Don't worry, boy. After a hundred or so years, you will see the world differently."

"What was that, Asya?"

"Nothing, boy, just the wine talking, and from the sounds of laughter, it looks like their make-out session is over. So, let us rejoin the party. Stay close. A hungry group of women could overpower you just like that." Asya snapped.

"Ladies, are we decent and calmed down?"

A few were redressing.

"I see that only two bottles have made it, so let us each have a small amount so we can share the last of the good stuff."

"Where were you two?" Sofia asked, standing on shaky feet. She smiled.

I sat down next to Topaz and Tova.

"Quick talk with Asya about how hungry you all are getting."

"I was keeping Slade safe from the likes of you six filthy-minded sirens. I worried you all would hurt the poor boy with the state you were in. His first time should not require a healer afterward, should it?"

Sunako laughed so hard she started to cough, then said, "I have no problem with that." Then, in a blink of an eye, she was between my legs with her hands on my knees. "I can heal you. Then, you can thank me over and over and over again." Sunako winked, and in a flash, she was back in her seat.

Cheri was next in my lap for a stolen kiss and back in her seat, all in under two seconds. It was a wonder no one ever got hurt running that fast.

They all laughed.

"Well, I think it is almost time for bed, and by bed, I mean *sleep*. I have a feeling that we will have a fun day tomorrow. Now, let's get the room ready."

We all got up and went into the bedroom.

"Watch and learn, ladies and boy." Asya laughed while calling out something in a strange tongue. She clapped. The beds rose and collided.

Asya looked at me and said, "Cool, huh?"

"I'm warm but thank you."

"No, 'cool' can mean awesome or good or a word you use to express excitement." Asya just smiled and shook her head.

"Okay, let us do whatever needs to be done to get into bed, and I might have one more story in me."

They all went back to the bathroom.

"Asya, why do they go to the bathroom so often and in pairs or groups?"

"I thought it was obvious. They're talking about you."

After everyone had 'used the bathroom,' they got into bed: Lucy and Sofia, Cheri and Tova, Sunako and Topaz.

"Asya, there is only room for one more. Please take my spot. I will sleep on the floor."

"Thank you, Slade. That is very kind. Your chivalry seems to know no bounds, but I prefer to sleep floating in the hands of the gods." Asya rose into the air and appeared to be floating in invisible water.

"Asya, that is very cool. Did I use that word right?"

"You did, and it is very cool. How about I let you earn a bed like this for the night? Are you up to a challenge?"

"How could I say no to an offer like that?"

"Good. Now first, give a kiss goodnight to these five little angels and then one to the naughty little demon Lucy."

Laughter erupted.

Lucy did her best impression of a demon voice. "Come here, boy, and let me taste your soul. I want to make you my slave. Now come have a drink from my wicked flower!"

More laughter followed, and I smiled. I gave each one a goodnight kiss.

"Okay, Slade, my challenge to you is to wow me with your silver tongue. Show me your command of speech. Bend your words in a way that will amaze me. Come on, wordsmith. Impress me."

"I have one request."

"Out with it, you big staller!" Sofia commanded.

"No one makes a sound above breathing while I do this, especially you, Sofia."

Everyone agreed.

I stood in the middle of the room, and I felt every eye on me. I dimmed the lights a bit and took a long, deliberately loud, deep breath. I closed my eyes and looked down. I extended my arms to my sides at shoulder height and faced my palms upward. I raised my head slowly and opened my black eyes. I heard a familiar gasp, and Sofia pulled the covers over her mouth and nose like a frightened child. I let out a long mournful sigh that wound down into a low, rumbling hiss. I stood in silence for a minute before I spoke.

"A glass of suicide raised in honor of a love lost to the abyss of loneliness. We sit back-to-back, isolated by time and regret. If only you could hear my plea. If only I had a voice that could reach you. Why have you gone deaf to my love? Will I ever see you again? Soon to embark on this lonely road to seek out your voice if only in a dying memory." As I twisted my silver tongue, I poured passion into those cold words, giving birth to sentences. I breathed life into them, just to give them away to an audience that hungrily devoured them like candy.

Asya clapped, and the others followed suit.

"Slade, where did that come from?" Tova asked.

"I just thought of what it would be like to lose someone I love."

"Well, I will tell you one thing, Slade. You know your way around words, and those were beautiful. When you speak, people want to listen. I'm happy that you ended up here where we can help mold you into a good person because a mind and tongue like that could cause a great deal of pain and suffering if wielded like a weapon."

"Thank you, Asya."

"So, are you ready to sleep in the arms of the gods?"

"Thank you, Asya, but I will share a spot on the bed. I don't think I will be able to sleep well knowing that my friends are below me."

"I see what you are saying, Slade. But why would you share your winnings? Don't worry. There is no right or wrong answer."

"I just think a prize like this one is better shared or not had because it could be a once-in-a-lifetime chance to feel something that cool. I would rather talk about it later than describe it as if bragging." I crawled between Sunako and Topaz.

"So, you will only take your prize if you can share it?"

Asya snapped, and seven bodies floated upward.

"Ladies, make sure you thank the boy tomorrow. Slade is a true gentleman."

"Asya, how does this work? Can we roll over? What if one of us has to use the bathroom later?"

"Sweetie, I'm a light sleeper, so if one needs to go to the ground, I will know. Then you will float down. As for rolling over, just roll. But I get the best sleep on my back. If you want to move somewhere, just think about where or to whom you want to go to. I will ask that you all refrain from having sex, at least while I'm in the room. I would rather not get any liquids on me while I sleep. I will give you all a few minutes to enjoy being weightless."

The lights got really low, and for about ten or so minutes, we all enjoyed floating and gliding around the room. Even Asya was in on the fun, but it was time to relax. Everyone said their goodnights to one another and paired up in each other's arms. Topaz and Sunako left space for me, and I floated toward them to enjoy their body heat.

The light went off, and darkness enveloped us. Asya wished us goodnight and pleasant dreams.

"Who would like to be sung to sleep?"

Everyone said, "Please."

"Okay, great. Then I have a special song with some help from Topaz and a pinch of magic."

Asya began, then Topaz joined soon after as she held me close to her bare chest. I felt her voice in my chest, and little lights started to blink and fly around the room. I was struck by the awe of it all: music with a light show. My eyes became heavy, and I tried to stay awake, but sleep pulled me away to the land of the dreamers, lovers, fighters, and those who sought enlightenment in the realm of shared unconsciousness.

"I see you're getting closer to me."

"Who are you?" I asked.

"Someone from your past, and I want you back. Soon, you'll be in my arms once more. Then you'll never become lost again."

Chapter 17

The House of Whispers

As I woke up, I felt amazing. My whole body was alive and comfortable. I was up before anyone else, but I was in the arms of Asya, and she was topless. I panicked at the thought of what might have happened, as my memory from the night before was hazy.

"You're okay, Slade. You drifted toward me about an hour ago, and I didn't want to wake you. You're a snuggly thing, and I enjoyed it. Now, I'm going to gently push you toward the ladies—let's keep this between us. Oh, and you might want to control that thing a little better because it woke up before you. So did your hips. If I were a slightly weaker woman, I would have guided you in."

"You're not making this easy, Asya." We were eye to eye as I whispered, "I dreamed of the green-eyed woman again." I stopped floating and slammed into the floor.

"Oops. Go to the bathroom and take care of that before it gets you into a tight spot."

I returned, then floated back up and over to Topaz and Sunako. I came up between them, lying on my back with my arms outstretched under each one's head. Soon, their bodies were snuggled tightly to me with their legs on my legs. Topaz's face was tucked in next to my ear, and Sunako's head was on my chest. Both pairs of hands quickly found their way in my shorts, firmly holding onto me—I was growing again. Out of the corner of my eye, I saw Asya and tried to catch her attention, but when I did, she only waved at me and smiled. I slipped my arm out from under Sunako and attempted to remove their hands from me, but they only tightened their grips.

I kissed Sunako, and she woke up. I did the same to Topaz, who smiled as she blinked up at me sleepily.

"Ladies, I desperately need to use the bathroom, and as much as I want to enjoy you two a little longer, I must regretfully ask you both to unhand me."

"Can I—I mean—can we have it back later?" Topaz whispered.

"Provided Lady Silk says it is okay that you and I can be together."

Sunako made a purring sound, and they let go at the same time. I tried to glide toward the doorway, but as I got within five feet of the bathroom door, Sofia walked by and blew me a kiss.

"A gentleman always lets a lady go first." She closed the door.

"Damn it."

I floated to Asya and meant to touch her hip, but I only got her behind.

She rolled over and said, "Bad boy!" With a snap of her fingers, I crashed to the ground. I immediately wished I were in a better position because hitting the floor face, chest, stomach, groin, and knees-first was very unpleasant.

Sofia walked back in and said, "I warned you not to swear in the house. Asya dislikes it the most." She then stepped on me rather than over me, and if that wasn't bad enough, I didn't think I was going be able to get up and not piss myself. So, I gathered my thoughts and willpower as I attempted to rise. Lucy walked on my back with her little feet and stopped with one foot on my lower back. With the other, she pressed down on the high center between my shoulder blades.

Lucy said, "Has anyone seen Slade this morning? Oh, hey, Slade. Whatcha doing down there?" She laughed.

"I fell, and now you are on me. Now, kindly get off so that I may use the bathroom," I requested with irritation in my voice.

She laughed again, stepped off, and walked into the bathroom. I took a breath, stood up, and walked in.

"Oh no! I was here first, cutie. So, piss in front of me or hold it." She smiled and peed in front of me, her eyes never leaving mine. "See, I'm not as shy as you." She stood up, and I relieved myself while Lucy watched from the back. "See, not too hard, was it?"

I kissed her cheek and walked out.

A little while later, Asya somehow made breakfast for all of us by herself.

"Magic?" I asked.

She smiled. "No, silly. My little helpers bought me what I needed and assisted me in the kitchen."

"Will they be joining us?"

"No, but you will meet them in about an hour when we go see Lady Silk. Now, everyone, let's eat."

We gathered around the table and enjoyed the eggs, potatoes, and small square pieces of ham. It was very delicious, and the conversations were light.

"I had a really fun last night with you all, and we are going to do that again very soon, hopefully, within the next week or two. But I will need Mr. Slade to escort me to the other two Houses, and I might borrow two of you as well," said Asya.

We finished our food and cleaned up.

"Slade, Topaz, Sofia, please come with me to the main house."

We gathered our things and made our way to Lady Silk's house, where we were greeted by Elma.

"Good morning, Elma. I'm here to see the lady of the House."

"Please come in, Asya. It's always a pleasure to have you. How have you been?"

"Thank you, Elma. I am well."

We entered through the main doors, and Lady Silk greeted us from the second-floor landing.

"Asya, please come up. No need to stand down there. You know my house is your house. Elma, please have tea sent to the north reading room."

We walked upstairs, and Lady Silk hugged Asya. Then the two little ones appeared.

"Asya, I do so wish you would come live here with us, like old times." Lady Silk seemed very happy. "Topaz, please take Sofia and Slade to your room. I will send for you soon."

Topaz smiled and took our hands as we reached another set of stairs to the third floor. Her room was filled with many books on her shelves but no bed in the room, only a comfy-looking chair.

"Where is your bed, or do you float when you sleep?"

"I wish I could float. I want to learn that spell first. Tell me it was not the best sleep. I have no use for a bed. I only have a hammock. I set it up right before I go to sleep. It saves me a lot of space. If you move in, you will have the room two rooms over."

***

In the reading room, Lady Silk said, "Asya, I see you have spent some time with Mr. Slade. Tell me: what do you think about him? I trust you were thorough, so please fill me in on what you have learned."

Tea arrived, and it smelled wonderful.

"Thank you, Elma." Lady Silk was always very polite. Asya deeply loved that about her.

Asya smiled. "Ah, yes, straight to the point. The boy is something of a mystery. A kind and gentle soul. He does not think of himself first, but what you really want to know is his abilities, am I right?"

"Please. Asya, don't tease. That boy is the only person I've ever met that makes me nervous and not just in a sexual way."

"First, is that because he can physically handle your shadows? Second, in a sexual way? Please, explain that."

"Besides my father, no one dares to challenge me or my sisters because of my shadows, and yes, the ability to fight off my shadows has me somewhat nervous, as I am defenseless in more than one way. As for the sexual feelings I have for him—haven't you noticed the way he smells, the way his eyes look right into you? To me, it feels like he is kissing my soul. It took all I had to not have him on the floor the other day. I'm convinced he is at least eighteen, and I am embarrassed of my feelings."

"Silk, let me stop you right there. Mr. Slade will be loyal. This, I have seen. Give him some trust, and you will see that you have someone whose only want is to further the wants and needs of this great House. I also believe that, even if he regains his memories—which, by the way, were not forgotten but were removed—he will remain loyal to you and the women who have adopted him as their consort. I feel you have nothing to worry about from him. And, yes, he does smell wonderful. His eyes are hard to look into as well because they burn with passion. My only fear is it will cause reckless passion on the part of the women who are falling for him."

"I have heard that he is quite taken with Sofia. Then, I have Topaz who is crazy for him, and I wouldn't be shocked if one of the others liked him as well." Silk laughed. "So many women and so few men.

I'm astonished that the men get any work done around here, and you didn't answer my questions. What can he do? Or am I just going to end up with another gifted fighter? Will there be more than just *wanting* him?"

"I feel that some females will fall all over him, and you will find out sooner or later. So, this seems like a good time to tell you that six have chosen him as their own. Shockingly, they're willing to share."

Lady Silk spat out her tea. "What the hell, Asya! How is that going to work? Two or three in one cottage and there are still problems, but six women sharing one man? Holy shit, that sounds like a potentially problematic situation, and I can't have that."

"Trust me, Lady Silk. I feel it will work. H does have a few abilities, starting with his strength. He is highly intelligent and has the silver tongue—it's almost as if a siren and a hypnotist had a baby, that baby being his tongue." Asya took a long sip of her tea as did Lady Silk. Asya casually said, "By the way, he has the Eyes of Nyx, and he is an oracle."

Lady Silk spat out her tea again, jumping up. "What? How is that possible? I mean, that statement is inconceivable!" With an astonished look, Lady Silk cleaned the tea off the table. "I say, Asya, you have told some amazing jokes in the past and pulled even better pranks, but this, I simply cannot believe!"

"Please, calm yourself, my love. I could not be more serious. I have been inside his mind, and there is no doubt at all." Asya looked Silk directly in the eyes.

"Asya, you have known me since I was a baby. I learned so much from you. When my mother died, you were there for me and my sisters. You and your sisters became our second mother of whom we greatly love. You were with us every step of the way when our abilities started to develop. You were there for us in every possible way, but this? This can't be true; no boy can be an oracle. Why would the gods let a man have that most coveted ability? After all, they're unclean. It's just that simple." Lady Silk wiped her mouth and sat back, folding her arms. "Besides, you told us that story when I was a child, albeit it was a favorite one of my sisters and me. Asya, it's just a story, isn't it?"

"My sweet adopted daughter, where do all stories come from? All lies have a speck of truth buried within them, and yet, here he is, the fabled male oracle in this very house. And he wants to live here. Topaz has seen it. I'm curious: why not have Saffron check him out?"

Lady Silk called for Elma, "Please call Saffron and tell her I need her right now."

A few minutes later, Saffron ran through the door. "Lady Silk, you have need of me. Is everyone all right?"

Lady Silk smiled. "Saffron, do you remember the boy Slade?"

"I do." She sounded unimpressed.

Lady Silk said, "Good, because I have a job for you, if you are up for it." Lady Silk neglected to mention Slade was an oracle; she only told her to go in and bend him to her will. "Force him on both knees and make him kiss the bottom of your feet."

Saffron only nodded.

"Please have a seat. I will call him in. Elma, go get Slade."

"Saffron, would you like some tea, darling?" asked Asya.

She accepted the cup.

"Two sugars, if I remember correctly?"

She nodded. Saffron was not a big talker.

***

Someone knocked at Topaz's door. Elma entered and said, "Lady Silk would like Mr. Slade to join them in the reading room. You two, sit tight. No doubt I will come for you two soon enough."

Elma did not speak in the short walk.

"Ah, Mr. Slade. You're looking well-rested today. I would like you to meet Mistress Saffron." Lady Silk gestured toward the young woman.

She was about my height at five-foot seven with long dark-black hair, brown eyes, and dark skin. Her eyes were half-open, and she wore an apathetic look.

"Hello, Saffron. I remember you from the first time I met Lady Silk. You're an oracle."

She stood up and walked toward me with great confidence, holding out her hand. "Take my hand, boy."

I smiled at her and said, "You mean Mr. Slade." I reached out and took her hand. The room fell away, and we were in a forest.

"Boy, you will kneel to me here and now and kiss the bottom of my feet!"

I started to laugh and turned my back on her.

"Boy! I know you heard me! On your knees and kiss my feet like the filthy lost dog you are!"

I started to walk away, but she made the land disappear, bringing us to a white room. She made many copies of herself who all commanded me to drop to my knees.

"Saffron, I will not touch the ground with even one knee, let alone both. One could consider your tone condescending. So, if you're going to talk to me, then you better be able to walk the walk!"

"How dare you speak to me like that, you filthy dog! I order you to take your right hand and bite it until you bleed. Then get on your knees, kiss my feet, and beg my forgiveness."

I raised my hand, making it look like I had no control, and the real Saffron got closer. "Saffron, what are you doing to me?" I placed my hand close to my mouth as she walked right in front of me.

"Bite yourself, dog! Your new master commands you!"

I opened my mouth, and she produced a wicked smile. Without warning, I took her arm. "Saffron, take me to your library. This, I command you!"

The room changed, and books appeared all around us.

"Now, show me what Lady Silk told you before I walked in the room."

A book floated over to us.

"Unlock it, please."

She did. I saw what she was told, and I smiled.

"What are you?" Saffron facial expressions softened, and she looked scared.

"Saffron, please accept my apologies, but it seems that you were not told anything about me. May we start over?"

She nodded.

"Excellent. How about we go to my library? Feel free to wander around. I'm an open book, but I do ask one thing of you. Please call me Slade. I really don't like 'boy,' and 'dog' is a bit much, don't you think?"

Saffron nodded, going from book to book.

"Slade, I can't believe it. You are like Topaz and me. Wow, this is crazy! Did you know that there is an old legend about a boy like you? This is amazing. Does Topaz know?"

I held out a hand, and a book came to me simply titled *Topaz*. I handed it to her, and she started to read. "What! That dirty bitch! Keeping such a secret from me. Wow. Look, I'm sorry I spoke to you that way earlier."

"It's fine. I guess we should wrap this up, but first, I want you to kiss me on the cheek."

"Sorry, Slade, I'm not into men."

"I still want you to do it right after we return to the reading room."

I clapped, and we were back.

"Saffron, do you have something for me?" I smiled as she leaned in to kiss my right cheek and sat down. I then took a bow toward Lady Silk, Asya, and Saffron. As I sat, I winked at her, and she tried her best not to smile.

"Mistress Saffron, what was that? What did you learn?"

"Lady Silk, I believe you understand what Slade is. I tried my best to bend him to my will, but he didn't even budge. Then, you saw he made me kiss his cheek. He told me to do that while inside of his head. We came out, and I was still compelled to complete his request, even though it was against my will. For lack of a better word, he is amazing. Not even Topaz can bend me to her will, and we are almost evenly matched."

"Slade, please fetch your two love interests."

I got up and left.

I knocked hard on the wooden door. Topaz opened it.

"Damn, boy, you knock hard."

"I didn't want you to think it was me."

We shared a quick kiss, and I took Sofia's hand.

"Did you think I was going to forget you, my sweet?" We kissed.

***

Asya asked, "Lady Silk, may we speak in private?"

Lady Silk motioned for Saffron to leave the room, and the two little ones followed and closed the door.

"I would very much like Mr. Slade to escort me for the next few weeks, if that is okay. I believe that these upcoming days will shape him into something far more magnificent. Either way, he will be close to me, and I wouldn't mind two others, if you can spare them."

"For you, Asya, anything. I must know, if you can tell me, why do you never name your young apprentices?"

"I was wondering if you would ever ask me that." Asya smiled. "They lose whatever name they had because we empty them of the distractions of individuality so that they can focus on studying. When the time is right, their true names are bestowed to them. Then, and only then, will they be ready for their final tests. We never changed your names out of respect for your mother."

***

"What's going on in the reading room?" Topaz asked.

"You two have been summoned by Lady Silk. Please follow me."

I saw Saffron and the two hooded little ones. We waited to be called in, and it did not take long. We all entered the room.

Lady Silk smiled and said, "Everyone, have a seat."

Asya continued what she was saying before we entered the room, "I think the field trip will be beneficial to all."

"I agree. Which two do you have in mind?" Lady Silk's eyes fell on me as she spoke, but her face showed no emotion.

Asya said, "I would like Topaz and Sofia. Topaz can use the travel experience, and Sofia can get some training in, as well as keeping Mr. Slade focused on his training. I will visit the other three Houses, and we will leave after this meeting if you have no problem with that."

"I see no problem with that. Ladies, go get what you need for your travels and hurry back. Slade, stay here."

Topaz and Sofia got up to leave.

"Asya, please give my best to Father. I expect that the House of Thorns is the third House you will visit."

Asya laughed. "Of course I will be visiting your father. He hates it so when I don't visit. Plus, I'm picking up a new student from him. It will be a busy next two months for me with my new little apprentices."

"Slade, as the newest member of the House of Ribbons, I expect nothing but the best out of you. Make me proud and earn my House colors."

"I will. Thank you, Lady Silk."

"Asya, I would like to keep his abilities a bit of a secret or at least the oracle part for as long as we can. We would not want words like that getting into the wrong ears."

"Lady Silk, you have my word on that. I, as well, would like to keep that under wraps as best as we can for now." Asya got up to give Lady Silk a hug. She murmured, "I miss the days when you were only as high as my knee. Like a squirrel, you would crawl up my leg and up to my shoulder where you would sit. You always knew how to make me smile, and I thank you for that, Silk. I love you dearly." Asya placed a kiss on Lady Silk's forehead before leaving the house.

My new friends were there to see me off, and I hugged and kissed them. After a few minutes, everyone was accounted for.

"How to travel? Should we walk? Or should we shift there?" asked Asya.

I asked, "What does shifting mean?"

"Think of it like teleportation."

"So, it's fast."

"Oh yeah." Asya smiled.

Topaz spoke, "Please, Asya, shifting is so fun. Hey, Slade, do you have a weak stomach? Don't worry. We will see soon enough."

Sofia and Asya laughed.

"Asya, those two there—why do they always stay silent?" I felt that, under their hoods, they would look like little goblins or some other creature.

"They speak, but only when I ask them to do something for me. They communicate with me and Topaz through thoughts. So, is everyone ready to leave? Slade, just do what we do." Asya said something in a foreign tongue, and she clapped. One oblong hole appeared in front of us. Topaz turned around and fell backward. Then, the two little ones and Sofia jumped into the hole.

"Slade, it is your turn. Just jump in."

So, I turned around, crossed my arms, and fell back.

It felt a little like falling, but it was too fast. Then suddenly, I was on my feet, and Asya appeared out of thin air next to me.

"How do you feel?" Topaz was studying me.

"I'm fine. Why?"

As I finished that statement and stepped forward, the world began to shake violently, causing me to fall over. It didn't allow me to get up, and gravity took hold. The best I could do was get to my hands and knees and empty the contents of my stomach. After a few minutes of heaving, one of the small ones came over and offered his hand, and I took it. Then he bit my arm and wouldn't let go. It felt like he was sucking while he clamped down, his teeth hitting the bone.

"Slade! What did I tell you about that one? He's a biter."

"He won't let go. What should I do?"

"Let him enjoy the meal or slap him off. Either way, we have to meet with Lady Velour, so stop screwing around."

I felt bad for doing it, but I had to slap him twice before he'd let go. He then growled and leapt for me again. Asya caused the boy to stop midair and floated him to her, scolding him. Sofia handed me a piece of cloth to wrap around my forearm, and I thanked her with a kiss.

"I see the boy thinks you taste like candy. Careful he doesn't attack you while you sleep." She laughed.

We walked about ten minutes until we were at a house that looked identical to Lady Silk's. The only thing different were the cottages. The House colors were blue and orange.

"Okay, people, wait here. I will return in a few minutes. Real quick, last-minute rule." Asya smiled. "No sex, period. To be very clear, I'm talking about Slade. He is off-limits until I say otherwise."

Asya wasn't gone long, and she came back with Lady Velour who had medium-length, reddish-blonde hair that looked almost like fire and complemented her blue eyes.

"Slade, tell me why you have a foot on that child's chest!"

"Asya, he bit me again and tried again after that. This was the best I could come up with. I apologize."

Lady Velour said, "I see you have brought the boy with you. How am I not surprised that you have taken an interest in him? Hello, Slade. I am Lady Velour. I have seen and heard some good things about you. The way you handled those pricks, William and Richter, was very enjoyable. Asya, will you be staying in my house?"

"Of course, my sweet. How else will we be able to stay up late and talk?" Asya pulled out a small book, seemingly out of nowhere, and handed it to Lady Velour.

"Thank you, Asya. I can't believe you found it. Oh, I can't wait to read it." She hugged Asya. "Mistress Topaz, I will have a room readied for you. I will have a cottage made up for Slade and his obvious love interest, Sofia."

Asya laughed. "Lady Velour, Mistress Topaz has decided to fall head over heels for the young man, as well as a few other ladies."

"Right this way, lover boy," Lady Velour said.

They escorted us into the main house.

"Put your belongings there. I'll have them brought to the cottage."

"So, Asya, how long do I get to enjoy your company?" Lady Velour closed the door.

"Only two days, I'm afraid, but I promise next time I will stay longer. I'm due at your father's house later in the week, and I will be stopping in to see Velvet, too."

"Sounds like you have a full schedule. Are you or anyone in your party hungry? If not, Topaz, you know people here, so feel free to show off your man—I mean—introduce him, if you like. Oh, I will have dinner ready at six sharp, so be back by then." Lady Velour smiled. "Wait! How is Topaz allowed to be with a man? She's an oracle."

"I said she was head over heels. I never said she was allowed to be with him."

Topaz took my hand and led Sofia and me outside.

Asya called us and said, "I want you to keep Slade's ability as an oracle a secret until I say otherwise, understand? When you run into Cyan, tell her Slade is off-limits. He is not to be touched, and that comes from me. Slade, if Miss Sneaky pants Cyan manages to touch you long enough to get in, block her in the library. Let Batch, and only Batch, interact with her. The book I gave him will help guard your secret by putting up a fake front. Now, go have a bit of fun, and do your best not to get any new love interests. Remember, we're guests here."

Asya walked away.

Sofia asked, "Topaz, where do you want to take him first?"

They decided to visit their friend, Kailee. After finding out where she was, we went to find her by the lake. When we arrived, Kailee was picking fruit from a tree.

"Slade, I bet you can't walk up to her and charm a kiss out of her." Topaz pointed at Kailee.

"What will be my reward if I win?"

Topaz said, "Whatever you heart desires."

Sofia laughed.

"Oh, and Kailee loves it when someone compliments her eyes, and her favorite flower is the tiger lily."

"Too easy. Watch a master at work." I walked out from behind a tree and said, "Hello, I am new here. You are Kailee, right? I am Slade."

"Yes, I'm Kailee. Where did you come from?" she asked.

"I'm from the House of Ribbons."

Kailee was around five foot six with wavy light-brown hair that hung just below her shoulders; she looked thin, but very fit. She had huge blue eyes, very light-tan skin, and a soft voice. I was embarrassed because she was very beautiful, which took me by surprise.

"Welcome to the House of Whispers. Slade, may I help you with something?"

"Well, I was hoping you could show me around. This is such a beautiful area with the lake and the waterfall in the distance. I would hate to get lost and be late for dinner with Lady Velour."

"Oh my, you must be an important visitor. Sure, I'll escort you around. Would you like to see the top of the waterfall?" Kailee sounded giddy.

"I very much would."

Kailee took my arm, and we walked. We talked about little things, and as we neared the top, she smiled.

"Slade, you're not afraid of heights, are you?"

"Not with such a beautiful woman like you on my arm."

"We are north of the House of Ribbons. This water feeds your lake." Kailee pointed to the lake fed by the tall waterfall. She told of other landmarks that could be seen.

As we reached the top, I appreciated the breathtaking view. I could see the main house, but it looked so small.

"Wow, Kailee, the view is almost as beautiful as you are. My only regret is that I don't have flowers to give you for sharing such an amazing sight, which is your smile."

"Oh my, I love flowers." Kailee was smiling and blushing.

"I would give you a tiger lily because that flower is unlike any other, like your smile."

Kailee smile grew. "Those are my favorite flowers."

"One would go perfectly in your hair, complementing your beautiful eyes."

"Oh, Slade, I think I could fall for you with all your pretty words, but I don't think you would fall for me." Kailee walked to the edge of the cliff. "You see, men ignore me because I'm too small and I like to read." Kailee walked back over to me. "I know this sounds crazy, but I feel like you honestly mean what you said about me being pretty, and I feel that you want to kiss me. Slade, do you really want to kiss me? Please tell me that I'm not wrong. Tell me that you hear my beating heart as it sings to you."

I looked Kailee in the eyes. "Yes, Kailee, I hear it. Let mine join with yours to make a duet that would make the very birds envious with our song. May I kiss you?"

Kailee stepped up into my arms and placed her face close to my neck.

"Slade, will you fall for me, or will you let me drop into a void of sorrow, only to spiral down into my own tears and throw my love into uncertainty?"

"Kailee, I will not let you shed a single tear other than that of joy."

"Slade, close your eyes. I don't want you to get dizzy from my kiss."

Kailee kissed my neck and my cheek. Then a dizzy, sickening feeling overtook me. When I opened my eyes, I was—for lack of a better word—*flying* through the air. She had thrown me up, and I was a hundred feet or higher than her. She waved at me.

I could hear her say, "Better luck next time, dickhead!"

I was falling, and I watched the cliff pass me. The fall was fast, and the water was not as soft as I'd expected upon impact. It took the wind out of me. When I rose to the surface, I merely floated, waiting to catch my breath. As I did, I heard one splash after another.

"Hey, Slade, you look better wet." Kailee laughed.

Then, I heard Sofia laugh along with Topaz.

Sofia swam up to me. "Don't be mad, my love. You can't win them all. How do you feel?"

"I feel a bit stupid, and my whole body hurts."

"Oh yeah, you hit at a bad angle." Kailee laughed some more.

Topaz said, "Sorry, but Kailee is a powerful mind reader. Please don't be mad at our little joke."

"I might be a little upset if my body wasn't on fire, but I did win."

"You must have hit your head because you lost." Topaz splashed me.

"The bet was to get her to kiss me, right? Kailee, did you kiss me?"

"Yes, but only on the neck and cheek," Kailee claimed.

"Then I win." I began to laugh. "I told you to watch the master."

"Oh shit, he's right!" Topaz exclaimed.

"Sorry, ladies, but I needed him to trust me enough to get very close, and besides, he smelled really good."

Sofia grabbed me, pulling us under the water where we shared a romantic kiss as we floated to the surface. When we emerged, we treaded water, almost nose to nose.

I said, "It was a very funny trick."

We kissed again, and Topaz came up from behind me and kissed my neck.

Kailee said, "Ladies, be careful that you don't drown that poor guy in the water or love."

When our kiss was over, we swam for a bit. Eventually, we got out and walked around to dry off. I looked at the height of the waterfall and laughed.

Kailee was very funny and laughed a lot. She was also one of the strongest. She could read minds through touch, which explained why she'd taken my arm when we'd walked. We went to find Topaz's friend, Cyan. We found her talking with a few small children.

"Topaz, my favorite friend, how are you? I thought I was going to have to wait two more weeks to see you. I see the rumors are true: Sofia has picked a mate."

They hugged and lightly kissed. Cyan was five foot seven with medium-length light-brown hair, deep green eyes, and very tan skin.

Sofia softly whispered in my ear, "Cyan is an oracle, and you know they can only have women as lovers. It is said that an oracle will lose her gift if she sleeps with a man."

"Is that really true?" I asked.

Sofia said, "Who knows, but they stick to women only. This is good for me and bad for you because Topaz is something in bed, real passionate."

Cyan saw briefly into Topaz's thoughts. "Oh! Topaz! How can this be? How are you in love with this man? You know the rules! Only women! Do you want to get in trouble? Well, do you? Besides, look at him. He looks like he might be stupid. Hey, stupid, we're oracles. That means we are divine, so hands off, you filthy ape. Come on, Topaz, look at me. These feelings will come and go. Trust me. Hey, ape man, stop looking at me before I make you lick the bottom of my foot."

I laughed.

"Why is he wearing a dress, and what the hell is so funny, you raggedy bastard?"

"Asya said that he's wearing something like the Greeks used to wear."

"Don't defend him, Topaz. Come on, I don't want you around him."

Topaz stood still as Cyan tried to walk away with her hand.

"Topaz! Come now!"

"No. Now stop embarrassing me."

"Cyan, what if I can make you think differently of me by night's end? Would you cease your seemingly endless show of dominance?" I questioned.

My question might have upset her because she punched me directly in the face. Luckily for me, strength was not her gift, but she did manage to draw a good amount of blood from my nose.

"Damn it, Cyan! We have to be at Lady Velour's for dinner in thirty minutes. Kailee, please show us to a healer. Topaz, we will see you at dinner."

I smiled. "Good day to you, Cyan."

We walked to the healer's cottage, and Sofia knocked on the door.

"Please come in. My name is Samantha. How may I help you two?"

"I think I may have a decent cut in my nose." I pointed at my face.

"Well, with that amount of blood, it looks more like you might have a broken nose. Sit down and let me do my job."

I sat, and she placed her hands on my face. "Kailee, I don't recognize either of these two, but I know the House colors."

Sofia spoke up. "I am Mistress Sofia of the House of Ribbons. My cottage boy, Slade, spoke to Cyan and—"

"Let me stop you right there. Boy, look at me. Do not speak to Cyan unless she speaks to you. She has a real dislike for men. Sofia, please keep your boy on a tight leash around here because he doesn't look too bright. So, if Cyan did this to him, then I can only imagine what Thomas would do. Boy, look at me! Avoid Thomas for the duration of your stay because he likes to throw his weight around. Kailee, see to it that this boy goes the rest of the day here without further incident. You know how much Lady Velour hates it when House-to-House violence happens."

Kailee laughed. "Yes, this would really piss her off."

"Yes, Samantha, thank you. I will heed your warning." I sounded congested.

"Call me Sam."

Ten minutes passed.

"You look all better. I hope that your stay will be better than it has been so far."

We thanked her again and left to walk to Lady Velour's house.

"Sofia, since I was pronounced a free man and titled 'mister,' why do you refer to me as a 'cottage boy?'"

"It's easier while here because it helps keep a low profile on you. I meant no offense."

On our walk, we saw three men walking by and eyeing Sofia. One called out to he using an unfamiliar word.

"Wait, are there more men here? And why are those men not afraid to speak to you that way?"

"Our House is the strictest pertaining to males. You will find different rules at each House. Be prepared for that." Sofia took my hand. "Ignore them. Just keep walking. You don't need the trouble."

I turned and made the hand sign that Cheri had done to me, the one where she raised her middle finger in the air.

"Shit! What the hell, Slade! What did I just tell you about that type of thing? That counts as dirty language!"

"But we are not in the cottage. He shouldn't talk to either of you that way."

"Good point, Slade, but you're with me, and I am the head of the cottage. As your mistress, I set the rules! Now be a good boy and play nice."

"Hey, bitch! We were talking to you, but now your friend has made a big mistake."

Kailee said, "Mind your business, Thomas. Go be a prick somewhere else."

Unbeknownst to the group below, Asya and Lady Velour were watching.

"Lady Velour, should we call them to attention to let them know that they're being watched?"

"Honestly, I really want to see how Mr. Slade handles himself. Don't you?" Lady Velour rubbed her hands together.

Asya said, "I am more worried about your guys than my boy. I bet you one gold coin and three silver coins that my boy stops all three."

"Oh, you have a bet, but no magic! Asya, you little trickster. What do you have up your sleeve this time?"

Thomas, the taller of the three, walked up to me and poked me in the chest, barking nasty words in my face. Before he could finish his diatribe, I grabbed his finger and jerked it with a forceful twist to the right. He went to his knees, and I kissed his chin with my knee.

"Would either one of you like some one-on-one time with me?" I asked.

One stepped forward with a puffed-out chest. I stepped forward, closing the gap between us. I snapped my eyes black and lunged forward, causing the bully to fall backward in his retreat.

As I stood over him, I smiled and went back to Thomas. "Would you like to apologize to my mistress, or shall I make you lick the dirt from her boots?"

Thomas said, "I am truly sorry, Mistress. My friends and I were just joking, and we let it get out of hand. Please forgive us."

I looked at the still-standing friend and bared my teeth. He backed up and looked away, placing his palms out at chest height like he wanted no part of it.

"Good. Now piss off before I become hungry and make an early snack of your soul." I stepped back, and the two picked up Thomas, who was holding his hand. "It was nice to meet you, Thomas. I hope our next meeting is just as fun."

They ran off toward Samantha's place.

I turned around with a huge smile, and Sofia scolded me, "No! What have I told you about those eyes? Never show them to me! Damn it, you're so thick sometimes."

I shifted them back and bent a knee. "My mistress, please forgive me. I have no excuse for my forgetfulness on that topic."

"Stand up, or you will draw attention to us!" I did, and Sofia grabbed me, kissing me passionately. "I will admit you're very sexy when you got all alpha wolf defending our honor."

Kailee said, "I don't care what you say, Sofia. I love those eyes. I bet Thomas and the asshole gang thought Slade was a vampire. This day keeps getting better. Sofia, he's a lot of fun."

Asya extended her hand, and Lady Velour placed one gold and three shiny silver coins into Asya's palm.

"It was worth it to be further impressed by the boy. I wonder if Silk will sell him to me?"

"It will never happen. Silk pronounced him a free man and gave him the title of mister. Then Mr. Slade swore loyalty to the House of Ribbons and was granted permission to have not one but six lovers."

Lady Velour laughed. "What? That is unheard of. What is he, some kind of god? Even Lord Allen only had three wives at one time.

I mean, six really is a bit much for a mere boy, unless he can maintain a lover's embrace for a supernatural amount of time. If so, I take it that Sofia is his number one?"

Asya sighed. "She is the number one and holds his reins—tightly, I might add. I think it was love at first sight for him, with her and Sunako."

"Then explain the other four." Lady Velour smiled.

"I don't even know if I could explain that boy right now. I say let them live and love as long as there is no fighting between any of the women."

Chapter 18

Dinners with the Ladies

Kailee, Sofia, and I approached a large, highly decorated wooden front door. Kailee knocked, and a male opened it.

"Greetings. I am Mr. Willock. Lady Velour is expecting you three in the dining room. If you will, please follow me."

We were led into a large dining hall with many tables that could easily fit fifty people. We were seated at one of the large round tables. Topaz and Cyan entered soon after and spoke with Mr. Willock.

Sofia told me, "Don't let Cyan rattle you. She is and has always been a bitch. She has a huge crush on Topaz, but Topaz will not be with her as a lover. So, I bet she is going to hate on you a whole lot more. I think you should seduce her, then leave her wanting what she will never have: Topaz and you."

"My love, that would not be very nice. She has every right to not like me. Just look at her: she hangs on Topaz's every word. I feel bad for her, but I will not make her heart want any more than it already does."

Sofia smiled. "You really are a nice guy. I want to kiss you right now, but it would be inappropriate and may be looked down on."

Lady Velour and Asya arrived with a woman.

"Ah, Mr. Slade, Sofia, and Topaz, welcome to my table. I hope you like roast pheasant. How has your day been, Mr. Slade? Anything that troubles you?"

"No, my lady, I find the people that I have met today to be very social, warm, and welcoming."

"Have you met Mistress Cyan yet?" Lady Velour smiled as if she knew the answer already.

"I have, yes. I found our conversation very striking and on point, but it was cut short due to a time conflict. But I hope to see a lot more of her very soon."

Lady Velour laughed. "Boy, I like you very much. I must say that was the best way I have ever heard a man explain being punched in the face by a woman who loves the one who loves you."

I sat there and said nothing.

"My dear boy, this is the House of Whispers. I have a large collection of whisperers and secrets. One is that you have won the heart of an oracle, a heart that you may never be able to possess. But still, she looks at you like she could just eat you up. You're a very lucky, and at the same time, unlucky young man."

"Dinner is served, my lady."

The food looked like little chickens; there was also an assortment of small potatoes, carrots, and tomatoes. We had a tangy yet enjoyable fruit drink. The talk was light with Asya and Lady Velour talking between themselves, occasionally looking over at me and smiling. Dinner ended, and Lady Velour asked me to come meet the young lady who had said nothing the whole meal.

"Mr. Slade, please allow me to introduce you to Mistress Portia."

I reached out to shake her hand, but Asya placed her hand on my shoulder. I could hear her in my head.

"Slade, I will take over because this one will just fish out information from you."

"Hello, Mr. Slade. I am Portia. Nice to meet you."

Portia was short, around five foot two and thin with brown hair and brown eyes, almost like Sunako. She was very cute. We shook hands, and I felt her enter my mind. Asya was hiding Batch and my thoughts from Portia.

"Asya, come. Let the boy enjoy his time with the oracle. Maybe he can win her heart as well."

"I think Portia has had enough time in there. Come back to us, Portia." Asya pulled me backward.

"*Aha!* He is special! I didn't believe it when I heard it! I had to see it with my own eyes. So, what can he do? Can he command with his voice? Is he a witch? A sexy vampire? I promise I will not tell. Better you tell me than rumors get out. He must be special to be greatly prized by the great witch Asya. It will cause Velvet to dig for the truth. You know how her curiosity gets the better of her every time. Wait! Is he unique like me and my sisters?"

Asya whispered, "Lady Velour, this is a very delicate subject. Let us find a spot with fewer ears if you don't mind. Mr. Slade, come with me. My ladies, you're dismissed for the evening. I will send Slade to catch up with you later."

We went to the fourth floor then into a large bedroom. Asya snapped, and candles ignited the room, flooding it with a soft glow.

"Velour, you will keep this to yourself. Yes?"

Lady Velour nodded.

"I believe Mr. Slade is an oracle."

Lady Velour jumped to her feet. "No! No way he is! That is an old witch's tale to make a long night shorter. I don't believe you, Asya! A male oracle? Okay, really, what is it? Can he read minds, fly, or run really fast? He's a vampire? I hope it is that one. Please tell me he's a vampire."

Asya waved me over to her. "Lady Velour, your hand, if you please."

She placed her hand in mine, and a minute later, she was shocked as she sat down. "Asya, he *is* unique. I'm sorry I doubted you, but sorrier that he's not a vampire."

"He's not a god, but he may very well be the child of one. So, for now, treat him like you would Topaz, Cyan, or Portia. Your mouth is closed about this to your sister. We will make it known soon enough, but only after Zyra meets with him in a week's time. What is it with you and the vampire thing?"

"I heard about his soulless black eyes, and vampires are sexy, mystical creatures who are great lovers."

"I take it you have been reading Galya's books again. Which one is it this time?"

"*I Am Dracula.* It's a love story and so enjoyable to read."

"I know the book well, but no, Mr. Slade is not a vampire. No one has seen a vampire since the Great War. Honestly, Velour, this obsession with vampires is borderline unhealthy. If what we think is true, then the old story may very well be true. That makes this time a special time. I think Topaz saw a vision of him years ago. I thought it was just a fever dream of a new oracle because she said to me, 'He will love me as I take him within me.' Mr. Slade, you're to say nothing about this conversation. Now, go find your lovers. I ask you not to give the finger to anyone for the remainder of our visit." Asya waved her hand.

I got up and left without a word and made my way to the first floor and out the door into the night air, bumping into Cyan.

"I have been waiting for you, boy. Tell me: why does she love you?"

I said politely, "I'm not supposed to interact with you."

"Okay then, I will dig it out of your head."

I yawned. "Go for it. You might fall in love, too."

Cyan grabbed my hand, then began to cry and passed out. Asya was going to be so pissed when she found out. I really needed some training, although I did learn where the ladies were. I knocked on the door, and Sofia opened it.

"I have a delivery for a Mistress Topaz."

Topaz exclaimed, "Holy shit, Slade! What did you do to Cyan?"

"She's fine. She was waiting for me outside of the main house and grabbed my arm and tried to force her way into my mind, so I put her to sleep. Speaking of, I would love to get into bed myself. Today's fall off the waterfall really took it out of me."

We put Cyan in bed, and the three of us pushed two beds together. I got in between Sofia and Topaz. We kissed and said our goodnights. I spooned Topaz as Sofia spooned me. I faded away and dreamed of a bronze-skinned woman with a blurry face, striking green eyes, and the voice of an angel.

"Hello, Slade. Which way will you fall: in love or over the edge? Both are deadly." She kissed my cheek. "I can't wait to hold you. I watch you when you sleep."

I woke up, still spooning Sofia, while Topaz was spooning me. I heard a small voice in my head. I had a stowaway, and it was Cyan. She was touching my ankle, and I snatched her by the hand, pressing my finger to my lips. Climbing carefully out of bed, I did not let go of her hand. We walked downstairs to the kitchen.

"Let go of my wrist—you're hurting me," Cyan said in a low voice. "Let me go, or I will scream. You don't want that."

I smiled and said, "Go ahead because you won't like what comes next if you do." I pressed her against the wall with my body. "Now, tell me, Cyan. What did you see while you we in my mind?" I called for Batch. "What did she see, Batch? Batch! Batch?"

"I know that you're like us even though no man can possess the power of sight. We are the chosen ones. Men are weak, pitiful, lust-filled animals that we have to put up with. No different than dogs." Cyan smiled in my face.

"Are you done? I get it you don't like me, and you can run your mouth all day. But the fact is, I have the sight, and you will keep that to yourself. If you run that petty mouth of yours, what will Topaz think of you? Will she turn her eyes from you forever, leaving you lovelorn? Do you want to risk that? Now kiss me on the cheek, and I will call this a misunderstanding. Or shall I wake my beautiful Topaz and kiss her the way you want to?"

I turned my face, and Cyan went in for the kiss. I rotated my head, and our lips touched as I stole the smallest kiss. "That is for my face yesterday. Now, we're even. Lucky for me, your lips are just as soft as your fist."

With a little laugh, I turned and walked out of the room. Cyan jumped onto my back and wrapped her legs around my waist and her arms around my neck. Lucky for me, she had the strength of a normal woman her age. I continued to walk upstairs to the bedroom.

"Good morning, ladies."

Topaz and Sofia sat up, yawning and stretching.

"Damn it, Cyan, get off Slade right this instant!" Topaz sounded annoyed.

Sofia stood there shirtless and spoke politely to Cyan. "Cyan, can't you see that you're having no effect on him? If he wanted, you would be unconscious, but he is showing restraint, so please get off him."

"This son of a bitch made me kiss him, then laughed at me." Cyan was squeezing her arms as hard as she could without the results she wanted, which upset her greatly.

"Is that true? Did you make her kiss you?" Sofia narrowed her eyes.

I told them what had happened from the start. When I had finished, they both laughed.

Sofia said, "Cyan, if I had Slade's gift, I would have made you kiss all of my ass for the rude behavior you've shown him. You know, Cyan, maybe you would be more liked if you were not such a bitch all the time."

"Cyan, you have to understand that I have chosen him. I am a slave to my heart and emotions when it comes to Slade, and the ruder you are to him, the more I might think that you and I should not be friends." Topaz turned her back on Cyan.

Cyan released her grip and climbed off my back. "I'm sorry, Slade. I just thought that one day I might win Topaz's heart. Then you walk in out of thin air, and without effort, you take hold of her heart. I have the right to be upset, but I shame myself with my undignified behavior." Cyan stood up and walked up me. "Mr. Slade, I am sorry. I promise you that I will say nothing to anyone about you, and I swear on my body that I will keep that promise." Cyan placed her hand over my mouth and kissed my cheek. "You're soft like a woman, and you smell nice, really nice."

"He always smells like that, even after a shower." Sofia sniffed my hair. "He is like a flower, wine, and candy mixed together."

A knock came at the door, and Asya walked in.

"Hello, my friends. I trust you slept well." Asya saw Cyan with her shirt off. "Slade, please tell me that you did not sleep with Cyan." Asya placed her hands on her hips.

"We slept in separate beds." I pointed to the other bed.

"No, I mean, did you have intercourse? Because we definitely said no sex while we were on this field trip." Asya looked unhappy.

"Asya, no, no one is having sex with anyone," Cyan spoke as she sat down.

"Give me your hand, Cyan."

"I would rather not, Asya."

"Then you admit you had sex? Give me your hand! I will not ask again, Cyan!"

"I'm sorry, Slade." She gave her hand to Asya. Moments later, Asya and Cyan laughed together.

"I see you have snuck into my boy's mind, you naughty thing. I thought I taught you better than to get caught doing things like that. Oh, well, Lady Velour knows about him, so go to her now with what you discovered so that you remain loyal and no promises are broken here."

Cyan left right away.

"Slade, it looks like you had a fun morning."

"I'm starting to think it might always be like this."

Asya laughed. "Enjoy these times. You will remember them fondly because this will settle down, and life for you will become a routine. Breakfast is in ten minutes. Then, the rest of the day is yours to do as you would like, but no trouble, no sex, and Slade, this applies to you: absolutely no new followers. A few more women and you might get the title of lord." Asya laughed to herself. "Enjoy this beautiful day, Lord Silver Tongue."

Asya left, leaving the door open.

Kailee and Portia stood outside. "Sofia, I hear you three are free for the day. Want to go on a hike with us and Cyan? I just saw Cyan on our way here, and she asked me to invite you three."

"That sounds like fun. What do you think, my mistresses? Shall we go?" I bowed and extended my hand.

Sofia laughed. "I think that if you are going to be a kiss ass, then allow us to at least pull down our pants." Sofia bent over and pulled her pants down. Topaz slapped Sofia's bottom, which made a sharp, loud sound and instantly left a red handprint and a raised outline.

"Ouch!" Topaz exclaimed while rubbing her ass. "Sometimes, I really hate your gift, Sofia!"

"Hey, I feel it as well, and that one stung really good. Maybe later you can do that again. Mr. Slade, do as your mistress asks of you, and kiss it better."

Sofia stayed half-bent, while she looked over her left shoulder at me.

"Oh, and me too." Topaz mimicked Sofia's pose.

"I see no mark on you, Mistress Topaz."

"But I still ache for your kiss. Would you deny a simple request to relieve this pain I have?" Topaz made a pouty face.

Portia said, "Go ahead, Mr. Slade. Your mistresses have asked a small thing of you, and I would very much like to see you carry out this task." Portia tilted her head to one side.

I walked up to Sofia and gently kissed her in the center of the handprint.

Sofia stood up. "Oh, that felt nice. Now, don't leave my sister waiting a second longer."

I gave the same kiss to Topaz. "I look forward to the sequel to that kiss, but somewhere else." Topaz smiled at me.

"What in hell is this?" Cyan stood in the doorway next to Kailee.

Kailee laughed. "Hey, Slade, you lose another bet?"

I said, "Kailee, I didn't lose that bet, and it was worth it. It's not every day one can say that a kiss sent you over the falls into a pool of love."

Portia laughed. "I heard about your little swim."

"Still trying to be smooth, huh?" Kailee winked.

"Cyan, Mr. Slade was helping us understand the importance of a good and proper ass kisser to his mistresses." Sofia laughed and placed her hand on my shoulder. "Besides, wouldn't you make him kiss your ass if you could?"

"More like the bottom of my foot or my armpit." Cyan held up her dirty, bare foot like a dancer. "Come on, boy, you can lick this all you want."

"Maybe later, my bittersweet friend." I reached out and wiggled my fingers on the side of her foot, and she laughed. "Oh, look at that, she can laugh. So, are we going to get some food, then hike, or am I going to have to kiss everyone's ass to properly motivate you all?"

"Okay, I'm getting hungry." Sofia patted her flat stomach, and we went to eat. The breakfast was very good, and I made a point to say thank you to Mr. Willock. I attempted small talk, but he seemed disinterested with my very presence. When everyone was finished, we left and started our walk.

"Excuse me, Mistress Cyan, can we talk to your friend?" It was Thomas with a group of men.

Sofia said, "Slade, I don't think it is a good idea that you talk to them."

"I think I have this. If I need you, I'll scream like a baby for its momma." I walked over to them. "Gentlemen, I bid you a good morning."

"Hello, I am Thomas, and I wanted to apologize to you in person for yesterday's misunderstanding."

I held out my hand. "Thomas, you have no need to seek forgiveness. If anyone were to blame, it was me and my rude gesture. For that, I am sorry. I am new here and should have shown more respect while a guest in your beautiful House."

Each of the six reached out and shook my hand.

Thomas said, "Either way, I'm sorry, and I would like to ask you a question. Are you really a vampire? If so, what's it like? Is that why you are surrounded by so many women?" Thomas seemed very curious about me.

"My master would frown on me for flaunting my gift, and a gentleman never reveals his secrets. I hope to have more time next time I'm here, and maybe we could get together and swap stories and abilities."

Topaz walked up to us. "Slade, we will fall behind in our day's planned activity if we don't leave now." Topaz paid the group no attention.

"Gentlemen, another day then? I bid you *adieu*."

They waved, and we walked away.

"Wow, I really thought they wanted another shot at you, Slade." Sofia took my hand. "Was that French?"

"Oui et ta belle."

"How do you know French?"

"How do you know English?"

"Don't be a dick," Sofia said with a smirk.

"All I know is, I know some things, but don't know others. It was my fault. I should have ignored them, but on the bright side, I may have made some new friends."

"Thank you for saying I'm beautiful."

"You are."

We walked for an hour and a half.

"Mr. Willock had sandwiches made for us." Portia patted her backpack. "Cyan has the drinks: honey wine and cold tea."

The area was beautiful, and our path led us to the top of the waterfall.

"Hey, Slade, would you like to see something?" Kailee waved me over to the edge of the cliff.

"No thanks, Kailee. That was only funny once, but I think I'll just stay back here."

Kailee smiled. "Come on, Slade. It's a game of trust. Now come play with me, or I could physically force you to come here."

I looked at Sofia, and she said, "Don't look at me. She is the strongest one here. I would do as she asks before the request becomes an order."

I walked over to Kailee.

"I knew you would see it my way." Kailee and I locked eyes, and she smiled. "You know, I almost feel bad for throwing you up and over this waterfall, but you came to me as an arrogant ass. So, to make it even, I will show you something you might like. Sofia, may I have him for a little while?"

"Yes, you can have thirty minutes, but he's not allowed to have sex. So, you will have to take a rain check on that—Asya's orders."

"Who said anything about sex? But thank you for the idea." Kailee looked me in the eyes and rested her wrist on my shoulder, her fingers playing with my ear. "Do you trust me, Slade?"

"Should I have reason not to?"

"Nope." Kailee lightly pushed me. I lost my balance, and gravity took me in its embrace like a lover.

I did my best to hit the water at a better angle, but it still stung a bit. As I surfaced, I watched Kailee cut through the air into the water with her hand above her head at a point. Before she came to the surface, Kailee grabbed my ankle and pulled me under. When I returned to the surface, she was laughing.

"Place your arms around my neck and hold onto me." I did as she asked, and she swam us over to the rocky wall. "Hold on tight. Don't worry about choking me." Kailee grabbed the rock wall and began to pull us up. She climbed the wall effortlessly as if she had done so a hundred times before. She made no noise as we ascended the cliff. About halfway up, she took us behind the waterfall, revealing an amazing view. Soon, we reached a cave.

"Wow, this place is very beautiful."

"I had to chip it out a bit more here and there to make the opening less jagged. I come here to be alone sometimes, and the rushing water helps me sleep. You are the first male to see the inside of my special place." Kailee walked up to me and pushed me against the wall. "Look, I'm going to come out and admit something to you." She took a deep breath. "I really liked what you said to me, but I think it was shitty that you would have used me for a bet." She backed up and sat on the ground, and I did the same. "I have feelings and emotions, but the worst part is I can see what people want from me before they open their mouth. Men are usually the worst of the two sexes. But when you spoke to me, you meant what you said to me, so I want to know: How did you do that? How did you lie so well that I believed it?"

I looked at Kailee and said, "I told you the truth. That is why you believed me. I really did want to kiss you. I still do. Yes, I'm stupid to have entered a bet to win a kiss from you because you're a person with feelings. I was arrogant, and I did not think of the consequences that my stupidity could have had. I would not have been able to go further than some kissing."

I stood up. "Kailee, I am sorry. Not because you can read minds and I was caught and not because I acted like an ego-driven fool—I am sorry that I did not put my best foot forward and wasted the only chance I would have to make a great first impression on you. I am sorry that you've seen me like that. I hope that, someday, you will see that I am more than some idiot eager to win a bet. I should have treated you like the lady you are. I will not ask for your forgiveness, but I will ask for a chance to earn your forgiveness."

Kailee walked back and forth for a few minutes. "I will ask you one question, and I want the absolute truth. Is it true that you are an oracle?"

I looked down and searched my mind for any trace that Kailee was snooping.

In an ill-tempered voice, Kailee said, "Slade! I'm not snooping. I saw it in Portia's mind first."

"Kailee, I should not talk of such things that I do not understand. I was told not to say anything."

"Slade, I am just as valuable as either Portia or Cyan. I don't need to touch anyone to read their mind. Lady Velour and the witches tell people that I am a bodyguard so that I can walk around and gather intelligence by just looking cute at a party, dinner, or a gathering. I can only read what they are thinking about in the moment. I can read a little more if I touch them, so I bump into people a lot, and by pretending to serve Portia, Cyan, and Lady Velour, no one gets upset at my clumsiness. The only reason that Sofia and Topaz know about me is because I have been intimate with them both, and we kiss every time we see each other. Topaz saw into my mind as I was reading Sofia's thoughts at the same time, and Topaz piggybacked from me into Sofia's mind. You know how to piggyback someone into another's mind, right?"

"Honestly, Kailee, I really don't know much about this gift, other than if the wrong people find out what I am, there might be a problem. Asya has shown me how we can connect multiple people in one mind."

"So, it is also true that you have a black hole where the first eighteen years should be. You seem to retain various memories regarding education, fighting, and a few other things. That is so weird. Why would someone take so much away, then just leave you all alone? Sounds like they didn't know what you were and gave you a bit of the old snip-snip then let you go."

"Yeah, it sucks to not know where I came from, but I try to think only on the here and now." I looked at Kailee.

"Hey, I thought you had to touch someone to read their mind."

"That's a cover story. Only a few people know the truth."

"That makes sense."

"Slade, I really want you to kiss me here and now. Show me what your pretty words were promising me yesterday. Remember, you promised that you wouldn't make me cry."

"Kailee, please understand. I'm with Topaz and Sofia."

Kailee laughed.

"You're also with Sunako, Cheri, and sort of Tova and Lucy." Kailee paced back and forth. "There is something about you. I've thought a lot about you since I met you yesterday. I could barely fall asleep with you on my mind and not in my arms. I must talk with Asya about you. Until then"—Kailee pushed me against the wall and breathed heavily in my ear— "I need you to help me with this fire you started within me." Her hand was heavy against my chest, not allowing me to move. She could easily crush me against the wall. "Kiss me. Give me the special kiss, the one I saw in Sofia's mind. The one you gave to that stray dog, Lucy."

"Kailee, you're crushing me." She took her hand off my chest, and I took a deep breath. "You're kind of scary. If you really want my kiss, then you will have to see me, truly see me as I am." I snapped my eyes black, hoping it would startle her, but Kailee was a woman without fear.

"Damn! This just makes me want you more." Just short of trying to run and jump out of the cave, I believed I'd tried everything, so I pressed my lips to hers. We held each other as we kissed long and deep. Kailee's arms held me in an iron grip, but I felt safe there. When we stopped, she bent her neck, and I gave her the kiss she desired. I thought about being with her in that cave. I imagined what she was thinking about and focused harder than I had with Lucy. When I was done, I laid Kailee down as she mumbled. I stood at the mouth of the cave, waiting for Kailee to emerge as I listened to the roar of the waterfall.

"Slade, you smell so wonderful, and your kiss was amazing. I really needed that." She laughed. "Wow, that was great, and you have never made love before, but you can do that? Wow, just wow. I want you to make love to me and do that at the same time. Let's get back to the group before they come looking for us. Now just take a running jump out, and I'll get you back to the top."

"Why not just climb up from here?"

Kailee rubbed her forehead in frustration. "Yeah, sure." Without warning, she pushed me out and into the waterfall. The water was softer than before, and she was right there with me. "Slade, what you should also know about me is that I only like to say something once." Kailee smiled and gave me a quick kiss. "Now, get into my arms. We have this spot that brings us up to the top." She swam to a place where the rocks were flat, where three people could stand side by side. We climbed out of the water and stood up.

Kailee said, "Up!" Then, we were floating up at a good speed. When we reached the top, it curved us toward the grass about ten feet from the cliff. It was very cool. "That is how we can dive, swim, and dive over and over again without it being a pain in the ass to walk back up to the top of the falls."

"Is that a naturally occurring thing?"

Topaz walked up. "Nope, that is something Asya and Galya did years ago. They call it a gravity lift."

Sofia smiled at me. "So, Kailee. Did he kiss you?"

"Yes, he did, and it was everything you said it was going to be." Kailee slapped me on the ass as she walked away. "I might need more attention, so this fire doesn't get out of control."

"Told you he would feel bad for trying to take advantage of Kailee," Topaz said as she laughed.

Sofia laughed as well. "Okay, Topaz, I will pay you when we get back home."

I sighed. "Sofia, can we stop the betting on this kind of thing? Remember what Asya said? You know how fond she is of hanging me upside down, which, I might add, I very much don't like."

"My love, all I bet was that you would kiss her neck, no harm in that." Sofia kissed me with her eyes open. "Slade, I should tell you that Kailee is someone that visits us regularly, and Topaz and I have been intimate with her many times. I really wanted to share you with her, but I promise I'll do my best for no more bets about you kissing anyone."

I led Sofia off toward the edge. "Sofia, I am becoming more and more confused about this romantic entanglement of ours. Why don't you want to keep me just to yourself?"

"Slade, we learned at an early age to love with our mind, not our hearts, because there are more women and so few men. We tend to have multiple female partners, and often, one man will be shared between two or three women in a single cottage. You're blessed in this way. I'm not saying that if, in a few years when our love grows stronger, that I wouldn't be opposed to wanting more from you— like marriage and all the rest that comes after that—but you can only have no more than six wives. No one in the House of Ribbons has more than one, but in the House of Thorns, I know two men that have three wives. I will introduce you to them if you would like. Maybe they can help you understand."

"Thank you, Sofia. I feel better now and not so confused. You know how to ease my mind."

"Hey, just remember that when it comes to cuddle time okay?" Sofia kissed me on the lips. "Now, let's eat so we can go swimming."

One of the ladies had laid out a large sheet, and we sat on it and had what was called a "picnic." We ate some sandwiches while we drank honey wine, which was very sweet. The picnic was my first in recorded memory, and it was a very pleasant one. The talk was light with many jokes, and they told me what to expect when we reached the House of Dreams and the two oracles there. When we were done, we lay down in a circle with our heads in the center. We called out what we saw in the clouds. A little while later, we packed everything up and hung the backpacks in a tree. Then, one by one, they jumped off the cliff with me being the last one standing on dry land. I heard them calling me and waving. I walked about twenty feet back and ran like Hell itself was chasing me. I jumped off into gravity's embrace, and soon, I entered the water more gracefully than before.

Portia said, "I thought you had second thoughts about jumping in."

Cyan laughed, and they all began to splash each other. I enjoyed splashing them back. We swam and floated around and exchanged kisses. The swimming lasted for about an hour, and we got on the gravity ladder two by two. We lay out in the sun, finishing the last bottle of wine.

Soon, our relaxation turned into a small nap. I dreamt of a woman screaming in extreme pain, her face begging to die. She lived on in darkness, saying, "Only you can help me reenter the light."

As we slowly woke up, the sounds of yawns and stretching surrounded me. I still heard the woman's voice for a few more seconds—she was weeping and begging for release. I rubbed my eyes and tried to shake off the disturbing dream.

"Who's up for the hike back? We can take the long way around the lake because it looks like dinner will not be for another two hours. We can take our time."

The walk was very enjoyable. They called out the names of the birds that sang in the trees and the unseen animals that spoke to one another in the forest.

Portia said, "Kailee, why don't you sing for us? Please, pretty please?"

Kailee walked up between Topaz and me, took hold of our hands, and started her song. At first, it was soft and low. Then, it steadily rose and leveled out to a smooth and almost hypnotic rhythm, spinning a tale of lost love, only to be saved by the lost lover. As Kailee sang, butterflies danced around us. I wondered if they were attracted to her singing or if we were just in the right place at the right time. We stopped to skip some stones.

"Hey, Slade, I bet you can't get at least six skips." Kailee tossed me a nice flat stone.

"I'm done betting, but I believe you could probably hit the moon with a stone like this. Besides, if I don't stop betting, I might accidentally bet myself into slavery."

Everyone laughed.

"I guess there goes my next bet. Thanks a lot, Slade. I'm sure I'll find a way to possess you, my sexy diamond." Kailee ran her hand through my hair and launched her stone. It must have skipped clear across the lake. I skipped mine with an embarrassing four skips. Everyone skipped their stones with at least ten or more skips.

Portia yelled, "Don't worry, Slade! You will get the hang of it in time."

I smiled at her, but I was a bit embarrassed.

Kailee said, "Don't worry. No one cares if you can't skip a stone. Just keep being you, and almost everyone will like you."

"Kailee, my sneaky little mind reader, what did I ask you about trespassing in my headspace?"

"You did ask, but I thought you should know that you should not be embarrassed by your skills compared to ours. Stone skipping is just something that you have to practice, and practice makes perfect. I'm more than confident that you will overpower our senses and bodies in the bedroom or maybe behind that bush, and I mean that bush right over there." Kailee laughed and squeezed my hand slightly.

"Kailee, please, do as I ask because I can feel you when you creep into my mind."

Kailee sighed loudly. "I will do my best to stay out, but I won't promise anything."

"The ground looks soft right here," Topaz declared.

The others laughed.

Kailee spoke, "You know, Slade, Asya said no sex, but she didn't say anything about a little playtime."

Topaz agreed, "She makes a valid point."

Sofia said, "Okay, let's get this straight. First off, Asya asked us a simple request: no sex with Slade, and I take that to be all kinds of sex. And second, I get the first time with him. No exceptions! No bets to win a night with him and no trades! To be clear, if it were not for Asya's warning and me not having my first taste, then yes, we would have had him by the waterfall. It would have been a very romantic location. I would lay on my back and have him start kissing me at my knee, then move slightly upward as the sun began to set. I could welcome the moon with cries of ecstasy as I gripped his hair, tightly holding him against me for a longer kiss.

"Then, I would pull him to my chest and arch my hips to meet his hips as I slowly take him into me. As I hold his shoulders, our eyes will lock, and we kiss. As I get closer to exploding again, he bites my neck, and in body and mind, I explode. He takes me there over and over, his body a slave to mine, as our hearts dance inside our chests. Our hips match the rhythm of our hearts until our bodies give out and all I can hear is his heavy breath in my ear with a single phrase escaping his mouth: 'I love you, Sofia.'"

"Holy shit, Sofia!" Cyan said abruptly. "Until now, I have never thought of him that way, but you might have made me a believer. But only if Topaz is involved."

"Yeah, Sofia, some of us are going to need a minute because your imagination and words were a little too intense. I may have lost myself in what you were saying, and now, I need a drink." Portia pulled off the lid of the tea and took a drink, passing it around.

"Now, I really want him underneath my hips." Kailee drank her tea slowly, but her eyes never left mine.

I spoke, "Excuse me, but don't I get a say in when and where?"

They all laughed. Sofia looked me in the face.

"Once Asya gives the okay, I'm going to treat you like a thoroughbred horse and ride you to the finish line. Then, I will allow you to give out rides to our little circle of friends with the occasional guest like Kailee here. So, when you ask if you get a say on when and where—after your first time, you will count the seconds until you can race again. And race you I will, my young stallion." Sofia gently kissed my neck. "Come on, my cutie, we have a whole world of feelings and emotions to show you, and once you get a taste, you'll want more."

I took a drink, trying to hide my nerves. "Well then, I believe I will have to take your word for it, but I will say this. I love the idea of the top of the waterfall and maybe inside it as well?" I looked directly at Kailee who just smiled and winked. We continued our walk.

Cyan said, "Have you ever heard about the talking squirrel?" Portia groaned as Cyan tried to contain herself, laughing at the joke she had not told yet. "He ran around always saying, 'Hey you! Have you seen my nuts?'"

Topaz, Sofia, and Kailee laughed loudly.

"Oh, Slade, you will like this one. A different squirrel was juggling a few acorns, and his mate walked up to him and she asked, 'Mike, what are you doing?' He looked at her and said, 'Cindy, can't you see I'm playing with my nuts?'" Cyan held her stomach as she laughed. "Okay, one more. Same squirrel. 'Hey, Mike, why aren't you friends with Bob the blue jay? Because that bastard won't leave my nuts alone!'"

Everyone was laughing except Portia. I asked, "Why are you not laughing?"

"Slade, I'm with Cyan almost every day. She loves jokes, but her favorites are dirty jokes. I mean, real groaners and awful puns. Sometimes, I wish I were deaf."

"I don't understand why the squirrel was funny in those jokes."

Portia made a strange face. "Because of his nuts. It's the whole joke."

"My apologies, Portia. Why are his nuts funny, or is the joke so bad that people are not laughing with but rather *at* the absurdity of the squirrel?"

"Slade, do you know what nuts are?" Portia waited for me to answer the question. I noticed that the other five were looking at me, silently awaiting my response.

"Nuts are some of the squirrel's food source." I look at the stunned faces of the women. "Am I wrong?"

Topaz said, "Yes and no, my sweet. I think it would be best to show you. Kailee, can you find some nuts?"

Kailee laughed. "You mean these? They're all around on the ground. As you can see, they fall from the trees."

Sofia said, "Slade, see these acorns? Now, hold them in your hands above your head and close your eyes until I tell you to open them. Understand?"

"If this ends up with you hitting me, then I promise I will seriously consider Lucy for my first time."

"I promise, no one is going to hit you. See, now you have my word." Sofia kissed my cheek. "A promise sealed with a kiss."

Kailee pleaded, "Oh, Sofia, please let me show him! Please! I will give you my dessert tonight. It's pie, lemon meringue pie, one of Asya's favorites. Please, Sofia, I'll also take you to my hidden place next time you come back. I took Slade; he will tell you how amazing it is."

I nodded and smiled.

"Please, Sofia, I will let you name one other thing, but nothing too crazy."

Sofia thought about it. "You got yourself a deal."

The two spit into their hands and shook on it. I noted the action as very odd but not worthy enough to ask a question.

Kailee stood in front of me and said, "Close those pretty blueish-green eyes of yours, and raise your hand high in the air. Whatever you do, don't move or drop your nuts."

More laughter.

"Wait a second, Sofia. May I kiss him again?"

"Why not? The pie alone is worth it." Sofia's voice was soft.

"Okay, Slade, you heard Sofia. Stand still while we kiss." She was gentle as we kissed, her left hand behind my neck. I tried to see her thoughts. "No! No, stay in your mind, Slade." Kailee's right hand reached up into my skirt, and she took hold of my manhood. We kissed for a few seconds longer as she held everything, slightly moving her hand. "Slade, what do you call these?" Kailee said while looking me in the eyes.

"I have no name for them. It is just the groin."

"Slade, these have many names. Most are hilarious, but the joke is funny because these are also called nuts. So, the squirrel playing with his nuts was an analogy for playing with oneself in public. It is not acceptable to play with your nuts in public, but that is why the joke is funny. Do you understand?" Kailee explained it well.

"I do now. Thank you, Kailee." My eyes were getting heavy but not from sleep. I was awakening to her touch as she moved her hand around. I wanted her right there, just like she said about the bush.

"By the gods, you're a big boy, aren't you? Sofia will definitely need help with this, and I look forward to that night." Kailee kissed me on the lips again and squeezed me lightly before removing her hand, then whispered, "I want you right now as well."

"That wasn't my nuts."

Kailee smiled. "I know, but you liked it."

"I did very much, so thank you." My head was cloudy, but one thought remained. It wanted me to give in to sexual desire and kiss and touch her right on the spot. The more that happened to me, the stronger the urges were. I didn't know how many more times I would be able to restrain myself.

Topaz yelled, "Okay, love birds, let's break it up before this turns into an all-out orgy! Asya will have our asses with a belt or her stick. Damn, I hate that stick."

"I think it would be worth it. You lucky duck, he has those sexy-as-hell black eyes and that tool of love. Honey, I envy you so." Kailee rubbed her hands together, biting her bottom lip.

Topaz asked, "Did he show you the eyes? Sofia hates them."

"I don't hate them. They're just scary, and I don't want scary mixed in with my sexy time. Besides, they don't give you the creeps?"

"On the contrary. I think it will make it hotter. So, remember I said that. Is that okay with you, Slade?" Kailee winked.

As I turned away from Sofia, I snapped them black. Portia covered her mouth.

"What in the unholy Hell's front gate is that? I just thought you were—well, I don't know what you were talking about, but I didn't think he could actually turn his eyes black! Sweet baby Jesus, make it stop."

Maybe Asya kept her black eyes to herself because of reactions like that. Cyan studied them up close, and I noticed that she had a tail, almost like Sunako. The thought of Sunako made me smile.

"Hey, Cyan, want to feel something weird?"

"Sure, demon boy, but keep your hands out of my pants, or you really will have black eyes."

I reached around and caught her tail, giving it a tug.

"What in hell was that?" Cyan jumped, then turned and walked toward Portia.

I held her tail and pulled her back to me.

She asked, "Slade, what was that? What are you doing to me?"

I changed my eyes back, and I felt her tail almost melt away. "I think it would be best if Asya explains it to you because it's hard to explain what you experienced, but I will say this: you're more than you know."

"Okay, well, damn, you're weird. Even among our kind, you're weird. Topaz, what do you see in him?" Cyan nervously looked around while she rubbed her bottom.

Topaz just smiled. "When you find out, you will want to love him as well."

We noticed the time and continued to walk homeward for dinner. Cyan told a few more jokes, and I understood a few. The one about the octopus and the blind man confused me a bit, but I would ask at dinner for someone to explain.

Topaz said, "Oh shit, you know who is going to love Slade? Molly, of course! She's weird and twisted like Slade. Yeah, I bet you're going to have to beat her off with a stick."

Cyan and Portia stopped walking.

"What? Hello, Cyan?"

"How do you not know?" said Cyan.

"Know what?"

"Molly is dead. She was executed when the three sisters gathered. Why weren't you and Saffron there?"

"Saffron and I were away with a ranger escort, which included Sofia, Cheri, Samson, and Victor to settle a dispute in the nearest town."

Sofia said, "We returned in the morning, and around midnight, Slade appeared."

Topaz's eyes were watering. "Why was she executed?"

"She had run away, and a couple days later, returned in the night to steal something or kill someone. That part is not clear. A few from the House of Dreams died. Molly, a young witch, and four men were caught. They stabbed the men in the heart and burned the witch, but Molly—Molly got the worst. I think it would be better if you were shown by Diandra. It was the most brutal thing I have ever seen, the way she screamed. I cried for days. I miss her so much," said Portia.

The rest of the walk was silent, and as we passed the first cottage, I saw two guys fighting. They looked my age.

"Kailee, is that acceptable here?" Sofia asked.

"No, Sofia. A hand if you don't mind?"

They went to break up the fight. When Kailee walked back, they each had a guy by the neck.

I asked, "What will happen to them?"

"Slade, these two will have to see Mr. Willock and receive punishment duties for fighting outside of the pit."

Chapter 19

A Castaway in the Mind's Eye

Mr. Willock took both men by the back of the neck and excused himself.

"I know that look. They are going to the pit." Portia pointed to the left. Mr. Willock made the men walk with bent backs.

I asked her, "Why does Mr. Willock bring them there? Why not someone else?"

Cyan spoke, "Mr. Willock is the head fight instructor."

"I thought he was the head caretaker, like Elma back home?"

Topaz took my hand and kissed it. "Oh, my strange flower. Mr. Willock and Elma serve one main role, and that is second-in-command. They're the most experienced fighters. This is a highly coveted position."

"I thought Elma was warm and gentle."

Sofia burst out in laughter. "Elma is scary strong. I once watched her pull a full-grown man's arm off and beat him with it before she pulled out his heart from his chest. I occasionally have nightmares about that. I mean, it was so gory. The way he screamed and begged for his life was nothing compared to when she reached in and grabbed his heart. She moved so fast that he was still alive to see his own heart. She even bit into it, then threw it in his face. Topaz was there to see it. Just ask her."

"Why did she kill that man?" I asked.

"He raped a woman. Rape is an automatic death sentence," said Sofia.

"It was really gruesome. We had to witness her execute more than a few people in our time." Topaz rubbed her stomach. "Great, now I'm hungry."

Sofia asked, "Wait, did that make you hungry?"

"Kind of—is that weird?" Topaz looked at Sofia.

"No, but it is funny that you said what I was thinking." Sofia and Topaz bumped hips and laughed.

As Asya came into the room, Kailee, Sofia, and Topaz walked over.

Topaz asked, "Asya, may we speak to you about Slade?"

Asya pointed at me, and I rose from my chair, high into the air. I crossed my arms as I floated over to them. Asya then put me on the floor. "I hope that he has maintained his manners since I last saw you all."

Topaz said, "That's just it, Asya. Well, I don't know how to say this, but Slade and Kailee were alone for a bit and when they came back—"

"Stop!" Asya materialized something she called her hickory stick.

Everyone suddenly backed up against the wall except for me. I was frozen in place; my limbs were not under my control. Asya looked more sad than angry. I could see Lady Velour come up from behind Asya.

"I see I might be just in time for a little pre-dinner excitement. Oh, I remember that damn stick. It has been a long time since that dreadful thing last tasted my backside. Oh, boy, you must have done something really naughty." A sexy, sinister smile grew on Lady Velour's face. "Let me get a good seat for this one. Pay attention, ladies, because this punishment is something you'll want to avoid."

"Kailee, is it true? Were you and Slade together alone?" asked Asya.

"Yes, Asya. I had him in my special place. Please don't be cross with him. I kind of blackmailed him into showing me what he had, and I just could not control myself. I let him take me right on the spot, and his kiss was as deep as he is. Feeling him inside me was honestly the wildest thing to ever happen to me. He is truly gifted in more than one way. I would let him kiss me like that right here if Lady Velour allowed it. He swims in my very thoughts, even now."

Kailee didn't hold back. Not even a little.

Asya looked at me and shook her head. Then she whacked me on the top of my head with the stick.

"Ouch! Damn it, Asya! My brain is in there!"

"Oh, really? Ask me why I didn't hit you in the ass? Go on then!" Asya said in a scornful manner.

I hesitated until she raised the stick again. "Why didn't you hit me in the ass?"

"Because I didn't want to damage your brain, you dumbass! See what I am saying? Because your brain is located in your ass! I specifically told you no sex while we were out, and I said no more followers. Who else has a crush on the boy? Tell me now, or I'll fish it out of your mind. I'll be more upset that you withheld information from me."

Portia and Cyan both raised their hands.

"Look what you did, boy! I will leave the remainder of the punishment to Lady Velour, but just so you all know, I'm very disappointed with all of you!" Asya was very upset. Her tone was direct.

"Why did you hit me? I didn't have sex."

"Are you deaf? I said no sex—and—or—no new followers! I ought to hit you again for not paying attention." Her tone had a bitter coldness as she gripped her stick.

"Kailee, do you really like him?" Lady Velour smiled.

"I do, my lady. I would like permission to further get to know him, inside and out."

Lady Velour smiled. "Granted. Portia, Cyan, now tell me how you both feel for him. Cyan, you only like women, so I don't understand. Plus, you both know that you must be with women only."

Cyan said, "Lady Velour, I have long crushed on Topaz, but she will not do anything more than kissing. I would be with him to have her. Plus, he smells really good, like a woman."

Portia replied, "I just want to know what all the fuss is about. Look at him! He is nothing special to look at. I swear I have not been touched by him."

Lady Velour smiled. "Well, Asya, I see no real harm done here. My oracles have their virtues intact, and we were both young and curious once. Besides, you did hit him pretty hard." Lady Velour raised her voice but not in a harsh way. "I hope you learned your lesson, young man. Now keep that little thing in your pants from now on."

Kailee started to laugh but tried to cover it with a cough, which caught Lady Velour's eye. Then, Kailee did something with her hands with a space between them.

"Oh, really? My, oh my. I believe I may understand why the ladies follow you around so much. Maybe I will, with Asya's permission, have you over later tonight to better understand the situation. Yes, I will have to further investigate this matter."

"Asya, I must confess one more thing," said Kailee.

The hold Asya had on me tightened, and I snapped my eyes black. An iridescent snake, at least ten feet in length and thick as my thigh was wrapped around me, its face in front of mine. It flicked its tongue against my nose. I wondered if it was real or just made of magic.

"By the gods, Asya, look at his eyes!"

The snake tightened, and Asya's hickory stick came down on my head again. I did not let out a sound, mainly because the snake granted little breathing room. Lady Velour looked shocked.

"Slade, what did I tell you about that?" Asya sounded cross, but she was hard to hear with my heart beating so loudly in my ears.

"Asya! Please let me explain!" Kailee stepped in between Asya and me. She sounded desperate. "I know what he is because I saw into Cyan's mind. The news of it had them thinking about him in great detail, and we never had sex. We just kissed in my secret place under the falls."

"You mean to tell me that your secret place is not between your legs?" Asya sounded confused.

Kailee laughed. "Oh my. No disrespect, Asya, but he said no to me when his body and mind wanted one thing. That one thing was to be in the arms of Sofia, making love to her. I had him all to myself, and he stayed true to Sofia and the others. That was the moment I really wanted him more, like wanted to be wanted *by* him—like the way he wants Sofia and the others. His loyalty is very impressive, and when tempted again, he did state that you said no. Believe me, his body was saying yes, while his mind struggled to say no. But he resisted because you said so. What does that tell you about him, Asya?"

"I see that I was too rash in my judgment, but I did say no kissing, no new followers, and to keep his gift under wraps. I told all who knew that." Asya awaited Kailee's response.

"You didn't tell me not to kiss him, and like I said, I came out and told him about his gift. I made it seem like he did not have a choice. That is how badly I wanted to feel his kiss, and I foolishly thought that I was mentally strong enough to shrug off his kiss. But I was not. But I'm happy knowing that I have feelings like these inside me."

"Slade, I will speak with you after I speak with Lady Velour." Asya waved her hand, and the snake uncoiled and slithered toward her, then disappeared. "Now, I want you to feel better." Asya extended her hand, and I took it. I felt her healing gift flow through me, and my head felt better. "Now eat and enjoy time with these beautiful women."

Lady Velour called out, "Mr. Willock?"

"My Lady, Mr. Willock has taken two lost souls to the pit for an attitude readjustment."

"Thank you, Beth. Have our dinner redirected to the Sunflower Room, please and thank you."

"Right away, my lady." Beth walked away.

Asya asked, "Who is that?"

"Asya, after your last visit, you brought Mr. Willock to that town forty miles away. He was buying a few rare spices and came across a young woman being abused. He offered to buy her, but her owner said no. So, the poor bastard bet Mr. Willock that he could beat him in a fair fight for her. If Mr. Willock lost, then he would give up his bag of coins. The other guy lost, and now we have a young woman with no abilities. But she can cook like a master chef, so I am happy that you dropped him off in that town. She is very pleasant to be around, and now she is free for the first time in her life."

Beth was short at five foot five and thinly built with medium-length, semi-curly black hair. She had very light-brown eyes that seemed to reflect the light at the right angle. She was close to twenty.

The dinner had been delivered to Asya and Velour—steak with sautéed onions and potatoes.

"Asya, we should talk about Mr. Slade, and I hope I can be very open and honest."

Asya raised her eyebrows. "By all means, be at ease around me, and always speak from the heart."

"Thank you, Asya. I think that trying to hide Slade's gifts may be seen as dishonest, like an underhanded power move. I personally do not see it that way, but I did have the briefest thought flicker through my mind last night as I laid down for the evening."

"Okay, then, I would guess you have a solution or suggestion. Come out with it before this wine causes me not to care so much about this business. Oh, by the way, thank you a hundred times over for last night's late-night gift." Asya smiled.

Lady Velour smiled as they toasted each other. "I take it that the two I sent you mixed well with the wine, and all was adequate?"

Asya laughed, wiping her mouth. "Those two ladies are very skilled at what they do, and the wine was almost like candy wine. But, yes, those two were amazing. I wouldn't say no to them tonight, if perchance, they were free to stop by and recreate last night's romp." Asya stood up, and walked a few feet over to a bag, and handed it to Velour. "Before the wine causes me to forget, here is something for you." She placed a large bag on the table and kissed Velour's forehead. "Please, my sweet little one, open it."

Lady Velour opened the drawstrings, and the bag relaxed and opened like a flower.

"Oh my goddess! Asya, I don't know what to say."

"Then say nothing, my child. Just enjoy them or gift them out. They're yours to do with them as you would like."

Lady Velour now had more candy than she had ever seen at one time—at least fifty pieces.

"This is not for last night, right? Because that was my gift to you," Lady Velour said.

"No, my sweet. That is because I love you and your sisters as if you were my own children, and you have become something that your mother would be so proud of, as is your father. So, when I see one of my daughters doing great things, I like to show them that they may have grown up, but they are still greatly loved. Now back to Mr. Slade."

"I love you, Asya." Velour wiped her eyes. "Yes, Mr. Slade. I believe that you stopped here first because of Portia, Cyan, and my little whisperer, Kailee. I think you were testing how well his secret could be kept, but the young man is fairly untrained. Something swirls around him that attracts those who get to know him, and I might add, that he seems like he is from a much different time and place. Nowhere close to this place. Sorry, I lost my train of thought. I think we should gather my sisters at my father's, and with the combined oracles, try to figure this out. It will show that Silk is not hiding a uniquely gifted person in hopes of more power. I hope that came out as clearly as I see it in my mind."

Asya leaned back and sipped her red wine, savoring the bittersweet taste. “I agree. You have a better idea than me, and yes, this is why I came here first. Velvet can get a bit overwhelming in times like this.”

“My sister is a bit of a control freak. She has always been that way.” Velour laughed and raised her glass once more. “To Lady Velvet! Hers is a blessed life as ours is. So, I will just come out and ask the burning question: being that he may be or is an oracle, what will happen if he sleeps with one of our oracles?” Lady Velour leaned in to hear the answer.

Asya laughed, almost spilling her drink. “More bluntly, you mean if he bends one of the ladies over the bed and unleashes the beast of passion, which, I might add, he is packed from head to toe with. I swear, it’s like he amplifies their passion, takes it into himself, and gives it back to the woman. His kissing making them melt reminds me of—” Asya paused. “Aw fuck!” She stood up, raised her hand, and turned into mist. Her voice came out of thin air. “I’ll be back soon; don’t finish all the wine.”

Cyan was telling another bad joke, which was poorly worded, and forgot the punchline. We did not speak of anything that happened before dinner or Asya’s stick. We just enjoyed each other’s company.

Lady Velour walked in and asked, “Is everything to your liking?”

We raised our glasses. “Here is to Lady Velour.”

Lady Velour poured herself a glass and said, “To my ladies and Mr. Slade: live, love, enjoy, and most of all, sing the song within your heart and care not what others think. Mr. Slade, may we see you in the other room? No worries, ladies. Asya is no longer upset, and we may have come up with a thrilling idea. Mr. Slade, if you would follow me?”

I said nothing and followed her into the Sunflower Room. Lady Velour pulled out a chair for me.

“Lady Velour, where is Asya?”

“She will be with us soon. She had to attend to something, and please, Mr. Slade, call me Velour. I can only hear *lady* so many times before I want to scream. May I call you Slade?”

“Please, I hate the *mister* part. It makes me feel uncomfortable. A title is the last thing I want.”

Velour smiled. “If things fall the way I believe they might, you might have a much larger title, like Lord Slade, one day soon. Wow, that does roll off the tongue! And speaking of… Your silver tongue and your smell are very enjoyable. I would very much like you to grant me one small request. Well, at least one for now."

"All you have to do is ask." I noticed Velour studying me intently.

"Slade, I want to know what it is that you did to Kailee."

"I kissed her lips then her neck. I'm sorry if I offended you, my lady."

"It's just Velour, if you please. Wasn't it clear enough for you, Slade?" She took a long drink. "I want you to do for me what you did to Kailee. I have to know what it is you do."

"I have already offended Asya once today. Please, I'm new and can't afford to make any more mistakes. Plus, I will offend Sofia, and I would sooner go blind before I hurt her heart."

Velour got up and left the room without a word. I felt the night could only get worse. She returned with Topaz, Sofia, and Kailee.

"Ladies, please be seated. Sofia, I will ask you something, and you have my full permission to tell me no. I cannot stress that any harder." She went on to tell Sofia about our conversation and asked, "May I have a kiss from Slade? First my lips, then neck?"

"My lady, I would be honored." Sofia placed her hand on mine. I could see into her mind. She really was honored to be given the choice to say no. Her love for me was young but very strong.

Velour looked at Topaz and asked, "And you, Topaz? What say you?"

"Lady Velour, I feel the same way as Sofia, but I have to ask: do you not see the state it leaves one in? Kailee stood in front of Asya to defend someone she scarcely knows, and I'm ashamed that I did not do what she did or stand up for her. Kailee, I want you to know that in that very moment, I knew that you should be given a chance to be with Slade. If he's as smart as he is cute, then he would accept you into his bed, but not before I have my first time with him. Lady Velour, if you want him, and you accept the risk of losing yourself to him, all I ask is for you to watch Slade work his magic." Topaz winked.

Velour said, "Agreed. I would not make him break his promise to you because I believe a promise in a sacred thing. I would look greatly down on you, Slade, if you did not fulfill that promise to your Sofia."

"I will, Velour, and thank you for those words, but I must add that no one is making it easier on me with all the kissing and groping."

They all smiled.

Velour laughed. "Well, you will just have to endure it again for the sake of scientific discovery. Now, please show me. Kailee, you have my permission to hold me back if I get out of control. You'll know if I lose myself to lust." Velour laughed and unbuttoned her shirt down to the middle, her cleavage bared as her breasts threatened to escape.

I walked up to Velour. "So, you want to know what they felt? You want to feel my kiss? Look at me, Velour."

I saw my reflection in her blue eyes and changed mine to black. She was glowing. Her hair moved like there was wind blowing through it, but I felt no breeze. Her eyes had something inside them, and as I looked closer, I saw her thoughts. I was not touching her, but I was somehow connected to her. She was sad, like she was missing someone dearly. Her mother. She had never healed from that horrible moment—no, it was worse than that! She was there when it happened, and she had never stopped crying on the inside for the loss of her mother. So much pain for so long, and it rushed into me. Twenty-three years of pain set loose, flowing from her into me. I was frozen, unable to stop the flow, unable to free myself from her sadness. It became overwhelming.

Batch, where are you? Damn you! I felt heat coming from my eyes as the tears freely flowed. There was nothing I could do as her pain attacked me. She was huddling by a large rock on a tiny island with one very tall, strangely shaped tree. I didn't know where we were, but I could feel the wind, the sun, and the ground beneath my bare feet. It was a light-colored sand, almost too hot. The tiny island couldn't be more than two hundred feet around and was surrounded by dark blue water.

"Velour, can you hear me?"

She looked no older than eight when she saw me and stood up. She began to age until I recognized her face.

"Slade? What is this place? Where are we?"

"I think this is a memory, something you had buried deep within you. I don't think we should be here without someone like Asya and maybe Topaz." It was full of sorrow and was dreadfully overwhelming. "Velour, are you sure you don't know where we are?"

"No, but I'm scared. Please make this stop. I want to go back to dinner." Velour walked over to me, and I took her in my arms.

"I don't know where we are or how I got into your mind because we were not touching. Without touch, I can't enter a person's mind. I don't know how to disconnect from you. Believe me, I tried as soon as I got here. Can you think of anything but this place? Maybe a happy place?"

"I don't know what's wrong. I can't make this go away—"

A green bottle floated to the shore. I reached out, picked it up, and removed the cork. It contained a rolled-up piece of white paper.

"Velour, here, this must be for you."

"No, I don't want to read it. Slade, you read it."

"What if it's really personal?"

"Slade, you are inside of my head, in a place I didn't know existed. So, please read it to me. But only if it is something good. If it's crazy, then throw it back in the water."

I turned over the bottle, tapped the bottom, and the note slid out. I handed the bottle to Velour and read the words.

"It's okay."

It seemed like a poem. It read:

These are my tears. I have cried so much; I have no more places to go. All that I love is there under the waves of my salty tears. I am alone, stranded, a castaway to my own thoughts and happiness. Self-destructive enough to dig this grave, but I lack the courage to lie in it. This place is a prison for something that should never get out. Run, my sweet. Run fast enough that the water becomes the stones that break the mirror that reflects what should be chained down. Run, my friend, before I devour you. Find the stairs before they turn into teeth that will drag you back to my stomach. Run. Run. Run!

After I finished the last word, Velour pointed out something in the water—another bottle, one made of red glass, had just popped to the surface. The letters inside contained Velour's mother's name: Haley. I remembered it from the story. More bottles rose to the surface, and each had only one word. There were at least four hundred little white pieces of paper, all with one word. But there had to have been a thousand more bottles that rose to the surface.

"Slade, what does this mean?"

"I think there is a message if we put the words in the right order. The problem is that all those unopened bottles have more words, maybe even a full letter. But until we decode this message, we will have no idea how or when we can leave. However, I think there is a bright side."

"Do tell, Slade, because I don't see one." Velour looked uneasy.

"Asya. How long did she say she would be gone for?"

"She said she'd be right back and not to drink the rest of the wine. How is Asya coming back something that will be useful to us in here?"

"Okay, so time moves differently in here than time outside of here. Time would appear to almost stop, so when Asya gets back, she will see something is wrong with us and jump in and save us. Problem solved. Now we just sit back and wait." I sat down and lay back. "I wonder if the sun sets here. I bet it will look spectacular."

"Slade, if time moves the way you say, then how long could we be here for?"

"It could be a while."

Velour lightly kicked my leg.

"Okay, but remember, I wasn't the one who did this because I didn't touch you. But I think every five minutes from there might be a year or so here. I'm probably wrong. It could be weeks. Too bad we were not in your library because we could spend our time really getting to know one another. That is what is really odd. I should be able to pull you into my library, but I can't seem to see it clearly enough to pull us there."

"Won't we get hungry in here?"

"Nope. Hey, we don't even have to breathe because that is just a way our mind makes us comfortable. So, let us check out how deep the water is, and maybe we'll find a passage down there."

Velour stripped off all her clothes, and I couldn't help but stare. "Like what you see?"

"Wow! You're really beautiful."

Velour walked back to me. "Get me out of this place, and I promise that you can have me in every way you can imagine. When you run out of imagination, I'm sure we will find other ways to increase your repertoire of newly acquired skills."

We jumped into the warm water, which stung my eyes at first. The farther we went down, the darker it got. I realized that I suddenly needed to breathe and saw Velour rise. I did as well. As I hit the surface, I gasped for air, even though it was not really there to breathe. We swam back to the island.

"I thought you said no air means we can swim underwater."

"It makes no sense. There is no air in here to breathe, but I swear, I thought I was going to drown. Believe me, I've almost done that. I wouldn't recommend it."

"Really? How did that happen?" Velour took my hand.

I paused. "Her name is Cheri."

"Say no more. Cheri is a huge pain in the ass. You probably don't know this, but I used to own Cheri. In the first month, she was nice. She kept to herself, and a few of the boys were picking on her as they had for a few weeks. One day, she lost it. She hurt each one of them, but the biggest bully ran from her. He ran right past me, but Cheri was hot on his heels. When she caught him, I thought she was going to kill him. It took a healer a full day just to heal his face. Now, don't get me wrong. The kid was a bit of an asshole. I did not fault Cheri for her actions, but only asked her to be stronger when it came to words instead of violence. But she had a taste for blood.

"Every sparring match ended with a knockout. Well, one day, my father came to visit. He brought a young man with that same blond hair you have. Long story short, he put his hands on Cheri, and she did not like that. They were evenly matched, and they fought until they were too exhausted to choke one another, collapsing onto each other. They would fight occasionally, and her mouth was awful, so she spent most of her free time alone. So, I gave her to my sister Silk. I did like her fierceness and quick wit."

"Cheri and I had an interesting first encounter." I drifted off into thoughts about the water and Cheri's grip.

"Well, are you going to share or just sit there looking good enough to eat?"

"Sorry, I was lost in thought." I suddenly started to laugh really hard.

"Are you okay, or is this place driving you insane?"

I did my best to calm myself. "I was lost in thought. Get it? *Lost* in thought? Because we are literally lost in your thoughts."

"That is funny, but I will save the laughter for when we get out of here. Now, tell me of this first encounter with Miss Cheri."

I filled her in with all the details about waking up to Sofia and Sunako.

"So, I passed out again, but this time, I woke up underwater with Cheri's vise-like grip around my throat. She was choking me while I was underwater. I think she was trying to double down on my death, but Sofia jumped in. Sunako began to heal me as she sang a beautiful lullaby. Now Cheri and I have become much closer."

"Oh yeah, now I remember. Wow, I would have thought she would have lost her head after the little spectacle you put on to save her from punishment, which was amazing. Between you and I, I really dislike the two young men, Richter and William. Seeing them get their asses handed to them and the way you did it made me want to buy you on the spot. But Silk said she needed more time to find out where you came from or if you belonged to someone." Velour threw one of the bottles back in the water.

"That might have not been my best idea to protect her, but I still believe that Cheri acted in the best interests of the House of Ribbons." I threw a bottle back in the water, where it crashed into another bottle. "Why do you dislike Richter and William?"

Velour smiled. "I just dislike those two pricks because of their pompous attitudes, the way they think they can talk to my women. I will have a talk with Silk next time about them. Does it feel like a lot of time has passed already?" Velour stood up.

"With the sun appearing to be stationary, it makes it difficult to mark the passage of whatever time exists here."

"Slade, while we are stuck here, would you like to broaden your horizon with some sex?" Velour hopped onto my lap.

"My lady, I think I would very much like to, but only if you will allow me to tell you what could happen first." I asked her to get up so that I could stand. "Lady Velour, you're extremely beautiful. The gods and goddesses have blessed you with a physicality that is stunning, but you should know that I am promised to Sofia, mind and body first."

Velour walked up, placing her naked body up against mine. "She will never know, and I could show you how to be a great lover."

"My sweet Velour, I would know, and my word would be like ash in my mouth. I believe that, without your word, no one would ever trust you again."

"You know, when you speak like that, it drives the ladies wild. I want you even more now."

I smiled. "What would Lady Silk would say? What would you do if you became like Kailee?"

As I walked backward, Velour matched me step for step until we were waist-deep in the water. "You mean a lovestruck young lady? To forget even if it were for a small time my responsibilities and to know that I'm being loved because I'm a woman and not because I am the lady of the House? So, does that answer your question? I'm all in. Why else would you think I called you to me in the first place? I know Sofia would want this for you. Now please make me feel alive."

***

The ladies looked at the two living statues.

Kailee asked, "Is this normal? I thought he was going to kiss her, not turn to stone. Lady Velour looks like she is in a trance."

Topaz ordered Sofia, "Sofia, go get Portia and Cyan right now. Something seems wrong."

"Good idea, Topaz." Sofia entered the dining room, where Cyan was laughing. "Portia and Cyan, we may have an issue. Please follow me."

Kailee brought them up to speed.

"Well, what do we do now?" exclaimed Portia. "Wait, are we sure they're connected and just haven't noticed the time difference? Hold on, I will go in and get them." Portia placed a hand on Slade, entering his mind quickly and coming back out. She did the same to Velour. "Holy shit!"

"What! What is it?" Sofia yelled.

"They're having sex, like really wild sex."

Sofia became very angry. She commanded, "Topaz, get me in there. I want to kick his mind's ass before I kick his real ass!"

Portia started to laugh and pointed at Sofia. "Look at her face. She's so mad." Portia laughed more. "I was just joking."

With a dour look, Sofia said, "Portia, tell me: what is funny about that? He made a promise, and if he breaks it, I will break his arm and not let him heal for a week."

"Wow, you're really adamant about that promise. Actually, I could not find them. They're simply not in either library. I even called to them, but nothing. Topaz, Cyan. Please. Let's go in and search different places. I will send out a call, and you two echo it back."

Both nodded in agreement.

They entered, two going into Velour's mind, while Topaz entered Slade's mind.

"Batch, find Slade."

Batch gave Topaz a quick kiss on the cheek, then flew off. Topaz began to call for Slade and Velour. A bit of time passed.

"Topaz, Slade is not in here, and I have no control of his body. It's like it is locked up. That means he is over there. Shall we?" Batch held out his elbow, and Topaz placed her arm through the space, resting her head on his shoulder.

"You're such a gentleman." Topaz and Batch found a sparkling door, which was bridged by Portia when touching both Velour and Slade. They opened it and were now inside Velour's mind library. They met up with Portia and Cyan.

"Oh good, you found them. Wait, where is Lady Velour?" Cyan asked.

Portia said, "Slade, Cyan just asked you a question. Answer her right now!"

Topaz stepped in front of Batch. "This is not Slade. Trust me. I will have Asya explain it to you."

Cyan tapped her foot. "What in the hell do you mean, that's not Slade? I'm looking right at him!"

"Topaz, this better be really good, or it's going to get really bad, really fast." Portia stepped toward Batch.

"Ladies, allow me to briefly explain." Batch introduced himself and told his story.

Portia looked at Batch. "Well, I'm calling bullshit on this one."

"Yeah, that sounds like bullshit to me," Cyan said. "Now, tell us what happened to Lady Velour."

"Topaz, I'm going to disconnect them, but I will come back with you until we figure this mess out," Batch said and snapped his fingers.

Portia said, "Oh, shit. This might be bad."

Cyan asked Sofia, "Who is Batch?"

Sofia told Cyan and Portia the story.

"Whoa, you mean, that really wasn't Slade?"

Topaz suggested to Portia, "I think you should call for Asya."

"Good idea, Topaz, but first, I need a really big drink." Portia took a glass off the table and drank it, pouring more drinks. She wiped her mouth. "Yes, I will go call Asya."

Portia left the room.

Sofia grabbed Topaz's arm and said, "What's wrong? Topaz, tell me now because I know that look."

"Neither Lady Velour nor Slade are in either of their minds. Sofia, I fear they're gone. They're just shells with a mind but no consciousness. I'm really scared."

Ten minutes passed, and Portia came back into the room and took another drink. "Okay, I have the crystal, but I was never taught how to use it."

"Give it to me! I have done this a few times for Lady Silk." Topaz went into the other room and held the clear crystal to her forehead. "Asya, hear my voice. Your child Topaz calls to you."

"Topaz? Why are you calling me, my dear?"

"Asya, I'm sorry to disturb you, but well, I don't know how to say it. I think Slade and Lady Velour are dead."

With a flash, Asya entered the room. Two more flashes came quickly after. Two women stood silently.

"What happened? Show me their bodies. What were they doing? Did they say anything before they died?"

"Asya, I don't know if they are dead, but I fear for whatever is happening to them."

"Topaz, you're not making any sense. Take me to them." Asya waved for her two companions to follow, and they entered the room.

Asya asked, "How long have they been like that?"

"Thirty minutes, give or take," Sofia said.

"Nothing that happens in this room will ever leave this room unless you seek an early grave, am I understood?" Asya's companion said. "I am Zyra. I am the great grandmother times nine to Galya here, who is great grandmother thirteen times to Asya. Now take a seat, young ones."

"Asya, is this the one you are so excited about? Hard to believe this child might be the grandchild of Nyx," Galya spoke softly.

"Shall we?"

Zyra, Galya, and Asya joined hands, creating a circle around Velour and Slade, and connected their minds.

***

"Velour, you make a great point, but if you catch feelings, will you be able to live with the fact that Sofia is the number one? There are no numbers after her, only lovers to be loved, so can we just kiss?" We were still waist-deep in the water.

"I think I can handle my love life, but yes, I will mind myself."

I took her in my arms, and we kissed. She was a bit aggressive at first, but she softened up. I ran my fingers across her cheek and down her back, and she shuddered. I took hold of the bottom of her buttocks, and she raised her leg, wrapping it around my back. I held her as she wrapped her other leg around me, and I walked us slowly back to the shore.

"Here, half-in and half-out of the water."

I lay on top of her as we kissed, gently grinding myself on her.

She rolled us over. "Just in case this happens, I want you to know that I have you, and all you have to do is keep your eyes on mine. Hey, can you make your eyes black for me and take off your dress?"

"I'm sorry. They don't work in the mind, and it's not a dress."

Velour grinded her hips back and forth while she bit her bottom lip.

"Do you like this?"

I nodded.

"Good."

The wave playfully matched her rhythm, and she reached down and unbuckled my belt. She undid my skirt, freeing me from its prison. Then taking me within her hand, she said, "Nice. I'm very happy to finally see why all the girls are so worked up over you. Yet another gift from the gods?"

"Lady Velour, please allow me to keep my promise, and I will come back to you. You have my word on it."

"Okay, I can get to where I want to go without you inside of me. I'll just glide on you with my body until I reach my destination. But I will hold you to your word. I will feel you, and I want it all. Now, place your hands on my hips or my breasts and just lay back and enjoy this little trick of mine."

Her skin was so soft. She steadied herself with her right hand on my leg and arched her back as she slid back and forth. It was a dizzying sensation and made me crave her more and more with each pass of her body. I reached up and took hold of her back, pulling her to me. I bit her neck as her movements quickened. She began to cry out, which turned into a deafening moan. As she arched her back, she cried out again and collapsed on top of me. Her reddish-blonde hair covered my face as we lay in the waves.

"Slade! Lady Velour! Get up now!"

We were shocked.

"Do I need to repeat myself?"

We both got up as quickly as we could. "Please cover yourself before you offend my eyes!" yelled one of the tall women.

I put my clothes back on. Asya didn't look mad, just a bit annoyed.

"Slade, this is Zyra, and this is Galya."

"Lady Velour, please tell me you did not have intercourse with this boy—and in this place, no less." Zyra waited for an answer.

"No, Zyra, we have been trapped here for what feels like ages. I didn't see any harm in enjoying myself with a little grinding with Mr. Slade."

Galya said, "My sweet girl, do you know where you are right now? Don't you feel the sadness that surrounds us?"

"I don't know this place, and yes, I could feel the painful sorrow, but then Slade touched my hand, and it went away." Velour stood there, naked.

"Slade, this is Zyra and Galya."

They both waved. Zyra had to be six foot four with a slender build and green eyes. Her hair had a long braid that was light brown with hints of blonde. She had very light skin with freckles on her face and shoulders. Galya was six feet tall with large green eyes and dirty-blonde hair in two braids that were almost down to the middle of her back. She was tan. All three looked like they could be real sisters, no older than twenty-five, and strikingly beautiful.

"Slade, I was only gone for the briefest amount of time. Please tell me how this all came to be."

I told her the story, and Velour added the other parts to make a whole story.

"What did I tell you about kissing? Listen, boy, I understand that you're young and horny, but we need to understand who you are more before you enthrall a small army of women with your kiss. You ought to listen to my words, lest you feel my hickory stick again!"

Zyra said, "Lady Velour, we created this place shortly after your mother died. It was designed to hold the pain you were going through. Honey, you were with your mother when she was attacked, and it put you into a bad state of shock. We rescued you and locked away your pain. These bottles have every word detailing what you saw and how it made you feel. We broke them up and placed them in separate bottles so they would never touch and become whole again. Child, we just wanted you to come back to us and not turn into a savage out for revenge. We suppressed your memory by locking it within your subconscious because we believe your mother would have wanted the best for you. We did it out of our purest love—we meant no malice." Zyra held Velour's hand and took her in her arms.

Asya asked, "Are you okay now that you know we did this to you?"

Velour said, “I see that you saved a child from immense pain, and as an adult, thank you for your loving touch. Now, can we leave this place?”

Asya clapped.

Chapter 20

A Magical Evening

Suddenly, we were back in the Sunflower Room.

Galya said, "While we are here, we should eat. Let's take this into the dining room."

"Great idea, Galya. Lady Velour, is Mr. Willock here?" asked Zyra.

Velour smiled. "No, but I can send for him right away."

"Please do, my child."

Velour picked up a small bell and rang for Beth to come in. "Beth, please send for Mr. Willock. Tell him he is wanted right away, regardless of what he may be doing."

Everyone sat down and enjoyed some wine. I thought everyone was just as scared to speak as I was.

A few minutes later, Mr. Willock hurriedly entered the room. "My lady, forgive my lateness."

From the shadows of the room, Zyra's voice boomed, "You mean, sorry you kept *me* waiting, my old friend."

Mr. Willock's face lit up as he smiled.

Kailee leaned over and whispered to me, "I have never seen him smile before."

"Zyra, my fairest. I was not expecting you. What a pleasure to see you with these tired eyes."

Zyra walked over to him, took his hands, and kissed him.

"Lady Velour, will you be needing me for the remainder of the night?" Mr. Willock asked.

Lady Velour said, "I think I am in very capable hands with Miss Beth. She can handle whatever may come up. Please, enjoy yourself, my dear friend."

Zyra and Mr. Willock left, and we could hear his laughter as it faded down the hall.

"So, ladies. I will say it has been an eventful night so far, but I will say, Sofia, you have a trustworthy man here. But I will expect him back here to fulfill his promise to me."

Sofia said, "Lady Velour, you can count on me to personally ensure that he does deliver on his good word to you."

"Thank you, Mistress Sofia. I hope you will join us for dinner on that night. I would like you to bring his six women, including my favorite little pain in the ass, Cheri. Please do send her my warmest regards." Velour was smiling.

"My lady, we would be honored to be your guests. Thank you." Sofia smiled back.

Asya asked, "Beth, may I have eight new bottles brought to the table? Have one of the bottles come from the back of the cabinet labeled 'Asya.' Thank you, my sweet. On second thought, three from mine for a total of eleven. After the night I've had, I want to forget, if even for a moment."

"My apologies, Asya, but with Mr. Willock retired for the evening, I will not be able to unlock your private cabinet."

"Well then, my sweet, I shall show you the way to open it." Asya moved her hand and whispered in Beth's ear. Beth giggled. "You see, we're not to be feared; we're good witches. Now, off with you. No need to hurry. I would not want you to fall. So, please be careful."

Beth walked off.

"So, Asya, what would have happened if you did not rescue us from that place?" I asked.

"You two would have lived there until your body starved or died of dehydration, whichever came first. But it would have felt like ten or more lifetimes. So, I guess you two would have gotten to know one another even better than you already had."

Sofia's face went from smiling to sour.

"Oh, my Sofia, I did not mean it like that. I simply meant better than they did before they were trapped. Excuse my clumsy tongue."

Lady Velour asked, "Asya, what about what we talked about before? You know, when it comes to revealing what Mr. Slade is to avoid my sister looking like she is hiding one such as him? Have you thought on that?"

"Both Zyra and Galya agree that it would be the best course of action to be open and honest. It will cast not a shadow of doubt on her loyalty to your father and her sisters. With that said, we three and all the oracles, will study him for a few hours to make sure he is what we think he is. We are due at Velvet's house tomorrow, so we will not make our determination until we get to your father's. Until that time, I suggest we enjoy ourselves. Hold on. Before we let the wine lull us into a forgetful state, allow me a few minutes to inform Lady Silk of our decision, just to make sure that we are all on the same page. Galya, would you mind keeping a watchful eye on Mr. Slade? Or more so, the ladies. We wouldn't want them all to get pregnant while I'm away." Asya laughed, winked at me, and *poofed* into mist.

Everyone was laughing.

I looked at Galya. "Galya, may I ask you a question?"

Galya laughed. "Do you mean, may I ask you two questions, or do you mean, may I ask you a question after the question I've just asked you?"

I looked around the table. "I am sorry. Yes, I should have said I have a question that you may be able to answer."

Galya smiled. "No need to apologize. I was not correcting you to embarrass you, only to help you refine your already advanced intellect. Who would say no to that? Now, feel free to ask me anything."

"Is it just coincidence that all three of you have green eyes and look no older than twenty-five?"

"Ah, in such a very small amount of time that we have been together, you noticed our eyes are all the same. To answer your question, no, it's no coincidence. We all have natural green eyes because we are related. All of us look twenty-five, which makes us appear to be sisters, and yes, we are sisters of a coven called Those of the Ageless Emeralds."

***

Asya appeared within ten feet of Lady Silk who, at the time, was engaged with a gentleman.

"Damn it, Asya! I hate it when you pop out of thin air like that." Silk covered the man beneath her hips and said wryly, "Great timing. I was almost there, if you catch my drift."

Asya laughed. "I'm sorry. I should have peeked first. I will be brief, and I'm sorry. This should be a private conversation, and I think you will agree when it is done."

Lady Silk uncovered not one but two lovers, one male and one female.

"Please give Asya and me a few minutes. Get a drink and regain your strength. Bring me some wine when you return."

The two naked lovers walked by Asya.

Asya said, "Again, I'm sorry about the interruption." Asya giggled softly and explained what Zyra and Galya had spoken about and what it would look like.

Lady Silk stood there, naked, while she thought about the new idea. "Yes, as always, you are right. I will see you at my father's house in a day and a half." Silk waved her two lovers back into the room, and they got into bed. Silk was handed a glass of wine. "Asya, how is my boy doing?"

"Rather well, I might add, but it seems that your sister has taken a real liking to him."

Silk shifted from standing to getting back on top of the man. "Well, you can tell her he is not for sale because I made him a free man. He did swear loyalty to my House, so for me to let him go to her, I want Kailee and Cyan in trade. Or she can kiss my recently loved ass."

"That's some very gross imagery, and you're a lady. But, no, I mean she wants to enjoy his company as you are enjoying your company right now."

Silk began to laugh. "That is more than fine with me as long as you interrupt them at least once. Now, if you don't mind, I would really very much like to go back to getting laid."

Asya smiled. "I will see you at your father's house. Happy trails, little rider."

Lady Silk threw a pillow at her, but Asya disappeared before it hit her.

Asya reappeared right as Beth was returning.

"Ah, Beth, did the lock give you any trouble?"

"No ma'am. The spell worked for me on the second try."

"Good. Trust me, you'll get the hang of it. Now, with Lady Velour's permission, I would like you to join us."

Velour raised a glass. "Beth, have you eaten yet?"

"No ma'am, I usually eat with Mr. Willock."

"I hear he gets grumpy fast." Asya held out her glass, and Beth got up. "No, my dear, sit. I prefer my wine to come to me."

Asya stood up. "Who here would love a story?"

We all raised our hands.

"Now, just so we are clear, part of this is not my original story. A very, very long time ago, I met an old woman whom I thought might have been stark raving mad. She said she would tell me a fantastic story that would amaze me for a bottle of wine, so I agreed. Her name was Rachelle. She told me a story of an hourglass that ran slowly and people who turned into specters that could speak. She told me how her master had been turned into a small dragon and something about true love lifting the curse. As you can see, it was a very fantastical tale. She was the head chef, while her best friend made candles, a man named Remi who would sing and dance. He was in love with a woman who would sing in the rose garden."

Gayla spoke, "You should have seen Asya, a young witch telling me this strange story. We set out to find this old lady and arrived in town only a few hours after Asya had left the old woman. Sadly, she had passed away. She was still clutching the very same bottle with only a small amount missing, and she had this eerie smile from ear to ear as if she were happy to receive death's releasing kiss. Asya wept deeply for her. She had no family and no loved ones, so we paid a local to carry her body to the town's cemetery, and we buried her in the name of the gods. The story plagued Asya's mind, but soon, it began to consume her. Until one night, a year later, we followed a rumor of a very old man named Remi. When we arrived, he was clearly on death's doorstep, surrounded by his family. He was in great distress, calling out to his long-deceased wife.

"The old man cried out aloud, 'Yvette, Yvette, come take me in your embrace. Set me free from this aching heart, as I long to hold you once again. Help me shed this mortal coil. I am ready to come home to you, my love!'

"As he spoke, we could sense something unseen in the room with us. We told the family we were sent by the local doctor to help ease the pain, but we needed the room cleared, giving us the privacy we needed. We worked a spell to ease the pain so that he could converse more easily with us. Asya asked him if he knew a woman named Rachelle.

"He smiled and said yes. 'She and I lived together for a very long time in a castle, trapped as specters along with my wife, my sweet gardener.' He said if he told us the story, we would think him crazy, but we told him that we knew and told him about Madame Rachelle's story. Then, Asya opened the window using only magic, and he knew that we would believe every word he would tell us. His heart had become very weak, so we used magic to keep his heart beating at a steady rate as he told the same story, only from his point of view. He asked one thing of us, and that was to keep the pain away until he passed. We informed his waiting family that he would not live past the rising sun, so we sat with him and held his hands. He said goodbye to his family, and as the rising sun shined its first rays through the window and onto his weathered face, I saw with my own black eyes a beautiful, dark-haired woman lean over Remi.

"He smiled and said, 'My love, you have returned to me at last. Please take me to our true home, to our friends, so that I may sing once more to you.' I watched his angelic wife kiss his lips. With his last breath, he said, 'I love you.' Then, she lifted him in spirit out of the bed. They waved to us and faded away. Both Asya and I cried the whole way home, not because of his passing, but because we watched him reunite with his most beloved. It was one of the most beautiful things we have ever witnessed in our long lives."

Asya wiped her eyes. "I still think of them to this very day, knowing we were the last people to ever hear that story. So tonight, I will recreate a small portion of that enchanted tale in honor of Madame Rachelle, Master Remi, and Madame Yvette. May your souls come and drink with us this very night. Children, are you ready to see something that will make you truly smile? Would you like to see the impossible become possible?"

Asya shifted away then back within a few seconds. Smiling, she held a jar of clay, then created a few small clay figures. With a snap, the lights went out, and only silence hung in the air. Then, an unfamiliar voice rang out. No one in the room spoke as the voice began the story and the lights slowly flickered to life. As the disembodied voice spun its little story, noises could be heard, coming from the top of the dimly lit table. It sounded like a few little mice were clumsily walking across the table, and as the story came to the people, the lights flicked on to their full brightness. More than a few gasps could be heard—everyone was shocked. Before us on the table was a small man in fine clothes. A few more people appeared. I snapped my eyes black to see if it was an illusion, but they were still there in front of me. I made my eyes return to normal.

Asya spoke, "Calm yourselves, my children. Relax your minds, and don't frighten our new friends. Let's allow them to finish this beautiful tale."

With a wave of Asya's hand, the man spoke, and I almost fell out of my chair. He spoke with a strange accent, singing and dancing around. Suddenly, he jumped from chair to chair onto Cyan's head and Topaz's shoulder. He sang softly in her ear. Then, he came over to me. I held out my hand, and he jumped onto it while hitting a high note that echoed off the walls. When he finished his song, he took a bow and thanked everyone. His bride, Yvette, came to his side. As they kissed, I could swear he winked at me.

Next up was the singing and dancing silverware. As they did their routine, the bottles of wine stood up on ghostly, glowing legs and danced to our glasses. They poured themselves into the glasses, and I could see the glasses giggle. The bubbles tickled their sides, but the best part of that was when I took a drink. As I removed my lips, the glasses made a loud kissing sound. It was truly something out of the most intense dream, but it was really happening. The last song was sung by Remi to his wife, a song of long love, starry nights, dreams, and roses. As the song ended, he kissed his love, and they were consumed in the flames of a fireball that raced around the room, laughing in both voices. It finally settled into Asya's hand, dimmed into a blue ball, and disappeared as her fingers wrapped around it.

I was so moved that tears streamed down my cheeks. The lights changed colors before returning to normal. We all stood up, clapped, and praised Asya for the magnificent show.

Asya said, "Thank you. It took me almost seven years to create and perfect that spell. Lady Velour, a word before this wine takes my thoughts away."

They left, and Gayla followed.

"Velour, I have reason to believe that Beth may have an undiscovered, magical gift, and if you would give permission after we see your father, we could test her, if you would like?"

Velour looked down. "I would lose a hell of a cook."

"No, you would gain the trust of a new witch that has a home right here. Wouldn't you be the envy of those around you?" Asya knew what she was doing—she was both cunning and intelligent.

"Asya, you are a very shrewd witch and a second mother to me. So, yes, take her and see if she has magic inside her. Now, let us finish those funny dancing bottles and enjoy our company before tired eyes steal our fun." Velour was happier than she had been in a long while.

We talked some and drank even more. The room was filled with warmth, happiness, and love. It made me miss Sunako the most, and I wondered if she was thinking of me. As the night winded down, Asya and Gayla stumbled and laughed their way down the hallway, and Beth went off to her room. So did Portia as she helped Cyan down the hall. Lady Velour gave a *good night* to all, staggered toward me, and sat in my lap.

"You know, blondie, you never did give me that kiss. Why don't you carry me to my room, kiss me, and tuck me tightly into bed before I have my way with you, Sofia, Kailee, and Topaz right on this table? By the gods and goddesses, you smell amazing. I want you inside me right now!"

I stood up with Velour in my arms, looking at Kailee as she carried Sofia into Velour's bedchamber with Topaz following. She had a large bed easily big enough for five people.

As I sat Velour on the edge of her bed, she noted, "Ah, I see what you want. Why else would you bring me to this room? Sofia, hold me down as Slade makes love to me. Sofia, you're so beautiful. Would you like to sit on my face while he takes me into the clouds?"

"Velour, this is where you will sleep. You need it more than you need my love inside of you." I looked her in the eyes as I spoke.

Velour said, "Yes, I sleep here, but only after I am pleasured. This is where I want you to—"

I cut her off with a deep kiss and moved her more toward the center of the bed as her legs wrapped tightly around my waist. I kissed her neck, and she relaxed. I started to feel something different, something deeply rich and more intoxicating than the wine. Velour's fingers became tangled in my hair as she held me tightly to her. She started to moan louder and louder until she screamed. I stopped kissing her, and she begged me to kiss the other side of her neck. Her body began to shake, and she pleaded for more. I bit harder as she let out a howl that I was sure most everyone in the house heard. I found it hard to stop kissing her neck. Out of the corner of my eye, I saw Kailee lying naked on her stomach with her face between Velour's legs. Velour's other hand was tangled in in Kailee's hair.

I looked over to discover both Topaz and Sofia were naked, tangled up while kissing—it was overwhelming. I felt I was losing control as my body reacted, desperately trying to take control of my mind to make those women mine. Thankfully, I had to piss badly, so I said I would be back momentarily, but my voice went unnoticed. I made my way to the bathroom within her room and noticed it felt like I was holding back a small lake. As I went, it really felt like it although it was a bit difficult to piss with it hard. When I was done, I washed my face and hands and dried them off. I must have gotten some water on the floor, because when I stepped away from the sink, my back foot slipped, sending my already unsteady body headfirst into the door frame. The last thing I remembered was a throbbing pain and the sounds of pleasure from the ladies. I tried to roll over, but I must have blacked out.

"Hello again."

"How are you?"

"Someone that likes seeing you in the Land of Dreams."

"Why can't I see your body?"

"Bodies are overrated. Besides, my face does all the talking. What else do you need?"

"You have a point."

"Damn, I never find you with enough time. See you soon, clumsy boy."

I awoke to Sofia on top of me and the rest of them looking down on me. "Slade! Slade! Can you hear me? Hey, Slade! Hello?"

"What the hell happened, and why does my head hurt so much?"

Velour said, "That is either the hangover or the fact that you busted your head open. Just look at yourself! You have dried blood all over your face and the floor."

Kailee laughed. "He must have hit just above his right eye, tried to get up, then fell on his back. Is it weird that I want to sit on his face with it all bloody like that?"

Sofia said, "Now that you say it, that would be nice since he never returned to bed last night."

"I think I have a good excuse for my absence. I wanted greatly to be a part of whatever you call it, but I had to use the bathroom first."

"Yeah, I tripped over you last night." Topaz laughed. "I just thought you were passed out. Also, that was called a small orgy."

"So did I," Velour said.

"I guess it's a good thing I didn't bleed to death."

Topaz lightly kicked my leg. "Oh, shut up, you cute baby. Now, get up."

"I can't. I think I might be stuck. Why else do you think I'm still down here?"

"What! Get up, or I will pull up your skirt and steal your virtue in front of these good women!" Sofia exclaimed.

"No, really. My head won't move."

"What?" Sofia bent down and said, "Oh shit. He really bled a lot. When it dried, it stuck his head to the floor."

Everyone in the room burst out into laughter.

"I don't see how this could be funny. Please, entertain me with why this is so funny, my loves."

"Aw, he called us 'his loves.'" Kailee knelt. "Well, it is funny, because while we were screwing our brains out, you almost knocked yours out. By the looks of it, hard enough that you glued yourself to the floor with your own blood. Oh, I have a great idea! Sofia, please allow someone to reach into his skirt and see if her hand unsticks his head when he tries to get up. I'll hold his hands, so someone can do the deed."

Velour smiled. "As the lady of the House of Whispers, I ask you, Sofia, if I may handle this problem."

Sofia smiled and said, "By all means, my lady."

Velour smiled. "Trust me, Slade. You're in skillful hands."

They all laughed.

"Here I come, Slade. Maybe you will too this time?"

I tried to protest, but Topaz covered my mouth. After a few minutes of me trying to free my head while Velour worked on me, Velour said, "Well, he must really be stuck, and he is gifted by the gods. Now I want you even more, you sweet piece of candy. Kailee, please get Mr. Willock. Tell him it is an emergency but say nothing more. Slade, I would make that go away before he gets here because that will only make this more awkward between you two." Her eyes hung low as she grabbed it again, squeezing gently as she bit her bottom lip.

A few long minutes later, Mr. Willock walked in and looked at me. "Boy, you better be dying to take me away from my Zyra, because if not, you're going to wish you were. Did anyone call a healer? Because he looks like he needs one." A few more minutes went by with Mr. Willock staring coldly at me. "Boy! Don't look at me. Look at the wall!"

I turned my eyes toward the wall.

The healer, Samantha, walked in. "What do we have here?" Someone explained the situation, and she laughed. "Holy shit, this is going to be great. Do your thing, Mr. Willock. You know how much I love to watch you work."

Mr. Willock went to grab my face and said, "You know, boy, I was enjoying a lovely meal with my beloved, and you interrupted that meal because you seem to be stupid and clumsy. So, I will spare you no gentleness, and I will enjoy your screams. And scream you will."

I smiled. "Well, Mr. Willock, I hope you enjoy my silence."

In the background, I heard Velour say, "Oh shit! Tell me he didn't just say that to Mr. Willock?"

Mr. Willock wore an ear-to-ear smile, grabbed my face hard, and rocked it left then right. He lifted my head straight off the ground and let go of my face, only to have my head bounce off the floor, which made me yell.

Mr. Willock laughed at me. "You almost made me go deaf with that high-pitched voice of yours. I'll be seeing you around, Slade. Lady Velour, will you need me further?"

"No, Mr. Willock. Oh, did Beth speak with you this morning?"

"She did, my lady. Worry not, this House will be under control, as always."

"Thank you, Mr. Willock, you truly are a godsend."

He walked off.

"I don't think he likes you, Slade."

As everyone was talking, Samantha was holding my hand and healing me. She also removed the hangover as well.

While we were having breakfast, Asya made a joke. "A party is not a party unless someone bleeds; someone has sex; and someone passes out. Slade, you almost did all three."

Everyone laughed. We finished eating, packed our backpacks, and headed out. Lady Velour took Kailee as her guard, while she brought Cyan, Portia, and Beth as her guests.

Zyra called our attention, "As we have so many and at least five or so miles ahead of us, I think a proper means of conveyance should be in order." Zyra clapped, and ten shadowy black horses with flaming eyes appeared. "I call these my Nightmares."

Galya said, "Very funny, Zyra. I bet you have been waiting to use that line."

A few people laughed.

"I have been waiting for a proper time, and it was right then." Zyra laughed with Galya.

"Zyra, why don't we just shift there?"

"Too many people at once puts a strain on the mind. Besides, aren't they lovely?"

We all saddled up and began our journey to see Lady Velvet at the House of Dreams. The horses felt super soft and seemed more like they were floating than walking.

"Asya, where are the little ones?" I asked.

"I brought them home last night due to the current situation. One of my sisters will take over for me."

"Asya, I have been thinking about our black eyes. They have to have a deeper purpose because we can see a different layer of reality. Simply put, to see an unseen world that somehow coexists with ours, but is just out of reach for everyone except those of us… What I'm trying to say is, I feel you know more than you're letting on. I feel you not only know, but you believe that I might be the key to a locked door that you want opened."

Asya said, "Well, look at you, my young friend. You're learning to feel with your mind as if you were in a dark room and had to touch everything to find your way out. Yes, there are stories in books that contain power, and it can only be seen with the Eyes of Nyx. Our eyes only let us see the books. We can hold these books, but we cannot read them. If we put the book down and change your eyes back to normal, the words would become invisible. If all of the books are found and properly read, it is said one could call down Nyx herself. That sounds like a job maybe for you. Your eyes might be able to read what we cannot. Oh, and so you know, we can see what those without these eyes look like—like Sunako being an angel—but even we cannot touch them as you can. This is another reason I think you're special. Slade, you can see and touch the unseen world."

"This is just a story, right?" I scratched my head where the cut was.

Asya smiled. "No, my child. I used to think so until Zyra and I found our first book about Nyx. Zyra had a dream, and we took a year searching for it. The closer we got to it, the louder it called to us. But sadly, a large portion of the book is in a long-lost language, so we only got so far in our research. Where do you think we got the story of child born of the gods and kissed by Nyx herself? We also found that this book is indestructible. Mostly due to an accident by a young witch messing with a magic that was beyond her talent. She burned down the place where the book was kept."

Zyra overheard us and asked, "Is Asya telling you about the time she burned down our research place and library? Thank the gods we studied every one of those books—it took a whole year to rewrite them."

Asya laughed. "Yes, at the time, I was a bit greedy for knowledge, and I was only eighteen, mind you. I wanted more than my hands could hold. A spell grew beyond my control, and I was too prideful then. I thought I could contain the spell, and that is where I got this mark." Asya showed me her bicep. "Some scars cannot be healed by normal means, but I kept it as a reminder to never bite off more than I can chew. Those black eyes can also see into the astral world."

I asked, "Asya, what is that?"

"The astral world is the unseen plane of existence, a realm that is only for those touched by the gods and no one else."

"What? Like whom?" I had so many questions.

"Oracles of a high level, witches of a certain level, angels and demons. Demigods have one parent. One is a god, and the other is human. Then, you have the Ghost Walkers, Void Walkers, and finally, dragons."

"Are you pulling my leg? Dragons? Come on, and what is a Ghost Walker?" I laughed.

"Boy, you have only been outside of the House of Ribbons once, and that was to come here. You have only ever seen the smallest part of this large world, so what would you know about the larger world and its inhabitants? For all you know, I could be a dragon in human form. The Ghost Walkers were only ever spoken about in Egypt. They could appear in one place then in another place as a ghost would."

"Asya, are you a dragon?"

"No, but I would love to be. If you pass our test, then someday you will become a magic user." Asya smiled.

I wanted to know more, but Zyra said, "In time, child. Do not rush to learn. Instead, take it in. Slowly understanding what you are learning is the key to more knowledge, lest you burn something down." She winked.

"Thank you, Zyra. I will do as you say."

"I have a good feeling about you, and if I'm wrong, I can always turn you into a frog or a songbird until I tire of you. Then, I can mix you up into a spell."

Zyra rode up ahead to where Galya was.

"She's funny." I smiled.

"She was not making a joke. She could turn you into a number of things, all of which you would be aware of while in your new state. I have a few rats I keep in cages, men who chose to be wild in life and now are caged animals." Asya looked up and sighed. "I do miss my parrot, Ron. Good old Captain Ron; he told the best dirty jokes."

"If you don't mind me asking, what became of Ron?" I was a bit scared to inquire.

"I let him go. He learned his lesson of his cheating ways, and I turned him human again." Asya laughed and mumbled something to herself.

"Oh, I get it. You two were lovers, and he wronged you. Punishment fits the crime. Do you still talk to him?"

"Good heavens, no! He was a card cheat, and I was playing fairly. Well, mostly, but he tried to cheat me out of one gold coin. He went on to spend twenty odd years as my parrot. I returned him to his former glory and sent him on his way with that very gold coin. Wow, that must have been two hundred years ago."

Galya slowed her horse, and we caught up with her.

"It was almost three hundred years ago, and he had a filthy beak on him. He was truly a foul creature as a human and somehow worse as that filthy mite-ridden bird." Galya spat on the ground and rode ahead.

Asya said, "Gayla hated him the most because of the dirty things he would shout at her, and she would zap him all the time. But he still persisted, even with his singed feathers, and I swear she almost killed him a few times. He was not mite-ridden, though. He was exceptionally clean and healthy, so much more than when he was a filthy pirate." Asya laughed and rode up to catch Galya and Zyra, giving Sofia and Topaz a chance to ride up on both sides of me.

Sofia asked, "Does your head still hurt?"

"No, Samantha did a great job. I'm sorry that I could not enjoy the show, but I would like to next time, only without so much wine."

Topaz smiled. “It’s a date. I want to ride you into the sunset.”

I said, “I hope that my riders will be able to break this wild horse.”

“Be careful, boy, because you’re in my stable, and that means many lessons. So, save your shit-talking for after I break you.” Sofia blew me a kiss.

Kailee took Topaz’s place, and we talked about the places she had been. She disclosed the incident that led to why she always chose to be with only women. She told us about Lady Velvet and how she could control dreams, thus, the House of Dreams.

I asked Sofia, “Why is the House of Ribbons called Ribbons?”

Sofia rubbed her hands together. “Oh, you have just asked a great question. You know how Lady Silk can make shadows come to life, right? Well, she is also known as the Shadow Lord in some circles. Yes, it is true. She occasionally goes to far-off places with Asya and fights for fun. She brings home foreign coins of gold and silver and other exotic gifts. As you have seen, she loves to fight, and watching fighters is her second love. But her one true love is to hunt down slavers and kill them. Her father, High Lord Dutch, named her Lord of Shadows after they ran into slavers in a distant land, and she summoned her first shadows. She commanded them, and they tore every person in the group to ribbons. She was only ten years old, and from then on, High Lord Dutch called her his little ribbon maker. When she was thirteen, they came across more slavers. She killed those people, and it gave her just the right taste to really embrace a deep hatred for slavers. She wanted to do something about it because of her mother, but that is a tale best told by someone other than me. When she turned twenty, she was given land and a House, which she named the House of Ribbons.”

“I was told that story about her mother by Lady Velour while we were trapped in her mind, and Asya told us the story of her father.”

“Nice, now you know all four of the stories.”

I told Topaz, “I don’t know Lady Velour’s story, and I still don’t know what her gift is. All I know is her place is called the House of Whispers and nothing more.”

Topaz asked, “What did you do the whole time you were in her head? Screw?”

“No, but that reminds me. Please tell Batch that I would like to know when he is going on a trip because I could have used him.”

Topaz smiled. "He says, 'You're not my master,' and that he can come and go as he pleases."

"Ah, very well then. Tell him to kiss my horse's ass."

She smiled and shook her head.

I asked, "Wait, if she hates slavers so much, why does she own people?"

Topaz smiled. "Please, don't become upset, but clones are not people. They are just copies. They're alive, but they are not real. That is why they all have a mark. So, everyone will know that they are the workers, nothing more. Yes, clones have gotten married because people fall in love with them, but people love their dogs, too. Clones can be bought from special places, and the rest of us are born naturally. Oh, I didn't tell you that the people the sisters own are clones, not true natural-born humans turned into slaves."

"Cheri is a person! She deserves the same rights! She deserves love. Human is human!" I rode up toward Asya.

Sofia said, "I have never seen him upset like that. He was so passionate in his conviction, and did you notice that as he became upset that you could smell him more?"

Topaz said, "I thought I was the only one to notice. The smell became so intense, it made me want to hold him."

"Why do you think it upset him?" Sofia was confused.

Topaz smiled. "Batch says that Slade thinks he's some kind of clone. He thinks someone made him and gave him all these gifts, and he somehow failed and was deemed worthless. So, most of his memory was taken, and like an animal, he was dumped out into the wild or just thrown away, like trash. Just the mere use of the word *clone* is upsetting to him. I think that is why he likes Cheri so much. Remember how well he got along with the twins at the lake? Oh shit, that must be why he risked his life for Cheri and dislikes William and Richter so much.

"Sofia, this is a deeply held belief to him. It may very well be the root of his pain, and he suffers a great deal. This is why Batch does not like to stay with Slade. Batch does not believe Slade is a clone." Topaz wiped her eyes. "Batch, you could have told me this sooner so I wouldn't have looked like such an asshole." Topaz openly scolded Batch as if he were right next to her, and her tongue was sharp. Sofia was silently trying to hold her tears back.

We arrived at the iron-front gate. I was told it was just for decoration, and it read "Welcome to the House of Dreams."

We were greeted by a few guards with copper-brown and pink stripes down their right shoulders. We were escorted in and directly to Lady Velvet.

"Welcome, my sister, I see you have brought us a good night's worth of company. Zyra, Galya, Asya, it's always a pleasure to see you. Shall I have rooms made up, or is this a quick visit?"

"Lady Velvet, we would like to stay the night, but we do have to be at your father's tomorrow. All of us, including you, my sweet dream weaver," Zyra spoke for the group.

Lady Velvet smiled. "Welcome to the House of Dreams, for any of you who have not been here before. Please, take a load off. Nice horses, Zyra. Did you go all the way to Hell to pick them out yourself?"

"Thank you, my child, I did. Maybe you can come with me next time. I have a devil of a friend that would love to make your acquaintance. I think you will like the name of my horses. I call them Nightmares." Zyra winked.

"Brilliant, as always. Zyra, you always know how to make me smile, and you know how much I love seeing one of my adopted mothers."

They hugged, and the rest of us dismounted.

"Gather up, people. Remember, we're guests here, so rule one is no one let any female near Mr. Slade. If one does get close, then watch the hell out of them. I really don't want to add to this group. It's already large enough," Zyra said, ending her speech.

Kailee raised her hand. "I hope everyone knows that I'm here because I am Lady Velour's bodyguard and not because I'm in love with Slade. I mean, a follower of Slade." Kailee cleared her throat. "I'm a bodyguard."

Galya said, "I'm most sure that we all know your role, but your wild, lustful thoughts about a certain Mr. Slade are hard to block out, due to your constant thoughts about him. Oops! Did I say that out loud and in front of everyone? Just look how my tongue got away from me with your little secret. I am sorry. I will try my best not to say such things out loud in the future."

Kailee rolled her eyes. "Thank you, Galya. You are most kind. Maybe the next time I get my period, you can announce that as well."

Asya stepped in. "Ladies, I think a little breathing room could do us all some good. Sisters, let us do what we came here to do."

Both Galya and Asya walked over to Zyra and Lady Velvet.

"We would like to have your oracles meet with us tonight at dinner. Is that okay with you, Lady Velvet?"

"Allow me to guess: it's about that strange-looking boy right there, isn't it?" Lady Velvet looked over her shoulder at me.

"How could you tell?" Zyra asked.

"Just look at how Topaz, Kailee, and my sister are looking at him. The other one is almost standing on his feet." Lady Velvet raised an eyebrow. "Wait, isn't he the one from Silk's House? The one that put a hand on her shadows and successfully fought them off? One does not simply forget something like that. Plus, he is in a dress. What is this world coming to?"

Zyra rubbed her forehead. "It's not a dress. As you can see, it has pleats and looks kind of like a tunic. Will you excuse us for a minute? People, do as Lady Velvet asks. We three will be right back."

The three witches turned into mist and disappeared.

Lady Velvet said, "Lady Velour, will you join me for tea? Alone, if you don't mind."

"It would be my pleasure. Kailee, you're to be Mr. Slade's personal guard. Make sure he is made happy and keep others away from him while we're here, except the oracle. She is going to find out anyway, but she is not to physically touch the boy. She may only speak with him. Thank you in advance, my most loyal." Lady Velour waved to me.

"As you wish, my lady." Kailee bowed her head slightly and walked over to me. "You heard her. I am to guard your body with my body. Wink, wink."

I asked, "Kailee, why did you say, 'Wink, wink?'"

"Damn it, you're just too cute sometimes. It's a figure of speech, and it is a cute way of saying one thing while meaning another. Topaz, Sofia, we will catch up with you later. I'm going to show him around. I feel that if he's followed by lovely women, it will arouse suspicion."

Lady Velvet yelled over to Topaz, "Please find my oracle, Diandra! Tell her about dinner tonight. I believe she is in the hot springs pool area. Take your friend with you and enjoy a nice soak."

"She doesn't even know my name, and I have met her like five times." Sofia was a bit upset.

"Come on, Sofia, have you ever actually spoken with her? No, besides, you're going to love where we are going—trust me." Topaz took Sofia's hand, and they walked away. About ten yards away, they both turned and blew a kiss in my direction.

***

The three witches popped back into their home and sat at a table.

"Asya, have you forgotten to tell us something about the boy wonder of yours?" Zyra was a bit upset.

"I was going to tell you tonight, but to be clear, I was not there to see it with my own eyes, but I did see his memories of the encounter." Asya placed her hands on the table, palms up.

"Damn it, Asya, you don't bury something like that in common talk. That is big news! I mean, huge news! Damn it, I don't even have a big enough word for it right now."

Galya added, "The word you are looking for would be *extraordinary*. That is extraordinary news, Asya."

Zyra said, "Thank you, Galya. Look, the kid clearly is an aberration, something not seen by us to date, and it will be up to us how he is molded into the best he can be. Being able to fight off Silk's dreadful handful is something that we think you should have shared with us as soon as you found out. I mean, he successfully fought off Silk's shadows. If that is not huge news, I do not know what is!"

Asya said, "Look at him! Eighteen, with no memories of people, places, his name, and so on, except he has a wealth of information on proper speaking and some fighting skills. He is strong, not to mention he can kiss like a vampire. Did I leave anything out? Oh yeah, he has the Eyes of Nyx! Look, the kid may very well be who we're all thinking he is, and it is up to us to raise him. If he is what we think he is, and since I found him, it's our sole responsibility to raise him up right. I vote to bring him back here and begin his training. And can you explain his smell?"

Galya scoffed at the idea. "Really, that boy training here? With us? Please. So, he has some gifts, but I have not seen him demonstrate one. What if these are just gifts that are being confused as divinely given? I vote no!"

"I vote yes. Asya, you have seen within him. Cast your vote." Zyra banged her fist on the table.

Asya said, "It's true that we have rarely trained a male in the ways of magic because we almost always send the males to be trained with

Asimov the Wise and Bill the Merciful. I really hate that name because it should be Bill the Horny Old Goat, but I digress. I see no harm in training the boy, but he is stronger than he looks. I believe his power comes from his passion, and we all know that passion can lead him into the fire. If he is who we think he is, then he has been set loose upon us with the passion of his mother, Theia, and the power and love of war of his father, Ares. Do you remember the last time Ares walked this world? The three thousand years of constant war in the old Middle East? With help from the god Lazorot, that war spread like a cancer and almost destroyed Earth.

"I cannot prove at this time that he is that child, but his abilities alone should allow him to be taught. On that same note, I do think a light touch should be used with this boy. Besides, he is bound by his passion to a handful of women that we know of. We have raised Silk as our own; she will allow us to take the boy here and there and never bat an eye. So, in closing, I vote no to taking him, but I vote yes to training the boy with a light touch just in case we are wrong about him. As for his smell, I think it's an ability or maybe something we have never seen before, but it is nice to be around him."

"Okay then, we have it. He stays within our sight, and we train with a light touch." Zyra looked content with the decision. "Now, let us get back before we bump into you-know-who. God, could you imagine if she knew about him?"

An unseen voice from the shadows stopped them. "Don't I get a vote? After all, I outrank all of you. Asya, my sweet. Give me your hand, now!"

Asya reluctantly walked into the shadows toward a shorter female.

Asya said, "I'm sorry. I was not aware you were home, and you usually don't like to be bothered by trivial matters such as these."

"I think I will be the judge on what constitutes as a trivial matter! Just hearing you three speak of raising a boy here has me intrigued. Now, give me your hand before I take it from you!"

Asya gave the unnamed woman her hand, who then saw the memories of Asya's time with Slade. The unnamed woman smiled, laughing as she watched Slade.

"He's so clumsy." She smiled again. "He's so beautiful. When the time is right, you will bring him here to Mother and me. We will decide what to do with him from then on. But the time is not right for us to meet. Soon, it will be. Now, am I clear about what I want?"

The three said yes.

"Proceed with your idea. Oh, and ladies, I will be watching very closely."

The three turned into mist and returned to the House of Dreams.

Chapter 21

The Head Knows Where the Body Is Not

Zyra said, "Great, now she is involved! She has not cared about anything in a thousand years. In fact, I don't think I remember her ever caring about anything since I was sixteen. She is unpredictable, and I don't like this one bit. Now that we are back, let us have some tea and try to relax. I swear, if anything else goes wrong today, I will choke someone. Now, let's speak with Velvet."

Galya replied, "How are we going to relax with her knowing now? Why did we go home to talk? We should have just gone down the road or behind a tree! I just do not think I can deal with her craziness. Her, of all people, who barely tolerates men? She is going to kill him, most likely on the first day. Why couldn't she have just stayed hidden like always? Asya! This boy is becoming a huge pain in my ass, and I just met him last night!"

Asya waved her hand. "Please stop, she might hear us! Look, she was going to find out sooner or later. Now Slade will not be such a surprise, and you know how she detests surprises. As long as she doesn't just pop in, we will be fine."

Zyra laughed. "Remember the last time she decided to go out and handle things herself? At least, they were the bad guys." Zyra, Galya and Asya shook their heads. "All those bodies. She didn't let anyone live, not a one. But the war did end soon after, so I guess it was a good thing."

A bell rang for teatime.

They knocked on the door, and Miss Kath answered the door.

"Well, good afternoon to you three. The ladies are expecting you in the Room of Keys. If you will follow me." The house was built almost exactly like the last two, beautifully ornate and tastefully decorated. The House colors were copper brown and pink. "Lady Velvet, your guests have arrived."

"See them in, Kitty Kath." Lady Velvet stood up, hugging each woman. "Good, I see your private business did not hold you up too long. We were just about to have our tea, then head off for a soak. Would you care to join us?"

Zyra said, "Yes, I think that will be an enjoyable place to talk about why we came here today."

"Ah, yes! You must mean the boy. My sister here has been rather obstinate about the subject, only to remark that it will cause quite a commotion when fully revealed and understood."

Velvet and Velour were brought the tea. The five of them sipped their tea, enjoying small talk before making their way to the hot spring.

***

A little while earlier, Topaz had said, "Mistress Diandra, how have you been?"

Diandra got up and ran to Topaz. "Oh my! Wait, has it been two months already? How are you, sweetness? I have missed you so much. Little birds have been chirping about a mystery man with powers unseen before."

Topaz smiled. "I am well. This is my friend, Sofia, and I haven't heard any birds." Topaz winked.

"Hello, Sofia, it is genuinely nice to meet you, and what a beautiful name you have! Please, will you two join me? The water is nice and hot. Just the right temperature to let the mind wander here and there."

"Diandra, we have a story of our own. Most of it will be told at dinner tonight. Lady Velour said it was okay to tell you a little bit about it before dinner. But first, why is there a black flag hanging on the post outside?"

As the ladies undressed and entered the water, Diandra sat back and said, "Do you know why the three sisters gathered together not too long ago?"

"I do not. Lady Silk has been closed off ever since, and that is very unlike her. Cyan told us a little, but she said you have the whole story." Topaz held her breath, waiting for the story.

Diandra said, "It's about Molly. She ran off with a few people from the closest town last month. At first, we covered up why she was gone. But then she showed up in the middle of the night with a few others and was caught stealing. One of the men she was with stabbed two of the new guards, and they died before the healer could get to him. They were all caught, and Lady Velvet had a special meeting about what to do with Molly. They had me read her mind. She had been involved with seven murders; one of them was a child. One of the people she was with was a young female witch, and poor Molly had changed so much in a month that I barely recognized her mind. She cut her beautiful long hair to half of what it was, and she acted wild like a beast. It was very hard to subdue her."

Topaz asked, "So, what happened to all of them?"

"The four men were held down and stabbed in their hearts by Kath. The witch was dealt with by Asya, who gouged out both of her eyes, cut out her tongue, and made her swallow it. Then, a few hours later, they set her ablaze, burning her to death. For a person without a tongue, she sure could scream. Asya says if she were better trained, she would have been more dangerous, but one of the guards got a lucky hit to the head and knocked her out. She was still unconscious when Asya arrived not too long after."

"What about Molly?" Topaz splashed Diandra. "You're keeping me in suspense on purpose."

"Lady Velvet punished her in the square in front of everyone. She let Lady Silk slowly torture Molly. Lady Silk cut off all her limbs, one by one, then cut off Molly's head. But that is not the worst part."

Sofia inserted, "Wait, how could that possibly not be the worst part?"

Diandra looked at Sofia, saying in a low tone. "Lady Velvet asked Asya to keep Molly alive. So, right before the first cut, Asya made an incision behind Molly's right ear and inserted a small blueish crystal into her head so she would not die after her head came off. She was still alive and in agony. You know how they say, 'A person with their head cut off, a foul thing they can no longer utter?'"

"I have heard that one." Topaz had a horrified look on her face.

Diandra moved closer. "Sometimes, that saying is just not true. So, Molly howled as her arm fell from her body, then her other one, then one leg, then the other leg. Her screams echoed off the trees as she begged to die and pleaded with Asya, but Asya turned her back on her. Lady Silk did not have the shadow cut Molly's head off. No, she had that wickedly foul thing pull Molly's head slowly off her shoulders. The screams and sounds made some who were watching throw up. I almost lost it when her head came off. The horrible part was she could still talk. Whatever Asya did made it so that she would not die and made that possible. At first, she screamed, but then she stopped and started to cry. I mean, really sob. It was truly heartbreaking to see my sister like that, but the truth is, she deserved it for her crimes."

"Holy shit! I mean, not to be morbidly grim, but you didn't finish the story." Topaz had wide eyes.

Diandra said, "Yes, I did."

Sofia said, "We both want to know about her head. What was done with it—I mean—her?"

"Lady Velvet keeps Molly in a box. I bet she will bring her out tonight. Why? Do you want to see her? I had to carry her in the house, and she was fully conscious. I bet she would love to see you. I really think the company would be great for her, but her mind must be like a prison right now. Oh, she smells like spices. It's the crystal Asya placed in her head so it will not rot and smell foul. I kind of feel bad for Molly now that I say it all out loud."

"I don't know if I want to see her, let alone hold her head." Topaz imitated gagging. "Maybe we can lighten the mood. Sofia and I are in love."

"Congratulations! Will you ask to be married or just stay as you are now?" Diandra smiled.

They both laughed, and Topaz said, "Yes, Sofia is a very generous lover, but we're in love with another person."

"Wait, you two are in love with someone else, and both of you are okay with that?" Diandra looked puzzled. "How are you two not going to fight?"

Sofia whispered, "We can't say much right now but trust me. You're going to fall over when you hear the news."

Just then, Lady Velvet, Lady Velour, Zyra, Galya, and Asya entered the hot springs.

"What news?" Lady Velvet asked.

Sofia replied, "Topaz announced that we are in love."

Topaz took Sofia's hand in hers.

"Great news! We shall toast to it tonight. But for now, let us enjoy the water. Asya, where is that strange boy of yours?" asked Velvet.

The thought of his face caused Lady Velour to smile. Diandra shot Topaz a look.

Asya said, "I thought Kailee could show him around, you know, help him relax. I fear the last week or so has been a little much for him. Last thing I need is for him to have a breakdown or worse."

"I believe he will be fine. He just needs a little time to adjust to his new life is all." Zyra rested her head on the rock behind her as she spoke.

"Why, Lady Velour, did you buy that young boy? Oh, let me guess." Velvet deepened her voice. "He has a power greater than any other, or his gift is to be an amazingly great lover, built like a horse and eats like a hungry dog. Am I right?"

No one said anything. Velvet tried to read the room. Topaz and Sofia sank just up to their noses into the water as Asya smiled.

"Oh shit! Please don't tell me he has a unique ability. Does Father know yet? Come on, someone speak."

"Lady Velvet, can't you see that I'm trying to relax a bit before dinner? Please save all your questions for then, my dear." Zyra smiled.

Velvet's eyes darted back and forth between all the ladies.

***

Kailee and Slade were walking and talking about everyday stuff.

"Kailee, where did you come from before the House of Whispers?"

"I used to live with my mother and father in the House of Thorns. You will get to meet them tomorrow. My mother is a healer, and my father is a fighter and head ranger. I also have a younger sister, Lizzy. She can move things with her mind."

"Kailee, may I ask you a personal question?"

"Of course, Slade."

"What's it like to have parents?"

"Well, I don't know the proper way to answer that question. They're just my mother and father."

"I wonder, sometimes, if I have a mother and father. Maybe I'm a special type of clone. If I was just a slave, I guess no one cared enough to look for me when I went missing. It's an odd feeling to know nothing about oneself. I feel so disconnected."

"I'm sorry. I didn't know. So, it's true that you just appeared out of the nothingness one night and Sofia walked into you?" Kailee stopped me and hugged me. I wondered if she could feel my sadness. My scent grew stronger as she held me tighter.

"I don't think I appeared out of nothingness. I must have had a part of my memory cut out, just like Asya said, and placed by the shore near the House of Ribbons. Then, I stumbled into Sofia."

"Slade, how do you feel now?" Kailee held both of my hands.

"Honestly, I feel confused by my feelings, but I feel safe with you. I am happy and sad at the same time."

"Can you explain so that I may better understand?" Kailee smiled and brushed my hair to one side. "Yeah, that is a good look for you."

"Confused because of the real love you and the others are showing me. At times, it's a bit overwhelming, but I want to make everyone happy and keep them safe because I really feel safe with you, Sofia, and Topaz. It's a warm feeling that I hope that I can give you all, and I thank you for it. What little I have is a treasure to me. Your friendship is more than I could have asked for. Kailee, I really feel bad about our first meeting. You're a wonderful person with a kind heart. You deserve so much love and respect. You deserve someone better than a fool like me."

"Slade, allow me to say what I want to say to you in its rawest form. I want to make love to you right here and now, not because of anything more than what you just said. It was so beautiful that it has made me feel in a way I have never felt before. Slade, may I kiss you?"

I reached out and hugged Kailee as hard as I could. "Kailee, from this moment forward, if you want to kiss me, then do so."

We kissed a loving kiss, like when new lovers just crossed that line and become old lovers. When we were done, we walked toward the hot springs. I felt happy, and I pushed my sadness down. Things would settle down soon.

Kailee said, "Come on, Slade. Let's see what Sofia and Topaz are up to."

A few minutes later, we arrived and quietly entered as we saw Zyra there asleep.

Lady Velvet waved us in and whispered, “Come on in. The water is just right.”

Kailee stripped off her clothes. I noticed everyone else was naked, but I was hesitant to get undressed.

“It’s okay. You’re with friends. Take it off and get in.” Lady Velvet watched me the whole time.

Right before I entered the water, Zyra opened her eyes and said, “One day—can I go just *one* day without seeing your manhood?”

Everyone laughed. I tried to hurry into the water but lost my footing and slipped, falling right into Lady Velour’s lap. I had to grab her legs to regain my footing and stand up.

“I was hoping you would find yourself between my legs sooner rather than later.” Velour smiled and stole a quick kiss.

Lady Velvet said, “Wait, are you two together?” Is that what the news is about? You know, sister, I don’t tell everyone when I find a new lover. Unless—wait! Are we going to Father’s so you can get married? Congratulations, sister.”

Velour replied, “My sister, do you really think all of us would come out here just to show off my attractive but clumsy lover? No, sister, we are not getting married. But don’t count that idea out just yet. No, the news you will hear tonight will have you in utter disbelief when you hear it. You very well might piss yourself.”

“Two more hours until dinner, and you all will keep me in suspense like this. It must be juicy.” Lady Velvet’s eyes were locked on me.

We enjoyed the next hour and a half. As I drifted in and out of sleep, I dreamt of the bodiless woman with her black hair. Her pale-white skin made her little blue eyes stand out in a brilliant way. She was the centerpiece on a dining table. When she was talking to people, she was able to turn herself toward the person she was speaking with.

To me, she said, “Beware the road that takes you to many lands. Beware the door that leads to many rooms. Beware of your heart—it beats for more than one. That is how many times you will die without them. Concern yourself not with anyone, and you will become the true hand of fates and a legion of reflections you will command. Embrace the eternal fire, take its throne, take it all, so nothing can be taken from you. Traveler, lover, preacher, killer, king of kings—you are all these things, and soon, they will know you are the taker of souls, harvester of tears. They will not be able to stop you because you are no one!"

Lady Velvet called to Mistress Sofia, "Please wake your boy. I fear if he stays in any longer, he will cook like a lobster. Why do I feel that some of you would like to slather him in butter?"

Lady Velour spoke, "Butter? I prefer honey for the sweet and sticky."

Zyra laughed as a few others did. "Thank you greatly on the insight into your deviant mind, but I will say, I never thought to use honey in a way that could be sexual."

Velour laughed. "You're welcome. It's very nice to be recognized for my genius and my deviant mind at the same time."

Everyone laughed.

"Hey, Slade, wake up. Slade!"

I woke up, making a loud, startled sound, and heard loud screams.

"What the hell is wrong with his eyes?" Lady Velvet backed up against the wall in terror and began to shake.

"Slade! What did I tell you about those eyes?" Sofia grabbed me by the back of the neck with a vice-like grip and dunked my head under the water. She pulled me up, and my eyes switched back to normal on their own. "Tell me what that was! Why did you frighten Lady Velvet so?"

I moved toward Lady Velvet. "I'm sorry that I frightened you. I was dreaming, and that is how I wake up sometimes. It was unintentional."

Zyra asked, "Slade, what were you dreaming about?"

I told them about the black-haired woman with blue eyes.

Galya took my hand. "Relax your mind, boy. I want to see your dream."

Zyra and Asya held on to Galya.

"By the gods! Boy, that was no dream. That was a vision. He has the gift! This is our proof." Galya was excited.

"Lady Velvet, calm down. He's no threat to you or this great House. I promise you on my name." Zyra hugged Velvet.

Velvet yelled, "Why would you let a Void Walker in my house, let alone stay with you? Have you all gone mad? When Father finds out, he will have harsh words!"

Gayla came up from behind Velvet, touched the side of her head, then said, "Sleep."

Lady Velvet's body went limp, but Kailee caught her right before she hit the ground.

Asya said, "She is going to be pissed when she wakes up."

Zyra requested, "Kailee, Sofia, and Diandra, please get Velvet dressed and bring her to the main dining room. I will wake her up there. Lady Velour, Slade, and Topaz, come with us."

Galya led us out into the cool air. It felt nice on my wet skin.

"I'm sorry, but she was about to lose her mind in there. I had no choice but to put her to sleep."

"Galya, you did the right thing," Asya said. "I had forgotten about Velvet's first encounter with the Void Walkers. They had recently made a young boy into a Void Walker, and he was maybe seven."

Zyra added, "That's when the three were about ten. Each of us took one girl and mentored her. We switched girls every month, so each girl could spend enough time learning from all of us. One time, when all of us were together, we went across an ocean very far from here. We came across a group of Void Walkers, who had recently made a young boy into one of them. But he was so wild that they had him on a leash. Sometimes, a new Void Walker can become unpredictable at times. Takes them around six months to adapt to their new life. So, this Void Walker child somehow gets off his leash and ran right at Velvet, who was frozen in fear. I waved my hand and rose the boy up into the air and just let him hang there while we spoke with the male and female heads of the group.

"They offered an apology and told us that they have been to three places looking to find someone to take care of a problem for them. That was the boy and the one that made him into one of them at such an early age. This is forbidden since they never outgrow the anger within, never able to come to peace with the truth of the universe. They're also forbidden to harm another Void Walker. So, to make a long story short, we executed the older male and the boy in front of everyone. They were very thankful to have them released back into the void, but it was Velvet that was the most troubled by the whole thing. I don't think that girl said a word for a whole week. This is why we never turn our eyes black in front of her."

Lady Velour spoke, "To be fair, we were ten, and that was the scariest thing any of us had ever seen before. Honestly, I still have nightmares about that boy."

"I pushed that so far back in my mind that I almost forgot all about that. Slade, be mindful of your eyes while around Velvet. We know you didn't mean anything but still a vision of Molly? Very strange," said Asya.

"Strange indeed," Galya said.

"Why is that strange?" I asked.

Galya said, "Because, my boy, I believe that Molly reached out to you, using the only thing she has left: her mind. That's beyond her skill. Zyra, what do you think?"

"Well, Galya, I think we are going to have to have a word with Mistress Molly, but I think it may have been both Slade and Molly. His sleeping mind may be unhindered and free to roam and who knows what else. Maybe it's time to send Molly off to the gods, so she doesn't infect the boy." Zyra shook her head.

"Zyra, may I be there when you speak with Molly? I would really very much like to see her."

"I don't see a harm in it. Not like you are going to get her to fall in love with you." Zyra smiled at me.

I said, "Well, if she did fall, she wouldn't be able to get up off the floor."

Everyone immediately started to laugh.

"May I ask about the Void Walkers? Who are they, and where do they come from?"

Asya smiled. "I will tell you soon."

"You know, kid, I like you a lot more now." Galya smiled at me. "You might just grow on me yet."

"Thank you, Galya."

"Save the ass-licking for one of your many loves, kid. Just do what I ask when I ask it, and do it in silence."

I didn't know what to say so I winked to let her know I understood.

"Don't wink at me, boy. Look, I say something to you, and if you don't understand, then ask. Other than that, keep the chatter down to a minimum when it is just you and me."

I just nodded.

"See, I knew I would like him. So, let us make our way to the food because I'm getting hungry."

We got to the main house, where Mistress Kath was waiting for us. She announced, "Dinner will be in ten minutes, and it will be served in the Wildflower Room. Lady Velvet thought it would be more casual, and if someone could wake Lady Velvet for me, that would be very kind. Please be careful. She has a tendency to be cranky in her first few minutes. I shall see you all momentarily."

"Well, let's wake her up and get this over with." Gayla sighed.

We walked into a grand room that could easily fit thirty people at just one long table. On the wall hung tapestries with brilliant colors and symbols. The chairs looked handcrafted, each different from one another. Clearly, one was the grandest of them all, and I hazarded a guess that was where Lady Velvet sat. I wondered what the main dining room looked like compared to the lavish room.

Zyra called for Kailee, "Kailee, please sit down in this chair. We will then set her down on your lap, and you are to hold her still if she becomes unpleasant."

"Lady Velvet, time to wake up from your nap."

With a snap of Zyra's fingers, Lady Velvet slowly woke up. "What, what happened?"

"My lady, you became hysterical. Galya helped you by easing you into a sleep. We hope you're not displeased with us, but we could not bear to see you in pain that way again. Forgive us," said Asya.

Lady Velvet patted Kailee on the leg, and she let her go. "No, thank you because I swear I saw a Void Walker in the pool with us. I must have soaked too long in the hot water." Velvet looked around the room, but no one made eye contact. "What is wrong? Someone speak up!"

I raised my hand, and all three witches shook their heads. "Lady Velvet, please accept my sincerest apologies."

Velvet waved me over to her.

"I believe you have mistaken me for a Void Walker." We were within touching distance.

"How so, boy? You clearly don't have the two main things that make a Void Walker stand out while amongst humans. One, the black veins and two, those dreadful, nightmarish-black eyes. So, how are you to blame?"

"My lady, I have black eyes."

Asya tried to interrupt, but Velvet held her hand up with one finger raised.

"Surely you jest, and I'm not known for my humor until I have had a glass or four of wine. You have beautiful, striking, blueish-green eyes." Lady Velvet went to walk away.

I said, "I would show you, but I'm afraid you will become unraveled again. I don't want that but just know that I didn't mean to scare you."

Lady Velvet replied, "Again, you say this. I like you, boy. You seem to not fear what comes out of your mouth, and you're as handy with your tongue as with your fists. When you demonstrated this the first time, I saw you. Now, with that said, I will ask you not a single time more to prove what you say. Or you can leave anything to do with Void Walkers out of any conversation from here to the end of time, and I will thank you for that."

Zyra said, "Lady Velvet, I think that would be unwise at this time."

Lady Velvet raised her hand and waved dismissively. "Well, boy, you have the undivided attention, which you have sought out. Now, go on. Shock me." She laughed.

"As you wish. Now come closer and stare into my eyes as I show you my truth."

I held out my hand, and she grabbed it. She came almost nose to nose, and I whispered, "The vast emptiness of the universe calls to you, Lady Velvet. Can't you hear the voices?" I snapped my eyes black.

Lady Velvet jumped back at least five feet. "Look at his eyes! Is he some new type of Void Walker? Stay away from me! I knew this would happen. They will come for us all!"

I brought my normal eyes back. "No, my lady. I'm something altogether different, and I promise you that I am no threat to you or anyone here."

"Velour, did you know about this?" Velvet leaned on the table.

Velour looked Velvet in the eyes and said, "I did, and I think it is sexy. Those cold dead eyes staring into your soul—it gives me the chills just talking about it. Besides, a Void Walker's eyes are different. Zyra, please tell her."

Zyra told Velvet, "My lady, a Void Walker's eyes are not like his. Slade, if you will, please."

My eyes went black.

"Look closely. See how black they are? Black as ink, black as Hell itself, not a hint of color as if they were feeding on the very light itself. Now, a Void Walker's eyes look more like the night sky. When you look closely, you can see stars, solar systems, planets, and more. So, you are essentially looking into the universe itself. They are touched by a being from beyond our realm and understanding. They seek to spread the message of their religion. They are cursed to see the space between everything. Like Mr. Slade's eyes, they can see the true form of a person and also see the unseen thing that lives between the planes of existence. They have black-as-night veins that run all over their body. Their hair goes white, which they grow long. They have their own god that they worship, and that god gave only a few the power to change new members to the faith. That person has to be willing to give up their old life and worship their god. It's more of a religion that physically changes you from the inside-out. The black eyes are important to them. We three can do the same as Mr. Slade, and we believe Slade was born with them."

"I need a strong drink." Lady Velvet called to Kath, "Kitty Kath, please bring me the small bottle of that clear drink your husband makes, the one that burns going down. I feel I will absorb tonight better if I can relax faster."

Kath was only gone for less than a minute.

"Will anyone join me?"

Everyone shook their heads.

"Mr. Slade, will you be so bold as to have a real drink with me?" Velvet poured a clear liquid into a tiny glass.

"My lady, can you and he at least wait to drink that until I tell why we are here?" Asya was trying to bring Velvet to focus on the meeting before she was intoxicated.

Lady Velvet said, "I have already guessed it. To my sister, first of us to get pregnant. May your children be strong and beautiful. Why isn't anyone cheering?" Velvet nervously looked around the room.

Asya smiled. "If it were only that easy. Please allow me to explain the oddity that is Mr. Slade." Asya told Velvet the story of our journey and why we were going to their father's house. Asya finished as the food arrived.

"Really? I mean, that is a wild story. I can believe the many women part because Velour is more into women, and now, she clearly likes this Mr. Slade, but come on. This boy might be the grandson of Nyx herself?"

Asya said, "One of the reasons we are going to your father's is so we can put all the oracles in one room. With our combined power, we will try to reach out to find the truth, or at the very least, study Slade from every angle. That is why we are going to respectfully ask you to bring out Molly tonight," said Asya.

Lady Velvet gasped. "You must be joking! You mean right now? What can she do besides scare people? I put her in a wooden box and into the back of my closet. A shame, really, because she smells so nice, but she would not shut the hell up. She would talk and talk and talk. She was driving me mad, I tell you! So, I had a nice box made and lined it with a soft pillow and closed her in it."

Zyra said, "Well, we're going to need her because she somehow made contact with Mr. Slade while we slept in the hot spring. He had a vision, and she spoke to him."

"Say no more! I just thought I was having nightmares about her, but it seems that she has learned to reach out. Interesting. Would anyone object to her dining with us? Funny thing is, she cannot eat, but she can taste. I tell you: it must be a fate worse than death itself. Kath, please pour everyone some wine, and I will be right back. Oh, Slade, drink with me." She raised her glass, and I did the same. "Trust me, drink it fast." We did, and I struggled to keep my eyes open as it burned on the way down. "Good boy." She walked away.

I asked Asya, "Am I a Void Walker?"

"Don't be stupid. I would have told you if you were!"

A few minutes later, Lady Velvet came back with a beautifully decorated box. She placed it down and put a finger to her mouth. "*Sh.*" Then, she slowly opened the box. "Hello, Molly. It seems that you have learned a new trick or two, haven't you?"

Molly's voice could be heard, and I noticed how pretty it sounded. "My lady, whatever do you mean?"

"Cut the bullshit, or it's back in the closet with you!" Velvet narrowed her eyes.

"Okay, okay. Let me start by saying, hello, Mr. Slade. I felt you the moment you arrived. Now, Lady Velvet, may I please come out of the box? I promise I will behave when I speak. Please, give me this chance, or grant me true death."

Lady Velvet took her drink in her hand. "Slade, you might want to have one more drink before you see this. Come on, do another shot with me." She poured two more drinks.

"I think I will be okay," I said.

Velvet took the living head out of the box and placed it on top of a large glass vase, like a morbid flower arrangement. I immediately reached down and drank my little drink. It somehow burned more. I must have made a crazy face because the whole room was laughing, even Molly. I walked over and sat closest to Molly.

"Hello, Molly. You're looking beautiful today." I was stumbling, and my words were harder to find.

"Mr. Slade, may I say, you're much more handsome in person. I would shake your hand, but I seem to have misplaced mine."

I started to laugh and found it hard to stop, even as a few tears came out of my eyes.

"It's okay to laugh. I bet when you thought you were going to meet me, you never thought I would be great head right out of the box."

I tilted my head while others were laughing.

Sofia got up and whispered in my ear, "That was an oral sex joke, and do remember it because guys joke about shit like that when they are together. Sorry, Molly, he is new to anything sex-related, and he is untouched."

Molly smiled. She was cute and horrible at the same time. "Whoa, someone place me in his lap, and he will have a funny story about getting a little head from a zombie or whatever it is I am classified as now. Hey, Slade, I'll let you hold the back of my head while I pleasure you. Trust me, most women hate it when a guy holds the back of their head, and as a plus, I don't think I have a gag reflex anymore."

"Molly, what is your life like now?" I asked.

"Great, except I can't scratch my ass, and it's super itchy."

I couldn't say why, but I laughed so hard, I fell out of my chair and almost pissed myself trying to get to the bathroom. It was in that moment I knew I liked Molly, while, at the same time, felt really terrible about her situation. When I came back into the room, people were laughing at a joke I had missed.

"Please forgive my rude exit. Molly, what I meant was, in your current state of being, how have you not gone insane?"

Molly thought for a bit. "It's true that I deserved this punishment, but I'm deeply grateful to Lady Velvet for this chance to live on in hopes that one day I can somehow make up for my misdeeds in the eyes of my lady and friends. Maybe the gods might look at my good deeds over my mistakes."

"Tell me how you visited me early today while I slept." I found it oddly easy to speak with her. One would think a talking human head would be hard to look at, let alone speak with.

Molly told me, "Well, you fell asleep in the hot spring, and it's a place of dreams. That spring has been touched by a goddess. I miss it so much. It's in that place I have learned to wander. You, Slade, are the only one who did not treat me like a nightmare. I thank you for that kindness."

Lady Velvet asked Molly, "Have you visited me while I slept?"

"My lady, I came to you a few times to beg for your forgiveness because I miss our talks, and I can still be useful, even with my obvious limitations, but you only saw me as a nightmare."

"Zyra, Galya, Asya, what do you think on this matter? Should Molly go back into the box, or should she be made useful?" Lady Velvet awaited their answer.

Zyra looked at Molly. "I vote yes. She can be made useful, but I want to see how the boy votes."

Galya looked stunned. "How will Slade vote? Since when does Slade get a vote? I vote no, but I do think she should be reexamined for usefulness."

Asya calmly sipped her drink. "I like the idea of Slade getting a vote because I think he will breathe some new life into our debates. As for Molly, I was most hurt and upset by your actions because I was the one that found you as a young child. I had a big hand in raising you, and for you to do what you did saddened and darkened my heart for you. I still love you dearly, so I vote yes, but I say that with this warning, my child. If you're given any form of a second chance and you waste it or betray us again, I promise you that you will live a thousand years in that box buried in the ground. Now what say you, Slade?"

"First off, thank you two for the vote of confidence. Galya, I hope to earn yours someday. As for Molly, I really don't know her, but I know that if her fate were mine, then I would do anything for a chance at redemption. So, I vote yes for Molly to get one, and only one, chance to regain her good name."

"Lady Velvet, Molly is yours do with as you please. We have only presented our opinions, and the final judgement is solely up to you," Zyra stated.

Lady Velvet sat and stared at Molly. "I will not make this decision on an empty stomach. So, while our food is hot, let us dig in as we enjoy one another's company."

I sat next to Lady Velvet, who was on my left side, and Molly was put on a table almost between us so that she could remain a part of the night's festivities. The table could have effortlessly fit six more people if need be.

Twenty minutes into the dinner, while people were telling jokes, Molly said, "Thank you, Slade, for your kind words. Whatever happens tonight, I will never forget them."

"We're all here now, so let us work toward a bright future." I raised my glass. "To life's many roads and bumps, may your horse carry you far, and may your journey yield you what you seek most."

Everyone's glasses went up, and a toast was given.

Lady Velvet told the table a story of a man who loved his reflection. "His name was Narcissus. One day, a wood fairy appeared before him, telling of her love for him and that she had watched him for many years. She finally built up the courage to tell him that she was in love with him. All he said was, 'Be gone, you filthy creature. Haunt my eyes no more with your disheveled look.' Well, she took it so hard that she let herself waste away until she woke no more. The goddess of the forest wept for her child and cursed Narcissus, so he fell in love with himself. He could not bear that his reflection would not reciprocate his love, so one night, after drinking wildly, he threw himself chest-first on his own sword. As he lay dying, the reflection in the mirror turned its back on him, denying Narcissus a last look at the beauty he'd so deeply fallen in love with. He was cursed because he was too arrogant about true beauty."

We all clapped except for Molly, of course, but she whistled. Velvet asked Asya to walk her to the bathroom, and off they went. Sofia was gently rubbing my right leg and whispering about how she wanted to steal a kiss. She wanted me to drop my napkin, so I did. I bent down and lifted my head to kiss her lips; it was warm and delightful. As we returned upright, both Topaz and Kailee had taken notice to our not-so-discreet kiss, each with a grin, most likely something wicked on their minds. Lady Velvet and Asya reentered the room and took their sets.

Velvet raised her wine glass, called the room to order, and said, "I have made my decision on what to do with Molly. I will allow her one final chance, but she must find a home elsewhere. Do I have any takers? After all, Molly has always been a very fine oracle. Lady Velour, would you take her in to live with you?"

Lady Velour jokingly said, "I don't know. Why not give her to the handsome, black-eyed Void Walker?"

Velvet threw a piece of food at Velour.

“I am sure his silver tongue could persuade Lady Silk to let her live there. Or better yet, Zyra, why not bring her with you on your travels? I’m sure she does not eat much at all, if any.”

Zyra shook her head. “We get into enough trouble on our travels as it is. I think a living human head would make us look more like users of dark magic than the good witches we are, besides the fact that we used dark magic to keep her head alive, lucid, and smelling wonderful all the time. But we can bring her along to your father’s house, and we can speak with Lady Silk then about it. Congratulations, Molly, on rejoining civilized society.”

“I have a better idea. Slade, will you accept Molly here and now? Besides, Lady Velour did call you out.”

“Lady Velvet, I don’t know what to say.”

“Say you will take her, or back in the closet she goes.”

“Then, yes. I happily accept Molly.”

“Excellent. Slade, you now own your first slave and an oracle to boot. What a score.”

“Molly, are you a slave?”

Molly nodded.

“Lady Velvet—”

“Boy, if the words you’re about to say has anything to do with not wanting a slave, then shut up and deal with it. I don’t take back gifts, and you wouldn’t dare insult me at my own table. Now what were you about to say?” Gritting her teeth, she stared at me as if she were choking me with her mind.

“No, Lady Velvet. I just didn’t know Molly was a slave.”

“She lost her rights as a free woman, so now she is property. Your property, I might add. Now, enough talk of this extraordinary gift, lest you offend me.”

“Thank you, Lady Velvet. For this chance, I will not fail you again.” Molly literally had an ear-to-ear smile. “Mr. Slade, I will serve you in any way I can. Thank you for accepting me. I will not let you down.”

Lady Velour suggested that we not drink as heavily as we did last night and told the wonderful story of how I knocked myself out and missed out on an amazing time. “Plus, my father will no doubt want to throw a feast because I think it has been almost four months since his three daughters have been together in his home, not to mention you three. For all three of you to come together and join his daughters just to lead us all to Father’s house, one can only assume that Slade here is clearly at the center of this great gathering. Now, with that being said, whose ass do I have to kiss to find out what Mr. Scary Eyes has to do with all this?"

Zyra spoke up. "Lady Velvet, you are very right! All of this has to do with this young man. We believe he is a gift from Nyx herself."

"Wait a second, please." Lady Velvet had another shot of the clear drink. "Are you going to tell me that this boy"—She pointed a finger, almost in my face—"May very well be the child from the stories you told us when we were children? I mean, those were just fairytales, right?"

"Velvet, my sweet, how many times have you seen with your very own eyes the very thing from a story been proven true? Besides, where do stories come from? Some are rooted in truth." Zyra waited for an answer.

"More than a few stories, but this is not just the gods. What we're talking about is Nyx herself, the very night sky in living form. Then that wasn't just a story; it was a prophecy. Okay, now I have to hear more about this."

Zyra said, "Well, you seem to remember the story about the boy with black eyes."

Zyra gave a fast overview of that story. "Now, we only have to tell your father that story and his oracle, Reveka. We believe that, with us three and the combined oracles, we might be able to learn something. We can have proof that he was a natural-born oracle and not enhanced to fool everyone. Hopefully, he is who we believe him to be, and also, we have two others coming. One of them does not know about the boy because I fear he is already much too excitable."

"Why?" asked Lady Velvet. "Why tell anyone? Just take the boy, train him like you did with us, and keep him a secret until his gifts and abilities are significantly developed. No one needs to know. I feel you're giving the upper hand to those who need not the temptation to steal the boy, then bend him into something used for their own wicked ways. Who else did you ask to study this boy? Anybody besides Asimov, whom I assume you called?"

Asya smiled. "Lady Velvet, imagine if your sister never told you about him, and you found this boy a year or more down the road. Are you going to sit there and tell us that this news would not make you think on why she had hidden him? Was it so she can gain power later on?"

Velvet replied, "I see what you mean, but still. Too many people seem to know already. Transparency is always the safest option, and you, Asya, have always preached honesty. So, I guess I have joined your merry little band of whatever you call yourselves. So, who will be meeting us at our father's tomorrow?"

"Lady Silk, Saffron and…" Zyra mumbled another name and took a long drink.

Lady Velvet exclaimed, "First off, can we suspend the titles just for this trip? I swear, I will bite off the finger of the next person that calls me lady!"

"Excuse me, Lady Velvet, does that apply to me?" Molly smiled.

Velvet laughed, and everyone did so after. "Oh, look at you. I see your quick wit has not left you. Ladies and gentlemen, I give you Molly. She literally is a head above everyone and quick on her feet."

Everyone laughed.

"Molly, if you do not mind, may I?" I asked.

"By all means, my hands are tied. Presumably in a shallow grave somewhere." Molly laughed.

"Velvet, I would have said, 'I give you Molly. She literally is a cut above the rest.'" I then pointed at her neck.

Portia booed me, and the rest gave a thumbs down at the joke.

Molly was laughing. "Hey, Slade, I thought it was very funny. Next time, don't ask. Just say it because I won't hold anything back and couldn't if I wanted to."

I laughed and slapped my leg.

"Why are you laughing, Slade?"

"Because you said you couldn't hold back if you wanted to. Because you have no arms." I continued to laugh.

"I'm happy to see you happy. Can you clap for me? You know, for being a huge ass about my disability."

My laughter came to a quick halt. "Molly, I am sorry."

The room went silent.

"Look at his face! He totally bought it!"

The room exploded with laughter.

"I got you good with that one. Wow, look how red your pretty face can turn." Molly was smiling.

"Very funny, Molly. I will get you back." I smiled.

"Wait, I still didn't catch the name of our yet-to-be-named guest." Velvet tapped her fingers on her half-filled glass.

Zyra came out and said, "The wizard, Bill."

Velvet yelled, "The Goat? You know that guy always grabs or pinches my ass every single time he walks by me. Don't laugh, Velour! I know he does the same to you and the way he stumbles into one of us just to grab our tits while he steadies himself—he's a filthy old fool. No, he is a filthy, old bastard, goat fool!"

"Well, Velvet, I will do my best to shield you from his smutty ways." Zyra walked over and kissed Velvet on the forehead. "Do you feel better now, my little ladybug?"

"Thank you, Zyra. I do feel a bit better."

For the remainder of the meal, more jokes were had with laughter overflowing the room. Some of the ladies were more inebriated than others, and as the night came to an end, Asya, Galya, and Zyra gathered the other girls.

Asya spoke for her two sisters, "Look, I know you all want a piece of Slade, but I ask you to wait until we have visited with Reveka and have attempted to ascertain what he is. We only ask that he abstains from intercourse, oral, or otherwise. I know asking some of you this sounds absurd, but we have to assume he's an oracle, and you all know the rule that an oracle can only be with a woman—"

"I will follow what you ask, but, Asya, if the rules states an oracle can only be with a woman, then I am following the rules, as I am only going to be with a woman or women," I interrupted.

Asya pinched the bridge of her nose and rubbed her temples. "Oh, my sweet, sweet dumbass. The rules are like that so no man will defile the sacred body of an oracle, and the fact that no man has ever been an oracle—at least, not to our vast knowledge so far. The next night or so, keep your manhood to yourself. They will still be in great wanting for you in the next few days. So I know that Mr. Slade will not be tempted by any of you wicked temptresses, I'm going to let one of you sleep in the same room with him. So, on the count of three, Zyra will pick the first person to raise their hand the fastest. One, two, two and a half, two and three quarters. Three!"

"We have a winner and just by a hair." Zyra finished the last of her drink and almost missed the table as she placed the glass back down. "Slade, I expect you to be an extreme gentleman with your lady partner for the evening. I present to you, the winner by a nose. Drumroll if you will."

The room was silent.

"I said drumroll, damn it, or he sleeps like a kitty cat at my feet for the night."

We all thumped our fingers on the table.

"Stop, stop, that is just terrible! The winner is… Molly. Thank you all for playing. Now, Slade, help a drunk old witch to her room." She threw an arm over my shoulder. "Ladies, get your goodnight kisses in fast."

I received a nice but short kiss from all but Beth, Diandra, and Velvet.

"I don't know where your room is, Zyra."

"Okay, but only this one time." Zyra was talking to something unseen. "This might feel strange at first, but worry not, I have you." We then started to float up. "Weird, huh?"

I answered, "This is how I met Asya."

"*Sh*. Just relax, and we will get to my room. Yours will be next to ours. Oh, I almost forgot. I swear, I would lose my damn head if it were not attached." Zyra snapped, and Molly floated up next to me and winked. "Ladies, lead the way, please."

We gently glided our way across the floor and up three flights of stairs. I set her on the bedside.

"Slade, I sense the good in you. Worry not who you might have been; only focus on who you are today. Be that person. The person people have come to know, so they can look up to you. After all, these could all be your people someday. Goodnight."

As I walked out of the room, Molly floated next to me.

"Molly, do you want me to hold you, so you don't fall?"

"Thank you, but Zyra spoke to me in my mind. I will be able to float around like this as long as I remain close to her. She said two hundred feet, but any farther than that, and I will fall to the ground. Shall we go to our room?"

Chapter 22

Because a Little Head Never Hurt Nobody

Molly and I walked to the next door and entered.

"Molly, what does it feel like being a floating head?"

"Well, I can tell you that being just a head sucks, but even though I don't fully remember what I was doing, I deserve this punishment. So, while it is terrible, it could have been worse. Hey, Slade, may I see you with your special eyes?"

I thought about it. "As long as you're not going to get scared and lose your head or anything."

Molly laughed. "Good one. I'm thankful to have met you. I don't feel like you care whether I have a body or not, and that is a good thing to know someone likes me for who I am and not have ulterior motives. So, I will do my best to keep my head around you."

I snapped my eyes black and looked Molly in her eyes. Molly had wings and a tail, like Sunako. Her tail looked a lot like a palm-sized snowflake, but the design moved around. I would have to share this information with the witches. "What do you think, Molly?"

Molly was silent for a few seconds. "I see pain in your future. Come touch my face and see what I see."

I reached out and touched her face, feeling her spirit hand touch mine.

"Slade, what are you doing? Whatever it is, I can feel it. By the gods, is this what I look like to you?" Molly could see what I could by looking through my eyes.

"Yes, some of you looks more or less like this, but you look most like my friend, Sunako. She has wings and a unique tipped tail. I find it beautiful and strange that some have a dual body, and others have none. Even Asya says she doesn't understand why that is. Molly, are you tired?"

"Am I tired? I was in a completely dark box for a long time. I never knew when I was asleep or awake. Why?"

"I was hoping you would welcome me deeper into your mind. I want to know you."

Molly said, "Sure, but I will do you one better. Why don't we get into bed, and you can rest your body and visit my mind at the same time as you hold me?" Molly smiled.

"Do you mean sleep and interact at the same time? I didn't know that was possible."

Molly said, "It is. I can tell that you have not started your training yet, and what better way to train the mind? While asleep, the mind is totally free from the outside world and its attention-grabbing annoyances."

We got into bed, and she turned her head away from me, laying her head down on my arm. "Slade, no funny business while you are behind me. I know you might be tempted to get a little tail in this position."

I reached down and lightly took her tail in my hand, tugging a few times.

"Oh, Slade, and on the first date! At least buy a lady a drink first." Molly laughed, and so did I. I rested my arm on her hip, and she welcomed me into her mind.

Molly was standing before me. Her skin was pale white, and she had medium-length black hair with beautiful blue eyes. She was five foot two and wore a long red dress.

"Do you like it? Is it too much?"

"Molly, that's a beautiful dress."

"I bet you never thought I was this short, did you?"

"I never gave a thought about it until now."

"So, Slade, where would you like to begin?"

"If you don't mind, I would like to research you a few months leading up to you leaving the House of Dreams and what occurred afterward. I can look up to when we first met, unless you have a better idea."

"We could do simultaneous research, me to you and you to me."

I thought of a good joke. "Don't you mean, you do me, and I'll do you?"

I laughed while Molly rolled over and moved closer, whispering in my ear, "Careful, Slade. Talk like that could make a girl think naughty thoughts. In here, anything goes since I have a body and the sensation of touch. But, yes, I will read your books, and you read mine. We can talk after."

Just as I finished reading the book that contained what I was looking for, I noticed Molly watching me. "Slade, I never thought I could ever feel sorry for anyone ever again, but you—you and everything about you all fits in one incomplete book. You have a chapter for each of your love interests, all of which were interesting to see how you love without knowing what love is. You just feel love in its purest form. No one taught you about love. You were very enjoyable to read, and I thank you for that."

"Molly, you have an impressive library, and if I may say, I thought you were eighteen. Due to your looks, I was surprised to find you are twenty-one, but not as surprised to see that you were really not in control of yourself after you left the House of Dreams."

"Slade, even I have never looked at why I did what I did because I was judged. What is the sense in retreading old ground when I can't do anything about it?"

"I understand, but I fear Asya might not have had the full picture and may have judged you too harshly. Wait here. I will be right back."

We disconnected, and I left the room, knocking on Asya's door. It opened right up.

Asya spoke softly, "Slade, what is it? If you wake Zyra, she might get ill-tempered, and that would mean she would surely hang you upside down for the duration of the night."

"Then, may I speak with you in the hall for a moment? It's very urgent."

Asya came into the hall and shut the door. "Okay, dumbass, this better be good, and if you are just going to ask if you'll become a zombie if Molly bites you, then the answer is no and goodnight!"

"Asya, I think this is serious. Did any of you research Molly's mind before judgment was made?"

Asya thought for a bit. “No, because Diandra looked into her mind and witnessed the events. Besides that, she was wild and admitted that she enjoyed killing the little boy, all the while trying to bite anyone that came close to her. Why do you ask? Go on. Get right to the point!”

“Asya, I believe Molly was under the control of a witch or wizard. I’m not really sure the difference in the classification, but you need to see her memories. You need to see them right now.”

Asya ran her fingers through her blonde hair. “I will tell you the difference in the morning, and yes, we killed a witch, but she was young and did not possess the power of mind control.” Her hand rested on the side of my face in a loving way. “So, I am sorry to tell you that you’re wrong, but you are a good person to look into the matter for her. Now, get some sleep. We will have a very long day tomorrow.”

“Asya, please. While I was in her mind for just a moment or two, I saw the face of a man who was not in the group that was executed. The weird thing was, I could feel him, and he was filled with hatred. Please check Molly now or take my hand and see what I witnessed.”

Asya took my hand, and her face went sour. She opened the door and softly called for Galya.

“Yes, Asya, what is it? Please don’t tell me dumbass did something stupid. Boy, you didn’t try and have sex with Molly, did you? You’re even move depraved than the old goat, Bill, and that is saying something!”

I was shocked. “Holy shit, Galya, why would your mind go there? I mean, it always goes to something sex-related.”

Galya waved her hand, and I became stuck to the wall as if gravity were different for only me.

Asya covered her mouth and laughed. “Yes, Galya, that was dark, even for you. But, no, Slade has brought me some new information that I think should be addressed immediately.”

Galya twitched her finger, and I became unstuck, so we could go to my room.

Molly’s head turned toward us on the pillow, and she sat up. I didn’t think I would ever get used to her disembodied head and the way she moved around.

“Hello, Galya, Asya. I asked him not to bother you. Please don’t be angry with me.” Molly sounded very frightened.

"Molly, you're not in any trouble. Mr. Slade believes he saw something, and now we need to see into your mind. Slade, come show us what you saw."

We entered Molly's mind, and I led them to the events just before she returned to the House of Dreams with the witch and the four men. Then, we saw a man for a brief moment, but his back was to Molly.

"Asya! That's the person I told you about."

They replayed the whole event three times and found a voice that I did not hear before. We exited Molly's mind.

"Oh my, this isn't good. No, this isn't good at all." Asya looked sick. "I think I'm going to be sick."

Galya sat down and started to cry.

I asked Galya, "May I do anything for you?"

But she shook her head.

Asya left the room, went to Velvet's door, and banged on it.

"What in the hell is so important?"

"Velvet, a word! Right now!" Asya pushed Velvet backward. She accidentally sat on a female hidden under the sheets. "Velvet, tell her to bring us some water. This is an emergency."

"My sweet, bring us some water from downstairs. Please don't rush because I need time to finish our talk in private."

The women walked off.

"Asya, can't you tell time? It's right about snack o' clock, and I'm the snack. So, for the sake of the gods, what is so damn important?"

Asya was direct with her question. "Velvet, what did you have done with the four bodies from the execution?"

"What? Why would you care about that and at this hour? I think you should cut back on the wine or that funny stuff that Galya smokes in her wooden pipe."

"Velvet, this is serious. Now tell me!" Asya's tone was cold and straightforward.

"I told Kath to have them buried. Why, Asya? What is wrong?"

Asya was silent.

"Asya, you're scaring me. Please tell me what is wrong."

Asya spoke mournfully, "We messed up, Velvet. We should have interrogated the witch and men, and most importantly, Molly. We should have read her mind." Asya wiped her eyes. "Velvet, I think we wrongly judged Molly. I believe the proof is buried in the ground out there."

Velvet sat back against the headboard. “Tell me you’re joking. Tell me anything but what you just said. Asya, Molly was my second most trusted next to Kath. I loved Molly as a sister. She was going to be a lady with her own House one day.” Velvet had tears in her eyes. “Okay, what do we do now? Shall I have the bodies dug up?”

Asya said, “No, I have a way to do that, and it will be safer and faster. Besides, we will need Velour.”

They both went to the second floor and barged through Velour’s door, who sat up on her knees.

Velour was startled. “Son of a bitch! Can’t you two knock before you enter? I’m in the middle of something, if you catch my drift. Just give me ten more minutes.”

Asya wiggled her fingers, and Velour rose from the bed, revealing Topaz who had been under her legs. Next to them was Kailee who was on top of Sofia.

“Velvet, is this all you and your sister do? Drink and have copious amounts of sex with many women?”

Velvet laughed. “I enjoy a very healthy sex life, and what I do is my business.”

Velour said, “I don’t always drink, but it helps to have a good buzz going while someone is going down on me. Now, I will kindly ask you to please put me down.”

Asya said, “Are you just going to stand there nude?”

Velour nodded with her eyes wide open.

“Velour, we will need your special skill at first light.”

“Why? Who died?” Velour looked shocked.

Asya replied, “The men from the execution. We will fill you in on the rest in the morning.”

“If this was going to wait until the morning, then why in the hell did you burst into my room?” Velour folded her arms.

Asya said, “Because this is urgent.”

Asya and Velvet left the room. “Velvet, I will see you at first light.”

Asya went back to Slade, Molly, and Galya. “Good news, I think. We can dig up the bodies and go through the minds of the men Molly was with. We should learn more then. Galya, we should get some sleep. It is only four and a half hours until first light. Slade, you and Molly should do the same. Molly, I will give you this.” Asya said words in a foreign tongue and clapped.

“I can feel a tingling where her body should be.”

"Give it a few minutes, and it will be like you have your body back, just invisible. Everything will work so you can eat and do other things," said Asya.

Galya inserted, "Think of it more like a spectral body. It will work just like a real body, so if you eat, you will need to use the bathroom, but you are to stay with Slade at all times. Do not leave this room or his side until we come get you. Goodnight."

Galya and Asya left the room. "Oh, and no intercourse or oral sex. Light touches, I don't mind."

"Molly, are you okay?' I asked.

"Better than okay. I can feel the floor under my feet. Come here."

I walked over to her.

"Do you feel my hand? Because I can feel your skin—it's soft and warm."

"I feel your hand. Asya was right. It's like you have an invisible body. Now it sounds like it will be a bigger day tomorrow, so let's go to bed."

"I was thinking the same."

We got into bed.

"Thank you, Slade. Even if this is just for tonight, thank you a thousand times."

I was face-to-face with Molly. "All I did was report what I saw. You deserved a fair trial, and you didn't get one. Even if you did what they say you did, what they did to you is still messed up."

"Slade, while I was in your mind, I noticed that you made a promise to Sofia and that you will not break that promise. You are allowed to kiss, though. Whoever you kiss on the neck seems to cause one to love you, so would you kiss me? Not on the neck, I mean mouth-to-mouth, or would that be too weird for you? I might never get a chance to feel another person like this again. I mean, even if my name is cleared, who would want to kiss a floating head?"

I kissed her before she could say another word. I placed my hand on her hip and pulled her close. "Molly, I believe a terrible wrong was done to you by the sisters and Asya, but it all started with the one who commanded your mind, making you their thrall."

"Are you just kissing me because you feel sorry for me?" Molly looked sad.

"No, I wanted to kiss you before, and now I'm very excited for you."

We began kissing again, and she climbed on top. I felt her whole body, but it gave off no heat as she grinded on me.

"Molly, would you mind moving to my leg? I don't want to lose control, and I'm getting foggy in the mind. I fear I will lose control and have you right here."

Molly smiled and straddled my right leg before going back to kissing. A little while later, she was moaning heavily.

"Slade, give me your hand."

I gave it to her.

"Can I bite you right here?"

I said yes, and she sped up her grinding. She began to lick my fingers, and as she reached the place she wanted to go, she bit down on the outside of my left hand and screamed with it in her mouth. I was worried someone would hear her. She didn't bite so hard that it hurt too much, and I didn't bleed—it was kind of enjoyable and weird at the same time. Molly slumped over me when she was done.

"Thank you, Slade, I never thought I would ever feel that sensation again. I hope I didn't bite you too hard, but your smell has made me so horny."

"No, it was nice. I really liked it."

"Good. If we can, I would like to do that when we wake up before we go, just in case they take this body away from me. Is that okay with you?"

"I would like that."

We kissed a little more and fell asleep in each other's arms. I dreamt of a man with a murderous stare and a black hat. He wore an emerald on a gold chain around his neck and a black mask that covered his face from his nose to his chin. He had stolen a baby he'd placed in a floating orb, and the kid disappeared. The emerald seemed to glow a little, and he took another baby to the orb, and that child disappeared as well.

I woke up to Molly gently rubbing herself on my leg just above my knee, her hand wrapped around my manhood.

"Morning, sleepyhead. I thought you might sleep through the whole thing. I got off on you three times already, and I am about to hit the fourth. Give me your hand."

I gave her my right forearm, and she clamped down, causing me to bleed. I was totally awake. Molly's eyes rolled back into her head, showing only the whites of her eyes. As she moaned loudly, the door opened to reveal Velvet, Zyra, Galya, and Asya standing there, staring. Molly was so enraptured that she kept going, unaware of our guests' arrival. I had no clue what to do and was frozen to the spot.

Velvet said, "Holy shit! Now I think I have seen everything! Are you two having sex?"

Molly's eyes rolled back from being white, and she jumped out of the bed. "No, my lady, but I was grinding on his leg." Molly sounded embarrassed.

Asya spoke up. "My sweet, why else do you think I gave you a spectral body with sensation if not to use it? Now, you two get dressed. The truth needs to be unearthed."

"Slade, I should have told you, but this used to be my room." Molly dressed in what looked more like combat attire. "At least, I will fit in and not look like a freak. Now where did I put those gloves? Ah-ha! Perfect. Hey, Slade, how do I look?"

"I think you look just as beautiful as you did last night."

"Damn, you're smooth. It's no wonder they follow you around like they do. I should be careful, or I might end up married to you. Oh, and I don't think it is just the kisses you give. I think it is the kisses and the way you smell; it is sexy and delicious at the same time." Molly put in small, dangly earrings. "Ah, it is the little things I missed. Your blood tastes as amazing as your kiss. Shall we go, my master?"

"Don't call me that."

"Slade, you own me. That makes you my master. Now, please, we should go."

We hurried and met everyone outside. Zyra had already been caught up to speed. The air was cold enough that we could see our breath.

Sofia and Topaz winked, and Velour said, "You missed an even better night last night, but we heard that you went to bed with a little head."

Everyone who heard the remark started to laugh, even the witches. I just stood there, and Velour whispered in my ear, reminding me what that meant. Then I laughed a little, seeing the humor in the double entendre.

Velvet delightfully announced, "Okay, let's dig us up some corpses."

Kath led us to the grave site and pointed at two stones.

Kath said, "This is where they're buried."

It was a little chilly, so Sofia and Kailee huddled close.

Asya said, "Everyone, stand back."

Zyra stood at one spot and Galya another, while Asya stood in the last spot. It looked like they'd formed a measured point, like a triangle. They began to chant and raise their arms, and when their chants grew louder, the ground seemed to rumble and shake. Suddenly, there was a bright light, and it caused a huge scoop of dirt to rise in the air. They were using magic to pull the ground from the earth into a large dirt ball. The three witches made the ball slowly rotate. As it did, dirt fell from it and back into the hole until four bodies hung in the air. Galya had water that encircled the men's heads, completely washing off the dirt. Then, they set the bodies on the ground.

Zyra patted Velour on the back. "Velour, it's your time to shine, honey."

Velour stood less than ten feet from the bodies and shouted, "Awaken!"

In the first few seconds, nothing happened. Then, the closest body started to spasm and flail its appendages. A few gasped, and the others were silent. But some of us laughed.

Sofia remarked, "The blond one looks like a fish out of water."

As he flopped around, he suddenly stiffened and sat up. The rest followed suit soon thereafter and lay back down. The whole thing seemed insane, but I guessed it was a common thing to witness for some.

I asked Zyra, "What would you call them? Are they considered human?"

"Good question. Does anyone here besides Velvet, Velour, or Kath know the correct answer?"

No one answered.

"The poor souls are the reanimated, and any high-level witch, wizard, warlock, mage, sorcerer/sorceress—whichever you want to call us because we're all just witches with fancy titles. Mind you, some like company. Some like isolation, and that is where these classifications come into play. Great, I lost my train of thought. Where was I?"

I raised my hand, and Zyra pointed at me. I said, "Your last words were, 'The poor souls are the reanimated.'"

"Good boy. If I had a cookie, I would give it to you. Yes, these are reanimated corpses, and they are only puppets right now. Using so many at once is very demanding on the user. No matter how high in the arts one can get, this spell can consume the user. So, only the stupid bring the dead to their feet, but not Velour—no—she was born with this gift, and she is in no danger. This is where our star of the day will shine. All eyes are on you, Velour. Finish the job."

Velour said, "For those who do not know, I can raise the dead. If I want, I can give the dead back their long-lost voice. Under normal conditions, I would have them just lay there and speak, but Zyra wants a bit of a show." Velour walked over to the cadavers of the mute men. "Open your eyes and tell me no lies. Speak to me with a truthful tongue. Return your voice. I will, on this day, suspend the judgment for which you must pay. Speak! Speak! Speak!"

Asya blurted, "Velour, stop being melodramatic and touch their foreheads already!"

As Velour touched each man, she shouted, "Speak now!"

The blond dead man turned his head, opened his mouth, and said, "I was dead, not deaf. What is it you seek?" Worms fell out of his open mouth. It was really gross. He stood up slowly and brushed himself off as did his three cohorts.

Lady Velvet said, "Why did you come to my House on your last night of life? What was your main purpose?"

One of the reanimated men said, "You have something we wanted. We were supposed to sneak in and grab it, but as you can see, we ran into a complication."

Velvet asked, "What was it you were trying to take?"

The blond man said, "You have the Eye of the Void, and we wanted it."

Velvet looked upset.

Asya asked, "How did you come to know it was here, and why do you want it? This time, make your answers more defined because you can feel pain while that woman over there animates you. I will not hesitate to start a fire for you and your friends. So, either you and/or your friends can speak clearly, or I will see how much pain you receive. That is solely up to you."

The blond man's friend said, "We don't have to tell you, witch!"

One of the men with long black hair spoke up. "Please, I will tell you what I know. Just don't burn me."

"You stand over here." Asya pointed to a spot closest to her. "Anyone else want a chance to do the right thing?"

One more man nodded and joined his friend.

"Good, I have two who will and two who won't."

The blond one yelled at Molly, “I see you cut a deal! You’re a filthy piece of shit!”

Zyra wiggled her fingers, and the man rose into the air. She spoke, “Listen to me, bastard, and listen well. You only need your head to speak, so will you apologize to Molly? If not, I will have to show you who the boss is today!”

“Eat shit, witch!” The blond man in the air had made a mistake.

Zyra laughed and said, “Wrong answer!” With a flick of her wrist, three fingers on his right hand fell to the ground, and he shrieked in pain. “Oh, I see you remember pain. Now how about this?” A few more hand movements, and next toppled his hand at the wrist, below the elbow, below the shoulder, and then his left foot. “Oh, I’m sorry. You wanted *me* to eat shit, was it? Anything else you want me to do before I remove your head? I will keep you alive and put you in a box back in the ground with your own prick stuffed into your mouth for a hundred years. How does that sound? As pleasant as eating shit to you?” Zyra was pissed with the man’s calloused and ill-chosen words.

“We will tell you nothing, bitch!”

Zyra opened her hand, and Galya placed two small, thin, blue crystal shards into her hand.

“Velvet, looks like I have more heads for you.” Zyra waved her hand, and his head came off. The body hit the ground and wiggled. She looked at the younger man beside him, and his head was severed as well—I hadn’t seen her move her hand. Asya and Galya picked up his head and placed one crystal behind the ear of each man.

“What can I say, two heads are better than one. Now, where were we, Mr.-Soon-To-Spend-A-Very-Long-Time-Locked-In-A-Box-With-His-Own-Prick-Stuffed-In-His-Mouth? Or better yet, each of you will enjoy each other’s prick in their mouth, you know, because you’re so tough. I think I’ll call that ‘Friends till the End.’” Zyra touched the blond one’s temple and entered his mind. “Thank you. I have all I need now. Enjoy your box. I will see you again someday.” She dropped his head face-first on the ground.

Galya said, “Kath, have someone dip his neck in wax and shove his buddy’s prick in his mouth. Put restraints in his mouth. We wouldn’t want him to chew on his new toy. Do the same for his friend and have two boxes made. Wait, one box with both of them in it. Thank you, Mistress Kath.” Galya handed Kath what looked to be three or four pieces of candy.

Zyra turned and walked over to the other two men. "Back to where you came from or a life like your friends?"

One man spoke for both, "The grave will do just fine, thank you kindly."

His buddy shook his head as well.

"Excellent, now this won't hurt a bit." She touched each man's face one at a time.

Asya said, "Oh my, this is a real problem. Now, all three witches have seen the minds of these four. We know that these four men acted not on their own, but instead worked for a master that controlled Molly's mind to try and steal the orb."

The blond man said, "Hey, witch, now you know what you were looking for. I hope my master finds you soon and fornicates your face to death."

But he didn't use the word *fornicate*, which set Zyra on fire with anger.

"Oh, really? Mr.-Soon-To-Be-More-Miserable-Than-You-Could-Have-Ever-Imagined. Enjoy this!" Then she kicked him like a ball, walked over to him, and kicked him again toward us. "Enjoying your return to life? Oh, I'm sorry. I seemed to have gotten you dirty. Let me help you clean up." Zyra undid her small dress slightly, pulling it up to squat over his face. She pissed all over his head. I could not help myself—I burst out laughing. It was the funniest thing I had seen so far. The man was full of curse words, some I had never heard before, but they seemed really foul.

"Slade, what is so funny?" Asya asked.

I did my best to calm myself. "She kicked him like a ball and pissed on his face."

"What would you have done?" Galya inquired.

"Nothing that awesome. I didn't even think anyone could use piss in a humorous way." I clapped for Zyra, and she took a bow for me.

Zyra said, "I will let you piss on him unless you're chicken. *Bok, bok, bok.*"

I accepted and stood over the male for a minute. He was cursing like a pirate, and I tried.

"Why are you wearing a dress? Are you a very ugly girl, or do you like men?"

"I'll have you know it's called a skirt, and it gives me easy access to doing this." I walked over to him and pulled myself out. "I can't go with you all gawking at me like that."

The blond man laughed at me. "Pussy!"

I heard someone yell, "Get on with it, you big baby."

I closed my eyes and thought of the waterfall. Then, I was pissing on a reanimated, foulmouthed imbecile's severed head.

As I finished, I said, "Sorry I got so much in your mouth. Honestly, I was trying to get more in your eyes." I stepped over his head and gave it a little kick. He called me a bastard, so I laughed and kept on walking.

Zyra spoke, "Kath, my sweet, you see that one with the foul mouth? After you do what I ask, I would very much like for you to have anyone you choose to shit in that box with them in it once every five or so days. I want them to know that I have feelings too, and he's being a big old shithead. Bye-bye, shithead. I will see you soon to do something even worse—well, when I think of it."

More curses flew from his mouth.

Kath asked, "Shall I do the same to his friend?"

The friend was praying to an unfamiliar god.

"No, his friend's prick in his mouth will do for now, so just stuff his mouth, wait, and keep his mouth free so he can talk shithead into insanity. Yes, that is what I want." Zyra walked up to the last two friends. "We have all we need from you. Thank you for your assistance. If you have anything you would like to add, this is the last chance you will ever get."

One of the men got on his knees. "Molly, I am so sorry that I lied to you. I am sorry I said my mother needed your help. I deserve my punishment, and I beg you, Lady Velvet: spare Molly. She was not in control of herself."

Molly unbuttoned her shirt, revealing a void. "Look at me! This is my fate for trusting you! I am like your friend over there. Nothing more than a head! Jacob, how long do you think you have been dead for?"

"I don't know. All I remember was the woman stabbing each of us. Then, it was my turn, and it hurt so much that I passed out. I woke up, so maybe five minutes, twenty at the most?"

Molly buttoned shirt and said, "Jacob, you have been dead and in the ground for almost three weeks."

"Excuse me, miss." He was addressing Zyra. "Why can't I remember where I was?"

Zyra replied, "The afterlife is a mystery. What secrets it holds is only known to the dead, and, son, you're temporarily alive. The great beyond will never give up its secrets, no matter how many we bring back."

"Thank you. Molly. Again, I am sorry." The man looked up at the sky, turned to the man beside him, and said, "Sam, I am sorry I took you on the wrong path in life. Mother and Father would have looked down on me for it. Forgive me, brother. I love you."

They hugged, and Sam said, "I love you." They held each other's hands and looked at Zyra. "Please, if you will. I don't deserve another minute of this beautiful day, but thank you for the chance to clear Molly's name and see my brother again. We're ready to die again."

Zyra said, "You have already been judged, so I will make this painless. Your words will hopefully shine on you wherever you return to. Now, take this." She handed each man a nice-sized gold coin. "Lie down and place this in your mouth. It will not be removed for an hour after you pass away. I give this to you so long as you tell Charon, the ferryman, that Zyra says hello."

Each man lay down, then placed the coin in his mouth.

"Dream well, boys." Zyra walked up to Velour and said, "They're yours. Send them back."

Velour touched their foreheads and murmured, "Back to sleep."

With that, both men were gone.

"Velour, I know your gift is unpleasant, but it's in the right hands, and today, I am proud of you." Zyra patted Velour on the back. "I have missed you, my little bunny rabbit."

"Lady Velvet, we three would like a word with you in private."

Zyra, Galya, Asya, and Velvet walked back into the house and into the Velvet's meeting room.

"Young lady, do you have something you would like to share with us? Mind you, I just pissed on a reanimated severed human head, so I would very much like only the truth!" Zyra was still a bit angry.

Velvet said, "Zyra, in all the commotion, I may have forgotten to mention that I located the Eye of the Void."

"Then why not tell us when the commotion died down?" asked Galya.

"I was trying to learn its secrets before you three could come and take it away. You're so secretive about items like that."

"You're damn right, we would've taken that dreadful thing away! Do you know how dangerous that thing is? Look what it drove them to do. Now five men are dead, one being your guard and your second, most trusted, who was wrongfully punished. The Eye of the Void is an incredibly dangerous thing that should only be handled by the likes of us. It should be hidden away and forgotten about. Thank the gods and goddesses you didn't awaken it."

"It was already awake when I received it. One of my rangers came back with it, and it was awake and started talking to me."

"What did it say?"

"It wanted me to bring it babies under six months old. The voice says it could give me things like power and knowledge. I became scared. I knew I should lock it up, so I did."

"Velvet, do you know what is in The Eye of the Void?" asked Galya.

Lady Velvet looked down and said, "No."

Galya said, "The legend goes, long ago, a witch gained the power of a demon, and all he obsessed over was how to gain more power until his dying day. Then, on that day, another demon traded him immortality for the lives of all his coven. He did so, and the demon placed him in that hand-sized orb. The only way he can reenter this world is have to a certain number of children, then the demon will be released, reborn in the flesh into an immortal body. Well, that's how the story goes because our mother wrote that story, and we passed it around to try and locate The Eye of the Void after it mysteriously disappeared. What is inside is much worse and far more dangerous than a demon. Now, I trust you still have it?"

Velvet turned around and opened a hidden space on the wall, bringing out a wooden box. Asya opened the box, and inside lay The Eye of the Void.

Zyra said, "Finally, we have it back." Zyra looked at Velvet. "Galya, Asya, take this wretched thing home, and lock it up before it influences anymore people."

Asya and Galya disappeared as Zyra and Velvet went back outside.

"Okay, people, are we ready to leave here soon? Do whatever you need now because we are on the road in thirty minutes. Slade, before we leave, I want you to bring me the coins from the dead men's mouths. Understood? Keep them and buy the ladies something nice with the money. Trust me, a nice gift is just as good as a kiss, and ladies love gifts. It shows you're thinking of them."

"Thank you, Zyra, but I have done nothing to earn those coins."

"Okay, you have a great point. When I signal, you go get those coins and bring them to me. I will find a task for you to complete so you may earn them. How does that sound to you?"

"Thank you, Zyra."

Zyra snapped, and thirteen Nightmares appeared and walked to their respective riders. "Molly, please ride with Asya so you two can talk about the man in the black hat."

Upon closer inspection, the Nightmares were black as night and full of muscle, larger than most horses. Their manes were so fine and black that it was like touching a cloud. They reacted to whatever their rider said as if they spoke our language. When I made my eyes black, I could see them as something strange: they were alive and not alive at the same time. They had a skeleton but no hearts or organs—truly something from beyond.

"Zyra, I don't remember meeting a man in the black hat, only a man's voice talking to Jacob the night we tried to get the orb. Jacob went into the other room to speak with him," said Molly.

Asya said, "Molly, we have what we need, and we now know who the man in the black hat is. So, let us finish this business at hand, then we can track down our target."

"I thought he was dead," Galya said.

Zyra sighed. "We all did, Galya, but now we know we were wrong. When I find him, he will be dead, even if I have to take him screaming to Hell, clenched in my arms."

"Zyra, when Bill finds out, he will join us, and we will overwhelm our target. Besides, it's been a good long while since we had to fight anyone, so I'm going to savor his pain." Asya laughed.

Galya insisted, "We should create an orb so that we can trap him!"

"Yes, we will create something like that out of a dragon's eye. It's something more akin to a prison, so he could never get out unless one of us releases him. Then, we will hide it forever, thus locking him away."

I asked Zyra, "Why not do what you did to those two men and lock him in a box as well?"

Zyra's responded, "He is kind of like us, and even as just a head, he would be extremely dangerous. By placing him in a magical sphere, he will not be able to access his powers, and his voice will enchant no one. So, you see, the sphere will be safer for all." She paused for a few moments. "On a different note, I want Molly with me because I think Sofia and Topaz are feeling a little neglected and require some attention from you. Now is the time for you to retrieve those coins for me."

"I understand now. Thank you, Zyra." I walked over to the corpses and pulled one gold coin from each of their mouths, delivering them to Zyra with a smile.

"Thank you, Slade. Now help me up onto this mighty steed and do the same for Molly."

I did not know how to help them, so I got down on my hands and knees, and each one stepped on my back to get on her horse.

Zyra said to Molly, "He's a true gentleman, a throwback to days long passed. Slade, give me your hand."

I gave it to her.

"Here, now you have earned one gold coin for the help you have given each of us. Now, run along and do the same for the other female friends who have just watched you do such a noble gesture."

I walked over to Sofia and got on my hands and knees. She stepped on me, and I did the same for Topaz.

When Topaz got on her horse, she said, "I like the way you look down on your hands and knees for us." She and Sofia began to laugh.

The way she'd said it was kind of funny. I mounted my horse, and we set out to our last stop.

I overheard the witches talking. Asya said, "It's not possible; it can't be him. He died. We all saw it."

"Asya, in our long lives, haven't we seen strange and amazing things? If anyone could beat death, it would have been Vorador," said Zyra.

Chapter 23

The Man in the Black Hat

On our ride, the talk was light and random. I couldn't seem to think about anything but what had just occurred. I wanted to know more about the man in the black hat, but I knew that it was not an appropriate time to ask. The ride was shorter than from the House of Whispers to the House of Dreams, as it only took about an hour before we arrived at the House of Thorns. The gate was large and made of iron, nestled between ten-foot stone walls. A guard said nothing as he opened the gate, and we rode in. As we approached the largest house, we stopped in front of a dirty man who was sitting down and eating an apple.

He stood up, opened his arms, and said, "Velour, Velvet. My daughters, I have missed your pretty faces."

Their father must have stood over seven feet tall with arms and legs like tree trunks. He had wild, dirty, reddish-blond hair that touched his shoulders and a long reddish-blond beard with hints of silver. I would guess that both daughters could have stood on his shoulders and he would scarcely notice their weight. We all dismounted, and he greeted those he knew before the rest of us. In my first few seconds of seeing the giant man, I understood how his gregarious attitude made him very approachable despite his mountainous size. His voice was deep and dark; his laugh was strong and loud; and he shook everyone's hand and addressed them as one would a king or queen.

Then, he came to me and said, "For those who may be new to my House, welcome to the House of Thorns. I am High Lord Dutch."

He looked at me for a long second, placed his hand on my shoulder, and held out his other hand. I placed my hand within his massive one, which was at least two times—if not slightly more—the size of mine. As he closed his hand around me, I watched mine disappear within his. He appeared more like a giant than a human.

"Boy, what is your name?" He leaned and sniffed me from ear to ear like a horse would. I didn't know what to say. "Boy, do you have a tongue?"

I nodded.

"Then speak your name, loud and proud!"

"My name is Slade."

"Where do you come from, Slade?"

"I come from the House of Dreams."

"Boy, I mean where do you live?"

"I live at the House of Ribbons."

"Slade of the House of Ribbons, you say?" He leaned over and sniffed me again while holding both my shoulders. He picked me up. "Slade, I can see you better now that we're eye to eye." His eyes were such a light crystal blue that I could have sworn they were made of ice. "Slade, where do you come from before my daughter's House? Did she buy you, and why are you wearing a dress?"

"That is something I cannot answer, my lord."

"Slade, were you dropped on your head as a child? Or, rather, would you like to, like, right now? Now tell me. Where do you come from?" He was not mad, but his voice was thick and scary.

"Lord Dutch, you have had your fun. Now put the young lad down before you make him piss himself, if he hasn't done so already." Asya's tone was not one I would expect from a tall yet thin woman making a demand of such a giant.

Lord Dutch asked, "Asya, my sweet. Where is this boy from? I want to know right now."

Asya smiled. "Then maybe inside will be the best place to talk, as this matter is sensitive. It is the reason we are all here. By the way, has Lady Silk arrived?"

"No, I don't expect her here for another hour or so. I will send a few riders out to see that everything is fine."

Zyra laughed. "Lord Dutch, I pity anyone that dare interfere with Lady Silk's journey. Now come. I'm thirsty, and I know you have excellent tea."

High Lord Dutch cradled me in his arms like a baby's ragdoll and walked off toward the house. I saw Sofia and Kailee doing their best to hide their grins as I was carried past them with a sideways view. High Lord Dutch's bicep was easily the size of my head. He walked us to a large hall with straight tables and set me down.

"Don't move, little man, or it's back in my arms you go."

Asya said, "High Lord Dutch, I would like to wait until your daughter is with us before we proceed. Trust me. You will understand why after. Meanwhile, will an old witch die of dehydration today?"

"Asya, for the love of all creation, stop calling me High Lord Dutch. That is a title I only use while hosting others that are not family. Please call me by my first name as my beautiful wife once did. Lord *this*, Lord *that*, so much so that I would almost forget my real first name. Besides, titles like that are for assholes who like their asses licked. With that being said, all in this room will now address me as Dutch until I say otherwise. Now, I will see about that tea. Hands up if you'd like some tea."

At least half the people in our group raised their hands. Dutch came back with his second in charge, Mr. Cyril.

Mr. Cyril announced, "Tea will be served shortly. I have taken the liberty of having sandwiches prepared for a small lunch, so as not to ruin dinner. The meal tonight will be turkey with all the trimmings."

Dutch said, "Mr. Cyril, come smell this boy."

Mr. Cyril walked over to me and sniffed. He stood back, looked around the room, and sniffed me again more deeply with his hands on both sides of my face just like Dutch had done.

"Witch! Is this some kind of joke?" Mr. Cyril looked at Asya. "Did one of you do this to the boy? If so, then it most certainly is not funny! Dutch, my oldest friend, this simply can't be. I mean, look at what he is wearing."

Dutch smiled. "Calm yourself, Mr. Cyril. I'm told that all will be explained when Silk gets here, and yes, I noticed what he was wearing. Now, until then, let me catch up with my beautiful daughters who I do not see nearly as often as I would like."

Mr. Cyril sniffed me again before walking off and mumbling. I got up to go sit with Sofia, Kailee, Molly, and Topaz. All leaned in for a sniff.

Sofia said, "Oh, you always smell so yummy, like edible flowers in full bloom that—"

I asked, "Can we just get this night over without anyone sniffing me again or any talk of sex? Because I feel I might explode with how you three smell."

Kailee said, "Slade, for the record, I bathed this morning." Then, she added, "Because of all the sex from last night, a little this morning, and a little while in the shower with Sofia." I tilted my head to one side, and she smiled. "What? I thought you should know that I like it in the shower, so remember that." Kailee was rubbing my leg while she spoke.

"Kailee, you're as beautiful as you are strong, but I see what you are trying to do. If I could stand right now, I would get up and walk over there with Asya and the others. But I see you just couldn't resist a bit of fun at my expense. What if Dutch the Giant asks me to come over to him?"

Topaz laughed. "No worries. He can just pick you up and cradle you in his arms like a small baby, like he has already done today." Topaz leaned over and kissed me on the cheek. "Hey, look at it this way. Dutch likes the way you smell, right? What if he falls for you the way we have? Oh no, I fear he would split you in two like a log. Good lord, I don't see you walking well after all that. No way will you be able to ride a horse with a sore bum." I received another kiss.

"Topaz, no way would he say or do something like that. That man is like a man and a large animal put together. He is a manimal, and the idea of him doing what you said is more than a bit frightening."

Topaz kissed my cheek again and said, "Good, now stand up."

"I see what you did. Well, it was better than when Lucy kicked me."

Topaz patted me on the back. "Lady Silk has just arrived, and tea and sandwiches are being served."

Lady Silk walked in and waved me over. "Slade, you look well. I hear you have been behaved and well-mannered. I thank you for that. Ah, Zyra, Galya, nice to see you."

Zyra said to Silk, "Molly is here. Why she is here can be fully explained later. Silk, promise us you will hold your tongue. Trust us on this. In the meantime, sit and eat with us. Tell us, how was your ride?"

"It went smoothly, as to be expected. I see my father is in a jovial mood as always, so that tells me that you have not told him about the boy or Molly. How is Molly sitting upright like that? What did you three do to her?"

"Ah! My last kitten is here. Silk, will you make this old man walk all the way to you?"

Silk stood up. "Hello, Father, you look enormous as always." Then she ran toward him, stepped on a chair then the table, and jumped into his massive arms. He cradled her like a baby, kissing her forehead many times.

"Wonderful! I have all but one of my favorite people under one roof, just like the old days." Dutch set her back on the table, and she retook her seat. "Everyone, thank you for being here today. For the reason, I know not yet, but still, I'm more than grateful to have my family together and with new people to get to know. Now, Zyra, Galya, Asya, and my daughters, please eat with me at my table and bring the boy because he's the reason we are all here today, am I right?"

Asya spoke first. "Yes and no."

Zyra went second. "Dutch, yes. At first, it was about the boy, Slade. But one more issue with a few things attached to the main issue has been discovered, and we owe our thanks to that discovery to Mr. Slade."

Galya waved Molly over and had her sit next to me.

Dutch said, "Hello, Molly, how have you been? I'm sure Reveka will be pleased to see you! She will be here shortly. She is standing in for the teacher who has given birth two days ago. A baby girl, a tiny little thing with golden locks, and I want the mommy to have all the time she needs to recover. Besides, Reveka is great with kids. When she is not terrifying the hell out of them with the crazy stories that she learned from you three, I might add. Oh, look at me, babbling on. Molly, why are you wearing gloves, and why are you are all bundled up with no exposed skin? Zyra, what is going on?"

"I think it best to show you. Molly, undo your buttons." Zyra looked around. "Dutch, please remain calm."

Molly opened her shirt, and Dutch covered his mouth.

"What in the unholy hell is wrong with her? Reveka is going to lose her mind when she sees this. You know how angry she can get." Then Dutch grabbed me by the back of the neck and slammed my head into the table.

Slade was out.

Asya jumped up. "Dutch! Why in hell did you do that to him? Have you gone insane?"

Dutch looked speechless. "Well, I put two and two together and—"

"Damn it, Father! You were never good at math. Oh, look what you did. I think you broke him!" Velour was upset as she held Slade's limp body in her arms. "I need a healer right now!"

"I'm sorry, my sweet. I did not think. I was simply overcome. He sure is a bleeder, isn't he? Mr. Cyril, a towel, please. Honey, give him to me."

"I think you have done enough, you big jackass." Silk pointed at her father.

"I said I was sorry. He does look dead. I hope he's not dead." Dutch nervously took a drink. He picked up Slade's right hand, but it slipped and fell, lifeless, to the table. "Oops, sorry about that. He's definitely going to need a healer or gravedigger, that's for sure."

Velvet yelled, "Damn it, Father! This is not a time to be funny! Give the boy some room before you breathe up all the air in the room and he suffocates."

Someone shouted, "Make way! The healers are here."

The two ran up and stood on either side of Slade, one male and one female—the twin healers, Demi and Caleb. Caleb bent down and placed his hand on Slade's face.

Dutch exclaimed, "I made a mistake!" He cleared his throat. "Demi and Caleb, please have Mr. Slade brought in the next room. Bring him to me the second he is awake and can say his own name. Save him, and I will have something for you both later."

Kailee walked up to Demi and said, "I will carry him for you."

Demi thanked Kailee. Sofia and Topaz escorted them to the next room.

Dutch noted, "They look unhappy with me. Why?"

Zyra told everyone to sit down and said, "Dutch, all three of those women want to be with Slade so much so that they are willing to share him with seven other women without any fighting."

"No, that is unheard of. You want me to believe that all those women would be willing to share that tiny man? What? Does he have a magic c—"

"Finish that sentence, Father, and I will climb all the way to the top of that thick head of yours and bite you on the ear," Velour snapped. "The very thought that you would use a word like that in front us and at a dinner table, no less? Shame on you, Father! Shame on you!"

Dutch looked around at the glaring women before him. "Well, I see that I have been rash twice in a row, so I apologize to those I have offended. I will apologize to Mr. Slade if he wakes up."

Silk squinted at her father. "You better hope he does."

Zyra knocked her cup on the table three times. "May I pick up where I left off? Good, I will start with Molly. Where did Molly go?"

Velvet said, "I saw her slip off when Father was being yelled at for trying to use a foul word at the table. My guess would be with Mr. Slade."

Zyra shook her head and rubbed her temples. "I might be getting too old for this shit. Okay, Molly's story first, and then I will tell you Slade's story. Try and be openminded, and if you have to ask a question, please raise one of your tree-like arms. You, of all people, know how much I hate to be interrupted."

Zyra began with Molly unexpectedly running away and finished with Slade finding out that Molly was under a strong spell. They'd discovered the identity of the man in the black hat.

Dutch raised his hand at the end of the story. "Are you telling me that you three rushed to judgment and made Molly into a walking abomination? Why would you do such a thing? Even under those circumstances, I would have still put her into the fire before damning her to a living head in a box. This, I find very disturbing, very disturbing indeed!"

"Dutch, had we burned her and the rest, we would not be aware of the man's continued existence. His name is Vorador. He used to be one of us, a true good guy, but his wife was murdered. He changed into a plague, and his only joy is collecting rare items and causing death. We had believed that he died a long time ago, but now we have proof he's alive. So, yes, nothing makes up for what we did to an innocent woman. Now all we can do is take care of her until a better option can be found."

"A better option? That girl is a walking head." Dutch sipped his tea from his oversized mug. "Have you thought of cloning her? The only problem is putting her head onto her clone body—would that even be possible?"

Asya leaned back. "That is a hell of an idea. I was just in a place not far from where they can now flash-clone a cow for food. It only takes two hours, and now the food production is so much faster."

"How would that help us? Whether it's two days or the standard two years, it will be a body, yes, identical in every way down to her DNA. But how to get Molly's mind from one body to another? Not even black magic has something like that, and Molly is not a magic user. It would take hundreds of years to study the spell, so that will not work." Galya tapped her fingers on the table while she thought. "We will come up with something. We have never had a problem like this, so we would have had no reason to solve it until now."

Zyra explained, "Keep an open mind, as we have yet to confirm or deny our story is fact or fiction. Asya will tell this story because she is the first of us to discover him."

Asya spoke, "It was Topaz and Silk who called me to look into the matter of a strange boy who seemingly appeared out of nowhere."

She spoke for a solid hour.

"Now, we are all on the same page, and we would like Reveka and each of the three Houses of oracles to combine with us in a way for something we have never tried before. We all will enter Slade's mind and scour every part of his mind for any clue that might have been left behind, accidentally or otherwise."

Dutch said, "I think I'm going to need something much stronger to drink to wash that story down. Look, I can almost believe anything because I have seen things that I would only tell you six about, lest I sound like a mad man, but that boy being some kind of god? Look at how easily I knocked him out. So, we can rule out that he's Hercules reborn."

Zyra said, "Don't be stupid, Dutch. Not everything is about strength. After all, he's a boy. For all we know, he was born right before Sofia found him, so that would make him less than twenty days old. But what is time to the gods? Nothing, nothing at all. Either way, we need to know where he came from, determine what type of gifts he has, and which direction we should take him in, if any. I will admit, if he is an oracle, he is a unique being, seeing as he is male."

"Fine. Dinner is in five hours. Will that be enough time?" Dutch looked at his daughters and smiled.

"That will be four hours more than needed." Zyra then asked, "Why before dinner?"

"Because, my beautiful family, between the two stories I have heard today, I want to enjoy tonight's celebration like it will be my last. That means bring out the magic wine you three made for me last year. Not to mention, if you find what you seek in the boy, it will be like he is the guest of honor. I am the lord of this House, so I set the rules as long as they are okay with my princesses. Now, let us see how Mr. Slade is doing."

They all walked into the room, and Dutch asked, "Demi, how is my guest?"

She looked at Dutch. "I am sure he was fine before you caused his brain to bounce around inside his skull, but Molly says she has spoken to him inside his mind. He's a little confused and is having trouble controlling his body. He keeps calling for someone named Batch?"

Asya looked at Molly. "Is it true? Is he calling for Batch?"

Molly responded, "Yes, but it is like he is super confused and not all there. He's foggy, almost asleep in his own mind. He's going to need some more time. Who is Batch?"

Asya looked at Topaz. "You will find out soon enough. Topaz, can Batch see and hear me?"

Topaz nodded.

"Batch, stop being a dumbass, and get in there and help the poor boy out."

Topaz bent down and kissed Slade on the lips, then stood up and backed away.

"Topaz, is that how he transfers between minds?"

"No, any touch will do. I was just hoping he would wake up and take me in his arms." Topaz sighed.

Dutch laughed. "Like in the fairytale books I used to read to my sweets angels. Yeah, she ate some poison grapes and slept for a long time."

Asya suggested, "We should give Batch some time to work with Slade."

Dutch said, "I don't remember you saying anything about Batch in your story about Slade."

"Because it would have made you more confused than you are now." Asya mumbled something to herself. "Trust us, we know what we are doi—"

Slade's arm flew up, and his hand grabbed Asya's wrist, who shrieked and jumped back, sticking to the wall like a spider. Everyone laughed.

"Gods damn it, Slade! You almost caused me to die of fright!" Asya climbed down as I sat up.

"Asya, I know how to fix Molly. Molly, come here." Molly walked over to me, and I kissed her deeply. "Now, Molly, sit down and speak with Batch. He will fill you in as I do the same here. Asya, I heard you say flash clone and that it works in two hours."

Asya looked stunned. "How do you know that? You have been unconscious for almost an hour."

"My body was, but I was right next to you the whole time. I heard everything, and, Lord Dutch, no need to apologize. It is I who am thankful to you because I did not know that I could leave my body while asleep. But back to Molly. Molly, give Batch back to Topaz when you two are done. Yes, about Molly… I think Batch and I together can move Molly's mind into a clone body. If they flash-clone her body, that mind will be in the infant stage. If I'm correct, then she would be free to take it over and suppress the inferior infant mind."

"That makes sense, but how do you know you can move Molly's consciousness?" Galya had a great question.

"The same way I left my body, then returned. Although I only have one body, I have two consciousnesses, and one can freely move from mind to mind, living outside the main mind. But if I leave my body, I must return to it to live. Molly would leave her body, then enter into her clone body because both are her bodies, her mind. She should be able to control the new body effortlessly."

Zyra said, "But she can't leave her body like you can. So how will that work? Besides, when did you learn astral projection? That is what you call the action of leaving your body, moving from place to place, and returning to it. It's a skill that takes many years to learn."

"Batch and I should be able to help her. She leaves her mind all the time when she enters another person's mind, and I know what you are going to say: she will return to her body when the physical connection is broken. This is the best part." I asked for water and drank it. "Without the physical connection, she will be stuck inside her own new mind. That is when Batch and I help her gain control. She might not even need any help, and there you have it, with a pretty pink ribbon on top. As for what you call astral projection, I took the time to learn what time is inside the mind. In the book Asya gave Batch, there is a story of how Asya left her body by imagining a door, so that is what I did. Then, I was free of my body."

Zyra said, "Slade, you're either batshit crazy or a genius. Only time will tell."

"Thank you, Zyra. I hope that I at least meet one of those expectations."

Molly kissed Topaz, and I could tell by Topaz's smile that Batch was with her.

Asya said, "Just keep being you, and everything will be great. So, we will put a pin in the Molly clone issue and address the meeting of the oracles. As for the story, you misinterpreted it. It was about freeing the mind from pain, not astral projection. I clearly would have used astral projection in the title. So that means he was taught that before Sofia discovered him, and my story led him to rediscover one of his abilities. He could have all sorts of hidden talents locked away. Ah, look who has arrived. Hello, Reveka."

"Hello, Asya, Galya, Zyra. I see the oracles from every House are here. I take it you have something interesting planned?" Reveka stood at five foot seven with small dark-blue eyes, wavy light-brown hair, and fair skin. "I know everyone in this room but you, boy." She extended her hand. "Don't be rude, boy. I won't bite."

Asya stopped me from shaking her hand. "Reveka, you may not want to do that just yet. He is not like anyone you have ever met. You could lose yourself to him, if not prepared."

Reveka laughed. "Asya, you almost had me there for a minute."

Asya said in a strong tone, "I'm not joking."

Reveka looked at me, then back at Asya. "Really? Look at him. He is what, eighteen? Barely a man *and* wearing a dress. His face is as smooth as my ass. So, *lose myself* to him? I think not. I bet you three gold coins that I could make him bark like a dog within ten seconds of entering his mind, and when I win, I would also like a piece of candy or two, if you so doubt my skill."

"You're on, but if he wins, he tells you what he wants." Asya looked excited. They loved to bet on all types of crazy things.

Reveka looked me in the eyes. "You have a deal, Asya. Slade, I'm going to make you my doggy. Then, I'm going to name you Spot, and you will lick my boot like a good dog."

Asya asked Reveka to wait in the other room, and we would join her there. "Slade, Reveka and I have this thing where we are always one-upping each other. I will give you one gold coin and two pieces of candy if you do what you do and turn her into one of your followers."

"Asya, with all due respect to Sofia, Topaz, Sunako, and the rest, please don't make me do this. Even I will admit that I have too many ladies who want to be with me, and that is a bit hard to take in. Plus, I can't sleep with any of them, and they are always having sex in front of me. I feel like I am going to explode, but I have to draw the line, if not for me, then for Sofia and the rest."

Asya thought for a minute. "Sofia, please call in every woman you know who wants to sleep with Mr. Slade."

Sofia was gone for a few seconds and returned with the ladies.

"Hello, ladies. Please raise your right hand if you desire at least one night with Mr. Slade. If you do not raise your hand out of embarrassment, then I will not allow Mr. Slade to entertain you in that way. I hope I am clearly understood. Now, all that I want from you is to raise your hand."

Sofia, Topaz, Saffron, Cyan, Molly, Kailee, and, last but not least, Lady Velour.

"My own daughter?" Dutch looked upset as he looked at me. "You better turn out to be a god, or you and I are going to have a problem in the arena."

"Ladies, I have asked you into this room because I have asked Mr. Slade to take Reveka down a peg or two because you know how she can get. But it involves him kissing her neck in a way where she will fall for him. He does not want to do it out of respect for all of you and the four who are back at the House of Ribbons. Would any of you have a problem with that? Raise your hand if you do. No one will be upset."

Sofia, Topaz, and Kailee's hands rose into the air.

"Ah, I see. How about I give each of you two pieces of candy right now? Would that change your mind?" Asya laughed. "Would that sweeten the deal?"

The three hands went down, and all seven held out their hands for candy.

"Please, Sofia, remind me that I owe the four back at your place two pieces each. Now, Slade, you have the blessing of your harem. Please go out there and do your thing for me."

I said, "I hope these candies are worth it."

Zyra chuckled. "Son, you have never had anything like these candies—they're out of this world."

I smiled and looked at the ladies who I'd become fond of. "If the candy is as sweet as the lips I have already tasted, then I will enjoy it, but I don't imagine a piece of candy could compare to the love of beautiful women."

All the ladies simultaneously swooned and gathered around me.

"Okay, cut the shit. You have a contest to win. Remember, you're to block her from your library and give her that kiss thing you do." Asya took my hand and stood me up.

Everyone in the room walked out and into the other room. I was last to enter. Everyone took a seat.

"Oh, I see you want an audience. Your confidence in this boy is maybe misplaced, or is this another one of your bluffs? Either way, I will collect my prize, so please, do have it ready." Reveka smiled and winked at Asya. Asya had no expression and no taunt to offer.

"Oh, Asya, pride goeth before the fall." She winked and made kissing noises.

I walked by without looking at her. "Hello, Reveka. I have heard many great things about the House of Thorns, but for some reason, your name was nowhere in any of those stories. Either way, now is the time to train you good and proper."

I might have crossed the line with that one because she slapped me with the back of her hand so fast, I didn't have time to react. No one had informed me she had the gift of speed.

"Can someone close a window? There seems to be a draft in here."

Reveka slapped me two more times with lightning speed, and with that, I was done talking shit for the moment. I swore I had tasted my blood more than I'd tasted kisses. Reveka reached out her hand, and I took it. The game had begun.

I imagined a field with lots of flowers.

"Hello, boy. I'll make it quick. You will wake up and lick my boots, and when I ask you to stop, you will bark and follow me around on all fours until I snap my fingers. Do you understand?"

"Yes, Reveka."

"Good. Now I will count to three, and we will be back in the main hall. One, two, three."

We were back in the hall, and Reveka looked at Asya and commanded me to get on all fours, so I did.

"As you can see, Asya, I have won. Your boy is my dog now. Pity he isn't flexible enough to lick his own balls, or I would have him do so. Spot, sit!"

I sat.

"Now lick my boot, you overgrown rat."

I began to laugh. "Overgrown, you say?"

I had a marvelously wicked idea. I changed my form into that of a wolf and grew until I was too large to leave the room and big enough to swallow her whole. As Reveka backed up and fell on her backside, covering her face, I growled and drooled all over her.

I said in a deep, gravelly voice, "You're almost too small to eat, but a snack is better than nothing."

Reveka stood up and tried to run, but as she did, I popped back into my human form and swept up from behind her. "When you open your eyes, I will snap my eyes black, and you will kiss me whether you want to or not."

I then made the ground disappear, and we both fell. I disconnected us. I snapped my eyes black, and immediately, Reveka was in my arms. I kissed her neck, her arms wrapped around my back. She went limp, with only a smile showing any trace of life. When I was done, I gently placed her on the table, but before I could wipe my mouth, Topaz was kissing me.

Asya started clapping, then the others did as well. "Slade, let us see what you did."

All three witches placed their hands on my arm, and after a few seconds, removed them.

"My, you're a clever boy—very scary, indeed. The way you used her fear of wolves against her—but will she want you when she wakes up?"

Dutch asked, "What was that? Did you bring a vampire into my great House? You know they live by their own rules, and to invite one into one's home courts disaster."

"Calm down, Dutch. Look for yourself. Is there blood on his mouth or on her neck?" Galya pointed to Reveka.

"But look at his eyes! He must be a—"

"But nothing!" Asya coldly cut Dutch off. "He just drained a little energy from her, caused her great fear, and then overwhelmed her with emotion." She laughed. "Come on, Dutch. We have matters to discuss."

At that moment, Reveka sat up.

Zyra asked, "Reveka, how do you feel?"

Reveka looked over Zyra's shoulder at me. "Are all of you mad? You dare bring a filthy Skinwalker into this House and play him off like he's normal? That's why he smells the way he does. To lure people to their death!"

Zyra said, "My dear, what you saw took place in his mind. It was not real."

Reveka walked up to me. "So, you were in control the whole time?"

I held up my hand and went to snap my fingers, but Reveka's speed had her fingers around mine instantly.

"No need for that because I want to kiss you. Anyone who can frighten me that way merits a kiss from me."

We kissed, and she put real passion into it. In my mind, we talked, and she told me that I was the first man she had ever kissed and how I was invited to her room after dinner and to bring my friends. Our kiss came to an end. As we looked one another in the eyes, Asya killed the moment by thrusting her open hand between our faces, opening and closing it rapidly.

"Can someone enlighten me as to what a Skinwalker is?"

"It's a human who can change into one or more animals. Their kind are very secretive."

Asya happily said, "I believe the bet has been won. I am the victor, so get on with it." Asya raised her voice, making it deeper. "Render unto Caesar the things which are Caesar's."

Reveka stepped back without breaking eye contact with me and reached into her pocket. Then, there were one, two, three clinks as the gold coins fell into Asya's hand.

Reveka, still locking eyes with me, said, "Asya, I'm sure I will have a chance to win at least one back before you leave. Oh, and, Slade, this will be continued after dinner. Those eyes are beautiful, and I hope to see more of them." She turned and sat down by Dutch.

Asya placed her arm around me and said, "Fine work, my boy. I am proud of you. Here you are: one gold coin and two pieces of enchanted candy. They're worth at least ten pieces of gold for one piece of candy, so eat it, cash it in for gold, or buy a few favors with it, but I urge you to try at least one. You suck on them; don't try to bite them. Just let them slowly dissolve in your mouth. Some put it in the cheek for a half hour at a time and then keep it in a jar for later because they never go bad. So, enjoy what you have earned because you're very impressive, but those eyes—change them back before you scare someone."

I told Asya, "I have three gold coins and my original silver one, but I never want to spend that one. So, what do I do with this money?"

"Slade, hold onto your money. You will have everything you need when you need it, but we will take you to a place that you could buy some gifts for your many loves. Now, I have some business to attend to. I'll call on you in two hours, so remember the rules: no sex, but you may watch. Ladies, come to me, please. May I have all the oracles over here for a head count? Good, all seven of you will be needed in about two hours, so I suggest a nap because the task at hand might be draining. I know dinner will be a hell of an event. Oh, and one rule. I will tell you all, and this goes for both oracle and non-oracle: Slade is off-limits sexually. He may watch, but that is all. Please, ladies. Do this one thing I ask. He may be all yours soon enough. Thank you, my sweets." Asya turned and walked toward Dutch.

He pointed at himself, tapped his eye, then pointed at me.

"Sofia, what does this gesture mean?" I showed her.

"It means 'I'm watching you.' Why? Who did that to you?"

"Dutch did," I said.

She laughed. "Well, good luck with that then. Come on. Reveka is taking us for a relaxing dip in the meditation pool, kind of like the one at the House of Dreams. I hear this one is really big, and there are crystals in the rock walls that flicker with soft lights." Sofia took my hand, and we followed the group. "Slade, how are you doing with all this stuff? It must seem a little crazy to you."

"Thank you for asking, Sofia, and yes, it does feel a bit odd, but I'm getting used to the feeling. I keep hoping that I'll see or hear something familiar, anything that will ring a bell."

Sofia added, "I really like how you stood up for that poor girl, Molly. I really hope you and Batch can help her with the clone body, mind-swap. Every day, I find a new reason to want you, and not just in the sexual way. I'm thankful that I found you because I feel you're going to do great things, and you make me feel loved."

We stopped walking.

"Sofia, I want you to know that it's you I think of the most. I love talking with you, and you make me feel safe and wanted. Thank you for being the one who found me."

"Slade, who do you miss second? Come on now. You can tell me anything."

"Sunako. I miss Sunako, and I miss Cheri a little as well."

Sofia smiled. "Cheri is a raspberry. Bitter at first, but then they become very enjoyable. Besides, she doesn't really want you, and that means more time for Sunako and me—that girl is over the moon for you."

We reached the meditation pool, and the ladies undressed and got in the water. I did the same, and the water was warm. We enjoyed small talk, and a few jokes were told with ensuing laughter.

Before the hour had ended, Asya, Zyra, and Galya arrived and announced, "Ladies, we will soon begin. I would like all the oracles to come outside with us. Slade, you will remain in the water. Sofia, Kailee, please move to the other side, and when we start, you must remain silent and touch no one in the group."

They all went outside.

"Slade, give us a kiss before they do whatever it is they're going to do."

"Sofia, are you just using this as an excuse to get a kiss?"

Sofia smiled and said, "Can you blame me?"

"Sofia, if you ever want a kiss, just do it. I will never say no. Kailee, same goes for you."

They both smiled and kissed me. They didn't know it, but I felt very loved, which helped keep unwanted thoughts away.

Asya and the rest walked back in. All the oracles entered the water, and Topaz took my hand, leading me to the middle of the pool. Asya, Galya, and Zyra undressed, and I noticed that Zyra had a tattoo from her collarbone down to her left knee. It was of a vividly colored snake that wound from her knee to almost her neck. Asya and Galya had tattoos as well but on their backs.

"Slade, we are going to have you float on you back while we each place our hands on you. This may feel different or even uncomfortable at times. Don't struggle if it gets weird with so many people inside your mind at once."

"Asya, you said that you have never done this before—is it safe?" I asked.

Asya smiled as she looked at me. "That is because we have never had the need to do this before today. So, it could get a little dicey with all these consciousnesses inside your mind at once. Ladies, inspect every part of his being. Review every moment of his life twice. Attempt to find anything that might have been hidden. Some trace of his old life must be in there somewhere, so find it, and be careful because, like I said, we have never done this before. We'll meet in Slade's library and start there. No one goes into anyone else's mind for any reason, and that goes for you, Slade and Batch. Topaz, can Batch hear me?"

Topaz nodded.

"Good. Batch, I expect you to be standing next to Slade the whole time in case I need you. Reveka, please start the fire and burn this in it."

Reveka walked over to a large metal bowl, where she placed something in it.

"What is she doing?" I asked.

Topaz said, "That is incense. She will make it burn, and it will fill the air with a nice smell. For most, it helps to relax as we meditate, so lay back and relax your mind, but try to stay between awake and asleep. Now, watch what she is about to do."

Reveka's arms shot out into the air. "Please hear my plea, oh great Pasithea, daughter of Dionysus. Help us reach the state of true meditation, so we can see clearly see the will of the fates. We seek answers about the boy named Slade."

Asya looked at Sofia. "You and Kailee might need to bring one of us to the sides of the wading area in case anyone lets go and slips under the water while appearing asleep. Don't try to wake that person. Just prop them up." Each woman placed a hand on my body.

"Okay, everyone ready? Reveka, you're the last one. Yes, just grab his ankle. We go in three, two, one. Okay, is everyone here? Nine. And I'm ten. Good, we are all here. Ladies, for those of you who have not met him, this is Batch. He is a part of Slade, but Batch is a separate consciousness. The two work in tandem, with Slade being the primary controller and Batch being able to come and go as he pleases."

"Batch can gather information in a way that Slade can later integrate into himself. Batch and Slade are identical in appearance, but they are different in speech and thoughts. This is an ability that has never before been witnessed, and he may be the first and only male oracle. So, he is unique with unique abilities, so we're here to see if there has been anything that has been left behind. This will also determine if he is a true oracle, and we have all had the test to determine if you're an oracle. So, go find me something because no one ever does a perfect job when they try to suppress a memory or memories."

"Asya, it feels cramped in here. It feels like a headache, and I can hear everyone's thoughts. Their voices all at the same time are too loud. I don't like this."

Asya said, "Slade, relax. You are safe. Three of the ten in here have love for you, and we three love you like a son."

Zyra laughed. "Yes, like a short son with a weird mind twin."

Galya looked at me. "Don't look at me like that. Slade, you're, at best, a nephew that I don't want to take care of because you're a boy and you pee standing up. That is strange to me."

Zyra and Asya looked at her.

"What? You all put me on the spot!" Galya smiled at me. She looked like it was probably her first time smiling.

Asya said, "Don't mind Galya. She hates most people. So, Batch, how have things been lately?"

Batch floated above the ground by a foot to meet their eyes. "Good. My small trip into Molly's mind was a bit of a horrific eye-opener and a huge reminder to never upset you. She has terrible nightmares, and if she could, it would have made her piss herself. You should be greatly ashamed of your actions. I, like her, am very grateful she was not executed because now we know the man behind her mental hijacking. I would very much like to get close to Mr. Vorador."

Asya sighed. "Slow your roll, Batch. We don't know each other well enough for you to chastise us. Vorador has kept his existence a secret for more than two hundred years. So that makes him good at hiding, and he is ruthless. He will slaughter many to get what he wants. Vorador thinks that those with power should rule those without power, and those who do not bend to his will should die."

Galya said, "He's also known as Vorador the Ruthless. We don't know how he escaped death. He was a good man until someone killed Isacay, his wife. Then he went mad trying to repeatedly bring her back. He found the most unholy book called *Naturom Demento*, a terrible grimoire that showed him the way to feel the Eye of the Void. On his last day with us, he grabbed hold of the orb with his bare hands. He began to scream, and he vanished. Then the orb settled on the ground, seemingly inactive, and we thought it had consumed him. Within that same year, it had disappeared without a trace until now."

I asked, "Galya, what is a grimoire?"

"A grimoire is a book of spells. We all have a few, but the *Naturom Demento* is one of the five worst grimoires in the history of magic. If it can be found, we might be able to lock it away because to read from it is to court one's own doom. No bargain can be made with any demon from that book, and they say the demons from that grimoire are not even from this dimension."

I laughed. "Who said that? Because it sounds like an old wives' tale."

Zyra calmly looked at Batch and me. "Abaddon himself told us that. He abhors that cursed, indestructible grimoire. He said that elder gods created that book to use people to help them breech their way into this world."

Batch said, "Slade and I thought that was a made-up story. The one about Abaddon and Kael."

Zyra laughed. "No, my child, they're very real, and if you are what we think you are, Abaddon and Kael will be asked to examine you next."

I said, "Wait. In my very short time since I woke up, I have heard some of you talk about many gods and then one God. Which is it? Because I have to say, it all sounds a bit contradictory to Batch and me—we only seek to understand. How can there be many gods and goddesses but only one God? Is that God a king of the gods?"

Asya nodded. "Slade, I explained this to you already, but I see you might have been too drunk. I will have to explain all of that later. Trust me. You will understand when we are done. Ah, I see Topaz and Molly have returned."

The rest showed up seconds apart from each other.

"Speak up if you have found anything at all."

Molly said, "I found a book that was blank. Now, look what happens when you open the book, then hold it upside down and face-down and shake it." Molly handed Zyra the book.

Zyra did it, and a slightly smaller book fell out of the book. "Well, shit, I have never seen that before: a book within a book. Mr. Slade, aren't you full of wonders!"

Asya picked it up. "The title says *My Fears,* then it lists things you're afraid of. Slade, I think you wrote this book as a child."

I stated, "Go on then. Show me a fear."

Asya created a swam of spiders that began to crawl onto me.

"Really?" I just stood there with my eyebrow raised.

Asya held up a finger. Then, a dog-sized creature appeared with the head of a baby, the body of a dog, and the tail of a snake; the dog's feet were made of small cat heads.

"Asya, that thing is hilarious! How could I ever be afraid of something that makes me laugh so hard?" I walked over and patted it on its baby head, and it whistled like a bird. "I have got to get me one of these things."

"Slade, this book has to belong to you because it has a picture of you on this page, only younger. I think you're afraid of yourself. Well, this doesn't make sense at all. Did anyone find anything else? No? Then, everyone, grab a book and shake it. There might be more mini books."

A few minutes later, three more books were found, totaling to four.

Zyra read all three in a flash and stopped halfway thought the last book. "Asya, Galya, look at this."

All three looked up at me.

"Slade, you saw Sofia, Topaz, Sunako, and Molly before you ever met them. I wonder why you drew them with wings. Sunako and Molly, I understand, but Sofia and Topaz? This can mean only one thing: Slade must be an oracle. He must have hidden this memory in this mini book then inside this book he called *Nocte Mater*. Who taught you how to use his *Lumina Noctem*? Slade, do you understand it when I say *Lumina Noctem* and *Nocte Mater*?" She handed me the book.

I smiled. "Of course; it's Latin. *Nocte Mater* for 'Night Mother,' and *Lumina Noctem* for 'Eyes of the Night.'"

"When did you know you could speak Latin?" Zyra asked.

"I've always known. You never asked."

"I believe we have all the proof we could ever ask for," Asya said.

I asked Asya, "Could that have been planted there for someone like you to find?"

Galya said, "Not likely. I believe you hid these books because you knew that you were going to lose most of your memories, and these three books meant something. They're so valuable that you were in great fear that you would lose them forever. The fears book might have been when you first learned to hide a book within a book, and you hid this book to have no fears of anything within this book. Clever, very clever. So, this book has the four ladies in it. They are only drawings, but there is no doubt who they are. Molly is on the page before as just a head. Look here: all the drawings are black and white, but look at this one. It's a woman standing in fire. She is colored red with black wings and a tail, and she looks like a demon. These drawings are so lifelike."

Molly came over and saw herself in the book. "Slade, we were destined, as was Sofia, Sunako, and Topaz. Two oracles and two regulars, but who is the demon? Zyra, how could he have seen so far into the future if he did this as a child?"

Zyra was just as shocked as everyone else. "I don't know, honey. Maybe his people are greatly gifted with sight. These books only raise more questions than answers."

Asya said, "He has to be from the gods. I mean, come on. He can speak Latin for crying out loud. That language has been dead for so long that maybe ten people in the whole world can read and speak it outside of us witches. Yet he did it with ease. We all know that Latin is one of the preferred languages of the gods, if what the books say are true."

Zyra laughed. "Speaking of dead Earth languages, don't forget Sumerian. There isn't a chance in Hell he knows that language."

I made a tablet appear, and I handed it to her. In perfect Sumerian, I smiled and said, "There must be many chances in Hell."

All three stood, shocked.

"Slade, who are you?" Asya moved closer. "How could he possibly know how to write in cuneiform, let alone speak Sumerian? We only know a few dozen sentences between us. It's a truly dead language, but he spoke it like it's the common tongue. Slade, tell me how you know Sumerian."

"I don't know. It just came to me when you said Sumerian. I wonder what else I know."

"He is a mystery, and I'm more uncomfortable now that I know he knows things we do not." Galya continued, "Slade, this book is your Latin language book, but the fourth book is in a language we have never seen before. Slade, what does it say?"

I looked at it. "I feel like I know the name of the language, but it escapes me now. I can tell you what the cover says: *A Guide to the Many Paths*. The first page reads, 'Not one world, but many. Beyond the gods, beyond time, beyond yourself, lies many faces that stare back at you the same. Four mirrors pointed at one another becomes an infinite. Find the House of Many Doors and become a true son of the Fates. Become their hammer and build. Become their scythe, and harvest souls when called to do so. Become the historian and teach. Kill with impunity but beware the House of Isolation and the rooms of madness. This House, you will build after the death of countless billions. Stay your hand when angry; control your anger. Never lash out in blindness unless prepared to feel a pain unending. Herald a change, and escape the path.' Asya, my eyes—I can't see. What is happening to me?" My mind was shaking and rumbling. "Asya, please help me. I feel sick."

Batch and I fell to our knees and were pulled into the floor by shadow hands.

Zyra screamed, "Everyone, get out now! His mind has become unstable."

Black, shadowy hands emerged from the walls and floor and started to grab some of the women.

Reveka yelled, "Asya, I can't disconnect!"

Molly said, "Me too! I'm stuck!"

Diandra screamed, "Get it off me! It's pulling me in." She was being tugged into the floor.

The other women disconnected. It took Asya, Galya, and Zyra everything they had to pull Molly, Reveka, and Diandra away from the shadowy hands.

"Ladies, is everyone okay?" Zyra looked at each woman.

They all nodded, but each woman who had been grabbed had a fiery red handprint. They added that they were frightened by what happened.

"Let's relax for an hour, and he should be okay by then. I hope."

Galya said, "He looks dead, and he's barely breathing. Should we leave him like this? What were those hands?"

Zyra said, "I don't know what they were… maybe a learned self-defense to stop people from doing what we were doing? What can we do? I have no clue what just happened in there, let alone what is happening to him right now."

"Slade, where did everyone go? They were just here."

I said, "I don't know, but you know how strange they are. One minute here, gone the next. On the bright side, I don't feel sick."

"Slade, this is something really great. We're so much closer to finding out who we are, but I swear I saw some shadow hands."

"Batch, I don't care who I was. I care about who I will become, and I like who I am right now. Yeah, I saw the hands, too. It must be a memory of Silk's shadows, and to be honest, her gift freaks me out. We were not meant to find these books; we hid them for a reason. Whoever I or we were stole and hid it away as a defiant gesture.

Whatever was taken away from us was done for a reason. Maybe I was bad, or this is a mission. This could be a reward for a job well-done. I mean, look around us: we have everything we could ever want. All I know is I want to be Slade, the person who woke up in Sofia's arms, and, Batch, I know how you feel about Topaz. Don't you want the same?"

Batch paced around. "I want to know the truth above all else! I want to know why there are two of us, and why I can leave while you stay behind. How can there be two of us? How can I be self-aware of my own wants separate from yours? I don't know if I am a reflection of you or if I were created to live in your mind for some purpose, but what would that be? I only know what you can recognize when I am with Topaz or when I hop into someone like Molly. I'm just a ghost without a body of my own. I feel like I am just a ride-along. If that is the case, then where is my body? Were there two of us at one time?"

I thought about that for moment. "Wow, the thought of it. There could have been two of us, and now we are together in one body. Wait… Molly! Molly is the answer to this question. If you want a body, then we can get you a flash clone. You and I can help Molly into her new body, and then we help you in one of your own. *Boom*! We're separate. I mean, if that is what you really want, because I want what you want."

Batch looked at me. "You would do that for me? Then you would lose the way we can gather information really fast."

"Batch, we can't lie to one another. Of course, I would do that. Plus, having all these women is going to really wear me out. Half will want to be with you anyway, but you have to take Cheri. She is a little too mean for me."

"Slade, I was going to say the same about her. You have to take her or no deal."

"Okay, but you owe me one. Time to wake up. Wake up, Batch. Our body is not responding."

"Hold on, let me see what I can do. Bad news, I'm not able to wiggle a finger. It must be the body; it must have been too much with all those people in here. We have no choice but to wait it out."

***

Everyone was starting to wake up.

Asya asked, "How is Slade doing now? Any better?"

Sofia said, "He is still asleep, and he won't wake up. What is wrong with him?"

"I don't know. We will just have to let him wake up naturally." Asya climbed out of the water. "When he wakes up, get him dressed, and bring him to the main house. No dillydallying, okay?"

Sofia gave a thumbs-up. Everyone got dressed and walked out into the fresh, cool air.

A young girl was waiting for them. "Asya, your guests have arrived and are waiting for you in the main dining hall." The young girl curtsied and ran off.

"Good, Galya, your favorite wizard is here. No doubt, he will be as charming as always."

Galya rolled her eyes. "That guy, I tell you. Always finds a way to piss me right off. He is such a lecherous old fool."

"Yes, that is true, but he is most trustworthy and honest. Ladies, we will see you all at dinner. Thank you so much for your work. You will all be rewarded tonight."

The ladies went their separate ways to get ready for dinner.

"Asya, I think this was a great time for the girls. They each did very well and should be proud of themselves," said Zyra.

Galya said, "I agree. They should be rewarded."

Asya looked up and spoke, "They did a wonderful job. Gathering together like that all in one mind, and no one pushed for dominance? We have done well with each young lady. Now, let's get ready for the talk before dinner."

Chapter 24

Old Friends and a Sharp Tongue

Zyra said to Galya, "Please do try to be nice to Bill for the time being, or at least, remain calm if he upsets you."

"I'll try my best, Zyra. Thank you for your concern."

The three headed to the main dining hall, and the smell of roasting turkeys hung thick in the air. The doors were already open, and the three sat and waited. Before they drew another breath, Dutch walked in with Bill and his lifelong friend, Asimov, who was a favorite and dear friend of all three.

Asya yelled, "Asimov, you old, back-alley card shark! It has been too long a time. I am grateful that Bill could reach you. You look well. How have you been?"

Asimov looked at Asya. "I'm well, but I think you three have grown younger and more beautiful. Now come. Let these arms remember you three."

One by one, they hugged Asimov.

Bill opened his arms and coughed. "Sorry, ladies, I must have accidentally made myself invisible, but now that you can see me, I will receive my hugs now."

"Go hug yourself, you old charlatan. I wouldn't hug you if I found out I was your mother." Galya threw her shoe at Bill. "Here you go. Hug that, you deviant old fool."

Bill laughed as he picked up the shoe. "Ah, Galya, one day you will see that your blind hatred for me was clouding your judgment. I know, deep down, you yearn to hold me in your arms, but you're afraid to show your true feelings. I'm fine with waiting for you, my love." Bill took a deep sniff of Galya's shoe. "My sweet, maybe you can throw your panties next?"

Zyra caught Galya in midair as she leaped at Bill. "Will you two stop your jabs for a second? I swear, you two are acting like stubborn asses. Do you think Dutch appreciates such bad behavior?"

Dutch laughed. "Please, by all means. I'm enjoying the show. Bill, is Galya the one you call Sweet Apples?" Dutch made the gesture of holding two apples to his chest.

Galya said, "You dirty bastard! You will show me respect, or I will show you your place, which is at my feet." Before anyone could stop Galya, she waved her hands and Bill floated up and turned upside down. He came to rest with his head a foot off the table. "Now you will stay like that until I let you go. How do you like those apples?"

Bill laughed. "This is a child's spell. I will have myself freed momentarily, but if you could climb on the table and stand a wee bit closer, I can see what color panties you have on, if you're wearing any at all."

Galya stepped up on the table and punched Bill in the groin.

Bill yelped. "See, what did I tell you? She will do anything to touch my dick."

Galya cut him off with another punch. "Would you like me to touch it again? Maybe you prefer I squeeze them until you pass out."

Zyra rolled her eyes. "Please let the old goat down."

Galya laughed. "Nope! I worked that spell in a way so only I can release him, and I say he stays that way until I say so. Now that we are all here, we should talk, and, Bill, for every dirty comment out of your mouth, I will bang your head on the table or stab you in the hotdog with a fork. It all depends on the comment." Galya caused Bill's head to hit the table.

Dutch was laughing so hard and so loud, it caused his eyes to water, and he began to cough.

"We have learned something terrible. Vorador is back among the living and causing problems," announced Asya.

Asimov said, "Please tell me you are joking."

Asya shook her head.

"I think I might become ill."

Asya spoke of how they'd punished Molly, and she didn't spare the horrible details.

"No, no, this can't be. You three are so good at your job. How could you have messed up so badly? We are so close. I consider you three family. But to hear that you were so reckless with the life of a young girl, let alone an oracle, makes me want to cry. I trust you have a way to make it up to her."

Galya said, "We did what we could, but a young, gifted boy has come up with something beyond what we could imagine or do."

Asimov's eyes opened wide. "Have you found us a male witch? You know they're becoming harder to find these days. I fear the gene is dying."

Zyra spoke for Galya, "No, but he does have it inside him to learn magic. This boy is nothing like anyone we have come in contact with before. He is so very unique, so much so, that on what little we know so far, we could write a book or two about him."

Bill said, "I'm sorry, maybe it's the blood rushing to my head, but did you say he is *unique*? How so? Because Galya is unique in a way to me."

Galya knocked Bill's head onto the table.

"Damn it, Galya. How in the world did you take that as *dirty*?"

Galya squinted. "I know your filthy heart, goat!"

Zyra clapped to calm Galya down.

Asya looked at Bill. "We believe this boy may be from the most famous story we know."

Bill looked funny, possibly because he was upside down, but he exclaimed, "The one about the boy hatching from a dragon's egg?"

"Really, Bill? You think that was a real story? You're such an idiot." Galya got up and walked to the door. "The air in here smells like a goat's ass."

Dutch laughed. "That might be me. I've lost count of the days since I last showered."

Galya crinkled her nose at him.

Asimov sat back and asked, "Ladies, please tell me you're not talking about the child kissed by Nyx, born of Theia and Ares. The one that has the black eyes gifted to him by his grandmother, Nyx. Please tell me you know that is just a story, a metaphor for something that was relevant thousands of years ago. Come on, look at the world and how mankind foolishly and almost completely destroyed it by chasing metaphors and magic items from old books. I don't think I need to remind anyone in this room of the Crusades."

Zyra said, "Asimov, we think we have proof."

Asya got up and sat across from Asimov to give him the backstory. She spoke for twenty minutes.

"See, now you two know what we know about the boy."

"Ladies, with all due respect, I'm having a hard time with this story. I will need to read the boy myself."

"We thought you would say that, Asimov. Unfortunately, he is unconscious, but I assure you he is unique."

"Take me to him, please." Asimov seemed anxious.

"Follow us."

Bill said, "Please, can someone let me down? I am feeling a bit unwell."

Asya looked at Bill. "Galya did this, so you need to apologize in a way that she believes you, and, please, no more dirty jokes. You know how she hates you so. I swear, you better set a perfect example of a well-mannered wizard for the boy because we're all he has for teachers. If he picks up rude behavior, I will be very displeased with you because we like him the way he is now. Besides, Galya will probably fly you like a kite in a thunderstorm."

"I heard that, and it's a great idea, but for now, you can hang around until we get back," said Galya.

Soon after, they began the roughly ten-minute walk, and drops of water hit Galya's forehead. "I didn't think it was going to rain today." More drops landed on them.

"There are no clouds." Asya held out her hand as the raindrops increased. Then, without warning, hundreds of gallons of water crashed down, sending the party to their asses.

"What in the hell was that?" They quickly got to their feet. "I'm soaked!" yelled Asya.

"We're all soaked, Asya. I bet that asshole, Bill, did this. I'm going to kick the shit out—"

Asimov called attention to his friends, "Ladies, is this the boy?"

Slade lay naked on his stomach. The four were stunned, and soon after, a half-naked Sofia and Kailee ran into them. They were talking much too fast. Asimov held up his hand.

"Young ladies, please put the rest of your clothes on and speak slowly."

Sofia said, "We were watching Slade, and we got worried because he started breathing in shallow breaths. Suddenly, he was pulled under the water, and it exploded, so we ran to get you. What is going on?"

"We know as much as you do. But answer me this: why are you two so fond of this boy?"

Kailee spoke first. "Galya, I have never liked a boy before because they're disgustingly foul in their thoughts, but Slade was pure when he met me. No gross thoughts, only kindness with a little stupidity. Just thinking about Slade makes me feel warm, and I smile."

Sofia said, "I feel very strongly for him. I felt that way the first time I laid eyes on him, and every time we kiss, I want him more. I want him to love me, but I also want to share him with my special friends."

"I just don't understand what you two see in him, but if you two have feelings, then enjoy him. Explore your feelings. Teach him the right way to love and treat a woman. Kailee, pick up the boy, take him home, and get into dry clothes for dinner. Dress him and bring him to us whether he is awake or not," said Galya.

"Yes, Galya."

"One day without seeing his junk is all I ask," Zyra said, shaking her head.

"Look at it this way, Zyra. He could have landed on you, and you would have touched it," Asya said.

She and Galya laughed.

"How would that be funny, Asya?"

"Asya, I think the boy shifted in his sleep!" Asimov exclaimed.

"No, I think someone did this to get our attention," Zyra speculated.

"We're halfway to the cottage. Slade looks like he's waking up," said Sofia.

"Kailee, you can put me down, please. My head is spinning, and I feel groggy."

Kailee commented, "Okay, you look kind of stupid when you sleep, and you drooled on me."

Kailee and Sofia laughed.

"Thank you, Kailee. I meant put me down on the ground. Not put me down."

She put him on his feet.

"Do I really look stupid and drool?"

Kailee said, "No, you looked fine, but you do drool. And yes, you did drool on me. But I will no doubt drool on you tonight."

Sofia ran back and got my clothes, while Kailee stole a kiss.

"Hey, I was only gone a minute. So, shouldn't I get more kisses?"

We kissed and got dressed to meet the witches.

I asked, "Asya, why is that man on the table upside down? Is he like that all the time, or is that another strange witch thing?"

The three witches placed their hands on their faces in frustration.

Asya introduced them, "Slade, this is Asimov."

He stood five foot nine and was thin, wearing round glasses. His skin was light tan like mine. His hair was white, and he had long white sideburns, leaving his chin and upper lip clean-shaven. I would admit, it made him look very wizardly.

I walked up to Asimov. "Nice to meet you, sir. Thank you for coming to see me."

Asya pointed. "This is Bill."

Bill's hair was white and braided in the back. It must have been two feet long. Bill was five foot seven and had a little bit of a husky build. He wore a long mustache and hair on his chin, but they did not meet. He also had tan skin.

"Hello, Bill, nice to make your acquaintance."

Bill smiled. "I would shake your hand, but Galya believes I might contaminate you with my charm like I have done to her."

Galya bumped his head on the table again.

"Woman! I am sorry, but you are acting childish in front of the boy! Now, I demand you release me, and slowly, I might add. I will do my best to keep a better hold of my tongue for you."

Galya hissed, "Next time you speak to me, it better be 'Yes', 'No,' 'You're the greatest,' and 'I am a worm at your feet.' Do you understand? Worm!"

Bill looked around the room. "Why, yes, Galya, you're the greatest. I am but a lowly worm under your foot. I am always wrong, and you are always right. I would be considered a fool if I were smart enough to spell my own name."

Galya slowly turned him right-side up until he was on his feet, but his face was still bright red.

"Now then, Mr. Slade, we have heard wonderful things about you. May Asimov and I see your eyes?"

Asimov walked over and sat next to Bill. I leaned in and snapped my eyes black as they both leaned in closer.

"Marvelous, my boy, simply stunning. But can you do this?" Bill made his eyes turn all red, and his tongue became like that of a snake's tongue.

I was impressed. "Wow, that is really cool. I can only make mine go black."

Asimov asked, "Can you keep your eyes like that for as long as you want?"

"Yes, for as long as I want, and sometimes, I wake up like that, but Mistress Sofia doesn't like them because they make her uncomfortable. I can see people's other selves."

"I see that you like her," Asimov noted. "Wait, did you say, 'other selves?'"

"Yes. Her face is my first memory and one of my favorites. Some people are different to my eyes. Some have tails and wings, while some have horns. Others look like things I have never seen before."

Bill said, "I see. That part, we will come back to, and yes, some people are two in one. As for your friends, the love of a beautiful woman, or *women* in your case, is a powerful thing and can be a great motivator. Always remember that love will be more powerful than hate. Never hate more than you love, and you will always be on the right path."

"We see that you have many ladies that follow you." Asimov looked over at Sofia.

"As I always say, ladies, ladies, ladies! What we need is more ladies."

Galya threw her shoe at Bill again and hit him in the side of the head.

"Damn it, woman! If you keep abusing our love like this, you will lose me someday! Someday soon, in fact!"

Galya held up both fingers in the shape of a V.

"Really, Galya, in front of everyone? Well, if that is what you desire."

Galya yelled, "You decrepit, filthy fool! I would not lay with you if I were on fire and you were made of water."

"Thank you, Bill, for that advice. I hope to show everyone that I will become of great use in whatever I do in the future."

Dutch inserted, "Moving on. How bad is this Vorador character?"

Zyra replied, "Dutch, that man used to be one of the best of us. No one knows what land he came from, but he is very old. Unfortunately, a tragedy caused him to give in to the dark side of magic and other unnatural practices. Now that we have proof that he is alive, and we know that nothing will turn him back to the light, I fear he is in league with a great evil. He must be stopped by any means, then burned to ash."

Dutch scratched at his beard. "Well then, we will put together a force and cleanse him from this world with fire. Besides, how hard can it be to find one wizard and kill him?"

Asya shook her head. "Dutch, Vorador walks like death, leaving none alive, when he is searching for magical items. I could only imagine what he knows now that we know he has cheated death itself. So, the answer to your question: I would not fight him one-on-one. It would take all five of us, and there is a chance we could lose two or three in the fight. But he must be stopped for two reasons. One, he is so evil, he needs to be put to death. And second, he still thinks that the Eye of the Void is at the House of Dreams. He will come for it at some point, and when he does, he will leave that place a graveyard."

Asimov asked, "How did Lady Velvet get her hands on such a unique item?"

Galya said, "One of her rangers found it, mistaking it for a jewel. Then, it spoke to Lady Velvet, so she hid it away. A month later, there was the incident with Molly, leading up to Mr. Slade seeing the man in the black hat. Then, we confirmed it was Vorador seeking the orb by using other people and enslaving Molly's mind. As of yesterday, the item has been locked away."

Asimov stretched his arms. "I see. We're all lucky she was not tempted into doing anything foolish with it."

Bill looked around and said, "Well, we certainly have our work cut out for us. On the bright side, you three have the orb locked away, and we are having roasted turkey for dinner tonight. I call that a double win, but Vorador will have to be dealt with sooner rather than later. With that, I'm going to use the little wizard's room." Bill was walking toward me.

I was greatly curious about Bill, so I asked him, "Excuse me, Bill. May I inquire as to why you and Galya seem to not get on so well?"

Bill looked at me, placing his left hand on my shoulder. "Good question. Now, walk and talk with me because I really have to use the little wizard's room."

Galya yelled over to me, "Don't believe anything that floppy old goat tells you!"

I laughed. "Wow, she has a real dislike for you."

"She certainly does. Asya showed Asimov and me your very short but interesting story. I especially like the parts that show you meeting and getting new women to like you. I would very much like to understand how you pull that one off because I have yet to tell if you're subconsciously using magic or if it is a built-in ability. Either way, it must be great for you."

I looked Bill in the eyes and said, "I really don't like it. Before I had time to understand what was happening, I had gained a few too many, and I don't want anyone to be upset or sad."

Bill laughed. "Boy, it seems that you can have almost anyone, so enjoy yourself, but not at the cost of someone's feelings. Take it from me. Sometimes, you never get a second chance with the one you want to be with because you're a stupid, horny old goat."

"Bill, were you and Galya together before?"

"Listen to me, boy, and hear me good. It's very true I hold a flame for Gayla, but the last time I said something about anything pertaining to her and me, she plucked out my right eye, which she still keeps in a jar in her room—or so I'm told."

I began to laugh. "Galya was right for me not to believe the things you say because I am clearly looking at both your eyes. How could she have plucked one out? Yet here you are with two."

Just as Bill was about to say something, Galya appeared out of thin air, startling us both.

"Damn it, woman! Look what you did! You made me piss on my leg, and these are my good traveling paints. Can't I have even one moment alone to have a piss without you stalking me?" Bill sounded more than a bit annoyed.

Galya wiggled her fingers. "There, you're all clean now, you big baby. To answer your question, Slade, I did remove his eye, and I do keep it as a trophy in my room. I know you can see through it, Bill! That is why I put a little cloth over it at night. I wouldn't want to keep you up too long, you big pervert. Remember what I said to you when I took your eye? I will take the other to have a matching set if you ever say what you said that night in any way, shape, or form."

I was shocked.

"Don't look so shocked, Slade, because Hell hath no fury like a woman scorned. You will do well to remember that phrase, boy, because you have more than a handful of women, and you only have *two* pretty blueish-green eyes." She laughed. "I will see you both in the other room." She vanished into thin air.

"Bill, does she always do that to you?"

"Son, let's not talk of the sweet, beautiful angel Galya without her being in the same room and surrounded by people that can help me. To completely answer your question on why I have two eyes, you will see, pardon the pun. When you learn and master the right spells, you can lose almost anything besides your head and regrow or acquire something like an eye. With a little magic, *poof*! You have a new but slightly used eye or hand." Bill flexed his left hand, and I noticed it was a bit darker than his arm. "Come on, son. I hear more people have arrived."

We walked out and into the main hall, where there was a large crowd. "Slade, do you see that young man there? Mingle with the group. Try to blend in and have some fun. It was nice talking with you, and we will speak more very soon."

I walked over to a group of ten men and five women. The tallest one saw me and said, "Hello, I am Roger. This is my brother, Kalth, and my sister, Hayth." He named everyone else in the group.

I introduced myself. "My name is Slade, and I'm from the House of Ribbons."

Kalth asked, "What is your position within the House?"

"I have not been assigned one yet."

Hayth said, "How are you here and have no assigned position? Where are your House colors? Did Lady Silk acquire you while on the road?"

I replied, "I'm not a slave or a clone. I have always been free."

Roger said, "We are sorry. No offense was implied, I assure you. I'm a ranger and fight instructor. My sister is a teacher for the young, and my little brother here just became a ranger. We're very proud of him."

I said, "Congratulations, Kalth. I hear that is a difficult job."

Kalth jokingly remarked on some of the new women, and he pointed at one. "She is yummy. I will ask her if she would like to spend some time with a ranger and maybe her friend as well."

I laughed. "You'll have no luck with either of them because they're with me as well as the women over there."

Roger said, "I call bullshit on that, my new friend. I bet you Kalth can—"

"Kalth, it would not be a bet. It would be robbery, so be my guest. Show me how it is done."

Shortly after, Kailee, Cyan, and Sofia walked up to me. Kalth had his arm held tightly by Kailee.

Sofia spoke, "My love, I believe your new friend here has the manners of an entitled brat. He believes that rangers are unequaled in skill. Maybe when he has been a ranger long enough, he will be able to spot other rangers, like the one who is talking right now."

Kailee laughed and spoke, "Slade, the six of us want to make sure that you know which room is ours, and we expect you there after dinner. No excuses."

Cyan said, "Yeah, Slade, I want you to put me into a nice coma, like the one you were in the other night."

Sofia smiled. "Leave our boy alone. It's not his fault his body can only take so much punishment. There were four of us and only one of him. If you need us, we will be over there."

Each woman kissed me on the mouth.

Roger smiled. "Holy hell, man. Four women at once? Come on, tell us what you really do for your House."

Lady Velour interrupted, "Slade, there you are. I have missed you. Which room is the afterparty in tonight? If I don't get a piece of you soon, I will drag you off into one of the empty rooms and have my way with you right there." Velour kissed me in a way that I swore her tongue was looking for hidden treasure. I told her that Sofia knew and that I looked forward to a kiss like that again.

Rogers and Kalth were stunned as was the whole group, but Hayth was unfazed as she asked, "Well, whatever it is you do, you must do it extremely well to have six, plus Lady Velour, drooling over you."

"I have four others waiting at home, which makes for eleven." I smiled at the group. "Please excuse me, Hayth. I didn't mean to sound like I was bragging about such things in front of a lady."

Hayth ran her fingers though her black hair. "No need to apologize. I'm not easily offended, but I am thirsty. Would you escort me while I get a drink?"

I extended my elbow, and Hayth smiled, placing her arm through it. We walked away, but not before I heard Roger say, "What just happened?"

We got a drink and engaged in small talk. She leaned over and whispered, "I think your friend Cyan is very cute. I know she is with you, but do you know if she likes girls? If so, would you invite me tonight? I like men as well, and I like what I see when I look at you."

"I will take you to her. I'm sure she would like to be introduced to a beautiful woman such as yourself. Come with me." I took her hand and walked across the room to Cyan.

"Cyan, my sweet. I did not get the chance to tell you that you look stunning. This is Hayth. She thinks you're very attractive. On that note, I will leave you two to talk."

Cyan said, "Remind me to show you the proper way to introduce someone, but yes, thank you. Hayth, I did notice you and your pretty blue eyes a bit ago."

They walked off, and I was alone in a room full of at least fifty people. I suddenly felt alone but without the terror part of being utterly alone. I felt watched, inside and out, as if someone were in my mind. The feeling passed when someone bumped me, and I went to find Asya.

I found her speaking with Asimov. "Ah, my boy, Asya has shown me everything about you, and she speaks so highly of you. I'm greatly impressed at the fact that you will make a promise and not violate that promise. That, my boy, is a trait of a true gentlemen, unfortunately carried by far too few these dark days."

"Asimov, how did you know you were a wizard?"

Asimov sipped his drink and said, "I was discovered by a witch who took me under her wing. I started off as a witch. I even lived with Tambry, Zyra, Galya, and Asya, among a few others, for a long time. It's a wondrous coven. Our goal was to locate and teach what we call special children. We find it easier if the child has an ability because the child's mind is already accepting of the idea of magic. Some people just keep their mind shut off to our world. As some of us grow in magic, we have a tendency to go off on our own and study nonstop. We, as males, like to call ourselves wizards, but it's just a name. We are still witches, but we no longer live with our own kind or in groups. Besides, the word *witch*, conjures the image of a woman, and it confuses those who are less than educated. I prefer to say a 'user of magic' or 'gifted.'"

I asked, "Asimov, where does magic come from?" I was hungry for any knowledge on the topic.

"Asya, you are right. This one is curious and knows how to ask the right questions." Asimov touched his hairless chin. "Magic comes in a few forms. Spell books called grimoires are a collection of knowledge handed by the gods and goddesses and written into powerful books. The other way magic comes to us is a bit hard to explain and easier to show. So, I will do my best, and please excuse me if I do it no justice. Slade, imagine a person made out of metal and wires; wires look like pieces of string. Now, see it walk and talk like a human marionette."

I raised my hand. "Asimov, you mean androids, robots, or the half-and-half, which blends humans with a machine called Cybernetic Lifeforms. If I lose my arm and have a robotic arm bonded to me, then I will have a cybernetic body part."

Asimov and Asya looked as if they had been completely frozen. "Holy shit, Asya! Gather the three others and meet us upstairs in two minutes. Slade, come with me." Asimov took me by the arm, and we disappeared and reappeared upstairs. It made my stomach twist a little. "We call that shifting from one place to another. It makes travel less tedious. Some people call it other things; I believe you've already been taught this."

The other three shifted in.

"I believe Slade has more information that he has uncovered since earlier today."

"I can't be too far away from Molly."

"I lifted that knowing we can trust her now. Sorry I meant to tell you, but you fell out of the sky on us," said Asya.

Asya, Zyra, and Galya entered my mind and exited it just as fast.

Zyra said, "Yes, someone or something removed so much but left more than enough for him to blend in and function as normal. But this devious little monkey must have overheard what was going to be done to him. I'm certain of it now, and he stored away a great deal. Why else would he know about cybernetics? Children are the most fascinated with automatons. I bet he was raised by one, or at least, one cared for him where he lived." Zyra paced around while she spoke to herself in a dialect unfamiliar to my ears. It was very nice to hear. She held her necklace in her hand as she spoke to someone not in the room. "Yes, I am sure of it. We all are. His knowledge was too vast to get every little bit, and he hid some of it. Can we bring him home for study? I see. Thank you."

When Zyra was done pacing and talking, I asked her, "What did she have to say?"

"I was talking to myself, boy. Now let me think."

I spoke up again, "Zyra, I mean no disrespect, but you were talking with another woman."

Zyra looked at me. "Yes, you're right. This is a magic item. Most would think it is an everyday monocle used to help a person read. Well, I can speak with the person on the other side of it. Understand?" She laughed. "I love his curious nature and his keen eye for details."

I looked at her then Bill, who looked away. So did Asimov.

"Asya, why are you all dreading what comes out of my mouth next?" I moved to the other side of the room, taking the doorknob in my hand and looking over my shoulder. I said, "Why did Zyra just lie to me? Zyra, that is a two-way communication device, and it's fairly common. You just fashioned silver and glass around it so that it looks like an everyday item."

No one spoke. I opened the door and went downstairs. As I turned the corner, Asya was there.

"Asya, how can I trust any of you if one of you is lying?"

"Please come back with me, Slade. We will explain." Asya shifted us back into the room where I took a seat in the corner.

Zyra said, "Slade, you are right. I was wrong to think you could not handle the truth, and I apologize. Yes, I was talking on a communication device, and the woman I was speaking to is dealing with a different situation. But she will find her way to us as soon as she can, or we will take you to see her, whichever comes first. But yes, we're witches, and most men like to be called wizards. We do have some magic, but we also employ technological devices that we hide in plain sight and play off as magic. Most here do not know the real world around them, so magic is the easiest way to explain away things. I promise you we would have told you."

I said, "Thank you, Zyra, but isn't any type of advanced technology indistinguishable from magic to the lay person?"

Zyra's eyes opened wide. "Again, you demonstrate your knowledge. Now we know how he understands technology. A long time ago, a very famous writer named Sir Arthur C. Clark wrote, 'Any sufficiently advanced technology is indistinguishable from magic.' So, Slade, it appears that you may have read his works, and this one quote has stuck with you. Good news for you is that Asimov is a collector of old and rare books of that time period and genre."

I stood up and asked one more question, "Who is this person coming to see me?"

Asya spoke for Zyra, "Her name is Tambry, and she is an expert in the study of enchanted items. She can tell if a piece of technology is in disguise, and we want to know more about your coin, that bracelet, the ring, and Mr. Batch, if more can be learned about him."

I asked, "What does Batch have to do with any of this?"

Bill said, "Imagine that Batch was a robot in your brain, a robot so advanced that it can love, reason, hate, and contemplate its own existence and so on. If this is true, then he should be able to lead us to where you came from. We believe you came from a wondrous place where science and magic dance simultaneously. Maybe even more than it already does for us."

Zyra spoke, "Slade, in our lives, we have met amazing people, angels, demons, and those above them, but we believe that some of the gods and goddesses have mingled with foreign technology to become something wholly new, more advanced than they were already. You could be the first of many children. Maybe you are all they needed to do whatever it is they needed done, or maybe you're just you, and you were left behind, lost, or stolen. All we know right now is you have been altered in a way where some memories just don't exist inside your mind. But you were clever enough to hide information that you did not want to lose from those who would have taken it from you. Plus, you have unique gifts that you seemingly had to have been born with because why would someone create a child straight out of some the oldest stories to educate him, just to take away some things? What purpose would that serve?"

Galya was the last to offer her opinion. "Slade, we will never ask you to do anything that you do not want to do. If someone does come get you, we may be able to learn from them. You're in the dark about a lot of things. Now it is our duty to bring you into the light of knowledge, and we will learn with and from you. Please, not to distract you from any other question you might have, but Sofia is looking for you. I believe she is worried about you. We will go back to the pre-dinner party, or I could bring her up here if you would like. One more thing: would you mind keeping your knowledge of technology to yourself? Not all around you will understand it. Just remember what Arthur said. Plus, we value our secrets. We hope you can understand."

"I will, and I would like Sofia here. Thank you."

Galya disappeared.

Bill said, "Sofia makes you feel safe, doesn't she?"

"Yes. Why do you ask?"

Bill smiled. "Because that is the way I felt about a special someone a long time ago, and that is a special emotion. I am happy to have met another that I can relate to."

Galya flashed back in with Sofia.

"Slade, I feared you left with the witches."

I walked over and took Sofia in my arms. "I wouldn't leave without you, no more than I would leave without my heart." We locked eyes, and I whispered, "I have this intense feeling for you that I can't explain, but I want it to be love. Sofia, I think I love you, and only death will keep me away from your kisses." We kissed in front of everyone.

Sofia's eyes started to water. "I think I love you, too. I really was so afraid when I could not find you and Asya. I thought you were gone, that I might never see you again. I felt like I couldn't breathe."

"No, my love, just a small meeting. I am sorry with all my heart that I caused you fright. Here, take this, and I will always be with you." I handed her my bracelet.

Asimov said, "Mr. Slade, that might be unwise."

"It's mine, and I will gift it to whomever I please. Thank you very much."

Asimov insisted, "Mr. Slade, what if the bracelet is an item like we talked about, and someone comes looking for you? That is how they might track you. But they find her instead in possession of your bracelet. I believe they would surely take it and interrogate her about you. They might discard her or use her as leverage."

"I see your point, Asimov. Thank you. I don't want to put you in danger, Sofia, so I hope a kiss will do for now."

Sofia smiled. "How could I say no to a kiss from you?"

Zyra clapped. "People, let's give these two lovebirds some privacy. Slade, I would like you downstairs with Sofia in five because I heard the ten-minute warning from the dinner bell. So, don't be late. Dutch will see it as very rude."

"Thank you."

They left, and Sofia and I sat and kissed.

"Sofia, I don't understand these feelings I have for you. I know I want to be with you, but you're accepting of me being with other women gives me an odd feeling. Are you sure it's not upsetting to you? Or am I understanding love wrong?"

Sofia took my hand. "Slade, you're new to us and our way of life. To hoard you away would be something I could only do if we were married, maybe not even then. I want to know you for a good amount of time before something like that, so I gladly share you with the selected few. The bonus is you will become a better lover with a few than just one. How else will you be able to learn the subtle intricacies of the female body and mind if I alone teach you? Besides, I've never been with a man, so I would just be stumbling around in the dark."

"Then, I look forward to stumbling around with you, because words do not describe how I really feel. But I'm happy to know that I will get to have my first time with you."

Sofia whispered, "Well, I was hoping Sunako and Topaz would be there, if that is okay with you."

"I think I really like that idea." We kissed a little more while holding hands as we walked back to the party. The first person we saw was Topaz.

Topaz smiled. "Where did you two sneak off to?"

Sofia laughed. "Nothing like that. Asya and her gang needed a word with both of us."

Topaz's eyes widened. "Oh, please tell me that Asya lifted the ban on sex with Slade." She exhaled deeply. Her grin suggested thoughts too dirty to say out loud.

I laughed. "Sadly, no. It was more about technological things versus enchanted items."

Topaz sighed. "Sorry, you lost me at *no*." Topaz hugged me and kissed my cheek.

Mr. Cyril walked in and said, "If everyone could find their seat so dinner can be served."

I sat next to Sofia and Kailee, while Beth and Topaz sat across from us.

Beth said, "This is so exciting. This is my first dinner party where I get to be a guest."

Kailee nodded. "I would assume this will be the first of many for you. Do you know when your studies with Asya will begin?"

Beth smiled. "Soon, I hope, because I want to learn how they do that thing where they float instead of walk. It looks so damn cool and hauntingly scary at the same time."

I looked at Beth. "I think you will make a wonderful witch." We raised our glasses, and Beth was rosy red.

The food was served. Dutch stood up to make a toast. "To my three wonderful daughters: over the years, you have brought me great joy and much laughter, and as ladies of your respective Houses, you have brought great pride to my heart. I know I can speak these words because they are true, and I know if your beautiful mother, Haley, were here tonight, she would say the same, only better and with a more beautiful voice. So, cheers to my daughters, and cheers to the people who live here in the House of Thorns. Now, let us eat and enjoy one another's company."

The turkey was so tender, and the wine was unlike the others I'd had before. Talk was light and random with laughter echoing off the walls.

I got up to use the bathroom, but before I entered, Velour came up from behind me and placed her hands over my eyes. "Guess who?"

I made a humming noise. "I would guess she is beautiful, smart, funny, and in a position of power. Her name would then be Lady Velour."

She removed her hand and spun me around, shoving me through the bathroom door. We both stopped as we saw a couple fornicating against the wall without a care in the world.

"Velour, I really have to piss, so could you give me just a little privacy or a little space?"

Velour laughed. "Just think of the toilet as the reanimated head you pissed on earlier. That should help your stage fright, you naughty boy."

Velour sounded a bit tipsy. When I was done, Velour pressed me against the wall and kissed me.

"Yum, you taste like wine and turkey, my two favorite things. You will soon become my third favorite thing." She softly bit my ear and grabbed ahold of me below the belt. "Soon, I will have you help me release all this tension." She got on her knees and pulled up my skirt as she took ahold of me. "I want to kiss you right here, right now."

I tried to pull her up.

"Please, just a little kiss. I promise you will love it."

I pulled her up and asked her to kiss my mouth, while the other two were reaching their climax, breathing heavily and moaning. Velour slurred a few more erotic things in my ear and a thing I did not know was possible and probably a bit unsavory.

"I will see you back at the table. You see what he is doing to her? I will teach you that move." She blew a kiss and walked out.

I washed my face and did my best to pretend not to notice the woman's high-pitched, passionate moans, but I would say she was definitely having a good time.

I returned to the table, and Sofia asked me, "How did you like my little gift I sent you? Did she help you in the bathroom?"

I smiled. "Well, two people were enjoying themselves up against the wall, and yes, I enjoyed it. My sweet, I mean no offense, but maybe that's not the place for me when it comes to intimate encounters because it smelled a bit off. Also, I do enjoy a little privacy while I piss." I leaned over and whispered in her ear, "Velour tried to put me into her mouth. Is that what you wanted her to do?" Sofia nodded and smiled.

Beth started to speak, and I politely stopped her. "Yes, I know I pissed in front of everyone today, but it is still weird to be watched."

Beth laughed. "I was going to say I like privacy, too, when I go to the bathroom, but I'm a lady."

I nodded. "Beth, forgive my rudeness in cutting you off."

She smiled and raised her glass with her pinky in the air.

As dinner came to a close, Dutch bid everyone a goodnight, leaving the room. He really did look like a giant compared to everyone else.

Asya walked by. "Ah, my boy, just the man I want."

"Asya, I'm over here." She was talking to the person at the table behind me. I'd never seen her so drunk.

"Hold still, boy, you're moving all about. I want you to know that you may partake in the activities of the women tonight on one condition. You must solve my riddle first. I am me. You are you. We are together. Can you take the reins and control this wild beast? Or will you be trampled under the weight of carnal want? I lead from the rear but fight at the front. Will you become the cup you so desire to drink from? Slade, solve this riddle and unburden yourself. Do you understand me? If not, play it safe and withhold your needs. Avert your gorgeous blueish-green eyes if you have to. Slade, have I told you that you're very cute? And the way you smell makes me want to—"

Asimov placed a hand on her shoulder, and Asya smiled, leaning over to kiss me on the forehead. "I will see you in the morning, my fairytale boy, child of the stars."

Asimov excitedly said, "Pay no attention to Asya. Our wine was stronger than yours was, and she is making no sense." Asimov was clearly holding his hand over Asya's mouth, so she could not speak to me, but she was winking.

"Should I ignore her riddle, as it sounded like drunken prattle?" I asked.

Asimov laughed. "No, because we were talking about that riddle before she became inebriated, and I believe she meant to deliver it earlier. Do you remember it word-for-word? If not, here." Asimov touched my temple with a single finger, and I could repeat her words and remember them as if I'd written the riddle. "There is one last thing. If you really want to impress Asya, solve it without any help from Batch."

I looked over at Topaz, who was listening, and we kissed. Batch slipped from me to her.

Asya began to fall over, and Bill caught her and said, "Slade, help Galya because if she knew I picked her up—well, just remember what I told you about my eye, right? Now come on."

I went to find Galya upright and fast asleep, so I picked her up and slung her over my shoulder, following Bill. Asimov was helping Asya and Zyra, who were a bit less drunk. We got to their room on the second floor, and I placed Galya next to Asya.

I asked Bill, "Bill, should I bring them water?"

Galya sat up and said, "Goat? Is that you?"

I floated to the ceiling.

"You can watch me sleep from there, you horny old goat."

I felt like gravity was three times heavier, and movement was all but impossible. I tried not to be too loud. "Bill, Asimov, help me."

Zyra said, "I got this." She raised her hand and down I went. Asimov used his magic to stop me from hitting the ground face-first and helped Zyra into bed. Bill, Asimov, and I left the room, quietly closing the door.

I was happy to leave the room. "Bill, why does Galya call you the Goat?"

Asimov and Bill chuckled. "Because my name is William, which can be shortened to Bill or Billy, as in, Billy goat. I look like a goat and love eating delicious things, including women, if you know what I mean. So, Galya rudely started calling me Billy goat, then one day, just old goat."

I sighed. "To be honest, that was a less exciting story than I thought it would be."

Bill looked at me and raised an eyebrow. He smiled. "Goodnight, Mr. Slave."

"It's pronounced Slade," I said.

Asimov exclaimed, "Now do you see how a nickname can be funny and insulting at the same time? Plus, my esteemed friend can be a very stubborn old goat at times, especially when it comes to dealing with Galya."

We said our goodnights and took our leave to go to our respective rooms.

I repeated the riddle over and over, not understanding it any more than the last time I said it. I turned the corner and saw Sofia standing outside a door.

She smiled. "I wanted to make sure you made it to the right room, but before we go in, I was hoping for a kiss."

We did, and while we kissed, I showed her, or rather, I *let* her hear the riddle.

Sofia said, "Okay, so we can ask everyone but Topaz because she is holding Batch. Well, let's get you into the room and solve this riddle. If not, you are on kiss-and-watch duty tonight."

We went into the room. There, waiting for us, were Molly, Kailee, Reveka, Topaz, Cyan, and Hayth. Sofia informed the group that we had a mystery riddle to solve.

I shared the riddle with everyone.

Topaz said, "I'm sorry, but I can't help, especially since Batch has been left in the dark about it."

After ten minutes of talk, I started thinking that Asya was drunk and had given me an impossible riddle. But I really didn't think that was the case.

As the ladies began their kissing, I thought about what the riddle could mean; it sounded like I would need to become a woman. No, that couldn't be right. Work together and take the reins, *control this wild beast*. If I jumbled the words, it sounded like I might be able to take control of someone's body or switch bodies. Was that even possible?

I walked over to Topaz as Kailee undressed her. "Topaz, ask Batch if he can control your body. Have him run that test for me, please."

Topaz nodded. "Batch tried, but he is unable to find the part of my mind that controls the body."

"Topaz, may I try?"

She said yes, and I entered her mind. I concentrated on her body to no avail. I left her mind and walked away.

"Hey, Slade!" Topaz called out. "Maybe it is because I'm an oracle. Maybe our minds are different. Try Kailee or Sofia."

We told Kailee about the idea, and she liked it. I entered her mind. I checked her library for anything on the body and how it was controlled, but I found nothing. How could everything be there, but not the controls to the body? Then, it hit me. The body was run mostly on a subconscious level. *I mean, how tedious would it be to have to think left foot, right foot, make the heart beat, breathe in and out*? So that meant there had to be a way to tap into it somehow, but that was beyond me unless… "Kailee, can you make your arm raise up?"

Kailee said, "No, I feel disconnected to my body while you're inside my mind."

"Kailee, I want to try something. Please hold on."

I jumped out and spoke with Topaz about what I was going to try. If anything looked weird, she had to go get the witches. I leapt back into Kailee and told her what I'd said to Topaz.

"Kailee, while I'm inside your mind, you can't move your body, but I can kind of move mine while I'm with you in my body. I think if you stay in my mind, I will be able to control your body. Is this something you want to try? If you can control my body, please honor my promise."

Kailee smiled. "I will, as long as you promise me that when we can be together sexually, you will wash my hair and give me a bath or shower anytime I ask."

"Deal, but I would have done that if you asked before, so come up with something else. I will agree to it so long as it does not add anyone else into the mix because, to be honest, I feel overwhelmed with all of you."

Kailee hugged me. "Don't worry, lover boy. You will grow to love the fact that you are shared because it's the single most thing men think about besides power and gold."

"Okay, Kailee, this might feel strange, but don't worry. Topaz will be right here for us. If something goes wrong, she knows what to do. I am going to leave, then see if I can let go of our hands and control your body."

I let go, and I was alone in Kailee's body. I began to concentrate, and I started to see out of her eyes. I could see my body, and I could move her head, but her hands were not responding. Then, a chair appeared from nowhere. I didn't think of a chair. I wondered if that was the way the mind and body connected. I sat down and felt instantly connected to her body. I could freely move. It felt different, like I was in a dream, but I knew I was not.

"Kailee, Kailee! Can you hear me? Topaz, connect to her and tell her to look for a chair and sit in it."

Topaz winked. "Kailee told me that it feels like a dream, and she can only wiggle a few fingers. She can hear and see you."

I smiled. Or, more so, I made Kailee smile.

"Kailee, the moment you want your body back, say so to one of us, and I will put you back, but keep trying. If you can wiggle those fingers, you should be able to move me around soon. Remember my oath about my body."

I turned around, walked up to Sofia, and said, "Hello, Sofia. The moment I saw you, I knew you would keep me safe, and I want for nothing but to make you happy. Now, how can I make you happy?"

Chapter 25

Trading Places

Sofia took my face in her hands. "Slade, is that you in there? Is this what Asya meant with her riddle? Because if not, then won't she be mad?"

I looked down at the feet that were not mine. "Well, she should have been clearer about the dos and don'ts."

Sofia said, "Wait, if you're using Kailee's body, then shouldn't you have access to all of her gifts?"

I thought for a moment. "Kailee is one of the strongest and can read minds, right?"

Sofia nodded her head. "Tell me what I'm thinking about."

I concentrated and began to hear whispers. "Kiss me, kiss me, kiss me here."

"Sofia, are you asking me to kiss you *there*?"

Sofia said, "No, that would be too obvious."

I started to feel dizzy, and the room lit up with noise. Everyone's voices were talking at once. I thought my eyes were going to pop out from the pressure. I stumbled over to my body and collapsed on my lap.

I connected to Kailee. "Holy shit, how to you do it? How do you stand the noise?"

Kailee laughed. "That's right. When my gift first manifested itself, it was deafening, but I soon learned to focus on one person at a time. Then, I widened it when I needed it. I would close my eyes, hum, and focus on the sound I was making. Oh yeah, I can almost stand up in your body."

I thanked her and went back. The noise was on full blast, but the pressure was not there. I walked over to Sofia and took her in my arms. She felt like she weighed nothing, which meant I did have access to Kailee's strength—the gifts were locked in the body. I found that strange, as I would have assumed all powers were mental.

"Sofia, you want me to dance with you."

Sofia winked. Cool, I could read minds. All I had to do was find a way for it not to feel like I was going deaf. I put her down and walked over to my body. Kailee was standing up but wobbly.

"Kailee, can you feel anything? I cannot feel much, almost no touch sensation."

Kailee smiled.

"I'm Slade. You're Kailee. I am a boy, and you are a girl. I can prove it. I'm a boy. All you have to do is look at my penis."

"Kailee, pull my skirt down. You don't see me just waving it around like that, do you? Kailee, you're going to make me look stupid."

Kailee took off my clothes and said, "Everyone! Look at me! I'm a boy, and I have this." She started dancing around with it bouncing around, and everyone was laughing and hooting.

I yelled out, "People, that is Kailee in my body, and I'm in hers! Please note that I would never do that. Please don't encourage Kailee to make me look anymore stupid."

Topaz yelled, "No one cares! Kailee, make it spin around. Yeah, like that!" She started laughing. "That is so damn funny. Slade, I want to be you, so I might see what it is like to have boy bits."

I looked at Topaz. "Good luck because neither her nor I have feeling. The body is numb, so Kailee and I can feel no pleasure with these bodies."

Sofia said, "No feeling at all?" She placed her hand between my legs, and I felt nothing. "That is a shame. Hold on, stay right here." Sofia walked over to my body and sat Kailee down in the chair. She sat on my lap and began to kiss Kailee, while she was in my body. It was the weirdest moment of my life, watching that happen to me, while I was not me. Sofia wiggled around on my lap and stood up.

"It's true. They have no feeling in the skin, but I can show you how to kiss a woman."

I smiled. "Sofia, we have been kissing for a bit now. I think I know how to kiss."

Sofia laughed. "I'm going to show you a way to kiss a woman that will make them scream. Now, get on the bed and kiss me right here. Be gentle, and I'll guide you when you need it."

I did as she asked, and I kissed her. Ten minutes went by too fast because I was lost in the sheer enjoyment I received from making her moan.

Kailee interrupted, "Slade, I want my body back, or I'm going to try and stick this inside of Topaz."

I looked at my body. She'd somehow gotten it to work.

"Kailee, how did you do that?"

She smiled. "I might not be able to feel much, but watching everyone is so very arousing. When I looked down, I noticed that your penis had woken up. So, give me back my body, or I will definitely take this dog for a walk."

We grabbed hands and switched. I suddenly felt everything, and the room was a great deal quieter.

Molly said, "Look, it's so—"

I covered myself with a shirt that was on the floor.

"Yes, Molly. We all saw it. Now please throw me my clothes."

Kailee smiled. "Clothes? I think you would make a better towel rack right now. Slade, it was so weird to feel so weak. I don't know how you do it. Now, come on and get into bed. We will promise not to impale ourselves on your spear of destiny."

Sofia laughed. "I don't know about any of you, but if he keeps that thing out, I will somehow find a way to back into it or mistake him for a chair. So, what I am saying, my love, is find a way to put it to sleep. Caress my shoulders, while you and Topaz kiss me."

Cyan called out to me, "Slade, I'll take a back rub when Sofia has her fill."

Sofia sat up. "I have a great idea. In case we are wrong about what Asya said, we could do something just as good as sex."

Topaz raised her hand. "This one is easy. A daisy chain of oral sex."

Sofia yawned. "No, you dolt! Full-body massages. So, we can pair up as he works on us one at a time but with a fifteen-minute limit. Oh, we have an extra, so one pair with one *ménage à trois*. That is how the fancy ladies call it in the town of Oxsettle. It means three-way."

I nodded. "I surmised that by counting the number of beautiful women in this room. Plus, I speak French."

Reveka rolled over Sofia. "I want to go first. Call me beautiful over and over as you kiss my neck."

Sofia smiled and winked at me, grabbing Topaz. I began to massage Reveka.

"Anyone seen Saffron, Portia, and Diandra?"

Molly said, "Saffron and Portia went off with Diandra and Beth. Saffron and Portia said they won't spend the night with Slade if he is not allowed to enjoy them like fine wine."

Reveka sat on her knees, and I held her from the back, kissing her neck and working my hands over her whole body.

When it was done, Reveka said. "Those bitches don't know what they are missing because Slade has some black magic in these fingertips of his. I mean, wait until he does this to you. I swear, I have never felt so relaxed. Thank you, Slade. That was amazing."

We kissed.

Next up was Cyan. "Hey, I'm going to lie on my stomach so I can feel the pressure. Don't worry. I will tell you if you're pushing too hard on my back."

A few of the ladies laughed and someone said, "Pushing too hard would be great right now."

I straddled Cyan's backside and began to work her back, arms, and neck. Then, her time was up.

"Oh, you're really talented. Wonderful work."

Sofia was next, then Kailee, Topaz, and Hayth. She kissed differently than the others, with short kisses that made up one big kiss. Her hands were all over my body as much as mine were with her. At one point, she was on top. The last was Molly, and by that time, four were asleep, and two were completely engrossed with one another.

I asked, "Are you okay?"

Molly simply replied, "Are you tired, Slade? Would you mind if we talk first?"

I said, "I would love to talk with you."

She took my hand and led me quietly out of the room.

Molly said, "I don't want Topaz or Hayth to overhear. Slade, thank you for standing up for me the way you did. I want you to know that I know I might never have a real body again, but I need you to know that I am yours whether or not I have flesh, blood, and a body. By that, I mean any way you want. A lover, friend, buddy, teammate, lover, best friend, or lover."

I looked Molly in the eyes and smiled. "You said friend twice and lover three times." I lightly kissed her on the lips. "Molly, be what you want to be. You owe me nothing. I did what was right, and you deserve to have the wrong done to you corrected. I want you to want me because I earned a place in your heart, not because I stood up for you. Besides, I think this look is sexy as hell. It's like I'm blind, and I can only feel you." I ran my hand all around her spectral body until I felt her between her legs. "Molly? Can you feel this?"

Molly said in a whisper, "Goddess, yes, please don't stop what you are doing."

"Molly, I thought this body was more like a ghost body."

Molly moaned for a bit as she bit my shoulder, moaning louder. "Asya made it so I would have feeling, so I could at least feel pleasure. Why? Did you like what you just did to me?"

"Yes, I would very much like to kiss you there."

Molly smirked. "Good, because I want you to do that. Then again after my back massage. To answer your question, and I am embarrassed to say, but I was strongly attracted to you the moment Velvet took me out of that hellish box. As soon as I smelled you, I missed my body because I wanted to hold you tight and sniff you. Even now, your smell makes me want you inside of me. Your smell is as intoxicating as wine itself, and with Sofia wanting to share you to make you become an excellent lover in and out of bed, makes it easy to tell you how I feel without fear."

"Molly, I have one odd question. I watched you drink wine, but I see no color in you. Where did it go? Does this body act like your last body? I mean, do you have to pee?"

Molly kissed me. "Yes, this body acts like a real body. Think of it like it is invisible, and I do have to pee. Why? Do you want to watch?"

I laughed. "Would that be too weird?"

"Slade, I would think you weird if you didn't say yes. Now, come on." Molly looked like she was standing. "Okay, Slade. You ready?"

I nodded.

"Here we go." And out of nowhere, the wine began to leave her invisible body at a high rate of speed. After a few seconds, she said, "All done. Cool, huh?"

I nodded and said, "I never thought watching anyone have a piss would be that cool, but when you drink the red wine, why can't I see it in your belly?"

Molly looked like she was washing her hands. "I don't know, but here: try something for me. It's just for scientific research only. Slide your fingers in me. Get on your knees when you do it, and you will be able to see dead-on."

I ran my hand up her leg and found the spot, then slowly watched my fingers disappear. "Molly, can you see this? My finger has become invisible."

Molly lightly grabbed my hair. "It's all very cool now, but do that a little more." She grinded against my hand.

I removed it and stood up. "Molly, the bathroom is such an unsexy place. May I take you back to our room and do as you ask there?"

Molly smiled. "Will you carry me?"

I laughed. "I wouldn't have it any other way, my sweet." I picked her up and walked her back to our room. We noticed the last two had fallen asleep.

"Slade, we will have to be extra quiet. Put me on that bed, and when we are done, get Sofia."

There were four beds in the room, and I placed Molly on the empty one. I crawled next to her, and we began to kiss as I massaged her between her legs. The first two times, she moaned, placing her face in the pillow. But the third time she bit my hand as she reached down and took hold of me. "Slade, I lack the words to tell you how badly I want you inside of me."

I said, "I will kiss you there."

I did, and after a time, I said, "Molly, I'm losing myself to an urge that I can't explain. I want and need to be inside you. It feels like it's taking over. I feel I'm losing control. Please be the stronger one and get up because, if you don't, I'm afraid I will make love to you right here, right now. I don't want you to be a regret. I want you to be someone I love, and I must keep my promise to Sofia."

Molly got up and stood next to the bed. "Slade, I think you just said the most beautiful thing I have ever heard. The fact that you would rather be in love with me than make love to me now is so much more romantic. I think I'm going to cry. Get Sofia."

I found Sofia and pulled her out of bed by her ankle, carrying her sleeping body in my arms.

Sofia barely opened her eyes.

"Hey there, savage, are you going to take me on the floor and make me your queen?"

I placed her in the other bed.

"Why is Molly crying? Molly, are you okay?"

Molly told her about what we did in the hallway and the bathroom and what I'd said a few minutes before. "Sofia, I could feel his words. He spoke the truth, and he has so much love in him. Please, may I officially be one of his lovers? I know a lot of girls want him, but I need him, like you want him, not just for sex. I promise you, Sofia, that I know you're the alpha, and I will respect any and all of your wishes. I know I can love you as well."

Sofia was quiet, then said, "Molly, if you love me, love me because we make a connection, but whether we do or do not, I will not stop you from loving Slade. With that said, I'm the alpha of this group, and I get the first night of love with this beautiful boy." Sofia kissed me. "Now, Molly, I would like for you to kiss me while Slade does what he did to you a little while ago. That is how I want to be put back to sleep if you both don't mind. Matter of fact, Slade, sit here between us and play with us both as we kiss."

"As you wish."

Soon after, the sounds of lust began, which started to push me into a heavy feeling of want and desire. The border of restraint was within spitting distance. Not too long after, they got into a position where they could service each other at the same time. When they were done, each one took a side next to me. We said our goodnights and shared a few kisses as we drifted off to sleep. Sleep ran from me, as all I could think about was what I'd just witnessed.

The next morning, I was woken by the first light of the sun on my face. Bill was at the foot of the bed.

"Good show, old chap. I see you were bedding the birds last night. Asya and Dutch wish to see you five minutes ago. So, chop, chop. I will meet you out in the hall. Oh, Zyra wants Kailee and Sofia as well."

"Bill, are they upset?" I whispered.

"At you? No. Maybe a little at me, but I will carry on." Bill walked out and closed the door.

I shook Sofia. "Sofia, Asya wants us. Get up, please."

She sat up, and her pretty, wavy black hair fell around her breasts.

I walked over to Kailee. "Kailee, get up, sweets. We're being summoned."

Kailee asked, "What's up? Why so early?"

"Asya wants us, and I want to try something."

"Slade, with you, I'll try anything, and I mean *anything*, no matter how dirty it is."

"Kailee, I want to trade bodies for a bit right now. I want to see if they notice."

Kailee laughed. "Okay, I said anything no matter how dirty, and you want to get inside my body the only way I don't get to enjoy. Okay, but I want something in return, and I get to name it later."

I rolled my eyes. "Deal, but nothing too crazy."

We held hands and switched. It was easier for both of us, but I still had barely any feeling. Thankfully, I could move around with greater ease.

"Kailee, I bet it was the wine that made it hard to control one another's body."

"*Shh.* Don't tell Sofia. Wait until after, and don't forget to speak the way I do."

We quickly dressed and exited the room. Bill led us to a heavily decorated room with paintings obviously painted by Dawn. There were a few animal heads, two of which I had never seen before, and strange sculptures. Dutch, Asya, Zyra, Galya, Velvet, Silk, Velour, Bill, Asimov, and Mr. Cyril were in the room, seated at various points. I was sure Galya, Velour, and Velvet were asleep.

"Good morning, Slade, Sofia, Kailee," Asya stood up and spoke. "We have called you here at this very early time to ask for your combined help. We have spent the last two hours talking about what to do next when it comes to you, Mr. Slade, and also the Eye of the Void and Vorador. We think that Vorador will no doubt make another attempt to steal the Eye, and we want him to get it. While we wait for him to try again, Slade, we also want to train you in fighting, education, and strengthening your abilities. We will not force you, manipulate you, or coerce you into what we are going to ask you. Before you answer, is there anything you would like to ask us? Because you have a funny look on your face. Are you well, boy?"

In my body, Kailee said, "I really have to pee. May I have a moment? Kailee, will you help me for a second?"

Zyra said, "Slade, you don't need any help. Now get a move on it." Her tone was sharp. I watched my body leave the room. "Kailee, what is up with you and Slade?"

I answered like I thought she would answer, "I have grown attached to that body, I mean, his body. I mean, he is clumsy, and I like to know that I can pick him up and dust him off if he falls over again."

Velour opened her eyes and yawned. "Kailee, are you still drunk? You sound a bit off."

I looked around the room. "Lady Velour, I just need a bit of water, and my head will be fine."

***

Kailee was having difficulty with Slade's anatomy. "How the hell do I work this thing?"

When she got everything working, her aim was way off. She overcompensated and pissed on the other side of the floor until she finally got it in the center.

"Hey, it's like a game of target practice. This thing isn't so bad. I look forward to getting full feeling in this body and taking this bad boy for a walk." Kailee walked Slade's body back into the room.

Asya asked, "Everything good?"

Kailee laughed and said, "Have you ever tried to piss with one of these things? I don't know how he does it."

Galya sat straight up. "What in the hell did he just say? Boy, come here!"

Kailee did not move, as she was too busy brushing things off her shirt. She must have forgotten what body she was in.

"Boy! Come here now!"

Galya looked at Zyra. "Boy, did you go deaf?"

I moved over to tap her shoulder and switch, but Zyra stood up, moving herself between us with great speed, preventing us from touching.

Zyra walked to the door, opened it, shut it, and called out. "Kailee!"

Kailee, in my body, turned around.

"Ah-ha! What is going on here?"

Kailee said, "Shit, sorry, Slade."

Asya stood up and took the hand of Kailee's body, of which I was in control. "Well, I see that Mr. Slade is a good riddle solver and a fast learner. I tip my hat to you, but this is not the best time to be a show-off. Today is very important. Switch back."

Kailee said, "Sorry, I sort of peed on your leg. I thought it was done." She smiled and raised her eyebrows in embarrassment. We touched hands, and the right minds went into their respective bodies.

Zyra laughed. "I thought that is what you two did but was unsure. Slade, how do you feel when you control someone's body?"

I looked around. "I find it a bit dizzying in the first few seconds, and I only have one concern. Neither one of us could feel anything. There was almost no sensation."

Galya laughed. "You take one of the most complex tricks and pull it off with ease, but you didn't figure out how to turn the lights on?" She laughed some more. "Oh, my boy, you will soon understand how easy that part of it is. The pleasure you will experience!"

Zyra said, "Don't pick on the boy. Slade, what you did was a very complex and dangerous trick. Most people never try it because you can get stuck. You don't know how much time you will have, because the longer you are in, the more the subconscious will fight the foreign consciousness. So, the max I can do is four days."

I smiled. "I thought this was the best way to show what I can do and see if anyone noticed."

Asya spoke to me, "First off, she stood in your body like she is standing now, off to one side. You stand very straight, with your legs shoulder-width apart as if you are ready to defend. You're always on guard, and you do not talk while using your hands. I bet it comes from your old life, but back to business. Slade, we want Vorador to successfully steal the Eye. Then, we want you track him, stop, and/or kill him. I just want it done away from any of the villages. We want the least amount of people to suffer. Vorador must know about everyone that lives in the House of Whispers, but you're not a member of that House, which makes you the perfect person for the job. Assassination is a skillset that is needed in times like this. I have a feeling that whoever taught you your skills also taught you to kill."

"If he's as bad as you say, then why not kill him yourself?"

Zyra replied, "He would feel us before we could get close enough to kill him."

I looked around. "I see. You want to make me the hidden blade and get close enough to end his life. What will happen if we ignore him and make it known that the Eye is hidden away?"

Galya looked at me. "Slade, Vorador is a force of nature. He will not stop; he will do what it takes to get his hands on the Eye because it will help him find other items of power. Vorador doesn't want to rule as a king. He wants to rule as a god, and he will kill anyone and everyone to achieve his goal. Vorador loves nothing but power and the misery that power can bring to others. Suffering is like music to him. Slade, you appearing out of thin air? This couldn't be better timing. Maybe you're a gift from the gods and goddesses to stop Vorador. That could explain why you were found at the House of Ribbons and not the House of Whispers. Maybe this is your purpose. Maybe I am wrong, but today, we ask for your help. So, will you help us? If not for us, then for Molly?"

"Wow, way to drive your point home, Galya. I get it. He's a bad guy and needs to be stopped. You want me to help with his premature exit from this plane of existence. Say no more. I'm in it for Molly. When do you think he will strike?"

Zyra looked around. "We believe that because of a recent attempt to steal from the House of Dreams, that he would wait at least a month, maybe two. He will most likely send more expendable people. You could capture one, interrogate him, and follow the surviving raiding party back to where they came from. Blend in, maybe get into the group—do anything that will get you close to Vorador. He would never expect such a young boy as an assassin. He is that arrogant."

Dutch shifted in his seat. "Look at this guy. He said that like he does not have a care in the world. Slade, are not you afraid of death?"

I looked Dutch in the eyes. "My only fear is that I might not be able to poke out one of Vorador's eyes and piss into his eye socket right before these five put him in the fire."

Dutch asked Asya, "Can the boy fight? No offense, Slade, but he looks tiny, like a girl in a skirt. Not to mention, he smells pretty."

"Dutch, why did you and Cyril sniff me so much when I first arrived? Cyril had said, 'This simply can't be.' I'd love to understand this."

"The man that stopped Haley's attacker was badly stabbed. We healed him. His daughter and him came home with us that day."

"I'm not following."

"Slade, he dressed and smelled just like you do now."

"You mean my skirt?"

"He called it a kilt, and yes. It was even the same color. Mix that with the same smell, and I think you both might be from the same place."

"What was his name?"

"Winter, Herrick Winter. His daughter was Ashley Winter. She and Silk were like best friends while they lived with us."

"What happened to them?"

"They left. A ball of light came for them, and I never saw him again. Hell of a fighter, that one was. Asya, I think you knew him."

"I don't remember the smell, but now that you mention it, I remember his dress. He had brown eyes and black hair." Asya shared her memories with Zyra and Galya.

"He definitely looks like he could be one of his people, maybe a cousin?" Galya proposed.

"Maybe Slade came looking for this Herrick?"

"Then how do you explain my memory loss?"

"Slade, we can't explain most things about you. This only raises more questions," Zyra stated.

"It answers what my skirt is called."

"I guess that's better than nothing. Kilt is such a strange word. I wonder if it's short for something else," said Asimov.

"Sounds like a made-up word if you ask me," Bill inserted.

"No one asked you, you old dummy. Besides, why make up a word for what he's wearing? I think kilt sounds very nice." Galya smiled at me.

"Dutch, may I see the memories of Herrick?"

"Oh no, I don't want you poking around in my brain. I don't let this lot do it, let alone a young man with new powers. I will thank you to stay out of my mind."

"I understand."

"Moving on. Slade, what do you say to a little combat with the old man himself? Will you be that brave in this moment, or have your words lost their strength?"

I smiled and said, "High Lord Dutch, I would hate to give your ankles a hell of a beating but thank you for the offer." As I stretched, I smiled. "Besides, what will people say when I win?"

Dutch laughed. "By Zeus's beard, you're a feisty little nob, aren't you? Okay, one round, and I will put up five gold pieces. All you have to do is stay conscious for three minutes. You could just run around on your little girly legs while attempting to avoid me."

I laughed and said, "Five gold coins for three minutes? Playing it cheap, I see. I would have thought it be worth more to take down a mountain, such as yourself, unless you have doubts. Maybe you're hoping your words will have more of an effect than your fists?"

Asya said, "Slade, enough posturing. Accept or decline."

Dutch smiled. "Since I'm going to win anyways, then I will up the bet to ten gold coins and a title within my House. Only a child or a fool would say no to that, but when you lose, you have to ride backwards on your horse all the way to your destination."

I agreed. "When I win, I would like one more thing. I want to have one ride on your shoulders."

Dutch extended his mighty hand, and we shook on it. "One hour. Mr. Cyril, ready the healers for Mr. Slade because I'm going to show him how to take a punch or ten." Dutch and Cyril laughed.

"Asya, why did you have Sofia and Kailee come to this meeting?" I asked.

Zyra answered, "I would like Sofia to select a team that will assist and cover you while you fight Vorador. We will be watching your every move, but we must remain at a distance. You will, no doubt, get into some dangerous spots where you will have only yourself and the ladies to help you. But when you wound him, we will appear and take control of him."

"I don't like the idea of taking Sofia."

Galya said, "Slade, do not let your feelings affect your judgment. Sofia's gifts make her well-suited to dangerous situations, not to mention she is an amazing fighter. In case you don't know, she is known in some of the towns as a serious fighter. Sofia, do you accept this mission?"

Sofia nodded. "Yes, I accept."

Zyra said, "See, Slade, she wants to be a part of this. You will need a healer, one more fighter, and Kailee for her strength and mind-reading skills. Kailee, what say you?"

Kailee stepped forward. "I am honored to be asked. I gladly accept."

Asya said, "Good. Now you two find a healer and one more fighter. Pick a male because I don't think you have any guy friends, so this will be good for you."

I yawned loudly while stretching and asked, "Dutch, would you mind fighting here in this room?"

Dutch looked confused. "Where will you run in such a small room? Oh, wait. I see. You want the least amount of people to watch me spank your face."

"Dutch, I will run straight into your arms and take you down. When it's done, your lips will say that I am the cleverest boy you have ever met. This body will stand over you while you lie on the ground, or you could forfeit now and save face."

Everyone stood up and moved to the side of the room as Dutch stood up. I thought I might have talked a little too much shit for my own good in the moment. Dutch removed his shirt, and I lost count of the muscles stacked on top of muscles. Dutch was truly a beast man.

"Slade, those words will not leave my mouth, but instead, I will sing you to sleep with Mr. Right and Mr. Left because I will defeat you."

Dutch lunged forward. For a guy that enormous, he moved fast. I narrowly avoided his arms and the chair beside him. He came at me again, and he was not holding back. I managed to jump to the right and leap on his back. I did my best to hold on, but he stood straight up, running backward into the wall so that I felt all my bones collide there—I yelled upon impact. Dutch was laughing. I would be done for with another hit like that. I managed to get a better hold and reached the titan's neck, wrapping my arms around his above-average-sized neck.

"Surrender now, and I will go easy on you!" I shouted. "Accept defeat with honor and dignity in front of your beautiful daughters." I winked at Velour, but I bet Silk thought I was winking at her because of the way she smiled.

Dutch laughed hard and loud. I felt his laughter in my chest. "Better luck next time, little mouse." Dutch then reached back with one hand, grabbing my whole face. That was all the time I needed to enter his mind.

"Hello, Dutch. Welcome to the inside of my mind. In here, I'm a god! I am untouchable!"

Dutch tried to grab me, but I grew much larger—he was the size of a little mouse.

"So long as I keep you here in my mind, I write the rules. You have no chance."

I made a door appear that read "Dutch." When he saw it, he ran for it, but I blocked his way with my foot. He ran the other way. I tripped and fell, giving him time to get to the door.

"No, Dutch, do not enter that door!"

He opened the door and slipped through, and I placed my foot against the door until I could gain control of his body. Seconds flew by, and I felt the subconscious giving over control. I disconnected Dutch from myself by throwing my body across the room and into the wall. Shit, I bet that was going to leave a mark.

Only a few seconds had passed for the spectators. I stood all the way up and noticed how small I really looked to the giant's eyes. My body moved around in an odd way as Dutch struggled to understand what was happening.

"I, Dutch, the High Lord of the House of Thorns, hereby say that Slade is the cleverest fighter I have ever met!" It had been just under a minute and a half. "Slade, I'm right here. Come get me unless you're scared."

Dutch looked mad, and he jumped for me. He climbed on, and I danced around the room, stopping to shake my butt at the ladies. I wasted more time. The crowd counted down the last ten seconds, and he hit me in the face. I fell back while he jumped off me, and I stayed there until the time was up.

Dutch stood atop his own body in victory and yelled, "I have won! I'm so great. I beat myself."

I sat up, grabbed my arm, and we switched back. Dutch stood all the way up and declared himself victor.

Asya spoke, "Dutch, we all saw it: you lost. Slade stood over you, while you laid on the floor."

Dutch said, "That is because I was in his body and he was in mine. I'm the winner! I'm a titan slayer!"

Zyra laughed. "Dutch, Slade's body won, and he said this body and his clearly won. Your body did say that thing about cleverness."

Dutch paced around. "Son of a bitch! That was a clever move. Slade, you had me beat the second I challenged you." Dutch walked up to me and shook my hand. "I'm greatly impressed with you. From now on, I will make sure no gifts are used in a competition like this. Slade, you truly are a clever boy. Here are your ten gold coins. Spend them well." Dutch patted me on the back so hard, I nearly lost my breath.

Everyone walked out to attend breakfast. Asya and Zyra stayed behind.

Asya said, "Slade, chat with us for a second."

I asked to sit, and she nodded.

"Slade, may we see what you did with Dutch?"

I held out my hand, and they both held on and let go.

"I will speak for both of us when I say that move you did on Dutch was magnificent. The way you seamlessly moved between bodies and how you made him believe he was in your mind—this is a thing that even we would hesitate to do, and yet, you do it as easily as breathing and with reckless abandon. Why are you not afraid of getting stuck or of what could happen to your body?"

"Until this morning, I didn't know I could get stuck. I never thought about my body, but now that you mention it, if I had Kailee with me and I swapped bodies with someone, she could restrain my body as I do whatever needs to be done. I could take over Vorador's body. Kailee will hold my body, and I will stab myself a few times while in Vorador's body. When I swap back, he will be too injured to put up a fight, and you five pop in and do what you need to do."

Zyra said, "Slade, I love the way your brain works! We now believe you're the perfect man for this job because that is a completely insane and genius idea at the same time."

"Why do you always say I am not allowed to have sex?"

Asya spoke, "Slade, I was going to bring that up later today, but now is a good time as any. First off, I just wanted to see if you would follow my rules. I find something like this has shown me great loyalty, honesty, and respect by keeping your promise to me. Secondly, the oracles: we don't know if they would lose their gifts. I'm an oracle and have been intimate with one man, and my gift still works. So, we would have to see which women are willing to risk their gifts and get permission from their respective lady of the House."

I asked, "Are you not worried I might lose my gift?"

Zyra said, "No, because we have never found one like you. You, Slade, are different. Women are greatly attracted to you, and I will admit, you do always smell wonderful. It makes the mind wander. So, to answer your question before you ask, you're now free to enjoy the pleasures of intimacy. No, we don't believe you will lose your gift of sight because one of your gifts attracts women. So, why have a gift that threatens another gift? It would make no sense."

I stood up and said, "I have agreed to trap and kill Vorador, but I have one request. I want you to get clone bodies ready for Molly and Batch. I will pay all that I have, which is thirteen gold coins. I'll work for the rest if I have to pay off my debt."

Asya said, "Slade, tell me. Why do you care so much? It should be us who rights this mistake."

"When I first looked at her, all I saw was pain. When I entered her mind, I saw, felt, and endured her pain, from the first cut to the last tear. I suffered with her."

Zyra stood up. "Slade, why would you do such a thing? Do you not know that when you're in someone's mind that you need not feel what they felt or experience their emotions? Did you think that you have to do that?"

"Zyra, I know I don't have to, but I felt to truly know her, I had to become her. I chose her worst day, and believe me, what was done to her should only be done to people you hate. She was so alone and frightened, and Silk cut her over and over again. She begged, but no one cared. No one took the time to beg on her behalf for mercy." I felt a strange anger wash over me. "Diandra took a few seconds to see into Molly's mind and condemned her." A chair in the room flipped over on its own as those in the room remained calm. "No, Diandra saw a small piece of the puzzle, and for that, Molly suffered and how she suffered was agonizing and intense."

The chair on its side instantly became crushed by an unseen force. Asya calmly looked at Zyra as they noticed Slade's smell had intensified slightly.

"The fire would have been kinder!" I spoke a few words in the foreign language that Asya had heard at our first dinner together when I'd put out her fire. I resumed in English, "If you really want to know, ask Molly. Enter her mind, and live her moments. Feel her skin open. Feel her life spill out of her body. Feel what it was like to have that crystal shoved in behind the ear, and feel her head as it was torn from its shoulders, away from the only body it had ever known."

My eyes became black as I was consumed with anger, and those watching were frozen. I felt an influx of power surge through me, and I could feel the emotions of those in the room. I could read their immediate thoughts without touching them. They felt my words as if they were razors. In their minds, they could feel their skin being cut open. With a wave of my hand, Sofia and Kailee passed out, their bodies lifelessly falling to the floor. Bill, Dutch, and Asimov became stuck to the wall with their arms out.

I pointed as I shouted. "Then the endless hours alive in a dark box not knowing if she were awake or asleep, if anyone would ever open it again was driving her into madness. She desperately begged the gods who ignored her pleas for release. 'Maybe they buried me. Maybe this is forever!'"

Asya, Zyra, and Galya were forced to their knees.

"You didn't care enough to research Molly's mind yourselves because you had become jaded and arrogant in your self-righteous judgment! You three damned her without forethought, the truth, and its many angles. You should be ashamed! Are you aware that Molly forgave each and every one of you because she was just so happy to know that her good name was cleared? She bears no ill will at all toward any of you. I will do what it takes to restore Molly to a full body because she was wronged twice—once by Vorador, then by you, who thoughtlessly judged her. Vorador will suffer in the lowest part of hell, while I will enjoy his pain."

"Please, Slade, release us from whatever you are doing," Asya begged.

My blue eyes returned. "Asya, why are you three on your knees?"

"We were using magic to reach out to someone," said Asya.

"Please take this gold and buy Molly a new body. I will obtain more if you need it."

Whatever had taken hold of the five let them go. The witches could feel the power leave the room.

Asya said, "Slade, keep your gold. We were already going to order her a new body, but it will be up to you to place her in that body. You have shown that you possess unwavering loyalty to those you love and care about. Slade, you're on your way to great things."

Sofia and Kailee woke up and said nothing.

"Slade, would you like to come with us to where they clone new bodies?"

I smiled. "I would like very much so."

Zyra said, "Good, then it is settled. Now, can we go eat? Because I smell bacon. Would you mind meeting us at the table so we can discuss the boring travel details?"

Sofia, Kailee, and I left.

"What in the hell was that?" Zyra rubbed her eyes. "You saw it, too, right?"

"You mean the smoky, gray figure behind Slade?" exclaimed Bill.

Galya said, "No, Asya, Slade had black-as-night wings, and his eyes were made of fire. He looked like the Devil."

"Galya, I didn't see wings or fire. I saw a shadowy person whispering in Slade's ear with its hand on his shoulder," said Asya.

Zyra paced around. "I'll mull this over, but what if Slade isn't one person? What if he is 'them?' It makes sense—the smell draws women in, the tone of his voice and magical words, the clothes and strange accent."

"Zyra, all I know is that I saw something holding his shoulders, and for a second, I swear it winked at me. My sisters, could we be wrong about this boy? What if Slade were a god that has removed his own memory to experience life? Wouldn't you say that this is how a god would act if they were—let's say—*removed* from most of their power to live a human life, unaware that human emotions are powerful in their own right?"

"I don't believe so, Asya, but that display of power was an eye-opener. A story to share with Mother, but I fear her reaction. What I fear most is the interest of our hidden sister. She loves dangerous things, and Slade could be the most dangerous person we have ever come across."

"Ladies?" Asimov interrupted. "That may have been an ability. I, too, saw a shadowy figure. He may be able to control his soul, controlling it as his avatar. What say you, Bill?"

"I don't think Slade was in control or total control. His eyes and the energy that dripped from him showed us that, but what confused me was why Sofia and Kailee passed out. Maybe his people are way further beyond our known universe. What if he is from closer than we think? Yes, that could be it." Bill walked back and forth. "Yes, what if he is from below us?"

Asya sighed loudly. "Come on, you old fool, not the hidden people from inside the Earth, *blah blah blah* thing again. Don't you think we would have made contact by now?"

"What if he is the first contact? He may have become lost, or his memory was tailored, so those like us could not gain information they don't want us to have. That would mean they know of our kind and may not trust us. Slade could be part of a recon team, and he is the one that was tasked to be found by us."

Galya looked at Bill. "I hate it when you make sense, and I applaud your conviction on the Hollow Earth Theory. Or is it the hidden people's theory?"

"Hidden, gifted people. It's theorized there are pockets within the earth. My last thought on Slade is: what if he is truly in love and is willing to do whatever it takes to hold onto this life? If they are dangerous, he could be our greatest ally."

Dutch sighed. "I don't think Slade was totally aware of what was happening. I believe it was him speaking but something else helping him."

With disbelief of what they'd just witnessed hanging thick in the air, they talked for a bit longer.

***

Kailee, Sofia, and I talked a bit more and walked to the dining hall. Laughter could be heard far down the hallway. A seat had been saved for me between Molly and Sofia with Topaz and Saffron across from us. We ate and enjoyed small talk.

A little while later, Zyra walked over to us. "Slade, you and Molly will come with us after the meal is done. Sofia, you, and Kailee are in charge of everyone for the House of Ribbons and Whispers until we get back. It should not be more than a full day at the most, maybe more. If so, I will come back to let you know we are fine. Velvet and Velour will be told as well, so enjoy the day. Molly, Slade, wait for us by the fountain in the square when you are done. We should be there shortly thereafter." Zyra walked away.

Topaz looked at me and said, "Field trip within a field trip? Must be nice to be the man everyone wants to meet."

I laughed. "Honestly, it is becoming a real pain in the ass. Oh, I have a small bit of good news, but it can wait. You probably won't care. I can just announce it later."

Molly touched my hand, then said, "Holy shit, that is great news."

"Molly, don't give it away."

Sofia said, "Out with it, Slade. We all want to know. Besides, I hate secrets, and you oracles are so damned secretive and sneaky. So, Slade. Do I have to ask you what it is you hid from all of us, minus Molly?"

I drank some of my juice. "I am now free to have complete sex, but an oracle has to volunteer to see if she will lose her gifts after she has slept with me."

Topaz said, "I will volunteer under one condition. If I lose my sight as an oracle, will you stay with me? Or would I lose two things if you don't want me anymore?"

"I want to be very clear about this: I am not with any of you because of gifts, powers, abilities, or beauty. But I will admit, I do love the way you all look because not one of you looks like the other. So, Topaz, if you're chosen, and you lose what it is to be an oracle, I will not abandon you. If you're chosen, you're taking a huge risk. So, don't do it for sex. Do it for love."

Molly said, "Aw, he's so romantic, but it should be me because I'm ready to not be an oracle anymore. Just look what it has done to me. A visible head with an invisible body, but I want you there with me, Sofia. I wouldn't feel right without you because I know you and Slade have the tightest bond, as does Sunako, of whom I have yet to meet."

I looked at Molly. "Sorry, but the decision is not mine. Asya is talking with the three sisters about who will take that risk. I don't think I get a choice at all."

Sofia said, "Watch it be Cyan or Portia. There are seven of you, and I don't think Reveka will get a vote because she is Dutch's oracle. So, then it is six of you. Who will mount this wild beast? Who will risk it all to orgasm so hard that she might pass out? Who will risk dying over and over in his arms? I know I would die happy in your arms."

Molly smiled.

I asked Sofia, "Will that happen? Will you die in my arms because of sex?"

Sofia laughed. "Lucy talked about how one guy made her pass out, but I don't remember how he did it."

Topaz smiled and made an odd gesture like she was brushing her teeth, which caused her to choke.

Saffron said, "Don't be gross, Topaz. I'm sure he was just choking her with his hands because she likes to be choked."

"No, Slade, there is a French phrase for orgasm," said Molly.

"*La petite mort*. It's French, meaning 'the little death.'" I smiled.

"How did you know that?"

"Shit, I forgot to mention that he can speak French," said Sofia.

"Okay, that makes him sexier." Molly slowly brushed her hair over her ear while gazing at me. "Yes, to orgasm is like losing one's soul as the body weakens during the great release. Before you ask, I know because we had a French girl for a few months. Her name was Sylvie. She was blonde, filled with passion, and she was a screamer in bed. I still have a crush on her to this day."

I asked, "Choked? Why would she want to be *choked*?"

Sofia smiled. "We have a lot to show you, but she does like to be choked really hard as she reaches climax and a little after. One time, I had to give her mouth-to-mouth."

Molly said, "I call bullshit on that story."

Topaz laughed. "It's true. Sofia was kneeling over her stomach while choking her as I was helping her reach climax by going down on her. Lucy was almost blue, and Sofia breathed for her. Sunako used her gift and started her heart. After that, we never got that intense again, but, damn, was it hot. Great! Now I want to get choked a little while I climax."

I said, "I have a feeling the world is going to get really strange for me, isn't it?"

Molly leaned over and whispered in my ear, "Why in the hell would I do that?" She laughed. "Trust me, that's not even weird stuff; that's everyday common stuff. Sofia and Sunako will school you. Oh, baby, I have a lesson plan for you when it's okay to sleep with an oracle."

Saffron said, "Okay, can I just finish my meal without being so horny that I might slide off of my chair?"

"Too late for me," Sofia retorted.

I started laughing, then looked at Sofia. "It might be a minute before I can stand."

Both Molly and Sofia grabbed me.

"Okay, maybe a few minutes."

Kailee walked up behind me. Her voice sounded like little bells in my ear. "I heard the good news, and I want to say that I look forward to taking you in for the night or three, if you know what I mean."

"We all look forward to that," said Sofia.

Asya walked by. "Slade, you and Molly finish up. I don't want you two to be late."

We finished our food, and I kissed the ladies goodbye.

Chapter 26

You're Going to Learn Today

Molly and I held hands as we walked outside.

"Slade, do you know where we are going?"

"I think I have an idea, but I don't really know. Either way, we will know soon enough."

We waited a few minutes and saw all six travelers walking toward us.

Zyra greeted us. "Look at these two, waiting on us, and so cute together. Are you both ready to go?"

"We are." Molly nodded.

Dutch asked, "Are you ready for that ride I owe you?" He leaned down, and I climbed up to his shoulders. He walked me around the fountain three times in front of his people.

"Dutch, may I ask why you were so cool with the way I won?"

"You showed me that I should not doubt someone in a fight, even if they are the size of a toothpick. I was getting a little long on the tooth anyway, and you have given me a reason to get back out there and train with my people. Oh, and that title. Slade, Master Tactician. No, it doesn't sound right. I will try to come up with something better, and you will have it next time we see each other."

Galya said, "Dutch, stop goofing around with Slade. You two can play when we get back."

I ran over to the witches.

"Slade, you're not ready for this, but the time is now. Let's all hold hands. Slade, this will be a longer jump, so take a deep breath in, and hold it so you don't throw up. Molly, you have done this before; you know the drill. We're going on five. One, two, three, four, five."

Everything became bright white, and it was very hot but only for a second or two. The stop made the world feel like it was moving under my feet, and my head was spinning.

I heard Bill say, "Molly, give him space. Let him regain control."

I felt dizzier, and my head was splitting. I struggled not to fall over, and I snapped my eyes black without thought. Everything felt better. I stopped feeling dizzy, and my head didn't hurt.

"How do you feel?"

I said, "I feel better." All I saw were trees. "Where are we?"

Asya said, "Change your eyes back and look."

I did as she asked. My head started spinning, so I snapped them back.

"We're just outside of a friend's place of business. Your first big jump is always the worst, but at least we don't have to carry you."

"Zyra, what do you think she'll say about Slade and his eyes?" asked Bill.

Zyra replied, "I don't think they'll care. This is a business. They conduct themselves in a very discreet and respectful manner."

We came out of the tree line and stood in front of a five-story building.

"If you think this is big, it's not. Most of the building is underground, and it goes at least ten levels down. They branch out into the water on the other side. Slade, you, and Molly are about to meet your first Jotanfo. No matter your first thoughts, just act normal as if you see them on a daily basis. We know more than a few Jotanfos. One could say that we are experts on them."

I said, "I believe Sunako spoke of a female Jotanfo."

Asya said, "Yes, she was lucky they were out that day."

We entered through the front door, and a voice came out of nowhere. A disembodied, metallic voice asked, "How may we be of service today?"

"I am Asya. I'm here with Zyra, Galya, Bill, and Asimov. We're here to see Tomok, Amoli, Vilina, or Vidya. Anyone of them will do." Asya then turned to me. "Slade, don't be so jumpy, and try to fix your eyes."

The voice said, "If you have been here before, and you are on file, please step one by one into the chamber and proceed into the waiting room. If not, please wait here."

The room had no windows and was very sterile.

Asya spoke, "Molly, you and Slade wait here until we come and get you or someone escorts you to us. Slade, just act normal, like this is an everyday outing and you have seen it all. Please, I can't stress that enough. Walk with confidence. Same goes for you, Molly."

We both nodded. I changed my eyes, thankful the dizziness had stopped.

One by one, they went into the chamber. A light turned red, blue, red, blue, then to green with some kind of smoke or steam surrounding them. Then, we were alone. Molly and I talked about what life for her was like before Vorador and how she liked to help people when she went into the other towns.

The voice came back and said, "Slade, Molly, please step into the chamber one at a time. Hold your breath. When the light turns green, the door will open. Then proceed to the next room."

Molly entered first, and I went in after. I held my breath, and it was done fast. The door opened, and Molly was standing there waiting for me.

She said, "Slade, don't freak out, but the person coming back to get us does not look all the way human, so just smile."

The door opened, and I just smiled.

Molly said under her breath, "Slade! You look crazy. Stop smiling like that!" She stepped on my foot.

An unidentified Jotanfo said, "Molly, this way. Asya is through that door. Mr. Slade, stay right here. Someone will be with you soon."

I stood, waiting for the door to open. I didn't believe Asya would've brought me to a dangerous place, but I felt uneasy. The door opened again, and two Jotanfos entered the room, one smaller and more my height, while the other was over six feet.

"Mr. Slade, I am Amoli." Amoli offered to shake my hand, and I returned the gesture. Their skin was cool to the touch. "This is my mate, Vilina. Asya wanted us to help you adjust, so don't panic. Slade, your heart rate is off the charts. Please calm yourself. This is a safe place."

I asked, "Then why have I been separated from the group? That is only done to the weakest to kill it or to the strongest to mitigate damage. So, which is it? Because your mate has not taken their eyes off me since he walked in."

Amoli said, "I'm sorry. I should have told you. Please sit and allow me to explain."

We all sat down.

"Slade, Asya informed us that you have never recognized a Jotanfo before, and we want to be the emissaries for our race. Please ask us any question you wish. We will not be offended. Please, anything."

"I would like to know why your mate is looking at me that way. If I have offended you both, I am sorry, but he is staring at me like he wants to fight. I'm not here for that."

Amoli said, "Out of all the things you could ask, all you care about is the way Vilina is looking at you?" Amoli turned to Vilina and made a strange sound. "Slade, my mate means nothing by her intense staring."

I asked, "Your mate is female?"

Amoli smiled. "It has been so long since we met someone that has never met a member from our race. I'm the male of my race, and this is my female mate. What you would call a wife." I must have had an odd look on my face. "The females of our race are larger and can grow a wide range of hair and skin color. Their tendrils are longer. They have six, whereas males only have four. We mate for life. Other than that, we look very much like humans of this planet, and we have ways of blending in. We have been on your world for thousands of years, in the time when Egyptians first came together under their first Pharaoh, Narmer." Again, I must have had a strange look on my face. "Is this too much for you?"

"No, I just know so little about so much that the thought of life from somewhere else has never crossed my mind. I am sorry. Vilina, why are you staring at me like that?"

Vilina said, "Your smell. Is it naturally occurring? I want to study him. Amoli, I want him on my table in my lab as soon as possible. I must understand why he smells this way."

Amoli said, "Slade, our machine decontaminates and samples the species for disease. It will catalog the individual if they are not in our records. It is a security measure—you can understand. But you, my very sweet-smelling friend, are not in any of our records. This is common for first-time visitors, but when I say you, I mean your *species* is not in our records. That is new for us, or rather, we have not for a long time encountered a new race. We just need to study you to ensure the safety of our personnel. Now, do you understand why we have to contain you? Vilina, I don't think he understands what is going on."

I stood up, looked around, and said, "I would very much like to see someone from my group now!"

Vilina asked calmly, "What would you do if we said no?"

I snapped my eyes black and waited for one of them to make a move. "I would leave and wait for them outside."

The disembodied metallic voice alerted, "Warning. Exit room immediately! Unknown substance emitting from hostile, unknown lifeform. Temperature of hostile unknown lifeform has risen ten degrees. Heart rate has risen from one hundred beats per minute to two hundred and thirty-five beats per minute. Containment in thirty seconds. For your safety, doctors leave the room now!"

Vilina stood up and extended all six of her tendrils. She looked like she was going to strike. "Leave? I'm curious how you would *leave*. That was the way you came in, and it only goes one way. The other door is behind me, and it only recognizes our DNA. You're our guest. Come with me and submit to my tests! This is not a request. You have no choice!"

"I will not submit to anyone! I am not a slave!" I acted purely on instinct. I would not lose Molly in there. I saw a strange symbol glowing faintly on the wall. Then, I touched it, causing a door to open.

Amoli asked, "How did you see the door, and how did you open it?"

"Let me see my friends, and I will tell you, or I will open every door until I find them and a way out. Please, I'm asking nicely, but I will kill to protect my friends!"

"Can he see in the ultraviolet spectrum?" asked Vilina.

"I can't see how that would be possible. He's human right?" quipped Amoli.

They just stood there. I walked through the door and down the hall. I opened another door, and a Jotanfo was sitting at a desk.

I needed to play it cool. "Pardon me, but I seem to be a bit turned around. Can you point me toward the way outside?"

The unnamed Jotanfo said, "The door you want is down the hall on the left, then down three doors. It will be the one with a yellow mark on it, and, Mr. Slade, I look forward to speaking with you later. I have so many questions to ask."

How did he know my name? I followed his directions and found the door. After opening it, I was faced with a male Jotanfo.

"Mr. Slade, so pleased to meet you. I am Tomok." He reached out and shook my hand. He had cool skin like Amoli. "Wow, just wow! Look at your eyes. So fascinating. Come, follow me, and I will take to Asya. Sorry, we were having a bit of fun with you."

"Tomok, are you okay? You are speaking fast, and I can hear your heart beating fast. That means you're scared or ready to fight. Please don't make me hurt you!"

"Ah, that would be my hearts. Males have two, while females have three. I'm just so damn excited to meet you. Asya dropped by almost a week ago saying she thinks she discovered a special human male, and I was instantly excited."

"I won't ask again! Where are my friends?"

"Right this way, if you will." He led me to a room with only one door. "This room will take us down. Trust me. Besides, you can open our doors, so what do you have to worry about?"

I smiled. "Worry at a time like this? No, this is me focused. If this is a trap, I might die, but you will die first."

Lights on the wall blinked, and the doors opened. Asya was standing there with her arms out. I ran toward her, and she hugged me.

Asya smiled. "You did a great job. I'm so proud of you." She took my hand and led me to a room where everyone was gathered, including the two Jotanfos from earlier and a new one.

"Slade, you know Tomok, Amoli, Vilina. This is my good friend, Vidya. She is most interested to meet you."

Vidya smiled. "Slade, I am sorry if we frightened you and made you uncomfortable, but we needed to know how you would react in such an alien environment with strangers. I needed to know if you were going to be a threat or if you would follow orders that made you feel threatened. Clearly, you're not hostile. Asya, I will have you paid before you leave."

"Asya, did you bet on me again?"

She nodded.

"Damn it, I could have killed Vilina or Tomok. He came the closest when he put me in the little room."

Asya smiled. "I will try to stop, but betting on you is just so damn fun! And not one of these fine Jotanfo were in any danger from you because you posed zero threat to them."

"Asya, I think if I grabbed one of them, they would have been badly injured."

Vidya laughed. "Asya, may I borrow two gold pieces?"

Asya handed her two gold coins.

"Slade, I bet that you cannot lay your hands on Tomok, let alone grab him. Do you want to try and impress us? I think my dear friend, Asya, has vastly exaggerated your skill. I mean, you're really small for a human male."

Tomok stood up and smiled, his four tendrils extending out of his back. He was close to the wall, so he could only go left or right. I jumped full force at him and only crashed into the wall. Tomok tapped me on the head with his tendril. I jumped at him, and he disappeared again. He could do what the witches could. Three more attempts failed, and I intentionally slowed down, trying to grab him two more times after that. On the third try, I moved forward and instantly pushed backward as Tomok reappeared. I got only one hand on him as he disappeared again. As we came out of it, I wrapped my arms around him.

Vidya stood up and clapped. "Excellent! You're terribly clumsy, but you did manage to grab Tomok. Here you go: two gold coins. Now, Slade, please tell me how you can see the doors and how you opened them."

"I can see the absence of light right here." I pointed to another door. "To open it, I just touched here. Anyone can do it. Molly, come here and touch there."

She did it, but nothing happened. I placed my hand on hers, hitting the right spot, and still nothing happened. I touched the spot with my finger, and it opened.

Vidya said, "Slade, now do you understand why I am so excited to meet you? There should be no way you could open any doors unless you have been here or have been given access to the common doors. It would not open for a human from the wild. That, and the fact that you should not be able to see any of the symbols because they're in the ultraviolet spectrum, which apparently you can see while your eyes are black."

Vilina interrupted, "Why not try him on a restricted door?"

"Good idea." Vidya did something with what looked like a skinny book. "That door is now locked and is a restricted door. Now only three members can open it, two of which are away on business. Now, Mr. Slade, continue to impress us."

I touched the spot, causing the door to open. Vidya's eyes went wide and seemed upset, but not with me.

"I guess that means something. With that trick done, may I have some water before you make me bark or roll over?" Water was brought to me. "Thank you, Tomok. Why was I called an 'alien' of my own race? Asya, is that true? Am I that different?"

Vidya said, "I knew who you were before you arrived, so I knew that you don't know who or what you are. We thought that would add to the tension by throwing you mentally off-balance, to see if you would resort to violent methods to get your way. But, instead, you chose to move peacefully through the hallway without harming anyone. Your restraint shows a lot about you. What I can tell by looking at you is that you're human. If you were Jotanfo, you would have tendrils, and you are not Sa-Teen, so human it is. That's not so bad, as I'm really fond of your race. Something unusual was detected, but it was just your scent. The machine you went through kills germs, bugs, external parasites. It deep cleans you. After all, it's a dirty place out there. Now, come stand in front of me and stay still."

I did so, and she placed her arms around me. All six of her tendrils found their way around my neck, back, and hip.

"Asya, he smells so good. It's almost intoxicating. I have never smelled anything like it." She let go. "Thank you, Slade."

I asked, "What is this place, and why are we really here? I don't believe that I was brought all the way here just to be tested to see if I am a violent person who can open doors and be sniffed. Asya, I swear I will lose my mind if one more person sniffs me—it's so weird."

"Zyra, you didn't tell the boy?" Vidya smiled. "Slade, we are this world's clone supplier. There are four other places just like this around the world. I run this one but own them all. Welcome to One Cell at a Time. It's a play on words. It typically gets a laugh because of the word 'cell,' as in, 'sell you a body,' and the body is made up of cells."

I smiled. "No, I got it the first time. It's just I would have called it Grow and Go, Clones-R-Us, or The Body Shop."

Vidya said, "Your people have an expression that I love to use and that is 'Holy shit!' Kid, how would you like a job? That is very clever. I have a group down on level three that will get a kick out of those, but on to business. Molly, I heard about you, and I'm very sorry to say that I can only clone you. Your mind is stuck in your head. We have yet to be able to move a human consciousness from one body to a new clone, and it's just humans that have that problem. Sa-Teen have the limitation where they can only be transferred once. We Jotanfo, on the other hand, do not have that limitation, but we can only switch twice. That is why we live for as long as we do. Each body lives for eight hundred years, which adds up to three bodies in just under twenty-five hundred years—give or take, injury or illness."

I spoke up. "I believe I can move Molly's consciousness into her new body and get the new body to adopt her mind."

Tomok said, "Are you willing to risk her life to try it? The last few humans who tried the procedure passed away. Molly, the risk is one hundred percent fatal in humans."

"I am willing to try. I trust Slade with my life."

Vidya said, "Okay, let's collect her DNA, and we'll have a clone in two years, due to last year's breakthrough."

"What about flash clones?"

"I am sorry. A flash-cloned animal is immediately processed as food. Flash clones have serious limitations because they only live for slightly more than three years. They are bred exclusively for work. Their training begins when they wake. We only sell those types of clones when a place is being rebuilt, like a very small town or city. So, I am sorry, but it is not a viable option for the long-term life that Molly requires. I am a bit worried that the procedure could be traumatizing if it works."

Molly laughed. "Trust me. Nothing will ever be as traumatizing as what has been already done to me." She took my hand.

Amoli asked, "May we see you to better understand what the problem is? You look well to us."

Molly took off her top and pulled her pants down.

"I'm at a loss for words." The Jotanfo in the room looked visibly shocked. "Child, are you in any pain?"

Molly smiled. "No, but thank you for asking. I trust Slade. We believe that I will be able to assume control of a body that has an infant consciousness. That might be even better because I will not have to fight for alpha rights to the body. I will, essentially, suppress and/or absorb that consciousness permanently."

Tomok said, "Actually, a standard clone, not pre-trained, would be an infant in an adult's body. Molly, you two have really thought this out in great detail in such a short time. How do you know that you will be able to take control of the new body?"

Molly smiled. "I am glad you asked, but, please, call me Slade. That is Molly. We switched bodies, and you didn't even see it because it happened so fast. I have something that she does not, and that is the ability to move between bodies. I have done it four times now, and I'm getting better every time. At first, I could not switch with an oracle, but I found out that I went about it the wrong way the first time. I can show you with greater detail if you allow me into your mind."

Vidya said, "I would like that very much. Our biochemistry matches close enough that it should work."

I switched back with Molly and took Vidya's right hand.

I was in. "Hello, Vidya. We're standing inside your mind. From here, I can study you in detail at great speed, but I'm a guest and will not poke around unless you allow it."

Vidya said, "Slade, this is so strange. Your kind is truly gifted. Are you also a witch? This gift in the wrong hands would be devastating."

"I guess it's a good thing I woke up in the arms of Sofia." I let Vidya see my first twenty-four hours of life. "Cool thing about this is we can spend what feels like days in here, and only seconds will pass outside in what I call the real world."

We talked for a good duration, then I exited.

Tomok asked, "Vidya, how do you feel? You were frozen for a few seconds."

"The same as a few minutes ago. Slade's idea is sound, but there is a problem. The upside: the three-year clone can be fitted with all sorts on information and skills. I can make Molly better than she is now. Stronger, faster, and—hell—I can change her hair and eye color. She could become a whole new ethnicity and even change gender, but that is when we clone someone, and that clone goes off to whatever life it was made for. Downside: a flash-clone body, as of now, will not live much beyond three years. The standard two-year clone can live up to a hundred and fifty to two hundred years with the new breakthrough we just had."

"How do I purchase two flash clones and two standard clones?"

Asya said, "Wait, why two?"

I said, "Batch. I want to give Batch a body. We both agree that he's a slave to the noncorporeal world. He's like a spirit, and we both agree that it would be better than a life as a librarian, never knowing a true and separate life. I can put Molly and Batch in their own flash-clone body and later into the permanent body. Now, how much will it cost?"

I pulled out all the gold I had.

"I'm sorry, Slade. We don't take gold, but if this works out the way you say it will, I can offer you a job. Come work for me. Help transfer others into clone bodies. For that, I will give you what you ask and more. Plus, I will extend your life if and when you need it later on down the road."

Asya said, "Vidya, that is one hell of an offer, but he has other obligations. Even though he is a free man, he vowed to help us in an already agreed-upon assignment of great importance."

Vidya sat back, tapping her finger on the little flat book. She said, "Slade, would you work for me if I gave you a way to get here in seconds and back to where you were? The only time you would lose would be the time it took to transfer a person to a new body. You could call it a quick in-and-out. I am also prepared to offer you your own office, workspace, and living space with us, and in case living on the outside loses its charm, all your needs and wants will be met here. You will earn what you call money."

I looked at Asya, and she nodded. "I will accept those terms, so long as I will be allowed to have guests while I stay here."

Vidya smiled and shook my hand. "Welcome to One Cell at a Time. Tomok, please escort Mr. Slade and Molly to the prep room. Enter Slade into the main system with level-seven access and title of Lead Consciousness Transference Officer. Then assign five to him; that will become his team after Molly has been prepped and the sample has been extracted. Amoli and Vilina, help Slade build a team if this works. Tomok will oversee all of Slade's work. Asya, how long do you and your party have?"

Asya said, "We have at least a day or more, if needed."

Vidya said, "Excellent, then I take it I can have him trained? It should not take longer than two hours, depending on how easily his mind accepts new information. From what I've witnessed, I feel he will do great. Tomok, assign Mr. Slade a room like yours. I'm sure he will love it. Notify me when his initial training is complete. If there is enough time, give Mr. Slade and Molly a tour of the facility."

Tomok stood up. “Mr. Slade, will you and Molly please follow me?”

We walked out and back into the box room with the flashing lights on the wall. I asked about the room.

“All will be explained in your training. It’s designed for members of other races to take in knowledge at an accelerated rate. What would take ten or more years in just one field of study takes, depending on the mind of the species, minutes to a few hours? Best part is you get a nap. Do you have any questions for me? You can ask about anything.”

Vilina and Amoli got out of the box at a different place than us.

***

Vidya said, “Good. We are alone and free to talk. Zyra, Galya, Asya, Bill, Asimov, we have known each other for many years; we have exchanged many ideas and information. We have supplied you with anything you need or asked for because of the amazing work you do for us, but I have to ask: where did you did you find that young man?”

Asya told her the whole story.

“Asya, you have to be shitting me! Really? I don’t know what to say. I’m truly at a loss for words. I mean, just that he can open any door here is nothing short of astonishing. I would have thought him some advanced AI, or well, I don’t know. I have never seen anything like him. I hope for the sake of that poor girl he can do what he says.”

Asimov said, “Vidya, we have known one another the longest, and we have witnessed astonishing things together. I believe we’re dealing with either a child of the gods or a child of the stars, from farther than any place you or I have been.”

Vidya sighed. “Asimov, surely this boy could be of an unknown classification, whether he be human or otherworldly. But the fact is, he came from somewhere, and if he is from the stars, he needs to be welcomed into The Fold, especially because of his uniqueness. I wonder why he has the blank spots. Maybe it’s to test whether his race can integrate with the rest of us. Or maybe he was abandoned to see how well he could survive. Or maybe he volunteered to have his memory wiped and what he kept he kept out of fear of memory wipe, like a backup plan if things go wrong. Or he is just a hybrid, and we have seen those before. I hope he is not a hybrid.”

Asya laughed. "No offense, Vidya, but you have been reading way too many science fiction novels."

"Oh, I do so love the written works from this little out-of-the-way planet. So quaint, so fascinating, and don't forget the mystery novels."

Asya smiled. "This is a mystery, no doubt, and one we may never know all the details of. What I do know is that he's fiercely loyal to a few of the ladies, including Molly. I have seen him take a savage beating, but nothing so far stops him. It's like he is programmed to never give up. We want to train him, but first, let's give him a few weeks to relax and enjoy the pleasures of the flesh before pulling him here and there."

Vidya laughed. "All I know is, if this really works, he can have whatever he wants. Nothing will be off-limits to him, and my company could soon enter into a new era of wealth and prosperity. We might be able to offer longer life beyond what we can now. No more medicine to prolong life, only to lose it in the end. Body to Body. That sounds like a great name for it. Oh, I bet the kid will come up with something better. Damn, I'm excited!"

***

The doors opened, and we followed Tomok.

"Hey, look. His eyes are blue." Tomok startled me with the way he said it. I didn't feel them slip back or even notice it. I could no longer see the doors, but I kept that to myself. "Here we are. Molly, please sit here, so I can take the sample. This might sting a bit. I have to extract your DNA and RNA. Plus, I have to extract some bone marrow. Normally, we do it from the leg or arm, but I only have your head to work with. That is more than enough, so again, I'm sorry for any discomfort I might cause."

"Tomok, have you always worked here?" I asked.

Tomok smiled. "No, I used to be a soldier. I fought in a large war that took many lives while ravaging a few worlds. I was badly wounded, and a day later, Vidya's team found me and stopped me from dying with an experimental procedure. I became fascinated with Vidya's work, and she saw something in me. Soon after I was fixed, I joined her team and worked my way up to her right hand. You will like her. She is very fond of humans. One might say that Earth has become her pet project, and her research has had a few important breakthroughs in her time here, even though the human race is extremely temperamental and prone to self-destructive behavior."

Tomok placed his tools into a machine. When he closed the door, it made a high-pitched whistle. "Great, your DNA, RNA, and marrow came up clean, and the process will begin in three minutes. Molly, I have to take Mr. Slade for training. Would you like to watch your body being made or come with us and watch him sleep in a chair?"

I said, "Yours sounds more exciting than watching me sleep. Tell me all about it when I get back."

Molly took me in her arms and kissed me deeply. She smiled. "Thank you for this."

We kissed again. Then we walked to a place with chairs and a large window that viewed a room with tables in it. Two women prepped a large, coffin-sized glass box.

Tomok said, "Molly, that is where your body will be created. That door leads to the bathroom, and it will open when you get close to it. I will be back soon to sit with you. Follow me, Mr. Slade."

"Tomok, please just call me Slade. When will you make a body for Batch? Can you get Asya before I begin my training?"

"If Molly is a success, then they will start a body for Batch." Tomok looked at me. "You're not having second thoughts, are you? Vidya, please send Asya to my location. Slade needs her."

I laughed. "No, I'm very excited to start training, but I left something behind, and Asya can get it for me."

"Good, I was worried for a moment. May I ask you something?"

I nodded.

"Please do not repeat this, but when you were inside Vidya's mind, did you happen to notice if she likes me as more than a friend and coworker? Because I am horrible at dating, and my last relationship went to shit because I said the wrong thing at the wrong time, so I'm single again."

"Tomok, while I was in her mind, I did not peer into her thoughts or gain any insight. I have to say, before an hour ago, I didn't know your kind existed. So I don't know the subtle signs when it comes to flirting. Hell, I barely know the subtle signs of my own race, and I might be human. At least, I think I am."

Tomok laughed. "I am sorry, you *might* be human? Trust me, you're human. I have been around your race long enough to spot you from a Sa-Teen. It's the way you move. We're very much like humans, except we mate for life. Before we find our mate, we can enjoy the company of others. But I see that is not a human thing. Although, in the history of this planet, men have fought wars to win a woman's heart and still not be faithful to her. If you don't mind me saying so, humans are a mess when it comes to mates. So, how did you and Molly meet? Did you know she was your mate right away, or was it over time?"

"Tomok, my new and hopefully longtime friend, I must confess that Molly is not my only mate; she is one of a few of my mates."

Tomok laughed. "You're bullshitting me. Having a laugh at my expense because I said that humans are a mess. Well, you need to work on your poker face because I see your eye twitching."

I laughed, and Asya came in.

"Ah, my savior. Asya, promise you will not be cross with me." I smiled at her.

Asya asked, "Why? Did you do something stupid? Or do you want something stupid? Which is it?"

I smiled really big, like a child. "Batch is with Topaz. He must have slipped when we kissed. I'm sorry, but he's a slippery one."

Asya made a silly face at me. "It's okay. I will just pop back and get him. I'll bring Topaz because I don't want him in my mind."

"Again, I'm sorry. Everything has happened so fast. I didn't even think to call on him. He is closed off when researching new info."

"Slade, are you sure you want to part with him? He is yours; you own him." Asya looked worried.

I said, "Asya, to imply that I would keep my brother as a slave is hurtful. Slavery should not exist. Trust me. You will see how much better it will be."

Asya winked and became mist as she shifted away.

"Asya should only be gone for a few minutes. Tomok, how cool is that? The way she shifts in and out like that? Magic is really something, don't you think? How did you do it? Was it magic?"

Tomok said, "Slade, if I tell you something, promise you will not repeat it."

I nodded.

"What she is doing is not magic at all. It's technology. Yes, some things are magic because we have yet to explain it, but that little trick is as easy as this." Tomok disappeared and walked in through the door. "See? We call it the envelope. It is simple teleportation, but you will soon learn about that in training."

Asya shifted back in with Topaz.

"Hey, Topaz." I smiled, and she practically jumped in my arms. "Hey, sweet lips. I heard you could not go another second without me."

We kissed, and Batch came over when I requested him.

"This place is strange looking. Are you okay?"

"I'm fine, Topaz. Thank you for bringing Batch to me. Would you like to see Molly?"

Topaz smiled and said yes.

"She is all yours, Asya."

They walked out of the room.

Tomok was silent for a moment. "Sorry about doubting you and saying humans are a mess. That is bad form on my part. I have a tendency to, as you humans say, put my foot in my mouth. So, it's true: you have a few mates."

I said, "Eleven, to be more precise. It's more like I'm *their* mate."

Tomok eyes were wide. "Shut up! Now I know you're bullshitting me. We bond with our mate on a chemical level, but we can talk more about your crazy ways later. Now hop onto my magic chair and let me put a spell of learning on you." He made a bunch of funny sounds while he pressed buttons, and we were both laughing.

"Tomok, I can't put my finger on it, but I like you. You're very funny." I got on the chair.

"Okay, Slade. I have to strap you down in case your body jumps out of the chair. We wouldn't want you to hurt yourself. Now, you'll drink this black drink. It will taste like I took a piss in your mouth, but that happens after you are out. Just kidding. Maybe. Now let me get something to sweeten it."

He placed the glass on the table next to me and turned around. I drank the liquid, and it did taste something awful.

"Oh, shit. Did you drink that already? This stuff makes it taste better. We have to mix it on the spot, and it tastes like grapes. Sorry about that. I should have told you to hold on a second. You should feel the effects in less than two minutes. When you start to feel weird, just go with it. Don't fight it, or it will make the learning process harder and a bit uncomfortable."

I laughed. "Tomok, I think we are going to be great friends, and I owe you one." I started laughing a lot. I felt really weird, like strangely happy. My eyes snapped to black, and my mind raced.

Batch called out to me, "Slade, what the hell is happening? I don't feel right, and I am having trouble thinking straight."

"Just do what Tomok said. Relax. Holy shit, I'm sleepy."

Slade was out, and Tomok hooked him to a machine with many wires. Tomok's tendrils placed some of the wires on Slade's face and neck. When he was done, he pushed a green button, and Slade's body tried to jump out of the chair as if it were hit with electricity.

"Vidya, Slade is out in the chair. I will check on you in thirty minutes." Tomok left the room and walked to the waiting room with Molly and Topaz.

I woke up to see a large floating creature before me.

"Greetings, I am DeJoule. Please don't be alarmed at my appearance, as I am much like your planet's octopus."

A picture came up.

"As you can see, the only difference is my race is very intelligent and much larger. We are the Vevaphon, a race that not only can live in your seas, but can fly as well. We have developed the technology that allows for the absorption of knowledge, in which you are partaking in. This manner is far superior to that of a sit-down classroom. Do you have any questions before we begin?"

I asked, "Are you real, or are you a mental projection from the machine?"

DeJoule replied, "I assure you: I am very real. I see in the records that Tomok has you as a level seven with the title of Lead Consciousness Transference Officer, pending Vidya's approval. Your living quarters will be in the next room to Tomok, so I'll be able to swim by. We can talk again then if you would like."

"I would like that very much. This is all so new to me, and I want to know all about it."

DeJoule said, "Great, because you came to the right place for learning. Now, before we get started, I have to ask some questions. Just nod yes or shake your head no to answer, except for the first few. During the learning process, would you like to float around in the water or stand? Which makes you most comfortable: day or night setting?"

"I would like at night, floating in the water."

DeJoule said, "Prepare yourself. This might feel a bit strange. If, at any time, you feel sick and have to throw up, please tell me. If the information feels like it is coming too fast and your head starts to hurt, tell me. Lastly, at any point of this or in training you feel like you are having difficulty breathing, tell me. So, if anything feels wrong, tell me. Don't try to push through it. Now, please hold all questions until the break where I will check to see if you are doing fine. I will be right here with you the whole time. I see here these are the standard work stuff and not much on the fun side. I will add further information on the species and races that you might come into contact with. We will begin as soon as you hit the water."

I was not aware that I was falling until I hit the water and swam to the surface.

"Relax and take a breath. In here, you will be able to breathe underwater."

I inhaled, and it was just like air, but I could feel the warmth of the water. It was very relaxing. I saw the stars in the night sky, and I began to feel some pressure. I was unsure where on my body it was, but it persisted.

"Slade, how are we doing? Your heart rate in getting a little high. Shall I back it off a bit?"

"No." I began to see colors and shapes. I saw humans of all kinds from all over the planet, and I knew all the names of the places. The planet that I lived on was called Earth. I knew how to deliver a human child and minor medical procedures like setting a bone, stitching a wound, and CPR. Animals of every kind, from the sky to the ocean, flew past.

"Slade, you're doing fine. Would you like me to increase the flow of information?"

"Yes." Next was language and terms for work used in the facility, then tools, computers, genetic materials, gathering and storage.

"Break time. Slade, how do you feel?"

"I feel fine. A little nauseated, but nothing that will affect training."

DeJoule said, "You're doing great. We're over halfway done. Honestly, the rest is boring."

"DeJoule, if we have time, can I learn anything else?" I asked.

DeJoule said, "I will ask for permission to allow you to pick from topics."

"Thank you."

"Here we go," announced DeJoule.

The history of clones, fighting clones, worker clones, loved ones, clone families, and rare DNA that had been unearthed at dig sites rattled through my mind. Next was clone wake-up and training, then assigned living areas, and release of the clone to the purchaser. Then, finally, the program disclosed clone disposal due to unforeseen anomalies. It introduced personality cloning, by which the living subject was placed in a chamber and analyzed in a manner similar to how I was learning. I learned how to use a tablet. The thin book that Vidya was using was a mobile computer. I learned names and faces of all historic places and artificial lifeforms from Earth's history.

"Full stop! Slade, are you well? I have located a second consciousness, and it seems to be parasitic in nature. I have quarantined it. Please wait while I'm advised on what to do next."

I said, "DeJoule! Don't worry. That is Batch. He's like a brother. Together, we share this body, and he's not parasitic. DeJoule, DeJoule. Can you hear me?"

"Tomok, this is DeJoule. I have a situation with Slade, and I need immediate advisement. I found a parasitic consciousness that was trying to evade detection. Slade is aware of it, and he says it has a name. Batch. Current status is… Slade is quarantined, as well as the parasite. I need command key-level-ten authorization to terminate the parasite, host, or both."

"DeJoule, this is Tomok. Please hold any actions until I speak with Vidya."

"Vidya, this is Tomok. We have a level-ten matter that needs your full attention right away. Slade appears to have a parasitic consciousness. Standard procedure is to terminate one or both. Either way, only your clearance level can put that into action."

"Tomok, this is Vidya. I'm on my way. Maintain the quarantine. Asya, Slade appears to have a stowaway, a parasitic consciousness, which Slade called Batch. I will be right back. We terminate all parasites after a group of clones became homicidal. Thankfully, they were never delivered. Could you imagine how embarrassing that would have been for me? Worst part is it was two hundred highly-trained military clones that became homicidal. All were lost, along with seven staff members. Stock would have taken a real hit if they were sent off a month earlier."

Asya spoke up. "Vidya! I'm sorry, I didn't think to tell you. Batch is not a parasite. He's a separate consciousness that needs a body."

Vidya laughed. "My dear Asya, that is the precise definition of a parasite. There are only two known species that live in symbiotic harmony with those we have encountered. The rest are just bugs that need to be routed out and destroyed."

Zyra said, "The second clone is for Batch, the noncorporeal librarian Slade mentioned."

Vidya said, “What? Really? I thought Batch was like Molly. I thought you three trapped Batch in a cube, and you had him in your bag or pocket. Come on, admit it. You have trapped a few in a pocket dimension, here and there.”

Asya smiled. “I will admit, it is a rather enjoyable way to punish someone while getting my point across. But no, I assure you, Batch is a separate entity. We believe Slade was either born with it or given Batch as a helper for whatever purpose. Perhaps it’s part of an ability, allowing his mind and consciousness to twin itself. Whichever the case is, both are very different in some ways, and you can easily tell them apart.”

Vidya asked, “Can you elaborate?”

Asya said, “Slade is more of a talker in the mindscape, as opposed to Batch, who is quiet and calculating. Slade is always excited because almost everything is brand new to him. Slade knew what the food turkey was but had no memory of ever eating it. He was very excited and enjoyed it. It was almost like watching a child. Batch can only catalog the real world through Slade but not feel, taste, or enjoy it—life behind glass. I believe that a parasite can enjoy what the host enjoys, whether it is food or feelings. Or at least, the parasites that are conscious. I might add that in my extremely limited knowledge of parasites, I believe they live symbiotically with the host with a negative effect or, sometimes, a positive effect for the host. But they cannot exist for a period of time without a host. Batch has lived for a time inside the mind of a young lady I brought here, Topaz.”

Vidya sat back in her chair. “You make a most fascinating argument. I will test Topaz, and if she shows any signs that a parasite would leave behind, I will either terminate Batch and continue training Slade, or Slade can take Batch and leave. We will tag him, so we may study the progression to see if it’s truly benign. If Batch turns out to be ‘other,’ then I will study him. So, let’s go meet this Topaz. Tomok, ready the chair. We will have one more.”

“Will do,” said Tomok.

“Hello. Topaz, I am Vidya, an old friend of Asya. Please come with me. I will take you to see Slade, and we would like to run some tests on you. I assure you it will be painless. Feel free to ask me anything.”

Topaz asked, “Are you human, and what are those?”

Vidya smiled. “I’m not human, but we’re a very close cousin to the human race. We share a good amount of DNA, and we can interbreed with humans. These prehensile tendrils are our cephalopod-like limbs. Please sit in this chair. Sit still and let me attach these things to you. This should only take a few minutes."

"Vidya, is Slade okay?"

Vidya smiled, "Honey, he's asleep. When he wakes up, he will have lots to tell you. While his body rests, his mind is hard at work. Now, relax. Tomok, run the test. Asya, would you like to see Molly's flash-clone progression?"

"I would, thank you."

"Then follow us. Tomok, if Topaz is clean, send her my way. If she is not, then send her to lab four and alert your team."

Ten minutes later, Tomok said, "Tomok to Vidya. Topaz shows zero traces of any known parasitic lifeforms on file."

Vidya said, "Good. Send Topaz to me and resume training with Slade."

Tomok said, "Will do. Topaz, what a beautiful name. Thank you for your patience; you are to join your friends down the hall and to the right. The door should be open."

Topaz smiled. "Thank you, but what were you testing me for?"

Tomok said, "Sickness, but your health is good. In fact, you're extremely healthy, so no worries. Tomok to DeJoule, resume testing. Batch is not a parasite. Will explain later. I will be home around seven. Trust me. This is a story you will want to hear."

DeJoule said, "Sounds great. I will be there. Slade, can you hear me?"

"Yes, where did you go?"

DeJoule said, "Sorry, Mr. Batch had to be triple-checked, but I will include why in your training as extra training. Resuming now."

The rest was just procedures and breakthroughs. Then, the history of parasites, including two that were well-received, highly intelligent, sentient, and sapient beings.

"Tomok, Slade is done, and we still have time to kill. Would you suggest extra training while we have him?"

Tomok said, "What do you have in mind, DeJoule?"

DeJoule said, "Slade has requested history and religion, one of my favorites, and human combat in its many forms, including edged and nonedged weapons, for starters. We can also do firearms. Does that sound good?"

Tomok said, "You're the trainer, but yes, I think he could use the combat upgrade, being that he lives out in the wild. Do the religion one as well. I don't think he is ready for the history part yet, but soon."

DeJoule said, "Slade, I want to see in your mind, if that is okay with you."

"That's fine."

"Ah, I see you're not that good with fighting skills. What you lack is compensated by your high pain threshold and endurance, strength, and ability to think at great speeds. Now, what if I told you that I, DeJoule, can make you into a real fighter, a very skilled warrior in less than a minute? What would you say to that?"

I laughed. "I would say hell yes."

"I see you are using the new language classified as slang. Here we go."

First thing I learned was human history of hand-to-hand. Then I absorbed information about bladed weapons, with extensive emphasis on the history of Japan and China. Then, it was Earth's many religions.

"Slade, I'm about to pull you out. Please understand that this part might feel uncomfortable, and you will undoubtedly lose the contents of your stomach. That is normal."

"Why does that happen?"

DeJoule said, "It has to do with a small bone in the inner ear. It will cause the sensation called vertigo. Oh, and please tell Zyra I said hi. I hope to see you again soon. It was my pleasure to make your acquaintance."

"I look forward to seeing you in the real world. Thank you for being a great teacher."

As soon as I was disconnected, the room began to spin.

"Slade, here. Throw up here; let me help you. You did an amazing job."

I started to throw up. I thought I was going to die. I threw up so hard that I pissed myself and continued to throw up for a least five more minutes, but it felt like an hour. When I was done, I was sweaty, cold, and shaking. I just lay on the floor.

"Slade, how do you feel now?"

"Tomok, my friend, I would feel better if you turned off the gravity because I fear I am stuck to the floor."

Tomok laughed. "Yeah, I remember my first time in the chair. Best part is, you won't always feel that way when you are done. The sick feeling is mostly the black drink, so maybe next time, you let me give you the thing that makes it tastes better before you drink it down like we were at a bar."

I laughed. "That black drink tasted like liquid shit, and I thought it was going to come out of my eyes. What other training is available with level-seven clearance?"

Tomok said, "We have an extensive library, and you have access to almost everything because you're a seven. That is good because I am a ten with total access. One other thing: you may experience unexplainable dreams, but I would not focus on them, as they're a side effect of the mass loading of information. I had them all the time, but everyone is different."

"What I am most interested in is the complete history of Earth and other worlds. I noticed there were times where the course would jump around. You said we finished early. Any chance I could get back in the chair? If I'm right, a subject can reenter the chair within ten minutes without having to consume more B.E.P.B.O. one-two-one-eight-two-zero-zero-one, and I would consider it a favor-worthy request."

Tomok rubbed his hands together. "Look, human history is super messed up. From the start, they killed each other. Are you sure? Not everyone that takes this course is okay for a few days afterward. That is why we toned it down with a few edits here and there."

I nodded.

"Get in the chair, and let's get you hooked back up." He hooked me back up to the chair. "Boom, you're all hooked up. I was wondering if you could get me one of these things that the witches hand out? It's called candy. Oh, we just call it B.E.P.B.O. You don't have to use the numbers. The system will recognize that, and you can only get it on this level in the whole facility."

I smiled. "Say no more, my new friend." I reached into my pocket and handed him one piece of candy.

Tomok jumped up and said, "Holy shit, you just had this in your pocket? Are you insane? Honestly, you must be crazy. Why have you not eaten it?"

"I've never had one. I just haven't had a minute to sit down by myself and eat a piece of candy, but I hear they're best shared with your mate or lover."

"Slade, you're missing out. I like to lay in bed and listen to old music and roll one around in my mouth. I can get one of these things to last awhile if you store it in a jar. Damn, it's going to be a fun night tonight. Thank you so much. Here, I have what you asked for loaded up. Would you like the overview or the deep dive? It's the most extensive lesson, and, in my opinion, your culture is a very rich one when it comes to its wars that intertwine with its religions. Sit back. You'll be asleep on my mark. Mark."

"I see you are back so soon and with an interesting request. Earth, religions, and wars. Time to let DeJoule tell you a tale of seemingly unending wars. Ready?"

"DeJoule, I want everything you have about the Greek gods and goddesses. I'm particularly interested on how they impacted human civilization."

"You have come to the right place. Here we go."

First up was the Sumerians. Then many more came and went, followed by the Egyptians, the Greeks. The Romans came to power and adopted the Greek gods and goddesses. The rest was superfluous because I had what I needed.

As the lesson came to a close, DeJoule said, "Tomok wants to know if you want the history of magic and witchcraft worldwide."

"Yes." It was fast, due to overlapping religions, but I understood some of the modern magic was nothing but concealed technology.

"Slade, Tomok gave me the wrap-it-up signal. I will see you soon, my friend."

"I look forward to it."

I was out and back in the real world, and the room was spinning again. I just dry heaved, which sucked so much more than the first time.

Tomok told me, "Well, you're done here. Remember, you will feel dizzy here and there for the next hour, so take it slow when you're walking. Vidya wants me to take you to her, so let me know when you are ready to walk. How are you doing, Slade? Slade, are you okay? You look a bit odd."

I snapped my eyes black, put up my hands, and moved toward him. He moved against the wall, and I started to laugh.

"Man, I got you good. You should have seen your face."

"Slade, they have a great term for that, and it is called a dick move. Shit, I thought you had a synaptic misfire that causes Neurological Homicidal Rage Disorder, NHRD for short. Not funny when it happens. Thankfully, it mostly only shows up in clones and only while training. Now, let's go see Vidya, Mr. Funnyman."

We both laughed.

Chapter 27

Two of a Kind

Tomok smiled as we walked through the door.

"Vidya, Mr. Slade is all finished. I will finish adding him into the system when you give the okay."

"Thank you, Tomok." Vidya smiled as she studied her tablet. "So, I see you have learned a great deal today. I really thought you would have only made it halfway through training before needing a day to recover, but you're an animal. I like that. Now show us what you can do. Molly's flash clone is nearly finished. I will observe and will only assist if you miss a step or do something wrong. So, don't worry. It can take up to a month to gain total access to all the new information you have been given, so take your time. I have the group you came with waiting in the next room. They'll be watching, so no pressure."

Vidya handed me her tablet, and I touched the icons in the right order. I said, "Molly, please completely strip down, hop up onto this bed, and relax. Molly, are you absolutely positive you still want to go through with the procedure?"

"I fully trust you."

"So, I can be sure you fully understand the risk, and for the official record, I need to inform you that this procedure has never worked on a human before. To date; it's yielded thirteen fatalities. Further attempts have been deemed too dangerous and not cost-efficient. All prior patients that have died were aware of the risk versus the gain. If this procedure is successful, you will be the first. Do you understand and agree? And are you ready?"

"Baby, in your hands, I'll always be ready."

I informed her, "This is for the record, and I need you to be serious."

"I'm ready. I understand the risk."

"Molly, I'll be ready to begin as soon as your body arrives."

Soon, a fully formed Molly lay naked and unconscious on the table.

"Molly, is that you and the body you wish to transfer into?"

"Yes, but may I make a request?"

I nodded.

"In case this does not work, and I'm lost to the void, please tell Asya, Galya, and Zyra that I forgive them and that it was a privilege to study under them. Slade, my only regret would be that I could not spend more time with you."

We kissed passionately until Vidya coughed. Vidya raised an eyebrow. "I'm sorry to interrupt, but we're trying to make history here, and you two are weirding me out. Please mate on your own time, but now, Slade is on the clock."

"Vidya is right. Molly, let us make history together."

First, I entered into new Molly's mind to see what was going on. I jumped out. "Wow, it's a ghost town in there." I placed my hand on Molly's arm.

"Slade, I'm scared. I want you to know that I love you. I know it is true because my heart sings your name."

I looked her in the eyes. "I love you, Molly. I'm not worried at all because this will work."

A tear rolled from Molly's right eye, and I kissed it away.

Vidya said, "All eyes are on you, Slade."

I entered Molly's mind. "Hey, cutie, this might feel weird." I took hold of what looked like a ghost arm and pulled her spirit from her body and guided it into her new body. "How do you feel? Does it feel normal? Tell me when you have control."

Molly smiled. "I feel just like when I'm in my old head. What do I do now?"

"Think about the space around us. Try to do what you do when you enter someone's mind. Show me anything."

We were standing in darkness with only a small amount of light. Suddenly, the room was blinding with sunlight and warmth. We were in a wheat field, and there was a bed. Molly was behind me about fifty feet away.

Molly called out to me, "Slade, I think I have control." She grew wings and rose into the sky, flying around in a large circle and landing next to me. "We have a bed and some time. It's a new mind, so let's dirty up the place."

I laughed. "Molly, show me your library."

We appeared in her library.

"Molly, is it all here?"

She looked around and nodded.

"Excellent. Now, we should make sure you can pilot your new body first."

She started to kiss me.

"Molly, we will have plenty of time to make love later. Now take this sexy body for a walk."

Molly made her new body sit up and placed her feet on the ground, steadying herself.

"Great. I'm going back to my body. If you think you're in distress, signal me. I will jump back in to help if needed." She kissed me, and I transferred back into my body. "Molly, can you hear me?"

She nodded.

"Excellent, you're doing wonderful. Now put one foot in front of the other, leap into these arms, and kiss me again."

Molly took one step and another. It was apparent she was in total control.

"Now for the real test. All you have to do is show me you can speak." I wondered what her first words would be.

Molly took a small drink of water, looked at me, and cleared her throat. "I love you. I love you. I love you a thousand times. Thank you for this."

We kissed.

"I love you, my sweet. What did I say, Vidya? I said it would work."

Molly jumped onto me, and we fell to the floor kissing as she held both sides of my face with her hands.

Vidya stood there silently for a minute or two with an unreadable expression on her face. Then, out of nowhere, she moved up close, picking me up with her tendrils, then took me in her arms, spinning me around.

Vidya said, “Excuse my excitement, but I can’t believe it. Oracles were the key this whole time.”

Asya walked in and said, “No, for some reason, only Slade can trade bodies and transfer people’s minds.”

Vidya said, “Either way, I have him on the payroll. Speaking of which, Tomok, finish entering Slade into the system and put some credits in his account.”

Tomok smiled. “While he was training, I entered everything. I was just waiting on the go-ahead to finalize. Great job, Slade.” Tomok started to whistle as he left.

I asked, “Now will you make the body for Batch?”

Vidya laughed. “Of course, I will prep you myself. Molly, I will have some clothes brought to you. Slade, come with me.”

We left and went to a room two doors down.

“Slade, get on the—what am I saying? You know the procedure.”

“Vidya, are you very excited because of the breakthrough, or is there something else that you haven’t told me yet?”

Vidya said, “You will understand better when you see the deep files, but this is a historical moment. You will make us not only the premier cloning company, but also the richest. I might wait a month to see how well Molly and Batch are doing, then test them and fully announce our breakthrough. This might sting a bit. Okay, I have your sample. You can go make your first flash clone. We will be in room one hundred and seven. Meet us there when you are finished, and welcome to my company. I hope you will consider this your home away from home or your permanent home, if you want. Oh, and before you leave, you need to be fitted with a spider that is preprogrammed. It will return you to this facility when we call you or any time really that you want to come here. Tomok will fit you and give you the tutorial on how it works. Well, I best leave you to your work because it’s time to celebrate.”

Vidya left the room with a bounce in her step.

“Batch, you have been awfully quiet today. Are you okay? Come on, brother. Speak to me.”

“Slade, I like it when you call me brother. This week, including today, has been so crazy with so much information that it makes my nonexistent head spin. Slade, we have gone from you not knowing who you are to us finding each other in Topaz, to women that can be everywhere and use magic, to a woman who was just a head, unjustly accused and now saved. Then the man in the black hat who we now know as Vorador, not to mention we might have a connection to Nyx.

"Then, if you thought it just could not get any more unbelievable, we come to this place and meet people from the stars, and they help to right the wrong done to Molly. I tell you, if this were a novel, I would say it has a bit of everything in it. All we are really missing is a space battle, like a war in the stars. Now, we have a job and a second place to live. Plus, we are building a body for me, and if this works, it will be the first time I will be able to physically feel, see, taste, and smell. It wouldn't just be me living like a parasite anymore."

"Hey, man, listen to me. Don't you ever call yourself that! Do you hear me? We don't know what we are, but I know one thing for damn sure: you are my brother, and I love you. That is why I want you to have a body. I want you to be able to live a life in the way you want to, love the way you want to, and to be with who you want to be with. Sure, I will miss you, but I would rather you be by my side than stuck in my mind. Besides, whoever we really were will be nothing compared to who you and I will become. I love you brother. I mean that."

"I love you, too, brother. What are we going to do about the women who like you?"

"Damn, that is a good point. Well, it is obvious that Topaz is your number one, like Sofia is my number one. I will say, I really like Sunako, Molly, and Kailee. And I kind of do have a thing for Velour. Although, in the end, we will not have a choice. They will pick who they want to be with, but you definitely get Lucy. She is a bit sexually aggressive for my taste."

Batch laughed. "Really? You must know that she will pick you. Under all the big talk and the sex jokes, I feel she can be just as loving as the rest of them. Okay, one hour and ten minutes until the flash clone is ready."

"Batch, will you keep your name or take a new name?"

"I never thought about that. I'll see what names are on file."

I walked, and we found Tomok in the room down the hall.

"Hello, Tomok. I have no access to the main data bank, and I'm looking for names."

"Place your hand here, and your hiring will be complete."

I did, and it took a skin and blood sample and a retinal scan.

"There you go. You're now completely in the system."

"Tomok, Vidya says to see you about being fitted for a spider."

Tomok laughed. "Excuse me for laughing. It could not be shown to you unless you were hired. Now I can, but I have to speak with Vidya. Now that I think of it, wouldn't Batch be fitted as well? Please sit down, and we will begin."

"Please, Tomok, not the black shit drink again. I honestly have nothing in my stomach to throw up besides what I drank."

Tomok laughed. "No, this is not that type of training. That type involves complete mental interaction with the way the Vevaphon interacts with the brain, filling it with knowledge. Without the black drink, you could die from the sheer volume of information in its many formats like pictures, written languages, computer skills, and the bio codes. Yeah, you would have had a mass overload, probably leading to a stroke then death. Your race is a bit on the delicate side." Tomok laughed again.

"I don't remember a course on bio code."

"It's not a course. It's something given to each employee after they're hired. Now you really need to understand this, and it's usually the thing people have the hardest time understanding. The building is, well, imagine the building as a huge creature, and we work and live within it. The bio code allows us to enter them, move from floor to floor and place to place. That is why we were so fascinated with your ability to open any door because that simply can't be done without a personal bio code, but you did it. It's like he knows you. This ship is what you would call a male."

"Tomok, is the building a living creature?"

"You caught that, didn't you? Damn, you're bright. Yes, that is why you will mostly find ships, submerged in water, enjoying the salt water. They can spend vast periods in any water or no water at all."

I sat down and said, "Of course, this is a living ship. Why wouldn't this place be alive? Then, I have to ask: do any of our fellow coworkers belong to a race that might be a little odd to me—say—a talking duck or raccoon? Maybe dogs that walk upright?"

Tomok looked at me and laughed. "No, that would be something. I think I saw that in one of the old movies your race was so obsessed with. Hold on. I'll check." Tomok spoke to the building's artificial intelligence. "Isaac, what Earth movie had talking ducks and raccoons?"

A disembodied man's voice came out of the room itself. It was smooth and sounded like the voice from earlier but without the metallic sound. "Tomok, your inquiry has yielded fourteen movies and two hundred seventy-four episodes of a children's cartoon show. One hundred and thirteen contain a talking duck named Fowl Drake, due to his foul language and temper. The raccoon was named Cheeto, the Garbage Panda. The movie he first appeared in was named *Protectors of the Universe* and the children's cartoon of the same name. Shall I have it placed on your watchlist on your personal viewer?"

Tomok replied, "Yes, please. Thank you, Isaac. Slade, why do you ask? Do you want to come over and watch a flick with me? That is what they called a movie: a flick."

"Yes, whatever that is sounds enjoyable, but another time. Batch and I were talking about how our life has taken so many insane turns that it sounds more like a crazy science fiction novel." I stood up, beginning to wobble, and fell over, unconscious.

"Tomok to med lab. I need someone with expertise in human physiology to my location immediately."

A female Jotanfo appeared in the room seconds later.

"This is Slade. He must have passed out due to exhaustion, but I need to know if there is anything wrong with him, anything that could lead to death. Have him directly into stasis. He is to be treated as a VIP."

She worked on Slade. "He appears to be dehydrated and extremely exhausted. Tomok, put him on the table. Wait! Slade appears to have a parasite."

Tomok said, "Doctor Rilla, I assure you, it's not a parasite. It's something else entirely."

"His brain pattern shows a parasite. Look, these readings are all over the place. Tomok, did you scan Slade for a nano-life mate? If it's not a parasite, then it has to be a bio implant. How you missed that is beyond me but obviously not you. I will run the scan. Watch and learn the correct way to do your job, fool!"

"Look, I'm sorry for the tenth time. I honestly didn't know you were in the room."

Doctor Rilla scowled at Tomok and scolded him, "Maybe you should have kept your mouth shut or at least been aware of your surroundings before you open your big, stupid mouth and say stupid things that your tiny, stupid brain thought up! I mean, who says shit like that? What I am saying is, you're an asshole! How could you say something like that? No! Strike that. You're a stupid asshole with a stupid face. I mean, what in the hell was I thinking, dating you? You're an idiot that watches too many of those old Earth movies! I would have said that they were making you stupid by rotting your brain, but you had to be smart in the first place to become stupid!"

I woke up to the doctor berating Tomok. I had just enough strength to say, "I'm trying to die in peace over here. Can you two just kiss and make up already?"

Doctor Rilla yelled, "Shut up, Slade! Go back to dying, and mind your business before you get something amputated while you're unconscious."

I closed my eyes and mustered a little more strength to say, "Like what? You already bit off my head."

Doctor Rilla stopped yelling at Tomok and walked over to me. "Nap time for Mr. Funny Guy."

She jabbed Slade with something that made him completely blackout.

"You see, Tomok, this is exactly what I don't like. Smart-mouthed, jackass behavior! He, I can understand, because he's just a talking hairless ape, barely a step up from monkeys and a big step down from dolphins and most whales."

Tomok placed his hands together and said, "Doctor Rilla, I am sorry. Please, let me make it up to you in any way you would like. Just allow me a second chance to show you my better side."

"Fine! Tomorrow at four in the workout center. If you can withstand three minutes in the ring, then maybe I will give you a second chance. If you pass out, it will be game over for you, baby cakes." She pinned him to the wall and whispered in his ear, "I believe that's one of the filthy Earth lingo things you called me: 'honey buns.' Or was it 'sugar tits?' What in the hell does that even mean? Tomorrow at four or no second chance. Now you do the scan and tell me if he has a bio implant. You do know how to turn it on, don't you?"

Tomok moved a handheld device over Slade's head and chest.

"Not a nano-life mate, but something much more advanced. You're right: his brain waves are almost unreadable. Tomok to Vidya, please come to my location. This is something you'll want to see."

Vidya shifted into the room. "Is the boy okay? Tell me he's okay."

Doctor Rilla said, "He is fine but needs at least two hours of sleep. While he is under, I will completely hydrate him. It seems that he overdid it and has had minimal sleep for at least four days prior to today, but he will be fine. The reason Tomok called is—well—you tell her Tomok."

"Thank you, Doctor Rilla. Vidya, you know how nano-life mates used to be very popular, and you know they're making a comeback, right?"

Vidya said, "Yes, for those out on long missions, lonely people, and young ones that are an only child. What about them?"

"I believe Batch is something like that, but super advanced. I mean far beyond high-end AI. If Batch is some form of AI, then we have never seen its kind before. It's a new type of synthetic lifeform, but instead of it being an implant, it must come from his nonremovable bracelet. Why else can't it be removed?"

Vidya said, "Good. That will be double good for us. Besides, his ability to do what he did with the subject, Molly, is too important to let anything get in the way. If Batch is some form of AI, then the flash-clone transference will not work because he cannot control a clone of Slade's body. That will prove he is a form of AI. So, call me when he wakes up, and maybe you two can stop fighting while on duty."

Vidya went back to Asya's group.

"Asya, I'm sorry, but Slade will need two hours of sleep due to extreme exhaustion. I can take you to see him if you would like."

"No, he couldn't be in better hands. Our business can wait a day or so. Would you mind if we stayed the night?

"Asya, I'm shocked that you would even have to ask that when you know you always have a place here with us. I will order up rooms for you. Would anyone prefer a private room?"

Asimov said, "Bill and I can room together."

Zyra said, "I would love a small room with a view so I can meditate."

Galya asked, "Asya, want to share a room?"

"Sounds great, Galya. I will pop back and inform the main group that we will be away, so no one has reason to worry. Galya, would you like to escort me?"

Galya nodded.

"Excellent. We will leave soon."

Vidya asked, "Would you like me to put Molly and Topaz in the same room?"

"I think Slade has earned his time with the ladies. Do we all agree?" said Asya.

All said yes.

"Great, that settles that. So, place them in Slade's private quarters. I'm sure they'll just eat him up." Asya chuckled.

Vidya said, "This works out perfectly. We will be able to study both Molly and Batch for twenty-four hours. Then, I will know for sure that the transplant took root, and that should give my report the solid foundation I need. Thank you so much, Asya. I will have someone bring you all to your rooms within a few minutes."

Zyra said, "Molly, my sweet. Tell me, is your gift still with you?"

Molly took Zyra's hand and let it go.

"I see that you are fully intact, body and mind. Now, are you willing to possibly lose your gift in the experiment by being with Slade? To lay with a man, lest she goes blind as her gift leaves her—or so the texts read."

Molly replied, "Something inside me drives me to want him, so I will risk it all to be with him. Besides, the gods must want this because he came into our lives and had the power to save me."

"Then, you will be the one that risks it all for love. I wish you the best, my dear."

An unnamed male Jotanfo entered the room. "If everyone will please follow me?" He took them to their assigned rooms, all on the same floor. "If you need further assistance, I am Isrum. Don't hesitate to ask for anything." He handed out bracelets. "This will allow you to contact me or each other. Just speak the person's name, and you will connect to that person." Isrum walked away.

Asya told Zyra, "Galya and I will be back shortly."

Then, Asya and Galya disappeared seconds later, reappearing at the House of Thorns.

"Galya, if you see Sofia, tell her I want to see her. Meet you back here in an hour."

"Okay."

Asya went to where she thought Sofia might be. She found Lady Velvet and Lady Velour with Sofia, Kailee, and Cyan. "Good, I found you, Sofia. Would you like to see Slade?"

"Yes, please, very much!" exclaimed Sofia.

Asya smiled. "Great, then stick by me. We will leave within the hour. We will return in one- or two-days' time. Velour, a word in private?"

"Yes, Asya."

"We will need Kailee to pair up with Slade to hunt Vorador. Are you still willing to part with her for up to a few months? I figure, with her ability, Slade could move from place to place without having to ask questions and rouse any suspicion."

"Of course. She is the perfect choice for a low-profile mission like this one," said Velour.

Asya replied, "I could not agree with you more and thank you. Kailee, I will be back for you when we are ready to start the hunt, hopefully three days tops. This may be the most dangerous thing you have ever done, so enjoy the next few days."

Kailee nodded.

"Since we're done here, I will leave tomorrow morning. My House surely needs me. I am sure my sisters will go home as well. Asya, how is Molly doing?" asked Velvet.

"Very well so far."

Velvet said, "Vorador will not get away with what he has done. Only when he's dead, will Molly be truly avenged. Can I get you to make us some horses to ride home?"

"Of course, I will, but I could just shift you and Diandra to your place. Velour, do you want to as well?" asked Asya.

Velvet shook her head. "No thanks. The horses will do just fine, and it will give me time to think on the way home. Besides, I'm only just under two hours away."

Velour said, "I'm going to stay at least a day or so longer. Thank you, though."

Asya smiled. "You're welcome." Asya walked outside, then made two large black horses. "Velvet, these horses will last you three days. More than enough time for you to really enjoy their speed, so enjoy them. They will turn white an hour before they disappear, so make sure you're close to home, or you're in for a walk." Asya walked with Sofia. "Sofia, I'm going to bring you to a very strange place, so grab what you came with. Later tonight, you will be able to be with Slade the way you want. So, wait for me here when you have what you need."

"Asya, is there any possibility that we can make a small stop back at the House of Ribbons? I promised Sunako that I wanted to share my first time with Slade with her," Sofia said.

Asya said, “Of course, and might I say that sounds very romantic? He will have to be with Molly at some point to see if an oracle will retain their gift of sight after being with him.”

Sofia smiled. “The more the merrier, but Slade is an oracle, and Molly is an oracle. Will that count as her being with a regular male?”

Asya said, “Shit, I never thought of that. Great point, Sofia. You just earned a piece of candy.” Asya handed a piece of candy to Sofia.

Galya saw Silk. “Silk, have you seen Sofia?”

“I saw her with Velour and Velvet about ten minutes ago; they should still be near the guest cottages,” replied Silk.

Soon, Asya came across Galya. Asya yelled over to her, “I found Sofia! Now I’m heading to the House of Ribbons to pick up Sunako. I’ll be right back.”

Asya disappeared, leaving only mist behind, and with a pop, she was in the House of Ribbons. Asya went to the main house and asked Elma if she knew where Sunako was. She informed Elma that Sunako would be away for a few days. Sunako was located as she was just finishing healing a broken arm on Mr. Treat, who’d fallen out of his hiding place in one of the trees while hunting deer.

Mr. Treat said, “Hello, Asya. It’s been awhile. How you have been?”

Asya smiled. “Jim, I am well. How is your lovely wife, Kim, these days?”

“Oh, happy as always. She just took in a new stray cat. You should see it, gray with tiger stripes. As long as she is a good mouser like the other three, I’ll be happy to keep her. I have smoked deer heart if you would like some.”

Asya replied, “This is why everyone calls you Mr. Treat because you always have the good stuff. I would like some, yes. But let me treat you as well. Here are six pieces of enchanted candy.”

Jim smiled. “Oh, thank you very much. Kim will be so excited. Here is that heart. I smoked it yesterday. Well, I best be getting on home. Thank you, Sunako, and thank you, Asya. I will give Kim your best.”

Asya smiled at Sunako. “Sunako, my sweet. How would you like to see Slade and spend the night with a few friends?”

Sunako smiled. “Oh yes, please.”

“Then grab what you need for two days, and let’s go.”

They walked back to her cottage. Sunako packed a little bag and took Asya's hand. They disappeared, only to reappear back at the House of Thorns to meet up with Galya and Sofia.

"I have to ask Kailee something." She found her ten minutes later. "Kailee, I will ask you to ride back to Velvet's house and wait for me there. What I really want is for you to find out if she has any other secrets or little items stashed away. I will tell her I'll pick you up in two days. Remember, very few know your true gift because of the way you can hide it from an oracle."

"Asya, you're asking me to spy on one of the sisters. I could be punished or thrown out. Then what?"

"Then you come live with us and have a life of adventure. Trust me. No one will know, not even Velour. Understand? You will be rewarded very well after this, I promise."

Kailee smiled. "I will do as you ask." She went to get her things.

"Velvet, I have a request for you. I need to pop to your house in two days to drop off something for you. I would like to pick up Kailee from there because I don't want to make Velour jealous that Kailee will have Slade before her. I'm sure you understand. Besides, what I'm going to bring you will make you very happy. It's something I know you have wanted for a bit of time."

Velvet's eyes opened wide, her smile growing. "I look forward to seeing you. I will need another horse."

Asya snapped, and it appeared.

Galya asked, "Did Velvet agree?"

"Yes. Once I said I had something to bring her, she knew it was the necklace. That is the perfect excuse to give it to her. Damn, I wish I never trained her so well as to be able to hide her memories. I really feel like the Eye is not the only thing she got her hands on, but I hope it was."

"Velvet was always the one who chased items when she was younger. We should have seen this coming."

Asya shrugged. "I agree. Well, we have everyone, so let's go."

They shifted away, reappearing outside Asya and Galya's room exactly where they'd left from.

"Zyra, we're back."

"Is Sofia with you?"

"I brought Sunako as well."

Zyra laughed. "They're going to injure that poor boy tonight."

They both laughed hard.

One hour later, Slade woke up.

"What happened?"

Tomok sipped his drink. "Man, you have to know your limits. That could have been bad if you were on the outside. Drink water when you can. You were dry as a sea sponge on a frying pan. While you were out, I had your personal bio code slipped into your wrist, so you're good to go. Time to put Batch in his body; the room is prepped and ready."

"Tomok, who was that angry woman?"

"That was Doctor Rilla. She was the one I made a mistake with, but that is a story for later."

We walked over to see a body lying naked on the table.

"Is that what I look like? It's so bizarre looking at myself. Batch, are you ready to dance?"

"I'm ready."

I lay on the table next to my naked self and took its hand, concentrating. Then, I was inside the body, and just like Molly's flash clone, it was just a shell.

"Batch, it's all clear. Come on over."

"Wow, it really is just a shell."

"It's all yours, brother. Just take control."

"I feel the eyes. I have them open. Now, I can move the right hand."

"I'm going back, so you can get total control."

I got back into my body off the table and watched Batch slowly take control of his new body. Batch sat up and tried to stand.

Tomok said, "Batch, take it slow. Give it thirty minutes. Trust me. You have to walk before you can run. Batch, can you hear me? Slade, I don't think he can hear me."

Batch spoke for the first time, "I can hear you." His voice was raspy, like he had been yelling. "May I have water?"

Tomok handed him some water.

"That feels better. I feel the coolness and how it is smooth when it went down my throat." On unsteady feet, Batch took his first steps. He looked like he was on a tightrope with his arms out to balance him. When he became steady, he stepped forward. "The floor is cold, and so am I."

Tomok handed Batch some clothes. "Tomok to Vidya, come in."

"Yes?"

"Batch is controlling the flash clone as his new body."

Vidya shifted in.

"I don't see how he could take over the body if he were an AI unless their race is almost indistinguishable from biological races. Maybe they live and die like us, or he is something else. We may never know."

"Should I give him a personal bio code?"

Vidya nodded. "Batch, how much did you retain in training? Can you do what Slade can do with your mind? I mean, can you go into other people's minds?"

Batch replied, "I retain one hundred percent of the training, and I would need to touch your hand."

Vidya gave her hand to Batch.

"I cannot see your mind. Maybe I need to adjust to this body."

"Tomok, give him his own personal bio code. Have them both implanted with the spider, the new kind with the envelope. Then have them trained on the uses of both at eight a.m. tomorrow. Gentlemen, it has been a very exciting day. You two deserve to relax, so go and enjoy yourself. Tomok, excellent work as always. Maybe I will put in a good word with Doctor Rilla for you."

"Thank you, Vidya. I do what I love and love what I do. Okay, boys, come into the next room. I will get you fitted, but I will warn you. This will be somewhat painful. Off with the shirt, Slade. This is the S.P.1.D.E.R. It will attach to your spinal column, and it has a built-in envelope with a neural implant. It will not activate until you take the training course with your favorite black drink. This time, maybe you will let me make it taste better." Tomok laughed.

I said, "Batch, you should drink it straight like I did."

"You mean, like an idiot?" Batch laughed. "I'll take you up on that challenge, as long as you do it again this time, knowing how bad it will be."

"Laugh it up, brother."

"Okay, boys, this is the part you will not like. Lie flat and stay still."

Restraints gripped us by the neck, hands, and feet, with one across the midsection.

"Tomok, is this really necessary?"

Tomok walked over and looked down at me. "I'm not going to bullshit you. This is going to be painful as hell, and you have to be conscious the whole time. I will make the incision right below your right floating rib. I will insert this flat oblong thing into the incision. I will go over there, enter a command, and it will spring to life, grow legs, and crawl its way to your spine, just behind the heart. The restraints will keep you from hurting yourself. I will step into the next room when the screaming starts. Batch, I have to give you your personal bio code."

Batch got a shot in the back of his hand. "You now have your bio code."

Tomok made an incision on both of us, and I felt the cold metal of the implant.

I asked, "Tomok, is it too late to have a piss?"

Tomok laughed. "Much too late now. You're going to piss yourself. I'll be in the next room. If you need me, just scream." Tomok laughed, and I wanted to jump off the table and kick him in the ass.

"On my mark… Mark!"

I felt the legs crawling inside under my ribs. There was a burning pain as it moved toward my heart. I heard Batch scream, which scared me, so I screamed. The sensation continued its painful journey up my back. That was when the real pain began as it latched on and locked itself in place. It hurt so much that I pissed myself as I screamed. My mouth went dry, then nothing. No pain at all. I was sweaty but fine.

"Batch? Batch, you okay?"

"I think I pissed myself."

"I did, too."

Tomok reentered the room. "Congratulations, that was the worst thing you will feel until they make a new one, which is about every five years. We all have to get the upgrade."

"Great, something to look forward to. Now, I have to get back to my room to shower because this is the second time today that I've pissed myself."

"Here, you can shower in this room."

We walked two rooms over.

"Careful with the heat—it can burn you. Some of our clientele can withstand water that would scald us."

Batch and I got into what appeared to be a six-person shower. The showerheads looked like flowers coming out of the ceiling and the walls.

We showered quickly and got out.

As I dried myself off, I remarked, "Man, I swear that was the best shower I have ever had. I don't think I have ever felt so clean."

Batch laughed. "Well, I don't know about that because it was my first shower, but it was amazing. I could feel the drops of water on my skin."

"Oh yeah, you're the new guy now. I will tell you in advance that if you eat the wrong foods and they don't agree with you, it could be a bad time in the bathroom." I laughed.

"What? Why not just avoid the wrong food?"

I laughed again. "That's just it! You will not know until after you eat and digest it. Then it's a waiting game. Welcome to being a biological being."

"You make it sound so great."

Tomok came back in with fresh clothes. "Okay, gentlemen. I just finished speaking with Vidya, and she has released you boys for the day. It is roughly eleven a.m., but you two will report back here tomorrow at eight a.m. The S.P.1.D.E.R will act as a two-way communicator. Batch, I will activate yours in the morning. Until then, Slade, keep Batch informed if anything comes up. I had you placed in the room next to mine. You will understand why when we get there. I will show you what is between here and our rooms."

We walked down a corridor. Tomok pointed out labs and workspaces and introduced us to a few people. We got on the elevator.

"Sublevel thirteen, please."

It only took a minute. We exited and walked down a well-decorated corridor.

"Okay, this is your room. To enter, place your hand here. Wait, what I am saying? You know how to open the doors. Sorry, I was in tour mode."

I smiled. "I was enjoying the tour."

"Thanks, man. Batch, I will ask Vidya about you getting your own room, if you would like. We have six open just on this side, so it would be no trouble."

"Thank you, Tomok. That would be nice. For the first time in my life, I can know what it is to be alone."

Tomok smiled. "I will call her right now. Trust me, Batch. A little me-time can do wonders for the mind." Tomok called Vidya, and Batch was assigned his own room two rooms down from mine. "Batch, follow me. Slade, wait right here at your door, and I will be back to show you in."

Batch walked to the room, and Tomok opened the door.

"Holy shit! The wall is a huge window! You can see how clear the water is. Look at all the fish."

Tomok smiled. "This right here is my favorite part, showing the rooms on these levels and watching the facial expressions. Well, I will leave you alone. Bathroom is over there; cold drinks are in here. Oh, it's empty. I will have some good stuff delivered in a bit. If it gets too much for you, feel free to call me. We could watch a movie or just talk because I rarely go outside and would love to hear some stories."

"Thank you, Tomok. I will call if I need anything, and I'm extremely interested in the thing you keep calling movies."

Tomok smiled and walked out.

"Slade, your brother is happy with his room. Now let's get you into yours."

Tomok opened the door, and we walked in.

Tomok yelled, "Holy shit! Wrong room!"

Four mostly naked women were lying on a large bed.

I laughed. "No, this is the right room."

Sofia, Molly, and Sunako smiled, and Topaz said, "Damn straight, this is the right room!"

I had almost no words. "Tomok, the wall is a huge window. Look how clear the water is and the fish—wow, this is very cool."

"Yeah, that is exactly what your brother said." Then, he kind of blanked out.

"Tomok, Tomok. Are you okay?" I tapped him on the shoulder. "Tomok, can you hear me?"

Tomok snapped out of his trance. "Oh yeah, sorry, man. It's just that you have four mostly naked women on your bed… and they are *naked*."

I laughed. "Yeah, you get used to it, and you said naked twice."

Sofia and the ladies covered up. "Slade, if you have company, announce them first, you idiot."

Tomok said, "Slade, a word outside, if you will please."

We walked outside my room.

"I thought you were bending the truth about your ladies. I though, okay, two, but more than that surely had to be bullshit."

I laughed hard. "First off, don't let them hear you say that because they're not mine. I'm theirs."

"What is that like? You know being with that many ladies at once?"

"I don't know. I have not been with them in that way yet, but I believe it will be really interesting."

"I heard this line in a move, and now I understand what it means. 'You're the man.'"

"You've said 'movie' before. What is it?"

"I will show you when you come over. Try not to hurt yourself in there, but you know where the med bay is. There is always someone on duty."

Tomok winked, then walked away. As I was about to enter my room, I stopped. I stood in front of my door, knowing the ladies were waiting. I was so nervous, but I took a deep breath and centered myself.

Chapter 28

Last Chance for a First Kiss

As I was about to open the door, Asya swept up from behind me.

"Ah, there you are, my boy. I have to say, once again, I'm proud of you. So many people here are so excited. I wanted to see you before I leave for part of the day."

"Is everything all right?"

Asya smiled. "Everything is fine. It's time for Beth to begin her training, and Tambry is waiting to meet her."

"Tambry? You spoke of her. She's an expert in rooting out if something is magical or technology in disguise, right?"

Asya shook her head. "You have a hell of a memory, and yes, that is her. I need to speak with Sofia and the ladies before I sacrifice you to them." She started to laugh, then pressed me to the wall, and whispered, "But we're waiting on a doctor. Oh, here she comes. Hello, Dr. Rilla."

"Hello, Asya. I have heard great things about you and your work in the wild. Did you bring Mr. Funny Guy here?"

"Yes, I did. Why do you ask?"

"I helped put him to sleep after he made two mistakes. One, he stuck his nose into my conversation. Two, he made a joke in a vain attempt to be funny. Ah, Slade, I see you are living next to Tomok. You two will make great working buddies. Dumb and dumber. Now, I just need to know which one you are." Dr. Rilla was poking me in the chest the whole time she spoke. "Now, Asya, my duty shift is about done, so let's get to it."

Asya opened the door. "Ladies, this is Dr. Rilla. She has something for you, so listen up."

"I will be blunt. Who is planning on having intercourse with Mr. Funny Guy at some point, whether it is today or in the near future?" Dr. Rilla grabbed me by the left ear with one of her tendrils and held it until she was done talking.

Sofia, Sunako, Molly, and Topaz raised their hands. I was incredibly happy they were mostly dressed.

"You have got to be bullshitting me. Really? All four of you? He isn't even that pretty, albeit he smells really good. Now, turn around and show me your ass. I'm giving you a shot. It will sting, but you will not get pregnant for thirteen months. If one or more of you wants to get pregnant before then, I have another shot that will negate this shot's effects. Does everyone understand?"

All four ladies said yes. Their voices combined to make a beautiful sound. Dr. Rilla gave each woman a shot.

"Asya, anything else before I take my leave?"

Asya shook her head.

"Good day, then." Dr. Rilla let go of my ear. "See you around, funny guy."

"Okay, ladies, here are the rules."

All four moaned and groaned.

"The rules are whatever you make from here on out. He's all yours, but if I hear of any fighting, I will be displeased. This is not the place for any type of bad behavior. Please act normal, no matter what you see while you're here. Don't worry; this is an extremely safe place. I am leaving now, so, Slade, enjoy yourself. Remember, love more than you are being loved, and you will become a great lover." She kissed me on my cheek and hugged me tightly. "Oh my, you do smell wonderful. Almost like flowers in full bloom sprinkled with sugar."

She walked out of the room and went to Beth. "Beth, my dear, are you ready?"

Beth smiled.

"Don't worry, you're going to a wonderful place, very safe. You will learn much there, and you will be loved. Now hold my hand."

Beth took Asya's hand, and they shifted away.

Dr. Rilla pressed the call button on Tomok's door, and he opened it. "Your one chance starts now, so you better impress me."

Tomok stumbled backward as Dr. Rilla pushed her way in. She stepped on him while laughing and sat down, crossing one leg over the other.

"May I take you to dinner? Maybe dancing?"

"How did you know I like dancing? Yes, I think I would very much like that, but first, come here and kiss me before I slam you into that wall and take a kiss from you."

Tomok rushed in to kiss her. When they did, each tendril intertwined as they caressed one another, causing intense pleasure to both.

Two rooms down, Batch was sitting on the floor and watching the fish swim by. He felt utterly alone for the first time in his short life, a castaway without an island or ship to call his own. The room was silent as his mind was quiet. He could hear and feel his own heartbeat as he contemplated life and his own existence. He was not sure if he was happy to be alone with just his thoughts. Then his thoughts drifted to Topaz. Would she still want him? Would she love him a thousand ways like she'd told him? Could Batch make her happy with his body? Life was easier when he was just a housecat in her mind.

Batch pulled his legs in close to his chest and said, "I think I am afraid."

The quiet of the room closed in on him, causing a rush of newfound emotions. Batch was completely overwhelmed. He reached out with his mind but found no answer. He lay on his side and silently cried as the word *alone* assaulted his mind.

***

The ladies were talking about details.

Sofia barked, "Slade, get naked and stand right there until we figure out what to do with you! Oh, I have been waiting too long for this."

"Remember, I'm a free man." I smiled.

"If you want to feel our bodies, you will obey, or you can stand there smiling."

My smiled disappeared as I started to take off my shirt. I began to feel strangely sad. I could hear my own voice, saying the word "alone" repeatedly with increasing sadness.

"Ladies! This not what you want to hear right now, but I have to do something. I will be right back. Stay in this room!"

I walked out and said, "Lock room seventy-four." The door locked.

I walked toward Batch's room, but the door was locked. I snapped my eyes black, and the door opened when I pushed the space on the wall. I changed my eyes when I saw Batch on the floor, and I rushed in to see if he was okay.

Batch jumped when I touched him. "Shit, you frightened me! Why didn't you just ring the door?"

"Batch, I could hear you in my mind." I hugged him. "I'm right here, brother. I won't leave you alone again. I'm sorry. I just thought that you would welcome some time alone."

"How do you do it? I mean, how do you deal with being alone? Damn, having a mouth as your main way to communicate is really inconvenient. Talking takes too long."

I looked at Batch. "I didn't know you existed until that time with Topaz. You were with her so much that I liked it when you were with me. What I am trying to say is, I got used to you coming and going. Wow, you're right. Talking is hard sometimes. The good news is, we are still connected somehow, at least on my end. Oh, shit. Stay here and wash your face. I'll be right back."

I ran back into my room. "Topaz, put your clothes on. We have to go."

Topaz said, "Baby, the only way I am putting those clothes back on is after I wake up from the coma you're going to put me in. Now, get on the bed before we have to restrain you."

I smiled "Then, why don't you try?"

Topaz bounced out of the bed. As soon as she was close enough, I grabbed her and slung her over my shoulder, making my way to the door.

"I'll be right back." I had a naked, yelling woman over my shoulder in the hallway.

"Slade! Stop right now! Please put me down." Topaz squinted at me. "Slade, where is Batch?"

"I will take you to him."

"No, stop! Listen, I can't be with Batch anymore."

"What? Why?"

"Yes, I fell in love with him, but he's not an oracle. I could lose my gift of sight because he doesn't have the sight as you have."

"How do you know that?"

"Duh! I read your mind."

"Topaz, what are you saying?"

"You're so damn cute, but you can be really thick sometimes. Batch spoke of slipping into another man's body. I don't want that, and now it seems he talked you into it. My gift means that much to me. Without my gift, I would be no one. I have no other real skills, and I have really thought about this in great detail. Cyan will push Batch to inhabit another man's body. Cyan will, no doubt, know such a man, and she will come on strong. Look, I am having second thoughts. At least, bring Reveka, Saffron, even Cyan. Let them host him in their mind. Wait, do you think he will be mad?"

"You have a really good point, Topaz."

She hugged me, and we locked eyes. "Slade? What if it's you that I fell in love with? What if I thought I was in love with Batch because we spent so much time together, but it was you during our first kiss? Slade, I have had the same dream three times now. In it, Batch had become quite different, and he had a body. Then, I lost you. This could have been just dreams, but I'm fearful of the future for the first time." She held me tightly. "Please don't let me go."

"Topaz, I will always—"

Her lips met mine, and we kissed. Next, we were against the other wall, and I was kissing her neck. Our minds were swimming as one.

"Topaz, is this right or wrong?"

"You don't feel wrong to me; you feel exactly right. Please don't push me away because I thought I loved Batch."

As we were kissing and pressing our bodies together, I said, "I will not push you away because I do have feelings for you. But please spend some time with Batch. I will bring Cyan and Saffron to make it more comfortable. See how you feel in a few days or a week. If you still feel the way you do now, then a home between my arms you will have."

We kissed again. As our lips parted, she bit the bottom corner of her lip. Then, we kissed again. Tears began to spill from her eyes.

"I am scared for you, Slade. I see suffering, pain, death, loss. You lose yourself in death. You leave us because you're consumed by a fire. Slade, I see you in the fire. You're on fire, yet somehow, you command the flames. Please don't leave us. I love you; we love you. I love you."

"You said I love you twice."

"Because I love you with my heart and yours, which has yet to give itself to me."

"Was it a dream or a vision?"

"Slade, I had that vision as we kissed. You were dead, and you were surrounded by six grief-stricken angels. You walked like a ghost, unseen and unaware that you were dead. One woman mourned your loss as do two others, but her face is unfamiliar to me. She has brilliant green eyes like Asya, Galya, and Zyra. She has so much power. It's like she is made of it, and she wields it as if she is out of control. But she is in control, and death seems to worship and haunt her."

"Have you ever had a vision that didn't come true? Why were there angels on fire?"

"No, I have only had three. Only Reveka and me, and we're always right. The fire was in my dreams; the angels were in a vision I just had. Please keep up. This is serious."

"Good, then I will meet my end knowing that I was loved. Wait, how would you have seen what happens after I die? How soon will this happen? How did you see me as a ghost?"

"I couldn't tell the time, but there were so many people I have never seen before gathered around you, so it could be in the far future. You moved through walls, so I figured you were a ghost, but you were like a demon. You were on fire. Slade. You looked like what I think the devil would look like."

"The future is always shifting, so you may or may not be right. But it seems I have plenty of time to plan my funeral arrangements." I laughed.

"Slade, this isn't funny. Something isn't right. I know you feel it as well. Wait! You know it's coming. You know you are going to die. You're going to go headfirst into death's icy grip!"

I kissed her. "I don't know or feel anything but a growing feeling to ask you to be mine."

"I'll say yes. Please just ask me."

"No, my thoughts are as clouded as yours are. Think on it a week. Tell me then, and I will accept whichever you choose. Now, let's get back to my room for your clothes."

We walked back into my room, and the ladies look shocked.

"Get dressed."

She did and kissed me before walking out the door. I got the funny feeling she did that to show Sofia that she was coming back.

"Slade, where are we going?"

I walked her to Batch's door. "Topaz, I love you. I want to hold you like you're mine, but I need to know that you're not confused." I kissed her one last time before opening Batch's door. Batch was sitting in a chair.

"I think this is the right place."

"I thought Sofia was going to be first?"

I turned her around.

"How are there two of you?"

I laughed. "Batch will explain the rest. Now, I have to leave. Batch, you will have more guests soon."

I ran back to my room to find the three naked women sitting on the bed.

Sofia got off the bed and spoke for them all, "What comes out of your mouth better be one hell of an excuse as to why you ran out of the room with Topaz while she was still naked, then came back in. And why did she kiss you?" Sofia had me against the wall, poking me with her finger. Two women had done that to me in the last hour. I hated being poked, but I loved the one doing the poking.

I pushed against Sofia's bare chest. "You will find out soon enough. Now get on the bed, or am I going to have to make you a woman right here on this very spot." Before she could say anything, I took her in my arms, kissing her deeply and passionately.

***

"Hello, Topaz. It's nice to see you with my own eyes. May I get you something to drink?"

"I didn't think it would work. Thank you. I'm not thirsty."

"Please, look into my mind. You will see and know the answers to your questions."

A few seconds passed before their hands separated.

"See, the world isn't just the House where we live or the land surrounding it. The world is much bigger."

"Why don't you have the gift of sight?"

"It was Slade's and Slade's alone."

"I know what you showed me is real, but I can't believe you have a body. You and Slade are like twins, right?"

"Yes, and unlike the usual clone, I bear no clone mark. Slade even calls me brother. It made me feel good hearing that. I never thought of what it would be like to be alone because I lived within the mind. Now, all I hear is silence."

"Where is Cyan? Will she be coming soon?"

"Why would I care if she is coming? You know me better than even Slade did, and I know you." He took her in his arms, gently kissing her neck. Then, he saw her eyes. "Topaz, are you okay? You look unwell. Here, sit. I know this must be a lot to comprehend."

Topaz smiled. "I just cannot wrap my head around this whole situation. Batch, I have reservations about us. I don't know what to do because you have a body. I know we talked about what it would be like, but this is so fast. What if I lose my gift of sight because you're not an oracle?"

"Topaz, how can you say this to me? It's me, just in a body of my own. So, what if I'm not an oracle?"

"Batch, I could lose my gift forever!"

"So what?"

"I am my gift. I was born to be this way, and I would never give it up!"

***

Slade and Sofia were kissing. "So, my sweet, shall we move to the bed?"

Sofia smiled and pulled me toward the bed. "Slade, you're mine, and I will share you with some of my friends. So, who are you?"

"I am yours."

"Sunako has not seen you in a few days, and I know that she missed you terribly."

"Sunako, my angel, did you miss me? I missed you."

Sunako eyes locked on mine. "I missed you this much." Sunako flipped me onto my back, sitting on my waist. Her hair tickled my face as she leaned in to kiss me. I could feel her passion; I could feel her desire. Mostly, I could feel her love.

"I want you to make love to me today. Asya gave us permission, and I crave you. I want to be one with you, now and always."

Sofia said, "Slow yourself, Sunako. Remember, I get the first time with him. Then, he's yours, then Molly's. Now, Slade, I want to feel you love me from within. I want you to take me to the places Lucy talked about. I want you here and now."

Molly turned off the lights, but the warm light from the water was still bright enough to see.

Molly asked, "Slade, do you want me to lower the blinds to block out all of the light?"

"No, I want to see you—all of you." I stood up, and Molly helped me with my boots and skirt. She ran her hand up my leg and over my manhood.

I was nervous. "Hey, I forgot to tell you that my skirt is called a kilt."

"How do you know that?" asked Sofia.

"Dutch and Cyril met a man twenty some odd years ago and her was wearing the same thing. When Dutch asked about it, he called it a kilt."

"That would be so very interesting if you weren't stalling. Come on, no need to be scared. I don't bite. Unless you want me to."

"How do you want me, Sofia?"

Sofia smiled. "I'm going to lie here, and you're going to kiss my feet while working your way up to here." She pointed to herself. "Stop here for a bit and kiss me. When I tell you to, work your way up to my neck, and I will show you my passion."

Sunako and Molly were on opposite sides of us.

I began to kiss the top of her feet, gently sliding my hands around them but not tickling. I moved up to her knee, and I saw her pointing at herself.

"What do you call it?"

Sunako said, "That is her butterfly; mine is a lotus flower. Molly, what do you call yours?"

Molly smiled, "I call it his, but he can call it a kitty."

I held in a laugh. Then, I began to kiss Sofia's butterfly. I could not describe her taste. To do so would do it no justice, but it was wonderful. Sofia lightly ran her nails through my hair, holding my head when I was doing something right.

She loudly exclaimed, "Yes! Right there! Oh, yes, I'm about to—Molly, hold me down! Slade, hold me tight, and don't stop what you're doing."

I wrapped my arms up under her hips and held her waist. "Oh yeah! Oh, yes, I'm about to! Molly, hold me down! Slade, hold me tight, and don't stop what you're doing."

Molly lay across Sofia.

"I'm—I'm!" She broke off and screamed.

After a long minute, Molly pulled me back. "Trust me, lover boy, she's going to need a second to breathe while she gathers herself." We kissed. "Damn, you taste really good."

Sofia said, "Slade, that was the best I have ever had. Now, do that to Sunako."

I turned and locked eyes with Sunako. With Sofia's taste on my lips, Sunako kissed me.

Sunako said, "I like the way you taste. Now drink deep my wine. Make me sing, so my ancestors can hear our song of love." Sunako lay back, and I kissed her feet. "Skip all of that, go right to my lotus."

I began softly kissing her as I held her like Sofia did. Sunako sounded different, more like whimpers and rapid breaths.

She suddenly grabbed ahold of my head with both hands as she moaned, "Oh yes!" She held on for a few minutes. "I think he almost stole my soul."

Sofia smiled. "Molly, your turn."

Molly kissed me deeply and said, "Sunako, you taste great on his lips. Now, lie on your back. I like it a bit different."

I lay on my back, and Molly stood on the bed, walking up to me and over my face.

She looked down into my eyes and said, "Slade, when I met you, I was nothing but a head, and you saved me, gave me new hopes and dreams. You even gave me a body. Now, I want you to enjoy my body because it is yours now. I want you to make me purr." Molly knelt over my face. "Show me the stars as you bring me over the moon."

I kissed her. The more I kissed her, the wetter she became. It began to drive me wild, as her taste was different than Sofia and Sunako. All three had different yet amazing tastes. It drove me to kiss faster. I looked up, and she was kissing Sofia then Sunako as she held me by the hair. I felt someone take me in their hand.

Sofia said, "I have you. Now just relax and let me do what I want."

Her movements were causing my heart to race, and I felt slightly dizzy. Sofia's grip became tighter. When I opened my eyes, Sunako was looking down at me with a smile. Molly was moaning loudly while moving her hips back and forth. Suddenly, she jumped up and walked around.

"Look at my legs! They're shaking uncontrollably. Holy shit! Slade, you give amazing head."

"Head?"

Sofia laughed. "We forget that you don't know all the fun words yet. What you did to us was going down on us or 'head.' As in, I enjoy watching you give head to Sunako and Molly. It was a huge turn-on. This is also called head." Sofia took me into her mouth and moved her head slowly up and down. "Yum, you can also say giving head. It is dirty but not filthy. I don't like filthy, so remember that. Now, make love to me." Sofia lay on her back, and I crawled up to meet her lips.

I whispered, "Sofia, I'm a little nervous."

"I am, too." She placed her hands on the small of my back, drawing me so close we were pressed together. "Grind yourself on me, but don't go inside until I tell you."

We kissed as our bodies grinded on one another. I started kissing her neck, and Sofia began to breathe hard and fast.

"Slade, I want you to bite me hard right as you enter me, like you did to Lucy. Just keep going until I say 'Stop' or I pass out. Then, make love to Sunako. Got it?"

I nodded.

"Now!"

I bit her neck as our bodies become one. She was so hot inside as I pushed myself deep into her. I pulled mostly out and repeated.

I bit harder, and Sofia said in a heavy, breathy voice, "I love you, Slade."

"I love you, Sofia."

Our bodies pushed and pulled, never disconnecting, to a rhythmic chorus of moans. Loudly, she expressed her want and need for me. I was a bit confused with the things she was saying because I was right there, and she had me in her arms. But I continued the dance. It felt so good. Sofia held onto my shoulders and neck. She must have said "I love you" a dozen times, and I loved the sound of each one. Then, I felt a bit strange, almost uncomfortable sensation, like I had to pee.

"Sofia, I have to use the bathroom."

"No, you don't."

I said it again, "I have to piss. Please let go and stop moving."

Sofia smiled. "Do you trust me? Just go with it. Where I get many, you only get one. Now it's your turn to give in to it. Just keep moving and relax. Please trust me. I have you."

I fought to hold it back as my whole body tensed up. I fought the urge to go to the bathroom.

Molly whispered, “Do it inside her. Give her your love; it is very natural. Don’t fight it. Now give in.” Molly touched my neck, and time began to crawl as she slipped into my mind. “Slade, you are about to give yourself to her in a way that you can only do once in your life. I will explain later. But relax and release yourself inside her. This is natural between lovers.”

“Molly, I’m about to piss myself, more to the point, *inside* her, and you’re going to tell me that this is natural?”

Molly laughed. “No, my love. You’re not going to piss inside of her. You’re about to have your first orgasm; it comes out of the same place. It is your seed, so give it to her. When it is my turn, I want you to do that to me. Oh, I really can’t wait for that.”

“I still feel strange about it.”

“I can’t wait to watch you climax. It’s time to reward Sofia and yourself for your hard work. Just give in and let it go.”

We disconnected, and I was right back in the moment. I was about to climax for the first time, and as I did, Sofia reached up and pulled my face to hers. We kissed as I felt myself throbbing inside of her. I could hardly control my thoughts. It was like every thought all at once, and my eyes became incredibly heavy for a few seconds.

When it was done, my body felt heavy, but my mind was sharp, much sharper than I’d ever noticed. I stood up, looking at Sofia.

She announced, “That was amazing! Lucy says that it will get better the more we’re together.”

“You were amazing. Any other words would insult the act, but I’m sure of one thing. I have to use the bathroom.” That was when I noticed. “Sofia, you’re bleeding. I’m sorry. Why didn’t you tell me that I was hurting you?”

Molly laughed. “Slade, calm down. This is perfectly natural. I know I keep saying that, but it is. Sofia has lost her virginity to you. This happens to a woman during her first time.”

“But she’s been with a woman. I don’t understand.”

“Yes, but for us, it’s oral, and our fingers don’t go that far in. I’ve never popped a girl’s cherry with my fingers,” said Molly.

“Okay, the cherry thing makes it sound gross.”

Sofia laughed. No, cherry is right. Also, when a person does something for the first time, they’re referred to as a cherry. Like the first fight you get into. You’re referred to as a cherry. After that fight, you’ve then popped your cherry, gaining experience. Also, when a woman has something inserted deep enough into her vagina, it will tear her hymen, which is a thin membrane. When torn, it causes the woman to bleed. I've never bled from being with a woman, but I bled because you broke my hymen. Therefore, you popped my cherry. This now concludes the boring sex ed portion."

"It's a rite of passage, and Sofia is now a woman. It's a special gift she bestowed upon you. A girl can only give that gift once in her lifetime. She chose you. Slade, we have all chosen you because we each love you in our own way. Remember this moment for the rest of your life. Keep it safe because you have lost your virginity to Sofia. She is, and will always be, your one, and you are hers. Soon, you will be *ours*. You're a man now, and before the sun rises again, we will give you our virginities," said Molly.

"So, what happened was me losing my virginity? I can only do it once in my lifetime, so I will never feel that feeling again?"

Molly replied, "No, my sweet. You will have that feeling every time, but you only get one first time. Trust me, you will begin to really love that feeling."

I smiled and went to find the bathroom. I laughed. "Holy shit, there is a whole other room over here with chairs and a couch." I stood in front of the toilet and had to piss really bad, but I couldn't get it to work, as it was still mostly hard.

"Molly, could you come here, please?"

"Oh, are you going to show me how you piss this time?" Her smile was huge.

"No, this is serious. I have to piss really bad, but the damn thing won't work."

Molly placed her hand on my neck and began to squeeze until I was able to go to the bathroom.

"Your body is to tense, so I hit the right pressure points in your neck. It has happened to Lady Velour a few times a month, but not when she has to piss. Wow, you really did have to piss. Look at you go."

She smiled and laughed as she left the room. When I was done, I noticed that I had blood all over me, but I didn't want to wash her off me.

"Tomok to Slade."

"Slade here."

"I hope you are not in the middle of anything. Dr. Rilla has invited you and your four brides to lunch with us, and between you and me, saying no is not an option. So, ready up and get Batch. Tomok out."

I walked into the other room and asked, "Who is hungry? Because we just got invited to lunch, and we have to attend."

All three were happy for the invite, and Sofia went to shower as the rest of us got dressed.

Molly discreetly said, "I noticed that you didn't wash off. I hope you wear me like that."

I looked at her and smiled. "I intend on sleeping with you all over me."

Molly bit her bottom lip and replied, "You're one hell of a sexy beast. I can't wait to have you inside of me as we sleep."

"Slade to Batch. Slade to Batch, come in."

"Shit, his communication device has not been activated. Girls, I will be right back."

I walked to Batch's room and rang the door.

Batch answered, "Brother, how may I help you?" His words were sharp with slight irritation.

"We have lunch with Dr. Rilla; it's a mandatory thing. Batch, my brother, you sound a bit off. Are you okay?"

His eyes darted back and forth.

"Let me have your hand. Maybe I can help you."

He shook his head.

"We can talk about it later if you like, but now get ready. We meet in five minutes." I then walked back into my room with an uneasy feeling.

Molly asked, "Why did you call us girls on the way out?"

I laughed. "Because I haven't made you and Sunako into women yet."

Molly threw her hands up in the air and said, "I should have waited until later to explain virginity to you. Sofia, your jackass is being stupid again."

"Would you have me any other way?"

Molly replied, "I will have you on your back. Then, you will see who's in control." She kissed me and slapped me on the ass. "I don't know where you learned that move, but I liked it."

Sofia walked out fully clothed. "Slade, are you being a jackass again? Remember, she is one tough cookie. After all, she was just a head for a bit."

I smiled. "Speaking of head."

Sofia said, "Remember what I said about the difference between sexy, dirty, and filthy? This is not the time to ask for head."

I laughed. "No, I want to know if your head became clearer after we made love because my mind did. My thoughts felt strong. Is that what happens to everyone when they lose their virginity?"

"All I know is that I love you more and feel closer to you. I feel like you're still inside me, and I have never cum so hard before. I still feel tingly."

Molly laughed. "Because he technically is still inside of you right now. Do you not know what happens when a boy orgasms?"

"No, I thought it was like us," said Sofia.

Molly smiled. "No, not at all. To put it plainly, the man has liquid come out of his, you know, and it goes into you. What are you people being taught over at the House of Ribbons?"

"Bullshit! Who told you that?"

Molly laughed. "Lady Velour teaches the class about the differences between women and men, and that is covered in the sex part of class."

Sunako said, "Sofia, what was it like?"

Sofia spoke, "I could feel him pulsing. I just thought it was his heartbeat, and it felt great. I did notice when I stood up that I was super wet."

The door rang, and I opened the door. Tomok, Dr. Rilla, Batch, and Topaz were together.

Dr. Rilla said, "You four must be hungry."

Molly, Sunako, Sofia, and I followed the group into an elevator and headed to an upper floor. It stopped, and we continued following Dr. Rilla.

We got to our destination, and Dr. Rilla said, "This is one of the restaurants. This one specializes and caters to those with exotic tastes and fine dining, of which I enjoy both. Everyone, please take a seat. Slade, sit across from me. I would like to speak with you."

We sat and a waiter informed us on what was available. Sofia, Molly, Topaz, Sunako, Batch, and I ordered eggs, potatoes, and bacon with orange juice. Dr. Rilla and Tomok ordered something I did not understand.

I asked, "What did you and Tomok order?

Dr. Rilla said, "It's a type of egg that has a half-developed, lizard-like animal inside, and it is unbelievably delicious."

Breakfast went very well, and Dr. Rilla asked basic questions after Sofia told her my story.

"Slade, I know you are not scheduled until eight a.m. tomorrow, but can I see you today for up to a half hour, maybe slightly longer? I want to look at your physiology. I can't put my finger on it, but I swear you're not human. I mean, no human has the capability to produce a smell like yours."

"Yes, of course. I am curious to know who or what I am."

"Very good. Besides, it will give you time to regain your sexual energy because you four smell like you were in an orgy."

I coughed out some of my food.

"Mr. Funny Guy, are you well?"

Tomok said, "Dr. Rilla, humans are often caught off guard with our bluntness. They tend to keep certain topics out of common, everyday conversation, as it can bring them to a point of shame. They don't typically speak so open and candidly, especially about intercourse. This has been the case in many points in human history. Sex seems to be a taboo subject, spoken almost in secret and not in public. This is often behind closed doors and with friends and lovers. They're very opposite when they talk, as opposed to us. They're a confusing group."

"Really? I will admit that I am new here and you, along with a few others, are some of the first humans I have met. Why do you feel shame about the sex you are having? Sex is natural and healthy. Slade, clearly you were with Sofia, Molly, and Sunako. Batch and Topaz have not been intimate. Batch, are you not attracted to Topaz?" asked Doctor Rilla.

"It's not that. We are waiting for Cyan, as per Topaz's request."

"Well, Tomok and I were engaging in… Tomok, what do humans call it?"

Tomok said, "It's called rough sex."

Sofia said, "We're not ashamed. It's that we are taught that it should not be in everyday conversation with those we don't know as to not accidentally offend."

Molly added, "But men are the double standard. They say we should be proper, but they speak like drunken whores when they gather, always telling sex jokes and noises to make one another laugh. We women are the only true adults."

Sunako laughed. "Yes, men are just tall boys. They get older but still act very immature for their age. Gold, sex, and violence is all they seem to want."

To which Topaz replied, "Some men are the exception to the rule, like Batch and Slade. I think that is because we are essentially raising them, and it helps that they have already been taught manners."

Dr. Rilla laughed. "That is the way we raise our men because a strong male is raised by a stronger female. In our race, the female is the strongest. It is nice to see that our distant cousins are like us in many ways. In any case, you don't know we are Jotanfo. We are distant cousins to you humans, and so are the Sa-Teen. They are more closely related to humans, and that is why we all look so similar and can easily blend in with humans. I find humans to be very fascinating. Did you know our DNA is compatible, but our blood types evolve differently? When our kind mix with your kind and create a baby, the blood somehow combines to make a whole new blood type. Your history is much like ours. Studying humans is like looking into our past. We hope to find who came from who. I mean, which race we all are descended from. Oh, look at me going on like that. I hope that wasn't too boring."

Tomok said, "Slade, Batch, I fear we're being ganged up on. I also fear that no matter our intellect, we would not stand a chance in a verbal fight to defend our side of the species."

I smiled and raised my glass. "I would say you are correct, my friend. Besides, what good would it do us? We are hopelessly outnumbered and outmatched in every way. Especially in the way of beauty."

Batch stayed silent and kept eating.

Dr. Rilla laughed. "My, you do have a way about you; you can certainly cast a spell with your words. Tomok, you would be wise to learn from this young man. Now, Slade, would you mind coming to my lab?

I nodded, kissing the ladies goodbye. I asked, "What about Batch?"

Dr. Rilla said, "The test requires the original, but he is welcome if he wants to join us and get some extra training."

Batch shook his head. "Thank you for the offer, but no."

We walked to her lab.

Dr. Rilla said, "Tomok, help him on the table. Slade, I'm going to take some basic samples that I see Tomok has not taken yet. I want to know you on a mitochondrial level. I want to see what your DNA looks like. I have to know how you are producing that smell. This will sting a bit, so please lie still." She swung a small arm of a machine over me and took a sample from my head, chest, and ankle. "Slade, this next part is painless."

A different machine scanned me from head to toe with a bright green light.

"Last one, Slade. Breathe in and out deeply into this mask for two minutes. Try and inhale as deeply as you can. Tomok, have that sample triple-checked. You're doing great, Slade. Keep it up. Thirty seconds to go. Tomok, what are the findings?"

Tomok just pointed. "No, that must be a mistake. I will retake the sample because it is obviously contaminated. I must have touched them or something in my excitement. Slade, I need to poke you a few times but a little deeper. Are you ready?"

"Yes."

Dr. Rilla took the sample and moved it directly into the machine. "Slade, you can sit up now."

"That one hurt a bit." I rubbed my temple.

Tomok laughed. "That is because the good doctor took a sample of your brain, heart, and bone marrow from above the ankle."

Doctor Rilla stepped out of the room.

"Dr. Rilla to Vidya. This a priority-one call."

Vidya replied, "This is Vidya. What's on fire this time, Doc?"

Dr. Rilla said, "You need to see this immediately. Nothing is more important than this. I will see you in my office."

Dr. Rilla walked back in, "Tomok, I need you. We'll be back, Slade. I just need to yell at Tomok in private."

They were gone, so I lay back down. I might have eaten too much, but it was so good. I'd just rest my eyes until they came back in.

Vidya stepped out of thin air. "Okay, Doc, what is happening?"

Dr. Rilla placed the tablet on the desk. "Slade is not human."

Vidya sat back, running her fingers through her hair.

She fiddled with the ring she was wearing and said, "No shit, I could have told you that. I figured he was half-human, half-Sa-Teen." Vidya rolled her eyes. "Call me when you have something exciting."

Dr. Rilla laughed in a strange way. "You're wrong, in a way. You will never guess what he is."

Vidya sat up. "What? Okay, now you have my full attention."

Dr. Rilla told Vidya about the triple test. "All come back the same. Slade has DNA from Jotanfo at twenty percent, Sa-Teen twenty percent, human twenty percent, and an unknown yet-to-be classified race—or races—at forty percent."

"You're joking! Oh, I get it. Slade has teamed up with you to play a joke on me because we called him an alien. This is to see how I would react. Very funny. At least, the kid has a sense of humor. I'll have to buy him a drink."

Tomok and Rilla went silent.

"Doc, you don't look like you're joking. Tomok, Tomok! Look at me. Is this a joke? I order you to tell me the truth!"

"If this is a joke, then it's on me as well."

"Doctor Rilla, what does this mean?"

Dr. Rilla sighed. "I believe we have found the missing race that we have all descended from. Forty percent of his DNA has never been seen before, and I don't know how long it will take to map it. It is so complex that the AI does not know how to examine it yet. I believe this is our first contact with his race. Exciting, don't you think?"

Tomok interjected, "Or he could be a cousin species, just like us."

Dr. Rilla snapped, "Thank you, Tomok. Vidya, look. His DNA is intact. He was born this way; the forty percent is dominant. I think we came from his race. You said he had blank spots in his memory. Do you mean amnesia?"

Vidya smiled. "No, it was removed. Someone did this to him, and no one we know possesses that level of technology."

Tomok said, "Maybe he is here to research the interactions between humans and all the other races. Every race is on this one planet for the first time in Earth's history. Someone took away his memory, so we could not retrace their steps. They need to be sure they want to be a part of our multigalactic community."

Vidya said, "Tomok, you're invaluable to me and our work, but I think you have watched too many movies and read too many goofy science fiction books."

"Really? Then someone explain the alien in the other room. Explain why it has been four hundred Earth years since the last race was discovered and joined us. The fact is, he may very well be the missing link we have all long searched for. My only question is, why? If he is here, why don't they don't reveal themselves to us? What would they gain by hiding, other than to observe? What better way than to live amongst the races you want to observe, just like we did with the humans in the beginning?"

Dr. Rilla had a thought. "Yes, maybe you're right, Tomok, but what if what was done to him was indeed on purpose? Maybe he was sent to observe something somewhere but not on this planet, galaxy, or universe. What if he is lost to them? What if we are so far away that he accidentally discovered us? Why would they send such a young boy?"

Vidya said, "How could he have evaded detection during his flight here?"

Tomok replied, "Some unknown technology, or maybe they don't use ships. Maybe he is not a young boy, and that is the way they all look, and he is hundreds of years old or older. Shit, my head hurts just thinking about the possibilities. Either way, we have a first-contact situation on our hands. So, what are we going to do about it?"

Vidya said, "Shit! You two dummies left him alone? He must know something is up by now. He is probably going through the system as we speak. Alabaster! Report what activity the systems have had in the last ten minutes in the lab where Slade is located and all surrounding labs."

Alabaster reported back, "Nothing out of the ordinary to report, Vidya."

"What is Slade doing right now? What, if any, activity is going on?"

Alabaster reported, "Slade is asleep in lab three. Itkis is playing music in lab two while running a test on samples B9 through D13, as per your request. Shall I shut off the music to increase his concentration and performance?"

"That will not be necessary but thank you."

Dr. Rilla asked, "How about we sit on this discovery for a month or so, watch his every move, and treat him like one of us? But we will have to announce the discovery to The Committee of Races to enter him into the galactic community. It's standard stuff as long as it is determined that he is not hostile or a threat. He may indeed be our missing link. Either way, this is extremely exciting."

Tomok said, "I hate to be the one to say it, but how are we going to keep this a secret from five mind-reading witches and Slade? Not to mention, if Slade is secretly observing us, he must know that we have the technology to detect unknown DNA. By not informing him, it could be a big failure for us, due to dishonesty. His race could just recede back into the infinite darkness from where they came from, thinking that we cannot be trusted. On top of that, look how everyone benefits from new technology and scientific discoveries every time a new race is welcomed into The Fold."

"Damn it. Tomok is right. There is no way to get around that minefield. We could lose it all if we look like we are being dishonest by hiding something from him," Vidya said. She paced. "The Fold and its council members can wait a month or so. Okay, we keep this to ourselves for now but don't exclude Slade, Batch, and the witches. Store all samples in the vault under the code name 'Lost Boy.' Any personnel working on this project will be told that this is hypothetical DNA, made up of many, to see who can crack the true genome. Now, wake the boy up, and send him on his way. Tomok, you're the point man on this, and you two seemed to have hit it off. Well, this is your chance to become his best friend. I give you authorization to go out into the wild with him from time to time, which should be no problem for you. You were a great soldier once. Time to wake up those skills again. Protect him at all costs. We may have made the biggest discovery, bigger than—well, just name a wonderful technology that made our lives better. Tomok, inform the boy on our findings to show transparency."

"Wait. How did you make a clone of Slade without the correct DNA?" asked Doctor Rilla.

"I let the AI do all the boring stuff. You should know that if any DNA is wonky, it fills it in with compatible DNA." He went to a screen and requested to see Slade's cloning information. "Oh, I see. The AI saw the DNA as unreadable. The unreadable forty percent was then changed to human DNA. So, Batch is now twenty percent Jotanfo, twenty percent Sa-Teen, and now sixty percent human. I will readjust the AI to inform us if this ever comes up again, even if the degree is within one percent."

It had been a long time since they'd come across new DNA. After the day they'd had, Tomok needed a strong drink. Vidya left the room, and Tomok winked at Dr. Rilla as he walked out.

Tomok entered the room where Slade was sleeping. "Slade, wake up."

"Sorry, I didn't mean to fall asleep. So, what is all the commotion about with Dr. Rilla?"

"She is excited about something that you and I should talk about. I'm just going to come out with it. Slade, forty percent of your DNA is unknown. Completely foreign to us. What I am saying is, you are the first of your race that we know of to make contact with us."

I sat in silence for a few minutes.

"Hey, man, are you okay? I know that is a lot to process. On the upside, you will be welcomed into The Fold with open arms. The Fold is what we call the multigalactic community of unified races. Vidya will announce you to The Fold in about a month or so. I'll tell you when she is ready. Well, you're free to go. Remember, I live next door, so if you want some entertainment, I can play a movie. Oh, and before I forget, I'm authorized to come out into the wild with you and Batch, if that is okay with you. I would really enjoy it, and I will blend right in so long as I don't need my tendrils."

"I would love that. I could show you my cottage, then where I woke up, and—well, that is it. But there are plenty of people to meet. Hey, that's right! You used to be a soldier and fought in a war before getting injured. I would love to hear that story."

Tomok smiled. "Yeah, sure. No one ever asks me about my time as a soldier. Hey, you should know that when Batch's body was created, it could not replicate the unknown DNA, so filler human DNA was introduced."

"I guess that is why he has no gifts. I want to know everything about that and you being a soldier later. I will see you at eight a.m., then."

Tomok waved goodbye and walked back into the other lab where Doctor Rilla was. "How was that?"

"I have seen better acting in the movies you watch. Just be yourself around him. In fact, be the Tomok I dislike with Slade. Besides, I should try to get used to your personality if our relationship is going to last. Wanna go for drinks then more of the rough stuff?"

"I would greatly enjoy that. Meet me at my place?"

Dr. Rilla touched Tomok's face with one of her tendrils and winked before leaving the room.

Chapter 29

Burning Butterflies

I made my way to my room and found it was empty. I enjoyed the emptiness and contemplated the new information as I watched the fish swim by.

"DeJoule to Slade."

"Slade here."

"Are you home, and may I come by? Or are you mating?"

I laughed. "I would love a visit."

DeJoule was at the window in a flash. "I was around the corner, and I thought I would drop by. I came unannounced earlier but felt it best not to interrupt your mating."

"Oh, you saw that? Sorry, it's just the way the light comes through the water that makes the room glow a beautiful, soft blue."

We talked for almost an hour before the ladies entered the room.

"Ladies, this is my friend DeJoule; he is my trainer."

The ladies said hi, and DeJoule spoke with all of us for another hour. He was interested in human life and life on dry land in the wild. Then, he was called away.

Sunako said, "I like your friend. Now, I would like us to take a shower so you can make love to me."

I smiled. "Sunako, I thought you would never ask."

We got into the shower, and I washed her body and hair. We kissed. Out of the corner of my eye, I saw Sofia and Molly watching us.

I whispered in her ear, "I love you," and we kissed again. We moved to the bed.

Sunako said to Sofia, "I want him, but I am nervous."

Sofia hugged Sunako. "I'm here, and soon, you will be too happy to be nervous."

They kissed, and Molly sneaked a kiss with me.

"Hey, if you want a kiss, then kiss me! Let these two lovers love," said Sofia to Molly.

I kissed Sunako's lotus, and she moaned, speaking in a foreign tongue.

She pulled me up to meet her mouth and said in a soft voice, "Make love to me."

I entered her, and she gasped. We kissed as we made love. A while later, my body told me I could go no further, and I orgasmed. Sunako held me tightly to her as she fell asleep. I felt her dragging me into her sleep and dozed off in her arms.

I woke up later. "Sunako, wake up, my sweet."

She woke up.

"I'm sorry. I may have drooled on your face."

Sunako smiled. "Baby, you can drool on my face any time. Thank you for letting me sleep. It just felt so good to hold you as I slept. I love you."

"I love you. How long were we out?"

Molly said, "You two have been out an hour. Batch had stopped by and told us about dinner, which will be in twenty minutes. He pointed at you and asked if his ass looks like that. We laughed, and Sofia made him show us his ass. We all said yes, and Batch thought that was nice. Then they left, but Topaz looked odd, almost uncomfortable. We can go to dinner and let our stomachs settle. Then I will show you what my friend, Keller, described to me that her husband does to her."

I got up to take a shower to wash off the blood, but Molly took me by the arm and said, "Oh no, killer. I want you just like that. All dirty with the smell of copper, and I want to add to that smell." She pulled me close, and as we kissed, she lightly rubbed my right earlobe.

I dressed, and we left for dinner. I had fish because Tomok suggested it. I liked the way he smiled when Dr. Rilla looked at him. I could feel his happiness. Dinner lasted an hour or so. We all went to a place where we could listen to music, and it was amazing, I would have no way to describe it, but it was everywhere and inside of me. Music had to be a form of magic. I was a lover of music from that night on. We were there an hour and a half. Walking back to our rooms, we wished each other a good night, but I noted that Batch seemed odd.

Sofia said, "Slade, are you ready for Molly? She described what she wants, and I can't wait to watch."

"Slade, I'm risking my gift for you. Will you stay with me whether I lose it or not?" asked Molly.

"We will be together so long as you want me."

Molly said to Sofia, "Last chance to say no if you are uncomfortable with what I am asking."

Sofia smiled. "Being with Slade is being with me. As long as it is what you want, then go for it."

Molly looked at me and said, "If you're willing to be with me until death, then you may kiss me down there. Don't stop even when I tell you to stop. Sofia will know when to drag you off me." Molly kissed me, then said, "Thank you for making me whole again. After this night, you will have my whole heart and body. Now make me scream with pleasure."

I kissed around her thighs and teased her until she took my head and placed it where she wanted it.

"Time to give me head. Make it so good, my head pops off."

Sofia, Sunako, and I started laughing really hard, but honestly, the image was very disturbing. I began to kiss her slowly at first, and then I picked up the pace. Molly's breathing was labored with deep moaning, while Sofia was doing something with her hand to her face and neck. Her body began to shake and move around. She yelled to stop, but Sofia and Sunako held her down as I continued to intensify my kisses. Molly loudly moaned in deep, heavy breaths and yelled intermittently. Then, the sound suddenly cut out.

Sofia yelled, "Keep going, Slade! She is about to hit her limit!"

As she reached her highest point, Molly's body struggled and strained before going limp.

"Slade, she is done. You can stop now."

I sat up. "Is she okay? Why is she like that?"

Sofia lightly slapped Molly's face and said, "Come back to us, baby. Come back and finish him off before I take over."

Molly sat up and gasped for air so fast that I jumped back off the bed.

I asked, "What in the hell was that?"

Molly replied, "Sorry, but I like it a bit rough. Sofia knows just how to choke me, don't you, Sofia? Now, come to me."

"How does she know that?"

"We've been practicing. Don't worry. We have Sunako," said Molly.

I walked toward her. She stood up, and we kissed. Then she lay on her back, and I positioned myself between her legs.

"Move with me, Slade."

I entered her. Each woman felt different just as they tasted different. We slowly made love, and she pulled her legs way back.

Molly said. "Will you choke me a little?"

I felt weird about it, but Sofia said it was okay. Sunako caressed my back as we made love, and I choked Molly.

She said, "Harder."

Sunako said, "She desires you to choke her until her eyes roll back into her head. So, choke her harder."

I did, and somewhere between my thrusting and squeezing on her throat, her eyes rolled right back into her head. Only the whites could be seen, and her body went still.

"Slade, let go. She is out."

"Will she be okay? I don't think I liked that."

Sofia woke Molly up.

Molly exclaimed, "Holy shit, that felt good! My whole body is still tingling. I really thought I was going to die right there with you between my legs. Oh, how I love you." Molly pushed me off. "Take me from behind."

Molly got on all fours and backed up to meet me. We were making love, but it felt wildly different. A woman's body was absolutely wonderful. I held her hips tightly as I neared my end. I finished, and we lay together. Sunako snuggled up next to me, while Molly was in my arms.

Sofia said, "We're now a family."

I lay there until all three were asleep. I got up and used the bathroom. Molly had bled the most. There was a tickle in my mind right in the very back of my skull, which I brushed off. I walked over to the window. I really couldn't believe all of it was my life.

"Slade!"

"Yes?"

I turned around, but the ladies were still asleep.

"Slade, help me."

I searched the whole room, thinking it might be one of the witches messing with me.

"Slade, I need you!"

I did not know where the voice was coming from. All I knew was it was female. One of the ladies must be dreaming. I bet it was Molly. I yawned, cuddled behind Sofia, and fell asleep.

I dreamt of Velvet and Kailee. They were fighting about something, and Velvet was bleeding badly. I woke up with Batch standing at the foot of the bed.

"Seven forty-five a.m. You slept though breakfast. Get dressed. We have stuff to do." His tone was cold and detached.

I dressed, and Batch and I walked out.

"You okay, brother? You seem off."

Batch laughed. "I had a bad dream is all."

"I had a bad dream as well."

We held hands in the elevator and saw that we'd had different dreams.

"Dreams are strange, huh?"

"Yeah, I wonder why we dream. You would think that the mind would rest."

Tomok was in his office. "Gentlemen, shall we get started? Batch, place your hand here and hold it. Great, now you are in the system, and your S.P.1.D.E.R is now activated. Your envelope is operational as well. Today, I'm going to show you how to use the envelope. Worry not; it's super easy. You know how the witches move from place to place? Well, today, you will learn to do that very thing. Follow me."

We stepped into the envelope, which looked like a slit in space that had been sliced in the air.

"See how, if we stop right at this point, you can make sure it is not something dangerous, like a room on fire."

I asked, "That is your room?"

Tomok said, "Correct."

We walked out of thin air and into Tomok's room. "See, your implant keeps track of everywhere you go, and with help from some technical things, we can go almost anywhere. We can travel planet to planet. I must warn you that for humans to shift too many times in a row could result in death, due to the great deal of strain it puts on the brain. Try and keep it below six jumps in an hour until you get really good. Then, it is much easier, so walk before you run."

Batch asked, "Can I jump from a cliff, open the envelope before I hit the ground, and come out the other side safe? Or will I be traveling the same speed as I went in?"

"Great question. You will stop as soon as you enter. Be happy because the early forms of travel did not have that safety guard, and people died."

I asked, "Isn't this just bending space?"

"I really like you guys. Great questions and answers. Yes, but it's called *folding* space instead. Imagine you fold a piece of paper, poke a hole in it, and boom you're tunneling through space. Now, into the chamber. Don't worry, the floor is soft, so you won't hurt yourself if you fall." The chamber was circular and fifty feet high. "You can only shift five times to get from point A to point B and so on while collecting flags. Make it in a few jumps. You fail if you hit the ground."

Batch went first, but I was not allowed to watch. Tomok said Batch collected four flags in four turns with two missteps. My turn. I studied where the flags were.

Tomok yelled, "Hey, pretty lady, do you want me to get them for you?"

I popped to the highest point and held onto the ledge. Two were below me, and I fell catching both. I popped to the fourth, and I got a foothold to pull myself up. There was one below but way off to the side, maybe twenty feet down, while the last one was ten feet from the ground. I leapt off the ledge and slammed into the wall, almost missing it. I let myself fall and pushed off the wall, catching the last flag right as I popped behind Tomok.

Tomok said, "Holy shit! You two were born to use the envelope. Slade, your score was three jumps. Now, time to celebrate with your favorite drink, the shit drink. I believe I remember a challenge that you both were going to take it straight?"

Batch and I drank it down while staring at each other.

"Damn, you two are nasty. Okay, boys, you know the drill. Time to train. School will be in session in three, two, one—"

We were in the training room with DeJoule.

DeJoule greeted us. "Today, we are going long because I know that you can take it. Some of this will be uninteresting, but I have been authorized to give you not two, but four combat-training models with simulations of pain. I turn on and increase the level you will receive. I believe you can't train without pain because pain will tell you that you messed up. It will teach you pain resistance. These are basic combat lessons, so don't go thinking that you will be able to dodge a sword or projectiles or anything foolish like that. Try it, and you will get hurt or worse. I wouldn't want you to get hurt out in the savage lands because you thought you were invincible."

"Why not train in the real world?" I asked.

"Because you would need time in a regeneration chamber to fix your injuries. The actual combat comes later, so this is the fundamentals. Now, I will send one man, armed with a staff, every two minutes for six minutes. Then I will send them in twos until you are defeated. The aim is to stay in the fight as long as you can. Know that it would be impossible to win because I have an endless army at my disposal."

Batch and I were separated. The first two went down with a few punches. The next three were tougher, but the staff I touched was the key. I was taken out by the fifth guy.

"Excellent. If you would have beaten one more person, you would have tied with Tomok."

"How did Batch do?"

"Defeated by his second opponent. Slade, I see that new information was entered about your DNA. It appears you may be more reliable than Batch due to your genetic differences, or he could be a slow learner. May I inquire as to why you have not told him about this difference?"

"How do you know that I haven't told him?"

"Slade, I can see into your mind as you see into other minds. My race is born this way."

"I think he is under too much stress. I will tell him when I feel the time is right."

"Moving on. These fights will be a series of stealth combat and open combat. Your goal is to rescue Sofia, who is being held. Fail, and she will be shocked. This will test your understanding of teleportation while fighting. Your opponents will also be able to shift around, and they will be equipped with stun sticks set to six out of ten. It will hurt, but not as must as you having to explain why you failed, and she was punished. You will start off with a knife. You may use anything you can find as a weapon. Good luck."

I was placed outside a large building with one guard patrolling the grounds. I shifted in behind him while thrusting my knife into his neck. I made my way into the building, but I was shocked as I attacked my sixth soldier. Soon, I saw Sofia tied to a chair and gagged. There were five guards, one being the size of Dutch. All rushed me as I stood still, but when they got close, I shifted in behind Sofia and shifted us outside.

"Great job. Sloppy with a dash of luck and a healthy dose of pain resistance."

Sofia disappeared.

"Where did Sofia go?"

"That was a simulation. You had to think she were in danger. If not, you would not have had the proper motivation. How did Batch do?"

"Failed three times. This is normal for most."

We trained for what seemed to be a few hours. The combat was educational and enjoyable yet painful.

"Gentlemen, that concludes the courses laid out for you. You both did a great job. Oh, and enjoy getting sick when you wake up, which is… Now!"

We were back in the real world, and I swore it was worse. I must have thrown up for twenty minutes straight, then on and off for another ten minutes.

Tomok laughed. "You two are animals the way you two take large chunks of information like that. Damn, that smells, and I bet it tastes awful coming up. The longer you're in the chair, the worse it is on the stomach. So, you both know where the shower is because I know you both must have pissed yourselves."

He continued to laugh. We showered and remarked how shitty we felt.

"I understand why they have us wear the training clothes," said Batch.

"Okay, boys, Vidya is happy with your training today, so you two are off. She says you will have your first client in a few days. You two will get a call from me, and you will have to report back. I hate to say this, but if you two fail to report in and go on the run, Batch and Molly will only live—at the max—three years. I'm sorry I had to tell you that, so you two understand the ramifications of jumping ship. Oh, and your S.P.1.D.E.R can be recalled, so you would end up back here but in trouble. But I don't see that happening with you two. Dinner tonight?"

"Why would people run?" I asked.

"Being able to shift from place to place is highly regulated. Very hard to get a permit for. To answer your question: imagine tech like this in the wrong hands. Assassins, thieves, and ne'er-do-wells could do whatever they wish. Now we can't have that, can we?"

"Why were we given it so quickly?"

"Earth is a gray area for this device. Not to mention that it will not help you leave this planet. It's local only for now."

Batch and I both agreed that it seemed to be a good way to test a person.

"I'll call you two when Dr. Rilla and I are ready."

We walked slowly to our rooms.

Batch asked, "Is it worth it to sleep with more than one woman? I mean, did you enjoy it?"

I said, "I really did, but you will find out. Remember, they're not ours; we are theirs. Freedom is just an illusion, my brother, but at least our masters are loving, kind, and beautiful."

We got back to our rooms, and Asya was there waiting for me.

Asya said, "Ah, Slade, I see that you have become a man. The girls won't shut up about it. So, how are you feeling?"

"I feel like hammered shit right now. The training really took it out of me. Hey, I had a bad dream. Come look."

We held hands and let go.

"It felt real, didn't it?"

"Let me get Zyra; we will be back to check up on things. Oh yeah, we will be here two more days. We can discuss Vorador in great detail. Hold on. I'll be right back."

I sat in a chair in the other room and tried to keep my eyes open. Asya and Zyra popped back in.

"Slade, you still with us?"

Zyra laughed. "He does look dead. Slade, you awake in there?"

I opened my eyes and inhaled.

"Velvet is fine. She should be going back home in a little while unless she stays another night with her father. Kailee will be accompanying her back to Velvet's house. I wouldn't suggest anyone picking a fight with Kailee because it could end badly for them. We brought you a gift."

Lucy, Saffron, and Cyan walked in.

Lucy asked, "Is he okay?"

Cyan laughed. "He looks half dead."

Saffron laughed.

Asya said, "Ladies, be nice. The good news is I've lifted the no-sex rule."

Cyan asked, "Where is Topaz? I will try him, but only if Topaz or Saffron is involved."

Lucy smiled. "I will nurse him back to full health after he gives me a shot in the ass."

Asya said, "Lucy! You filthy little thing! If you keep talking like that, you will become a bad influence on the others. Please mind your manners."

Zyra laughed. "Lucy, what you do with your ass should be private. Just don't get it all over the sheets."

Asya yelled, "Gross, Zyra! You know I hate humor like that. Slade, Dr. Rilla has given all three of these ladies the shot for birth control, so feel free to have at them."

I said drowsily, "Asya, I feel something is wrong with Velvet and Kailee. It's like the space around them is vibrating."

Asya smiled. "Slade, Zyra and I were just with Velvet. She is still with Dutch as he talked her into staying a little longer. They will head home later. She is fine. I think you're just pushing yourself way too hard. Plus, you have all these brand-new emotions. Sex itself is a powerful form of magic for the right people, so try not to worry." Asya kissed my cheek. I heard her say, "Zyra, do you think we're pushing him too hard?"

"I think he can take it. Besides, I pushed you past your limit a few times, and you became so much more than I imagined. I think he is doing wonderful; we're lucky it was us that found him."

Asya spoke to the ladies, "Listen to me. Slade's mind has been under a great deal of stress, so let him sleep. I know this place is strange, and, yes, I know it's underwater, but you are completely safe. You will not leave this room without Slade. I will show you the shower, but you will let him wake up on his own. Slade, honey, they can sleep over if you feel up to it. They will stay with us until we leave. If one or more becomes too much to handle or someone gets aggressive or if you are unsure, call one of us, Bill, or Asimov. Then, report to one of us. If you still feel unwell, I will take them home for you. Ladies, listen to me. Sofia is here with a few others, so best behavior and no fighting. Remember, you are a guest here. You will act like the ladies we know you to be."

Zyra said, "Asya, I think if he made a jump that far on his first time, it could be a little too much, not to mention the jump back. Slade, get one of us, and we will bring them back, okay?"

I nodded, as I was too tired to care about anything other than sitting down.

"Great, we will see you later."

Asya and Zyra left the room.

I called for Alabaster.

Alabaster replied, "Yes, Mr. Slade, how may I be of assistance?"

"Will you please wake me in one hour? And is there any way you can have six apples sent to my room?"

"I can and will. Red or green?"

"Three of each please, and please, just call me Slade."

"Your apples are on their way. May I be of any further assistance?"

"No, thank you, Alabaster. I appreciate you helping me this way. I owe you one."

Soon, there was someone at the door.

"Come in."

A human male came in and said, "Mr. Slade, I have your apples."

"Please put them over there, and thank you for coming so fast."

He said nothing but bowed his head slightly before leaving the room. I could hear the ladies in the shower, laughing. I slowly walked myself over to the apples and ate one red and one green. I just needed to rest my eyes.

Chapter 30

Unexpected Love

I sat down, trying to focus my thoughts. I'd thought the apples would give me a little boost, but it was no use. Sleep rushed in like a lover's kiss. Rest brought me no comfort. I saw fire and the dead strewn about. My hands were covered in blood, and I was crying and angry. I could feel my hatred. I could feel the blood.

"Slade! Wake up, Slade!" Alabaster's loud voice was suddenly in my nightmare, and he was screaming my name.

I sat up.

"I'm up, holy shit! I asked to be woken up, not go deaf."

Alabaster replied, "Slade, I upped the volume after the seventh time I called your name in compliance to what you asked me to do sixty-two minutes ago."

"I'm sorry, Alabaster. Please forgive my rudeness."

"Slade, there is no need to thank me; this is part of my job. Have a good day."

His voice was gone. I felt better, and I found Lucy, Saffron, and Cyan talking in the other room.

"Hey, Slade, do you feel better?" asked Cyan.

I smiled and nodded.

"Cyan, Saffron. I have a surprise for you. Please come with me."

I took them to Batch's room and rang the door. "Keep your eyes closed."

Topaz opened the door. "Hi, Slade. Batch is just waking up. Would you like to come in?"

"Yes." I took Cyan's and Saffron's hands and led them into the room. I yelled, "Hey, man, rise and shine!"

Rubbing his eyes, Batch replied, "What's up, brother?"

Cyan exclaimed, "Holy shit! There are two of you?"

Saffron was stunned.

"Batch, you can explain all the details. I will see you later."

I left the room and returned to mine. Lucy was naked, lying chest-down on the bed.

Lucy smiled. "Good news! I'm ready to go if you want me. Or do you want me in a different position? Maybe like this?" She got on all fours, while she looked over her shoulder with a half-smile.

"Lucy, put your clothes on. We're going for a walk."

Lucy dressed, and we left the room. I was silent until we found Asya. She was in a common room speaking with others, including Vidya, Dr. Rilla, Bill, and Asimov.

"Asya, a word, please."

Asya got up. "Yes, dear? Did I not bring you enough women? Did they not slake your lustful desires? Wait, don't tell me. You're still horny?"

"I'm not like other men that take women like wine, many glasses at a time. Well, that might have been a bad analogy. I don't want sex right now. I want to know why I keep seeing death."

I extended my hand, and Asya took it. She then waved over Bill, Asimov, Galya, and Zyra. They entered and disconnected in a matter of seconds.

"Way to go! Three in one day and another waiting—I'm impressed," Bill remarked.

Galya slapped Bill across the back of his head, knocking his hat off. As he bent down to get it, she kicked him in the ass, and he fell over. Then she put her foot on him.

"Bill, you dirty old fool. I have told you repeatedly not to speak in my presence. Now, you better watch your tongue. Stay there like the filthy worm you are, under my foot!"

Zyra said, "Galya, I think Bill likes what you are doing, but on to you, Slade. Dreams are just that; some are good, while some are bad. Yes, yours seemed very real, but to think that you are having visions at such an early stage in your development is a little much. Yes, I know that Molly reached out to you, but I was with Asya when we visited Velvet, and she is fine. We just think that you're under too much strain. That is why we are staying a few days longer because we need you and Batch well-rested before we set out to track Vorador down. So, relax. Enjoy this because we are going to be back in the wild soon enough. After a week out there, you will be wanting to get back here."

"But it felt so real."

Asya hugged me. "Slade, if Molly or Topaz had the same dream, I swear we would be on high alert, but this is what stress does to the mind, and anxiety follows. Just breathe. Enjoy Lucy, or I will take her home later after we're done with our meeting. But it'll be a few hours." Asya walked me to the other side of the room to talk in private. "Slade, Lucy is crushing on you something awful, and handsome men like you don't just fall out of the sky every day. If I were her, I would want you to kiss me. I mean, *her*—kiss her."

"Most of you think I fell out of the sky. I have heard their thoughts on the matter."

Asya smiled. "I will admit, how you arrived is still up for debate. What I'm saying is, she is clearly beautiful, and she really desires you. Men would kill for the attention you get, so enjoy it, but treat them well. Now eat, drink, and be merry, because not too long from now, you will wish your biggest problem was who to sleep with and in what order." Asya hugged me again, and I could hear her slowly sniff me. "If you still feel worried in two hours, come get me."

"Where is Sofia?"

Asya smiled. "I thought they deserved a spa day. It's like the hot springs but better. Sofia wanted to let you have time with Lucy, Saffron, and Cyan. Where are Cyan and Saffron?"

I smiled. "Cyan and Saffron are with Batch and Topaz. Well, thank you, Asya. You're exceedingly kind to me. I'm sorry I have disrupted your gathering."

"No, you were right to trust your instincts. Finding me made you feel better, so good job." She smiled and walked away.

I could hear Galya berating Bill as he picked himself off the floor. He saw me from across the room, smiled, and winked. Galya saw what he did and started poking him in the chest. He had to really like her a lot to deal with all that because I hated the poking thing.

Speaking with them had made me feel better. I took Lucy's hand as we walked.

Lucy asked, "Slade, are you not pleased to see me?"

I stopped and asked, "May I kiss you?"

Lucy smiled, then nodded, and we kissed.

"Lucy, I had a bad dream and needed to see Asya. She assures me that it was just a dream, and now I feel better. Tell me, are you hungry?"

She nodded.

"Will you be my late lunch date?"

She said, "Of course, I will."

"Wow, it's only one in the afternoon. Feels more like ten at night." I laughed and held out my arm, and Lucy took it. "I hear there is a place five floors up that is romantic for couples. Does that sound good?"

"I think that sounds wonderful," Lucy said.

Her blue eyes seemed to sparkle as her smile grew. We walked to the elevator. I told her some of the work I was doing, and she seemed happy. We arrived at the place.

"Welcome to Candles, Shadows, and Kisses. Table for two?"

A female Jotanfo seated us at a table. She told us what was best on the menu when we asked. We ordered chicken, carrots, and potatoes. We had water that tasted better than the last time I'd had water. Lucy told me where she was from before the House of Ribbons. A place just like this, so Ribbons was a step backward. She revealed to me that she was a clone, and it did not bother her. She was designed to have the strength and speed gene.

"Slade, was this your home before you became lost?"

"No, the witches brought me here, and to tell you the truth, I haven't a clue where *here* even is. For all I know, we could be ten miles away from home."

"Wow, that is a bit unsettling. Not knowing." Lucy smiled a lot when she spoke.

As a waitress was walking by, I asked, "Excuse me, Miss. I'm new here and was embarrassed to ask my coworkers, but where exactly are we?"

She smiled. "A dirty, little out-of-the-way place called Earth. It's fairly backwater with very few major cities, but the people are rebuilding this world. I hear it used to be really nice."

"I'm sorry. I mean, where are we on this dirty little rock?" I acted like I was not from the planet.

"Oh, I'm sorry. We are in Sydney. An island far removed from the savages of the rest of this planet. The people here have a funny way when they speak, but they're very friendly. Side note: Australia, New Zealand, and a handful of other island nations were the only mostly untouched places after the war."

Lucy said, "Thank you. You were extremely helpful. Be with all."

"And all will be with you." The waitress replied, smiling as she left.

"Lucy, my sweet, how did you know to say that to her?"

Lucy laughed and excitedly said, "I'm from Sydney! She is Jotanfo. They're a kind race from the stars, and what I said is the polite, religious way to say goodbye. The necklaces she was wearing has a religious symbol, and my words shows respect to her goddess. You know, I might have been born in this very place. Did no one tell you that almost all the cloning is done in Australia?"

I smiled. "But the women said this was Sydney."

"Sydney, Australia. Sydney is the new Ruling House of all Australia." Lucy seemed incredibly happy as she told me about it, providing answers to questions I didn't even know I had.

"So, if you're a clone, then there are many more of you out there?"

"You are correct. Hold on, you went to the House of Dreams and didn't see anyone with my face?"

I laughed. "I think I would have remembered that. Do you all act the same? Like in your personality?"

Lucy smiled. "Why? Do you want a super nasty three-way? I don't think you could handle two of me."

We laughed. I noted that she was so much more than just a sexually aggressive girl next door with gorgeous eyes.

We ate, enjoying one another's company. Lucy couldn't have cared less that she was a clone, unlike Cheri, who seemed to hate that fact and herself. After we were done, the waitress handed me a tablet.

"I'm sorry. I'm new here. What do I do with this?"

The waitress said, "Touch the tablet, and it will pay your bill from your account. Sir, do you work here, or are you a guest?"

"I work here. Please hold on. Slade to Tomok."

"Tomok here."

"Tomok, we finished lunch, and the waitress handed me a tablet. I don't know what to do because it's not responding to my touch." I had to sound so stupid. I tried to hold a smile.

Tomok laughed. "Give me a second. Sorry, I forgot to activate your account. That was my fault. Now place your thumb on the tablet, and you will be good. Was the waitress nice to you?"

"She was very nice and helpful."

"Great, see the spot that says 'tip?' Push that, and give the waitress ten, no, twenty. That will complete payment of the meal. If you need anything else, just call. Tomok out."

The waitress was incredibly happy. "Thank you very much. Next time you come by, ask for Olmar, and I will personally take care of you." Olmar smiled and left.

Lucy said, "Wow, you really made her day. That must have been a lot of money, and I think she liked you before the tip. Now I bet she wants more than the tip."

She laughed, and I laughed with her. Her dirty mind was a bit humorous at times, and I liked that she was free with her thoughts and words. She just spoke her mind. I felt closer to her.

"I don't know how much it was. I have yet to learn about money."

As we walked, I told her about the things I had learned, and she told me how they trained clones was the same way: the chair, black drink, and the sick feeling. We both laughed as we gazed into one another's eyes. I stopped, took her in my arms, and kissed her.

"All clones are blank slates, and we're trained for one month, most of which is training on your particular ability, abilities, or skillsets. Some clones are just workers for rebuild projects; they're always the strongest. We develop a deeper personality from interacting with everyone, but when we first wake up, we know nothing, so our first training session gives us intelligence and a minor personality. We kind of act the same way because of the partial personality given to us. Then, we develop the rest on our own, so we think alike. But with us living apart from one another, there are differences. Living with other people helps us develop our true personality."

We got back to the hallway and saw Batch, Topaz, Saffron, and Cyan.

"Hello, brother. If you are going for food, call Tomok and ask to have your account activated. See if we are on the same account."

Batch looked confused.

"It's how we pay for things here."

We shook hands, and I instantly shared the info with him. I saw that he had been with Saffron and Cyan sexually but nothing with Topaz, not even a kiss. I sensed an anger deep within that he was trying to hide. I gave no reason to let him know I was aware of his anger. We parted ways, and Lucy and I were alone in my room. There was a note that read:

My Dearest Slade,

I will be with Asya in something called a spa. I want you to give Lucy whatever she asks. Lucy and I are super close. I want her to have you. Learn what you can from her when it comes to intimate things. I want her first time with you to be private, enjoyable, and full of passion. Do this for me.

Love,

Your Alpha Kitty

"Lucy, I'm yours if you want, but we don't have to do anything. We could keep talking." I felt weird without Sofia being there. It was almost like I was doing something wrong—it was a strange feeling.

Lucy smiled and said, "Anything I want? So, if I said shower and massage me, you would do it?"

I smiled. "Lucy, whatever you desire. So long as I am capable, I will do what you ask, and if I don't know how, you can teach me." I extended my hands to her. When she took them, I spun her around. We danced as she sang a soft-sounding song.

When she was done singing, she said, "Will you wash me? I want to know what a princess feels like when she is showered."

"May I carry this princess to the shower, so I may do as she commands?"

"Oh my God, you are incredibly sexy when you talk like that. Yes, please. My feet are tired, so you may carry me."

I lifted her off her feet and carried her into the shower. I got the water to the perfect temperature and slowly began to massage her shoulders in the warm water. I washed her body and rinsed her off as we began to kiss. I did my best not to see her thoughts, but they were very loud. I really did make her feel special, and being in my arms right at the moment was her favorite moment so far. Love was a funny thing. It couldn't be held, but it could be given. It couldn't be lost, only rediscovered. It would always override logic, and to utterly lose oneself to love was to be blissfully ignorant of the chasm of pain that lingered just below our very feet, waiting to swallow us whole.

We got out of the shower, and I dried her off.

Lucy said, "Kiss my neck. Do it like the first time, making me lose myself between what is and what isn't real. Then make love to me."

I kissed her neck and caused her to drift between her mind and reality. I went down on her, and she thrashed about, but emerged with a hungry look in her eyes.

"I'm going to tell you how to do something that will make Sofia explode over and over again." She whispered it into my ear, gently biting my ear when she was done. "Now, do that to me, so I know you understand."

We got into the position she wanted, and we made love nice and slow at first, then a bit faster. Lucy grabbed a pillow and screamed into it. I took the pillow away.

"No! I want to hear you. I want to see what I am doing to you while our eyes are locked."

I held both of her hands with one of my hands over her head and lifted her leg with the other. Her eyes rolled back as she climaxed. Just as she was about to explode again, I took my free hand and started to choke her. Her body writhed beneath me, and I noticed she fought it harder than Molly. I let go to give her some air.

"Get off me!"

I got up.

"Who taught you that?"

"Molly showed me that. Is that not something you like?"

Lucy rubbed her throat. "No! Not on the first time, and I only really like it when Sofia does it."

"When we first fought, you said, 'I hope you choke me harder than that in bed.' I thought that was what you wanted. Lucy, I'm sorry. I'll get your clothes." I was so embarrassed, and my face felt hot.

Lucy said, "I was being dirty to make me sound cooler in front of my friends, so I guess that was my fault. I wanted you to stop choking me, not stop making love to me. Choking comes with trust because it is so dangerous. Now lay on your back, and I will control our love."

I did as she asked, and she got on top, slowly moving back and forth.

"Oh yeah, baby, that's how I like it. I'm going to ride you all the way to the gates of Heaven."

She said a few other incredibly filthy things, some of which I understood. Some, I did not. She exploded as she screamed a few more times. I couldn't hold my body back any longer. I told her I was about to release, and she increased her motions, arching her back to show me how much she was enjoying it. So, I released within her as she reached the peak of her lust-filled cries.

She fell onto my chest. "This time, I'm really going to need you to carry me to the shower because I can't feel my legs."

We lay there for a while before I got up and picked her up.

Carrying her to the shower, I asked, "Was it what you hoped for?"

"Slade, you're worth more than just candy, but yes. You gave me something that I did not expect. I would have to say that was, hands down, the best sex with a man I have ever had, I'll help you be better at oral. I love the way the water feels on my neck. Maybe next time, I will let you take me from behind."

"I did that, and it's very enjoyable."

"I mean, I will let you take me from behind." Lucy winked.

I laughed. "You said that twice."

Lucy turned around and pushed her backside against me. "From behind, I mean my ass. That is where I want you next."

"Why would you want that?"

She laughed. "You will understand when we do it." She knelt down and took me into her mouth. After a few minutes, she said, "Good, you're ready to go again. I like a hard worker, and you're about to put in some overtime."

I took her against the shower wall, then on the floor with the water raining down on us. When we were done, we dried off and moved to the next room to finish, and as I got close, the ladies came back to the room.

"Oh, look, we get a show." Sofia grinned.

"Sofia, he's amazing in every way."

Sunako walked up and kissed me. She whispered to Molly, "Oh my, he's in her—"

"That is what my friend likes with her husband."

Sofia asked what they were talking about.

Molly said it out loud to Sofia, "She likes it in the ass."

"What? I don't know if I want to try that," said Sofia. "Slade, make sure you shower very thoroughly."

"Sofia, you like it when I put my finger in your—"

"Woman! Stop talking! I know what I like, but your finger and his thing are very different sizes."

"Sofia, you sound like a child. It's called a cock."

"Gross. That's too rough on the ears. What about the other things?"

"Dick."

"That's the one. I like his *dick*."

"Ladies, I'm finding it difficult to finish this debate."

"Sorry, baby. Now I'll help make her scream." Sofia slid her hand under Lucy and started to rub her kitty. "Come on, baby. I want to hear you scream."

Lucy and I achieved orgasm simultaneously.

"That was so hot, sexy, and dirty at the same time."

We kissed, then we showered.

Lucy said, "I told you it would be fun. Sadly, not every woman will want or enjoy it. Now give me a little me-time in the shower. I bet Sofia wants more kisses."

"It was really exciting in a dirty way, being with you like that."

I got out of the shower, threw a towel on, and hugged Sofia. I whispered, "I missed you three, but you the most."

Sofia said, "If I were any more relaxed, I think I wouldn't be able to walk. Where are Saffron and Cyan?"

"I brought Cyan and Saffron to Batch. Cyan is not really into Batch, but they had sex. Cyan and Saffron did look happy with him, but I think Topaz has second thoughts about Batch. Lucy is still in the shower."

Sofia smiled. "So, how was she?"

I kissed Sofia. "We enjoyed one another very much. I think Lucy will make an exceptionally good addition."

Sofia smiled and said, "Slade, Lucy just wants to get laid. Plus, she has a difficult time letting someone in. She just has sex to have sex. It's fun, and she enjoys herself. Being with you last night was something I thought of all day and not in a dirty way. The way you make all of us feel loved is special to all three of us, and we talked about it in depth. Slade, I don't care where you came from. As long as you are with us, I will be happy. Now, I'm going to take a nap, but I fear these lazy days are spoiling me."

She kissed me, and when Lucy got out of the shower, they cuddled. Sunako and I talked for a bit before she went to bed, but Molly and I stayed awake and talked about a wide range of stuff. I liked speaking with her. We both agreed we had a strong connection. She confessed that she had fallen in love with Sofia but was terrified to tell her and swore me to secrecy until she knew if Sofia loved her as well.

"Why not look into her mind?"

"No, that would be an improper use of the gift. Besides, it would spoil what good times we could still have. What would you say if I told you that I loved you as well?"

I kissed her deeply. "I know you do because I saw your thoughts as you drifted off to sleep. I didn't mean to, but you were against me, and I was curious. But, to answer your question, I would say I had feelings for you when you were just a head. I don't think that love has anything to do with sex. I love you for you, as I love Sofia for being herself, as I do Sunako. Molly, is it wrong to love more than one person?"

Molly thought for a bit. "Well, as an oracle, love is only between a woman and a woman. I have seen more than a few women fall in love with multiple women. They usually ask to live together. Before I met you, I never desired a man in any way at all. But the way you looked at me the first time, you seemed to see what I could be and not what I was. I believe I saw love in your eyes."

"What about Jacob? I thought you ran off with him?"

"Vorador was behind that. I had been enchanted. I never did anything with any of them. I was used, not for my body, but to gain access to Lady Velvet and the Eye of the Void. But you knew that already."

"I did, but I wanted to hear you say it."

I took Molly in my arms. We kissed and held each other until the ladies woke up. Molly announced it was dinnertime. I watched the ladies stretch and get out of bed.

Lucy said, "I'm so hungry I could eat Slade, but it will take a few big bites, and I will probably choke on him a bit."

The rest of them laughed. I called Batch and we made plans to meet for dinner. We all met up, and as we ordered, Batch and I were called away to see Tomok on an important issue. As I got up, Topaz slightly reached for me with a pained look. I wanted to take her hand, but I needed to know she wasn't confused. I didn't want Batch to get his feelings hurt.

Chapter 31

Bound by Blood

Tomok greeted us as we walked in.

"Hello, boys. Some of the tests have come back, and we think it best to just tell you now. Batch, have you tried again to use any of your gifts or abilities at all?"

"I don't have any, but Slade and I can speak directly with our minds when we touch. Does that count?" Batch added, "Why? Is everything okay?"

Tomok replied, "Batch, take my hand, and tell me what I'm thinking."

Batch took his hand and let it go. "I can't hear your thoughts, and I cannot enter your mind. How is that? I could have moved between two different people before coming back to Slade."

I said, "Batch, you didn't get all of my DNA."

"What? Are you saying you messed up my body? I thought you knew what you were doing. Tomok, you'll get it right for my permanent body, right?" Batch was upset.

Tomok rubbed his forehead. "Batch, you were transferred into a clone body, and a clone is one hundred percent a perfect copy of the host. But since forty percent of Slade's DNA is unknown, you were given filler DNA for the unknown DNA. The information I have is that it was split twenty percent Jotanfo, twenty percent Sa-Teen, and sixty percent human DNA. I was not even aware of the change because we have never had unknown DNA before. Then, I had a thought about the forty percent of unknown DNA, then went into the records. It is common to mix another DNA when the host has a fatal disease or they want new abilities. Then, there is something specific they want to add or any number of other reasons. Slade, have you ever had Batch out, then you leave?"

"Yes and no. Yes, I left my body while Batch was away, but I switched bodies with someone else."

"Why would you do that?" asked Tomok.

"I was demonstrating my ability." I stood up and paced around, saying directly, "Will we be able to read the forty percent DNA in time for Batch's permanent body?"

"Batch was given increased strength, stamina, and a rapid healing rate, which is very useful. But the forty percent is where I believe all of your abilities come from, like the black eyes and being able to hijack someone's mind, which—if I might add—must be very cool to do. Slade, whatever race you come from has such complex DNA that it literally caused the AI to have a problem. Upon further examination, your mystery DNA does not remotely look like any other DNA. It does not follow a pattern or a blueprint, if you will. If it did, we could begin to understand it. Take, for example, the Trilexen, the distant cousins to the Oncari. Their DNA is not able to be copied because it's always in a state of flux due to the fluidity of their race, but it can still be studied. On the Trilexen home world, there used to live a turtle-like species that is sentient/sapient, a race called the Rosemalty. They later moved to a world better suited to their lifestyle and studies of their religion. Due to their hermit-like nature, they shy away from the rest of us, but there are a few Rosemalty scientists out there. An interesting race but not very talkative."

"Tomok! Man, I fear you are way off point." I did not mean to be rude.

"Yes, right. Sorry about that. The Rosemalty had the hardest genome to understand of all races. It took many years to decode it. Without the accidental find of an ancient stone tablet on their original home world, we would have never been able to interact with them, due to the way they communicate. Also, the angels and demons of this world and other worlds have DNA, most which is on record, so everything that has DNA that can be studied. We just need to unlock yours now. Damn, I am excited. I'll finally get a published, worthwhile paper in the science community."

"Tomok, if you have DNA on record does that mean you can duplicate it?"

"No. Take a demon's DNA. We understand it but cannot duplicate it."

Batch asked, "So what does all this mean for me?"

"I don't want to get your hopes up, but let's say I crack Slade's DNA tonight. I believe I would be able to replicate it. You would be a one hundred percent perfect clone of Slade and, in theory, have all of Slade's gifts. I honestly couldn't tell you when that would be—anywhere between now and forever. Good news for you, Batch, is I have put in a request for you to become my lab assistant because you meet all the criteria, and we did train you."

"And the answer is?"

"Sorry, my head is all over the place today. Batch, you got the job, if you want it. You will be on my team as I'm the lead person studying the foreign forty percent. If we code your mystery genome, we will become famous in certain circles. I will have you trained on the physiology of all sentient and sapient races, including the essential information to be able to understand everything we work with."

"I think I would like that very much."

They shook hands, and we returned to dinner. Along the way, we talked.

"Congratulations on the job, brother."

"An interesting job that gives my life purpose. Cracking this genome and understanding our DNA could help us understand who we are and where we come from. I want to know just as badly as you because we're essentially twins. Don't you want to see if we can get back home?"

"No, no, I don't! Why would I want to go back to people who abandoned us? I like it right where I'm free with endless possibilities. I will hunt Vorador alone if I have to. I will have his head as a trophy. That is my purpose. Will you help me kill him?"

"So, you're really willing to kill someone over this? Listen to yourself, Slade. Molly is better than ever, thanks to you. The witches said he was extremely dangerous, so no. No, I will not go to my death to right a wrong that has been righted."

I took a deep breath. "Batch, I would like to just stay here with you where the air is cool and we are safe, but I feel I'm being pulled toward something bigger. In a few days, when the witches leave, I will go with them. I will return for work when needed, but I have to stop Vorador before he hurts anyone else."

"Why? Why you?"

"Because of the vision. I can't let that happen! I won't let it!"

Batch shook his head in disapproval as we sat down with the ladies. They ordered for us, and we ate and talked. I was angry with Batch, but he was his own person. I had a man to hunt. Vidya stopped by to talk.

"Slade, I'm about to announce the procedure, and I wanted you to name it."

"I'd call it 'Threshold.' I would say 'Welcome to Threshold,' or 'Step across the threshold. Where life would hold you back, we'll pull you forward.'"

"Holy shit, kid, you're a genius. This kid is brilliant. I love that brain of yours."

I noticed her top two tendrils looked like they were vibrating.

"Vidya, may I speak with you?" I stood up, and we walked into the adjacent room for more privacy. "Vidya, I hope I'm not overstepping my bounds, but what will I make for each transplant?"

"Oh. I thought you wanted to ask something else." Vidya looked to the left. We sat at an empty table. "I'm not going to lie. You're going to make me beyond rich and famous, and I will need you every step of the way. You will always have what you need when you need it. Long story short, you will be very wealthy. You can have your wives live here, so you'll know they're always safe."

"Really?"

"Slade, I'll be blunt. If I have to kill to get women for you, then consider it done. I will have two more rooms opened for you, so you can have your own space. Like I said, I need you and your unique gift. Now, tell me really why you asked."

"I was thinking of creating ten highly trained fighters to help me find someone that needs to answer for his crimes."

"Slade, please hear me. 'Before you embark on a journey of revenge, dig two graves.' Confucius said that. The quote is a warning to not take revenge. If you go looking for death, be prepared to find it." She hugged me. "Please, you're the only one of your kind, with one of the most unique gifts ever seen. You stand to save those who are facing the grave, but what good will you be if you're in a grave?"

"Amoli to Vidya, come in."

Vidya said, "Yes, Amoli."

"We found one for you, and we lucked out." Amoli sounded excited. "Shall I bring the client into the lab?"

"Lab six will do. We will meet you there. Good work." Vidya smiled. "Slade, I have your first job. It's time to earn your paycheck."

I went to inform my friends. "Ladies, duty calls. My brother and I will be back as soon as we can."

Amoli and Vilina were waiting for us.

Vidya said, "Slade, Batch, you have the floor. Show us how you work from start to finish."

"Vidya, you can't be serious. You're really going to let them work without backup?" said Vilina.

"Yes, I sent you two out to find a client, someone with influence, and you brought me the perfect person. Now, let's watch." She pulled me aside. "Slade, her name is Detra. She's Jotanfo. The machine that is attached to her is the only thing keeping her alive. If she is lucky, she will get another month, maybe two. This is your chance to save the life of a good person; all eyes are on you. Now, go make history."

I smiled and walked out.

"Batch, you run controls, while I escort her into her new body."

He nodded.

"Hello, I am Slade. You must be Detra. I have to take some samples. I apologize if I cause you any discomfort." I took the three samples, then put them in a machine. "Detra, you may get up."

"Thank you, Slade, but with my age, I don't move so well. Is it true? Can you really extend my life? They have tried before, but I am one of the unlucky few who cannot transfer to a new body. Slade, I am scared. Please, I don't want to die. Not here, not now. Please help me."

I took her hand and helped her up. "I will do more than just help you, but I don't want to ruin the surprise. Your flash clone will take two hours, and your regular clone will take two standard years." Tears ran down her face, and I gently wiped them away. "I will be back in two hours. Then, you and I will do something that will make you a young woman again."

"To be young again is beyond a wish, my boy."

"Good news is, you're already beautiful. And you'll do more than walk."

"You're too kind, but I'm old and weak. The best I can hope for is for this to work well enough to be able to walk without pain. Might I say whatever you're wearing smells so wonderful. What is it called?" Detra's smile was kind and warm.

"That is my natural smell."

"Gene-edited to smell nice. Where were you four hundred years ago? I would have bought you in a heartbeat just to have you sleep at my side. Ah, an old woman can dream, can't she?"

I carried her to the next room and got her a drink.

"How did you know I wanted a drink?"

"Every beautiful flower needs to be watered, and you, my dear, are no exception." I kissed her on the hand and walked out of the room as Vidya entered.

Amoli and Vilina were in the next room.

Vilina said, "Hey hotshot, don't screw this down."

I smiled as I replied, "Don't screw this *up*, not down. I have no intention of doing anything but my job."

I sat down, and Vilina walked out. As she did, she snapped me on the top of my head with her tendril.

Amoli said, "Please excuse my wife. She has a real dislike for humans in general, but I think she will warm up to you soon enough."

I sat back and closed my eyes. Vilina kicked my feet. I thought I had just closed my eyes but had been out for two hours.

I walked back to Detra, who was on her back. Next to her lay her clone. It was covered up, as it could be a disturbing sight.

"Detra, my sweet, are you ready to see yourself as I see you?"

Detra smiled. "You're too kind to this old woman. Flattery will get you everywhere."

"Please hold my hand. I will do something that may alarm you, so please remain as calm as you can."

I entered her mind, and we spoke for a bit there. She told me that she had a degenerative disease that began early in life. It weakened her bones and made her sick a lot. I told her that my brother found the gene and edited it out of the new body. I escorted her consciousness into her new body.

"Here we are, Detra. Please focus and try to move your hand. It may take a small bit of time, but I promise you will take control of this new body."

Her hand moved.

"Very good. Now I have to return to my body, but remember to make small actions. As soon as you have full control, sit up. I will be right by your side if you become frightened."

I left and reentered my body, standing up. Ten long minutes passed with only Detra's hand twitching. Then, she sat up and took her first steps.

"Welcome to your new body, Detra."

Detra stood there, naked. She started to cry. I took her in my arms.

She said, "No pain, I feel no pain. I have lived with the pain for so long, and it only became worse in the last hundred years. You took the pain away, and you saved me from death." She hugged me tightly with her arms and tendrils.

"Detra, I only helped you into this new healthy body. May I get you some clothes?"

Detra said, "No! I want to see this body. I need a mirror." She entered the bathroom and screamed, running out and picking me off the ground. "I am young again and beautiful. You really did see how I used to look. Name it, boy, and I will give it to you. Anything at all. Just ask."

"Thank you, Detra. I'm well-paid, but I am honored by your offer. Your smile is the most important thing to me right now."

She smiled. "Slade, you really don't know who I am, do you? Because I could give you an entire planet if you wish. I could buy you this planet. Just ask. I know this world isn't much, but you would own it and the rights to its moon. Please just ask."

"Detra, thank you again. Maybe later, but I don't think I am ready to own a world just yet. Detra, I look forward to seeing you again." I kissed her hand. "Now, I must go, unless you have anything for me, Vidya?"

She shook her head. Vidya said, "I will see you later. Slade, amazing work."

I left with a smile and a sense of accomplishment.

"Vidya, how did that boy not know who I am?"

"I'm sure he is just trying to be professional. So, look at you. I must say, you're stunning, and you get the permanent body in two standard solar years for this sector. I will be in touch before then."

"Vidya, I know that boy didn't know who I was. Now give me the boy's account number."

Vidya handed her a tablet. Detra spoke with a woman that she came with and began to type something.

"This is the tip I have left him. Be sure that he gets it and this note." She handed Vidya back the tablet and a piece of paper. Vidya slightly bowed. After a few minutes of talking, Detra left.

"Vidya to Slade. Meet me in room 1A in five minutes."

"Yes, Vidya."

I waited for Vidya for a few minutes, and she walked in with a smile.

"Slade, this is from Detra. She wanted you to get this immediately. You should know what you did looked like a miracle. Wow, look at me! I'm shaking."

"Are you okay, Vidya?"

"Slade, what you did with Molly and Batch was one thing, but that was Detra. A real mover and shaker. Slade, you could become the most famous person in all the known galaxies. I need a drink. Here, read this." She handed me a handwritten message, which read:

Slade,

Thank you for the gift of renewed life. I cannot thank you enough. Now please accept my gift to you, along with this tip. I look forward to seeing you again. If you want or ever need anything, please don't hesitate to contact me.

Detra.

"Vidya, what is this? I can't accept this, and I still don't understand credits yet. And what am I going to do with a whole planet?"

Vidya smiled. "Slade, it's a planet, and she just made you rich enough to buy two good-sized ships—much like the one you're in right now—and staff them for a few years. You will, no doubt, find out who she is. Be proud of yourself and your abilities."

"Vidya, I only did my job. I don't deserve any of this."

"Slade, Detra is a woman of immense wealth and is known to never take no for an answer. She is greatly loved by many races for her contributions and inventions, of which she makes available to everyone, not just the rich. If I were you, I would talk to her about this planet/gift. Maybe your smooth-talking ways will get her to take it back, but I will warn you. If I were her, I'd be offended. Learn to accept a gift here and there."

"Vidya, a planet isn't a *gift*. I mean, it's a whole planet! A country, I might understand, but this is a whole planet."

Vidya laughed. "Don't forget its moon. Slade, individuals like Detra can and do what they wish. I like you, kid. You're humble. Always be that way, and the galaxies will love and adore you. Who knows, maybe one day I will work for you. I'll see you soon. Great work. I am so impressed."

"Vidya, I'm serous. What do I do with a planet?"

"It's a status symbol, but you own the right to its gross domestic product and a shit ton of other things. I'll have a law team drafted for you, and they will manage it. Think of it like a company. I know you'll be very busy, so I'll keep a tight eye on this for you."

"Thank you, but I don't want to think of it at all," I muttered. I left the room to find Batch.

"Batch, I don't know about you, but I'm going back to my room to make love to Sofia, then hold her tight all night. Then, I am going to hunt and kill a man. Hey, man. Learn about credits because I have a lot of them, and I want you to have what you would like. What's mine is yours."

"Thank you. I will take the course tomorrow. Slade, does Sofia make you happy? Because I feel for Topaz the same way you feel about Sofia, but I fear she doesn't want me at all. I mean, she won't let me get close to her."

"I'm sorry, brother. I don't know what to say. Maybe she will come around. Either way, I fear we will have too many women soon enough. I suggest you give her time."

Batch stopped in the hallway and hugged me. He smiled. "I love you, brother."

"I love you, too."

We went back to our respective rooms. Sofia was looking out the window.

"Sofia, I want you to know that I have strong feelings for you. If I were never with another woman, it would be enough just to be with you."

"Slade, I am yours as you are mine, but I was Sunako and Cheri's before you, and I want to share you. I am not a jealous woman; none of us are. I want to be with you for as long as our road takes us, but I will not keep you to myself, if that's okay. Are you okay with what I want?" Sofia slowly brushed her hair to one side, exposing her neck.

"Yes, I just wanted you to know that I love you, even though love is new to me. I feel it the most in my chest when I see you, Sunako, and Molly. Is that strange? I feel that it might be wrong to feel that way."

Sofia kissed me. "Slade, you're mine. If you didn't have some kind of love for Sunako, then I wouldn't like you as much because she means a great deal to me. I love you, Slade, so please stop worrying. Oh, and I kind of lost a bet a little while ago to Lucy, and she gets first turn with you tonight."

"Sofia, please stop betting, or at least, stop using me like currency. It makes me feel weird. You're just lucky Lucy is so amazing in and out of bed."

"What did you say?" asked Sofia sharply.

I laughed. "I knew you wouldn't like that. By the way, your jealousy is showing."

Sofia pushed me to the bed, getting on top and calling the ladies in.

"Anyone here know what I am to Slade?" Sofia was loud as she spoke.

The alpha, the head mistress," they replied.

"See, Slade, I come first every time, except tonight, because I lost you in a bet. But I will always come first in your life—understand me?"

"Yes, but you will remember I am a free man with a title, so no using me as a coin to be lost in a bet."

She smiled while she slowly got off my lap. Sunako kissed me. She told me what happened at dinner, and I told her what I did with Detra. Molly and I talked for a bit before Lucy walked up to me.

"I think you know what time it is. Now I want what I won, and I want them to watch. You will focus on me the whole time, so get in the shower, and I will join you soon after."

I got to the shower, and the water felt great on my skin. I heard Batch, and it sounded like he was wrestling. I pushed that out of my mind as Lucy entered the shower.

"Lucy, after tonight, there will be no betting or trading for my time. If you want to make love, just ask, and make sure Sofia is fine with it. I am confused about my feelings toward you, so I wanted to be upfront with you. I hope you understand."

Lucy smiled and said, "Slade, I really do like you, but love is not my thing. It's like you say, messy and complicated. Not to mention confusing. With you, I just want to have fun, and you're incredibly fun. So, let's cut the heavy talk and fool around because I am getting a bit tired of waiting. Oh, they expect a good show. Don't let them down."

We kissed and caressed one another. I bit her neck a little, and we became aroused. Soon, we were slowly drying each other off.

I carried Lucy to the bed with the ladies chanting, “Slade, Slade, Slade.”

I placed her down and kissed her all over. We began to have sex, at first on her back, then on her side, then on all fours. She ended up on top, but at some point, it turned into making love. It was strange and furious, passionate and confusing. Lucy caught me trying to sneak a peek into her mind, and she told me to stay out. Soon after, I swore I saw a tear, but she touched her face too fast.

“Slade, I got what I wanted. Now give me you. I won’t stop until you achieve yours, and hurry, because I can’t feel my legs.”

I flipped her to her back, kissed her, and I helped her to achieve bliss one more time as I finished inside her.

She wrapped her arms around me and whispered, “I think I love you.”

Then, she passed out. The room was silent, and I held Lucy as she slept. Later, I got up and stood at the window and watched the fish. Most that swam by I had never seen. Soon, Sofia joined me, while Molly and Sunako were busy tangling themselves up with one another.

Sofia asked, “Are you okay?”

“Yes, I just need to get used to this life. Everything is so bright. There are people everywhere, and almost everyone wants to talk to me. It has been nonstop since the fight at Silk’s house with William and Richter. I would like to just go back to the cottage with Cheri being mean, Sunako being cute, and you taking charge while being beautiful.”

Sofia took me in her arms. “*Sh...* You just need some rest to clear your head. You have done so much in so little time. Come lay next to me and let me help you sleep.”

I saw that it was 8:15 p.m. I happily fell asleep in her arms.

I was woken by Sofia’s hands on me. “Sorry to wake you, but now that you are up, can I try something?”

Sofia got on top of me and slowly moved around. Sunako and Molly were asleep next to us, and I noticed Lucy was awake, watching us. She sat up.

Lucy and Sofia started to kiss, and Sofia said, “Slade, kiss Lucy for me.”

Lucy got on top of my face, and the two were riding me. This was different. The more I kissed and the more Sofia moved back and forth, the more it caused me to focus. I wanted more. I felt what Sofia and Lucy were feeling, and I looped it through us like electricity from body to body, faster and faster until Lucy stood up and tried to walk off her shaking legs. I grabbed Sofia and rolled her to her back, and we made love until I had nothing left to give.

I had to have lain there at least ten minutes before I could get up and walk. I went to the shower, and a few minutes in, Lucy joined.

"Holy shit, Slade. I think we may have created a monster."

I smiled. "Just be thankful I need to gather myself, or you would be up against that wall right now. The spirit is willing, but the flesh is weak."

We kissed as the hot water cleaned us.

"Careful, lover boy. Don't go hurting yourself. You have other ladies to tend to." Lucy was clever with her words.

"Lucy, did you mean what you said before you fell asleep?"

She said, "I don't remember saying anything."

As we kissed, I showed her the memory. She just stood there as the water ran down her face.

"Yes, okay? Are you happy? Yes, I kind of love you." She rolled her eyes. "I didn't mean to catch feelings for you, but I have thought of you every minute since we first met. There is something strange and fascinating about you. I have loved Sofia for a while now. I was just too scared to tell her how much I love her. Then, you came along and stole my heart. Yes, Slade, I strongly like you a lot."

I said nothing, just standing there looking at her. "I understand."

She started to walk out, and I took her in my arms.

"I, too, have feelings for you. The way you think about me makes me smile. I want you to be in my life. I want to know you more, so when I tell you I love you, you'll know that I mean it. But I do, in a way, love you."

Lucy pressed her face to my chest. "I love you."

We finished up and dried off in the room. We spoke for a bit, and we made love again slowly, without words and with locked eyes. Her tears looked like little diamonds with the way the light touched them. As we finished, in her mind, I told her I felt strongly pulled to her. We got dressed, and I put on some sleep pants in hopes it would ward off anyone with any ideas of waking me up. The clock showed it was 10:35 p.m. I climbed into bed next to Sofia. Lucy and I held each other until we fell asleep.

Chapter 32

When the Future Calls, Don't Open the Door

I didn't exactly know when I became aware I was not in my body or if it was a dream, but it seemed real.

Lady Velvet was screaming. The smell of burnt wood was in the air, and Kailee had blood all over her face. She jumped toward Velvet but was thrown against the main house, quickly rebounding. Velvet was being yelled at.

"Where are my things?"

Then, a masked man hit her in the face.

"I'll kill you if you don't give them back!"

As he went to kick Velvet in the chest, Kailee jumped to shield Velvet, but with a wave of his hand, the man pushed Kailee through the wall, knocking her out. A large hole was made between the windows.

"Where is the Eye of the Void and the Emerald Cane? Give it to me now, and I will not push in both of your eyes and cut off your hands."

He was choking her. I could see that her feet were off the ground.

I woke up, covered in sweat. I jumped up so fast that I woke Lucy and shocked Sunako, who had come from the bathroom.

"Slade, you just did a flip while getting out of bed. That was amazing."

"Go back to sleep, my loves. I have to check something. It is one a.m." I went into the sitting room. "Alabaster?"

"Yes, Slade, how may I help you? Your heart rate would suggest you're in need of medical attention."

"No, I'm fine. Bad dream is all. Where was I before Asya took us here?"

"Slade, you were outside. Asya shifted you and six others to a point just inside the tree line."

"Where were we before that?"

"You were in ancient America. The exact location is 39.7675° N, 94.8467° W. It is nine thousand six hundred and thirty-nine miles from here. The place you seek is not on any current map due to such a sparse population, nor does it have a name anymore. Did that answer your question?"

"Alabaster, what would happen if I jumped that far with such little training?" I concentrated on my breathing to steady my heartbeat.

"You would die. Your score indicated that you passed level one through five in training. You're cleared to shift without further training, but as of now, you can only shift within a five-mile radius."

"Then how do the witches make such long jumps?"

"They are trained."

"So, what you are telling me is, there is no way to get there on my own?"

"I didn't say that."

"Please, Alabaster, tell me what I need to know to shift to this place."

Alabaster took a full minute before saying anything.

"Slade, you will need to see the place you want to be and hold your breath as you step into the envelope. Even then, you might miss your target destination. If you do make it, you will not be able to do it again for at least two hours due to the exertion it will place on your brain. If you try, you will certainly have a brain aneurysm, which will be fatal. There is one other way, but the risk is greater in the beginning."

"Please, what is it?"

"Slade, you can jump into the water. At this depth, you will be able to make your jump safely, but you may drown in the process. That is your final test with the envelope. To shift into water and shift out."

"How do I get to that depth and hold my breath that long?"

Alabaster said, "It requires two shifts from the room you're in into the water while holding your breath. Focus on where you want to go. If you do it right, you will live. If not, you will be saved while in training. And at this depth, you will feel like you have up to three hundred pounds on your chest at once due to pounds per square inch. Slade, I don't recommend this course of action. It will be fatal, and you are not prepared. I strongly recommend you do not attempt this."

I walked to Bill's door and strode in. "Bill, wake up. I need you now."

"Kid, do you know what time it is?"

"Please trust me on this. Velvet needs us now, and if I make a jump that far, it could be fatal."

Bill got up, slipping on his boots and shirt. "Okay, kid. Let's go."

"My room first."

We shifted in, and I laced up my boots.

"Do you have everything? Don't forget your purse," said Bill.

He laughed, and I felt a slight hit as we shifted. When we arrived at The House of Dreams, there was smoke in the air. Lucy was hanging off my back.

"Damn it, Lucy!" I spoke in a low tone. "Stay with Bill!"

"Slade, take this." Bill handed me a short sword that he'd pulled out of seemingly nowhere.

I saw people I did not recognize, but I did not know half the people that lived there. I saw one man break off from the group of five and walk behind a cottage. I followed him as he walked toward a girl tied to a tree. He ripped at her clothes, while I shifted behind him. I grabbed him by the neck as I pushed my sword through his back. I did my best to see who he was and why he was there.

That's when I saw him: Vorador. The man had to have been working for Vorador, who was with four other men. I shifted back to Bill.

"Bill, Vorador is here looking for the Eye of the Void. What should we do?"

"We need everyone. It's not safe. We will go back, get everyone, and attack him together from different angles."

"I'll stay and keep an eye on him."

"Kid, watch, and do nothing more until I get back."

Bill shifted away.

"Shit! Lucy, you should have gone with him."

Lucy smiled. "I've never shied away from a fight. Plus, Bill gave me a sword. So, let's go stick this in a bad guy."

I reminded her what Bill had said.

"Don't pussy out on me, Slade. Come on, let's baptize our relationship in blood."

We moved to the girl who was tied up and cut her loose. We found the next guy choking a man who had his hands tied. Lucy ran up and took off his head in one clean cut. She smiled and waved to me. We found the next two. One was pissing, while the other was going through the pockets of a dead man. Lucy and I reached both men at the same time. Mine died right away, but Lucy's guy tried to make a run for it with her on his back. He soon succumbed to his injury.

"One left, then Vorador." She kissed me deeply.

"What was that for?"

She smiled. "I'm sorry I lied to you in the shower. I honestly do love you. You make me feel like I'm worth something, like I'm special. If I could, I would steal you away and marry you."

"Now might not be the best time to do this, but I'm really happy that Sofia wanted you to be part of the group. You're special to me. When we get back, I'm going to show you just how special you are. Look, there is the last guy. Damn, he's big, almost like Dutch big. You run by, and when he chases you, I will come up from behind him."

Lucy laughed, "That sounds sexy. Okay, here I go."

She took off, getting the guy's attention. I shifted right by a tree she was about to pass. When she did, I caught him in the side with my sword, but I didn't expect his momentum to knock me down. Lucy put her sword through the guy's neck.

"That still counts as my kill." I winked.

Lucy smiled. "I just wanted him to choke on his own blood, and I believe you meant to say *our* kill, thank you very much."

"Okay, let's get into the main house."

I told her to stay behind, but she was as stubborn as she was beautiful. Soon, I could hear Vorador yelling at Velvet.

"Return what you have stolen for me! Return the Eye of the Void, or I will kill you!"

I tried to sneak up on him, but the hardwood floor squeaked, rudely announcing me. Vorador turned around and looked right at me, tipping his hat. He picked up Velvet and tossed her though the large front window.

With an amazing leap, he sailed through the shattered window and started kicking her repeatedly, yelling, "Last chance, Velvet! Where are my things?" He bent down, picking her off the ground by the throat and choking her, just like in my dream. He looked as if he wasn't going to stop. I shifted out and back into the air about ten feet and came right down on him, knocking him off his feet. Lucy rushed in and grabbed Velvet.

He stood up, looked right at me, and said, "Well, look at you. Nice move, by the way." He cracked his neck to the left and walked toward me as if to greet me.

"Give it up, Vorador. We have you outnumbered."

He laughed. "Kid, if you live through this, learn to lie better. I figured the witches would be arriving any minute now for backup, but until then, I'll have you to play with." He walked casually toward me. "What name do you go by now, so I can add it to my list?"

"I will be called The Man Who Killed Vorador."

As he got close, I swung my sword, hitting nothing. He kicked me from behind. I swung again, only to be kicked from behind again. I spun around to catch him, but he was not there. He was behind Lucy, holding her by the back of the neck. He raised his free hand, and a high-pitched sound rang out as the backup arrived.

"See, you've lost. Now put her down!" I shouted.

He laughed. "How are they going to get in? I put up a force field. By the time they break through it, I'll have what I came for."

I saw the witches trying to break through.

"Look at their feeble attempts to get in and save you. Hilarious, really, when you think about it. They might as well be on the moon with that shield, so I have some time to play." He shook Lucy like a ragdoll. "Girl, is this your boy?"

Lucy said, "Drop dead, asshole!"

Vorador squeezed harder, and she screamed. I felt so helpless. I wanted to just get a hold of her and shift away.

"Bitch, I asked you a question!" He must have loosened his grip because she stopped turning red. "Is that boy your lover? Tell me now, or I will crush your neck."

Lucy looked at me with tears in her eyes. "Yes. Yes, he is."

"Do you love him?"

Lucy started to cry. "Yes, I do. I love him. Slade, I love you!"

"Slade!" Vorador said with shock in his voice. "But you're so young. Stay there, boy! I'm going to kill Velvet. Then, you and I are taking a trip."

"Why don't you stop being a coward and get me now? Or are you going to hide behind a little girl all day while you talk me into a slow death?"

"Girl, anything you want to say to that boy before I take him away?"

He squeezed her harder, and she slapped at his hand. He let up. Lucy gasped for air as he dropped her to the ground. He walked up to me.

"I really can't believe you're Slade. Any last witty remarks now that I am out from behind the girl?"

As I went to say something, he grabbed me by the throat and squeezed so hard that I dropped my sword. I couldn't feel my hands.

"What's the matter boy? You seem all choked up."

I tried to grab any skin, but he was covered from head to toe.

"Now you understand why I'm covered up. I learned from others' past mistakes, and I had a really good teacher. I won't be caught off guard again." He slapped me hard across the face. "Don't die on me yet. Maybe in your next time you'll train better before you square up with me, but I'd defeat you there as well." He tightened his grip. All I could see were stars, but he let go, and I couldn't take in enough air; my lungs were on fire.

Lucy had jumped up and stabbed him through the back right shoulder, his wound spraying me with blood. He screamed and turned toward her. I took my sword and did my best to yell for him, but my voice was hoarse and did not come out. He caught her as she tried to run.

"You know, girl, I was in love once. She was so beautiful, it made me weep. I would have killed for her. I would have died for her, but someone did this to her." The look in his eyes was of anger and sadness. A sword appeared in his right hand. As he looked over her shoulder at me, he stabbed her through the stomach. With his sword sticking out of her back, she cried out in agony. "These are the parts that I hate the most. Goodnight, pretty flower." He put her gently on the ground.

I threw my sword at him, and he moved to one side. I shifted behind him and finally was able to grab some skin just above his mask, near his right eye. I made it inside of his mind. It was empty and gray when he walked into view.

"Excellent job." He started clapping. "Look at you. You know, I have to hand it to you. I didn't know you had natural skill. It would really be a shame if you die here. Besides, I really can't let that happen, and I could really use a partner—someone just like me. What do you say, Slade? Wanna go be pirates? I will give you this one chance to go anywhere and do anything. Almost nothing will be beyond your reach. Just give up this life."

"I'm nothing like you. When I'm done with you, I'm going to violate your corpse."

Vorador laughed. "You're, in so many ways, exactly like me. You just don't know it yet because you lack the proper motivation. Consider my offer, then come find me. Well, shit, look at the time. I should be going."

And with that, I felt a terrible pain.

"See, kid, when you get as old and as skilled as I am, you learn to completely control your body while the mind is occupied. Now, enjoy that feeling because when I pull it out, you're going to wish I left it in. Oh, and don't die on me. I want you to watch me cut off Velvet's head in front of those filthy witches. Now, take a deep breath."

He pulled it out, and he was right. I wished he'd left it in. Then, he kicked me out of his mind.

"Sorry, kid, there is only enough room for one of us in here, but you're the first to get in."

I could see my friends using brightly colored beams of light in their desperate attempts to breach the shield with thunderous blasts. I watched him pick Velvet up and stab her through the midsection. He must have been squeezing her throat hard enough, so she couldn't scream. Then, he pulled something off her neck and put it in his pocket. When he dropped Velvet, I could finally see his face clearly. He had a few scars across his face. He looked so familiar. I knew him from somewhere. He was the first person I partially recognized.

He winked and said, "What's the matter? You don't like my face? Or do you just hate yourself that much right now?" He laughed hard while grabbing Velvet's unconscious body by the hair, holding her up.

"Leave now, or I swear I will cut off your head, keep you alive, and torture you for as long as I live."

Vorador lowered his sword and said, "See what I mean? We think alike. That is just what I'm going to do to her. Now, shut the hell up. I want to get her head in one slice."

While he was talking down to me, Lucy managed to get up and rushed him. Before Vorador could cut Velvet's head off, he dropped Velvet and spun around, stabbing Lucy again.

I heard him say in a low voice, "Damn it, girl! You were supposed to just barely survive!" He angrily threw Lucy at me. I did my best to catch her, but she was moving too fast. Her body sent us tumbling to the ground. Just then, the shield broke open. All I could hear were shouts and other loud noises with blindingly bright flashes of light.

I pulled Lucy close to me, and I felt her hanging on—she was so weak.

"Please, Lucy, don't die on me. Not here, not today."

"Slade, tell Sofia that I love her. She was my best friend. I love her, and I love you."

"I love you. I love you. Please don't leave—please don't leave me. I love you."

She coughed up a lot of blood, and I rolled her to her side so that she wouldn't choke.

"Slade, I can't feel my legs or arms, and I am so cold. Thank you for making me feel loved. I wish I could have been your wife."

We kissed, and she tried to say something. Her mouth was moving but made no sound. Only blood came out. Then, she was gone. I felt her slip out of her body. My eyes snapped black on their own. I could see her standing there. She blew me a kiss and disappeared.

I was so filled with rage that I couldn't feel any pain. I stood up, grabbed my sword, and charged Vorador while he was fighting my friends. I ran the sword through his side, then I caught the full blast of something that sent me flying through the air and crashing through the side of the house. I passed out on the floor.

"Damn it, he's gone!" exclaimed Zyra.

"Asya, is he dead?" asked Galya.

Asya said, "No, he is still with us, but he'll be dead soon. Asimov, take him back. They might be able save him. I will bring Lucy and Velvet. Galya, take Kailee. By the looks of her, I think she's dead as well. Bill, bring me the Eye of Night and Day. I will need it soon enough. I'll inform Tambry of what has happened. We will meet at home."

***

I woke up completely naked in a cylinder glass tube, much like a cloning case. I could see Tomok entering the room.

"Where is Lucy?" It hurt to speak.

"We're working on her in the other room. Please relax. Your body has been through extreme trauma. In fact, I amazed you're alive at all. Dr. Rilla, his brain is showing an unusual pattern of fluctuations."

"I have to see Lucy." I struggled to open the glass cover as Dr. Rilla came in.

Dr. Rilla said, "I'm sorry, Slade. I have to put you to sleep for your own good."

Something poked me from inside the case, and I could barely keep my eyes open as they spoke.

"Tomok, Slade stabbed a man named Vorador." The witches were whispering about him; they knew something. "Test all of his clothes for DNA. I want to know everything about Vorador's DNA. I saw Slade's memories. Vorador spoke to Slade as if he knew him. I wonder if he is part of Slade's race or if he a rogue assassin clone. If he has the same DNA, it will have a tag telling us who made him, what personality type, and who was the original. Maybe that will shed some light on him or how to track him."

"Asya, Vorador could be Slade's father. Did you see his face change when he spoke to Slade? The face we know was a false face, but why?"

"Vorador was always secretive, but he was good until his wife died. No, he and Slade cannot have a connection. I think he was messing with Slade. The face he showed Slade must have been the false face. Hopefully, we'll find out soon."

Chapter 33

Dawn of Mourning

I woke up in my bed. Sofia was looking out the window and crying softly. My head throbbed as I got up. Sofia took hold of me.

"The doctor says you are to stay in bed as long as you can. They brought you food. It's on the table." Sofia's eyes were red and puffy.

"Sofia, I have something for you, if you want it. It's a message from Lucy."

I entered Sofia's mind, showing her Lucy's message and thoughts as she died.

"Sofia, she died thinking of you in her arms. The thought made her incredibly happy as she passed."

I left Sofia's mind, and we held each other and cried until I passed out again.

When I woke up, Sofia, Sunako, and Molly were sitting and waiting for me to wake up.

"I'm so hungry."

Molly said, "I'm not surprised. You have been asleep for three days."

"Really?"

"The doctor came in every two hours to take readings," said Sunako.

"You were doing good, but she did not know why you would not wake up. We tried everything, and I mean *everything*."

"You wouldn't wake up, and we were so scared that you were dying."

Molly said, "Sofia didn't leave you unless she had to use the bathroom. I tried to wake you in another way while you were unconscious, but, at the same time, you responded to touch, and I thought it would wake you up. We all did, and that was yesterday morning. I hope you're not upset."

My thoughts were foggy. "Where is Lucy?"

Sofia took my hand and said, "Lucy died. They did all they could to bring her back. Asya says she was not in her body. Her mind was gone, so they turned off the machine that kept her body alive."

"Now I remember. She died in my arms." My eyes filled with tears, and Sofia held me tightly to her chest. "I love you, Sofia."

"I love you, Slade, but don't ever leave me like that again, or I will go crazy."

Molly said, "When you feel up to it, you can say goodbye to Lucy, so they can lay her to rest properly."

All the memories came flooding back. "How is Velvet and Kailee? Did they survive?"

Just then, Kailee walked into the room. She was drying her hair with a towel.

Kailee got excited. "You're awake, finally. Why didn't one of you come get me?"

"Kailee, how is Velvet?"

"She just about died before they could save her. She's messed up pretty badly in the head. When she talks, she yells and makes no sense. The doctor used words like brain damage and a few words I didn't understand."

"Slade to Tomok."

I received no response. Soon, the door opened as Tomok ran into the room.

"I thought we lost you."

"Take me to Velvet."

He helped me up and into clothes to visit with Velvet. Along the way, Tomok told me Asya and her friends were away and should be back tomorrow. We got to Velvet. Tomok advised me to not go into the holding room because she had a tendency to bite. I disregarded the warning. As I walked in, Velvet was naked and screaming in the corner. When she saw me, she rushed me. I hit her once, and she was out.

"I could have put her to sleep for you."

I ignored him and entered her mind. It was so loud, and all her books were on the ground. She had gone mad and couldn't communicate, just incoherent jumbles of words. I grabbed her.

"Time to put your mind back in order."

She stopped struggling. I concentrated as hard as I could on her library, and all the books floated up and moved to where they belonged.

"Slade?"

I let her go.

"What happened?"

I showed her memories before she was knocked out, how Lucy lost her life saving her. I left her mind.

"I see why Vorador personally came back. You were stealing things that did not belong to you."

She pleaded, "Please don't tell anyone. I will give you anything you want within my power. You can even have me in any way you want, I promise. I will be loyal to you. I will marry you, and my father will make you a lord. You can have anything you want."

I looked her in the eyes. "Can you bring Lucy back? Can you find her soul and steal that as well? No, you can't. She is dead because of you and your greedy ways."

"I didn't ask you to save me!"

"No, you didn't, but I saw you and Kailee in trouble. Then, Lucy was in trouble, and I went to save you both, but Lucy paid the price for your greed!" I walked out of the room. "Alabaster, lock this room. Send food and drink, but she is to remain locked down."

Alabaster said, "You don't have clearance to detain."

"Tomok, please keep her locked up until I speak with Asya."

Tomok smiled. "Consider it done."

I went to find Zyra, but she was not in her room. There was a crystal and a note that read, "Call us when Slade wakes up." I picked it up and called Asya's name. Galya answered.

"I need to speak with Asya."

Asya asked, "What's wrong?"

"Asya, I have information that you will want."

"Slade, I can't leave right now. Can you tell Zyra?"

"Yes."

"Go back to your room."

Zyra was waiting for me in my room.

She remarked, "Slade, you look much better. What information do you have for me? I don't mean to rush you, but the Vorador thing caused a gathering. We're waiting on our last members to arrive."

"What happened to Vorador?"

"I'm sorry, but he slipped away."

"I know why he was looking for the Eye of the Void."

"Out with it, then."

"Have you ever spoken to who or what is inside of the Eye?"

Zyra smiled. "Slade, what are you on about?"

"The story you know is total bullshit and for a good reason."

Zyra made the gesture to get on with it.

"Vorador didn't know it, but I could see some of his thoughts and memories. The Eye does not have a witch in it. No, it has something from another place and time, something far more dangerous than you may know. Vorador intends to get it. He thinks it will help him change something or alter something in the past or future; that part keeps switching. All I know is, it has to do with a woman, a woman he feels he cannot live without. She was his beating heart, and now it has gone cold. But here is the thing I don't understand. He kept saying, 'None of them are you with your face. None of them can restart the fire in my heart because you are my heart.' Zyra, what does that mean?"

Zyra sat still for a few minutes before speaking. "Sounds like the rantings of a madman who has lived too long and gone too crazy. Well, if that is all, then I will report what you said. Thank you again. You have done a great job." Zyra stood up. "Now I will take my leave. Ladies, make sure Slade's every need is tended to and he rests well."

I grabbed her arm. "No! Ladies, I need the room! Zyra, tell me things and tell me the truth, or I would hate to be you."

Zyra spoke in an almost threatening yet friendly way. "Slade, remove your hand from me at once. Don't ever touch me again unless I ask you to. Do you understand me? To think you, of all people, would act in such a manner. Slade! You're still holding my arm. Let go, or I will be forced to—"

"Force me to do what exactly?"

I was in her mind. It took a minute, but I'd slipped in. The walls and floors were made of marble. "Of course. Even in your mind, you enjoy the finer things. So, Zyra, pick a wall and watch me tear it down as I unlock your most guarded books."

"What do you want, Slade?" Zyra sounded nervous.

"Want? What do I *want*? How about you bring Lucy back for starters?" I rose into the air and looked down at Zyra.

"By now, you know I cannot do that. I am sorry you're in pain. I'm sorry that Lucy is dead. We did everything that we could to get in and stop him to save all of you. Slade, I am becoming uncomfortable with this display of power. Stop now, and I will overlook it as grief-stricken insanity. Slade, please stop this now!"

I shattered a wall and took hold of a book. Zyra moved toward me, but I summoned chains to hold her arms and feet.

"Oh, look, a lock. Oh no, information I will not be able to access. Oh, wait. Yes, I can." I unlocked it. "Well, look at this. I should have figured with the green eyes, your height, and your incredible beauty—you're Jotanfo. You hide your tendrils by retracting them under your skin. Very clever. Look at this. It was your race that introduced abilities to humans through genetic implantation and gene editing, and you were born with a rare one, I might add. Even among your kind, you're an oddity and with so few like you. So, you left and came to Earth. I must say, the ability to self-repair on a molecular level, making it so you stopped aging, is amazing. I take it your group is made up of people that have this ability or gene?"

"Not all of them. But, yes, some of them. I would have told you that someday, and it's a gene, not an ability."

I took another book. "Now this is fascinating. Zyra, I hope we can see past this day one day soon because this right here is exciting. Three worlds with people that worship the same gods! The best part is Earth, being the younger of the two, is not influenced by any race not of this Earth. So, the gods are real? Nice, now I know that there is another Eye—or shall I say—we both know now, since you knew that already. I bet there are ways to speak with them. Yes, that must be it. I see it was stolen, then lost. Excellent, just excellent. These eyes are out there, just ready to be found."

"Slade, I will not put up a fight. Please release me, and I will show you what you don't know that you should see." Zyra smiled.

"Why should I trust you?" I came down to eye level. "Lies, tricks, and deceit roll from your tongue, so maybe you just keep them in that overly beautiful face of yours. Although I do appreciate the offer."

I turned my back and got another book. When I turned back around, Zyra was gone.

"Oh shit."

"*Oh shit* is right, boy." She grabbed me. "Now sit down, so we can talk, or I will really be embarrassed for you. If you want to square up with me, I promise I will turn you inside out and make you kiss your own ass."

I sat down.

"Yes, you had me for a second or two, but remember, you're in someone else's mind, and they will always have the upper hand if given time. Get in, get out. Don't monologue like some cheesy supervillain. Men, I tell you. You're dumb as hell. Look, Slade, I really didn't know Lucy. That is not my area to govern; it's Asya's. But I feel your pain as if it were mine because we are sharing. Speaking of sharing, you should know that it is not the mind that lets you do what you do; it's the soul. Not all races have a soul, but only a few know this. If the public at large found this out, could you imagine the wars that would happen again? On a galactic scale this time? So, keep that to yourself. We will talk about why in depth later. You're not moving the mind to a clone body. You're moving the soul, and it holds everything about that individual. This will not work on some races because they have no soul, so you better come up with one hell of a bullshit story to cover the fact that you will not be able to relocate some from those races."

"Zyra, why do I feel this way about Lucy? I didn't love her nearly as much as I love Sofia, but it hurts so bad."

Zyra put her arms around me. "Slade, you watched her die while she was in your arms. She was not even able to say her last words as you watched her soul leave. I'm astonished you can even speak, let alone take me hostage in my own mind. This will not make you feel better but take it from me. Everyone will die someday, so enjoy the time you have with them. It is a gift from the gods."

"It isn't enough. Why should they, with all their power, not let us have more time to love?"

"What is time to the gods that count no time? What is enough? What would you do with all the time of a god? It can get really lonely more often than not. Now, I think it's time to return to the real world if you don't mind."

"Wait, Velour! She can bring Lucy back!"

"Let me stop you right there. First, we will not let that happen—please trust us on this. Second, she will rot, so long-term sustainability is not within our ability."

"But the crystals?"

"Slade, it only works for the head. Do you really want her to suffer like that, like Molly did?"

"I could give her a new body."

"Honey, look at me. Molly was alive. Lucy is dead. What if it doesn't work on the returned? You must know you will have to watch her die again. Is it worth that to say goodbye or a last kiss?"

"You're right. That would be selfish. I'm sorry for my actions. I will accept any punishment you deem fit for my trespasses against you."

Zyra kissed me on the cheek. "No, it is I that allowed this to happen, in so many ways. I should have told you the truth in the beginning and not thought of myself as superior."

I exited her mind.

"See, Slade, even I make mistakes from time to time. Now, I should be going." She kissed me on the cheek again and smelled me. "I just can't get over that smell. So nice. Get some rest. We'll be back soon as we can."

"Zyra, I should come with you. There is more to tell, and they're going to want to meet me."

"I don't think this is a good time with so much going on." She shifted away.

I called the ladies. "My sweets, I will be back soon. Tomok says he has entertainment, something called movies. Would you like to see what that is about?"

They nodded.

"Slade to Tomok."

"Tomok here. Slade, are you feeling better?"

"Getting there, my friend, thank you for asking. May I ask a favor of you?"

"Depends on the nature of the favor."

"Tomok, you have mentioned movies a few times." I took a drink of water. "I have to go somewhere. Could you show the ladies what a movie is?"

"Of course. I have all kinds of movies from the archive. Humans were crazy about movies. I can come down and show them how everything works. Will you join me when you get back?"

"You know what, Tomok, that sounds like it would be enjoyable. Besides, I have to find out why you speak so differently than other Jotanfo."

Tomok laughed. "That is Earth movies rubbing off on me. The way humans use slang in everyday life makes things funny but embarrassing at times. I will be down in a few minutes. Tomok out."

I laughed. "Tomok, please never say 'rubbing off.' It means something different than you think." I kissed each woman, saving Sofia for last. "I will be back soon. I love you."

Sofia said, "I love you, too."

Then the ladies sang, "We love you, Slade. Hurry back to us."

I concentrated and saw the slit in space made by the shift. I entered it and arrived right in front of Asya.

"Holy shit!" Asya jumped back. "How in the hell did you get here?"

"I could see the slit in space and stepped into it."

"Okay, kid. Only speak when spoken to unless otherwise directed. They might be mad at your little stunt. The person in charge here is Khalyla, so pay attention to her when she speaks. What am I saying? I have to get you out of here."

Just then, Gayla and Zyra came from around a corner.

"What is this? Asya, did you go get him?"

She told them how I did it.

"I was just about to bring him home."

"Shit, he's here now, so let's just deal with it. No doubt, he will shift right back."

We walked into a large hall with artwork on the walls and ten round tables in the room. Each table could seat five. A woman was speaking to a group of men and women.

"Slade, hold my hand."

As we approached the group, they all went silent as they turned to face us. We walked through the crowd. I noticed more than a few women were tall and had green eyes. We climbed a few stairs until I was standing in front of Khalyla.

She raised her hand to her face and tapped on her upper lip with her index finger.

"Hello, Slade. It is nice to finally meet you. I would have done it sooner, but I seem to always have matters to attend to." She looked at Zyra, and Zyra looked down. "Zyra, explain why Slade is here today with you at this meeting."

Zyra went to speak.

"Never mind, I was going to ask you to invite him here after our talk, but now is as good as time as ever." Khalyla faced the crowd and raised her hands. "As I was saying, a real and dangerous threat has come to us once again. Vorador has somehow returned. We believed him to be dead, but he is very much alive and hunting for certain items. His lust for power will only leave a path of devastation. I believe this boy will lead us to Vorador, where I will kill him myself for his crimes against this House." She lowered her hands and walked off the stage.

Zyra said, "Follow me at all times."

We sat at one of the middle tables with Khalyla, Zyra, Galya, Asya, Asimov, and Bill. They brought a chair from another table for me.

Khalyla asked, "Slade, may I get you some wine?"

"May I have water, please?"

She smiled and said, "Mahalia, seven glasses of wine and one water, please." She gazed at me intensely. "Okay, Slade, do one thing without speaking that will wow me."

I snapped my eyes black and put my hands above my head like I was holding a ball. I put my hands down, making my eyes normal in the process.

"Very good. Now tell me what you saw and what you think it may be. Don't worry; there are no wrong answers."

"You have a silver ball that floats above your head. Judging by the size and close proximity to you, of which you're aware, you have a floating AI companion. If I had to guess, it is with you, possibly, at all times. Might I inquire if you have named it, and if so, what did you name it?"

"Excellent, young man." Khalyla clapped. "You're a true find. His name is Bowmen, and he's an excellent AI companion. You would do well to purchase a high-end model." The wine was placed at the table. "Drink what you like, Slade, but I recommend this wine. You could say that the taste is out of this world."

They all laughed. Zyra brought Khalyla up to speed.

"So, Slade, I hear you have something to tell the group." Khalyla waved to someone out of sight. "Mahalia, will you bring us a plate of cookies, please?" She rubbed her hands together. "Sorry, Slade, you simply must try these cookies, soft and gooey. And they go perfectly with the wine. Okay, Slade, please share your information."

"Velvet has been acquiring magical items for the past three years. She used a young woman to purchase what could be bought. She had hired a thief to get what she could not purchase. She believed no one would ever be able to trace the item to its true destination. Velvet knew that some of these items were beyond dangerous. The Eye was not found by a ranger, like the story she originally told. It was stolen by the thief Velvet has in her employ. The thief's name is Jercil. He is a rogue by trade.

"This next part is fuzzy because it was when Velvet's mind was jumbled. I hope I don't sound incoherent. A man named Malik introduced them. She has known him for a little over two years. He is part of the October Men, one of the heads of the organization. He promised her something called the Shard of Life, a vial with a drop of Genesis, and the use of the four-way mirror." I took a drink. "I told you some of it was jumbled." I could see them whispering while Khalyla studied me. "Is everything all right? Have I offended you?"

"No, the opposite in fact. You have brought us something that would have rather remained in the shadows of rumor. Children, as we can tell, our ways have grown lax."

"What is wrong?" I asked.

"Velvet seems to have friends in low places. Malik was a witch hunter from before the war who cleared this world of most of its humans. He, along with others, were thought long dead. The October Men is a group of people first formed in the Crusades. They were looking for magical items, like the Holy Grail, along with other anomalous items, people, and/or technology that does not exist in the current century, like that of a downed UFO, as they called them back then.

"A great example—and we have Bill to thank for this one—took place in Earth's history in nineteen forty-seven. An advanced and heavily modified star glider was showing off by flying rings around the current aircraft of the U.S. Air Force, and while the pilot was busy making an ass out of himself, he flew right into a weather balloon, then was shot from behind by a P-fifty-one Mustang's fifty cal rounds. The damn plane crashed right into the star glider, sending both to the ground in Roswell, New Mexico. Now, this showoff, for some reason, did not have any shields on, let alone the rear shields, which had to be manually turned off. These shields would have allowed the ship to sustain no damage upon crash. Long story short, this jackass crashed my brand-new gift with the help of another young witch, who will not be named. Bill, would you like to tell the story?"

"Not really in the mood. Pass." He was zapped by Khalyla. "You've aroused my mood." He was zapped by Galya. "Damn it, woman!" he yelled while rubbing his backside. "So there I was, flying a magnificent state-of-the-art star glider. While yes, I was showing off a bit, I was heavily encouraged." Galya's hand shot out, but Bill dodged it, then smirked. "Have to be quicker, bunny rabbit." She gave him the evil eye, and I suppressed a laugh.

"Where was I? Oh yes. I was flying literal rings around the other pilot while kissing one of the most beautiful women I've ever seen. So my attention was not at its peak, but my arousal was." An unseen force pushed him from behind and caused him to stumble.

"Bill, stick to the story, or it's going to get painful." Zyra snarled.

"Don't listen to her, Bill. I like your story—don't forget the details," said Zoolee. Zyra gave Zoolee the finger, then Zoolee made a rude gesture with her finger and her other hand.

"I was about to engage the plasma thruster."

He winked at either me or Galya, who was next to me, and she vanished only to appear while bringing her fist down on his head, but he shifted a foot to the right then they were seemingly everywhere at once. Fists and flicks were thrown while Bill laughed and said things like "almost got me," and "tag, you're it." At one point, I was knocked off my feet by a blur of colors and shouts.

"Children, stop this stupidity!" commanded Khalyla. Both came to a stop. "Bill, continue with the story, but I warn you, the innuendos are wearing thin on me."

Bill pushed himself up while helping me stand. "Sorry, kid. I didn't mean to knock you down."

"It's okay."

"I was showing off while enjoying one of the galaxy's sexiest women." A sudden thwack brought Bill to his knees.

"My daughter is not to be spoken of in such a way." Khalyla had him by the ear. Stop rubbing yourself; it looks obscene."

"But it makes it feel better."

Bill winked, then Khalyla and Galya shot yellow lightning until he yelled, "Okay, I give up!"

"Tell another joke, and I'm going to beat you like the little dog you are." Galya placed her foot on his face. "Now, bark!"

"Woof, woof, babycakes."

"You motherfucker!" Galya and Zyra started to kick Bill until all three disappeared.

"I will continue the story when they get back."

Soon, they reappeared. Bill came out looking the worse for wear.

"Although rumor has it that the shield was switched off by the young witch's bare ass. But, then again, that is just the rumor and certainly not by video logs, which had to be manually switched on. I could only guess it would have been for later use as to rewatch it for instructive purposes and not for something recorded because it would be—oh wait, might someone have said, 'Oh, yes. It will be sexy, baby. Trust me. No one will see it but us.'"

"Both were lucky they were wearing their ZGCB, Zero Gravity Crash Bubble."

I asked how the crash bubble worked.

"It places the user in an instant bubble of frozen time at the moment of activation. While activated, it causes armor to envelop the body to stop any and all damage, and it holds forty hours' worth of oxygen."

"That sounds like a really good item."

"It is. Maybe we can crash our own ship soon." Zoolee's smile spoke of mischief.

"May I continue? Asya, Zyra, and I had to augment the minds of thirty-five men, six female secretaries, and two prototype androids. The androids suffered a complete meltdown, which set the Americans back eight years in android/early A.I. development. So, one could imagine how embarrassed I was and still am. If memory serves me right, their punishment duties lasted for two months." She took a long drink. "So, Vorador is alive. The October Men are still a thing. What next? Let me guess: Elvis Presley has returned and has remade his songs into disco music. If so, I'll be needing the check and a ship to anywhere but here. I'm sorry, Slade. I was rambling. Is there anything else?" Khalyla asked as the cookies arrived; they smelled wonderful.

"Vorador turns most of his victims into remote drones, like he did with Molly. They make the perfect infiltration tool and spy. If they're caught breaking a law, like murder, you have to kill the person, not knowing that they're a slave to Vorador. You're essentially killing a friend, relative, or loved one because the individual has become trapped in their own mind, but most would never know it. I believe the use of that spell was outlawed three hundred years ago, cited as cruel and unusual punishment. If one is caught using or have used that spell, they will face a stiff penalty, and sometimes death is demanded."

Khalyla smiled. "Well now, aren't you a little mole digging out the truth when others would try to bury it in a pile of lies and bullshit? I also heard you survived a direct blast from Asimov. You, Slade, are a curious one. As for Molly, I was recently made aware of the tragic mistake that befell her. Slade, will you bring her to me the next time you come over? Molly deserves proper compensation for her unjust treatment. Good work getting her into a new body. I have been left speechless by that ability. I'm sure you're happier with Molly having a full body. Not much you can do with a slave that is just a head."

"Molly is not my slave!"

"You own her; that makes her your slave. Oh, you do hate that word, don't you? Then call her your companion if that helps you sleep at night. Now, what else do you know?"

"I think it should be said in private. I don't know if you want Bill and Asimov aware of it," I spoke softly.

"They sit with us for a reason, Slade. I hold no secrets from them." Khalyla studied me with her green eyes. I felt her probing me.

I moved my chair close as I spoke. "I see that you are indeed the mother, in the truest sense of the word. Shall I go on?"

Khalyla nodded.

"I believe you're possibly the first in your unique family line. If so, Khalyla, you carry something like an immortality gene."

I was interrupted by laughter from covered mouths. Gayla's hand waved, signaling to continue.

"This gene is passed down sometimes and skipping many generations, with it selecting Zyra, Galya, and Asya. I don't know how Beth fits in, but there is one other. She holds a secret that many would fear. She, too, is a secret to many; her name is Zoolee, Zoolee the Destroyer. Or, as she is more commonly known as, Zoolee the Hidden or Zoolee the Unseen."

Khalyla leaned over the table. I saw my face reflected in her jade-green eyes. "Slade, I will only ask you once to explain how you know that name, or I will reach into your chest and pull out your heart, special boy or not!"

I smiled and raised my cup of water. "She comes to me in my dreams. She told me her name and to come find her. She sang me the same song that Lucy sang to me as we danced in my room. She told me that she is your daughter. That is how I know Zoolee. Now, may I see her?"

"What is that wonderful smell? It's amazing, like flowers and spice."

Asya pointed to me, as Khalyla smelled me all over.

"Now I am glad I didn't throw you off the balcony or pull out your heart."

I smiled. "It wouldn't have done you any good because I can do this." I disappeared and reappeared on the far end of the room. I heard a soft, feminine voice come from behind me, and I felt the heat from her breath. I turned to see who was speaking, but no one was there. The voice stayed behind me no matter how many times I spun around. I had to have looked stupid.

The voice said, "Slade, everyone here can teleport, but can you do it with style and grace like us? Or are you going to stay a clumsy, beautiful boy your whole life?"

I walked back to Khalyla.

"That wasn't you speaking to me, was it?"

She slowly shook her head.

"So, should I explore until I find the source, or is everyone going to stare at me like I am an idiot?"

Someone was tapping me on the back of my head, but I didn't bother to turn around. Then, I was flicked hard on the tip of my ear, which made me annoyed. I slowly turned around.

"Hello, Slade."

When I saw her beautiful face, I immediately felt an extremely deep sense of déjà vu. She was just slightly taller than me with brilliant green eyes and long braided black hair.

"I thought I was going to have to kick you to get your attention."

I couldn't say anything.

"Are you always this quiet or just on first encounters?"

I just stood there staring, like I had never seen a woman before. My thoughts drifted to Sofia and how I felt ashamed to be so instantly attracted to the woman in the same way.

"Hello, Slade. Come back to the here and now." She snapped in front of my face.

I didn't know what to say; her beauty was so unsettling that it made me embarrassed to look at her. But I couldn't look away.

"I, I, I am—I am Slave. I mean, my Slade is name. Me, Slade."

I sounded so very stupid.

She laughed. "I am sure that is a well-established fact by now. Can that pretty mouth say other words? Maybe a full sentence or two?"

I could hear the people behind me trying to suppress their laughter, which furthered my embarrassment and shame.

"Well then, I should just go ahead and get this out of the way sooner rather than later." She took hold of me, and we kissed deeply. I melted in her arms as we kissed. It was like being reunited with a long-lost love. She introduced herself to me while we kissed.

When we stopped, she said, "Now, what is my name? I want to hear you say it and say it slowly."

I went to speak, but nothing came out. I was embarrassed again. My face felt hot, and I was sweating a bit.

So, I cleared my throat and said, "Zoolee. You are Zoolee the Hidden."

Zoolee smiled and sat down. "Well now, I know four things about him. He's not mute; he has beautiful eyes; he smells wonderful; and he can kiss. Rather well, I might add."

Khalyla asked, "Zoolee, why did you do that? That was so out of character for you. If you're going to do things like that, at least do it in private. Slade, stop staring at my daughter, or at least, tell me why you're so transfixed."

"I think I know her, and not from my dreams. Zoolee, you're so beautiful. I have never seen your skin color before. What race do you belong to, and where are you from?"

Her skin was a light bronze, which made her eyes stand out like shining emeralds. Forbidden jewels I had to have. I felt shame again.

Zoolee smiled. "I like compliments. Please, keep them coming. Would it surprise you to know that I'm human? Well, half-human and half-Jotanfo. I'm the first of my kind. As for my skin, I am half-Egyptian."

"I must know: have we met before? That kiss is so familiar." Her eyes were so hauntingly beautiful, and I swore I had kissed her before.

"I didn't think you would've remembered our true first kiss or the kisses I have given you in your dreams."

Khalyla said, "Zoolee, is this him? The one you have been talking about all this time? He has been the one you have waited for?"

Without looking away from me, Zoolee said, "Yes, Mother, this is him. I could never forget his face, and it's been a long time."

Khalyla said, "Great, the introductions are out of the way. You two can make eyes at one another later, but now, we have business to attend to. Slade, give me your hand. I warn you: any attempt to learn anything about me while you are in there, and you'll be sorry. I ask you politely not to snoop. Just relax and let me work."

I gave her my hand, and she took it and let go just as fast.

"Well, that is very interesting. Very interesting indeed."

"Will you share?" asked Asya.

Khalyla smiled. "Sorry, Asya. I think you should have gotten the boy laid sooner. It would seem that after his first sexual encounter, it has somehow made Slade physically stronger and made the oracle gift within him stronger as well. Slade had a vision of Vorador; he saw parts of it happen before it happened. He saw how Vorador was going to kill Velvet in search for the Eye and other items. He had an intense dream where he saw a woman. He saw me. I also think the Eye of the Void may have reached out to him." Khalyla tapped her fingers on the table. "Slade, tell me. Have you heard any unusual voices in your head, maybe even just whispers?"

As Zoolee was eating a cookie, she suddenly got up and walked out of the room. Even the way she moved was unreal and hypnotic as her hips moved side to side.

Khalyla snapped in my face.

"No, not that I'm aware of." I didn't know how to tell her that sometimes I heard lots of voices yelling, screaming, whispering, or just talking. None of it had ever made sense; it just came and went. A few minutes later, Zoolee shifted back to the table.

"I hear you have an interesting coin. May I see it?"

I took it out of my satchel and handed it to her.

"My my, this is oddly heavy. Slade, you have no memory of how you came to own this coin?"

"No."

"Bowmen, analyze this coin."

"Yes, ma'am." After a few minutes, Bowmen made a beep. "It's forty-four millimeters in diameter. It is comprised of copper, iron, silver, and an unknown metal with a unique atomic structure."

"Yes, that is all very boring, Bowmen. How about the humanoid face or this symbol and the letter and/or marks?"

"The human face is not in any known database. Khalyla, what do you think the symbol looks like?"

"Bowmen, why would you ask me that question?"

"I believe we see something different. Could you draw it for me?"

Khalyla went to a large screen, then traced her finger around until it made the symbol.

"Slade, show us what you see," Bowmen ordered.

I drew what I saw with both my regular and black eyes.

"Interesting. Khalyla, it seems that Slade sees it differently than you. These marks are not letters, and these marks over here are part of the symbol, which makes a different, larger design. Here is what it looks like:

"Bowmen, how do you know that it's supposed to look like this?" I asked.

"This was created by a machine. I can see the differences between international cuts and unnational cuts—or as you would call it—marks, the wear and tear that coins go through."

"This symbol looks somewhat familiar," said Khalyla.

"It closely resembles that of the Void Walkers. The only difference is in this cut and that cut."

"I see. Slade is clearly not a Void Walker, and they don't have their own currency. This must be a coincidence."

"I agree with you. There are many different cultures, for many worlds have inadvertently created symbols, languages, art, music, and various other things that are identical—all which were done by coincidence," Bowman stated. "That and the fact that there are under a thousand Void Walkers on four different worlds. They seek only religious enlightenment as to awaken the one they call the 'Silent God.'"

"What about the unknown metal?" I asked.

"What about it?"

"What do you know about it?"

"Almost nothing because it's unknown. What I think is it could be heat resistant."

"Why would you think that?" asked Asya.

"This type of metal is in a crystalline pattern, much like a diamond. This metal with its crystalline lattice would be a great find in large enough deposits. This metal is defined by its lattice points, in turn, making it incredibly strong and heat resistant."

"Thank you, Bowmen. Slade, the unknown metal could be from deep space or a rare asteroid from deep space. Slade, we catalogued three new metals five years ago. One can be molded like rubber; it's clear and heat resistant. It'll be used in highly radioactive areas. So, this raises an eyebrow, but only slightly."

As Zoolee reentered the room, I was transfixed again, which irritated Khalyla.

"Zoolee, please come over here, and give me your hand now!"

They touched hands, and the color drained from her face.

"No! How can this be?"

"Mother, please don't say. It would spoil the surprise."

"I just can't believe it. Moving on. Asya, I take it that you took control and secured the Eye. Where is it?" Khalyla tapped her fingers rapidly.

"It has been stored in the vault, in my section. I was hoping to study it a bit under controlled conditions, so I have yet to catalog it."

"Who or what is really inside that orb? How did it get in there, and how did it get to this planet?" I asked.

"I can't tell you who the entity inside it is because there are no records of it that have ever been discovered. Most times, a Dragon's Eye is used as a prison. How it got to Earth is easy. I brought it to Earth, and no one could understand it or be influenced by it. Therefore, it was deemed harmless. Then, I gave it as a gift to a man named Narmer, who became the first Egyptian pharaoh and the father to my daughter. Zoolee is that child, and she is the first Jotanfo/human hybrid. But interbreeding with humans would soon be frowned upon due to humans' range of violence and warlike behavior. Humans were below us, but one day, we would stand shoulder-to-shoulder with them."

Zoolee called out, "Hey, Slade, catch!"

She threw something in the air. I had to drop my cookie and move fast to catch it. Zoolee was standing in front of me two seconds later and placed her hand on what I caught. She raised her other hand and snapped; a high-pitched whistling sound was made. I'd that before when Vorador had created a shield. I could see everyone in the room banging their fists against the invisible barrier, but I could not hear them.

"Do you think they're going to be mad?"

"They can be whatever they want." Zoolee wore a wicked smile as she said that, but the looks on the other witches' faces were not so happy.

"Slade, I was thinking we could see what's inside this Dragon's Eye together. Are you with me? Are you willing to call out to the Void? It could be dangerous or even deadly."

"So, our first date could result in death? Count me in. Zoolee, why are these things called Dragon's Eyes? Is it just a fancy name?"

"They're a dead dragon's eye. When a dragon dies, their eyes crystallize into an unbreakable orb. They can be used for a few things."

"Dragons are real? I thought they were mythical creatures."

"None are left on Earth, but a few different species can be found native to dozens of different worlds. Now, let's see what prizes are inside this Cracker Jack box."

I had no clue what she meant, and I was beginning to think she might be slightly off in the head. She pulled the Eye out from a little bag she wore with a shoulder strap, and I placed my hand on it. Soon, we were inside the Eye.

"Hello, I am Kelsomta, and welcome to my corner of reality."

"Where is this place? How can all this be inside such a tiny orb?"

Zoolee held my hand, but I could not hear her thoughts.

"The Dragon's Eye is the entrance to this place. Think of it as a doorway."

Zoolee asked, "How is it that you can communicate with us in our language?"

Kelsomta laughed. "I am speaking directly with your mind using your language to communicate, but I can be verbal, if that would make you feel more comfortable."

Zoolee asked, "Why do people think you're dangerous?"

"On occasion, I have had visitors, such as yourselves, become—as you say—unhinged after meeting me."

"What does 'unhinged' mean?"

Zoolee whispered, "Crazy. Kelsomta, can you see our thoughts, and where are you?"

"Your thoughts are safe. My species is noncorporeal. That is why you cannot see me and only hear me."

Zoolee asked, "What is it like not having a body?"

"I can no more explain what it is like to not have a body than you can explain what it is like to have a body."

I said, "So, you're not trapped in here?"

"No. This is the place I meet with those I deem worthy to speak with. I come and go as I please. You might call it a pocket dimension."

We spoke for what seemed like hours.

"Can you affect anything in our world?"

"No, I only speak with those who would gather what we want."

"What do you offer those who come here, and what do you want in return?" asked Zoolee.

"I don't always want something; sometimes, it is wisdom I impart. Others come because I can return them to any point in their past. Or they can stay with me, learning things that are beyond themselves, and return many years later in your future without aging a day."

Zoolee asked, "But how can that be? Our bodies would die of starvation if our minds—" She froze. "Wait! Are you telling us that we are physically here in mind and body?"

Kelsomta laughed. "How else could you travel? You're here, are you not?"

"No, we would like to be returned to the point in which we left," I said.

Kelsomta said, "I'm sorry to inform you, but that is simply not possible. Even as we speak, others of my kind are studying you both to better understand you in a more comprehensible way."

"Are we stuck here?"

"No, you will go home."

"Why are you studying us?"

"Your species seems so preoccupied with what you call time; some were obsessed with it. Including you both, I have spoken to thirteen of your species, and most are very pleasant like you both. But some were pushed out and not allowed back."

I asked, "Why and how were they pushed out? Who controls the doorway?"

"My kind has no need for violence, love, hate, greed, and envy. Your species seems to thrive on it, but I have seen a few exceptions. As for the doorway, I accidentally found a path into your plane of reality—or universe, as you call it. Some of your kind learned to open a doorway, and we found other doorways."

Zoolee asked, "Were there any visitors that you liked?"

"Oh, yes, a few. Leonardo da Vinci was a joy and a credit to your species. He spent two of his years with us. He had an amazing mind, and we gifted him with knowledge of the future. We learned your mathematics, which is still being debated. Another was Nostradamus. He was obsessed with the future, so we took him to many points in this time."

Zoolee said, "I know those two men. They were considered geniuses, years ahead of their time. Now, I know they had help. Tell us of the ones you pushed out."

"Genghis Khan was so obsessed with conquering, so he was deemed too radical, but he gave us what we requested. So, we brought him to where he requested in your year eleven thirty-two. Did he achieve what he wanted?"

Zoolee said, "He conquered and created the largest land empire in Earth's history. To some, he was a hero; to others, he was a monster. He was, no doubt, a brilliant general."

"The one who was most difficult and confusing was Adolf Hitler. Did he change the world with his art?"

"You unleashed a monster upon the world. The amount of suffering he unleashed—he started a world war that killed so many, and the suffering was still felt for hundreds of years after his death."

"Kelsomta, you said, 'He gave us what we requested.' What exactly does that mean?" I asked.

"We have found that your newborn children can be studied easier than at any other time in the human lifespan. We only have one request: six newborn children. Three male and three female under the age of three months. For that, we will gift you knowledge of future or past events."

"Did you ever interact with a human male named Vorador?"

"A multitude of times. He's the only one to repeatedly make it back to us. Do you know him?"

"I've had the displeasure. Can you tell me about him? What does he get from you?"

"He only ever wants one thing, and we don't understand how he doesn't get it. He goes back to save his wife. Since he is already in that timeline, he can only be there for a short amount of time before he is pulled back to us. Every time he arrives, he is in terrible mental pain. We struggle to study this emotion, as it creates an energy that we have learned about. The last time, he was so filled with sadness that he stayed here with us for what you call two hundred years. He left to find the one who killed his wife. He has never been able to prevent her from dying, so we sent him to where he can stop the one who did it. As he would say, 'I will kill the one who has stolen my heart.'"

"Can you show me right before she dies?"

"Which timeline? Vorador is the only one of your species to intentionally split a timeline into branches. Each one brought him more pain than the last."

"Can you show me them all?"

"Prepare yourself. Now showing one thousand one hundred and seventy-four times. Tell me when you're done."

I felt like I was being turned inside out over and over again.

I asked, "How can we go back to where we came from in time?"

"If I send you two back to your time, you will bounce back to us and split your timeline. Please pick a time you are not in. Before you were alive or after you leave. But we require what we have requested."

"Do people make this agreement before they get here or when they get here?"

"Before. You two are the second that have come here without being invited. The first being an accidental opening of the doorway and meeting a member of your species. Now, it is you two."

"Bring us to two minutes after we came here, and I will bring you what you have requested."

"See you soon, young Mr. Slade."

We returned by coming out of thin air behind the witches. Khalyla and Asya were crying loudly.

Zoolee said, "Have we come at a bad time? We could come back at a better time."

All of them turned around, and Khalyla took Zoolee in her arms. Zoolee filled them in on where we had been.

I told them about Vorador and why he wanted the Eye back. "He is obsessed with his wife's killer. He believes that by killing the murderer and himself that one of him will be happy. He is willing to kill himself to make his dreams come true. He just wants to have his love back."

Asya told me how she was close to Vorador and his wife and how he went mad after she was murdered. He was never right after that, becoming more and more unstable. Until one day, he went wild and killed many people because he thought the killer hid among them. After that, he turned on them and disappeared for two hundred years. She thought he was dead until recently.

"Asya, the only way we could come home was to give something we did not have in our possession. I need to get it and deliver it to Kelsomta."

Khalyla said, "I feared you both were trapped forever, but you came out and brought home my daughter. You can have whatever you want."

"I need six infants—three male and three female."

Maybe I should not have said that in such a cold and unfeeling way.

"How could you make a deal like that?"

I filled her in on why.

I got a great idea. "I don't like the idea of taking babies away from parents. So I have what I think is the perfect solution—flash clones."

Asimov said, "Brilliant. Can you tell us how you came up with this idea?"

"The moment I heard about flash clones, I was fascinated. Then, when Kelsomta asked for babies, I thought, 'Why cause anyone misery when we can create parentless children?'"

"Don't you fear what he's doing with these lives?" asked Bill.

"No. I sense his love for them. I can't explain it further, and if I'm wrong, then they'll be too young to understand what's happening."

"I still find wanting babies a bit disturbing," said Khalyla.

Soon, all agreed it was the best course of action. Asya went back to the cloning facility and placed the order for six flash clones.

Chapter 34

Pride before the Fall

Zoolee walked up to me and said, "Looks like we have two hours to kill. Allow me to give you the grand tour."

Khalyla pulled Zoolee aside. "I don't like your interest in him."

"Mother, I rarely, if ever, ask you for anything. I ask you now to allow me to do what I wish with Slade because I will do it, regardless of your approval."

Khalyla sighed. "I am already tired of this conversation. Do what you would like." As she walked away, she cast an icy glance at me.

"Slade, did you know that when we were inside the Eye that Kelsomta could talk to both of us separately at the same time?"

I asked, "What do you mean?"

"While you were asking your questions, I had my own. I'm from Earth's past, but from what I've been able to glimpse of the future, it was amazing. The sad part is that he would only show me a small bit."

"So, what did you see?"

Zoolee said, "That's private, Mr. Slade. I always keep to myself because I usually can't stand people. Because of the way I was first treated by the Jotanfo, I hid myself away. I read, and I explored, and existed, enduring an endless life while I waited to meet someone I could love. Please, don't get me wrong. Humans are nice. Back in

Egypt, during the old times, I could be open and free to be who I am—Zoolee, first of my kind, and for a while, it was good. People were accepting, but the future brought more wars, hatred, and bigotry. People became a great deal less tolerant of those who were different, and I was shunned by my own people. I was an orphan of two races. I was truly alone. I couldn't be who I was born to be, so I became Zoolee the Hidden. As time moved forward, after having to hide who I was, I grew angry and sometimes vengeful. Some called me crazy, and I still hear them say it. It hurts, but they didn't know what it's like to truly be alone. To be the only one of their kind, but you do. You know the sadness and pain. You felt it from the start. Slade, I think we were made for each other because we are the only ones of our respective kind."

I stopped and hugged her. "Zoolee, I never thought I would meet anyone like me, and now that I have, I feel angry that people would shun you for being what you are. We didn't ask to be born this way, but I feel better about it because I've met you."

I took her hand, and as we walked, she showed me around a large place that looked like a ship.

"Slade, what is it like to be in love?"

"I'll be honest. I'm not sure how to explain it. I love being with Sofia and Sunako, but I am confused as to why she had me take her friends as lovers. I feel a strange feeling, like it is wrong, but I don't understand why."

"An awfully long time ago, there was a thing called monogamy. That is what calls to you. It means to take one lover and stay bound to that lover. Although, in certain instances, people would secretly take a different lover behind the back of the one they had sworn loyalty to, and it would sometimes drive the wronged person mad. They would kill over cheating hearts. Love often caused death—a crime of passion, they called it. What Sofia practices is polyamory. It means to have many lovers. You're lucky. A lot of men would kill to have many lovers."

I laughed. "I think Asya said that very same thing. So, what else did you see in the future?"

She smiled. "You. I see you, and I kissed you the first time without your permission. May I have permission to kiss you this time?"

I leaned in to meet her lips, and we started to kiss and didn't stop until my jaw became tired. I wasn't sure how long we'd been kissing.

She kissed my neck, and I saw a flash of her and Sofia standing in the hall. Both had wings.

I pulled away, feeling a bit dizzy.

Two hours passed like minutes as we talked.

"I think the babies are here."

We walked back to the main hall where everyone was waiting for me.

Asimov said, "Six babies. Tomok says it was the first time he heard of someone buying a flash-cloned baby, let alone *six*. Vidya says it's a weird way to spend your credits. Batch said hi and wanted you to know he made these himself. Tomok said the blood and DNA from the fight came back as only yours and Lucy's. The samples were taken from yours and Lucy's clothes, and they are trying to find out anything about Vorador."

"I was covered in his blood. I will run the tests myself when I get back."

All six babies were nestled in two baskets.

"I'm going with you," said Zoolee.

"No, just in case this is something sinister." I held out my hand.

Gayla floated the Eye into my hand right as I called to Kelsomta.

A second before I entered, Zoolee yelled, "Don't talk to your wife that way!" She got a hand on my shoulder as I entered the Eye with the two baskets.

"Welcome back, Slade. Please place the children here."

A space opened seemingly out of nowhere. Clean, white light emanated from it.

"Kelsomta, I want you to know that those are clone babies, and their lifespan will be a maximum of three years. Is this acceptable? Will they work like natural-born babies?"

Kelsomta laughed. "Yes, they're the same, you know that. Besides, we can fix the three-year limitation. Honestly, I'm surprised the flaw hasn't been found and corrected. What good would these children be to us if they only live three years? Dissecting them for study would be barbaric. Wouldn't you agree? Rest assured, we have found a way to extend their lives well beyond that of any normal human. We would never hurt our children. They have taught us to care for others."

I put the babies in one at a time until all six were gone.

"Thank you, Slade, for staying true to your word. You'll always be honest with me, and I should always enjoy our time together. Oh, by the way, we have created a device that allows us to perceive you in the way you see things around you, which will make communication much easier. We also created something that shows how long your time is from the start. Your species has just started and look at how far you have come."

"Will you call out to me as you do to Vorador?"

"Of course. I always call out to you as I have done in your dreams."

"I think your words are mixing up. This is only my second time here."

"No, I believe I am correct."

For the first time, I could hear others of his kind speaking in the background.

"Now, this is your first time, but for me, I have seen you many times since we first met. Hello again, Zoolee. My wife calls you Zoolee the Ageless. She is enjoying Earth history and has seen you many times throughout it. You have also become a favorite among the students, along with the newcomer Slade."

Zoolee asked, "Where do the children go?"

"We have built a perfect artificial world that can sustain them with none of the dangers of a normally created planet. Their every need is taken care of. We study and work with them always. Each child grows to become very intelligent. Due to the fact they are such a fragile species, we have enhanced them. We are working on a way to make them live to eight hundred years or more. As of now, they only live five hundred years."

"Kelsomta, if you can see forward and backward and all things between, please, can you tell me who I am? Who are my parents, and why has someone taken my memories?"

"First off, my sight is not what you make it out to be. I honestly don't have the answers you are looking for. If I did, it is not for me to reveal to you or anyone else, and I am talking to you, Zoolee. By the way, Slade, congratulations on the promotion and new title. Now, you have to go. I am due to expect you soon, and two of you cannot occupy that same space at the same time. See you two soon."

We were returned to the hall thirty minutes later than our original leaving time.

"Zoolee, what did he mean about promotion and title?" All at once, it hit me like a ton of bricks. "Wait, what? Did you say *wife*?"

"Come here with me."

We walked to the balcony.

"How high do you think we are?"

"A mile or more. Enough that the air is a bit thin, and I cannot see through the clouds."

Zoolee smiled. "We are six and a half miles in the sky." She played with my ear. "It doesn't scare you to be so clumsy and this close to such a terrible fall?"

I laughed. "I'm standing still, so I am not worried about falling. Besides, I have an implant that makes falls nothing to worry about. You know that."

Zoolee kissed me again. She said, "Do you? Do you know one of the things I love about you the most? You're so stupid. It's cute, like a baby is cute." She kissed my cheek. "No, this type of fall can kill. I promise you that. Wait here. I have to get something from our room."

She walked away, her hips swinging side to side. I couldn't help but stare, and it caused a stirring within me. Before she took the corner, she looked over her shoulder and blew me a kiss.

Bill and Asimov popped up next to me.

Bill said, "This is not what you're going to want to hear right now, my boy, but Zoolee is crazy."

I laughed and patted Bill on the shoulder. "No shit!" I smiled. "I got that impression."

Asimov said, "We're not joking. She is the most dangerous amongst us. She is hidden for a reason. Run now and find Vorador because you have a better chance fighting him."

"I will kill him even if I have to walk him through the gates of Hell. He will pay for what he did to Lucy." I spit over the side. "How can Zoolee be any different than the others? I mean, she is beautiful and smaller than the other witches."

"For starters"—Bill took a deep breath—"she has been around longer than any of us. She is Khalyla's firstborn daughter. It was almost six hundred years before another of their kind was born, and that was Zyra. But Zoolee was the only half-human ever born to Khalyla. She carries what you call the immortality gene, but the human side has had an effect. When Jotanfo women have a child with a human, they have to use gene editing to tone down the human aggressiveness gene. When it mixes with the Jotanfo gene for aggressiveness, it creates an incredibly aggressive child who is near fearless. At first, these children were created to be the soldiers who would end a brutal war. When the wars were over, they never gave up their ways. Most were put down, while the last remaining lived in captivity and were studied. But not Zoolee. No, she could not be contained, and she cannot die. Planets feared her until she faded into the history files, folktales, and legends. She is a story almost every Jotanfo child has heard, and it frightens them to stay in bed and be good. She is also a course to be studied."

Asimov said, "Just watch your ass with her. I really like you, kid, and it would be a shame to lose you this fast. Bill and I really want to train you so you can adjust to what comes of this life."

Bill said, "We can help hide you if you want, maybe on one of the outer moons of Jupiter. Europa has a thriving civilization with mixed species, very forward-thinking people. You would like it, and you could bring your ladies with you. Oh, shit. Here she comes. Remember what we said. Asimov, act casual."

Zoolee walked up and said, "Do you two old fools need something?"

They shook their heads.

"Then get lost. Become like dust and fade away." Zoolee's words were sharp, cold, and dismissive.

Asimov and Bill said, "Yes, Zoolee. Our apologies, Zoolee." They hurriedly walked away.

"Did you miss me?" Zoolee played with something in her hand. "So, have you thought about what I said, or did those two idiots distract you?"

I smiled and moved some of her hair over her ear. I lightly kissed her neck as I said, "The fall. Well, I'd have to be afraid of heights to worry about a fall." I gently slid my lips over hers as I ran my fingers from her wrist to her neck.

Zoolee whispered, "Tell me you love me. Tell me you need me. Please. Tell me anything. It's been so long since I heard the words 'I love you' in my ear."

"I can't."

Her eyes opened, and I could see them lightly glowing. They were fixed on me.

Then, I was falling.

She'd shoved me over the balcony. I would just pop back and say something witty like, "You made me fall in love with you," "Looks like I fell in love with you," or "I guess I fell for you." Yeah, that could work. Oh, I could say, "Baby, I could fall for you all day."

Wow, I'm really high up. Maybe I should enjoy the feeling for a minute or two. Not like I get to do it every day, though I guess I could pop super high in the air any time I want.

"Hey, Slade, you know what they say about people who talk to themselves, right? They say they are crazy. So, do you enjoy the view?" Zoolee's voice rang out in my head, but it felt more like it was in my ear.

I said with a smile, "I was just thinking that I didn't think I would fall for you so fast."

Zoolee replied, "Holy shit, that was a terrible pick-up line. Try again, smooth guy."

"You have really turned my world upside down?"

Zoolee appeared next to me and laughed. She took hold of me, and we started kissing. It was really something of a rush to kiss her mixed with the speed of the fall and our unknown proximity to the ground.

She said, "Tell me you love and pledge yourself to me and me only."

"No!"

Zoolee took my hand, and time slowed to a crawl as she spoke to me inside of my mind.

"Slade, I disabled your S.P.1.D.E.R." She showed me what she got from her room. "I meant what I said. This type of fall can kill you. I promise you that. Give me your heart, and you will live. Or you will die here today."

"I cannot. I promised Sofia that I would not take a new lover without her permission."

"Silly little dummy. You're not going to take me as a lover. You're going to take me as your wife. Maybe I will bring Sofia to you now and then, but you will be all mine. Pledge your love to me now!"

"Who would I be if I broke my promise? I would be nothing and no one. A liar, that's what I would be. Zoolee, in the little time I have been with you, you have been really enjoyable and strange. But if you are giving me an ultimatum, then I will have to say I'm sorry I could not have more time to get to know you, and I'm sorry I could not kiss Sofia's lips one last time."

I kicked her out of my mind and drifted away. Zoolee looked sad and disappeared, leaving me to my chosen fate. I tried to shift away, only to confirm that my S.P.1.D.E.R. was indeed nonresponsive. I could see the ground. It was still very far away, but I could glimpse the end. My thoughts flashed to Sofia, Sunako, and dear sweet and sour Cheri. I thought about what would happen when it ended. Would Lucy be there to welcome me? Was there even an afterlife? I would never get a chance to get that bastard Vorador.

I started to twirl, which was not enjoyable. I didn't mind hitting the ground, but getting sick before would add insult to injury. I peered at an unfamiliar landscape in greater detail, even though the rushing air caused my eyes to water badly. I saw what looked like tall landmarks all clustered together and things moving around on the ground like ants. Ah, the ants were actually people, and I'd just missed one of the glass-covered landmarks with grass all over the top.

I said out loud, "I love you, Sofia."

I could see the people on the ground had noticed me. Many were pointing. I had never seen so many in one place before. I turned around, looked at the sky, and closed my eyes, thinking of Sofia's face. I held the image of her the first time I saw her. In the distance, people were screaming.

I felt the impact, and it was not what I expected. As I opened my eyes, I could see Zoolee holding me, but we were still falling. She entered my mind, and time slowed again.

"Zoolee, this fall was long enough. Please let this end."

"Slade, we have ten minutes inside your mind before you hit the ground and two seconds in the real world, so choose your next words very carefully. This fall is more dangerous than you know. Pledge yourself to me! Love only me! Tell me you will love me more than Sofia! Choose her and die! Choose me and live!"

"Zoolee, how could you believe I love you if I break my promise? You would never be able to trust me because I abandoned one love for another. I will say thank you for this because I now know that, at heart, I could have been a really good guy. For that, I thank you. Now please let me go. I have somewhere to be, and I don't wish to be late."

Zoolee went to kiss me, but I backed away, shaking my head.

She said, "You're better than I could have ever hoped to have. Goodbye."

Zoolee squeezed me tightly. I felt sick and could not see anything. Was I dead? I didn't feel dead, and I could think, so I had to be somewhere. Maybe I was about to be judged. Then, I felt something. A hand on my face. A light flicked on, and Zoolee was standing there.

"Come on, Zoolee. Is this your idea of a sick joke?"

"No, I think I will just throw you over again and again until you finally break and give yourself to me."

I laughed. "Baby, I could fall for you all day, but Sofia holds my heart. I will not betray her, no matter the circumstance."

"Oh really?" Zoolee had a crazy look in her eye. "You should learn to pick your words better than you pick your nose." Her eyes darted wildly around the room. We were alone, but I felt watched, and it was unnerving. "What if I make her fall? Do you think she will be so noble? Do you think a woman who shares you like candy will be so hard to break? I bet you your hand in marriage that she will break less than halfway down, but I will wait until she can see the ground and get her to be mine, and only mine, then and there. I will have her pleasuring me in my bed, and she will be lost to you."

"Well then, I meant nothing to her. Yes, it will hurt, but it will give me all the motivation to risk life and limb to kill Vorador. I will have nothing to lose. Zoolee, you're really sexy when you're desperate. Either way, I lose to you in your mind. But in my mind, I gain either way."

"Slade, what if I let her fall all the way while watching her? And give you that memory so you can always see what you did to her and how she screamed?" Zoolee eyes were beautifully icy as she spoke. "What then, smart-ass?"

"I don't know because you will be the only one with the memories. When I find Vorador, he will die, or I will be killed. If I die and if I am the grandchild of Nyx, then I will ask to have my soul weaved into Sofia's. Zoolee, you're so very beautiful. You could have almost any man. Why me? I'm no one." My eyes never left hers as I spoke.

"What do you mean, 'almost any man?'"

I replied with a smile, "You can't have me."

She moved toward me, then slapped me across the face. She did that two more times.

"Slade, if you don't give yourself to me right here and now, I will burn her alive! Then, I will burn the rest of them! You have one minute to get undressed and into our bed! You have never seen a person burn. You will wish I killed her in any other way!"

I shook my head.

"She wouldn't do this for you. None of them would! Why give yourself to someone like that?" Zoolee looked angry, sad, and desperate all at the same time.

"Zoolee, I am nothing without my word. Please don't punish someone for my actions. If you have to punish someone, punish me because I am the one telling you no. I was born no one, with nothing but the ability to speak, and I will not split my tongue with a lie. Zoolee, you're so beautiful to look at, but I'm done with this conversation."

I walked past her.

She yelled, "Don't you walk away from me!"

I marched out the room toward Bill and Asimov, who were outside, close to the balcony.

"Slade, I command you to look at me."

I ignored her.

I heard a familiar voice say, "Please, Slade. Look at me?"

I turned around and saw her holding Sofia.

"Slade, I like you, but I can't be with you the way you want. Now that you caused Lucy to die, I don't think I can be around you. Now I know that you would let me fall—or worse—burn because of your prideful tongue. Zoolee is right. You're a selfish, prideful bastard! Helping you was a mistake. I should have let Sunako drown you!"

I looked down and walked slowly toward Zoolee. "You win." I opened my arms and said, "Will you take me in your arms, or should I leave?"

Zoolee tried to hide her smile and opened her arms. "I told you I will have you. You just needed proper motivation." She embraced me. "Now tell me what I want to hear. Tell me that you love me and only me."

"Zoolee, my sweet. I was a fool. You offered me something, and I stupidly pushed you away because of pride. Thank you for showing me that I was wrong. Thank you for giving me this last chance to show you my love."

Zoolee smiled. "Then show me your love."

I took her by the arm. We disappeared and popped into my room at the facility. Sofia was lying asleep in my bed.

"Zoolee, there is my love. It's too bad you could not open your heart just a little and see that I can't love if I can't live honestly."

Zoolee grabbed my hand as Kailee walked in the room. We shifted near the balcony. Zoolee walked toward Bill and Asimov and yelled at them, pushing Bill down. Khalyla and the rest came out.

Khalyla said, "Zoolee, my sweet daughter, you were right. You have met the right man, but you have lost the bet, so pay up."

I saw Zoolee handing a few people something.

Asimov and Bill jogged over to me. Bill said, "Shit, that was intense! You, my friend, have the biggest balls I have ever seen."

I said, "What?"

"Never mind, you're made out of stone."

Asimov said, "What Bill is trying to say is you have an iron will and a steadfast heart. I'm proud to call you my friend."

Zoolee walked up and said, "Hey, idiots, let's play a game where you both screw off!"

They quickly walked away.

"So, Slade, are you upset with me?" She batted her beautiful emerald eyes at me and made a pouty expression. Damn it. She was so weird and sexy, unlike anyone I'd ever met.

I smiled. "No, but I will admit that you had me fooled into believing that you loved and wanted me. I'm new to love, so it was a good learning experience, and I thank you for it. Maybe I can take you to dinner sometime."

She smiled. "How did you hijack me? You got into my mind and used me to get back to your room? Why did you take me there?"

I leaned up against a post. "I meant all the things I said. You messed up when you had the Sofia lookalike speak to me because it was Cheri who tried to drown me. I just chose to change that memory and make her sweet. I just think of when I first looked into Sunako's eyes and how it would be nice to drown in them."

Zoolee said, "Stop being so sweet. You're going to give me diabetes."

"Isn't that a good thing?"

"No. No, it is not."

"Why do you use so many words that I don't understand?"

Zoolee laughed. "I have lived for a very long time. There was a time when people were assholes to each other in a funny way they spoke and acted to one another. It was my favorite three hundred years."

"That sounds like shit. Why would you interact with someone acting like that?"

She took my hand and showed me the time between 1990 and 2035—a small sample of human history.

"Wow, it was a planet of assholes being shitty to one another and using swear words all the time. This made them lose meaning and impact. So many swear words."

Zoolee laughed. "Do you want to try on a few dirty words to see if you like them? Go ahead. Call Bill a name."

"I like Bill. He is always nice to me," I said.

"Okay, I've got an easy one for you. Tell me what you think about Vorador and be colorful." Zoolee waited for my answer.

I replied with, "I feel sorry for him. He's a broken man. He wants his love in his arms one more time, but I will give him what he wants most: to be with his wife once more. But he'll be in the afterlife after I repeatedly run a sword through him in a way that will look almost like I am fornicating him to death with it."

Zoolee looked at me and said, "It's a start, but we need to work on it a bit. Oh, and I have to confess: I was not faking the way I feel about you. I still want you in every way and more so now. I needed to know you were real and that you could love in the face of death. You have a true heart, and I would very much like to earn a place in it. So, I was thinking I could ask Sofia since she is the head of the pack. Feel free to look around, and I'll meet you in our room." Zoolee held up both hands, snapped, then disappeared.

Zyra, Galya, Asya, and Khalyla came up to me.

Asya said, "You have to be as crazy as Zoolee. I have never seen anyone stand up to her like that."

Galya laughed. "He might be crazier with the way he took on Vorador, the Eye, and Zoolee."

Zyra said, "Slade, my sister is not like us. She has been all over many different worlds. She has never found one man she has ever liked, but she looks and moves differently around you. Slade, I'm genuinely afraid for you."

Khalyla added, "Slade, I'm very happy with you. I believe you will do well when you meet our guests when they arrive. As for my daughter Zoolee, I love her, but she is crazy and unpredictable at times. She has never taken a male lover, so if she chooses you, take that into account." Khalyla put her arm around my shoulder. "The bet you saw her pay was not about you. It was about her. But you can hear about that from her. Slade, you don't seem to be like anyone, not even us. But you're officially one of us. You're now family."

"Thank you, Khalyla. May I share something with you?"

She nodded. I gave her my hand, and she saw that I was forty percent unknown DNA.

“I want to be honest and transparent at all times. I don’t know who I am or what I am. As of now, I am no one. The name Slade is written on this bracelet, but I don’t know if it’s my name.”

Khalyla hugged me. “Slade, your race could be a warring race, but you have this chance, this life. When you’re no one, you can be anyone or anything. Our ways might not be the right way or best way, but if you stay true to yourself like you are now, race will mean nothing in the end. Hell, you’ll make a great ambassador for your people, and hopefully—fingers crossed—they all smell as wonderful as you do.”

“Khalyla, is Asya Jotanfo? Or are all of you Jotanfo?”

Khalyla smiled. “Yes, those with green eyes are Jotanfo. However, green eyes are not naturally occurring in Jotanfo genes. The gene that gives me extraordinary long life also gave me green eyes. I believe someone did this to me, and it was passed to Zoolee, my first and only daughter to have the gene. None of my other Jotanfo children had the gene. Six hundred years, later, Zyra was born, the second child with green eyes born on my home world. I received word and raised her as my own. Then it was Tambry, Galya, a few others you’ll meet later, and lastly, Asya. Most live here with me. Zoolee is the one who discovered the hidden gene. She named it the Green Eye Gene. After planetwide testing, we did not find the gene in its dormant state, which only proves our theory that I was implanted with this gene. But by whom? What race out there can cause someone to live so long as I have? Why don’t they make their existence known? Who knows, Slade? Maybe you are them, and this is their way to make contact.”

“No boys?”

Khalyla laughed. “I know! It is weird, right? No males except Asimov and Bill, along with a few other males, but they are Sa-Teen. Asimov is Bill’s great grandfather times four. Yes, to answer your next question: they have the same exact gene, which is why we believe someone did this to us. How could we both have the same gene when they’re not in my family tree? They are a different race, and they don’t have green eyes. So, the gene affects them slightly differently, but that could be the Sa-Teen DNA mixing differently with the foreign gene. Someone out there chose us for something, whether we have done it or have yet to do it. I was chosen, and they received it. Slade, we will need to test you soon to see if you have that gene. If you do, you will need to train to understand so you do not end up like Zoolee. I was young and did not understand this gift, let alone help someone learn to adjust to eternity. I love her so much, but she can be extremely dangerous. One of her gifts is a unique one. That's why everyone fears her. Lucky for us, she feels this is her true home and keeps her rampages to a minimum. Now that she is falling in love, I worry. I worry that she could truly become unstable again, so be careful, my child."

"Great, so no pressure at all. None whatsoever, except she could destroy a city with a temper tantrum."

Khalyla hugged me. "Slade, worry less and trust us more. We will discover what your mystery gene is. Oh, and it's a world. She could destroy a world, not a city. Now walk around, then wait for Zoolee in her room."

Chapter 35

Love and Tendrils

Two and a half hours passed, and I had spoken with many new people and walked around until I found myself in Zoolee's room. Her bed looked super soft with lots of pillows and flowers on the nightstand. The room had a single window. The temperature was just right wherever I went. She had a bathroom attached to her room, so I took a fast shower and dried off with a towel. It was so soft and reminded me of clean clothes. I sat on her bed, lying on my side. After a few minutes, I pulled the covers over me.

I dreamt I was falling. Lucy was there, and she told me that everything was all right, that she loved us, and that we would see her again. Then, she flew away. While I was still falling, Vorador was there.

He said, "Hey, kid, nothing hurts like losing a loved one. The best is yet to come if you don't join me."

Then, he was gone. I felt like I was shaking while I was falling.

Zoolee yelled, "Wake up! You missed dinner. Everyone thought you went home, and some people are looking for you." She called to her mother. "I found him. He was asleep in my bed." She started laughing. "Hey, sleepyhead. I have two people who would like to say hi."

I rubbed my eyes and saw Sofia and Sunako.

"Nice try, but you got their hair wrong."

Sofia said, "You ass, we worked hard to look nice for you, so get the hell up!"

I jumped out of bed and hugged her.

"Slade, why are you naked in Zoolee's bed?"

"This is not what it looks like, I promise. I took a shower, and my clothes were dirty, so I sat down and must have fallen asleep." I smiled and rewrapped the towel around me. "You two look beautiful with your hair braided like that."

Sunako walked over and said, "I have missed you."

We kissed, then Sofia kissed me.

Sofia said, "Zoolee showed me things. Things about you and what you said. I don't have the words to express how it makes me feel watching you say those things. I do love you, and I want you to still be a part of our group. Sunako, Molly, Kailee, and I have seen what happened and agree that we would like to bring Zoolee into the group but only with your permission. I don't want you to feel passed around like candy."

I asked, "Zoolee, are you sure you want this? I know that you have saved yourself, and I could understand with Sofia and Sunako, but you have gone a long time and never been in love. What I am trying to say is, how did you do it and why?"

Zoolee said, "He is so pretty to look at. Then, he opens his mouth and becomes clumsy and stupid. Whoever said I have never been in love?" She grabbed my towel and tugged on it, but I held it tightly. "Slade, if it's going to be a tug-of-war, you'll lose because I am very strong, and if you rip one of my favorite towels, I swear to God, I will be so pissed. Besides, I have something for you to change into. They should do until your dress is clean. Oh, and put it on in front of us. Or I'll shove you out of our room naked. And what will Mother say?"

As I dressed, they watched. Zoolee smiled as they whispered amongst themselves.

"How do I look?"

Zoolee said, "Like a pirate. A sexy pirate. Would you like to board one or all three of us?"

"You can take me as your love slave," said Sunako.

Sofia looked at her and laughed.

"Okay, my beautiful friends. I will gladly be whatever you want after I get some food in me."

We went to eat and talked. I felt safe, comfortable, and relaxed. I asked how they defended the place. Zoolee said that the only way to get to the house was to have a special mark or be brought there.

Sofia took me aside as Zoolee and Sunako were in the middle of discussing a large painting on the wall.

"Slade, I want you the way you want me, but in time, like I have said before. Seeing you stay true to your promise to me makes me love you more. I'm going to ask you to do two things for me without question. First, Zoolee is from so long ago—my head hurts just thinking about it—and she has waited for you. I know it sounds crazy, but I saw her memory. She didn't know your face, but she knew that she would recognize you. So, I want her first time to be with just you and her. Be there just for her. Make her know she is the only one in that moment. Secondly, kiss me."

"I will do what you want, but last time I was with a woman privately, she died soon after."

Sofia smiled. "We all miss her. She was my first love and lover, but I know her well enough to know that she meant what she said. She loved you. She meant it, and she died in your arms. If that were me, at least I would have known that you held me until the end because of love. You don't have to be *in* love to love someone. I love you, and I feel Zoolee will make a great addition, but I have to ask you: is Zoolee all there?"

"Do you mean is she crazy? Like when she deactivated my envelope, then tossed me over the balcony? It was a really long way down. So yeah, she is a bit touched in the head." I held her hand and showed her my thoughts. "See, I can't explain why I feel this way about you, but the feelings make me happy."

"Your thoughts are horrible and beautiful at the same time. Sunako and I will be going home tonight, so you will do what I have asked, yes?"

"Sofia, please don't leave this place without me. I will do whatever you ask of me. Just don't go."

"Is this about Vorador?" asked Sofia.

I nodded.

"We will stay but in another room. I want her time to be like mine but without the distractions."

We kissed, and she hugged me. Zoolee walked over, and Sofia told her about what I had asked. She thought it was a safer idea if we all stayed as well. We walked to their room and kissed goodnight.

Sunako whispered something super dirty in my ear. I smiled, and Zoolee and I went back to her room. We sat on her bed and talked for a bit.

***

In the room down the hall, Asya and Galya were speaking with Sunako and Sofia.

Asya declared, "So, ladies, you should know our sister can get strange at times. When that happens, give her space. A lot of space."

Galya said, "She can become dangerous at the drop of a hat, and now she wants Slade. I fear she will bleed him before the week is through." Galya and Asya laughed. "He will say something stupid, and she will hit him or worse. I wonder if he will fight back? Oh, I would love to see Slade kick her ass. Either way, she will make him bleed. So, Sunako, be ready to use your gift."

Galya, Asya, and Sofia laughed.

"I would love the chance to drink his blood again," said Sunako.

Galya and Asya suddenly stopped laughing.

Asya asked, "Say what? What did you say, Sunako?"

"Sunako, did you say you drank his blood, or is that a sexual innuendo?" Galya leaned in toward Sunako, awaiting her answer.

Sunako smiled and said, "Yeah, we all drank Slade's blood. It was on our first night together. That is when I knew I was falling in love. His blood made my whole body tingle for an hour. I even felt good when I woke up. Great, now I can't stop thinking about his blood."

Asya asked, "Sofia, you drank it as well?"

Sofia smiled. "Yes, it's so good. Better than any wine I have ever had and just as delicious as your candy. It made my body tingle as well, and I was so horny. I had to fight the urge not to make love to him right there that night. It was so bad that I used the bathroom to take care of myself, and all it did was make it worse. Sunako, you think he will give Zoolee a little before they make love?"

Galya asked, "Who is Slade making love to?"

Sunako and Sofia laughed.

Galya grabbed Sunako. "Tell me, child!"

"Zoolee. Slade and Zoolee are becoming one tonight."

Asya asked, "Why did you two drink his blood?"

They told them the story about Cheri biting Slade.

***

"Slade, would you brush my hair?"

I smiled as she handed me a brush. I slowly ran the brush through her hair. After five minutes of talking and brushing her super silky hair, I kissed her neck.

I asked, "Would like me to wash your hair in the shower?"

"That sounds like it would be amazing."

I undressed her and saw that she had two scar-like spots on her back, near her shoulder blades.

"Zoolee, may I ask you a delicate question?"

"Yes, you may."

"If you are half-Jotanfo, where are your tendrils?"

"Mine are retractable, but I only have two. They are not like other female Jotanfo tendrils. I am the first and only unaltered hybrid of my kind left. All other hybrids were euthanized to stop their madness and destructive behavior. We hybrids are born with only two. Even the altered Jotanfo human hybrids are born with only two tendrils, whether they are male or female. Mine are much stronger and longer than a standard Jotanfo."

"I really want to see all of you."

"Okay, but please don't get scared."

She stood facing away from me, and two snake-like appendages emerged from her back. They looked like smooth, cylindrical tentacles with six thinner, three-inch, fingerlike appendages that worked exactly like fingers. When held together, they were inconspicuous until they were utilized. She turned around to face me.

"This is the part that might look weird or scary." They began to grow. "See, mine are longer than my mother's and sisters'. I can extend mine up to a little more than nine feet, but theirs can only extend to six feet. I can put them away if you don't like them."

"No, please. I think they're beautiful. May I touch you? I mean, may I have the freedom to touch you anywhere?"

She nodded. I touched her neck and ran my hand down her spine and back up beneath her hair. I caressed one of her tendrils, and she make a sound that told me I'd found a pleasurable spot.

"Zoolee, you're beautiful."

She took hold of my hands with her tendrils and led me to the shower.

"Here. I would like it to begin here. Show me love."

We stepped into the running water as we began to kiss. I glided my hands softly around her body, and she did the same to me.

"Slade, may I touch you with my tendrils?"

"I would enjoy that very much. Zoolee, you look like an angel, and your tendrils are your wings. When I first looked into your eyes, I couldn't speak because you look like an angel. Even now, I feel hypnotized by you in a way that I don't understand. I feel I have known you from a time before. Zoolee, would you tell me if you knew me?"

Zoolee said in a sweet, soft tone, "I do know you, and I feel the same way about you. I've always wanted something beautiful, and I know my wait is over. We know one another from our shared dreams. Most of which you don't remember, but don't worry. I will help you remember them when we study dreams together. That is something I greatly look forward to doing with you."

Zoolee ran both her tendrils down and up my back, which felt so amazing that I shivered, even though we were standing in the warm shower. We kissed, and I thought about her eyes, the first second I saw her, and my desire to kiss her.

Zoolee said, "Slade, did you really want to kiss me the first time you looked into my eyes?"

"Zoolee, my angel, let my thoughts be my thoughts, but yes. I can't explain it, but I want you. Not in just a sexual way. I want more. I want something I can't explain, and it makes me want to burst into tears. I can't say it, and yet there it is, on the tip of my tongue. First of all, I have to say, I hope you like your name because it makes me smile every time I say it. So, I will be saying it a lot because it is so very beautiful."

Zoolee kissed me deeply and passionately. She whispered in my ear, "Slade, I'm falling in love with you. Please be there to catch me. Please don't let me hit the ground."

I smiled. "My sweet, are you sure you can love me knowing that I'm with Sofia, Sunako, and Molly?"

Zoolee laughed. "Don't forget Kailee. Yes, I will love them as well. You will be ours because your hearts are big enough to love us all without hurting any one of us. That's very special. You're special, and I want to be with you."

I kissed her.

"Slade, will you have me if I give myself to you? Will you hold me like only you can? Will you let me show you the love that I have for you that has built up over these many generations?"

"Yes to everything you just said and more. I hope to make you happy because you deserve love and happiness. If I can be that that for you, then I look forward to being with you from this day forward."

"Slade, I love you. Thank you for finally finding your way to me and these arms. It's been too long a wait. Now kiss me until I can't breathe." We kissed until I felt like we were one person as our thoughts intermingled.

"Zoolee, you're so intense. I hope I can make you happy."

"Slade, you already make me happy, and it keeps getting better. Is it true that Cheri, Sofia, and Sunako tasted your blood?"

"Yes, Cheri bit me really bad. She noted that I tasted good, and the rest wanted to try. Why? Is that not normal?"

Sofia had clearly told Zoolee they'd tasted my blood and the story of how Cheri bit into my arm.

Zoolee smiled. "Would you let me taste you?"

"Yes, if you want. I will give my life to make you smile."

She pushed me onto the bed, then got on top of me. "Kiss me the way you did Sofia. Kiss me here."

I rolled her onto her back and kissed her, using my newfound skills to send her into sexual bliss. Her hand danced atop my head, occasionally grabbing my hair and pulling me tightly to her as her leg crossed over me, holding my head in place. I was enjoying what I was doing. Her tendrils held a pillow against her face as she screamed. I liked watching her tendrils move. I was a bit jealous I didn't have a pair. After all, I was twenty percent Jotanfo.

"I love you, Slade." She loudly reached her height of ecstasy again and pulled me to her mouth for a kiss.

"I love the way I taste on your lips." She was strong as we held each other. She whispered, "Please make love to me. Make me yours. Make me a Slade. *Zoolee Slade.* Yes, I want that, and I want your blood. Will you taste me at the same time?"

I smiled and nodded.

"Okay. Soon after you are inside of me, we will share."

I entered her slowly, and we stared into each other's eyes. Slowly, we made love. It felt nothing like the others. Our bodies and thoughts became one. She wanted the black eyes, so I obliged. She glowed like Sunako. Her tendrils caressed me and coiled around my arms and neck. It never became scary, but it was otherworldly. She rolled me onto my back and gently swayed back and forth.

She said, "You feel right. You feel like home. Slade, I waited so long for this moment with you. I love you." Then, her eyes went black. "Mine are like yours. I was born with them as well. We were meant to find one another. Drink from me, and I'll drink from you."

One of her tendrils plucked something from her nightstand. "Slade? May I?"

I handed her my arm, and she cut me midway above my wrist. She sliced her forearm, and I tasted her as she tasted me. It was unlike anything I had sampled—so sweet, so salty, so unbelievable. It felt like electricity was flowing through my whole body, and I tingled all over.

"Oh, Slade. You taste so good. It makes me tingle, and I have never felt this alive. I love you."

Zoolee's door opened, and Galya and Asya rushed in with an astonishing speed to reach our bed. Zoolee's tendrils moved faster than the witches and caught both by the throat. They encircled their necks, and the ladies were helpless against Zoolee's power. Both Asya and Galya dropped to the floor, unconscious, and we continued to make love, sipping each other's blood like crimson wine.

"Slade, I feel you are so close. Please release your love inside of me. Let me have you while we are connected. Give me your essence. Tell me you love me as you do."

Soon, I was unable to hold it back. As much as I strained to savor just a minute more of the pleasure, I overflowed.

My passion spilled from me into Zoolee, and I said, "Zoolee, I love you. I love you now as I have always! Take me home!" I didn't know why I'd said that, but it felt right. I felt Zoolee knew me but was holding something back.

"Slade, in my arms, you are home. You have come back to me after all this time, and I will never lose you again."

I lost consciousness in the darkness of the room, and a voice asked, "Hey, Slade. Can you hear me? You should not have shared your blood with her. You're just going to lose that much more. This is how it all starts. You should have taken Vorador's offer."

I woke up to Khalyla, Zyra, Galya, and Asya yelling at Zoolee, but she was just ignoring them, looking at her nails.

"Hey, sleepyhead. You were so amazing that you knocked yourself out."

Khalyla demanded Zoolee answer her. Khalyla brought out her tendrils, all six of them moving almost too fast to see. One grabbed Zoolee by the arm, while Zyra, Galya, and Asya brought out theirs. Twenty-four tendrils and anger hung thick in the air—so much so, it started to make me angry. They were ruining Zoolee's experience. I stood up and felt sick, like I had a stomach full of snakes. Then I fell to my knees. I couldn't breathe, and no one noticed I needed help. My insides were *moving* and felt like they were on fire.

Suddenly, I could breathe, and the pain was gone. I stood up, and the witches stopped fighting and stared with sudden looks of shock. Shit, I was naked in a room full of women. The ladies might be right. I could be stupid.

I said, "I'm sorry. Let me put my pants on."

Zoolee was covering her mouth and pointing at me.

"Why are you all quiet? Someone say something."

Asya stepped forward. "Slade, when did you get those?"

She pointed, and I looked up. There, just above my head, were four tendrils slightly moving as if they were watching the witches. As Asya took another step closer, two of them opened and inspected her, almost like they were sniffing her.

"Slade, stop doing that to me. It's rude, and you're making me feel deeply uncomfortable."

I looked at her. "Asya, I'm not controlling them. I don't even feel them. Asya, make whatever this is stop."

I stepped backward onto the bed, and the witches matched each step. I finally made my way to the bathroom and closed the door. I looked in the mirror, and I saw them: four nine-foot tendrils moving like they were listening to music I could not hear. Two came down to eye level and opened at the end, then closed. Zoolee walked in.

"My love, can you retract them, please? You're scaring me."

"I'm scaring *you*? You have got to be kidding me! I mean, really? Zoolee, what is happening to me?"

She moved closer, and my tendrils gently took hold of her and pulled her to me. We kissed.

"Zoolee, do you still love me, or shall I leave?" My tendrils tapped her on the back over and over until she brought out hers.

"Please don't leave me. Slade, I don't want you to go. I think you're more beautiful like this."

Two of my tendrils entwined with hers. They slowly slid and coiled with one another. I started to feel it. It was like sex, just different, but still very intense. We kissed while our bodies talked, speaking a language just out of reach of my intelligence. I was lightheaded and lost consciousness.

I woke up a few hours later in Zoolee's arms.

"Zoolee, I had the strangest dream… I dreamt that I had tendrils. It was cool and scary."

We kissed, and I got up to use the bathroom. Then, I saw them, and I stumbled backward, falling over. But I didn't hit the ground. My tendrils acted like legs and held me up until my feet touched the ground. I peed, washed my hands, and walked back into our room.

"Zoolee, my love. It wasn't a dream."

"Slade, don't freak out this time. Just breathe. In, then out. In, then out. Please, I don't need you passing out again."

"Zoolee! I know how to breathe, damn it!"

Zoolee stood up and poked me hard in the chest with one of her tendrils.

"Slade! Don't speak to your wife like that. It's just plain rude! Don't be a rudey head!" Then, she threw her hairbrush at me, but one of my tendrils caught it before it hit my face.

I handed it back to her.

"That is what I thought. You have not gained control of them. Your subconscious is in full control. Slade, you're like a baby. Khalyla has to see this. Come with me."

She led me back out to the meeting area close to the balcony. Every witch I knew and a few I didn't gathered to see me. I was standing in Zoolee's pink sleep pants. Everyone was staring, and I just wanted to run away. Zoolee spoke with them for a few minutes.

Khalyla said, "Slade, you're just full of surprises, aren't you? What's next, wings? She kissed me on the cheek. "Go relax. We will talk soon. Oh, and welcome to the family, son."

Zoolee took my hand, and I saw Asimov and Bill standing there with shocked expressions.

"Zoolee, I can't control these things. How am I going to do my job? What if Sofia and Sunako see me like this? They will be frightened of me and won't love me anymore. How do I retract them? I have to hide this from them."

Zoolee smiled. "Too late."

She pointed, and I turned around. Sunako and Sofia were standing about ten feet away.

Sofia smiled. "Zoolee brought us in while you slept, and your tendrils caressed our faces, heads, and our hands. It was very romantic. Even while you sleep, you're loving and gentle. Please don't think this makes us love you even a small bit less than we already do. We still love you and want you to be ours. We want to be Slades like Zoolee. Sofia Slade, Sunako Slade—I think that sounds so sexy."

They kissed me and went back to their room. I was speechless for a few minutes, trying to take it all in.

Zoolee took my hand, and we talked about important things.

I asked, "Why do humans and Sa-Teen call them tentacles?"

She said, "It's a derogatory term. They're like arms, just not human, yet they're not like a cephalopod's. More like something in between and very strong. You will find fighting will become easier once you learn control of them, and they have the same power you do. So, think of it as you have two short arms and fists and four really long arms and fists that can choke the shit out of people."

We fell asleep in one another's arms. As we slowly woke up, we began to make love again. The morning was starting out very pleasurably. When our tendrils touched, incredibly intense feelings emerged. Well, if I had to have them, at least they looked cool and felt good.

"Wait! Why were you three using my name like a last name?"

Zoolee said, "Slade isn't your first name." She kissed me and smiled. "My beautiful stupid fool. I love you so much. Slade is your last name. But I will not tell you anymore right now. Maybe later if you are a good boy."

I knew she knew more about me than I know. Who is this heavenly creature?

"Vidya to Slade."

"Slade here."

"I have two here and prepped with clones ready in thirty minutes. I trust I will see you here in six minutes. Or are you between the legs of one of your pretty friends? If so, make it seven minutes."

"I will be there in four, but I need to see you first and in private."

I got up and dressed. As I pulled my boots on, Zoolee caught my wrist with her tendrils. "Zoolee, my love, I have to go to work."

Zoolee sat up, uncovering her breasts. "I have work for you right here between my legs."

"My sweet, I have an obligation to fulfill for the next two years. That is how I pay for things. Well, once I learn how money works."

Zoolee smiled. "I'm your only obligation, and I have more gold than most. Not to mention enough galactic credits to buy this planet. So, come back to me. My skin grows cold without you cuddling up against me."

"I will come right back, or you could meet me there, but I will fulfill my arrangement. Now, please let my wrist go. Oh, and I own this planet."

Zoolee smiled again. "You're lucky I love you, or I would pitch you out of my window for leaving me with the 'I have to go to work' line." She laughed. "Wait, what? You can't remember your name. How do you own Earth?"

"I don't know what that means. Is that one of those things you and Tomok keep using? What's it called? Oh, a reference. Yes, a reference. And I do own this planet, along with its moon. A woman named Detra gave it to me as a tip for my work. You can have it if you want."

"You don't know who Detra is, do you, honey?

"No."

"You can be funny, but you don't know what humor is. Yes, it was a reference to something. Someone would say that after they had sex and wanted the other person to leave. It was commonly called a one-night stand."

I laughed. "Instead of having sex, they would stand all night with each other. Then, one would lie to make the other go away. People back then were super weird, and you call me stupid."

Zoolee kissed me. "My dear sweet idiot, I will explain in great detail what that means later. Now go do whatever job it is you do, but think of me with Sunako and Sofia. That should make the time go by fast."

I tried to shift away in a cool way like Asya but fell backward. My tendrils stopped me from hitting the floor. I lay on the floor and asked, "Zoolee, can you please reactivate my S.P.1.D.E.R.?"

"Slade, you have to get that one taken out, and take the kind that we use. It's more stable, and you can jump many more times without getting sick." Zoolee pointed a little black thing at me. "May I watch you work?"

"Sure. It's boring, but I'm in charge, so I guess I make the rules in the lab." I heard a clicking sound. I looked at her and winked as I fell into the floor. It would look cooler if I'd done it the way I wanted. I reappeared in my room.

Kailee said, "I haven't had a chance to properly thank you for saving my life."

I gave her a deep kiss and said, "I have to work now."

On my way out, I saw something that was not in my room before. It looked like a really large tablet or a bright painting with moving, talking people. I would have to ask Tomok if that was his painting. I met Vidya in her main office.

"Okay, Slade, what's up?"

I pointed up and said, "Look, I didn't have these the last time we spoke."

Vidya looked at me. "Slade, your hair looks fine. Are you feeling well?"

"Vidya, don't you see my tendrils?" After I said that, I noticed they were gone.

"Slade, work now. Be funny later. Oh, Slade, you would be much more attractive if you had tendrils. Now go work your magic and make us rich and famous."

I arrived in my lab and shook Tomok's hand. I ignored Batch's attempt to shake my hand.

"So, I have two, back-to-back."

Batch said, "You must be used to that by now, if you know what I am saying."

"Batch? What was that?"

Batch replied, "I was using humor."

I smiled. "Let me guess. Tomok told you to say that?"

"No, I saw it in a movie. It's an expression. A long time ago, they used the wrong words to express themselves in really funny ways. As soon as you have an hour to sit down, you have to watch one with us. You will be blown away."

I laughed. "Honestly, since I opened my eyes for the first time, I have been on the go. I would welcome a few full days that I had nothing to do. Maybe after I transfer our two clients, I will show you what a six-and-a-half-mile fall looks and feels like."

Batch said, "You just seem to find trouble wherever you go, don't you? Room one-A is the first client."

"Slade, I wrote a bunch of information on your personal tablet, but would you like me to tell you about the Sa-Teen race?" asked Tomok.

"Sure."

"The Sa-Teen race has a wider range of ethnicities than humans. They are either black, white, purple, yellow, or red, with varying shades. They have no tendrils. Instead, they have a thumb where the pinky would be, which looks like a thicker pinky and is spaced more like a thumb. They can easily pass as human. Their lifespan is around five hundred to six hundred years. Gene editing at birth allows them to not be infected with most known diseases. Their skin is slightly more resistant to fire and heat, but no resistance to cold beyond that of a standard human. Both male and females have two hearts. They also look young, never appearing older than thirty. Sa-Teen physiology prevents their race from transferring into a clone body more than once. All attempts for a second transfer have resulted in death. Some Sa-Teen could not transfer at all due to a particular gene that Jotanfo scientists are working closely to solve. Your client has this gene."

"Thank you. That was very informative."

I walked in, and a light-green Sa-Teen male was sitting in a chair. He stood up to shake my hand.

"Ah, Mr. Slade. I am Redril Ra'th. I have been told you can work miracles."

We talked for about fifteen minutes. He was very worried, and I did my best to calm his fears. His new body was brought in, covered with a sheet.

"Could you please take the sheet off? I want to see what it looks like."

I pulled the sheet back.

"It looks exactly like me when I was in my early fifties. I was so handsome then, strong and virile."

They had to have a way to perceive age because they looked identical in my eyes.

"Slade, I am ready but scared. I don't want to die. I am five hundred seventy-four. My health is fading, and this is my only chance to regain health and my youth. I want to live, and I mean *really* live."

"Mr. Ra'th—I hope I said your name correctly?"

He nodded.

"Mr. Ra'th, I will be with you the whole way as my brother has informed you. It will be strange at first, but the more relaxed you are, the faster it will work. I promise that you will be able to take control of your new body, and I can always bring you right back to this one if you wish. I will not leave your side until you're comfortable."

I took a seat next to him, and we interlocked fingers. As we held hands, we had some interesting conversations about his home, world politics, the expansion of the city he governed on Earth, and his children, of whom he was very proud of. A few minutes later, he was sitting upright, and I was shaking his brand-new hand.

"Look at me. I'm a boy again, almost a man. You have given me the greatest gift. The gift of time."

"I am happy for you, Mr. Ra'th. I will see you back here in two years, Milky Way time. I think that's the correct term. It was a pleasure to have met you. I must attend to my next client. Vidya should be in soon."

Mr. Ra'th said, "Thank you again, Mr. Slade."

I smiled and exited the room.

Chapter 36

Work Stress

Tomok prepared all the pertinent information on the Jotanfo for me on a table. I read it before walking in.

A Jotanfo female differs greatly from their male counterpart. Females have six tendrils and will grow six to seven and a half feet tall. The males have four tendrils and reach a max height of nearly six feet. They come in four main ethnicities, a color combination of mixed colors, which are not seen as a separate ethnicity, and one rare color—white, black, red, green, and an extremely attractive, rare light purple. Jotanfo can pass as human when they have their tendrils retracted. If they have their shirt off, they will look to have four to six scars but would still pass as human. Hybrids only have two tendrils. Interestingly enough, the hybrids are born with one or two hearts. This is random.

Sidenote: Khalyla is the first Jotanfo to discover Earth. Jotanfo live up to eight hundred years, longer in cases in which they upload their consciousness into a special computer. Due to a flaw that caused many of the uploaded to become corrupted, many had to be deleted. In essence, that person is digitally euthanized. Jotanfo skin is soft as human skin but more durable. On a cellular level, Jotanfo skin is reminiscent of a great white shark due to placoid scalelike tissue, which makes something like a sword slash do little to no damage. Sharp objects cause less damage but not straight on.

Blood coagulates much faster, and endurance is twice that of a well-trained human athlete. Jotanfo can become overweight. The use of nanobots for weight loss is common. For an unknown reason, Jotanfo can only transfer once, due to a rapidly fading conscious. In the second week, subject succumbs, then enters a vegetative state. We have yet to overcome this difficulty. Jotanfo and Sa-Teen scientists are working to solve this problem. Both races are greatly fond of one another, and now they live more in a symbiotic relationship with many marrying.

Addendum: Hybrid's skin is twice as strong as a full-blood Jotanfo. Before a hybrid is six weeks old, DNA manipulation is performed by nanobots that cause normal skin strength along with any modifications the parent/parents want. The gene for aggression is dialed back to a standard human. Gender, skin color, eye color, height, and an intelligence booster are all standard with all Jotanfo embryos. No modifications can be made after nine weeks.

I walked into room 1D and saw the client. I had to take a breath, as she was a sight to behold. She was a light-skinned red Jotanfo female with long raven-black hair and brilliant ice-blue eye. She stood at seven and a half feet tall.

I had to focus as to not be entranced by her beauty. "Hello, I am Slade."

"No, you're not!" She walked toward me. "I was told Slade was a male. You're clearly a tiny female. Are you the nurse?" She poked me aggressively in the chest with one of her tendrils. "I want to see Slade now! Do you know who I am?" She poked me hard enough that it pushed me backward. "I don't appreciate being kept waiting like a common slave! Bring me Slade, or I will become very cross with you!"

I said nothing as I picked my table and read her chart. "Miss Elfano, I'm sorry to have kept you waiting. I was away on business but came straight back as soon as I knew you were here."

"Don't give me pathetic excuses, tiny girl. Just get me Slade now!" At that point, all six of her tendrils were in an aggressive, shaking posture.

Without making further eye contact and continuing to read the tablet, I calmly stated, "I assure you, Miss Elfano, I'm Slade, and I am a male."

She used her tendrils to grab both my wrists and my throat, lifting me to eye level with her. She caught me off guard, and for some unknown reason, I was having trouble entering her mind. She was depriving me of oxygen, making it awfully hard to concentrate on anything but breathing.

"Male, huh? We'll see about that right now!" She used her free tendrils to pull down my pants and take hold of my obvious male appendage. She loosened her grip slightly, allowing me to breathe. I snapped my eyes black, and her eyes went wide as I took control of her mind.

I explained, "You're being very rude and out of line with the very person who decides whether or not to relocate you to a new body. Rich or not, I will not tolerate any type of verbal, physical, or sexual abuse from anyone. Am I understood?"

I was unaware Tomok, Batch, and Vidya were watching.

"Now, Miss Elfano, kindly unhand my genitals and put me down."

She did as I asked, and I released her mind. Vidya began yelling, but I raised my hands.

Vidya walked in. "Everything is all right, just a simple misunderstanding between races. Nothing that should be noted or otherwise thought as bad behavior of an entitled, insert-whatever-your-title-is, queen, duchess, or ruler of the sky and all things below. While I'm your attending specialist, all titles along with attitudes are checked at the door. Otherwise, I will refuse service, and you can face your mortality, knowing that entitlement is for the dead. The dead are the only ones entitled to be honored. With that said, please sit down and regain your composure."

Vidya and Elfano started yelling at one another in their native tongue.

Tomok said, "I hope you didn't get offended by the way she called you a tiny female. How were you so calm? She grabbed you and your package, and you were still calm. This is just another day for you, isn't it?"

I smiled. "I must not have seen her grab a package. Did she put it back? So, you know who sent it? And to answer your question, yes, this is just another day in my life."

Batch laughed. "You're killing me, Slade. That's your package." Batch pointed at my groin. "Or a funnier word for it. Remember what I said about wrong words? They have a course on the history of language for Earth and its many forms, and the best stuff is slang and their meanings."

Vidya said, "Sorry for the misunderstanding, Slade. Elfano will be very cooperative from here on out."

Elfano nodded.

After the team left the room, I sat down to explain the processes and how she needed to be totally relaxed.

I smiled. "I have nothing planned in the next hour, so if you would like, we can sit here and talk. I could give you privacy, or we can begin the transfer. Either way, I need you to be very relaxed."

She opted to sit and talk. She was very interested in my black eyes. We spoke about that, and I brought my blue eyes back. I told her that the body would be sensitive to touch in the first week. Forty-eight minutes passed before she was ready. We held hands as I entered her mind, escorting her to her new body. I left her mind when I was confident. Ten minutes passed before she was able to sit up. She asked what we did with the old body. I told her she could take it, or we would cremate it while she watched to ensure the DNA was not misused in anyway, as per the contract.

Elfano said, "Maybe I could take you to dinner to apologize for my behavior. We could talk more then. Maybe you could help me christen this new body the right way. I have never been with a human male before, and you seem to have what I need. So, what do you say?"

She slowly licked her lips, and my heart and something else jumped.

"I promise you a night that you will remember for two lifetimes. Not to brag, but I am one of the most famous models and actresses to date."

I swallowed, and it made a weird sound. I did my best to play it cool. I replied, "That sounds amazing. You're extremely beautiful, but I must decline your incredibly tempting offer. I believe I may have recently become married to a green-eyed beauty, someone of your race. Well, she is half-human."

She looked uncomfortable. Then, with a shaky voice, she asked, "The green-eyed woman's name—what is it?"

"Are you feeling well?" I asked as the color drained from her face.

She prompted again, "Please tell me her name."

"Zoolee."

"Please tell me it's anyone else in any of the known galaxies. Please, anyone but her."

"Yes, Zoolee. Why?"

She began to look sick, so I laid her back so that she could rest. I rubbed her temples to relax her.

Elfano begged, "Oh no! Please don't tell Zoolee how I treated you and what I did to you. I will give you anything you want. I can make you very wealthy. If she lets you take a lover, I will give myself to you in any way, any time you ask. Please don't tell her. Please. I beg you in her name."

"Calm down. Why are you so afraid?"

"On my planet, many thousands of years ago, a green-eyed woman was born that outlived every generations of Jotanfo to date. Her name is—"

I said softly, "Khalyla."

Elfano slowly nodded. "Yes, that's her. She left to explore the stars and discovered Earth. A long time ago, she had a daughter that was the first half-human, half-Jotanfo. They lived on Earth for a long time until things started going bad. She, along with her daughter Zoolee, started the Human Restoration Project or HRP. Khalyla and Zoolee singlehandedly saved the human race from extinction. Those in power at the time thought she was crazy. Her visions of the future were not believed, so they turned their backs on Earth when humans needed them the most. Khalyla was the first to discover Earth and loved this place. She also owns the third-largest mining operation in this galaxy."

"How do you know this?"

She smiled. "Every child knows the story of Khalyla the Immortal and her daughter Zoolee the Hidden. It's a course all Jotanfo and Sa-Teen children love to take, and it's one of the most enjoyable because they're heroes. Not only to Earth, but with their many breakthroughs in science. There is a religion based around the green eyes and an even bigger one based on Zoolee, as it was Zoolee who changed everything for so many when she fought the Splice and won. She led an army and pushed them back. Our faith is in her, and she has billions of followers that are completely devout. Please, don't tell her what I did. Just name it, and I will give it to you. I will leave my contact information. Please call me, even if it's just to check on me."

"Miss Elfano, you are forgiven. If and when she finds out, I will ask her to disregard what happened today. But I will say, your beauty is so striking that, if I were single, I would have taken you up on your offer within a heartbeat. I promise, I will contact you. Besides, I will have you naked on my table in two years from today, Milky Way time."

Elfano smiled. "Thank you, Slade. So much." She kissed me on the cheek. "Wow, you smell so good." She breathed in deeply again. "That smell will have me thinking about you for some time. I don't think I have ever smelled anything like it. It's amazing. May Zoolee's love be with you."

"Thank you, Miss Elfano. Vidya will have everything you need. It was a unique pleasure meeting you. Please have a good day." I walked out then into the room with Batch and Tomok.

Tomok said, "Slade, you have to tell me your secret. Elfano was throwing herself at you. How in the galaxy did you say no? And are you insane? Batch, your brother may have suffered a brain injury at some point."

I rolled my eyes. "It's easy, and it sounds like this: no thank you. As for me being insane, maybe."

Tomok yelled, "Slade that's Juniper fucking Elfano! She is one of the galaxy's most attractive actresses and models. You must be insane. Five of her exes committed suicide when their relationships ended. Batch, your brother is nuts. Totally bonkers. I can't believe I'm having this conversation."

I started to feel the weight of Lucy's passing in a crushing way. The gravity of it was too much, and the pressure in my head was becoming overwhelming.

"Tomok! I get it. She's sexy, but she will not lie on her back any better than any other woman! You place too much emphasis on exterior beauty! She is a shallow, self-entitled brat who doesn't deserve her new life, if not for the fact that she has money. I'm sensing some common themes: money, sex, power, and enslavement of others in various ways, and it's disgusting!" I was about to become angry, and I didn't understand why. "I want you two to cover for me. I really need some time completely alone. I just need a small room with a bed and no windows, something completely dark. Please tell whoever asks that I left the facility, and I will be back in a few hours. I don't care if the king of the galaxy or a god is asking for me. If they need me, they can wait a little longer. Just take a message and tell them that I will be back."

Tomok and Batch could see something was wrong.

Batch said, "Are you okay?"

"I don't think so."

Tomok said, "Sure thing, buddy. Room one-K is unlocked and vacant. Just so you know, there is no such thing as the king of the galaxy."

I was walking out and didn't care to respond.

"Batch, you know him. Is he okay?"

Batch replied, "I don't think I ever really knew him that well at all, to be honest, but he appears to be suffering. Did you notice the way he wouldn't touch me or my hand at all since he got here? How his eyes went black while his tone was aggressive with a hint of sadness? I wonder what's going on. He's usually very open and friendly. He probably just needs a good nap."

I entered room 1K and lay on the observation bed.

"Lights off."

I welcomed the darkness as it enveloped me. I was alone, finally alone. I had killed. I would lead others to their deaths and cause others to die. People I loved would die because of my actions. The things I had set in motion with Vorador could change everything. I'd let her die because I was weak and unprepared. Others would die because I was weak. No one loved me because no one knew me because I was no one. I was alone, discarded like trash by my own people. What could I have done to be abandoned? Not a single person had come looking for me. Didn't anyone miss me? My head was pounding, and my eyes were heavy.

I heard a tiny whisper. *"I do."*

I was tired of playing that role, acting like I was okay with everything that had happened. She died because of me, but she would not die without me. Vorador had killed Lucy. No, Lucy died because I'd gotten her killed. I'd led her to her death. I could have saved her. I could have taken her a few miles to the House of Thorns before engaging. I killed her. I was the reason she was dead. I was the problem and the solution in one. I shifted outside three miles up. Sofia would not die if I were gone. None of them would. He would not bother with them. I listened to the wind rushing past my face. It would be better this way. I would barely be missed. I watched the ground rush up toward me for one final kiss.

Then, I felt nothing. Nothing at all. All I saw was darkness.

"Slade," an unseen voice called to me. "Do you think I would allow this? Every time you try to extinguish your light, I will stop you. I love you so much. Soon, you will be in my arms, and we will be whole again. Just hold on a little while longer. Soon, we will leave everything behind and be like new. I can't wait to kiss you again. I love you."

"Who are you to control me like this? I make my own decisions."

"You are free to do anything, but this is the only decision I will oppose. You will not die until I wish it, and I would never wish that. I am always watching, and you will never die."

I woke up as I hit the floor. I was sweaty. It had to have been a dream. *I must have fallen asleep as soon as I laid down and fallen off the bed.* What a terrible nightmare. I hoped I could find a way to turn dreams off or have no bad dreams at all. Why would I fall to my own death? That would have given me way too much time to think. Besides, I'd told Vorador that I would kill him, and I wouldn't want him to think I was a liar.

I drifted off again. I was standing in tall grass, and the wind was on my face. As I looked up, I saw three moons rising. The ground began to violently shake.

"Slade! Wake the hell up!" The lights were blinding as Tomok stood over me. "Slade, get up! Now!"

"Tomok, I told you. I don't care if the one of the gods wants me! Tell him or whoever to piss off. I'm on my time!"

Tomok said, "Funny you said one of the gods. You're close because it's one of the goddesses. Look, man. Listen to me. Someone incredibly important is here looking for you and only you."

"Tell them to go away! Please, Tomok! I don't want to be rude, but get out! Lights off!"

"Slade!" Tomok stood in the dark.

I snapped my eyes in hopes that if I turned on the light, he would want to leave me alone.

"Look, man, people are frantically looking for you, and that is not even the craziest thing. Not by a long shot! There is a goddess in my office claiming to be your wife, demanding to see you."

"Oh shit!"

Tomok replied, "Oh shit? What do you mean, 'Oh shit?' Are you saying you know who I am talking about? Because there is no way you know who this is! Not a chance in all the galaxies that you will guess who it is!"

"Tomok! Calm down and take a deep breath! It's just Zoolee. I might have married her or something. I'm a bit foggy on the details of how that happened. Just tell her that I will see her and the witches later, and I'm fine. I will meet her later in our bedroom."

Tomok said, "How the fuck do you know her? How in the fuck did you *accidentally* marry her? Zoolee is straight out of the pages of history. She is a living goddess! There is a whole religion based around her! Her just standing in my office made me almost piss myself."

I laughed. "I get it: she is a big deal. So just tell Big Deal that I'm off somewhere, and you're having difficulty pinpointing my location because my locator is not working. Say whatever you want to say so long as it fits my desire to be left alone."

The door opened, and Batch came in.

I said, "What the hell? This was not meant to be a social event. I just want some alone time and a nap."

Batch said nothing but was breathing oddly.

"Batch?"

Tomok began to make a strange sound as well. Tomok dropped to his knees, and Zoolee stepped over him.

Zoolee's eyes were glowing. "I was looking for you, and that idiot said he would be right back. Then, I saw who I thought was you, and he brushed me off when I called you. He made me choke him, and I pulled what I needed from his mind even though he fought to keep me out." She laughed. "Child." She slammed Batch's head into the wall, and he fell to the floor. "Now come along. Zyra said you are needed at the House of Thorns."

"Zoolee, you can't go doing shit like that. These are my friends."

She smiled. "You're so cute when you're mad. I'll try to be gentler in the future."

Zoolee's tendril grabbed my arm. She snapped, and we were at the front gate where Zyra was waiting for us.

"Zyra? What? Is it bad news?"

Zyra said, "Dutch has summoned you. Asya will be here soon with everyone else."

She disappeared, leaving just Zoolee and me.

"Zoolee, will you please follow me?"

She smiled and walked with me. We saw Dutch outside with Velvet. She looked up at me and jumped into my arms, hugging me tightly and kissing my face.

Velvet said, "Thank you, Slade. You saved my life. Thank you so much."

I said coldly, "Lucy died saving you! If it were not for her sacrifice, you would be minus a head right now. Vorador said he was going to keep your head alive."

"That sounds awful," said Velvet as she rubbed her neck.

I gave her a disapproving look while raising my eyebrow, and she looked away.

Dutch said, "I'm glad you made it, my boy. First off, thank you for saving my daughter's life. I am deeply sorry for the loss of Lucy. She will be greatly missed but not forgotten. Second, you will sit next to me at dinner tonight, about three hours from now. I have an announcement, and I need you at my side when I make it."

"Thank you, Dutch. May I ask: is there a place I can lie down?"

He waved someone over to me, and we were escorted to a cottage.

After I closed the door, I said, "Zoolee, please don't choke anyone again, especially the ladies. If we're going to have a relationship, I have to be perfectly honest with you."

Zoolee smiled and said, "I wouldn't want it any other way."

"Zoolee, my sweet. You're so beautiful. You could have anyone, but here you are, in my arms. I am no one, while you're an actual living legend. Tomok said you're a goddess, but I think you're a bit scary at times. I'm afraid that you will hurt Sofia, Sunako, Molly, or the others. There! I said what I needed to say. Please don't be upset."

She grabbed my arms with both tendrils and held them out like Elfano had earlier.

"Zoolee, this is the shit I was talking about. It's unsettling, to say the least."

She brought me close while wearing a smile that would suggest impending pain. Then, she kissed me.

"You talk too much, Slade. Why would I hurt Sofia and the exquisitely beautiful Sunako? They're mine, after all, and I don't hurt the ones I love. Well, it's super rare when I do. Think of me as if I had been waiting for you to come home after a great span of time. I just want to crawl all over you. Can you blame me for my desires?" She did the pouty face again.

"I guess not when you put it that way. May I have two things? Let my arms go and another deep kiss?"

She did just that, and when we lay down, she took me to her chest.

"Zoolee, is it true that there is a religion built around you and they believe you are a living goddess?"

Zoolee laughed. "It's weird, I know. Is it too weird for you?"

"Well, you definitely have the looks to be a goddess. Maybe I can worship you before dinner?"

"Slade, you say the most romantic things. I love you." She hugged me tight, and I felt safe as I fell asleep. My dreams were jumbled and confusing. People were talking over me while I couldn't move, and a tall man had eyes that glowed like hot coals.

Chapter 37

This Is Just Not Happening

I woke up in Sunako's arms.

"Hey, Slade, you know you still drool in your sleep."

"I've been told. Sorry."

"It's okay. I kind of liked it. You were really out. Zoolee had to do something with Zyra, so she asked me to hold you, so you would wake up in the arms of an angel. She is so sweet. I really like her."

Someone opened the door. "Dinner in thirty minutes, and Dutch wants to see Slade ASAP."

"Looks like we have to get up." I rolled her to her back, wiping my face and kissing her. "Sunako, I missed you. I think of you a lot. Are you really comfortable being with me, Sofia, and the rest of our little gang?"

Sunako smiled. "Yes, I really like it this way. It feels safe, and Sofia told me about how you feel about being one man with many lovers. Please don't worry because none of us care about that. Some of us have loved one another for years, and with you, it makes everything even better. Thank you for telling me that you think of me a lot. I think of you a lot, too. You don't know how happy it makes me to hear that from you."

We kissed again as Sofia walked in.

"Hey, we should be at the pre-dinner party, not kissing. But I will have a quick kiss while I'm here," said Sofia.

Cheri walked in after and laughed. "I hear you became some kind of big shot. Don't expect me to come over there and kiss your ass or anything."

I walked up to Cheri, took her in my arms, and spun her around. "I missed you and your witty comments."

She hugged me tight.

"Cheri, may I kiss you?"

She smiled, and we kissed.

She whispered in my ear, "I missed you, but if you tell anyone, I will drown you. In kisses." Her smile was tender.

We kissed again. I felt very happy that I had the three of them back together.

"I heard some bullshit about you might be married to a goddess. You better not go getting a big head or anything, Mr. Bigshot," said Cheri.

Sofia smiled. We kissed and then walked to dinner.

"Slade, I want you to know that I missed you." Cheri was kind when she spoke.

We walked inside. The place was packed, including Khalyla and all three sisters. Dutch waved me over to him, then bear-hugged me, his beard tickling my face.

I saw all the green-eyed witches, Bill, Asimov, Tova, Kailee, Molly, Cyan, Portia, Topaz, Diandra, Saffron, and Reveka.

"Slade, we need to have a meeting before dinner." Dutch looked sad. "We received a message from Vorador in the form of a messenger. Slade, be prepared. The messenger is an eleven-year-old girl who is under Vorador's control. We have agreed to hear him out."

I stood wanting and ready for the petite child to transform, explode, or do something threatening, but her voice started out soft and small. Her eyes were shy with a hint of nervousness.

"Hello. My name is Cora. My mother and I have been paid very handsomely for me to act as the vessel to deliver this message and to establish dialogue with Slade and the Emerald Enchantress. I have been promised no harm will come to me. Please honor this promise, as I am only a messenger."

"Cora, may I hold your hand to see if you are being forced to do this?" asked Asya.

Asya took the child's hand and let it go within a few seconds.

"Cora speaks the truth. May we speak to Vorador?"

From the petite child's mouth, Vorador's voice arose, giving the child an eerie, almost nightmarish demeanor.

"Slade, I want you to know that it was not my intention to kill Lucy. For that, I'm sorry. Zyra will attest that I always mean what I say. With that said, the Emerald Cane and the Wooden Man were found by me while off world. Therefore, they are mine, and I want them back. I also want the Eye of the Void back. You will deliver it to me, and in return, I will tell you something about you that you don't know. And I will prove it. I would also like you to hear me out on a proposition."

"What if say no?"

"Asya, you still desire the Mirror of Truth, if I'm not mistaken?"

"I do. Why?"

"Then this is a token for being there for me when Isacay first died. You stopped me from harming myself, and I am thankful."

"You went on to kill a few hundred the next week. Then you disappeared into the Eye."

"Yes, I killed them. They were holding something that belonged to me, and you know they were item hunters from Children of the Fallen Leaves. You remember them? The crazier version of the Starlight Catchers?"

"But you killed every man, woman, and child," said Zyra.

"Do you think they would have spared one from a thousand? No, they wouldn't have, and you have always said, 'If the fruit is rotten, cut the tree down, then burn the ground.' You said that every time we found pirates, item hunters, slavers, or Splice. So, please come down from your high horse. By the way, nice horses you got there—very rare, very cool."

Zyra rolled her eyes. "Turn yourself in, and we will be lenient. We'll even take the death penalty off the table."

"No deal right now. I'm too close to getting her back."

"How will getting your wife back help you against me? Because I will make her a widow," I said.

"Slade! Hold your tongue!" yelled Asya.

"No, it's okay. I like Slade's fire, and I'm sure he will come to understand in time. Zoolee, you're awfully quiet. Has your husband left you speechless?"

Zoolee stood up and grabbed the child. "You bastard! How do you know about that?"

"First off, unhand this child. She is only a messenger. Second, I already said I know Slade better than any of you."

Zoolee let go of the child. "You must have overheard me call him my husband, and when I find your spy, I will kill them with fire."

"Zoolee, have everyone leave the room except for Slade, and I will prove to you what I know."

"Everyone get out!" yelled Zoolee.

Everyone left.

"Shield the room."

Zoolee raised her finger, and a high-pitched sound rang out.

"Excellent. I know how you treasure your privacy."

"Get on with it!"

"Slade, you're married to Zoolee. It just hasn't happened yet."

"No shit," I said.

"Zoolee, Slade is your Ghost Walker, just like your mother was to her husband, the king."

"How the fuck do you know that?"

"We all have our secrets. Some are just buried in the past, and some are yet to be made. Are you satisfied?"

"I am, but if I find you're fucking with me, I will kill you!"

"I have never lied to you. Why would I start now?"

Zoolee lowered the shield and opened the door.

"Well?" asked Zyra.

"Vorador knows something that is unknown to most."

"Now that I have proved myself, will you give back what I have asked in return for information about Slade?"

I said, "I don't care if she is or isn't my wife. No one will bend me to their will. You will pay for Lucy's death. If you want the Emerald Cane, I'll be happy shoving it through your chest."

"Boy, you wouldn't speak to me that way if you knew who I was. Now I asked nicely for what is mine. I will return the Eye of the Void immediately after one use. As we all now know, it's just a way to make contact with our mutual friend, Kelsomta. Information for my things is a good deal."

"Vorador, what if we decline?" asked Khalyla.

"I will be forced to get what I want through other means. That could mean unnecessary deaths. Lady Velvet has stolen from me. If these things are brought to me, I will have no need to hunt for them, and lives will happily continue. Or would you rather me leave a trail of bodies as I hunt for my stuff? Zyra, I know you have the Wooden

Man sitting on your desk. Give it to Slade, or tell him what I'm capable of. Now I will give you two months to consider my very generous offer."

"Two months? I thought you wanted these items?" I said coldly.

"If you must know, I'm meeting with the one person who knows you better than anyone else. That person will help in my quest to bring my wife back. Khalyla, once I have Isacay back in my arms, you can have the items back. I'll throw in a few that I know most of you want from my personal collection. Maybe the Ruby earrings?"

Galya laughed. "They're just a myth. Maybe you try harder."

The rest of the witches laughed.

The young girl reached into her pocket. "You mean these? I mean, if you don't want them, I could just throw them into a sock drawer. Go on. Take them and verify."

Bill reached out, and they were placed in his hand. "I'll be right back, Asimov. Galya, please come with me."

They shifted away.

"So, Slade, have you figured out that your skirt is called a kilt?"

"I have."

"Ask Kelso. He will give you the different histories of the outfit."

The three reappeared.

"These are real. Khalyla, how can this be?" Asimov questioned.

"I don't know."

"Mother, these have power. Tambry confirmed these are authentic. Vorador, why would you give us something with this much power?"

"Galya, it's my way of saying I'm sorry for my actions. I know nothing can make up for my transgressions, but these were on the top ten most wanted items, and what better a home than with the Emerald Enchantresses? Either way, there's a gift."

"Vorador, did you know Slade while you lived with us?" asked Zoolee.

"Did you ever wonder why no one could enter my mind? My secrets have secrets. Besides, you of all people know what it's like to live with a secret. Just look at Slade. Don't you want to tell him things that would ease his mind, if even just a little? Maybe you unburden yourself by telling him his real first name."

Those in the room gasped, and all eyes snapped toward Zoolee.

I stared most intensely and said, "Zoolee? Is there something you would like to tell me?"

"No."

"Do you know something, or is he a liar?"

"He's telling the truth."

"Then don't you think you should tell me?"

"No."

"Zoolee, it's my name, so if you know it, then I think you should give it to me, now!"

"First off, check your tone, lest you get your face slapped!" Zoolee spoke through gritted teeth while leaning toward me. "Second, you will have it when the time is right, not a second before. Am I clear on this topic?"

I leaned in. "You and I are going to have a talk real soon. Don't think for a minute I will back down. I'm not afraid of you. If you really knew me, then you would know that I don't take shit from anyone."

"You're exhausting at times."

"I hate to break up the lover's quarrel, but I'm waiting for an answer. This child shouldn't be late for dinner. Now, Slade, what do you think of my offer?"

"I think you can kiss my ass, then fuck yourself, because I'm not giving you anything but an early grave."

"Slade, eventually, you and I will square up, but I whooped your ass the first time. What makes you think you'll do better next time? I had an amazing teacher who taught me to never give up, so I would watch yourself before you get spanked, again."

"Vorador, please. Provoking Slade is counterproductive." Bill added, "I would like to know what will happen if your offer is ultimately rejected?"

"Well, I will have to search for them while leaving a trail of bodies in my wake. Ergo, those holding my items will bear the burden of what could've been avoided, and I would hate to involve the October Men. Maybe the crazier Children of the Fallen Leaves or the Starlight Catchers. You know how they get about technology infused with magic. Oh, and before I go: Dutch, you might be interested to know that Malik survived the plane crash and is now one of the heads of the October Men."

"I don't see how that should interest me."

"My mistake. I thought you two were once colleagues."

"Your only mistake was coming for my daughter."

"Yes, well, maybe she should have known how dangerous magical items are. I hope you can teach her about the dangers of such things."

"I look forward to teaching you about how dangerous I can be."

"No need. I already know. Now, will someone bring this young lady to the main gate of the Gladstone village? See into her mind and know that her mother was paid well for the service that is being provided. Her house will be the place you can contact me."

"How do we know this is not a trap?" asked Asya.

"I would have placed a bomb on this young lady if I wanted anyone dead. I thank you for your time, and good evening." The young girl's voice returned to normal.

"Did I do a good job?"

"Yes, you did. We are very proud of you. Here is a gold coin and two silver coins as a tip. Now let's get you back to your mother."

All the witches shifted away, then were back ten minutes later.

"It's true. Vorador is taking very good care of the mother and child for future communication with us. Now, Slade, tell us how you feel," said Khalyla.

Everyone sat silent while all eyes fell on me. I thought of the appropriate words without letting my passions spill over.

"Slade, honey?" Zoolee touched my hand. "You have a look."

"Slade." Asya smiled. "We're all eager to hear your thoughts."

"I think he can kiss my ass. I'm not giving him anything but cold steel as I ram it into his chest. Then I want to watch the light fade from his eyes while I spit in his face."

"Well, I think I can get you a sword," said Zoolee. "I might have a few in my closet."

"Zoolee! This is serious! Vorador may know Slade. This could be a trap," Zyra cautioned.

"We know Vorador very well. I think he would take the items and leave."

Galya said, "Bill has a point, and not on the top of his head. The Wooden Man is mostly harmless. I mean, it is a meditation tool. I don't see how the Eye of the Void, the Wooden Man, and the Emerald Cane can make a dangerous combination."

"Galya, what does the Emerald Cane do?" I asked.

"It helps one astral-project, which Vorador can do, so what is the point? I mean, it's a teaching tool."

“Galya has a point. There must be a few dozen items like the Emerald Cane,” said Asya.

“It must be something more than you know, just like the Eye of the Void. What you think is benign could be deadly in the right hands.”

“Slade, I hate that you’re so young while still making a great argument.” Galya sat back. “Mother, what say you?”

“I think Slade is the key to it all. I also think Velvet overplayed her hand, and it should be slapped. Dutch, your daughter, who was trained by us, caused people to die because of her lust for dangerous items. Now, I’m sure I don’t need to tell you how to parent or do your job, but she should be punished.”

“I agree with you, Khalyla, and I have a great punishment in mind.”

“Slade, what would you like to do?” asked Asya.

“I will not give Vorador anything but death. The three items in question should be studied in depth by Zoolee and me. Perhaps Kelsomta can see what has been missed.”

“Yes, I like that. I will call Tambry to get her on the first round of studying the Cane, and the Wooden Man.” Khalyla called out to Tambry. “She is on it. Now, I’m getting hungry. Is there anything else?”

Asimov chimed in with a thought, “What if the child was a way to distract us? Other than Dutch and Slade, we know Vorador fairly well. The lengths he went to secure some of our most dangerous items was astounding. In fact, Slade reminds me of a young Vorador. Look at his intense stare and the way they almost share the same eyes. Even the way he sits, ready to strike. Not to mention his single-mindedness with the way he speaks.”

“Okay, we might all be thinking it. What if Slade is a son to Vorador? Slade had his mind scrubbed of certain places, people, and other odd things. What if Vorador found something or a combination of items that caused Slade to forget?”

“Asya, what purpose would that achieve?” Zoolee asked coldly. “No, I refuse to believe Vorador is my husband’s father!”

“Zoolee, why do you keep calling me your husband? Did I miss something?”

“Because you are! Slade is something no one can explain. Vorador must have seen it inside Velvet’s mind. Now he wants Slade, thinking he could be a useful tool, but Slade will not be made to do another's bidding. He is his own man."

I stood up.

"Sit down!" yelled Zoolee.

"Zoolee, I only got up to stop someone from pressing their ear to the door." I moved to the door, then pulled it open very fast. Velvet fell through the opening. "Hello, Lady Velvet. I hope the floor wasn't too unkind to you as it kissed you."

"You insolent fool! How dare you speak to me in such a manner! Father, will you let your daughter be insulted, or will you do something about it?"

Dutch stood up while stroking his reddish-blond beard. "I will do something about this. Unbecoming behavior like I've seen will not be tolerated. Slade, Velvet, I need time to think of a proper punishment." Dutch walked out.

"Oh, you're going to get it now! I bet he has you whipped. Maybe you'll lose your free-man status. Then I will buy you and work you. Oh yeah, I have a job in mind."

"Lady Velvet! Do you really think your snooping will be rewarded? Are you that stupid?" asked Khalyla.

"I will not dignify that remark with an answer because I'm a lady."

"When are you going to start acting like it instead of a snobby bitch?" Khalyla walked out as did everyone but me.

When the door closed, Velvet snapped, "What are you looking at?"

"I don't know, but a lady I know it isn't!"

She crossed the room and slapped my face. "You miserable fuck! How dare you speak to me like that? Yeah, you saved my life, but you will respect me and my title, lest you get another slap!"

"Respect is earned, and you have not earned mine!" I went to walk away, and she grabbed my arm.

"I better get an apology, and soon, or I'm going to—"

"You're going to take your filthy paw off of me before I make you drink your own piss while I laugh." I pried off her hand, then left, slamming the door.

Dutch was making his way down the hall. "You okay?"

"No disrespect, but your daughter knows how to get under my skin."

"Yeah, she has that effect on me sometimes. Slade, I'm going to need you to sit beside me at the head of my table for an announcement that I'm sure none will want to miss.

Dutch's table was at the front of the room about two feet higher than all the other tables and was sideways.

Dutch spoke loudly so that everyone could hear him, his voice booming with a deep pitch, "Tonight, we will drink to Lucy and Slade. They risked their lives to save my daughter, Kailee, and the survivors of the House of Dreams. Lucy paid the heaviest price. We will never forget her sacrifice. Slade had no loyalty to my daughter, Lady Velvet, but risked his life to save her and those of her great House because it was the right thing to do. In doing so, he almost died in the process. Slade looked death in the face and said, 'I'm busy. Now piss off!' Now, here he is at my side."

Someone yelled, "Cheers to the boy who smells like flowers!"

The whole room yelled, "Cheers!"

Then, we all drank. I felt all eyes on me, and it made me a bit uncomfortable. I hoped things would start to calm down a bit in the next few days. I wanted to go back to the House of Ribbons, find my place, and live a happy life with those I love and those I'm growing deeply found of.

Dutch continued, "Tonight, we honor Lucy and Slade, the only way I can. It will never cover my debt to them for giving me more time with my daughter, Lady Velvet. Tonight, I, High Lord Dutch, bestow the title of lord and lady to Slade and Lucy. They will be henceforth known as Lady Lucy and Lord Slade. Lord Slade will also be known as Lord Slade the Unflinching. He will be granted a House of his own, but until it's constructed, Lord Slade will take over the once great House of Dreams. I trust he will rise to the challenge of being a lord and everything that comes with it. This is not a demotion for my daughter. She will still be known as Lady Velvet. She will guide Lord Slade for a period of time so that he can one day soon lead a new House in his own name." He went silent as everyone stood while clapping and stomping their feet. I thought to myself, *This is just not happening. This has to be a bad dream.* After a few minutes, Dutch elbowed me and whispered, "Get up and say something. They're all waiting."

I was nervously spinning my silver ring around my finger.

I took a huge drink and stood up. I saw those I loved and those who were my friends. My brother was sitting next to Tomok, and there were a few more people I knew and lots who I didn't. I raised my glass. *Screw me, if I didn't have the absolute worst luck, I wouldn't have any luck at all.* I cleared my throat and steadied my hands.

"Thank you, High Lord Dutch. I hope to make you proud. I hope to make all of you proud. I raise my glass in honor of Lady Lucy. May the gods reward her sacrifice." I didn't know what to say, so I was making it up as I went. "And we are going to keep on doing what we do."

I thought to myself, Stop talking, you fool! Stop talking. You sound stupid, and everyone will know you're an idiot! Say cheers and sit the hell down!

"Cheers to Lady Lucy, cheers to High Lord Dutch, and cheers to the great people of the House of Thorns." I sat down and finished my drink.

Dutch leaned over and said, "Don't worry, Lord Slade. My first speech was much worse than yours."

He laughed loudly and patted me on the back.

To be continued in book two: *The House of Sleepless Dreams*

Acknowledgements

I'd like to dedicate this book to:

My wife, Lesley Slade. We were soldiers when we met in Baghdad, Iraq, and we soon knew we would create a life together. Now, fifteen years later, we're still madly in love and happily married. This book would have never seen the light of day if you hadn't saved its beginnings contained within a notebook from the trash. Lesley, you've stood beside me throughout this entire process, never letting me lose hope or focus. You've always believed in me, this story, and my dream that has now been realized. No words could ever thank you enough, other than I love you.

Ashley Winter Slade, your laughter, love, and constant smile never fail to brighten any situation.

Victoria Frostflower Slade, you're always a delight. Your imagination is key to unlocking your future.

Huxley Ignatius Dracula Slade, your giggles, kisses, and tiny hugs make the best days even better.

Silph, Isla, and Sunako. My oldest friends. I became who I am because of you three, and I love you all dearly. Some of the places we've been and adventures we've had made it into this book series because they were too cool to let them fade into memory.

Stephen King, Isaac Asimov, C. Dean Andersson, and Anne Rice. I grew up on your delightfully entertaining books. You and many more writers were, and still are, my heroes.

To Allen, Olivia, Chrissy, and all the fine people at Write my Wrongs editing. I don't know where this book would be with you.

To all the people who supported me in any way throughout my life. I thank you. Maybe it was a passing comment, some well wishes, or a good joke.

Lastly, but just as important. I thank you, the reader. Thank you for taking the time to enjoy my work and the art of reading. From the bottom of my heart, I thank you.

About the Author

An Army veteran with two combat tours in Iraq under his belt, Keith Slade decided to settle down and craft his own sci-fi fantasy universe. With degrees in both criminal studies and legal studies, he is fascinated by human behavior and what influences our choices. When he's not writing, you can find him lounging with his wife, Lesley, and their three children in their beautiful home in Missouri. *The House of Ribbons* is Keith's first book in a series of five.

Made in the USA
Columbia, SC
08 August 2021